AGAINST THE FALL OF NIGHT

by

Michael Disney.

Being the first of a quartet of novels *"Written in the Stars"* covering man's escape out of the atmosphere to see, for the first time, the Universe as it truly is. This (190 k-words) covers 1964 to 1975. The others are:

> *"The Whispering Sky"*, 1976 to 1983
> *"Crouching Giant"*, 1983 to 1995
> *"Beyond the Western Stars"*, 1996 to 2011

> *'Here, on the level sand,*
> *Between the sea and land,*
> *What shall I build or write*
> *Against the fall of night?'*

> Anon.

2

COPYRIGHT PAGE

© 2020 Michael Disney

Published by Kindle Direct Publishing.

ISBN – 979 862 294 75880

i

PROLOGUE.

After dawn, Banana Creek, Cape Canaveral. April 24 1990

They waited on the edge of the lagoon looking across two miles of swamp towards Space Shuttle Discovery, standing beside its gantry waiting for launch. For them, the astronomers, this was the most exciting moment in all their long history. Cocooned inside the Shuttle lay The Hubble Space Telescope. For seventy years men had dreamed of this moment when their eyes would be carried above the atmosphere at last, to see far further outward into Space, much further backward into Time. In the Mediaeval ages men built cathedrals to storm the heavens. Now the Space Telescope represented the spire of all their hopes.

It was an exciting moment, but a tense one too. Ten thousand of the most highly skilled astronomers, engineers and computer scientists on Earth had toiled for fifteen years to put the technical marvel together, and now was their Moment of Truth. Everyone remembered the Challenger disaster when a shuttle had blown itself and its crew to smithereens just after launch. At a cost of billions of dollars not even the United States and Europe together could afford a backup for the telescope if things went wrong now.

Everyone was there, that is to say everyone in world astronomy who could wangle a coveted seat on the bleachers and be as close to launch as men were ever allowed to go. They comprised the elite of astronomy, particularly those who had contributed to what some had called " the most exciting voyage of discovery ever undertaken by mankind." Only the first Moon landing had aroused so much enthusiasm.

The tannoy echoed:

"Hullo, this is mission control at Kennedy Space Centre. The time is T minus five minutes and holding. The software has now been configured for launch. The inertial guidance system is nominal. Houston has asked control to set the pre-flight uplink commands. The astronauts are going through their last minute checks.

" The forecast predicts only a five per cent chance of violating the launch weather rules at 08.24 a.m. However there is now concern about the winds at Banjoule, the crosswind factors are at margins. These are being assessed at this time."

Sir Frank Cotteridge, a very tall distinguished looking man, bearded, but bald on top, strolled along the water's edge, forgetting the warning about alligators. He'd worked so hard for this, toiled on so many boring committees to get the Europeans on board. And now they were. The leader of the European Space –Science delegation, which had been specially flown over from Paris on the Concorde, he now sought a little solitude to savour the moment.

"Mission Control announces that the weather conditions are now Go for a launch 08.24 a.m. Repeat. Go for launch."

The scientists and engineers behind him, even the Vice President of the United States, clamoured like children. They shook hands unnecessarily, punched each other on the shoulder. Then they checked their cameras and tape recorders for the final countdown, knowing that one day they'd be proud to tell their grandchildren.

The solitary Englishman strolled on until the shoreline ahead was blocked by another man standing alone, a man almost as tall as he was, but far more heavily built. That man wasn't elegantly dressed like Sir Frank, didn't wear a Savile Row sports jacket or the coveted orange and gold MCC tie. He wore a fisherman's smock and a Russian tank driver's hat with the earflaps turned up. His face was grim, the face of a man who'd had to fight, and to fight hard for whatever life had yielded, though it was a face not entirely without humour. Hands in pockets he was staring up at a Turkey Buzzard, marvelling at its ability to thermal on the tiniest fountains of air.

"Just look at that." he said, more to himself than to the other. "We may fly to the Moon, but we'll never be able to emulate that. Never."

Then the two men recognised one another. Both made as if to speak. But no words would come. Too much had happened between them. Far too much.

"T minus ten and counting.

Nine
Eight
Seven
Six
Fahve
Fower
…."

The two men, grateful for an excuse to look away from one another, stared out across the water as Space Shuttle Discovery rose from its cloud of white steam and thundered heavenwards on its pillar of fire.

CHAPTER ONE
1964
FALL

When Morgan woke up there were stars above his head. He could see them in between the branches of the trees. But were they real stars, or just stars in a dream? He watched intently, and sure enough, when the wind blew, the leaves moved and some of the stars went out while new ones appeared. Dream stars wouldn't do that.

So what was he doing under a tree in the night? And so thirsty? So very thirsty. His tongue felt swollen and cracked. It rasped when he rubbed it against his teeth. He must get up and have a drink. His legs though wouldn't cooperate. He placed his hands on the ground beside him to push, and passed out again.

When he came round it was daylight. Low clouds were scudding over the tree tops. He seemed to be lying, head downwards, on a steep slope covered with mossy boulders, bilberry bushes and stunted oaks. His climbing rope was coiled round his chest, his legs seemed to be tangled up in a recently felled sapling. Who had he been climbing with? He looked about for other bodies but the wood was gloomy and deserted. Thirsty. So bloody thirsty. Then he remembered the night and the stars. Of course he had been going to get a drink. He must have been lying here for ages. He tried to move again but his legs wouldn't collaborate. Heaving with his arms the legs broke free from the sapling and, unsupported, he tumbled backwards and downwards onto the forest floor.

Thirst reawakened him during the night. He had never been so thirsty in his life before. There were no stars this time but the branches were darker shadows against the darkness overhead. He had to go and get water. Had to! But when he tried to get to his feet his legs collapsed. Time and again he managed to stand, only to crash over when he tried to walk.

What was wrong with his legs? He couldn't see them but he could feel them with his hands. No blood. No pain. But nevertheless there *was* something wrong. That was it; his hands could feel his legs, but his legs couldn't feel his hands. He pinched his right thigh through the corduroy trousers; nothing. Not even the slightest sensation. He pinched his left thigh, and he could feel that. Good. What about lower down? He crooked the leg and pinched the calf. Nothing. The lower part was dead too. He tried to wriggle his toes. Nothing. It was as if his brain didn't know, or couldn't remember how to control them.

"I'll have to crawl. Can't die of thirst, not here in Britain." He giggled.

But once he'd turned onto his front, his legs were useless. All he could do was use his elbows, digging them into the ground, to shuffle forward a few painful inches at a time.

"Oh God, I'm passing out again. What's wrong with me......"

Spots of rain falling on his neck, woke him next day. Rolling on his back he held his parched mouth agape, hoping to catch a droplet or two. The branches overhead were thrashing and hushing about in the wind. He felt even weaker than before, presumably due to his thirst. And his head ached badly. Reaching upward he felt crusted dry blood on his scalp, lots of it. A head injury.

He closed his mouth and tried to remember where he was, or what he was doing here, but could not. He felt faint, disembodied, awful. If he didn't get water soon he knew he was going to die. Rolling over on to his belly he began inching forward again
.

His life was saved by a cowpat, a dried crusty cowpat on the grass at the edge of the wood. Grunting and gasping past it he noticed the rainwater gathered in the depression on top of it. It looked so delicious. He twisted over, lowered his head and sucked it up; not a third of a cup but it slipped down his gullet like ambrosia. He could literally feel himself coming to life. And there must be more. He lifted his head and searched about.

Then he heard them: men working in the wood to his right; the thud of axes; the staccato buzz of a power saw; voices calling; branches crashing.

"Help. Help. Help…." He could manage little more than a dry croaking. But it worked.

"Where are you?"

He passed out, only to wake again in the night. They'd left him, or more probably failed to find him. Surely they would come back again next day ? Surely? And if not? Dying didn't seem too painful, merely frustrating.

He woke on an operating table. Some one was holding his head up to give him water. Other figures in white were cutting off his trousers. Other hands stuck a needle into his wrist. His body was their problem now, not his any more. He could drift away again.

The surgeon was matter of fact:

"As you can see the right leg is dead almost up to the thigh."

Morgan was astonished to see that it was indeed black, black as a black pudding.

"And the left leg to just above the knee. After the fall you must have been lying unconscious in an awkward position for several days, which cut off the blood supply. The nerves are dead, the flesh is cold. We'll probably have to amputate to prevent gangrene."

"Your head wound is superficial, but you've had serious concussion. We did an angiogram and there's no sign of internal blood loss within the cranium. To be certain we'll give you a lumber puncture."

The surgeon looked at him quizzically, before resuming:

"I could operate on the legs now, but you are very weak, mainly due to serious dehydration. In any case there's just a chance of returning circulation. You're a very fit young man and there's just a chance. But don't rely on it. We'll wait for twenty-four hours and take another look."

For Morgan those twenty-four hours were one long sweating nightmare. But he tried to appear calm when the surgeon reappeared:

"Try to move your toes."

He tried with might and main.

The surgeon grasped the toes in his fingers.

"Try again."

"And again."

Nothing happened; the legs were paralysed.

"That's encouraging. I can feel a little movement in this left foot. Some nerves at least are alive and the flesh is warm. Circulation is returning. You will probably keep the left leg. Keep it moving as much as you can. The right leg isn't so happy. It's definitely warming up though – which is a good sign. That means circulation and no gangrene. But the nerves seem to be completely dead and the limb is paralysed. It could be more of a hindrance to you than a help. How old are you?"

"Twenty six."

'Mm. Marginal. A nerve can re-grow at up to one millimetre a day if you're young enough. In your case, in a couple of years they'll stop altogether. You might just be lucky. We'll check again tomorrow. By the way, you *were* climbing alone. They searched the area. No more bodies. Found your motor bike. Never climb alone; its foolish. I'm afraid now you'll never climb again. The very best you can hope for is partial recovery of the right leg and foot."

A couple of days later Morgan felt well enough to feel really sorry for himself. He couldn't remember the fall but he did know that his whole life was, or indeed had been, about mountaineering. He and Steve had been about to go out to the Dolomites, to do Cima Grande direttissimo. Then on to Chamonix and some big Alpine faces: the Walker Spur on the Grand Jorasse, the North Face of the Matterhorn and, weather permitting, a second recce of the Eiger Nordwand. They'd tried last year. Now it was all as far away as the surface of the Moon. And his right leg was agony. Someone had strapped an electric fire to his skin, just below the knee, and turned it on.

"I'm afraid it's Causalgia. " the surgeon had said. "The nerve is trying to re-grow itself, but the end is short-circuiting. Every tenth of a second your brain is sending a signal down to find out where the leg is. But when the leg responds the signal comes back up the pain nerve."

"It's bloody agony."

"I understand. It's the third most painful condition known to medical science, after child-birth and tic doloroso."

"Can't you give me anything?"

'We could. We could give you pethedine, which is what we use on terminal cancers. It's a strong morphine derivative. In your case anything weaker would be ineffective. But you'd soon become a drug addict, and in any case the relief it would give would wear off within months. And your leg is going to hurt for as long as the nerves keep re-growing; a year or two at least."

"My God!"

"I'm afraid we can't do much for you. Believe me we would if we could. We'll give you some crutches and discharge you in a few days time. I'd look upon the pain as the price you have to pay for getting your legs back. But I'd like you to see a psychiatrist before you leave. Good luck."

Suicide seemed the only logical way out. People would forgive him, even his mother, knowing about the agony in his leg. No one could stand being in labour for three years. But you couldn't commit suicide in hospital. Not with all those earnest nurses and doctors. And patients all hoping to get well. It would let down the whole side. And anyway how could one do it when they were watching you all the time? Drown oneself face down in a bed pan? But Christ, the agony was crucifying. His entire limb hummed with electricity and scorching heat. They'd put a cage over it to prevent the unbearable torture when a sheet brushed against his skin. He couldn't read even. All he could do, apart from feel sorry for himself, was watch the comings and goings of a hospital ward: operations, emergency admissions – often head injuries after a traffic accident; a death in the night. Being a neuro-surgical ward, brain operations were routine and many patients were semi-conscious and under intensive care. Both patients and staff were far too occupied to pay much attention to him.

With one exception; seated beside his bed on the opposite side of the ward was a man so hideous that Morgan was both repelled and fascinated. One side of his face was normal but, when he turned, one could see that the other side was grotesque, had collapsed. It was the contrast between the two profiles which was so shocking. Seated there in his dressing gown, with a walking stick in one hand, he appeared, when turned to his left, a normal, rather intelligent looking man in his forties. Turned to his right he became a gargoyle, a grotesque circus freak. His mouth and cheek hung loosely from his face, as if without animation or musculature; his left eye-lid and eye-brow had collapsed over his eye, hiding it from sight. He could walk, but only with an extreme limp, as if the entire left side of his body was paralysed. When he turned towards Morgan, Morgan quickly looked away. The last thing he wanted now was to see that nightmare visage close up.

But evasion didn't work. He heard the clumsy tap-tap of the walking sick approaching and steeled himself to look up.

" 'ello, 'oim Ernie." The voice spoke with the thickest Birmingham accent.

"Moind if I sit down?" he pronounced 'down' with half a dozen extra vowels normally not included.

"Please do."

"Oi'll turn the other way so yow dain't see it."

Morgan didn't know what to say, but was silently grateful.

"Aint a pretty sight am I? Yow daint 'ave to say nuthin', I'm used to it."

Ernie lowered himself clumsily into the visitors chair beside Morgan's bed.

"Looks worse'n it is. S'only Bells Palsy – paralysis down one side on me fice. They say yow'm in agony. That's mooch worse."

Morgan told him about causalgia, then about the climbing accident, and that led back into his earlier life. Somehow it felt much easier to talk to another cripple like himself. Ernie wanted to see the legs:

"Bleedin' 'ell! Warra bloody mess. This'n is a black puddin' whats turning purple and yeller like a black eye."

Morgan tried to look at Ernie's face without flinching. Once he realised it was just paralysis it didn't seem so bad. The left cheek and lips sagged downwards, exposing the teeth and gums on that side. From time to time Ernie would wipe the drool away unconsciously with the sleeve of his good arm.

"How did you get that?" Morgan asked.

" Brain Choomour. It's a growin' in me 'ead like a cabbidge."

"My God" Morgan couldn't help himself exclaim.

"T'aint that bad reely. Ad it more'n twenty year already. Grows ever so slow loike. Every few year I coom in 'ere and Mr Small, that's me surgeon, 'ee goes in there and chops it back a bit. Ee's bloody good 'ee is."

"So the tumour causes the palsy?"

"Not reely. It's mostly the dammidge left by them early surgeons. They dain't know what they was a'doin. 'Ow could they? They adn't been inside anybody's live skull afore. Oim one on the very first in Britain to survive a brain operation. And then only 'cos of the war."

"How do you mean?"

"'Cos of all them 'ed injuries they was expectin', some surgeons decided to train theirselves on patients what was going to die anyroad, loike me. I was eleven then. They took me down to Roehampton near London. And they operated on three on us on the same morning. There was a young woman, a girl about sixteen called Valerie, an' me. They parked us outside the theatre in wheel chairs. First of all they took the young woman in and she was gone two hours. Me an' Valerie was nervous like, and we chatted. But when they wheeled the woman out of the theatre, still in 'er wheelchair, she 'ad a sheet over 'er 'ed. Then they took Valerie. She was cryin'. Quietly like, but brave. She lasted four hours before they wheeled 'er out under a sheet 'an all. Right past me, poor kid. As you can imagine poor Ernie was a'shittin' 'isself."

"How bloody callous!" Morgan was indignant.

"They 'ad me in there, in the theatre, thirteen bleedin' hours. An' only a local anaesthetic 'cos they needed to talk to me. Ask me what sensations I was a getting when they prodded about inside me brain."

"It must have been terrifying."

"Ar, it was an all. Specially when they cut inside me skull bone with a 'lectric saw. Oi could smell the smoke on it, and the burning flesh. But I dain't feel a thing. I could 'ear them talking like – the surgeons. I was under this table see, with me 'ed a pokin' through an 'ole in the top. There were a nurse down there with me, moppin' me face, and talkin' to keep me awike. I could 'ear the surgeons a' talking to each other about what to do next: 'Ay think we've got to go down through that tissue Lennox' one on them said, all posh like. 'Oy don't like the look of it' says Lennox 'Too many blood vessels.'. 'Oy don't see any other choice' says the third 'The neoplasm must lie deeper because there's no sign of it up heah.' It's amazing 'ow much I kin remember about that operation. Natrally I thought it was me last moment you see. But 'ere I am twenty four year later. Not loike them other two; not like Valerie. I can't complain can I? I got a full pension. I never 'ad to work. I'm on 'oliday for life."

"Rather you than me. What do you do all day?"

"Model aeroplanes. I design 'em, build 'em an' fly 'em. Radio Control. I'm Midlands champion in the open class and runner up in the British Championship. But the champion, 'ee flies one of my models too. I've got me own wind-tunnel see. Me dad and me built it in our garridge. Gives us an edge. If I get through this next op' 'oim aimin' to break the World Endurance record. 'Eld by a German. Over seven hours. Bet you could understand aerodynamics – with all that science you done at university. I've tried. Got out the books. But it's all in mathematics."

"I suppose I could try" Morgan admitted "But they never taught us that kind of thing. I built a model when I was young. But I'm clumsy, and impatient, and it crashed on its first flight."

"Tell you what" Ernie sounded excited "I'll gi' yer one of me books. Yow study up on it while I'm 'avin me 'op, then yow can teach me when I coom out. And then I'll teach yer to build a real flyer. It'll take yer moind off yer pain. I guarantee."

"When's your 'op?"

"Any day. Mr Smart's lookin' at me latest X-rays. When they shave me 'ed I'll know its next day."

"You seem amazingly calm about it."

'What else can I bleedin' be? I gotta live the best I can. Not just for me but for Valerie, and that other girl. I call 'er Shirley but we never knowed 'er real name."

Morgan's left leg recovered quickly, so that he could hop about the ward on crutches, but the pain in his right increased with every day until he could barely stand it. The electric fire buzzed with electricity, getting hotter and hotter. He tried to gauge it against other pains he had suffered, albeit briefly. Like dislocating his shoulder on the rugby pitch. Or being flogged at prep school. Or being stung by wasps. That came nearest. Like being stung by twenty wasps at once, right up his leg. Relief came only in brief snatches of sleep which visited him unpredictably. The leg felt enormous, far bigger than himself, as big as a cow, as an elephant, as big as a roaring, stinging, burning whale attached to his thigh. At night, when the lights went out in the ward, it crushed down on him like a weight of tons until he wanted to cry out; to seek some kind of relief in a scream of protest.

His mother, who came every visiting hour, cried when she saw the suffering etched on his face, the sweat trickling down his temples. His step-father, more practical, left a bottle of illegal Scotch which certainly helped the sleep to come, but then woke him again with ghastly nightmares. On balance it wasn't worth it. All he could do, when the agony became unbearable, was imagine the leg floating away from him, off into the darkness, carrying its pain further away from his being. Sometimes it helped. Just a bit.

"Ah Mrs Morgan, thank you for coming to see me. The elderly psychiatrist got to his feet and ushered the woman into a chair. He could easily see the resemblance: a large frame, proud dark eyes, a powerful nose.

"It's about your Tom. I've been asked to see if I can help him."

The woman passed a hand across her face as if trying to brush away some intolerable strain:

"I hope you can Doctor Cole. I don't think I can stand much more of this, let alone Twm."

"I'll do what I can. But Tom isn't very forthcoming."

"No. He wouldn't be. I'm afraid he's got a very low opinion of the medical profession. But then he's got a low opinion of a lot of people."

"I see." The psychiatrist jotted imperturbably in his notes, "Now what I want to know about are his other interests – besides climbing."

"Not so much recently. He's become such a fanatic. He reads of course, but if he isn't actually away climbing then he's earning money for his next expedition. He's got a physics degree and yet he works as an ordinary machinist in a car factory. Can you believe it?"

"When did he start climbing?"

"Immediately he came out of the army. I think he found life very tame after Malaya – there was a war there then. Twm used to lead his men out on long patrols into the jungle."

"He enjoyed that?"

"I suppose he did. They were going to give him a medal."

"They were?" he left the question hanging in the air.

"There was some kind of scandal about it. That's all I know. Twm doesn't tell me …. man things. We're close…but he's kept that side of himself to himself – ever since his father was killed in Normandy."

"How old was he then?"

"Not quite seven. He adored his father. I'm sure that's why he did his National Service, when all his pals avoided it. He wanted to get into a war, any war, before it was too late you see."

"Didn't you find that odd?"

"I blame myself. When Evan was killed I built a shrine. But Evan was a hero. They gave him a decoration for gallantry."

"Did Tom have other interests – before the Army."

"Oh yes. For instance he was mad keen on science, and mathematics. He was very precocious you know. Used to read enormous tomes on history and philosophy even before he went to grammar school. He specially loved astro…astro….not astronomy, 'astrophysics' he called it. The boys called him 'the Prof'. His maths master said he was a prodigy. They were predicting great things – but then something went wrong."

"What?"

"I wish I knew. He clammed up but I know he turned against the masters – all except one or two; his maths master was his favourite. He didn't bother much after that – only games. He was very competitive. All his friends went to Cambridge, whereas Twm got rejected."

"He got a physics degree at Bangor I understand?"

"He went there because of the climbing in Snowdonia. I don't think he worked much."

"This maths master that Tom liked at school; do you think there's any way of contacting him?"

Coles rang the bell. "Edgbaston Residential Care" it said above the door, then in much smaller letters "The home for elderly gentlemen."

The matron paused before opening the door into Maurice Carter's room:

"He's had three strokes you know. Perfectly lucid most of the time. We all love him. But he does wander off onto the past sometimes. Just be patient – bring him back to the point. But a very educated gentleman. Do you know he used to play Bridge for England?"

Carter was seated up in bed, crossword on his lap, looking out of his expansive bay window. With a large domed forehead, a bald pate with white curls behind his ears he reminded Cole of a benevolent Roman emperor in old age.

"I like to watch the clouds you know, sailing by like galleons. Funny to think I never bothered to look up when I was younger. It's part of the wonder and wisdom of old age I suppose. Remember that when they ream out your prostrate. It's not all bad you know. Sit down."

As Cole explained the situation the older man became agitated:

"Of course I remember Tom Morgan. He and Frank Cotteridge were the two most brilliant mathematical scholars I ever taught, and I had plenty at King Henry's. The closest of friends – but the bitterest of rivals – at anything, from cricket to mathematics. Boys can be like that you know. Queer cattle. But those two were special, very special. They fought like cat and dog for first place in my mathematical set."

"Who won ?"

"It was fascinating; two quite different minds. Cotteridge: fluent, effortless, economic, accurate. Morgan: careless, tortured, deeper. They kept on getting one hundred per cent. So I'd set them fiendishly hard problems on Fridays to do over the weekends. Cotteridge usually managed them first, but occasionally failed. Morgan was often late – but he did them all in the end. But it was Morgan who gave up the battle first and conceded the palm to Cotteridge. Claimed, rather grandly, that *he* wasn't going to waste any more time doing 'trivial mental gymnastics'. He taught himself differential geometry instead; Ph.D. stuff, way above my head. But look at Cotteridge: he was top mathematical scholar at Cambridge in his year. The admissions tutor sent us a letter of congratulation. And he's gone on to even greater things. Graduated with a double First, then top of Part III. Now a Fellow of Trinity College I understand. All predictable. All predictable…..and yet his parents were complete oiks. I hate to use that term, but do you know they wanted to take him out of school at sixteen and put him in an office. Can you believe it?"

"But what about Morgan?"

"Morgan, yes…… now that's a sad case, very sad….we let him down badly I suspect. One can't be sure of course. One never can be with a nasty thing like that. We used to argue about it terribly, both then and afterwards. I remember especially the day of the Manchester Grammar School match. We were sitting up in the pavilion, Kay, Major and I watching Morgan and Cotteridge batting for the school…….." He looked out of his window again, his mind drifting off into the past………

Cole eventually managed to coax the old boy back into the present, or partly so.

"Well you see we were speculating about what would become of those two brilliant lads batting out there for the school. It was virtually their last day at Harry's. Morgan's tactic of stealing the bowling from Cotteridge our star batsman infuriated the others, and that restarted the row over Morgan's plagiarism."

"Plagiarism?"

"Yes Morgan handed in this extraordinary essay for the James Watt Science Prize when he was less than sixteen: Einstein's General Theory of Relativity you know, Tensor Calculus, Differential Geometry, Christoffel symbols – the lot. No one at school could understand a word of it – nor in the physics department at the university. So they sent it to the professor of Cosmology at Imperial College. He said it was brilliant, quite brilliant. But when they told him it was by a fifteen year old boy he flatly refused to believe it. Flatly. Said it must have been copied from somewhere. So they declined to give Morgan the prize. Unfortunately our new Chief Master, the Reverend Hunt, got wind of it and accused Morgan of plagiarism, cheating. Morgan challenged him to locate the original source. And nobody could – not even the professor. If you ask me it was completely genuine – the boy was just too brilliant for us to comprehend. It's bound to happen sometimes, especially in a school like ours used to be. We used to draw the brightest boys from the entire West Midlands. After all there must have been more brilliant boys in that catchment area than lived in Restoration England, or Renaissance Tuscany. It follows that we ought to stumble across the odd Isaac Newton, or Galileo Galileii don't you think?"

"Sounds reasonable."

"Unfortunately the majority opinion held that Morgan must have been cheating – though he did have his champions, among them myself. And his English master claimed that he'd read the whole of Gibbon's Decline and Fall before he even came to school at age twelve. The Chief master was adamant however. He couldn't punish the boy of course; proof was entirely lacking. But I do know he wrote Morgan the most frightful leaving report. A real stinker. I'm surprised he got into any kind of university with that on his record. Mind you he didn't help himself – Morgan I mean. He was always outspoken, and he made the Reverend Hunt to seem a fool in public, which he certainly was, and I believe still is. Morgan was the boy who coined the nickname "Schweinhundt" for him; it sticks to this day. And now you tell me Morgan is suicidal?"

"I didn't quite say that….."

"What a tragedy. What did we do to the poor boy? You know I can see the two of them vividly now, strolling out to resume the innings after tea……….

……….I watched the umpires go out and replace the bails: then the opposing team in their white flannels, led by a boy who, they all said, would one day captain England. Finally Cotteridge and Morgan, talking as ever. I borrowed Major's binoculars to watch them stroll to the wicket amidst a ripple of applause from around the ground; Cotteridge very tall, willowy and lackadaisical; Morgan, powerful of buttock and shoulder, his bat like a toy in his hand. Cotteridge, at the non-strikers end, leaned elegantly on his bat, as a duke might rest on his shooting stick. At the wicket Morgan took guard then stood up to survey the field. Bat on his shoulder, his left hand on his hip, I noticed him glaring arrogantly at the fielders one by one as if daring them to catch him out. Quite unnecessary of course, quite uncivilised. That was Morgan all over; arrogant, combative, truculent, certainly not English. A Welsh pirate perhaps, like his infamous namesake……"

Some one entered with two cups of tea – recalling the old man to the present:

"I've always wondered what would become of Morgan. I wish he'd kept in touch – but you can't blame him can you – not after what happened. But in a way, you can't blame us either. We were Lilliputians perhaps, first faced with Gulliver. Just you tell him from me that anything that Cotteridge can do – in mathematics I mean – he could do better. You don't lose that kind of brain. But you can misuse it of course. Yes , and I now remember a third boy. Not in the same intellectual class of course, but they were like the proverbial Three Musketeers. What was his name…..yes I've got it; Cockle. That's it: Tom Morgan, Frank Cotteridge and Jack Cockle. They were inseparable. I wonder if they're still close friends."

As Cole was leaving the old man called him back:

"You know I was much in the minority. Why don't you talk to Harry Major. He's still Head of Physics. He'll have a very different point of view."

Major grew cautious on the phone when Morgan's name came up.

"Yes of course I remember the incident. Very awkward all round. Typical Morgan if I may say so. Brilliant but awkward. Of course Carter took his side – he's an old darling."

"And you didn't?"

" To begin with I did. After all he was my brightest pupil. Miles beyond the rest, even Cotteridge. That's why I consulted Professor Dempster, a true expert in the field. But his opinion was unequivocal. It simply couldn't have been written by a fifteen year old. That had to be decisive didn't it?"

"Is that still your opinion?"

"I've heard no evidence to change it. And from what you've just told me he's done nothing much since. Hardly the mark of a genius."

"He might have become disillusioned."

"That is to argue in a circle."

"So there couldn't have been a mistake?"

"It's always possible – but highly improbable. We had to decide on the basis of the evidence at the time. And as I recall he already had some bad marks to his name."

"Such as?"

"Violence for a start. Always fighting as a younger boy. Then he was banned from playing Rugby for the school after he deliberately dislocated some boy's finger in a big under-16 match. The boy's mother fainted. Then again he was opinionated, disruptive, arrogant…just plain insolent at times. He had this chip on his shoulder about religion as I recall. It didn't worry me, but it infuriated the Chief Master who taught the boys Divinity. Morgan should have had enough sense to keep his head low on that. But there was something inherently self-destructive about that boy, something….ungracious, erratic, unlikeable. Many of the staff, though not I, thought he was bumptious and conceited."

Just before Morgan was discharged from hospital Dr Cole came to see him again. He came straight to the point:

"As I see it you appear to be an extreme character. An ordinary life doesn't satisfy you. You need to challenge yourself, push to the limit, get the adrenalin flowing, live on the very edge. If I told you that that isn't normal it wouldn't help. You don't want to be normal do you?"

"I'd hate it!"

"Climbing was an easy way to supply the adrenaline rushes you seem to need. But it's all over. You may get your legs back but, from what the surgeon says, full control of the right foot is highly unlikely. So you'll have to forget about climbing altogether. What with the pain, and the loss of your obsession, you are going to feel suicidal."

"I do already."

" The only advice I can give you is 'Find an equally absorbing challenge. And find it fast!' With all that pain you are going to need a strong distraction. You've got to get your mind away from it, out of your body."

"Easily said."

"Easily said indeed. So what are you going to do? Take up macramé, or flower arranging?"

"I might as bloody well."

"You might as bloody well not. I think I'm going to be rude to you young man."

"Feel free."

"I think you are a coward."

"Oh?"

"I've made a lot of enquiries. The thing people all mention about you is your brain. 'He's brilliant' they all say 'Absolutely brilliant.' And if they know it, then certainly so do you. And if you do have a big brain you've got to use it. That's one of the few things

I've learned as a psychiatrist. If one doesn't use an extraordinary gift then it tends to eat you away from inside. That's why I call you a coward. You know your gift but you're frightened to use it. Just in case it turns out to be less wonderful than you suppose. Climbing? Pathetic. You might as well play golf. You've got a physics degree. Why not use it? Do something more challenging than climbing the piddling Matterhorn. A monkey could do that – without a rope."

CHAPTER TWO
MUSKETEERS

The Midland Red bus dropped Jack Cockle on a steep hill in the Worcestershire countryside. Apart from the roof of a large house, mostly hidden amongst the trees, there was no sign of life. But there was the red pillar-box just as Tom's mother had indicated. Mrs Morgan hadn't come yet because he was early.

Jack was extremely nervous. Tom had been his guiding star at school, as well as his closest friend. Even now, when he did something good, Tom's approval was what he most craved. And yet Tom had barely spoken a word to either him or Frank Cotteridge, the third of The Three Musketeers, since they had both gone to Cambridge while Tom joined the army. And God knows he and Frank had tried. There hadn't been a quarrel. Tom just never responded. It was as if he'd moved on, left his school years behind him. Frank reckoned Tom was bitter at the way he'd been treated: the headmaster's report that had barred his way into a decent university or an exciting profession. Jack felt it wasn't bitterness so much as reluctance to confront just what he had missed out on. That vindictive priest at school: Jacks hands clenched at the mere thought of The Reverend Hunt. Tom, if any of them, was the one who should be out there exploring the universe. He'd been the one who'd fascinated them, taught them about cosmology and stellar structure; and yet it was he and Frank who now had PhDs in astrophysics, while Tom was a cripple. Tom would never forgive them now. Either of them. Jack feared Tom's withering scorn more than anything. He should never have come. Never. But Mrs Morgan had been so distraught in her letter, practically begged him, shamed him even. Frank should have come instead. He had more self-confidence, could turn Toms ill moods with a jest or a riposte. Frank had been even closer to Tom than he had. They were more nearly equals for a start. But Frank had his pride too. Tom had spurned him once too often. Only last week, over the phone, Frank had said:

"If Tom can do without a friendship as close as ours was, then he's either very lucky, or very foolish."

Jack felt so agitated about the approaching encounter that he didn't notice the car pulling up until Mrs Morgan greeted him:

"Oh Jack I'm so grateful." She put her arms round him, then held him at arms length;

"It's years isn't it? Do they still call you 'Mussels'? Twm tells me you' are 'Doctor Cockle' now. Mind you haven't changed a bit." Jack picked up the underlying Welsh lilt. She was a striking looking woman with large dark eyes and a powerful nose.

"Neither have you Mrs. Morgan."

"I'm not Morgan now. Remarried. Mrs Straight would you believe. But call me Blodwen. Oh I'm so glad you've come Jack." and she began crying, resting her elbows on the roof of the car.

"Aren't I silly then." she blew her nose and laughed. "I never cry. Never. Let's sit in the car and talk on the way."

But when they got inside she didn't start the car. She sat gripping the wheel, twisting her hands.

"I have to confess Jack. I haven't told him you're coming. I meant to. Kept on screwing myself up. He's in such agony. The doctor told us. They can't do anything for him. Nothing. They're worried about suicide; and God knows I am. He sits there, with his teeth clenched. Hour after hour. Night after night. I can't bear it. So how can he?"

"I'm very worried about this meeting Mrs Morgan…I mean Blodwen."

"You must be. I'm putting you in an awful position I know. Awful. But even if it all goes wrong, and he hates me and you for it, things could hardly get any worse than they are now. Really Jack they couldn't. The psychiatrist said Twm's only hope is to become absorbed in something outside himself. To get obsessed."

"Tom always was obsessive."

"There you are then. It's your job Jack to get him obsessed. I'm counting on you boy. Surely there's something out there in that great firmament of yours. You and he and Frank never talked about anything else much. Not even girls as I remember. Daft you was, daft as tups."

The Straights' 'cottage' was rather splendid, half timbered with a long garden which sloped down to the South-West and a distant prospect of the Malvern Hills. They stood in the conservatory looking down the garden to where Morgan could be seen sitting in a deckchair with his back to them. His crutches were resting on the grass; there appeared to be a crow perched on his head.

"That's his jackdaw see; a young one that fell out of the nest in our chimney. Twm's teaching him to fly. That's all he's interested in, that and Ernie his funny new friend that he met in hospital. Ernie's going to die soon, Twm says, so they're building a model aeroplane together; it's to break some record. You better ask him yourself. Come on Jack; lets get it over with."

The jackdaw it was who first sensed their approach. It hopped onto the back of Morgan's deckchair and called out in greeting.

"That you Mam?" Morgan didn't turn.

"You'll never guess who's come to see you".

Morgan turned around as they approached.

" My God if it ain't Mussels." – he sounded ironic.

"How are you Tom?"

" As you see; totally fucked."

Jack was shocked by the gaunt face, the wasted appearance of the big frame. The jackdaw launched itself into the air and flew around calling.

"Stand still Mussels! He's checking you out. If he lands on your head don't bloody move. It means he approves of you. And if he really likes you he'll shit in your hair."

Jack stood petrified until the bird settled on him, the claws teasing his scalp. Blodwen fetched him another chair and Jack sat gingerly so as not to unduly stimulate the birds bowels.

"Relax Jack, we've got plenty of shampoo, haven't we Mam?"

"I'll get a pot of tea for you boys, and some barrabrith. And get that bloody bird out of his hair."

Morgan reached across until the animal hopped onto his wrist, up his arm and went to sleep on his shoulder.

"Taught him to fly myself. Not bad for a bloody cripple."

Jack was at a total loss for words, as he usually was whenever he and Tom first met. He picked up the book Tom had been reading, quoting the title aloud:

" 'Fluid Dynamics' by Landau and Lifschitz. It's a stinker I believe."

"So it is. Jack here didn't understand a word of it, did you Jack?" He fondly teased the animals crest. "But you learned to fly all the same, didn't you boyoh?"

"How do you know he's a boyoh?"

"Now there's a question. Does he look like a bloody Daphne?"

"You look awful Tom."

"I don't feel all that wonderful."

"Why the hell didn't you get in touch? Frank and I would have come at once."

" Frank? How is our Frank?" Morgan didn't sound very interested.

"He's landed a job with Bellfounder. You remember? He was your hero."

Morgan looked pained. Cockle resumed:

"Do you remember teaching us stellar structure at school out of Bellfounder's book?"

"A bloody genius."

"Frank's just landed this plum job with him at Cambridge. A three year Carnegie Fellowship, half at the Palomar Observatory in California."

"Clever old Frank."

"Frank sent a message. I met him at the Royal Astronomical Society meeting in Piccadily last week. He wants you to go up and stay in Cambridge with him. And he'll introduce you to Bellfounder."

Morgan didn't reply.

"Oh Tom why don't you join us now? Astronomy's so bloody exciting at the moment. Almost every week there's an amazing new discovery."

"Don't tell us."

"Well I *am* going to tell you." He rummaged in his haversack, "In fact I brought you a paper."

"I don't want to read it."

" There are these staggering new objects which Fred Hoyle has called 'Quasars'."

" I suppose I can't stop you."

"No you can't. Right now none of us astronomers can think of anything else. You remember those mysterious radio sources in the sky that were first picked up by radars during the war? Well some of them have finally been identified. A brilliant fellow called Cyril Hazard thought of an ingenious way of pinning down their positions exactly; wait until the Moon passes in front of one of them. You track the source with a radio telescope and note the exact moments, first when it switches off, and then again about an hour later when it re-emerges from behind the far side of the Moon. Since we know the Moon's track very precisely we can infer the exact position of the radio source."

"Ingenious indeed. What then?"

"You look to see if there's anything visible there; a star or a nebula say. In one case, '3C-273' it's called, Hazard found a comparatively bright star."

"And?"

"Hazard sent the position of that star to his collaborator Maarten Schmidt who works at the Two-hundred Inch optical telescope on Mount Palomar in California. Schmidt took an optical spectrum of it – which looked like no optical spectrum he'd ever seen before. None of the spectral lines was in the right place. For three days he was totally mystified.

Then it hit him. The whole spectrum had been shifted, by an absolutely staggering amount, towards the red. It's been redshifted as they say. You get the significance of that?"

Morgan looked puzzled:

"If it had been a galaxy, not a star," he responded eventually "I would have attributed the redshift to recession. Said the object was receding away from us at a speed close to the speed of light. And that the recession, in turn, was owing to the known expansion of the universe. Owing to that expansion the further an object is away the faster it appears to be receding. So your radio object must be a truly vast distance away."

"Precisely" Jack continued, "But it looks far too bright, ten thousand times too bright, to be situated so far away. It would have to be thousands of times more luminous than the most luminous galaxy ever seen."

"But you said it looks like a star not a galaxy."

"Yes it's a sharp bright dot in the sky, not a fuzzy nebulous thing like a galaxy."

"Then what the hell is it?" Morgan, forgetting the jackdaw, sat up intently.

"That's what the Royal Astronomical Society meeting was about in London. It was packed out. All the Brits were there of course; and radio astronomers from Australia; optical astronomers from California; and famous astrophysicists from around the entire world all trying to come up with an explanation. Bellfounder chaired the whole thing. He was masterly. What a brain! He even managed to put Fred Hoyle in his place once. Oh I so wished you'd been there with me Tom, you'd have loved it! All those brilliant minds throwing up ideas then shooting them down again. You had Fred Hoyle leaping up onto the stage and writing equations on the black board. Then someone else leaping up to contest them. And people in the audience getting to their feet and shouting. It was one long sustained argument that went on for five days and nights. Nobody wanted to leave in the evenings. Bellfounder practically had to throw us out. And Frank was in the thick of it all."

"Lucky bloody Frank."

" 'Lucky bloody all of us' you mean. 'Quasars', as Fred Hoyle calls them, are a problem we can all share Tom."

"You mean there's more than one?"

"Half a dozen at least. The Americans have just found one with three times the redshift of 3C-273! Frank gave a talk estimating that there must be several thousand in the sky. There was a big row about that, but in the end most people seemed to think Frank must be right."

"So what was the general conclusion?" Morgan accepted some barra-brith from his mother absent-mindedly , "I mean people must have had some ideas after all that discussion."

Blodwen winked at Jack as she returned to the cottage. Jack bit into his barra-brith which was a soft sort of fruitcake. Morgan fed some of his to the jackdaw which was now fully alert.

"He likes hard boiled egg, barra-brith, mature cheddar cheese and lean beef mince, in that order. I'm returning him to the wild. God knows where he's going to get barra-brith out there. What do you think of it?"

"Delicious."

"Mam's a fair Welsh cook."

"I never knew you were called Twm. It was always Tom before."

"It still is – to everybody else but mother. Obviously I had to anglicise it at school."

"What is on your birth certificate?"

"Twm Ianto Morgan. A real Welshie see. But I covered it up when we came to Birmingham. Saved bother. Mam was on pain of death to use 'Tom'."

Morgan raised himself awkwardly to his feet with the aid of his crutches, the bird flying into the nearest apple tree. Cockle could see the agony etched on Morgan's face.

"You stay here. Got to give this bloody leg a turn, otherwise it grows unbearable." He stumbled off down the lawn and into the kitchen garden with the jackdaw circling round his head calling excitedly.

When he came back Cockle could see that Tom was white as he collapsed back into his deck chair.

"What does it feel like?" he couldn't forbear asking.

"On a good day like a crocodile's jaws clamped on my leg. On a bad day, like its frying in scalding hot fat. Now about those Quasars. What is the most popular theory?"

"At the beginning of the conference it was supergiant galaxies."

"But that wouldn't account for the radio emission."

"No, not unless there was some additional source of relativistic electrons."

"Synchrotron emission you mean?"

"Probably. Or at least I think so. A lot of it was too complex for me to understand. But anyway it didn't matter in the end."

"Why not?"

"Because somebody reported that two of the quasars are varying in brightness on a time-scale of weeks."

"Phew!"

"Amazing isn't it. It means they cannot be larger than a few light-weeks across. They are far too small to be galaxies. A giant galaxy is a hundred thousand light years across. Vastly bigger. By comparison quasars are absolutely minute."

"So how come they are so bloody luminous?"

"Precisely. That has got everybody stumped. Even Fred Hoyle. At the end of the conference he said that entirely new physics must be involved."

They discussed quasars for hours, with Cockle trying to recall everything he'd heard at the conference. With that topic exhausted they turned attention to their mutual friend Frank Cotteridge. Morgan tried to deflect him, but Cockle wouldn't be turned aside.

"No Tom, you've got to listen. Frank is very hurt by your treatment of him. He thinks you're bitter; jealous even."

"I don't want to know."

"You're going to listen anyway. Just so I can tell him you're not envious."

"It seems I've got no choice."

"You are a shit Morgan, sometimes. What has Frank ever done to you? Except admire you, follow you and even…..even love you. Now I've said it."

"Well?"

"Frank's turned out to be all the things you would have wished to be yourself. Admit it. Starred First Class Honours in the Natural Sciences tripos at Cambridge. Then top of Part Three – the Mathematical Physics diploma. That's an absolute stinker Tom. I nearly failed it. Even you would have struggled. Even you. They pile it on top of you, week after week, until you can barely stand. But Frank did OK. He beat them all. Then a brilliant PhD with the Radio Astronomy group at The Cavendish Lab. And the final accolade; a Fellowship at Trinity College where Fellows are more or less expected to get a Nobel prize in time. And on top of that he's won this Carnegie fellowship to work mostly in California, but partly back in Cambridge with Bellfounder. Isn't it wonderful? Go on be honest Tom. Isn't it?"

"I suppose so."

"Don't be so bloody grudging – or I'll tell Frank you're jealous."

"Oh all right then. And I am jealous. Why shouldn't I be. Here I am crippled, teaching a bleeding jackdaw to fly while Frank is at Mount Palomar using the most powerful telescope in the world. Yes, if you want to know, I am hideously, unbearably jealous. That's why I can't face Frank."

"Well thank God that's out in the open. Perhaps now we can move on."

Morgan waved his crutch : "Frank can, I can't ."

"Look Tom, Frank is the Great White Hope of British astronomy. But what does he say about you? You know you could knock spots off Frank when you tried. You know you could. And so does he."

"That was true. It was." Morgan gave a ghastly smile, looking into the past.

"Well then. You still could. Now's your bloody chance. That leg could be the making of you. You can't climb any more, so turn your mind to something sensible. Astronomy for instance. You were crazy about astrophysics."

"And how the hell am I going to do that? I've got a lousy Two-Two degree in physics from Bangor University. I've got a headmasters report so toxic that I've never passed an interview when a report was required. Did I tell you how I found out?"

"No."

"It was in the Army. After I'd done my basic training I applied for a commission. I had to go before a preliminary panel, USB or Unit Selection Board it was called. When it was over they called me back into the interview room and the major in charge said: 'We're passing you Morgan, to go forward to the full War Office Selection Board. We're doing this in spite of the worst headmaster's report any of us can remember. Indeed it is so bad as to be obviously unbalanced, even vindictive. What did you do to him? So we've decided to set it aside. But we think it only fair that you should know about it. By law I cannot show it to you because it was sent to us 'In Confidence'. But if I should now read extracts of it aloud to my colleagues here, and if by chance you should happen to overhear, I think we will have stuck to the law' And so he read it out. I wish I could remember the exact words – but it went something like this: 'This boy is a born trouble-maker and barrack-room lawyer who will infect and suborn any community which is misguided enough to make him a member. Superficially brilliant, with a facile gift of the gab, he is only too able to lead his fellows astray. Indeed it is this evil, almost irresistible influence which makes him so very dangerous....deee dah deed a deed a deed dah....' "

"He's never forgiven you Tom, not since you humiliated him in front of the class."

"I didn't humiliate him. I argued with him."

"I know. I know. But he didn't stand a chance. You made him seem like a buffoon."

"Not deliberately. He condemned himself by his own ignorance and inconsistency."

"I remember. But he got his revenge – the vindictive swine. And behind your back too. It was decent of the army board to tell you."

"Wasn't it though. The major said, with a smile 'Any boy so capable of leading his fellows astray should be capable of leading soldiers into battle'."

"Well it doesn't matter any more Tom, it really doesn't. If you were to apply to do a PhD nobody would ask for a headmaster's report. All they'd want to know about is your research potential. And what the hell would 'the vindictive vicar' know about that?"

"But who else would?"

"Frank for a start."

"Frank?" Morgan sounded incredulous.

"The word of a Fellow of Trinity College Cambridge counts for a lot, believe me, when it comes to scientific matters. And you know what Frank thinks about you."

"He thinks I'm a shit. And perhaps he's right."

"He thinks you've got a great scientific and mathematical brain, and an even greater imagination. And he's right. Even I can see that and I'm not in Frank's league, or yours. More important still you've got that driving curiosity which takes you out exploring new territory. It was always you who lead us Tom. Frank and I followed - when we could. Remember that time you went mad about seismology? Showed us how one could miraculously infer the properties of the Earths core from the mathematical properties of earthquake waves on the surface? You read every book on the subject in Birmingham Central library."

"And in the university. I sneaked into their library as well."

"And you taught us all that fiendish stuff about the 'Theory of Elasticity' using Cartesian tensors."

"So I did. That was fun."

"Research *is* fun Twm, the greatest fun there is. Imagine waking up in the morning and thinking 'All I've got to today is research'; spend the whole day wondering how Cepheid stars pulsate – or whatever. And being paid to do it. And to go on doing it all your life. But it's hard too; hard hard hard. At the end of a months' intensive thinking you may have got nowhere at all. Or worse still find you have been following a false lead, and have to start all over again."

"Sounds like rock climbing." Morgan mused.

"I wouldn't know about that. But you've got to be dogged, tenacious and ambitious to win. That's my weakness. I love learning about things, reading what others have done. But I want to lead a balanced life too. Frank says you need an obsessive bastard like Morgan to be really good at this game. Which reminds me." Cockle reached in his rucksack and handed Morgan a book.

"It's from Frank. There's a note inside from him. It's a prepublication copy of Bellfounders latest book on stellar evolution and structure."

Morgan opened it. A one page letter headed 'Trinity College Cambridge' fell out. He read :

'Tom
      I heard about your accident and I'm sorry. You may need something challenging to read, so here it is: Bellfounder at the summit of his powers. As far as stars are concerned he's left us nothing left to do. I

helped in a small way with some detailed calculations and am proud to appear in the Acknowledgements.

I now have rooms in Trinity, just down the corridor from where Isaac Newton used to live. My life here is exciting beyond my wildest dreams, but not beyond yours, as I recall. I shall always have you to thank for all this. Always. You inspired Jack and I. Please come to stay. If I could share with you some of the excitement at The Institute of Astronomy here it would be a small recompense. I could even introduce you to Bellfounder, your old hero and now my boss. Heal quickly. Your old friend

        Frank Cotteridge.

Morgan skipped through the pages of the book, which were covered with mathematical formulae:

"Here, you have it Mussels." he pushed it towards Cockle "More in your line of country."

Cockle shook his head in despair and refused:

"You are a shit Morgan, you really are. If I was Frank I'd tell you to shove it. But I've got a better idea. Why don't you read the bloody book and find something wrong with it. That's just the kind of thing you used to do all the time. Then you can write back to Frank and tell him his great Bellfounder has feet of clay. You might even be able to forgive Frank then."

"You've become a hard man Mussels."

"Now you're a cripple I can bully you back. It's my turn for a while."

"Since you're here why don't you tell me about yourself. You've moved to London University haven't you?"

Cockle talked about his research on stellar atmospheres, about the department of astronomy at University College London where he worked, and about computers, which were coming in to use for scientific research. He explained:

"Everything has changed since Sputnik Tom, everything. The Yanks are pouring money into science, especially anything to do with 'Space Research', however remote. My boss for instance has got more money from the US Office of Navel Research than he's got any idea what to do with it. Money for travel, money for computing, money for assistants, money for new graduate students. My God, that's an idea! Why don't we get you on to his grant?"

After Mussels had left, the crocodile's jaw clamped on to his leg tighter than ever. As if sensing the pain Jack flew out of the orchard to perch on Morgan's shoulder. He chirred affectionately, softly fondling the lobe of the man's ear in his beak.

"There's a lovely boyoh." Morgan tickled the crest of his head. Wood pigeons cooed from the oak wood on the far side of the lane. A blue damsel fly landed to drink from the bird-bath which his mother always kept filled. He would have been in the Dolomites by now.

Suddenly Jack tensed, perceptibly pinching Morgans shoulder between his claws. A flock of jackdaws was sailing overhead, flying home to roost for the night in the bell-tower of Alvechurch Abbey. Then one of them spied Jack and called to his fellows. The whole flock wheeled and circled frenziedly, emitting distress calls, obviously calling to their brother below.

Jack twisted his neck to look upward with one eye, his whole crest ruffled with alarm. The distress calls grew louder, ever more insistent, the birds came lower, twisting and tumbling through the sky:

"Jack Jack Jack......" they cried.

Morgan tottered to his feet.

"Go on boyoh. It's time to go. Now's your moment. Go with them. They're your kind. Not me. Go........"

He shook his shoulder so vigorously that Jack flew into the air, circling above Morgans head, visibly disturbed and confused.

"Go on boyoh, you're a bird not a bloody man. Be free. Go with them. Join your kind."

And almost despite himself Jack began to rise until he was lost among his swirling sweeping calling fellows who wheeled as one and sped away to the South West.

Morgan slumped back into the deckchair, tears flowing freely down his cheeks. He wiped them away on his arm.

"I'll miss you boyoh. I'll miss you so bloody much."

Absentmindedly he picked up Bellfounder's book and turned to the first page.

CHAPTER THREE
PAIN

The Salts' workshop was a study in total absorption. Ernie Salt, wearing his watchmakers magnifying glasses, was doing something exquisitely precise to the control mechanism of the model aircraft which stood on the long table before him. He wore a red woollen bobble hat to cover his recently operated on skull. At the work bench behind him his father Bob Salt stood, with his back to Ernie, working on the aircraft's engine using calipers and a miniature lathe. On the far side of the model, opposite Ernie, Morgan was spraying the wingtips scarlet. He had Bellfounder's book open beside him and would jot in the margins during the intervals while he waited for the latest coat of paint to dry.

Following the bad news about Ernie's tumour the construction work had had to be speeded up. The tumour had apparently now started growing downwards towards the brain's core, rendering it inoperable. Whether Ernie had months to live, or just weeks, the surgeons couldn't say. Outwardly at least Ernie didn't appear to care, just so long as he could challenge for the World Endurance Record in time.

Morgan's intervention in the project had proved to be a mixed blessing. Too clumsy to help with the precision engineering, he had been assigned to the theoretical aerodynamics, which had turned out to be very hard, though fascinating. What he had learned there had proved to be something of a surprise for all of them. The model's performance would be dominated not by Profile Drag, in other words by imperfect streamlining, but by Induced Drag which was quite another thing entirely. To keep itself up the aircraft wing had constantly to deflect air downwards, just as a helicopters rotor blades did. But that deflection cost the aircraft energy, which showed up in the form of 'Induced Drag'. The only way to reduce that drag, so Morgan had learned, was to increase the aspect-ratio of the wing – that is to increase its span in relation to its area. That had the effect of deflecting more air down, but at less speed. The Salts had of course known this but they also realised that a higher aspect-ratio wing would weigh more, and so reduce the amount of fuel that could be carried, and hence the endurance, by a corresponding amount. Their design had therefore been a compromise. What Morgan had been able to add was a detailed mathematical calculation which appeared to show that Ernie's original Mark III design was sub-optimal, that the wing-span was slightly too short. The Salts couldn't understand Morgan's mathematics while Morgan couldn't gainsay the Salts immense practical experience and past success. In the end the matter had been decided by Ernie who, at amazing speed, carved two one-third-scale models out of balsa wood, one of each design, and tested them in the home made wind-tunnel, a long structure made out of tea-crates which occupied the full length of the workshop. The results slightly favoured Morgan's theory, but not in the decisive way he had claimed. As Bob pointed out, the results were really inconclusive because model-carving could never be perfect. They had left the final decision to Ernie who had thought about it for twenty-four hours, before opting for the extended wingtips. It was, he admitted, a gamble, but if it came off to the extent that Morgan had calculated, then they could hope to break the record by such a significant margin that it might stand for years. Without the wingtips the improvement could be at best marginal, leaving the record vulnerable to an early challenge. The modified airframe, now dubbed The Mark IV, would however cruise at a lower speed, which meant that Bob now had to modify and retest the engine so as to extract the maximum of performance. With Ernie's tumour it was, as they all realised, an unpredictable race against time.

Morgan was grateful to the Salts for sharing their obsession with him. Not only did he like and respect them both, but in their company he felt much less of a freak than he did in the company of normal people. More importantly he'd learned that mental absorption was the one way to keep the crocodiles teeth at bay. The jaws didn't clamp the less but the agony seemed to come from further away so that if he couldn't forget it, at least it wasn't the foremost preoccupation of his mind.

This lesson had led him to pick up Frank's present, the Bellfounder book on stellar astrophysics. He had found it hard, but utterly fascinating. Bellfounder had collected together his own and other peoples research to present the full life-history of a typical star, from its birth condensing out of the interstellar gas, to its final dissolution either as a dimming White Dwarf, or in a titanic explosion, depending on its original weight. Every step of the story was mapped out logically, using mathematics, from the fundamental physics involved, to the inevitable conclusions: the initial condensation out of diffuse gas; the stabilisation at immense internal temperatures and pressures; the outward flow of heat by means of radiative diffusion; the replacement of energy thus lost by thermonuclear reactions started up in the core; the gradual transmutation of light elements there such as Hydrogen into heavier ones such as Carbon and Iron; and then the final dramatic episodes in the star's life when it eventually ran out of fuel. First the enormous swelling into a Red Giant which would radiate so prodigiously as to hasten its own end; pulsation perhaps and expulsion of the outer envelope leading to subsidence of the core into a dim dying White Dwarf star, finally arrested in its collapse by the weird effects of Quantum pressure. But for heavier stars no such peaceful end was possible. In their case Quantum pressure would never be enough to overcome the effects of Relativity, and a catastrophic collapse into a superdense Neutron Star must ensue, with the associated release of gravitational energy leading to a titanic detonation of its outside layers which would briefly be seen half way across the Universe as a Supernova explosion. Not even Neutron pressure could however sustain the cores of stars five times or more massive than the Sun. According to theory their collapse, once started, could never end. Dragging Space and Time and light in with them they were doomed to become the hypothetical Black Holes of popular legend. Whether such exotics really existed, remained for professionals a matter of continuing debate.

What intrigued Morgan was the intellectual adventure involved. No one had, or ever would, see inside a star. No civilisation had, or ever would, survive for long enough to see out the history of a single star. And yet by means of logic and inference, applied to the flimsy clues appearing on a stars surface, men like Bellfounder had travelled down into the stellar deeps, into furnaces billions of degrees hot, and emerged to explain not only a star's past history, but to predict the entire fascinating story of its future and eventual fate. Such men, and women, used mathematical physics like a magic carpet to carry their minds away on such adventures as no Marco Polo or Ferdinand Magellan ever imagined. And they returned with jewels of understanding more precious by far than Spanish argosys loaded down with rubies and gold. Starting from imagination and speculation, they proceeded by mathematical calculation to inference and prediction, and they closed the cycle by comparing their predictions with minutely precise observations of real stars sailing by in the cosmos. And when prediction and observation didn't exactly match they knew that some argument along the chain of inference was wrong and had to be modified. And so by a process of trial and error they finally reached truths both profound and certain. For instance no one could have imagined, nor did imagine, that The Origin of the Elements could be the subject of human understanding. How could puny man ever explain the origin and proportions of the very atoms out of which he was made? And yet, according to Bellfounder, Fred Hoyle and his collaborators had done just that in 1957, the year that Morgan had left school for the army. Geoff and Margaret Burbidge, Willy Fowler and Fred Hoyle had together calculated the rates at which stars cooked light elements like Hydrogen into heavier elements such as Oxygen, Nitrogen, Carbon, and Iron and then expelled them back into general circulation. And there could be no doubt about the results because they matched so perfectly the relative proportions of hundreds of atomic isotopes observed either in the laboratory or in the visible outer atmospheres of stars by astronomers using spectroscopes. It was a staggering achievement, an adventure of the mind exceeding in audacity the boldest voyages of mankind. Bellfounder's book made Morgan realise that even had he and Steve conquered the North Face of the Eiger it would have been a pimply, almost laughable achievement beside the work of true modern adventurers like Hoyle. He realised that, while he had been swinging about on rock faces from ropes, Frank Cotteridge and Jack Cockle had aimed much higher , climbing above him into the stratosphere and far beyond. Back in 1956 he'd taught them all that was known about stars from Eddington's famous book "The Internal Constitution of the Stars". By 1959, when he left the Army, the whole picture had changed, thanks in part to the advent of the digital computer and the nuclear accelerator. Astrophysicists like Fred Hoyle and Martin Schwarzchild had used computers to solve the equations of the stellar interior much more generally than Eddington and his successors had been able to do by hand, enabling them to include the nuclear physics recently discovered in accelerators, and so to travel onwards far beyond the early pioneers. In their computers they 'saw' hypothetical stars swell up into Red Giants just like the real stars in outer space. They 'saw' stars cook new elements, and then blow up as titanic Supernovae, spilling those same elements back into the interstellar medium, out of which new stars, enriched in oxygen, carbon and gold, might form.

Patrolling the jungles of Malaya, then climbing in Snowdonia, Morgan had missed it all. He hadn't read a single serious astrophysical paper for eight years, or even learned to program an electronic computer. Thus Bellfounder's book had come as an astonishing revelation.

But it was hard, hard, hard. Bellfounder made no concessions to the inexpert reader. Whole branches of modern physics and theorems in advanced mathematics were taken as understood. The dreaded phrase 'It is trivial to prove......' had several times cost Morgan more effort to overcome than climbing the crux pitch on 'Cenotaph Corner'. It was exhausting yet exhilarating to claw his way past each difficult inch of the climb only to find even steeper, even more holdless pitches stretching to seemingly impossible overhangs far above. He had persisted because he knew, from his climbing experience, that where one man could lead, another must eventually be able to follow. And the views he gained over Space and Time exceeded by far what he had ever enjoyed from the dizziest ledges of Llanberis Pass or the Dolomites. Nights of agony had turned into nights of struggle and adventure. He had never extended himself so far or, he realised, enjoyed himself so much. Indeed he dreaded the end of Bellfounder's book, now only a dozen or so concluding pages away.

He had conceived a project, and mostly carried it out: to translate Bellfounder's work, not into a popular volume excised of all mathematics, for Bellfounder himself was famous for doing that, but into a mathematically solid but still readable version, accessible to any hard-science graduate. It would contain all the physics and mathematics necessary to carry the argument through, but not in the forbidding format employed by Bellfounder. It was as if Bellfounder had set out to prove just how hard the subject was, and just how much cleverer he was than ordinary mortals. Morgan aimed to do the opposite: to find the simplest, most intuitive arguments at every stage; to replace the steepest mathematical techniques with simpler approximations, but avoiding none of the real physical difficulties when they formed an essential part of the argument. So as he read he had been making notes, then transcribing them into a 'shadow' book as he went along. Finding the 'simple way up' had been a challenge in itself, and a very rewarding one, because once he had found it he felt he had had a much firmer understanding than one reached through Bellfounder's mathematical convolutions alone. It seemed to him tragic that an intellectual achievement as profound and as satisfying as anything in Bach or Shakespeare should be reserved for a tiny coterie of expert astrophysicists. It would be all very well Bellfounder writing a popular account, as he certainly would, but it would be like a critic's account of a symphony, with no possibility of the reader ever hearing the music; in other words a profoundly dissatisfying experience. Morgan felt, or rather hoped, that his own account would be accessible to anyone with an A-Level in Physics. He aimed to write explanatory appendices to cover all the required modern developments in quantum and nuclear physics, and where necessary mathematics, that were not presently taught in a good modern grammar school. Indeed he was aiming his book at Frank Cotteridge and Jack Cockle, as the sixth formers they had been at school with him eight years before.

There was one impasse however. Bellfounder's book was an account of many mens work; of Eddington's at Cambridge in the twenties; of Chandrasekhar's at Chicago; of Saha's in India; of Cecilia Payne's at Harvard; of Opik's in Ireland; of the Burbidges with Hoyle and Fowler in California; of Martin Schwarzchild's at Princeton. All had added profound chapters to the story. Cecilia Payne for instance had proved, while still a student, that stars were mostly made of Hydrogen, which came as a complete shock to her seniors. Chandrasekhar, at the time even younger than Payne, had argued, against fierce opposition, that the heaviest stars must end up as Black Holes. What Bellfounder had added himself, was a masterly explanation of why all stars, as they began to run out of fuel, must swell up into colossal Red Giants. Hoyle and Schwarzchild had seen in happen in the computer, without understanding why. It was Bellfounder, with his elegant mathematics, who had finally pinned the explanation down.

It was this last crucial piece of the puzzle which Morgan was struggling to turn into a comprehensible argument. Out of Bellfounder's fearsome theorems, lemmas and corollaries he was aiming to distill a direct, intuitive proof. It had to be there. Bellfounder claimed it was 'obvious', but had then concealed it in a pyrotechnic display of the differential equations and infinite series for which he was rightly famous. Morgan accepted that sometimes such pyrotechnics were necessary to close out every avenue of doubt or possibility of refutation. Watertight mathematical arguments, like legal arguments, sometimes required contorted technical language.

Bellfounder's theoretical work on Red Giants had been hailed around the astrophysical world, earned him the Presidency of The Royal Astronomical Society, and ultimately a knighthood. Red Giants produced most of the light in the Universe and were scattered like orange jewels among the constellations. Betelgeuse in Orion was ten thousand times more luminous than the Sun while Antares in Scorpio was so colossal that had it been sited at the centre of the Solar System, in place of the Sun, the Earth would have been orbiting beneath its surface. Man could never claim to understand the stars until they had explained Red Giants – and that had been

Bellfounder's towering achievement. Morgan's ambition was now to translate that achievement out of arcane mathematics into arguments that ordinary scientists could understand.

Having broken down all the remaining stellar astrophysics in such a fashion Morgan had been confident he could do the same with Red Giants. But it had proved infernally, impossibly hard. Whole nights and days of calculation, hundreds of pages of differential and integral equations and jottings, had all ended in blind alleys and nightmare thickets of algebra from which he had had to retreat.

As they worked on the Mark IV Morgan explained his progress, or rather lack of it, to the two Salts. Both were born engineers and fascinated by science. Bob Salt, a small man of nearly sixty with iron grey hair, and steel rimmed spectacles, was a 'toolmaker', one of the master craftsmen of the engineering profession. He built or modified the machine tools at Austin's Longbridge factory, the largest car-making plant in Europe. His lathes, grinders, mills, stamps, drills and presses carved the engines and chassis out of which hundreds of thousands of cars, vans and lorries were made every year. He had done his apprenticeship at the Rover works in Solihull, worked for a while with Frank Whittle on the first jet engine, and then been transferred during the war to Rolls Royce's West Midland aero-engine plant. He loved precision instruments of all kinds, from chronometers to jet engines, and could talk for hours in his Midlands accent about the men who had first invented or constructed them. One story in particular struck Morgan. They were talking one night about the Mark IV's tiny diesel engine when Bob had remarked:

"Yow probably dain't realise it but the Second World War were won not very far from 'ere. Not ten mile in fact."

"Radar?" Morgan hazarded a guess.

"That's what they all say o'course. An' its partly true – the cavity magnetron devised by Randall and Boot at Birmingham University. Partly. But what's the good o' knowin' where the enemy is if yow can't defeat 'em in aerial battle? What were the good of Hurricanes and Spits knowin' the enemy was a'coomin' if the Messerschmidts could then shoot 'em down?"

"And ' Ernie added "The Jerry airframes was jinerally better'n ours – at the begginin' at least. Weren't they Dad."

"Ar they was. There were a lot of propaganda about the Spit in the British press, we needed it to keep our peckers oop, or so the government reckoned. And she weren't a bad machine. Good climb rate, manoeuvrable at 'igh altitude. But she only 'ad bloody machine-guns when the Jerries 'ad explosive cannon. And the engine cut out when she dived. A carburettor she 'ad when Mercedes Benz 'ad moved on to fuel injection, a better system for an interceptor aircraft manoeuvring at 'igh g. But the Rolls Royce Merlin engine beat the 'ell out on 'em in the end. And Jerry never twigged out why. We 'ad it in nearly all our best aircraft: Hurricanes and Spitfires, Mosquitoes , Lancasters and Mustangs."

"So what was the secret?" Morgan wanted to know.

"It was sort of an accident reelly." Bob looked up from his lathe, dreaming about the past. "It were this engine fitter at Rolls Royce. 'is job was to strip down Merlin engines after they was knackered. All them piston jobs was worn out after several 'undred hours and needed reconditioning. New bearings and piston rings for a start. Well 'e noticed as all the gear wheels in the used engines was worn asymmetric – as you might expect because they always run in the same direction, with the loading on one side of the gear teeth. So they allus 'ad to be replaced. So 'e begins a wondering;

why not cut the teeth asymmetric in the first place? Then when they revved 'er up, an' the load come on the gear wheels they'd mesh perfectly, not be out of true."

"Sounds obvious when you think about it." Morgan agreed.

"Ar" Ernie intervened "But that's joost it. Nobody did."

"So our bloke" Bob resumed "decided to do somethin'. They 'ad this 'Suggestions Box' like they 'as in most factories. So 'ee writes down 'is idea and posts it off loike, not expectin' to 'ear of it ever again. But the follerin' week the Chief Engineer called 'im to 'is office, and 'ee says 'Let's give 'er a go.' An' they did. An' the first time as they cut the asymmetric gears, and that was a bit of a game an' all, an' revved 'er up on the bench, they got thirty per cent extra power. Thirty per cent! Think on that. Put 'em miles out in front of Mercedes Benz. Miles. German aircraft was never competitive after that. Never. More power meant more speed, more altitude, more range, more armour, bigger guns, and much 'eavier bomb loads. Lancs could carry ten-ton blockbusters."

"That chap ought to be famous." Morgan remarked.

"Ar 'e should an all." Ernie agreed "If any one man won the war 'e did."

"But it 'ad to be kept secret." Bob countered " Dead secret. If the Jerries 'ad ever found out they'd 'a done the same thing inside of a week. And we'd 'a lost the 'ole advantage."

"But after the war surely."

"It were all forgot. What with the atomic bomb and that. Anyroad in Britain engineers never get the credit." Bob sounded slightly bitter. "The British press prefers dashing public school pilots. We dain't want 'oiks getting' the credit now do we? Might 'ave to pay 'em properly."

"Now dain't start on that again Dad. Tom knows what a bloody Red yow are."

"I ain't a Red son, I'm a radical. S'quite a different thing….."

And so they were off into the political debates which sometimes lasted half the night. only to start hotly again next day. Bob Salt was a shop steward at the Austin factory, battling with the bosses on the one hand, and with communist sympathisers on the other. Morgan found it hard to discern which of the two sides Bob detested the most. The bosses he despised for their short-sightedness and greed, the communists for their stubborn inability to change their minds. And both for their susceptibility to cheap propaganda. Ernie, for undecipherable reasons, was a high Tory.

The following morning, when Bob was at work, Morgan raised the Rolls Royce story again. Ernie was conspiratorial:

"If yow ask me it was our dad 'oo made the discovery. 'Ee denies it but our mam is certain it were 'im. She say as 'ee told 'er , in confidence loike, at the toime. Then 'ee clammed up. Official Secrets Act perhaps."

"But why would he keep it a secret now?"

"Yow guess is as good as moin. But 'e were there workin' on engines, in that very plant, at that very toime an' all. And if he knowed it were someone else 'eed 'ave give their name now wouldn't 'ee? To give them the honour loike. But 'ee never 'as, and I've asked 'im many a toime. If y'ask me 'ee can't. 'Ee can't cos 'ee dain't know that name, and beein' Bob Salt 'ee can't lie. It was 'im orl right."

"Surely the Official Secrets Act doesn't apply now?"

"'Course not. No I reckon they 'ad some kind of row at Rolls. That's why Dad left. They never give 'im the credit when they should 'ave, and 'eed never ask for 'isself. Barmy if yow ask me. It's 'is pride see. Ee'd rather be bitter than ask for what is 'is b' right. An 'e despises all them toffee nosed manager types with their titles and decorations."

Whether or not Bob Salt was "The Man Who Won the War" Morgan had come to like and respect him. For a start there was the way he had dealt with his son's illness. Largely thanks to Bob, Ernie was no tragic figure. He had an utterly absorbing if unconventional 'profession', a strong sense of self-respect, and a high, almost world wide reputation in his chosen field of aero-modelling. He was sometimes invited abroad to give lectures and demonstrations. As Bob said:

" 'Ee 'as a good life 'as our Ernie. Only thing as he's missed is love and a family. But his sisters kids are that fond of 'im, and 'ee of them, it's loike he's their second father. Saves 'is pension to take 'em on holiday every year 'ee does. 'Ee taught 'em to swim at the seaside last year. Imagine that."

Then Bob had a mind independent to a degree that Morgan had never encountered before. He read widely, particularly in politics and history, having educated himself in the Birmingham Public Library system. He read 'The Daily Worker', the 'Economist' when he could get hold of it, and the 'Daily Telegraph' to 'Find out what the enemy is oop to.' The Telegraph drove him into alternate fits of derision, fury, and laughter:

"Joost yow listen to this" he exclaimed one night, barely able to contain his rage. "A headline on the front page of this poisonous rag reading 'BIRMINGHAM CAR WORKERS KNOCK OFF TO ENJOY THE SUN'. Says it has brought the entire British car industry to a halt. That Britain's exports are threatened. That foreign importers are cancelling orders for our vehicles right and left. That the country is facing financial ruin, An' o course it's all on account of 'Communist Shop Stewards aiming to bring capitalism to its knees' Now what d'ye think on all that Tom?"

Morgan's political opinions had been forged in an elitist grammar school atmosphere which, if anything, was more right wing than its private school equivalent. Then in a county regiment where most of his fellow officers, educated in minor public schools and Sandhurst, had regarded flogging as too good for most trade unionists, never mind trades union leaders. And the left-wing politics at university had appeared so puerile to Morgan as to drive him even further to the right.

"What yow think on that Tom?" Bob Salt repeated.

"Well I have to confess we take the Telegraph at home. Always have. And my stepfather was reading that article out to us at breakfast, It does seem pretty scandalous – you've got to admit."

"God bloody preserve us." Bob looked up to heaven, holding his palms together in mock prayer. "A university ejjicated fellow like you and yow can believe this childish pap. What 'ope have we got? What bloody 'ope?" He danced about the workshop in despair. "Dain't yer ever use your critical faculty? What they bleedin' taught you at that posh school you went to?"

"I couldn't see anything wrong with the article. And surely they wouldn't just lie?"

"Lies! There's more'n one ruddy way of lying. Lying by omission. Lying by distortion. Lying by exaggeration. Lying by implication. It's all bloody in 'ere." He threw the Telegraph down on the bench in disgust. Then he waved his finger angrily at Morgan:

"Yow've worked in a car factory. 'ow are the blokes paid?"

"By 'piecework'. They get paid by the amount of stuff they turn out. So many shillings for so many holes drilled. And so on."

"Right! And 'ow long hours does they work?"

"Far too long if you ask me. Most of my fellows worked 8 to 6.30, then all day Saturday, and Sunday mornings as well.'

'An' why should they do that?"

"I suppose because they needed the money. Our pay packages were only thirteen pounds or so a week. Not enough to bring up a family. Not by a long chalk."

"And yow were prepared to believe, just because yow read it in this rag, that 'ard working men loike that would just knock of for some lunch-time sun? Any road, since they're on piecework, it'd all coom out of their pockets, not out of the bosses. Not out of the governments. Not out of Britain's. Isn't that true?"

"I suppose it must be."

"But there's no mention of that in 'ere is there? Oh no. And why should such men work inhuman hours? Why should factories pay double toime of a Saturday and triple time of a Sunday? Why should they?"

"I don't know."

"I'll tell you why. Because of sheer bloody management incompetence. They never plan ahead. Everything comes as an emergency. Not enough floor space. Not enough machine tools. Not enough training. Not enough stocks for emergencies. Not enough workmen. Not enough bloody investment. That's what. 'Ow we beat the Germans I've no bloody idea. All, I can tell yow as it weren't British industrial management. We out-produced the Jerries only 'cos we 'ad all our women working and they dain't. An that's the only lesson our management learned. Lots 'o cheap labour, and overtime. Yow jist watch the Jerries knock the British motor industry for six. Not by better engineerin' but by better management."

Bob came round the table and wagged his finger at Morgan as if he was personally responsible:

"D'you know as the export manager of Austin Motors hates travellin'? I know fer a fact that 'ee 'ates foreign food. What does 'ee do? 'e takes a brief-case full o' sandwiches with 'im, what 'is missis 'as made. Won't eat wi' them foreign business men. Oh no. 'Ee locks 'isself up in 'is 'otel bedroom with 'is bleedin' sandwiches. What impression is that going to make? 'ow are we going to sell buses and lorries to the foreigners if we treat 'em loike that?"

"I have to say" Morgan replied "That that sounds like cheap union propaganda."

"Ar I suppose it does." Bob smiled " I can't prove it neither. It just 'appens to be true.'is secretary told our Beryl. Tell yow what though; I can prove to yow as every word in this Telegraph article is a lie. That dispute is takin' place at the Burman's plant where they make steering boxes and gearboxes for us at the Austin. I've been on their shop stewards committee an' I'll show you the papers tomorrow."

Bob brought them. Morgan was able to verify for himself that the dispute at Burmans was of long standing. The plant, which was only twelve months old, had been constructed without a thought to proper ventilation. Inside, over a thousand men and women, working at piecework rates, crouched over machine tools turning out components. In warmer weather the temperature in the giant shed soared above one hundred degrees Fahrenheit. Men sweated like slaves, unable to keep up with their piecework schedule, although they tried. They lost wages if they didn't. Women fainted and fell into their own whirling machinery. The factory couldn't keep up with its contracted demand and had to enforce even more overtime. All that was needed was to hinge the glass panels in the shed roof, and open them in hot weather. But this the management had flatly refused to do. Time and again the plant manager, a stripling of twenty six, had refused to even meet union representatives, let alone discuss the matter.

" The amount of money" Bob explained "Were trivial. It were less than the cost of one extra days overtime. But this little creep in charge daresn't lose face dares he? After all 'is only qualification for the job is 'ee's married to the boss's daughter.

Eventually there were accidents. Stands to reason. One feller put a 5-bit drill straight through 'is hand trying to keep up. Then, in a temperature of one 'undred and seven degrees, a young lass bending over an auto-lathe pitches into it face first. Yow should see 'er face now. It'd put you off your lunch for a week. But that's not the worst on it. She fractured 'er skull and no one can say if she'll ever recover properly. So that was it. The shop stewards committee sent this to the manager – 'ee still wouldn't meet 'em mind. 'Ee dain't even 'ave the grace to visit 'er in hospital, though it were 'is fault entirely. I can tell you that wi' a face loike hers nobody'll marry 'er now."

Morgan read the union's ultimatum. It began with a reasoned plea to have the roof windows opened – pointing out the cost to everyone of lost production. It concluded:

"If, within one month of this letter, work has not commenced on the ventilation, the shop stewards committee will have no choice but to call out union members whenever the temperature in the shed rises above 100 degrees Fahrenheit. Members will turn off their machines and wait outside, at their own expense, until such time as the internal temperature falls back again below 95 degrees. We do so reluctantly, but we can see no other way of preventing further serious, and possibly fatal, accidents."

"Dain't you think that's reasonable?" Bob wanted to know.

"Well of course it is." Morgan agreed "In my opinion they shouldn't go back until the temperature is well below ninety. Or even lower."

"Did you see any o' this in the Telegraph? Did yow? Course not. Doesn't fit their manifesto of 'Lazy British workmen' and 'Agitatin' commie unions' does it? They bloody know what's really going on, know for sure. But they ain't going to say it are they? It's 'British workers knock off to enjoy the sun.' An' yow believed all this rubbish young Tom" he hurled the Telegraph on the floor:

"Yow should be ashamed on yourself."

"Oh dad, come on. Lay off Tom. It's nuthin' to do wi' 'im."

"Ee's been to university hasn't ee? And that posh school. What's 'e bloody learned if 'e ain't learned to recognise low grade propaganda for 'isself?"

Ernie tried to switch the subject back to aerodynamics, but his father was relentless:

"I'll bet all them teachers at that posh school yow went to was Tories. An' yer soaked it all up. Even the kids from workin' class 'omes. Specially them. They didn't want to feel left out did they? Oh no; they sucked up all that snobbery like babbies. Turned on their own class. All wanted to go to 'Orxford' and mix with them toffs. Why didn't yow go Tom? Yow'd 'a been at 'ome there. All them dreamin' spires and arf-priests an' Daily Telegraph readers."

"Dain't yow take no notice of our Dad Tom. 'e's just upset about that girl what fell in the lathe, ain't yer Dad. He went to the 'ospital on behalf of the union to try and get some compensation for 'er an 'e ain't been the same since. Mum says he's enough to turn the milk sour. An' 'e is an all. Knock it off Dad. We gotter lot of work to do."

The conversation lapsed but the following day Morgan found himself looking at the family Telegraph a lot more thoughtfully than had been his previous wont. And when he was leaving the Salts the following night Bob silently pressed a parcel into his hand. When he got home he found it contained a book entitled 'Battle for the Mind' by William Sargent. It was about brainwashing. Despite himself, Morgan found he couldn't put it down. It was to start an argument with Bob Salt that really never ended.

Henceforth the workshop became the site of three separate endeavours; Ernie's attempt to finish the Mark IV; Morgan's attempt to finish his simplified précis of Bellfounders book; and Bob's attempt to re-educate Morgan:

"Yow'm a tragedy Tom. All that sitting at lessons and listenin' to teachers droning on for twenty years 'as destroyed yer critical faculty. Yow gotter learn to question yer own opinions. Base 'em on evidence not fairy stories." Bob loved nothing better than a good argument.

For his part Morgan found the older Salt a stimulating irritant. An autodidact himself, who'd had no father to challenge his opinions, he began to relish the nightly jousts with Salt the elder.

At the same time the Bellfounder project had ground to a halt. He'd failed to simplify Bellfounder's Red Giant theory. Worse still he was coming to the belief that he couldn't understand it at all. Some subtlety in the chain of inference had evaded him. He borrowed Ernie's drawing board and traced out a flow-chart of Bellfounder's byzantine logic. And to clarify his own thoughts he used it as the basis for his own explanation of the subject to the two Salts. They didn't need higher mathematics to follow the general line of argument. He also lectured them on the newly discovered 'Quasars' , which they found fascinating. He had the material to do that because, almost every week, he received copies of the latest papers on the subject from Jack Cockle.

"Seems to me you ought to concentrate on them quasars." Bob opined "They're brand new and exciting. Yow could make your reputation there. I reckon as how you should concentrate your research on them. You'm more likely to make enemies tryin' to explain an old subject like stars. For a start your Bellfounder chap might not like it."

" It's all very well to say that" Morgan replied "But before you can do research you've got to have a new idea. And I've got no original ideas about quasars."

A week later, thanks to another batch of papers from Jack, he did have an idea. A very original, an extraordinarily exciting idea which robbed him of all sleep.

CHAPTER FOUR

DISCOVERY

Morgan had been able to get rid of his crutches and hobbled about with the aid of a rubber-tipped walking stick. His left leg and foot were back in perfect working order whilst his right leg was fine down to just below the knee. That meant, even if they were to eventually amputate the lower part, he would be adequately mobile with the aid of an artificial foot.

There were times when he thought of amputation longingly. He dreamed that with the lower leg removed the agony he felt would suddenly cease. He dreamed of waking up from the anaesthetic to float away on painless ecstasy.

But it was only a dream. An amputated leg could be even more painful. According to the doctor 'phantom-limb' pain was one of the most dreaded and incurable agonies known to medical science. While his own agony was almost unendurable at times, he could at least look forward to a time, two or three years ahead maybe, when the nerves would stop re-growing and the causalgia would hopefully abate. In the mean time the crocodile had its teeth firmly clamped through skin and bone. And at the same time the electric fire strapped to his skin grilled the flesh like scorching bacon. He'd been to see a pain specialist who had suggested a 'stimulator'. An electric device was placed against the flesh where its vibrating rubber teeth were designed to actually stimulate the pain nerves to the point of exhaustion. It certainly stimulated Morgan's agony to such indescribable levels that the subsequent 'relief', if there was any, never managed to compensate.

The way the weight was dropping off his bones was a measure of his suffering. At the time of the accident he'd weighed fifteen stone and ten pounds exactly. As a rock climber he couldn't afford to carry a spare ounce of flesh and so he had exercised and dieted to keep his weight to the absolute healthy minimum. Even so fifteen ten was far too heavy for a top climber to bear on his toes and fingertips, and Morgan had had to reconcile himself to the fact that he would never become an acrobatic artist of the rock face such as Joe Brown or Don Willans. He had tried to compensate with his enhanced load-carrying abilities; his climbing partners had referred to him as 'The Donkey' because, especially on long Alpine climbs, his strong second-row forward's frame enabled him to bring up valuable extra ropes, ironmongery, food and bivouac equipment. Now he weighed less than thirteen stone and, despite eating like a horse, his weight was still melting away. To a small extent it was due to the wastage in the paralysed lower right leg. With no nerves to exercise them his calf muscles had simply wasted away. But his whole body was being consumed by his suffering. When he could bear to look in the mirror he could see his ribs and clavicles sticking out, while his elbow and knee joints appeared unnaturally large because they had lost the normal muscle surrounding them. The pain specialist said 'it was to be expected in the circumstances' and reassured him that his flesh, or most of it, would return one day. To prevent his calf-muscle evaporating entirely he paid weekly visits to an outpatient clinic where the physiotherapist attached electrodes to either end of the muscle and made it twitch involuntarily.

Sleep was his only respite from the otherwise relentless torture. But sleep came grudgingly. When he turned off the light and tried to close down his mind the pain would grow remorselessly until it inhabited his entire being. So he gave up darkness altogether and sought distraction in books and calculations. Then sleep might catch him unaware for an hour or two before he woke again, even more exhausted than before. When he shaved in the mornings the face looking back at him in the mirror was gaunt, almost emaciated with pain. 'This can't go on.' he thought: 'I can't go on.' But he had to. And somehow or other he did.

Bellfounder's book had come as a lifesaver. First because it had revived his old fascination with astrophysics: the idea that, almost by pure thought alone, man could delve deep into the universe and come out with real understanding. Second because of the masterly, almost poetic way in which Bellfounder marshalled the arguments, weaving classical physics, quantum physics, and astronomical observations seamlessly together. Almost every page contained a delightful surprise; a discussion of atomic ionisation would suddenly double back to an earlier chapter on opacity and then leap forward to the unavoidable conclusion that stars at certain stages of their evolution must pulsate in a very particular way – which accorded exactly with the observations. And then it was hard, extremely hard. Bellfounder made no concessions. He was writing for his equals, seeking out adamantine certainties that would last down the centuries so that men of the distant future might still appreciate his work, as they still appreciated Euclid's. And Morgan had always enjoyed pitting himself against hard things: the most fearsome climbs, the deepest dives, and the fiercest mathematical problems. It was in his nature to push himself to the limits. He realised it had something to do with ambition and ego; a reassurance to some deeply held but otherwise unadmittable belief that he was special, that someday he would, indeed must, reach a pinnacle where no man before had ever dared to go. But it was more than that. Stretched to his very limits he made discoveries about himself that otherwise he could never have imagined. Like the time when, as a schoolboy, he'd fought a professional heavyweight boxer at Butlin's holiday camp. He'd been terrified of making a fool of himself in front of a crowd of thousands of jeering Teddy Boys, to say nothing of the girls who worked with him in the camp kitchen. But when he had turned to face his brutish looking opponent, and the bell sounded for the first round, there had been nothing he had wanted more to do than fight, and fight to the death if necessary. And he had fought the man to a standstill, enjoying every hook and savagery. But it wasn't the outcome that mattered to him, but the wonderful discovery that beyond fear there lay a completely new world of gladsome battlery. Without that fight he would never have known that under his civilised exterior there lay a radically different Twm Morgan. Only by pushing himself to the very limits could he find out who he was, what he was really made of. Now Bellfounder's book had stretched him in a completely different and far more satisfying way. Stretched between the stars and the atoms on a slender thread of mathematics he had heard, carrying from another world, the horns of elfland faintly blowing And he knew, with rare but absolute certainty, that this was a sound he would crave for all his life. It was his call. It sang to him like the remembered scent of the nascent stream called out to the homing salmon.

When he closed Bellfounder's book he picked up his pen and wrote to Frank Cotteridge:

Dear Frank

I want to thank you, from the bottom of my heart, for your inspired present. At a very bad moment it has reminded me of what I loved, what I could and should have been, and what I foolishly threw away in my feud with Schweinhunt. He didn't beat me; he didn't need to; I beat myself.

Even more foolishly, I threw you away too, my closest friend. It was in no way your fault. You had done, were doing, and will do, all the things I had imagined and dreamed of for myself. I couldn't bear that you were so successfully living my ambitions while I was shut out of them by Schweinhunt's revenge. As you know I scarcely remember my father. I possibly needed one to kick the shit out of me from time to time. Now I have acquired one, an improbable foster father called Bob Salt who I see most days. But Bob makes me want to talk about myself in a way I have never talked to anyone else before. For instance I told him all about our life at Harry's, and in particular about our friendship, yours and mine. He didn't say anything at the time, but a week later, as is his wont, he delivered himself thus: 'Yow Tom' he says 'Yow'm a great fool. Yow'm a peculiar sort o' chap at the best of toimes and there's not many as'll ever bother to understand you. Then providence gives yer Frank, another mad bugger if you ask me, but an identical twin to you in 'is head. Yow and 'e shared everything, talked about everything, fought over everything. What a wonderful piece of luck to find each other. Most people never get a present loike that. Never. And yow won't get another one loike 'im neither. It dain't happen twice in a loifetime. And what yow done yer silly bugger? Yow'm thrown Frank away loike an empty fag packet. Yow'm a bloody fool, and that's a fact I ain't going to argue over. Only Frank could've understood as yow needed Bellfounder. Yow dain't deserve 'im. 'e's far too good fer you.'

I find that Bob is usually right about people, and I'm sure he's right this time. I don't know if you can forgive me but I want us to be friends once again. You invited me to Cambridge, and I'd like to come, mainly to see you, but also if possible to meet your boss. Having read his wonderful book I'd love to meet Bellfounder in the flesh – if only for a moment.

And talking of the book I'm enclosing a roneoed copy of my much-simplified version of it. I'd value your comments. Unfortunately it still lacks a simplified version of the argument for a Red Giant phase in stellar evolution. I find Bellfounder's arguments about that as obscure as they appear to be brilliant. We can talk about it when I come - if you'll have me.

Mussels has been enthralling me with stories of the amazing new quasars. How lucky you are to be working on them yourself. I want to hear all about your research and what it is like to use the giant Two Hundred Inch telescope on Mount Palomar. In the old days, when I dreamed about astronomy, I dreamed about using that particular telescope more than anything. And it hurts like Hell to think I never will. But I know all about pain now and I'm not envious any more of you. Perhaps I can share the thrill with you at second hand.

Looking forward

Tom

That was the letter he wrote. But somehow he couldn't bring himself to post it.

Completely stuck as he was on the Red Giant problem Morgan began, in the long sleepless nights, to take an increasing interest in quasars. Every fortnight or so thick envelopes would come from Mussels in London containing the latest papers on the subject. These were real research papers, published in journals such as 'Nature' and 'The Astrophysical Journal' of a kind that Morgan had never encountered before. They were written by professional research workers in the front line of discovery, and aimed mainly at their rivals and peers. They assumed readers already had wide knowledge of the background, and employed so much technical jargon that sometimes Morgan couldn't understand the titles of the papers, let alone the contents. Titles such as 'Interferometric positions of flat spectrum 408 MHz. sources.' hardly whet the palate. Nor, as an undergraduate scientist, had he ever been exposed to such cryptic research communications. Fortunately however Mussels had, here and there, appended explanatory notes in his pathologically neat handwriting: 'A bombshell- if correct'; 'Coded attack on Cambridge Radio Catalogue'; 'A premature claim for glory'; 'But it all depends on isotropy, i.e. shining equally in all directions'. As Morgan's understanding of the technical terminology increased so he began to understand two things. First that quasars posed a threat to the whole of contemporary physics; that an enormous scientific revolution might be lurking just round the corner. And second that astronomy was viciously competitive. Despite the cryptic language it was clear that the authors were in a race for fame, even immortality, and were happy to trip or elbow their competitors aside. To Morgan, an arch competitor himself, it made astrophysics even more exciting. His teachers, both at school and university, had portrayed science as dispassionate, scientists as disinterested philosophers. But to judge from the quasar controversy, this was obviously nonsense. Astronomers were hurling criticisms, ideas and observations at one another like tribesmen in the heat of battle. One paper would often be a direct attack on another, questioning the data and undermining the conclusions.

Broadly speaking there were two camps. There were those who believed that the quasar redshifts were 'cosmological', that is to say a consequence of the general expansion of the entire universe. They argued that the light from quasars was so highly redshifted because quasars themselves lay in distant outposts of the cosmos, outposts receding away from Earth at velocities comparable to the speed of light. 'How ridiculous', their opponents replied; 'To be so far, and yet look so bright, requires enormous luminosities beyond the power of physics to explain. There must be' they argued 'Some other, some unspecified origin for the redshift of their light.'

Morgan was intrigued by this last possibility. As a long-standing enthusiast for Einstein's General Theory of Relativity he knew that light escaping from strong gravitational fields could also be redshifted. He was familiar with Einstein's fearsome calculation, a calculation which had been confirmed by observations of certain super - dense White Dwarf stars. But their redshifts were minute compared to the redshifts of quasars. Having nothing better to do he dusted down his notes from his schoolboy romance with Relativity. He wondered if, and how, Einstein's calculation could be modified to produce the much larger quasar phenomenon.

It was almost ten years since he'd studied General Relativity. The humiliating rebuff by Dr. Major, the physics teacher at school who he had once so much admired, had spoiled the whole subject for him. And, surprisingly, no one had taught The General Theory of Relativity at Bangor University. His tutor, when tackled on the subject, admitted that no one in the Physics Department understood it. He'd defended his colleagues by pointing out that The General Theory, quite unlike Special Relativity, was of interest to no one but astronomers, and he doubted whether there were more than half a dozen people anywhere in Britain who were truly conversant with it. If that was still true then Morgan felt he might have a head start in tackling quasars. Frank might know all about the observations but, at least at school, he'd given up on the fearsome mathematics.

Wandering through his old notes Morgan fell in love with the subject all over again. Einstein's central idea was so bloody beautiful; he'd arrived at his eponymous

Field Equations not by elaborate physics, but by demanding such mathematical generality that only one set of equations could be found to work. The equations simply comingled out of the air, proclaiming their own uniqueness, their own inevitability. They were one of the greatest coups of the human imagination, belonging with The Sistine Chapel and The Messiah. And what was miraculous, after such a philosophical conception, was that they actually bloody worked. The precision of their fit to the observed advance in Mercury's perihelion never failed to stagger Morgan.

In two nights of struggle and calculation he recaptured the art of Tensor Calculus; he could contract tensors, carry out covariant differentiation, and manipulate Christoffel symbols. The whole symphony came to life once again like a long lost gramophone record.

At this point the vital Strittmatter paper arrived amongst another batch of reprints sent on by Jack. It was a very short note to 'Nature' pointing out that quasars were not scattered randomly across the sky but were concentrated in one preferred direction.

Morgan realised at once that the implications were enormous. To be so concentrated the nine known quasars had to be associated with some particular structure in the universe: but the largest structures were Clusters of Galaxies, a mere million light years across. That in turn meant that the quasars couldn't be much more than a million light years away, a mere trifle in comparison with the universe at large and with the distances implied by their redshifts. The 'Cosmological' hypothesis had to be wrong! The hypothesis that the redshifts arose instead in intense gravitational fields now seemed the only reasonable alternative.

Morgan was electrified; he gave up working on the Red Giant problem; he gave up going to the Salts; he even gave up sleeping altogether. He didn't wash, he didn't dress, he demanded his meals be sent up to his bedroom. His mother, realising that he was at least distracted from his agony, supplied trays together with copious ink and paper. The floor of his bedroom became covered with a snowdrift of screwed up paper balls that Morgan had hurled away in disgust. Meals were often left untouched. The room began to smell of unwashed body. When she protested he screamed at her to get out and leave him alone. His eyes were wild, his cheeks gaunter than ever, his face unshaven, his fingers covered in ink, his hair dishevelled. Was this the breakdown about which the psychiatrist had warned her? From his demeanour she found it impossible to tell whether he was possessed, miserably unhappy, or breaking into pieces. She forced him into taking a bath by refusing to fetch him any more writing paper until he did. But he was only in it a minute or two before staggering upstairs again stark naked and dripping, muttering to himself about 'radiative transfer'. Her husband, when consulted over breakfast said "If you ask me Tom sounds extremely happy" a judgement she dismissed as "Typical male nonsense."

The fact was that her husband was absolutely right. Morgan had never done anything as fascinating or as exciting before. Climbing in the Dolomites, fighting in the Malayan jungle, paled by comparison. He had the quasar problem in his sights and he wasn't going to give up until he had squeezed the trigger.

The Einstein part of the problem had turned out to be comparatively simple. When a particle or 'photon' of light escaped from a heavy body such as a star it lost energy like a man climbing the stairs. The energy so lost weakened the photon. Weakening a photon reduced its frequency, that is to say reddened its light. So far so good. With a large enough gravitational field you could then 'redshift' a photon as much as you liked. Einstein's equations led to a simple formula relating the redshift to the strength of the gravitational field from which it had escaped. The strongest fields known to science lay on the surfaces of White Dwarf stars, some of the most extraordinary phenomena in Nature. They were the glowing remains of dying stars more massive than the Sun, collapsed into volumes no greater than the Earth's. A million times denser than rock their interiors consisted of, or were thought to consist of, exotic supercrystals of quantum iron. Being so massive, and yet so compressed, the gravitational fields on their glowing surfaces were staggering. The strongest known structures, even diamond, would be crushed in an instant. Ordinary gas would be compressed until it reached a billion degrees and erupted into a thermonuclear explosion. Even so, photons escaping from their surfaces underwent redshifts of a mere hundredth of one per cent. To explain quasars Morgan needed redshifts of ten, or even fifty percent.

His first thought had been to compress White Dwarfs even further but, as Bellfounder's book had reminded him, this had been ruled out in the 1920s by the young Chandrasekhar. Travelling to Britain from India by ship the nineteen year old student realised that if you squeeze White Dwarfs too far they would collapse completely – possibly to become Black Holes. Chandrasekhar was one of the first to take account of Einstein's other theory, the Special Theory, as it affected stars. He'd found that if you compress a star too much its electrons would speed up towards the speed of light and become heavier in consequence, This extra heaviness would increase the self gravity of the star acting on itself, leading to irreversible collapse.

But, so Morgan discovered after days of fruitless calculation, there was an even worse problem with super-dense stars so far as quasars were concerned. He calculated that they would pulsate, rotate or whatever in a matter of seconds. There was no way they could vary on a timescale of weeks, as some of the quasars appeared to do. Every object controlled by gravity, whether it be a butterfly or a star, has a natural timescale dictated by its mass and size, and the natural timescales of dense stars were far too short. Reluctantly he had to abandon the whole idea of quasars as dense stars.

Returning back to Einstein's original redshift formula he was excited to find that there was an alternative, if unexpected way out. He wanted a huge gravitational field, to provide the redshift effect, but a relatively low density to avoid the Chandrasekhar collapse. The solution he found was to postulate a giant "Superstar" weighing ten thousand million times as much as a normal star, and with a diameter one hundred thousand times larger than the Sun's million kilometres. The mass and size would provide the requisite redshift while the comparatively low density would provide timescales in agreement with observed quasar variations.

But there were two challenges to face. Would his Superstar have the luminosity of a typical quasar, supposing it to be situated at the distance of a nearish Cluster of Galaxies – the maximum distance permitted by their preferred direction in the sky? And would they be stable against both collapse and explosion?

Morgan's hypothetical Superstar was just that, an ordinary star, but of titanic proportions. In other words it was a supermassive globe of gas held together by self gravity. The great mass of overlying material would squeeze the gas in the centre to the point where it would heat up to no less than a trillion degrees. Since heat always moves from a hotter to a cooler place the interior heat would leak outward to the surface and be radiated into space. How luminous the Superstar would be depended on how easily the heat could leak out: rapidly through a transparent material, slowly through an opaque one. Morgan decided to calculate the opacity of his Superstar supposing it to be largely made out of Hydrogen and Helium, by far the commonest elements in the universe.

With the opacity to hand as a formula he set out to build a model of the Superstar's interior. Everywhere gas-pressure had to balance gravity: heat flow had to match temperature gradient – and so on. It was tricky but it wasn't impossible provided he used plausible simplification at every step. After all he only needed a rough answer. In astronomy, he knew, an answer was likely to be either roughly right if your hypothesis was correct, or wildly wrong if it was not.

Thus he was thrown into despair when the Luminosity turned out to be wildly wrong. His whole theoretical card-house had collapsed. He threw his writing pad at the wall and sank into exhausted sleep, a sleep that lasted for almost twenty-four hours.

During that time his unconscious mind must have been at work because when he awoke he knew with certainty what he had to do next. He checked back to the earlier opacity calculation, and sure enough a Boltzmann factor was missing through a careless mistake. Slipping back to the Luminosity calculation, but using the newly corrected opacity, he was dazed to find out that the Luminosity came out just right.

While the first calculation had been wildly wrong this second seemed to him to be too suspiciously right. Ignoring his mother's pleas to eat 'just something' for the first time in thirty-six hours he went back to the very beginning, and meticulously reworked the calculation from first principles.It was enormously satisfying when agreement turned out to be perfect. He had to be on the right lines. He had to be – otherwise it would all be too much of a coincidence.

Having eaten, slept again, and sorted out the wreckage of his room, Morgan set out to tackle the second, and what he had always known would be, the hardest step in the challenge. His model stood up, but it was like a pencil balanced on its point. The slightest perturbation and it would fall over, to one side or another. The question was whether his Superstar, if disturbed – as it certainly would be in the real universe – would return to its point of equilibrium. Or would it, more probably, either expand or explode, or else collapse into black oblivion. Morgan knew that Eddington had proved, long ago, that massive stars were predominantly supported by radiation pressure, not gas pressure, and so were inherently unstable. On the other hand no star was as simple as the ideal model which both he and Eddington had supposed. There would in practice be other complicating physical forces at work: convection, rotation, electro-magnetism and turbulence for a start. Each force could either add to or diminish the instability of a radiation-supported globe. Since that instability was so finely balanced, it might easily be true that one of the additional forces could do the trick – one way or the other: either break the camel's back, or keep it upstanding forever.

The mathematical task he faced was forbidding. He had to add the effect of the new forces to the equation, one by one, then he had to perturb his already complicated model solution ever so slightly, and see whether it would return to its equilibrium, or run away to destruction.

It took Morgan four days and four completely sleepless nights to calculate the instability effect of a single force. During that time he scarcely noticed the pain in his leg. Then he slept and tackled the second force, and so on. In three feverish weeks he'd done them all. Some, as he had suspected, were stabilising, some destabilizing. The combined effect – which is what he really needed to know – would only be calculable if he knew all the properties of a Superstar through observation – which was quite out of the question for the present. But what he could say, and that was the crucial point for now, was that Superstars with plausible combinations of physical properties would indeed be stable. They would have the luminosities observed, and they would appear to have redshifts as large as one liked.

When Morgan had finished, the sense of satisfaction was enormous. He knew something that no other man, perhaps no other mind in the universe, understood. The satisfaction was more acute than the exhilaration he'd felt on the last pitch of an Extreme climb, and far longer lasting. It was an oceanic, transcendental feeling that he could slip into happily when he woke in the morning. He could savour it in the middle of a conversation, retreat to it comfortably in a moment of especial pain. He felt as Johannes Kepler described in 1607 when, after fifteen years of lonely struggle, he decoded the Laws of Planetary Motion: " I have attested it as true in my deepest soul and I contemplate its beauty with incredible and ravishing delight."

In fact he felt 'real' for the first time in his entire adult life. Since he'd been a boy of only seven or eight Morgan had felt he was cut out to do something special, to be something special in life. For fear of ridicule he had told nobody, not even Cotteridge. And there were times when he'd chided himself for a megalomaniac, immature fool. But the feeling had never left him, if anything grown stronger with the years, torturing him, mocking him at every wrong turning or failure. Now he could acknowledge it, greet it as a friend. He was special, but only in a particular kind of way. He was an astrophysicist, a deep thinker about the cosmos, and a good one at that. He felt like a young albatross that, after nine months as an earthbound nestling, had soared into effortless windborn flight at last. From his new eyrie in the high air the entire world looked far more expansive, far more exciting. Everything was possible, everything could be done, great voyages and great deeds would be achieved. All his twenty-seven years had been a mere preliminary to this. He was, he always had been, and now he always would be, an astrophysicist.

His mother, his stepfather, and especially Bob and Ernie, had to be told about his new Superstars. He spent hours with each of them, drawing diagrams, and trying to find simple analogies which would make sense to them. While they couldn't understand his astrophysics they could all feel the profound change that had come about in Morgan. He didn't have to say anything; they felt it immediately. Blodwen in particular detected a sense of calmness, of self-confidence, of patience in a son who, from the very beginning, had been moody, impassioned, and unpredictable. She was thrilled for Twm, but wondered, at the same time, how long the new mood would last.

Armed with his new self-confidence Morgan sailed back into the Red Giant problem and tried to find a simple explanation for Bellfounder's theory. But he couldn't. It wouldn't yield. Not an inch. But whereas before he had become frustrated he now felt the equal of Bellfounder, was certain he could follow every pitch of the climb which Bellfounder had led. But when he came to it, he could not. Some vital, undetected move in the climb evaded him. Time and again he fell off the precipice and swung about on the rope.

It occurred to him, eventually, that rather than follow exactly in Bellfounder's mathematical holds, he should carve a way to the top on his own. He decided to manufacture an imaginary mathematical star that was running out of fuel in the centre, and show, by his own arguments, that it would swell up into a Red Giant. It was all a bit like his earlier work on Superstars, but with the process of thermonuclear -energy-generation added. He simplified the calculation because, if Bellfounder was right, the star must eventually swell up, irrespective of the details.

He failed. His mathematical star worked perfectly, but when he switched off the fuel it failed to swell. In fact, if anything, it shrank.

He assumed the problem must lie with his mathematical simplifications. So he changed them, built a second star, but it too failed to swell up. A third likewise. And a fourth. He simply couldn't get Bellfounder's mechanism to work.

Formerly he might have given up the problem as too hard. But now that he felt himself Bellfounder's peer, he would not capitulate. He sunk his teeth into it, like a bulldog, and carried on the fight.

It was always possible that in simplifying so much he had thrown out the baby with the bathwater. To demonstrate to himself that this was not the case he needed to manufacture at least one model star that was capable, under plausible circumstances, if not the ones envisaged by Bellfounder, of swelling to enormous size. This time he succeeded. As the interior fuel ran out the outer envelope was forced to swell dramatically. But it did so for artificial and unrealistic reasons, not at all those championed by Bellfounder.

At this point Morgan began to suspect that Bellfounder must be wrong. That somewhere, in his long chain of reasoning, a slip had been made. There was nothing for it but to reconstruct that whole chain, testing every link in it for himself.

Starting at the beginning he worked forward until he lost himself in a thicket of propositions, theorems and corollaries. So he used the old trick of working backward from the end towards the beginning. This too petered out in the very selfsame thicket of reasoning.

But now he was in a position to force himself into that thicket from both ends simultaneously, to the point where he might identify the very step in the argument that was causing all the difficulty. Doggedly he pushed in from one end, then from the other until he could identify the crucial step, that keystone in Bellfounder's arch of inference.

Having located that keystone his next task was to locate Bellfounder's argument for believing it to be sound. That proved fiendishly difficult because Bellfounder had divided the keystone argument into two stages, stage one in his Introduction, and stage two many chapters later amongst his investigations into dying stars.

This time Morgan was in a deckchair in the garden with the cat in his lap when the Eureka moment dawned. Bellfounder had made a mistake. Bellfounder had deceived himself – before deceiving everybody else. He had employed a deeply concealed circular argument. Near the beginning of the book he had "for reasons of simplicity" made a crucial assumption, an assumption which, much later in the book, he claimed to "have rigorously proved". It was, in principle, an undergraduate howler: but in practice, and in the particular circumstances, easy to forgive. Morgan threw the cat off his lap and did an awkward but transparently triumphant jig on the lawn.

There were now, he realised, two possibilities. The proposition itself might be wrong, in which case Bellfounder's whole Red Giant theory stood in tatters. Or it still might be right, and all that was needed was a sounder proof than the one offered in Bellfounder's book.

Morgan was instinctively attracted to the former possibility. To prove a great man wrong would be to make his own reputation. To merely improve the great man's argument would, if anything, bolster Bellfounder's reputation, not his own. In any case, from a purely logical point of view, it was generally far easier to disprove a theorem than to prove one. All one had to do was find a single exception where it didn't work. The discovery of a single triangle, anywhere in the universe, which didn't contain two right angles, would suffice to bring the whole edifice of Classical Greek geometry tumbling down. And after all his modelling experience it took Morgan less than half an hour to construct a single exception, a theoretical model star which should have been a Red Giant, according to Bellfounder's argument, but which so clearly was not.

He danced another lonely jig on the lawn, frightening the cat to hide among the raspberry canes. He was ecstatic. He'd done it not only once, but twice. He was not only an astrophysicist, but possibly a great one. In a single attack he'd brought down fundamental work which had dominated the whole field for a dozen years. The future was his, he was certain of that now.

"What yow a 'a goin' to do next?" Ernie wanted to know when the great news had been explained to him.

Morgan hadn't exactly thought about that. He supposed he would have to write a scientific paper, two papers in fact, and submit them to eminent scientific journals for publication.

"If I was yow" Bob Salt opined " I'd show 'em to your scientific mates first; Frank and that other fellow Cockle. Yow never know; yow might'er made a mistake."

Morgan tried to explain the impossibility of that; its preclusion by the interlocking nature of his argument. "It's like a jigsaw puzzle. You've only got one gap and one piece left over; it has to fit."

"I dain't know about that" Bob was stubborn "I do know as 'ow most revolutionary inventions dain't work; there's some practical problem as their designer aint foreseen. Like them Perpetual Motion machines. Sound good, sound marvellous in fact. But they dain't ever work."

Morgan rang up Jack Cockle, who laughed when he heard the news:

"I knew it Tom! I knew it. Didn't I say you'd find something wrong with Bellfounder's book? When I gave it to you?"

Morgan grudgingly remembered.

"You've always been like that. You couldn't be told anything at school. You had to verify everything for yourself. Every bloody thing."

Morgan tried to defend himself but Cockle interrupted:

"I'm not criticising. It's just you. And it's how a great scientist probably has to be. Never believe anything without the evidence. But if you're going to take on Bellfounder you'd better be right. I've seen him arguing in the Royal Astronomical Society, and he's ferocious. The other professors are all terrified of him – and rightly so."

Cockle explained that to get a research article accepted it would first have to be typed, including all the mathematics – which meant a specialised typewriter. Then the journal would send the article out to 'referees', that is to say to astrophysicists with a proven reputation in the specialised area of the article. They might suggest amendments, or reject his paper if they thought it unsound or not original enough. The author would then have chance to respond to the referee's criticisms, and amend the manuscript if he thought fit. The second round of refereeing would then commence. Only when the editor was satisfied that the paper was sound would it go forward for printing in a future edition of the journal.

Morgan was appalled. He'd been looking forward to becoming famous in a week or two.

"Good lord no" Jack laughed "Publication could take anywhere between six months and two years. Even three in tricky cases."

Morgan's plans for an illustrious career in astrophysics were shattered. If he had to wait another two or three years to even begin, he'd be nearly thirty, and too old altogether.

"It's not as bad as all that" Jack responded. "All you need is for someone who carries weight, a real professional, to approve your work. If he does, then his written reference could get you a studentship to start up the PhD ladder. Frank would carry some weight, and me, but we are only post-doctoral fellows. I tell you what though, there's a fellow at Birmingham University near you. He's retired now but he wrote an admired book on stellar astrophysics. His name is Dr Martin Johnson."

"I know it" Morgan exclaimed " 'The Physics of Stellar Energy and Decay'. Not bad. Not bad at all – though out of date by now. I read it at school."

"Well why don't you send him a copy. See what he has to say. A very nice chap. I've met him at the RAS."

Morgan's mother bought him a mathematical typewriter: "An investment." she said "To get you on your way. When you're a professor you can pay me back."

Morgan felt that day wouldn't be too far ahead. Five years at the most.

He wrote up two papers, one on "Quasars as Superstars." the other entitled "The Red Giant problem; still not solved." He sent copies to Dr Martin Johnson, to Jack, and two copies to Frank, one for himself, the other for his boss Sir Adrian Bellfounder. And into Frank's envelope he finally slipped the letter written several months before. Now that he'd really done something himself he felt that he and Frank could finally resume relations on equal terms. No others were possible.

CHAPTER 5
1965
TRINITY

Morgan lay in his bed at Trinity College Cambridge. The lights were out but through his open window he could hear, echoing off the ancient buttresses, the chimes of college clocks tinkling across moonlit quadrangles. No sooner had one finished chiming than another commenced. There were dozens, some near, some far off, each with its distinctive timbre and cadence. No two were in synchrony. The fastest had already chimed the quarter past before the slowest announced the hour. He was in agony as always, but extremely happy after his first thirty-six hours staying with Frank in the ancient university. Firstly because of his reunion with Frank. After a few moments of awkwardness at the station they'd fallen back, or so it seemed, into their old relationship, arguing from morning to night about everything under the sun, and indeed in their case, above it as well. He'd missed Frank profoundly – for almost eight years. How profoundly he hadn't recognised until now. Frank opened sunny pathways to his inner life that no one else apparently could. It wasn't just past history, or shared interests, but a fundamental and rare affinity of two souls. Everything was more fun when he could share it, and argue about it, with Frank. And Frank seemed to feel the same way. Indeed he'd said so. Their paths had diverged so far, so much had happened to them both, that it would have been natural, even healthy, to grow apart. But, on thirty-six hours evidence so far, it seemed they had not.

Then there was Cambridge itself, almost overpowering in its ancient scholastic atmosphere. Across this very courtyard were the rooms where Isaac Newton had invented calculus and first split white light into its spectrum of colours. The rooms where Hermann Bondi and his friends had invented the Steady State Theory of the Universe were just down the corridor. Frank had taken him for a pint of Abbot ale at 'The Eagle' where, only twelve years before, Jim Watson and Francis Crick had unravelled the structure of DNA. Then yesterday, at the Institute of Astronomy, they'd seen, but not spoken to, two of Morgan's own superheroes: Fred Hoyle the astrophysicist and Harold Jeffreys the geophysicist, taking coffee. Then, dining at High Table last night they'd encountered Bellfounder, also in the distance, entertaining The Minister for Science. At school so many of the wrong people had wanted to come to Cambridge for all of the wrong reasons, that Morgan had rather discounted the place as a haven, like Ascot, for the snobbish parvenu. In consequence he'd never shared with his mother, or with some of his schoolmasters, a sense of tragedy that he had never come here as an undergraduate himself. All the same it was awe inspiring to think that he might have been taught by titans such as Hoyle, Dirac, Bellfounder and Jeffreys.

Then there was Heffers bookshop. Heffers was an absolute Aladdin's cave for a bookworm like himself. Never mind the history, Morgan would have come to Cambridge simply to visit Heffers every day. Frank had practically had to drag him out by force, like a donkey reluctant to leave its feed.

What was even more poignant was the contrast between Cambridge and Birmingham. Not twelve weeks before he'd been a common worker in a car factory; clocking in at eight; standing all day in front of a vertical drilling machine; working frantically like an automaton to keep up with his piece-work rate; deafened by the sound of machinery, the clanging of completed components being hurled into metal pallets by his thousand fellow workers; half stunned by the smell of oil and swarf;

dehumanised and unable to converse with anyone because of the din. Cut off from the sky, the trees or anything of Nature, he had worked like a piston in the fierce glare of incandescent lighting which fell on rows and rows of identical machine-tools and identical fellow operators like himself. He, and all the rest of them, had been no more than slaves, chained to their machines by their need for wages, despicable creatures who had acquiesced in their slavery and denied their own humanity. Whereas here in Cambridge, men no different in flesh and blood, spent whole lives chatting about philosophy, or practicing choral music, or measuring the stars. He had crossed a gulf wider than the Pacific Ocean, wider even than a millennium of Time.

He was too excited to sleep. Today he was to meet Bellfounder, the man who would surely grant him his passport into this cultured and exciting world.

Frank Cotteridge had been horrified by Morgan's appearance when they first met at the station. The normally burly form was skeletal, the face emaciated, the eyes glaring out of his skull like the eyes of a holy man scarified by his own suffering. But there was a jauntiness too in his limp – and the old Morgan mockery:

"Frank Cotteridge – if I'm not a Dutchman. Or do I have to call you 'Dr. Francis Cotteridge' now? The secretary at your institute was absolutely insistent; 'We don't have a Frank Cotteridge here' she said, all hoity toity, 'Perhaps you are mistaken. We do have a *Doctor* Francis Cotteridge though.' '' But then he had thrown his free arm round Frank's neck.

The source of Morgan's jauntiness, as he quickly discovered, was Tom's confidence in his own new research. He talked about it constantly, switching between Superstars and Red Giants with bewildering speed.

"Hold your horses!" Cotteridge had had to insist in the end "I've no idea what you're talking about half the time. Remember I only got back from California the day before yesterday. Yes I've got your papers of course – but I haven't had time to read them yet."

Morgan looked stunned, as if the notion of anybody having something more important to do than read his work had never occurred to him.

"But I did give Bellfounder his copies before I left for California. And he promised to read them. I still think you should have kept the Red Giant stuff back. From what you told me over the phone it's likely to be a red rag to a bull."

In truth Cotteridge was worried about Bellfounders reaction. He should have read the papers himself before he left for California but he'd been so busy preparing for his observing run at Mount Palomar that he had had scarcely time to eat let alone wade through pages and pages of Morgan's mathematical astrophysics. He would, he certainly would, but there'd been no spare moment in weeks. Cotteridge was in any case trying to come to terms with BF himself. It had never been his intention to work for BF; he'd wanted to work with Fred Hoyle Everybody said that BF was a difficult man who intimidated his peers and dominated his collaborators. Colleagues had pointed out that Bellfounder's assistants rarely ascended to professorships themselves but tended to fade into obscurity. And it wasn't clear that he was actually Bellfounder's assistant anyway. The prestigious fellowship he'd won at Trinity College came with no official strings attached. It was Bellfounder himself, a very big noise in the college, who had intimated to Frank that his good fortune had come about entirely through his, BF's, influential offices, and that a quid pro quo was now expected. But was that actually true? Bellfounder's enemies, led by Fred Hoyle, referred to him as 'The Senior Wangler' – a jibe at both his mathematical background and his Machiavellian reputation. Whatever the justice of that nickname Bellfounder's patronage had certainly opened many doors for Cotteridge. In America Bellfounder was practically worshipped as a genius and Cotteridge had no doubt that his other, Carnegie award, with its generous allocation of observing time on the giant Two-hundred Inch telescope was more a tribute to BF than to himself.

It was a glorious summer morning as he and Tom cycled out along Madingley Road towards the Institute of Astronomy. Overnight mist hadn't burned away from the fields yet, while dewdrops in the grass beside the cycle lane decanted jewels of ruby, gold and emerald light. Tom, with his walking stick poking out of his rucksack, seemed as carefree as any man with causalgia could be. He took it for granted that Bellfounder would be convinced by his Red Giant work and bowled over by his Superstar Theory. And that was what was making Cotteridge feel so uneasy inside. Tom had no idea how professional astronomers operated. In Frank's experience they fought like cats and dogs, and never ever conceded defeat. With every furlong they cycled the idea of Bellfounder tamely capitulating to an amateur like Tom Morgan's ideas on Red Giants came to seem ever more ridiculous. So as Tom cycled along , chatting gaily, Frank was desperately trying to find a way to warn him of what might lie in store. And how to do it without disturbing their new-found friendship, or Tom's fragile equipoise. The collapse of his mountaineering ambitions and the agony in his leg were only tolerable because of his renascent astrophysical dreams. If he Frank was to bring them toppling down now, Morgan might never forgive him. But to send Tom into Bellfounder's office like a lamb to the slaughter was unthinkable too. He still hadn't solved this dilemma by the time they wobbled up the observatory drive and past the telescopes before chaining their bikes to a tree.

"What a fantastic way to get to work Frank. Bloody marvellous. Better than clocking in at the Longbridge factory with with thirty thousand other poor bloody slaves. And all you've got to do here all day is dream about the universe. You have no idea what a lucky sod you are."

"Oh yes I have." Frank was sharp "Remember Mum and Dad?"

"Good Lord I'd forgotten Frank. I even forgot to ask how they are. Forgive me. How are they? Are they still working at the Austin?"

"Dad died three years ago. Sudden heart attack. And Mum followed him a year later with lung cancer."

"Oh Jesus Frank! What can I say….."

Morgan trailed his friend into Fred Hoyle's new Institute of Astronomy, a low-slung, sunny building. Frank's office, which he shared with an absent American astronomer, had a floor-to-roof window which looked out over some flowerbeds to a field. There was a blackboard covered with equations, loads of books and astronomical journals, a microscope and, on Frank's desk, thick packets of punched cards held together with rubber bands.

"What on earth are these?' Morgan picked one up.

"My word Tom you are a cave-man. They're computer cards you chump. We program our computers with them."

Morgan stared at the cards, utterly puzzled as to how they could be of any use:

"And the microscope? I thought you were an astronomer."

Frank laughed:

"Come on. Pinch Schwartz's chair and I'll show you my research project."

Cotteridge began by showing his friend a photo of the Cambridge radio telescope out at Lords Bridge:

"Martin Ryle's group uses that, first to find cosmic radio sources, and then to measure very accurate positions for them. They give me those positions and I plot them on an optical atlas of the sky." He reached up to a shelf and brought down a square two-foot wide photographic print of some piece of night sky. It was a negative, showing hundreds of black stars and galaxies imposed on a white sky. He placed it on the desk and handed a small magnifying eyepiece to Morgan.

"My God" Morgan exclaimed "I can see millions of tiny little galaxies like germs on the film. The smallest ones must be enormous distances away?"

"Yes and No. Yes, in the sense that they are indeed four hundred million light years away."

"S'truth. That means their light is older than the oldest dinosaur" Morgan looked back through the eyepiece with increased respect.

"But on the other hand they have redshifts of only about zero point one. In other words, thanks to the expansion of the universe, they are receding away from us at zero point one, or ten percent of the speed of light. Some of the quasars we're looking for have redshifts of zero point five. They're five times farther away still, and receding at nearly fifty percent of the speed of light!"

"Not if my Superstar theory is right." Morgan laughed, glad to be in the thick of it.

"No. Well I don't know about that." Frank avoided the challenge. "Lets look at a quasar and then at its spectrum."

He looked thoughtfully at the print again and pointed to a tiny dot, a single dot among thousands:

"Take a look at that. What do you see?"

Morgan looked through the eye-piece:

"It's much brighter than the faintest galaxies. Maybe a hundred times brighter."

"And?"

"It looks more like a star than a galaxy. In fact exactly like a star. Just pointy, with four diffraction spikes sticking out of it. Whilst the galaxies are all oval, or disc like, and they're spread out on the sky."

"Exactly. Hence the name 'Quasi- stellar radio star' or "quasar" as Fred Hoyle has dubbed them. But don't use that name in front of Bellfounder. He hates it. Just use 'Stellar Radio Sources' or 'Stellars.'".

"How do you know this isn't just an ordinary star?" Morgan tapped it with his finger.

"First because it's a radio emitter, and it lies exactly on top of the measured position of a strong radio source. Ordinary stars don't emit radio. And second, and more important, look through the microscope here."

Morgan sat down at Frank's desk and peered through the microscope.

"That" said Frank "Is the spectrum of that very star. I took it last week with the Two Hundred Inch."

"But it's tiny – absolutely minute. I can hardly see anything."

"That's because a spectrum needs a thousand times more light than just a simple picture. We daren't stretch it out any more. If we did the the signal would be lost against the noise in the photographic emulsion – caused by the grains."

"What signal? I can't see anything."

"If you look hard, very hard, you'll see three slightly darker patches. They're emission lines. You don't see those in stars."

Morgan stared at the tiny elongated smudge within which individual dark photographic grains were visible. There was one patch only minutely darker than the rest. Was it a signal, or just a random extra grain? He was incredulous:

"You mean to say that's it? All our wonderful theories, even the expansion of the universe, hanging on pathetic little smudges like that?"

He looked up and stared accusingly at Cotteridge as if he were an imposter.

"That's the name of the game Tom. Digging the weakest of signals out of noise. That's all the universe gives us. We try to make the best of it we can."

They talked and argued excitedly for an hour before someone stuck a head round the door and said "Coffee?"

Morgan found himself standing in a sort of open library amidst a press of about thirty people, mostly about his own age, all discussing astronomy. He learned that even quasars were old hat compared to the new buzz - the 'Microwave Background'. Apparently two radio engineers in America had accidently discovered, but a few weeks ago, a whisper of short-wave radio radiation coming from all directions in the sky. Cosmologists had seized upon it as the first solid evidence that the Universe had actually expanded out of a superdense, super hot state. When Morgan gravitated toward a group around Fred Hoyle, the famous astrophysicist was expounding on the subject in his thick Yorkshire accent:

'It's a daft idea if you ask me – the whole universe growing out of a single explosion. It's no better than The Book of Genesis. Nobbut magic. The 'Big Bang' I call it. What was going on beforehand?"

"Yes" piped in one of his young interlocutors "But what about the new Microwave radiation? How do you explain that?"

"Dust" Hoyle replied. "Dust in space, in between the galaxies. Dust absorbs light and re-radiates it at its own temperature. I've worked it out. The dust temperature out there should be only two to three degrees Kelvin. And that emits microwaves exactly as observed. There's no call for this Big Bang nonsense."

Morgan was dragged away from the fascinating discussion by Frank.

"Come on, it's time to see Bellfounder."

As they walked through the gardens towards Bellfounder's solitary house in the observatory grounds Frank, now nervous himself, tried to warn Morgan:

"Bellfounder can be forbidding Tom, Not at all the public persona he projects in his popular books."

"Quotes from 'Alice in Wonderland' you mean?"

"Actually he's a batchelor. Lives with his sister. Can cycle a hundred and fifty miles non-stop. And he swims in the Cam before breakfast; winter and summer."

"I like him already." Morgan was not to be put off.

A bird like figure in her sixties opened the door of the small Edwardian house:

"Good morning Francis. And Mr…..?"

"Morgan." Frank replied.

"Sir Adrian can see you now. But not for long. He's got a Royal Society conversatzione up in town this afternoon."

As they walked along the dim hallway, past a coat and umbrella stand, Morgan noted that the walls were occupied with bookshelves loaded down with ancient leather-bound volumes of "The Astrophysical Journal", "Observatory" and "Monthly Notices of the Royal Astronomical Society"

Miss Bellfounder listened intently at the door of her brother's study before knocking timidly. When she opened it Morgan found himself staring at the great man himself seated at his desk with his back to the French windows. He appeared to be eating an apple core, pips and all.

"Adrian" Miss Bellfounder quavered, "It's Francis Cotteridge, and that young man you promised to see."

"Ah yes" Bellfounder stared coldly at Morgan. He was bald with a large head shaped like an egg, not an upright egg but one lying on its side with the blunt end foremost. His deepset eyes were melancholy, somewhat mystical and very cold. Amidst a clutter of papers he had the Times Crossword folded open with a large gold fob watch beside it.

"I've just started the crossword. I should be but a minute or two." He popped the last of the core in his mouth but didn't look up again. They crept into the room as Miss Bellfounder crept out. There were no chairs; they had to stand.

Morgan was happy to see his two papers, the Superstar one and the Red Giant one, on the great man's desk. But his eye was drawn to the speed with which Bellfounder's fountain pen raced across the difficult crossword. There was not a single pause for thought; no hesitation whatsoever. His brain obviously flew faster than, more accurately than, his racing pen could write. Morgan sometimes helped his stepfather to do the Times, which they never finished, if they finished it at all, in less than two hours. Bellfounder put down his pen and picked up his watch.

"Two minutes and thirty five seconds." He announced. "A trifle worse than average." He wrote the time into a tiny black diary and screwed the top back on his fountain pen. Then he looked up at Cotteridge:

"A good observing trip I trust Francis? How many redshifts?"

"Fourteen Sir Adrian."

"And how many of those were stellars?"

"I'm not certain yet. Probably two."

Bellfounder frowned:

"Most disappointing. Most. If you're not careful Francis those wretched Australians will beat us. What about the other twelve?"

"They look like radio galaxies. Low redshifts."

Bellfounder looked even more displeased.

"It's Martin Ryle's fault. I told him to search for stellars at higher frequencies – like the Australians."

He reached across his desk for Morgan's papers.

"Now Mr. Morgan I agreed to see you only because of Francis's eloquent pleading. Normally I never do this sort of thing. Never! It only wastes my time and makes more enemies."

He opened the Superstar paper. Cotteridge closed his eyes and prayed. Morgan leaned forward confidently on his walking stick as the great man flicked through the pages of his mathematics.

When Bellfounder finally looked up at Morgan his eyes were frosty.

"Did you really believe we professionals would have missed something as obvious as this – if it were really sound?"

Morgan froze. He didn't know what to say.

Bellfounder turned to Cotteridge:

"I must say Francis I'm extremely disappointed in you. And surprised. I would have expected any assistant of mine to have spotted the fallacy in an instant."

Frank opened his eyes. He wasn't going to admit that he hadn't even read Tom's paper before apparently wasting Bellfounder's precious time .

"Well?" the great man sounded coldly furious. "You are supposed to protect me from this kind of thing." He pushed the paper distastefully back at Frank as if Morgan wasn't present.

Frank still didn't reply.

"What happens when plasma is pushed up to temperatures of a million million degrees?"

The penny suddenly dropped.

"Neutrinos." Frank gasped.

"Exactly so." Bellfounder looked at Morgan "Your so called Superstars would lose their energy in a trice and collapse. In a trice. They'd be transparent to neutrinos – as everyone, except apparently Frank – knows".

Morgan was stunned. Absolutely stunned. Before this moment he'd never heard of neutrino emission. But it sounded plausible. Neutrinos could penetrate anything; even light-years of lead. His mind raced for a way out of his blunder. All he could come up with was :

"Red Giants. What about my Red Giants paper?"

Bellfounder pushed that in Frank's direction as well, using his fountain pen as if it was contagious.

"I'm afraid one paper was quite enough. I'll leave Frank to find the fallacy in this other one. And I'm sure there will be at least one. At least. It's a punishment he deserves."

Bellfounder smiled up sunnily at the two friends for the first time. Morgan looked as if he'd been bayoneted. Cotteridge closed his eyes again.

"Ah yes Mr Morgan, Francis did ask me about your prospects as a putative astrophysicist. Do you really need me to say?"

Morgan couldn't move from the spot. And so long as he was silent Frank couldn't bear to open his eyes.

"How old are you Mr Morgan?"

"Twenty seven."

"And where did you go to university?"

"Bangor."

"And what class of degree did you get?"

"A Two Two."

"Well you won't thank me for my advice. Not now. But you might in twenty years time. You might. Look at it this way" Bellfounder sounded gay, as if he was rather enjoying himself. "What would you say to a man of twenty seven who suddenly announced, never having played association football professionally before, that he intended to play for a First Division Club? Wanted to play centre-forward for the Tottenham Hotspurs ?"

There was no answer to that.

"Or what would you say to a woman of twenty seven who decided, on the spur of the moment, that she was going to lose four stones and become the principal ballerina at Covent Garden?"

Nobody laughed.

"Because you see that is the analogy here. Look at Francis even. Scholarship boy. Top in the Part Three mathematical-physics Tripos at Cambridge University no less. Fellow of Trinity. Now a Carnegie Fellow. Even he's not guaranteed a place playing in the First Division. He's got to score his goals first, regularily. And not own goals either, as he has done so egregiously today. In astrophysics you see, many are called but few are chosen. Very very few. Even if you once had the potential, as

Cotteridge seems to think you had, it's far too late now. Far far too late. You've lost what – seven of your most creative years? I'm afraid Mr Morgan you are deluding yourself if you're thinking of astrophysics."

Morgan turned on his stick and groped toward the door.

"Oh dear," Bellfounder sighed aloud "I've made another enemy. No don't go Francis. We need to talk for a few minutes. About Stellars."

By the time Cotteridge managed to escape from Bellfounder there was no sign of Morgan. He ran down the driveway into Madingley Rd to see a distant figure hobbling furiously towards Cambridge. Running back up to the Institute he unchained his bike and raced after his friend.

As he caught up he could see that Morgan was struggling dreadfully. He swung his paralysed leg in exaggerated strides like a pendulum and then reached far forward with his walking stick.

"Tom stop! Stop Tom. Take my bike at least."

But Morgan gave no sign of hearing. His face, ghastly white with pain, was set in a rigid grimace, eyes slitted, mouth open and panting.

"Tom stop. Please!" Cotteridge had to run himself to keep up. He could see drops of perspiration dripping off Morgan's nose.

"Don't take it so to heart Tom. I tell you its just Bellfounder's manner."

Morgan speeded up, as if punishing his leg to the maximum.

"What about your bag and your stuff? In the college I mean."

Morgan reached the main road leading into the town. He looked right and left, his face that of a madman desperately trying to escape from his asylum.

"Tom please. For God's sake let's talk."

Morgan raised his stick. He'd seen a taxi. The cab drew up.

"Please Tom." Cotteridge threw his bike down and pleaded, approaching as if to seize Morgan's arm. But he drew back when he saw the response on Morgan's face. The car door slammed, the taxi drove away. Morgan didn't look back. Cotteridge   watched the vehicle until it was lost in the traffic, fairly certain that he would never see Tom Morgan again.

When Blodwen picked up her son at New Street station the look of thunder on his face was enough to quell her curiosity. All he said, as they entered the driveway was:

"I've made a blundering fool of myself Mam. And I don't want to talk about it. Ever!"

He went upstairs, came back down again, and started a bonfire at the far end of the garden. Curious next day she found a pile of burned papers and the half charred remains of Bellfounder's book. By then Twm had retreated, almost full time, to the Salts' workshop.

He found he could talk most easily to Ernie Salt, and told him the whole story. Ernie looked thoughtful before pulling them both a quart of his home made ale.

"Yow should talk to our dad about it. 'Ee's the one."

Morgan had to screw himself up before repeating the tale to Bob Salt. Bob's reaction was immediate:

"Warra 'bout this other feller, that other astronomer as yow sent your stuff to? "

"Martin Johnson. I don't know. I haven't heard."

"Well then. Yow need a second opinion 'afore writing off your dreams entirely. That feller Bellfounder, 'ee could be wrong couldn't 'ee?"

"No way! He's *the* world expert. I blundered. It's as simple as that."

Salt was thoughtful for a while.

"Dain't sound like a blunder to me son. More ignorance. Yow know what they say? 'It's not what he don't know as makes a man a fool; it's what he do know, as just ain't so."

Morgan digested that.

"But what about being too old?"

Salt bent over his lathe.

"Depends. If yow was startin' out, raw like, 'e could be right. I dunno. But yow ain't. You'm already done original research, age or no age."

"But it's wrong."

"Yow need a second opinion on that. Dain't 'ee Ern?"

"Ar 'ee does an all. We ain't told yer yet Tom. 'Eard while yow was away. Mr Small, my surgeon remember, 'ee got a second opinion on me latest X-rays. They reckon my chumour ain't growin' downward after all."

Morgan staggered up and hugged Ernie. Then Bob.

"How wonderful!" There were tears in Morgan's eyes.

"There y'are then." Ernie was shy. "Dad's right – fer once. What yow needs is a second opinion."

In the circumstances Morgan could hardly argue.

It was torture for Blodwen to watch Twm deteriorating, as he now definitely was. He became apathetic, something alien to his entire personality. Didn't argue all the time. He gave up doing the crossword with her husband. Went seldom to the Salts. Opened books, but never read them. Sat in front of the television staring at his feet. Stopped listening to music. Ignored the dog. Ate little, and without interest. Threw his post away unopened. Grew thinner by the day. Worst of all he smiled passively at her from time to time, something he'd never ever done when he was happy.

Blodwen was a Welsh woman, not averse to telling her men folk what to do – when the necessity arose. But now she was flummoxed. What could Twm do to get himself out of his own mess? He'd tried so valiantly – and failed. She would have fought with him willingly, as she had in the past. But what was there to fight about now?

One thing she did do was rescue Twm's post from the waste-paper basket. He might want it one day. There were cards from his mountaineering friends, mostly showing distant peaks and snow-clad faces. Long, very long letters postmarked 'Trinity College Cambridge', obviously from Frank and obviously unopened. Out of curiosity, which she justified to herself in view of her son's plight, she opened one and found it was full of encouragements and apologies. Apologies for not having read Tom's papers. Apologies for Bellfounder's arrogance. On and on. Blodwen felt sorry for Frank and sealed the letters up, mostly unread. She knew how uncompromising, what a hater Twm could be. But what a tragedy; two young men who would never find closer friends in life than one another.

One day she thus found in the waste paper a small, unopened envelope marked 'The University of Birmingham'. She recalled Twm sending his two papers to some astronomer there and opened it:

Martin Johnson ;Dept of Physics.

Dear Mr Morgan,

Thank you for sending your two most interesting papers to me. I am semi- retired now and rather out of touch.The quasar paper was way above me. However I found your Red Giant analysis quite fascinating, and close to my own interests once upon a time. I wonder if you'd like to call in at my house for tea at 4pm next Saturday, and perhaps we can have a chat.

Yours sincerely

Martin Johnson.   R.S.V.P.

Blodwen's heart missed a beat. Perhaps Twm was not wrong after all. She got up to go and challenge Twm who was sitting listlessly in the garden. But she stopped at the conservatory door and reconsidered the matter. Twm had obviously recognised the source of the letter, and rejected it. She certainly wouldn't be able to change his mind. Who would? Some instinct told her that her best hope was Bob Salt. Twm had developed an almost filial attachment to the odd little man, something he'd done with no one else before. She looked at her watch. Bob wouldn't be back from work until six.

Late that evening, to Morgan's great surprise, Bob arrived at their house for the very first time. He looked uncomfortable in his best suit, and smaller than ever. But he wasted no time in coming to the point.

"Tom I want a word with yow. Private loike."

They went upstairs to Morgan's room.

Blodwen heard raised voices, Bob's more often than her son's. But when he came downstairs again Bob was alone:

"'Ee's a goin' to see that Doctor Johnson and that's that. 'Ee needs a second opinion. I'm a coomin' tomorrer to pick him oop meself. An' drive him an all. That way missis there won't be any 'anky panky."

And drive Tom in to Selly Oak Bob did, though shoe-horning Tom's large frame into the tiny Austin Mini proved a challenge. There was a determined look on Bob's face which brooked no opposition.

The Johnsons lived in a leafy drive not far from the university. Mrs Johnson, a cheerful white haired lady, showed Morgan in.

"Martin's waiting in the garden. I've made an orange sponge-cake. We thought you could have tea together out there."

Martin Johnson turned out to look exactly like Morgan's imaginings of a retired university don: thick white hair, a cardigan, intelligent grey eyes and a friendly face. He was podding peas at a garden table in the orchard.

"Nice of you to come Mr. Morgan, or shall I call you Tom?" He made it sound as if Morgan had done him a favour.

"I can't get up until I've finished these peas for Margaret. Darling I'm nearly through."

Morgan sat down opposite and offered to help.

"Good show. By the time the teapot comes we'll be ready to talk astronomy."

Morgan had already decided on his tactics. The quicker it was over the better.

"Look I'm wasting your time." and he explained about his blunder.

Johnson only smiled when Morgan finished.

"Bellfounder's a bit of a terror isn't he. Too much of a holy man for my taste. They seem to thrive at Cambridge. After all it was little more than a seminary until recently."

Morgan looked up sharply. It had never occurred to him before that Bellfounder and Schweinhundt came from the same stable. But they did. Mogan loathed prelates of any kidney.

"But it's your Red Giants I'm interested in. I think you've got something there. In fact I'm sure you have. I got stuck on the same problem myself when I was writing my book. Then Bellfounder's famous book came out, and that seemed to be that. While I wasn't convinced by his argument, everybody else was, and I couldn't put a finger on any definite suspicion. You have. This stuff" and he tapped Morgan's paper "Needs to be published at once. Mind you it needs to be completely re-written but, if you like, I could help you with that."

Morgan sat, staring at the chirpy old man, wondering if he was in a dream.

"B…b…but I've burned it all. I don't even have a copy myself."

Johnson laughed: "My, you have taken this to heart. Did it ever occur to you that our friend Bellfounder may have finessed you?"

"What do you mean?" Morgan was quite out of his depth.

"Well put yourself in Bellfounder's shoes. He gets two papers, one attacking his own pet paper – the one on which his world renown depends. Which one would you look at first?"

"The Red Giant one of course."

"Naturally." Martin Johnson's eyes twinkled. "But as you've just explained to me, he denied ever having read it. What does that tell us?"

Morgan shook his head.

"It tells us that Sir Adrian is worried your paper might just be right."

Morgan couldn't speak.

"Otherwise he would have demolished it. I imagine it's far more important to him than quasars."

"Are you sure?" Morgan was incredulous.

"Of course I'm not. One can't be. But, in my view, the balance of probabilities point in that direction. Bellfounder was never a scrupulous man. He tried to frighten you off. And has apparently succeeded."

So dramatically did the weight come off Morgan's shoulders that he almost shot out of his chair.

"Of course the real challenge lies ahead of you. Now you've shot Bellfounder's theory down it's up to you to find out what really makes stars become Red Giants. A fit ambition for your astrophysical career."

"But I'm….I'm….."

"Oh but you must be. You were born to do astrophysics. Born to it. I expect an illustrious career. There's not a minute to waste. We've got to get you started at once."

Two weeks later, having been briefed by Blodwen, Jack Cockle rang Morgan up; he sounded excited:

"There's a PhD studentship going at my place – London University Observatory. The chap who occupied it has just pulled out and gone to America. But it has to be filled within a matter of days – or they lose the money for it. No time for them to advertise. Just apply to the director, get Johnson to send him the best possible reference and you should stand a good chance. But don't waste a minute Tom! "

CHAPTER 6
LONDON
1965

To Dr Francis Cotteridge   From Jack Cockle
Trinity College   London Observatory
 Cambridge.

Dear Frank
You asked me to keep you abreast of Tom's progress. In two
words he's going 'great guns' – and of course, being Tom
Morgan, upsetting a lot of people – including our director, of
which more anon. Within a week of arriving he told me, over a
pint, that he 'feels like a young albatross that had flown its nest at
last and is winging the great world for the first time'. He's often
in his office well after midnight when I close the telescope domes
after teaching the undergraduates.

Coming from a great astronomical factory like Cambridge it
will be difficult for you to envisage a tiny place like this. Our 3
telescopes are set in a park on the far outskirts of London, though
light pollution has long since encroached to the point where they
are useless for research, useful only for teaching students from the
University of London the rudiments of observing. We are a mere
outstation of the department itself which is situated down in
central London. Thus the academics are seldom here – only
Professor Wilson the director. We have a workshop full of bolshie
technicians with nothing to do; a good library thank God; a
secretary for the Prof and offices for half a dozen graduate
students like Tom and post-docs like me. And no computer on
site! You can imagine the effect on a sleepy little place like this of
a whirlwind like Tom.

He upset the technicians, never a difficult thing to do, by
pointing out, during communal morning coffee, that the silvering
on our biggest telescope's mirror is so bad that it's throwing away
at least ninety per cent of the starlight. The Prof was there so the
Chief Technician felt he had to respond by saying that Tom
simply didn't know what he was talking about. To which Tom
responded that as he'd never seen a technician at the observatory
after dark (a very sore point because they are supposed to be
here) he didn't see how on Earth they could possibly know, one
way or the other. You can imagine how that went down.

He upset the director in quite a different way. The London
University Student's Union has just started the UK's first
computer-dating scheme for its students – imported from
America. Tom amused us all by filling in his form so as to
'maximise the prospects'. The result was that our telephone
system has been inundated ever since by thousands of calls for
Tom from lonely young females. The secretary is fully employed

in answering them, so cannot do the director's typing, while the director himself can scarcely get any of his own calls either in or out. He was, and still is, livid with Tom. As a punishment he's awarded Tom the ghastly job of answering all calls from flying-saucer freaks.

Tom also annoyed some of the senior post-graduates by talking all the time in the office he shared with them. The real problem, as you well know, is not so much the noise he makes, as the fact that he's so bloody entertaining. So much so that he and and another of them wrote together a really amusing spoof called 'Impure Mathematics' which I am sure is destined for immortality.

The upshot was that Tom was ejected from there and now shares a room with me and another congenial soul called Alan. With us he is a continual source of good ideas, daft ideas, and just sheer tomdrollery. At the moment we are in daily fits of laughter as Tom describes his encounters with the females who picked him out of the computer. Among the preferences he put down as part of his optimal strategy was a preference for females with a weight 'slightly above the average'. He makes assignations to meet them, one by one of course, under the clock outside Baker Street tube station. He says he can now tell them approaching from a quarter mile away. They are, he swears, the fattest young females in the London area. Grossly fat because, as he has found from the bitter experience of entertaining them to dinner, of their elephantine appetites. He keeps us in fits of laughter over every single one.

But being Tom he does have amazingly original, and occasionally sound ideas too. You know the Russians and the Americans are racing to soft land the first television camera on the Moon, and then on Mars, to see what they are like. And all crashing so far. Well Tom's idea is to use balloons –no less. These tough 'Maloons' as we call them (yes Alan and I have been roped in too) will cushion the shock of impact, then deflate and let the camera out. We gave a seminar on it down at the college. Most of the audience were incredulous. Some of the senior physicists even walked out and our director was furious. Who with and why I am not sure. But we've done our calculations –and maloons work! Anyway we have sent the idea to NASA. Let's wait and see.

What Tom is supposed to be doing for his PhD is find out how stars form, using the University of London computer down in Bloomsbury. It's a Ferranti Atlas and right now the most powerful computer in the world. According to Tom his supervisor, a certain Doctor Hood who Tom insists on referring to as 'Knight', is a bit of a twit. I think Tom's wrong, but you know what an arrogant sod he can be. I wish he wouldn't be so free with nicknames – which redound on his head in the end. Remember 'Schweinhunt'? Tom paid for that with almost five years of his life. And he's nicknamed the secretary here, who has a wry neck, 'Isiah'. When asked why, he quipped 'because one Isiah than the other'.

He's still in an awful lot of pain, which seems to build up during the course of the day. But he's eating like a horse and, as I was able to reassure his mother, putting some of his weight back on. He's living in digs in nearby Mill Hill which are ' very comfortable' except that, so he says, and I never know whether to believe him, he has to have 'intimate relations' with his landlady once a week. Having met her, I don't think that would be too much of a hardship.

Now, about Tom's feelings toward you. He doesn't blame you, at least not much, for his humiliation at Cambridge. It's just that he measures himself against you, he always has, and was found wanting there. And you were close at hand to witness his failure. That rankles. His real hatred is directed at Bellfounder. He's very definitely out to 'get him' by discrediting his Red Giant work as publicly and as humiliatingly as possible. In some illogical way he's equated Bellfounder with Schweinhunt and he's dreaming of wreaking a bloody revenge on the pair of them at the same time. From your point of view it would be good if he succeeds. He might 'forgive' you then. Personally I believe, and I've told him so, if it ever came to a public debate, Bellfounder would make mince-meat out of him. Tom of course doesn't agree. When did he ever take good advice? I'm coming up to Caius for a feast soon and hope to see you then.

All the best

Mussels.

Morgan's PhD project was to find out, by means of computer calculations, how stars formed. It was widely assumed that stars were born out of the huge clouds of cool gas and smoke which could be observed floating about in the immense voids of space between the visible stars. It was a plausible assumption, not least because no alternative assumption had been suggested. However there was no positive evidence in its favour. While some stars were unquestionably young, no astronomer had ever seen a new one being born. And there was a plausible explanation for this too. The densest clouds of interstellar gas, the very clouds where gravity had the best chance of compressing the gas into new stars, would be totally opaque thanks to the smoke of old stellar bonfires mixed inevitably with the gas. Thus stellar nurseries kept their secrets hidden. Yet without an understanding of the star-formation process astronomers would be powerless to tackle some huge questions such as: 'Is the Solar System unique? If it was, then there might well be no other intelligent beings out there in the Universe. On the other hand if planets were the commonplace outcome of star formation then, with billions of planets to thrive on, cosmic life might be abundant, and so contactable in time.

With observations impossible, calculation was the only way forward. Dr. Hood, Morgan's supervisor, had imagined a star being born out of the gas, collapsing under the force of its own self-gravitation. He had written down all the equations which could control the behaviour of such collapsing gas. The solution of those equations would then lead to predictions which could be tested against observations. For instance how many of the hypothetical stars would be double stars, orbiting around one another, instead of single stars like the Sun? If hypothesis and observation checked out so far, then one could hope to advance more confidently toward bigger questions, such as the ubiquity of planets and so of life.

Unfortunately neither Hood, nor anybody else in astrophysics, had been able to solve the complicated partial differential equations which supposedly governed the whole process. What Hood had been able to do was persuade the US Office of Naval Research to support a PhD student, namely Morgan, to 'have a go'. Hood had probably succeeded in this quest for funds because he would have access to the world's fastest computer, the new Ferranti Atlas recently installed at London University.

Hood didn't expect Morgan to solve the equations by brilliance, but by sheer brute force; to break the equations down into a series of simpler and simpler steps until even a computer, which was little more than an ultra-fast switching device, could carry out trillions of trivial additions, subtractions, multiplications and divisions. It would be brutal, and it would only be approximate: thus a smooth collapse in the real universe would be mimicked by a long series of jerky steps, like a film run too slowly. To Morgan, who had never encountered a computer before, it all seemed a wild fantasy. But, so Hood convinced him, similarly complex problems, for instance the explosion of an atomic bomb, had been successfully tackled by the same general methods. He had then given Morgan two papers to read, and told him to get on with it.

Morgan, though greatly excited by the problem, was daunted by the difficulties, difficulties which had caused his predecessor in the post to lose heart and emigrate to America. Instead of the few hours he had expected, the first paper cost him a struggle of six weeks to read. Being a technical paper for experts, it bristled with jargon, and with concepts he'd never heard of before. He passed days and nights in the library tracing back references to try and make sense of what had been argued in a terse line or two. The vastness of the subject, and the desert of his own ignorance, seemed to stretch away to infinity. There were occasions when he got completely stuck for weeks at a time. But it did occupy his mind completely, almost to the exclusion of his pain. He thought about the problem when he first woke in the morning, and as he was gong to sleep at night. It might catch him in mid sentence, or while forking food into his mouth. On the bus, in the cinema, even in the pub with Mussels, Star Formation came to haunt all the labyrinths and interstices of his mind.

What was so stimulating was having the Aladdin's cave of an astrophysical library next door to his office. Here were the journals describing the latest advances in all fields of science. Here were thousands of specialised books covering every aspect of astrophysics, mathematics and computing, as well as bound back-copies of all the great technical journals stretching back to the beginning of the century and beyond. Moreover there was a copying machine which enabled him to extract crucial papers to read in bed at night when he would otherwise have been wrestling with his causalgia.

In contrast computing was more like a crossword puzzle or an addictive intellectual game, by turns infuriating and then rewarding. He would break down a mathematical problem into more and more elementary steps, then program the machine to carry them out using a long set of precise instructions written in the baby language , or code, which was all it could understand. The code he then punched, using a sort of typewriter, onto a long strip of paper-tape to be despatched to the Atlas down in town. To begin with it invariably came back with a thick stack of paper printout covered in technical gibberish, a so called 'octal dump'. These papers he would pore over for hours, only to find out that he'd misplaced a bracket in his program, causing the computer to go into an infinite loop. The program had to be amended, the tape cut and repaired, and submitted again and again and again. But then one day the paper would come back with an answer, accurate to sixteen places of decimals if necessary, an answer which could not have been reached by any other method known to mathematical science. That was magic. That was exploring the unknown. That made all the frustration of little failures seem infinitely worthwhile. In principle all the great problems of science that could be formulated as equations were now within range of attack. He found that an awe inspiring thought. He determined to become an ace, better even than Frank and Jack, in the art, and it was an art, of using computers to solve differential equations. As a start he would do a proper job of optimising Ernie's wing design.

The outcome of that wing investigation was extraordinary, and was to have extraordinary repercussions. Morgan used the tireless computer to generate a whole series of different model aircraft designs, each with different characteristics, and each with its performance, calculated from those characteristics. From that series he was able to pick the one with the optimal design, one which had an estimated endurance and range well beyond anything Ernie, or indeed anybody else had envisaged. The estimates of range, in particular, were startling. In some cases they came to more than a thousand miles.

Initially Morgan supposed that a mistake had been made. After all it was his first serious computer investigation. So he tried to reproduce the most dramatic results without the computer, using pen, paper and algebra alone. And when, after a long struggle, he managed to do so, there emerged a startling, simple, and previously unknown formula. He rushed back to Birmingham to explain his findings to Ernie and Bob:

"So you see that the maximum range of an aircraft has nothing to do with its size. Nothing whatsoever! Nor its speed. It depends on only two design parameters.Firstly on is its lift-to-drag ratio – essentially its wing design and its streamlining. Secondly on the fraction of its total take-off weight that it can carry as fuel. What's the range of a Boeing 707 airliner?"

"About four thousand mile." Ernie responded immediately, "That's fully loaded with passengers and freight."

"Well then, you ought to be able to build a model with the same range. Four thousand miles!"

"Never!" they both responded in harmony.

"But you can! The formula, the computer, and the mathematics, all tell the same story. Range is independent of size! I know it is a shocker, but it's true. Understandably you modellers have been barking up the wrong tree – looking for maximum endurance, not maximum range. After all you've wanted to keep your models flying in sight. So you've tended to build relatively light, relatively slow machines. Sure, they stay up all day, but they don't go anywhere much. But if you went for maximum range instead, you'd need a much higher speed design, and you could go a thousand miles at the very least and four thousand if you really pushed it; after all you're not going to be carrying either freight or passengers."

After a thrillingly argumentative weekend in the workshop the Salts were finally convinced. And Ernie had a new dream:

"Oy am going to be the first designer as flies an aeromodel non-stop across the Atlantic. Yow'll help with the maths won't you Tom? And Dad of course will do the engine. And we're a going to call her Wild Goose. We got to keep it all secret for now, though, dead secret. I've started on the design already. Dad and me are going to 'ave to build a mooch faster wind tunnel."

There was a fanatic light in Ernie's eyes that Morgan had never seen there before.

To Dr Frank Cotteridge   From Jack Cockle
Trinity College Cambridge.   London Observatory

Dear Frank

I promised to keep you up to date with Tom's progress. I don't think we need to worry any more. He's an octagonal peg who has found an exactly octagonal hole into which he perfectly slots. His sheer enthusiasm, and his delight in small achievements, other peoples' as well as his own, are waking this place up.

As an example I'll tell you about his Flying Saucer escapade. After taking all too many 'saucer' phone calls from the general public he concluded that most reports are based on real but natural phenomena, and are not sheer lunacy. To prove his point he acquired several dozen of those long transparent plastic bags that dry cleaners return your cleaned clothing in. One fine evening, when the sun was low in the sky, we inflated the bags with coal gas and released them into the sky. In no time the observatory was inundated with phone calls, which we took in turns to record. Many reports were accurate – if uncomprehending. The floating bags caught the setting sun in the most convincing way. But other reports were so fantastical, mixing fantasy with fact, that they rivalled the wildest saucer stories ever recorded. It was great fun and resulted in a report which we sent off to 'Observatory' magazine. As a consequence Prof. Wilson has relented and shared out the Flaying Saucer chore amongst us all, instead of landing it all on Tom. But perhaps he relented only because all the computer dating calls have come to an end. Which reminds me: we don't see so much of Tom any more. After a few dreary weekends in our suburb, which to be honest is rather sedate, he announced that Mill Hill is a 'dump' and has gone to live in central London, in Bayswater. Through one of his climbing friends he's inherited the tenancy of a bed-sitter, which I have to admit is amazing. On the top floor of one of those Georgian mansions in Lancaster Gate his window looks out and down over Kensington Gardens, the Round Pond, the Serpentine and in the distance the rotunda of the Albert Hall. The area's full of pubs, restaurants, single people and Bohemian life. And girls. Thousands of them. Tom says there are five single girls in central London for every single man: secretaries, nurses, saleswomen, students, tourists and so on. According to Tom the Pill has released an absolute flood of pent up female sexuality and he's trying to get washed away in the outflow. He claims, and he should know, that no nice girl can resist a man with a walking stick. At all events when I've met up with him in town he's usually accompanied by a stunning mini-skitted dolly-bird, so far a different one on each occasion. I don't expect the sexual revolution, which has turned us into "Swinging London" has reached, or will ever reach Cambridge. You poor devils! Never mind, you've got 'each other'.

But it's not all frivolity here. Tom decided, since we have no post-graduate lectures in the observatory, that we would start a program and lecture one another. And I must say it's been a roaring success. Tom led off by giving a superb course on Special Relativity, Alan did Complex Analysis, I did Radiative Transfer, and so on. What an enjoyable way to learn, and to learn fast.

In addition to his PhD project Tom is noisily writing up his anti-Bellfoundfer stuff on Red Giants. He has no idea of the refereeing difficulties he will face here in Britain, with Bellfounder's cronies on the editorial boards of all the important journals. I warned him to try an American journal but he's determined, as he put it 'To beard the ogre in his den'.

And he might just do that. I heard the story of Tom's army exploits from Mick Wyverne, who I ran across last week and who you may you remember was in the Geography Sixth at school. Apparently he went into the army to do his National Service at the same time as Tom. He also finished up in Malaya but in a different regiment. Apparently, as a platoon commander, Tom was an absolute madman. He led his thirty men into the jungle on a long patrol which lasted for three weeks, instead of the scheduled one week. When they emerged many of his men were so exhausted, hungry and mosquito-bitten that they had to be hospitalised. Tom had set them up in ambush on a jungle trail and refused to leave until the enemy showed up. He threatened to shoot any soldier who left his post or made a sound. Eventually the enemy walked into the ambush and the platoon wiped out nearly 50 'CTs' or Communist Terrorists. There was talk of awarding Tom a DSO, like his father. But then, just when an armistice looked like being signed, he tried to do it again. After two weeks in ambush, and very badly bitten, some of the soldiers, led by a corporal, mutinied. Tom shot the corporal through the leg for cowardice; he nearly bled to death before he could be evacuated. There was a most almighty row when they all emerged from the jungle. Tom demanded the corporal be court-martialled for spoiling the operation, while there were some, including his own sergeant, who thought Tom should be court-martialled for brutality. Tom, of course, did his best to bring both court martials about. However, in the euphoria over Britain's victory, the whole matter was hushed up lest it raise a frightful stink in the press, and divide the Army. To some Tom was a real hero: to others a fanatic and a villain. So Bellfounder had better watch out. And so had Tom if you ask me.

Anyway you won't need any further bulletins on Tom from me. He's in his element in astronomy. It gets his blood up in every sense of the word. And Bellfounder is certainly an enemy worthy of Tom's steel. Who comes alive out of it is anybody's guess. Normally the odds would be overwhelmingly on Bellfounder, but Tom is nobody to be trifled with – as Schweinhunt found out. I only wish Tom had Schweinhunt in his sights again , not Bellfounder, who could really crush him flat.

    Best wishes
     Jack

*

Morgan had been brought up within sight sound, smell and indeed feel of the sea. As a boy he would lie in bed on stormy nights and feel their house in Pembrokeshire ever so lightly shake as Atlantic combers thundered against the cliffs of their cove nearby. The seethe and rattle of its boulders, and the gale moaning in the chimneys, lullabied him to sleep. Until they were snatched away from him, when they went to live in Birmingham, Morgan never realised how much his soul belonged to those storm tossed headlands, those inaccessible beaches, to the heather, the gorse and the crying gulls. He no more belonged to the brick suburbia of the Midlands than a wolf belonged in a cage at the zoo. For years he pined for his home, comforting himself in moments of despair by closing his eyes and imagining himself in his den in Swallowtree Wood looking out over St Brides Bay; or fishing for bass in the moonlight off Monkstone Point, or rabbiting with his dog Goch in the dune burrows behind Coppithall Sands. Goch literally pined to death when they took him to Birmingham. Morgan survived by launching himself into an imaginary world of books and fantasy, suppressing all sense of his physical environment, of pavements, trams and shop fronts. The municipal library became his saviour and from there he travelled the oceans with Slocum, the jungle with Quatermain, the reefs and trout streams with Mitchell-Hedges and Negly Farson, the snow trails of the Yukon with Jack London and his wild extravagant breed. When he could stand bus-stops and class-rooms no more he would turn his inward eye towards Yeat's Lake Isle of Inisfree

        "…And a small cabin build there, of clay and wattles made,
          Nine bean rows will I have there, a hive for the honey bee
          And live alone in the bee-loud glade."

or take Kipling's Long Trail through
        ".. the blazing tropic night, when the wake's a welt of light
That holds the hot sky tame,
And the steady forefoot snores through the planet powdered floors
Where the scared whale flukes in flame"

Even the mountains had not assuaged his thirst for place, his longing for 'home', what the Welsh call 'Hiraeth'. For all their occasional beauty, and they could be ugly and terrible at times, mountains had been the arena for a different kind of struggle with his soul. Now that he had found himself he didn't need that any more. And at last, in a village in Central London, he found a sense of place, an atmosphere which fed his spirit, and a home to which he could proudly belong.

His village was centred on Kensington Gardens, stretching to the West as far as Notting Hill, and to the East along the Bayswater Road as far as Bloomsbury, Soho and the West End. Paddington station, and St Mary's Hospital, where Fleming had discovered penicillin, marked the Northern extremity, while to the South it stretched through Hyde Park, Green Park and St. James' Park to Westminster and the river. The heart of it, between Queensway and Craven Terrace, consisted of Georgian mansions looking out over quiet streets and squares. Their cream coloured stucco facades had seen far better days when the carriages of the Victorian bourgeoisie, such as the Forsytes, had drawn up at the porticoed entrances. In amongst them were sandwiched discreet squares, and mews so hidden away that one could pass their arched entranceways a dozen time before recognizing their existence. Now the mansions were divided and subdivided into dozens of bed-sitters while the mews housed garages, discreet businesses and the pieds-a-terre of the super-rich.

The inhabitants of Bayswater were mostly young, mostly single, mostly educated, mostly hard working, and mostly poor. Half were foreigners working or studying in London, but tourists were relatively rare. There were dozens of pubs to choose from and even more restaurants of every ethnic variety and musical provenance. Tom's village included a West Indian dance hall, a Chinese gambling den, two large lakes – The Serpentine and The Round Pond, – the open air Portobello Road Market, Kensington Palace and the Soviet Embassy. It was a thronging, polyglot, exciting village where dreams and ambitions made for encounters and adventures of every kind. To Morgan it felt like the heart of a gracefully hopeful, pleasant world, and in many ways it was. The snobberies of the past were fading away, while a future ruled by talent and not capital, was coming into psychedelic focus. John Lennon was becoming more important than The Duke of Westminster; Mary Quant than Princess Margaret. The future had been a very long time in coming, but it felt as if it was breaking into the sunlight at last.

Tom's bed-sit was on the top floor of a mansion in Lancaster Gate whose frontage lay on Bayswater Road overlooking Kensington Gardens. For the ridiculously small sum of two pounds ten shillings a week he had one of the best views in London, a South facing window just above tree top level looking towards the Round Pond half right, and The Serpentine half left. The window gave out onto a balustrade from which, with the aid of some climbing rope, he could reach the roof and sun himself in total privacy, except for pigeons, enjoying a view which stretched from the pavement artists right below on Bayswater Road, to Marble Arch, Westminster and Kensington High.

The long thin room, which must have once housed a governess ,or perhaps a poor relation of the family, was partitioned by a large wardrobe, behind which lay the wash basin and the antediluvian gas stove which constituted the cooking arrangements. Somehow all the pots and pans and condiments left just enough room in the 'galley'for Tom to cook a decent dinner when he felt like it. Strings of onions and garlic, and bags of oranges hung from hooks driven into the wardrobe, whilst the 'larder' was a wooden box out on the balustrade where it was conveniently cooled by fresh air and protected from the pigeons by a zinc dustbin-lid.

The narrow but comfortable bed lay under the window, with a single radiator, made unnecessary by all the free heat seeping up from the five floors below. His dining arrangement and office consisted of a semicircular table which could seat two at a pinch and which folded against the wall. Opposite his bed was a comfortable armchair, a reading lamp, and an old dining trolley which supported his record player and radio. All his remaining belongings, including books and gramophone records, had to be stored either under the bed or in the wardrobe. He shared a bathroom, with an enormous long bath, just along the corridor.

The room was perfect for Tom. When he closed the door he was in his den, hidden away from the hurly burly of London, snug in his bubble of solitude. And yet it was large enough, just, to entertain a girlfriend for the weekend, or, if he borrowed a chair from a neighbour, to give a dinner party, served on laps, for four.

His neighbours, usually met going up or down the stairs, included Gretl a German girl who enjoyed her orgasms so much that her screams could be heard through his thick wall; Smithy a bachelor who had flown off aircraft carriers in the First World War and spent the rest of his life in China; Rod from Australia who was using a British computer to design the roof support of the Sydney Opera House; Clive who was gay and did something hush-hush in the Admiralty; and Janet a gorgeous art- student who was always dressed in exotic creations of her own design. They all had strong legs acquired from climbing the five flights to the top floor.

Of the pubs in his neighbourhood Morgan frequented two. Saturday morning usually found him at the White Hart in Craven Mews doing the Times crossword over a pint with his neighbour Smithy and Smithy's friend Geoffrey, another old China hand who had served in the Ghurkhas for 30 years. If they hadn't succeeded by noon then Jerry, a schoolteacher of Tom's age from Scotland, via Tanzania, would certainly finish it off for them.

With two pints and a pork pie inside them Morgan and Jerry would catch a District Line tube train from Bayswater to emerge on the Thames Embankment at Putney Bridge amidst a buzzing crowd of football fans making its way through the park to Craven Cottage. Fulham Football Club, then in the First Division, would be taking on the giants of the day such as Tottenham Hotspur, Wolves or Manchester United. Morgan, who'd never attended a professional soccer match until reluctantly dragged along by Jerry, was hooked from the moment 'his' players ran onto the pitch to the roar of the Fulham fans. For ninety minutes the pain in his leg was entirely forgotten as he watched Johnny Haynes sweeping passes from one end of the field to the other, George Cohen racing down the wing from full back, or Alan Clarke diving full length to head the incoming ball into the bulging back of the net. It was the Greek Theatre and the Roman Forum rolled into one. Fulham were always the underdogs, rarely expected to survive such illustrious opposition. This alone was enough to get Morgan's blood up, to get his powerful battle cries echoing round the terraces at the Craven Cottage end, especially when Fulham were a goal in arrears. According to Jerry, Morgan's bloodcurdling roar was worth half a goal a match to the home team.

On Sunday at noon, when he was frequently entertaining female company from the night before, Morgan would take them both to his other regular pub, the Swan on Bayswater Road. The Swan claimed a gruesome history for it was the last pub on the road to the gallows at Tyburn. The hangman's cart had usually stopped outside and many a poor wretch had been helped on his or her way to eternity by a stiff tot from the hostlery's cellar.

The clientele of the Swan were various, changing with the hours of the day. At lunch times the bar was often propped up by actors such as Peter Cushing who played Dracula in horror films, or Ian Carmichael who had made his name playing Bertie Wooster. In the evenings came rowdy medical students from St Mary's Hospital, including a stunning Indian girl who had just become Miss World. On sunny days it was a great place to eat lunch outside and watch the world go by. On Sundays the pavement on the opposite side of the road for half a mile in either direction was entirely occupied by artists who hung their paintings for sale from the railings of Hyde Park. They, and their psychedelically dressed clientele, would wander past, or drop in to celebrate the sale of a painting.

The Swan provided an excellent cold buffet, the centrepiece of which was always a monstrous roast turkey, allegedly the largest from Smithfield Market, weighing sixty pounds or more. Morgan had discovered that, for ten bob extra, the chef was willing to sell him an entire turkey ham, weighing several pounds, which made a tasty lunch for two, leaving enough meat over for curries and risottos later in the week. Surviving as he was on a student grant, such contrivances were necessary. Indeed Morgan's Bayswater idyll nearly ended in financial tragedy. A postgraduate student grant like his was designed to do little more than provide sustenance for a mendicant scholar. Living by the Park, entertaining women in restaurants, visiting the opera, going to West End theatres and night-clubs, none of these were budgeted for in a student stipend. But the Universe came to his rescue again. Scattered through the metropolis were sufficient minds with the curiosity and enterprise to demand part-time classes in Astronomy and Space Research, and to pay well for them. So he signed on with the WEA, the 'Workers Education Association', to deliver a course of evening lectures which he entitled "From Quarks to Quasars" that covered every aspect of astronomy and astrophysics. And what a stimulating challenge they were, both to his knowledge and to his ability as a teacher. He first had to learn about all of astronomy, not just his narrow area of research. And what a fascinating study that had turned out to be. Having a professional library in the observatory he almost lost himself in a succession of open ended investigations which he could share with his audience; how old was the universe; what caused the ice ages; could we communicate with extra-terrestrials – supposing them to exist; where do meteorites come from; is space curved; how were the elements created….. and so on and so on. And he had to know what he was talking about, really know. Audiences with the curiosity to turn up at an evening class after a hard days work could ask extremely penetrating questions and wouldn't be fobbed of with flannel of any kind. A naturally arrogant young man, Morgan found teaching them a humbling experience. Here he was, masquerading as a professional astronomer, when some of his audience had been grinding their own telescope mirrors and wondering about stars long before he was born. The questions and arguments which sparked in class often raged on in the pub for hours afterwards. He wasn't always sure how much they learned about the universe, but he learned an enormous amount himself.

The fees for these lectures were good – but precarious. If ever the class size fell much below the original enrolment, they were forfeit. It meant that week after week, come flu'come Christmas, he had to draw his audience back to hear the next thrilling episode. Any signs of dozing off, or whispering in the back row, threw him into a financial panic. He quickly learned three hard lessons: that he was there to inspire, not to instruct; that his fellows were more interested in ideas than facts; and that the unknown is far more fascinating than the known. The magic phrase "Nobody knows why……." was sure to wake up the sleepiest audience. Being a born show-off with the blood of Welsh preachers in his veins, Morgan was a natural teacher who looked forward to his lectures, was stimulated by his audience, earned his fees and enjoyed the spending of them. Delivering the same lecture twice in a week, once in North London and once in the South, funded a free and easy, if not extravagant lifestyle.

After lunch in The Swan a stroll through the Park was mandatory. Directly across the road from the pub the fountains at the North end of the Serpentine gushed in front of Inigo Jones' magical, ridiculous ha-ha. Seated there on a bench in the sun was a good place to catch up with the Sunday papers or watch the nannies feeding the ducks. From there he and his companion would stroll on, usually past the statue of Peter Pan, past the sparkling waters of the Lido where Morgan himself swam on unbearably hot days. To Tom the entire park from Kensington High Street to Marble Arch and from Apsly House to Queensway, felt like his own private garden. After all it was right under his window so that, one way or another, he was in it almost every day: strolling to catch the 88 bus to work; lying reading in the shade of the chestnut trees, walking to the West End to see a film, or passing down the side of the Serpentine on his way to the Royal Astronomical Society meetings in Burlington House off Piccadilly.

The "RAS" as it was called by its members was for Morgan a source of excitement and delight. Here discoveries were announced. Here he heard the great astronomers in lively debate. He was never to forget a battle there between Martin Ryle the great radio astronomer and Fred Hoyle the protagonist of the Steady State Theory of the universe. It began when an officious young henchman of Ryle's announced that observations by their group conclusively ruled out The Steady State Theory. To Morgan his arguments seemed incontrovertible. But then Hoyle leaped up onto the stage and thanked the speaker for having proved, beyond doubt, that The Steady State was actually correct. He then wiped away every trace of the offender's equations from the blackboard, replacing them with an equally conclusive set of his own. Seeing his champion humiliated Ryle, until then concealed in the audience, leapt onto the stage himself and expunged every last one of Hoyle's equations as he might have exterminated a nest of poisonous snakes. Then the two antagonists went for each other like Tweedledum and Tweedledee, to the immense entertainment, if not enlightenment of the packed audience.

At another more sedate meeting a tall man swept into the room, climbed up onto the dais and whispered into the secretary's ear. The secretary, looking astonished
, whispered in his equally astonished chairman's ear and the chairman called the meeting to order:

"Ladies and Gentlemen, I'm sure you will all forgive me for interrupting the proceedings when you have heard what Professor R. J. Davies from Jodrell Bank Radio Observatory has to tell us, and in particular what he has to show us afterwards."

Davies told them that the Russians had just made another attempt to land a television camera on the Moon. And this time, after so many failed attempts, they had succeeded. Having no radio telescoped powerful enough to detect the signals returning from so far away they had requested help from the team at Jodrell Bank with its 250 foot dish. Yesterday they had succeeded in picking up the faint signals and relaying them on to Moscow. But somebody on the Jodrell team had recognised the format of the signals as that used by newspapers to transmit their pictures around the globe. Accordingly they had rushed the signal to the Daily Express offices in Manchester and he was now proposing to show us the very first picture sent back from the Moon.

The lights dimmed. And there, all of a sudden, it was. The audience sat in silence, stunned by the sheer impossibility of it. Morgan pinched himself to see if he were really awake, or merely participating in a dream.

In 1967 another team from Ryle's lab picked up metronomic radio pulses from the heavens. The entire world was agog for they resembled nothing so much as the long awaited signals from Little Green Men. Morgan was at the RAS meeting in Burlington House, which was packed to the rafters, when the team showed their first results. The pulsating radio sources, or "Pulsars' as they came to be known, were an even greater mystery than the "Quasars" he'd been working on. Too fast to be emitted by a star, their erratic strength nevertheless suggested a natural rather than a deliberately engineered phenomenon. But if they weren't Little Green Men, what in heavens were they? The whole room, indeed the whole of scientific society buzzed with speculation and rumour. Radio antennae across the world were trained on them. Telegrams flashed back and forth. Professional astronomers couldn't talk about, could barely think about, anything else for a while.

The Park also turned out to be the starting point for other excitements of a non-astronomical kind. Morgan found out that it was a wonderful place to pick up the young women who teemed in central London. What could be more natural than striking up a conversation when you both were seated on the same bench enjoying the sun, or feeding the ducks on the Round Pond. Women came to London from the provinces or the Empire in search of romance, and where better to find it than strolling through the Park? Almost without trying Morgan found himself the object of more female desire than he could comfortably handle. Never having thought of himself as a particularly attractive man it was exhilarating to be practically chased into bed by desirable women of all ages and nationalities.

It was partly a reaction to the contraceptive pill which had just come on the market. Previously most young men of Morgan's generation faced the unpalatable choice between abstinence and siring unwanted children. For Morgan, who would have married the girl as a matter of conscience, it wasn't really a choice at all. But remaining almost celibate through his early twenties had been agony. Twice, in Malaya, he'd been forced into seeking relief from prostitutes, only to recoil from the degradation.

Now came the chance to compensate for all those years of lonely masturbation. He made love to school girls and he made love to grandmothers. He made love to nannies *and* their mistresses. He made love to women who never opened their mouths, and to others who couldn't stop talking. He made love gently and he made love savagely, he made love to them over the table and in the bath, and he made love in almost every position known to sexual science.

He made love to them but he didn't exploit them. He tried to give pleasure, and mostly he succeeded. The glory in a woman's face after she'd been pleasured to satiation was, for him, a pleasure in itself. And they gave him peace too. He became a calmer more patient character who could look back at his own wildness and wonder just how much of it derived from sheer sexual frustration. He recalled Somerset Maugham's remark that our bodies owed us a big debt of pleasure in return for all the pain they inflicted.

He never lied to a woman nor pretended to feelings he didn't possess. He kept their confidences and never boasted of his conquests to anyone. Indeed they weren't conquests at all, but liaisons between equals. He found he liked women and learned much from them. They would tell him, on the pillow, things he had never dreamed of, of their own shameful desires, about their husbands, about the shocks and compromises of marriage. To begin with he felt guilty about having intercourse with other men's wives but he found there were certain things a woman might desperately need which she felt she couldn't demand from a beloved husband, such as a good hiding, or being treated like a whore, or being subjected to obscene language. With his own conventional background it came as a relief to find just how huge the gulf could be between sexual passion and married love.

Once it peaked, his high flood of sexual gratification gradually ebbed away. There was an unsatisfactory sameness about liaisons which began in bed; they seldom led anywhere. Without some meeting of minds or hearts how could they? Fucking was well, just fucking. Pigs did it, ducks did it, a male lion did it three thousand times a year before he was killed by a more powerful or less exhausted rival. Always an early waker Morgan would sometimes wonder who it was sleeping heavily in his arms, with her face hidden from sight. He would search her clothes, resting on a chair, or scattered all over the floor, for reminders of who she was or where they had encountered one another. Usually it was fine, but sometimes it was not. Rarely, but all too often, he woke with self disgust. He then dreaded her waking, dreaded the thought of having to make polite, let lone intimate conversation. Thank God some experienced women did not; knew better than to spoil a great fuck with a banal pretence at chatting. Once he was in the corner shop looking for his supper. She was in her mid thirties, wearing a fur coat, very desirable in a dark, foreign sort of way. He'd seen her walking on her husband's arm, an older distinguished looking Latin. She turned, saw him staring at her. Startled, she dropped a paper bag of groceries on the floor. They squatted, heads together, silent, embarrassed, picking up her packages one by one. Their hands met on the last item, a small carton of eggs. His eyes came up, then hers. Quite unconsciously, almost imperceptibly, he gestured with his head. She didn't have to reply. They climbed his stairs, she a flight in arrears. He opened the door, grateful that he'd cleared the place up that morning. She arrived, quite breathless, and handed him her groceries. He took off his coat, then hers. They looked into one another's eyes, as if to speak, then looked away again. There was nothing to say. He led her to the bed, where they fell upon one another.

When the storm was over he opened his mouth to speak, but he couldn't find the words. She neither. Instead she kissed him gently on the forehead, extricated herself from his bed and was silently gone before he could really get his breath back. They hadn't even smiled at one another. But they did grin, weeks later, when they met in the street by accident. She had a little girl with her dressed in school uniform.

Whereas that was fun, another such encounter ended in anger and recrimination. Morgan loved female bums; he couldn't resist them. He dreamed about bums, lusted after bums, turned his head to watch bums jiggling by in the street. Sometimes he followed bums, entirely unable to resist. And after he'd fondled a naked bottom it was never forgotten. He collected them in his mind and enjoyed them afterwards like a stamp collector picking through his album. Some bottoms he remembered long after the face attached to them was forgotten. He loved thin bottoms and he loved plump ones; he liked girlish bottoms and he liked womanly ones; he liked pert bottoms, bottoms that stuck out, creamy bottoms, black bottoms, bottoms of almost every shape size age and kind. He loved bottoms that were proud of themselves, and bottoms that shrank away. Best of all he admired surprising bottoms, bottoms which when dressed , concealed their delights entirely. He knew what a fool he was over bottoms, realising that one day, like a moth, he would be lured into danger and consumed by the flame.

Suzy had a transcendental bottom. He noticed it one day, shown to advantage under a light blue pleated miniskirt, as she was stepping into a tube train. Although it wasn't his train he followed. When she got out at a remote station, miles away from his destination, he got out too. She changed lines, descending by a long escalator into the deeper catacombs. Hearing a train approaching on the deep level he realised she'd be in it and away before his limp allowed him to follow. Without thought or calculation he reached into his pocket and scattered pound notes into the air, crying 'Help' as they fluttered down towards her. Turning she saw the first one disappearing into the machine and bent to save it. Within minutes he had her telephone number. She was extremely pretty, with grey eyes, an engagement ring and an exaggerated upper class accent.

Her bum naked turned out to be every bit as gorgeous as he had anticipated. He was captivated by it, entranced by it, hypnotised by its silky seductive proportions. Unfortunately it was attached to someone with strong opinions, someone who liked to talk even when she was lying face down after intercourse. Morgan, lost in wonder, wasn't really listening.

"…..and daddy says all of them, all of those beastly trade union leaders ought to be shot. If you ask me, shooting is too good for them. If I had my way I'd flog them first. Every single one of them. Daddy says……."

Morgan recoiled. The only trade union leader he knew was Bob Salt, gentle Bob Salt. What did this ignorant little tart know of men like Bob, or indeed of the millions of other souls who had toiled alongside him in Britain's primitive factories. He bristled with anger; anger with Suzy, anger with daddy, but above all anger with himself for guilt by association. He felt contaminated.

"Your daddy" he said, pinching her bottom hurtfully "Sounds like an ignorant, greedy, arrogant, fascist swine."

The subsequent row woke up not only the neighbours on his own floor but tenants all the way down the five floors of the circular stair well.

CHAPTER 7
ANN

After eighteen months in London Morgan threw away his walking stick. His ankle worked normally so that he could walk with an almost imperceptible limp, although his toes remained paralysed and the bottom of his foot still hummed with electricity. Either the pain had greatly subsided, or else he had got so used to it that it didn't bother him much any more, although it was always there at the border of his mind. He slept normally and his weight had returned almost to its original fifteen and a half stone.

As his suffering subsided so did his sexual frenzy. Whether the two were connected, or whether one too many Suzies was responsible, he couldn't decide. He found that waking up with a stranger was scarcely better than visiting a prostitute and resolved to sleep only with friends in future.

Moreover time was flying by. His enormous computer programme, called 'Ethel', designed to investigate the formation of stars, still wasn't working. Week after exasperating week it returned from the Atlas computer accompanied by a printout of gibberish signifying yet another trivial programming mistake. It wasn't astronomy, it wasn't science, it was scarcely better than typing – an extra bracket here or an illegal comma there could waste an entire week's endeavour. Since the machine always stalled at the first grammatical mistake it encountered, he could identify and correct only one such error at a time, one single error a week. That panicked him eventually. There were six thousand lines of code in the programme, each line with an average of fifteen symbols, totalling ninety thousand symbols altogether. He was told that the very best programmers expected to make at least one mistake every hundred symbols, implying in his case at least nine hundred mistakes, or eighteen years of work.

He was appalled. Having sneered at his predecessor, who had become disheartened and left after twelve months, he now understood why. The project was simply impossible. His hopes of becoming an astronomer were dashed into smithereens. Unless he could work at least twenty times as fast, or more accurately than he was at present, he had no hope of producing a working programme, and hence a PhD thesis, within the remaining eighteen months of his bursary. Now he understood why the Americans had been willing to farm out the project abroad, and why no one else had taken it up. Morgan felt himself to be a complete and utter fool.

And yet there had to be a way! Or had there? When he talked to knowledgeable people they pointed out that huge programmes like his were usually the work of large teams, not of individuals. And anyway, before the days of massive machines like Atlas, no computers could handle programmes of such a size, so no one had written them. In other words he was exploring unknown territory.

Morgan's supervisor was unhelpful and unsympathetic while the professional 'advisers' at the university computer centre, because problems like his were of such recent vintage, knew even less about large scale computing than he did. For the same reason the library was no help either. The logic of his position was inexorable. He had to work twenty times faster. Or fail.

The solution, or at least the outline of a possible solution, came to him on the top of an 88 bus one morning as he was travelling to work. He must split the programme up into at least twenty self-contained modules, each one carrying out a separate task, each one testable by itself. If that could be done then he could submit twenty separate programmes to the computer every week, and proceed with error correction at twenty times his present pace. But could it be done? Could such a gigantic mathematical task be broken down into twenty such entirely self-contained programme modules?

It could. It took him only a week to establish, in principle at least, that the intricate logic could be broken into two dozen separate 'routines', with some of the 'routines' subdividing yet again. But all his previous work, over twelve months of it, would have to be scrapped. And the risks were enormous, the equal to anything he had faced in his climbing days. If he was wrong then his astronomical career, and with it all his dreams, would be over. He hesitated.

Weeks passed in an agony of indecision. He found himself looking for signs, like a superstitious Roman general examining the entrails of a chicken before going into battle. One week he decided to go ahead. The next he recoiled. The stakes were so great.

Finally he was left with no choice. For trivial grammatical reasons Atlas rejected his programme time and again. In fact it stuttered and faltered so consistently that all hope of it working had to be abandoned.

Morgan threw himself into the rewrite, working fourteen hours a day. He wrote programme modules in the bus, on the tube, in bed, while eating, in the park, even in the bath in his head. He wrote at astonishing speed, partly through necessity, partly through total immersion, but mainly because the modular approach was so much more transparent than the old way. Whereas before, when writing every single line of code, he had to worry about its repercussions throughout the entire six-thousand-line programme, now he could confine that worry to the module itself, and to its single simple purpose. Thus he wrote modules in days, and tested them to successful completion in weeks. He barely went to the observatory, haunting the university computing centre in Gordon Square, sometimes submitting and resubmitting a dozen program modules a day. Now at last he could feel a sense of progress as the modules proved out one by one. And when the last emerged successfully from the computer, all that remained was to write a brief 'master programme' which would shuffle the modules through the machine in the requisite order over and over again. Higher level modules were to call on lower level modules which in turn relied on slave modules to do the brute calculations. And because the same slaves could work for many masters, the final program, with all its modules, was much less than half the length of its nightmare predecessor.

With the air of a gambler throwing his last card on to the table Morgan finally submitted Ethel, down to her humblest slave routine, to the electronic leviathan. And she worked. Instead of reams of garbage, out came neat columns of pressures, densities, gravities, velocities and temperatures. His collapsing protostellar cloud had come to life. It was no longer computer programming, nor mathematics, nor even astrophysics; it was Nature speaking to him from the Cosmos at last.

The relief was enormous. He took his friends from the observatory out on a binge and slept afterwards like a hibernating bear. Although twenty-one of his allotted thirty-six months had slipped away, he seemed to be in sight of hope at last.

About this time Morgan began to fall in love — with somebody else's fiancée. Worse still that somebody else was one of his evening class students that he rather liked – Adrian Braithwaite. Ex public-school types never came to Workers Education lectures – with the exception of Adrian. Pin striped financiers wearing MCC ties never showed wild enthusiasm for anything so plebeian as astronomy – except Adrian. And nobody who earned tens of thousands of pounds a year in The City spent his evenings in the grubby occupation of grinding telescope mirrors – except Adrian. Adrian had absolutely no side to him – in fact he was a very nice man. It was not surprising therefore that he should have a very nice girlfriend – though she never came to the evening classes herself.

Morgan's main method of teaching, emulated from Dr Major his old physics master at school, was by means of posing questions. He liked to manoeuvre his classes into a position where they had to debate their way forward towards a possible answer, or alternative possible answers, for themselves.

"I want to demonstrate to you" he said at the end of one such class "That almost all our knowledge is second or third hand. We don't really know that the world is round. But we believe it is round because somebody told us when we were young. And that somebody had been told by somebody else, and so on. Although it is our conceit to imagine so, our brains were not, I believe, evolved to work things out for themselves. They are like sponges, designed to uncritically soak up vast amounts of second-hand information transmitted via tongue and ear. While it is a magnificent strategy for controlling our world, it renders us all dangerously vulnerable to false ideas. How do we know, since we know almost nothing at first hand, that our heads are not still packed full of false information, as we know now that the heads of all our predeceasing generations have been? The Victorians, for instance, ingenious though they were, believed that the Earth was no more than six thousand years old. Indeed the date of its birth had been worked out very exactly through biblical studies to be October 23 in 4004 BC."

"So here is my challenge. If you know anything of value at first hand, you ought to be able to demonstrate it to other intelligent people who do not share your preconceptions. So imagine that, by some quirk of a Time Machine, you have been transported back to central London as it was in the fourteenth century. You'd be wandering about in your pyjamas, looking odd if only because you were clean, sounding odd because you spoke with an unfamiliar accent, and using words that none of those bygone inhabitants had ever heard. In fact, to them, you would appear as a strange and suspicious being, possibly a witch. Almost certainly you would be picked up by the authorities and slung into gaol, there to suffer the terrible fate of witches in mediaeval times. But first you would be given the chance to prove that your fantastical story, about having come from the twentieth century, was true. All you have to do is prove to a panel of magistrates, who we shall assume to be fair and intelligent people, that you know something valuable, the fruit of seven hundred years of subsequent history and progress, that they do not. Your head is crammed with knowledge they do not have, knowledge of science, of technology, of geography, of history, of…of….oh of a million billion things. If you can only demonstrate one startling, useful piece of knowledge to them your story will be believed and you will be set free, might even be honoured. But if not then you will be condemned, as a witch or a madman. You have a week to think about it. Next Thursday we'll hold a mock trial. One by one you will have five minutes to plead your case, with the rest of us acting as the judiciary. I bet nobody succeeds."

The following Thursday Adrian Braithwaite was waiting outside the lecture room with a very pretty young woman in tow:

"I say Tom can I ask you a favour. This is Ann, Ann Cloudesly my fiancée. Can she please sit in on this evening's session. I mean we're happy to pay and all that……"

Morgan stared at Ann. She blushed, before taking up her fiancee's plea:

"It's just that Adrian comes back from your classes with such interesting questions. Since we spend half the week talking about them I thought I ought to come too."

"I'm afraid it's a bit late to join the course now. Anyway it's full. Officially."

Ann Cloudesly looked at the floor.

"But I tell you what, you could attend as Adrian's keeper-cum-medical adviser. See that his blood pressure doesn't get out of hand when he finds my lecture too interesting. Some of them die with excitement, don't they Adrian?"

"Ab..absolutely old boy."

"But what shall I do if he gets overexcited?"

'She really is lovely' Morgan thought 'Lucky old Adrian'

He probably stared at her too long because she blushed again.

"I tell you what" he said, recovering himself "I'll stare at you from time to time, and if Adrian is blowing up, you must wink at me. Then I'll talk about 'The Precession of the Equinoxes' a topic guaranteed to send him, you, and the rest of the class, to sleep in fifteen seconds flat."

The ensuing debate was lively. One by one the class came to the front and tried to prove that they came from the twentieth century. And one by one they were quizzed by their fellow students and found unconvincing. One wanted to make gunpowder – but couldn't explain where he would find the ingredients. Another wanted to quote the value of pi to seventeen places of decimals. But who in the fourteenth century would have been able to check whether he was right or wrong? A third wanted to make some spectacles, but the class were almost sure that they were already known by the fourteenth century. And so it went on until the janitor threw them out at ten, when they reconvened in the pub.

Although Morgan had used his licence to stare at Ann a great deal more than was strictly necessary, she never winked back. But she did ask some very perceptive questions which neither he, nor anyone else, could answer.

"I think I know a way." she offered eventually.

"Go on." Morgan sounded sceptical.

" I should demonstrate to them that a boat could be made to sail to windward. That would have seemed both amazing and extremely valuable to them. I'd do it by making a small model that would sail on a pond. It wouldn't take more than a couple of hours to make it and more than a couple of minutes to demonstrate that it would work."

"By God she's got it! " somebody opined, in imitation of Professor Higgins.

And by God she had, was the general opinion, after some discussion.

During the ensuing week Morgan found himself thinking about Ann Cloudesly a great deal. And he was bitterly disappointed when Adrian turned up for the following lecture on his own. Had he bored her? He was sorely tempted to ask Adrian where she was. He realised he'd been preparing his lecture with the sole aim of impressing Ann.

The following week she was absent also, but Adrian let drop in the pub that she was away in Washington on some hush-hush job.

"What does she do?" Morgan wanted to know.

"Don't ask me old boy. I've only known her ten years. Even her parents are mystified. We know she works in the Admiralty, off Whitehall, and that's it. If you ask her direct she says she can't say any more. Official Secrets Act and all that."

"But what's her training?" Morgan persisted.

"She got a double First in Maths and Russian."

"Odd combination."

"Isn't it just. Real brain box our Ann. God knows what she sees in a simple chap like me."

Now Morgan was really intrigued. He found himself fantasising about meeting her, on her own, by accident. He walked down Whitehall trying to locate the offices where she most likely worked. He spent a sunny lunchtime hoping to meet her eating her sandwiches on a bench in St James's Park. The reformed roué found himself behaving, and feeling, like a callow schoolboy.

On her return from Washington Ann Cloudesly became a regular fixture in the evening class. Morgan, a big show-off at the best of times, tried to weave a spell around this girl who obsessed his thoughts more and more. He gave outrageously brilliant and stimulating talks bringing in the whole breadth of his eclectic learning, his humour, his mimicry, his natural Welsh ability to preach, his hypnotic powers of persuasion, and his capacious memory for quotation. He held his audience bedazzled, fascinated, entangled in a wonder of enchanted anticipation. They even broke into spontaneous applause at times, having no idea that they were bystanders in a piece of outrageous male courtship. But did Ann? That was the question. And what would he do if she did fall for him? Morgan was nothing if not romantic and the idea of pinching another chap's girl, especially another chap he liked as much as Adrian Braithwaite, ran against his entire grain.

Ann Cloudesly wasn't the only distraction from his PhD project at this time. His paper on Red Giants, undermining Bellfounder's work, had been returned by the top British astronomical journal to which he had submitted it. The letter from the editor said:

Dear Mr Morgan

Your paper "Red Giant Stars: still not understood." has been read by two expert referees in the field. Neither of them recommends it for publication in this journal. Their comments, written anonymously, are enclosed with this letter.

Normally we recommend to an author in such a case that he re-submit his paper in an amended form, taking into account the referees' comments. Unfortunately here the referee's comments are so uniformly negative that we must reject the paper as unsuitable for publication in this journal

Yours sincerely

It was signed by a distinguished astrophysicist.

Morgan had felt so sure that he was right that the rejection came like a full-blooded kick in the stomach. He had to compose himself before tackling the referees' technical reports:

Referee A:

"This paper purports to prove that Bellfounder's classical work on the origin of Red Giant stars is wrong. If sound, this proof would amount to a very significant piece of astrophysics, fully worthy of publication in 'Monthly Notices of the Royal Astronomical Society'

Unfortunately the proof is not sound for a number of separate reasons. To begin with it relies on several crude assumptions, such as the discontinuous core-envelope boundary, which are nowhere justified, and are not convincing. Second, it purports to solve crucial differential equations using linearised approximations when it is obvious that second and even third order terms should be retained. Consider only the radiative transfer equation (17) on page 9......."

and the letter degenerated into a mass of technical algebra before concluding;

"Containing as it does such elementary and transparent mathematical mistakes it is hardly necessary to go into any further detail. Suffice to say that this paper should be rejected by The Royal Astronomical Society."

Morgan was appalled, supposing himself to have made some foolish mistake or mistakes. But then he skimmed his paper again, taking the criticisms one by one. They were outrageous. He leapt into the air and slammed the letter down on his desk with a cry of fury. Deliberately he had made no simplifying assumptions that Bellfounder had not made before him. All the charges levelled at Morgan applied therefore to Bellfounder's paper with equal force. And as for the approximation he had used to solve the differential equations, they were standard practice and used by Bellfounder too. Morgan felt sure that on closer analysis he would spot a fallacy in the referee's algebra.

Referee B wrote very differently:

"This paper attempts to discuss Sir Adrian Bellfounder's classical work on the theory of Red Giant stars. It is of a wholly negative character, and one easily detects here and there an unscientific frisson of personal spite.

Be that as it may the text largely consists of page after page of involved mathematics which may be, or more probably may not be, correct. Therefore before making the effort to plough through it in detail any sensible referee is going to ask himself whether it merits the effort. And I have to say that in this case it does not.

A mathematical theory in astrophysics is all very well, but at the end of the day a shrewd scientist will tend to believe it or not on more intuitive grounds. The elegance, the spareness and the compelling beauty of Bellfounder's theory, to say nothing of its agreement with the observations, all immediately appeal to the trained astronomical mind. 'Of course' one says after having read it for the first time 'Of course – so that is how it has to be.'

Even so I would be prepared to tackle all the ugly algebra if the author offered us an alternative to the theory he is so intent to undermine. But he does not. There is not the scrap of a better idea in the entire 27 pages.

Thus I decline to study in detail a paper so negative, so narrow-spirited, so unimaginative, and so unlikely to be right. I recommend rejection by The Royal Astronomical Society."

If Morgan was angry about the first referee's report he went hopping mad over this second: literally. To the astonishment of his office mates he tore it to pieces with a howl of execration, threw the scraps on the floor, and jumped up and down on them as if he was destroying a poisonous snake. It was a week before he could stop quivering with indignation, could think about anything else, could glue the offending letter back together again, and could sleep properly.

He decided to go back to the Midlands and consult his mentor Martin Johnson. His mother was delighted to see him looking healthy again while the Salts filled him in on their progress with the Mark IV, and its attempt on the world endurance record. The first attempt had failed when Ernie became so mentally exhausted after piloting the craft remotely for over four hours that he had crashed it into the ground. He blamed himself. Bob though disagreed:

"It's a design defect what we've got to put right. An' we will an' all. She pitches oop an' down a lot as the tanks empty. We're fittin' a trimmer, an'another RT channel to control it, as'll take care on that."

The Salts wanted to know all about Morgan's project so he showed them his huge computer programme as well as the referee's reports on his Red Giant paper. Bob's immediate reaction was:

"They dain't sound right to me. Sounds like they enjoyed a'writing 'em. An' they shouldn't. T'aint scientific."

Martin Johnson agreed:

"But what did you expect Tom? Bellfounder is on the editorial board himself, and more than half the rest are ex- students of his. Probably the referees are too. I told you to submit it to an American Journal. You'll have to now."

"But I've proved the first referee's algebra is wrong. Surely that will make a difference?"

"It might. You could try. But they're not bound to consider it again after an outright rejection like that. My advice is to submit it to The Astrophysical Journal in Chicago. Its editor, Chandrasekhar can't stand Bellfounder. I know."

" I can't beat a retreat. I want to beard Bellfounder in his own den."

"Good for you." Johnson laughed" But don't expect it to be easy. Alas the Cambridge establishment has got British astronomy in its pocket."

"I'll resubmit it, with a strong riposte to the editor."

Morgan invited Frank Cotteridge, on one of his infrequent visits back from California, to stay, and Frank slept on an air mattress for a week. It was a marvellous reunion on both sides. They both had so much to tell one another, that there was barely time to sleep. Frank, who was growing to resent Bellfounder more and more, had disturbing news from that quarter:

"He's out to get you I'm sure Tom. Which means he fears you are right. Why else would he worry about an obscure student from London University? He drops me hints from time to time, knowing full well I'll relay them to you. He's trying to put the frighteners on."

"He's got the wrong man for that."

"I know, but he could destroy you instead."

"How?"

"By undermining your PhD project. By beating you to the answer. In fact that's just what he's doing now. He's put this brilliant fellow Guy Tinker onto it. Tinker's a fluid dynamics whizz with years of experience in the defence industry, particularly in the States. He's acquainted with a lot of dodges that you are not. Your coordinate mesh is fixed in space, with the gas flowing through it. Tinker's mesh is locked to the infalling gas, collapsing in with it."

"My God, what a brilliant idea!" Morgan was thunderstruck.

"It's well known among the cognoscenti apparently. Your boss should have told you. But that's the least of it. Bellfounder's got his hands on the Los Alamos code."

"What on earth do you mean?"

"Who do you think knows most about spherical configurations of hot gas moving inwards and outwards?"

Morgan looked puzzled.

"The nuclear weapons people you mutt. For the last twenty years some of the best brains in the world, including all those brilliant European exiles, have been working at Los Alamos, their bomb research lab. developing hydrodynamic codes to compute nuclear bomb blasts – both implosions and explosions. That's hundreds of man-years of skilled effort, as against one from you. It's all classified of course. But somehow Bellfounder's got his fingers on it. One of his Machiavellian deals I suppose. And Los Alamos has agreed to do the actual computing. Tinker's gone over there for six months. Their 'black' computers probably make your Atlas look like a toy."

Morgan was temporarily lost in admiration for Bellfounder's plan:

"The cunning swine!"

"He'll delay your Red Giants paper, destroy your PhD project, and before you can say 'Jack Robinson' you'll be out of professional astronomy, and no threat to him any longer. You've got to work fast Tom, bloody fast. For a start you've just got to resubmit your Red Giant paper to a top American journal, 'The Astrophysical Journal' to be specific. It's got to come out fast enough to save your career." Morgan eventually submitted to this advice.

The following Saturday Morgan took his evening class for an all day visit to Stonehenge. Ann Cloudesly came too. Hawkins and Hoyle had recently written papers claiming that the ancient monument was actually a stone-age astronomical observatory, its huge megaliths aligned with important celestial events. After debating this hypothesis his class had decided to go out to Salisbury Plain to see for themselves. Morgan managed to borrow some sextants from his observatory so that the class could make their own measurements.

The great stones, brooding under a lowering sky, wove their spell as ever. He'd brought another class the previous year but he was no less awed by the spectacle. A line of Shelly came to his lips unbidden:

"My name is Ozymandias, king of kings…."

He was groping for the next stanza when a voice behind him continued:

"Look upon my works, ye mighty and despair."

He turned , and it was Ann Cloudesly. She continued:

"I always find this place more impressive than the Pyramids."

"You've been?"

"My father is an archaeologist."

She stood beside his shoulder, and they turned back to soak up the atmosphere together. The class, struck dumb themselves, had moved off among the Sarson Stones.

"Some scholars believe these stone circles predate The Great Pyramids. In which case civilization moved from North Western Europe to Asia, not vice versa. It all depends on controversial dating evidence."

He stared at her. She stared back. Drops of rain spotted on their anoraks. To break the silence he said:

"You know, we astronomers might be able to settle the issue. Constellations precess around the sky every twenty- six thousand years. If this ever was an observatory then by now it will be misaligned with the stars. How far it is misaligned will tell us exactly when it was built."

"How ingenious you are." Then she added hastily "Astronomers I mean."

"The problem is that these massive stones will settle and lean in the wet soil. That alone could destroy the alignment. That is what the class is going to try and measure today. They'll compare their measurements with Atkinson's taken a decade or so ago. If there's any difference in such a short time it would have to mean settling."

"I know. Adrian's very excited. It's his first chance to do some real research. He hasn't talked about anything else all week."

"He's volunteered to take charge of the surveying. So that lets me off for the day."

"And they're old enough to go to the lavatory on their own." She smiled.

"Well most of them. I'm sure Adrian will do the honours if necessary."

The rain stopped. A beam of sunlight illuminated the plain in the distance.

"Have you heard of Avebury?" she asked.

"No."

"It's just a few miles away. I find it even more impressive than the Henge."

"Never."

"But you haven't seen it."

"No."

"You should go then, while they're busy. Take the minibus."

He stared at her.

She said "I'll come with you if you like."

He held his breath; could feel the blood pounding in his neck:

"What about Adrian?"

"I'll tell him first of course. But he'll be too excited to notice."

She walked off towards the Sarson Stones. Morgan watched her, his heart racing. He felt faint inside. They'd be alone together, perhaps for hours.

Avebury knocked him flat: it was an immense stone circle half a mile across, composed not of faceted stones like the henge, but of rough cut megaliths of enormous size standing on their ends. Their sheer primitiveness bespoke a civilization altogether alien, altogether strange, whose thoughts could not be shared, however hard a man tried. Other avenues of stones marched away from it towards the horizon and towards Silbury Hill, a mysterious man-made monument of massive proportions. The far side of the circle included the village of Avebury, obviously constructed out of vandalised megaliths. Everywhere the grass was sculpted into barrows and ditches betokening the industry of tens of thousands of forgotten men, working thousands and thousands of years ago.

"But why don't we all know about this?" Morgan demanded. "It's bloody breathtaking. It beats Stonehenge, Westminster Abby and St Paul's Cathedral knocked into one. It... it..it it is staggering."

"And do you know it was all dug out with antlers? Archaeologists find them everywhere here, often worn out. Can you imagine the organisation that must have been involved?"

"What the hell was it for?"

"Of course nobody knows. Probably nobody ever will. But they buried men, possibly alive, under some of these megaliths."

"Oh God! Religion. How I hate religion. I loathe it."

Ann laughed:

"You see, you have to appeal to God even to forswear him."

"Are you religious?" Morgan looked at her abruptly.

"Do I believe in a specific religion? Yes, I'm a Christian of a sort. Am I fascinated by religion? Yes of course I am. Men are by nature religious maniacs. All archaeology and history tell us so. Did you know……"

They wandered round the site, marvelling at its grandeur, arguing about its significance, sizing one another up both physically and intellectually. When the rain began to come down steadily they huddled under a leaning stone and shared Ann's sandwiches.

"We are Stone Age people" Ann maintained "Man was cradled and evolved over a million years at least, all but one per cent of it lying in The Stone Age. To understand ourselves we have to understand them – before they are all gone. By the end of this century the last of them will be extinct. No Bushman will be left who can kill an elephant with his spear, no Eskimo woman who can make polar clothing out of skins, no poet left to tell their stories or sing their songs...."

Morgan was startled by the depth of sadness in her voice.

"I'd never thought of that." He stared down at her, desperately wanting to kiss her eyelids but terrified of making a wrong move. He looked down at her engagement ring. She followed his glance, half moved her hand to hide it, then left it resting on her knee.

"I suppose we'd better go back." he said, trying to conceal his cowardice. "If the rain gets any worse the others will want to shelter in the bus. Come on, lets run for it."

Driving back through the downpour he felt so tensed up that he nearly tore the steering wheel from its column. If he didn't speak now he might never get a second chance. But if he did speak, and it was too early, and it definitely was, he could drive her away altogether.

As they drove into the Stonehenge car park and stopped, the downpour turned into a deluge. Anoraked figures began running towards the bus:

"Ann, I've got to say this. I'm obsessed with you. I must love you". He looked straight ahead, not at her. "Since I first saw you I haven't been able to think about anything else…"

At that moment the first refugees reached the bus and flung open the sliding door:

"It's a cloudburst out there. We're all coming...."

The following week Adrian came to class on his own. And the week after that too. Morgan, cursing himself for a clumsy fool, could barely sleep at all. When he did nod off he woke again minutes later, his heart pounding like a pile driver. The only resort was to throw himself into research.

His big computer programme was now producing sensible results. His artificial protostars were collapsing under their own self-gravity, and as they collapsed cooling. This puzzled him for a while until he realised that they were completely transparent, and that transparent gas radiates its heat away faster as it contracts. But if that was so then the whole story was obvious, and a computer calculation was almost superfluous. The centre would fall in upon itself until, billions of times denser than it began, the central gas would become opaque to its own radiation and heat up to high temperature. At some point the gas pressure might rise high enough to halt the collapse and form a radiating protostar. So much was obvious. He could even make a rough back-of-the –envelope calculation to estimate when and how that would occur. All that remained was to calculate the outcome in detail with his programme.

And this is where things began to go wrong. All the action was taking place at the very centre of his protostar which was plunging in upon itself at ever increasing speed, whereas the outer parts, containing ninety nine point nine per cent of the material, barely moved at all. In other words his computer programme was wasting ninety-nine point nine per cent of its effort calculating numbers which barely changed whilst devoting zero point one percent of its energy to the central region where all the action was taking place. He could see now that the whole computational strategy was misconceived. He'd never anticipated the centre running away so fast, whereas Bellfounder and his henchman Tinker obviously had. Their programme, so Frank had reported, was ingeniously designed to follow the collapsing gas inward, cleverly reassigning its effort to the very place where it was most needed.

Morgan fell into despair. He knew what had to be done now, but he knew he had no time left to reformulate the mathematics in new Tinker-type coordinates and then virtually re-write his programme from scratch. He essayed all kinds of ingenious tricks to cheat the system, but they only put off the inevitable breakdown by insignificant amounts. The programme would come back from the Atlas computer showing ridiculous non-physical numbers such as negative temperatures in the centre. Deprived of the increased effort it needed there, the unavoidable approximations involved in representing smooth motion by a series of discontinuous steps broke down and then blew up. The more he desperately schemed, the more he thought about it in the night hours, the more certain it was that he was facing total defeat. The whole bloody scheme was misconceived. He'd set out to cross the Atlantic in a coracle and now, two years later, he'd been blown back onto the beach. He cursed his supervisor Hood for dreaming up such a misbegotten scheme, but most of all he cursed himself for not thinking properly. He'd been so involved in the mechanics of the computing, in other words rowing the bloody coracle, that he'd forgotten the navigation altogether. It was a complete and utter fiasco.

The only thing which puzzled him was why the gas in the very centre of his sphere behaved so dramatically, whilst the rest hardly moved. What was so special about the centre? How did the stupid gas there know that it was in a special place and behave accordingly? His boss had told him to start to start the whole thing off from rest, and in pressure equilibrium. But to achieve that equilibrium he'd had to make the gas in the centre slightly denser than the outside, so as to balance gravity. So it was obvious. Left to itself the denser gas cooled faster, lost its pressure first, and so collapsed first. It was as simple and mundane as that.

This however raised a philosophical question. If the behaviour of the gas was entirely dictated by the arbitrary initial constraints imposed upon it at the beginning of the calculation, then the outcome was the inevitable consequence, not of cosmic laws, but of arbitrary choices, made for his convenience, by the computer programmer in charge. By himself in fact.

To check that this was so he slightly modified the starting conditions for the gas, and sure enough it collapsed in a different manner altogether. He was playing an utterly capricious god.

The obvious next step was to put in no arbitrary information at all: to let the gas start off from a completely uniform, utterly structureless state. He did so, and the results surprised him. All of the gas collapsed, save that clinging to the outer boundary. And a strange pressure wave moved inward at exactly the speed of sound, dividing the collapsing gas interior to it, from the static clinging gas without. Huge densities developed at the centre, which the programme could now calculate since they were uniform, while the rest remained unmoved and unmoving. By the time the pressure wave reached the centre there was a tiny protostar there comprising one thousandth part of the original mass.

He could have been excited, but he was not. The tiny protostar was so obviously an artefact of the initial uniform conditions, that it had no physical significance. And the pressure wave was another artefact of holding the outside boundary of the calculation, and hence of the gas, absolutely still. To check that that was so, he allowed the boundary to drift inwards under the influence of gravity, and sure enough the mysterious wave vanished.

He'd learned nothing, absolutely nothing about the real cosmos, but he'd learned a great deal about the perils of simulating it with a computer. It was simply a case of GIGO, as it was known in the trade; "Garbage In, Garbage Out." Whatever he or anyone else fed into such a program in the beginning, it would be more or less garbage because no one knew at this stage what protostellar material looked like before it collapsed. A programmer's arbitrary choices would pre-determine the outcome. Nor would Bellfounder, and his henchman Tinker, despite the promised sophistication of their programme, be any better off. They could not know, any more than he could, what the detailed conditions were like in interstellar space, and it was the details which appeared to matter. An elaborate computer simulation, like his, of the hairs on a unicorn, would only be of interest when a unicorn had been sighted for sure.

At least he had something to say in his thesis, even if it was disappointingly negative, and rather meagre. He could point out that an understanding of star formation could come only after the physical properties of interstellar space had been mapped in detail by observers. His calculations could at best demonstrate what physical parameters would have to be measured, and with what detail and precision. Astronomers of the future, designing the satellite instruments that would be needed to map the interstellar medium, could look at his work for guidelines. "Anyway" said Mussels in the pub, trying to console Morgan "Most scientific projects end in failure. And a sound negative result can be useful. It tells one's successors 'Don't waste your time following this path again. Try elsewhere' ".

For Morgan himself the story had a different moral: in astronomy observations count far more than theories. If he was going to be a real astronomer he had to become an observer, not a theoretician. And that meant moving abroad. Because of its climate Britain no longer had a single competitive optical telescope.

When Ann Cloudesly failed to turn up at his evening class yet again, Morgan could restrain his impatience no longer. He tackled Adrian in the pub:

"Oh she won't be coming again. Bit awkward really Tom."

Morgan's heart stopped.

"Why not?"

"She's broken it off – our engagement I mean."

"I'm sorry." His heart raced on again.

"Thanks old boy. But not to worry. Best thing really. Both parties can move on and all that. Do you know we'd been engaged for nine years? Not healthy."

"Good Lord!"

"This gorgeous little thing of seventeen in the tennis club set her cap at me. What could a chap do? Bowled over completely. But then we grew up – or rather Ann did. And things didn't develop – if you know what I mean. Blamed herself. Good sort our Ann. Didn't want to let me down and all that. So it rather dragged on. Both relieved really. Good friends still. Said I didn't mind a bit if she continued to come to your class. No probs at all. But she said 'Better not'. Smart girl our Ann. I'd always rely on her judgement. Always did. So we won't be seeing her again."

"I'm sorry."

Adrian sank his pint with evident satisfaction before concluding:

"Well old boy you won't have to answer those fiendish questions of hers."

"That's why I'll miss her."

Morgan fled away to think on his own. What could it mean? Either she didn't want to see him again. Or she did. Surely it was too much of a coincidence that she must have broken with Adrian almost immediately after his clumsy declaration. That had to be significant, it had to. He couldn't wait to see her again.

But he was forced to wait. The awkward fact was he had no idea where she lived. And he could never ask Adrian. Never. He looked through the enormous London telephone directory. There were pages of Cloudeslys, not one of whom was obviously Ann.

The one clue he had was her father's profession. Archaeologists must be rare, especially professionals. But how to find them. He began digging around in libraries, lists and directories without much success. The obvious British Archaeological Society turned out to be mostly for amateurs. Then one Friday afternoon he walked into the courtyard at Burlington House to attend an RAS meeting. Around the courtyard were situated the premises of many of the most learned societies in the land: the Royal Academy with its famous art gallery; the Royal Geological Society which housed on one interior wall the first ever geological map made by man, the masterpiece by William Smith; and, most famous of all, the Linnaen Society to which in 1858 Alfred Russell Wallace and Charles Darwin had submitted their earthshaking papers on The Theory of Evolution. It always gave him a thrill to look around and see so much learning concentrated in one glorious building. If there was such a thing as a centre to 'The Thinkers' World' then this had to be it. He was glancing round when his eyes caught a notice; "The Society of Antiquaries of London". Of course that had to be it! This was where the professionals would probably hang out. He walked straight in and accosted the frosty looking lady at the reception desk. The name 'Cloudesly' however thawed her out a bit and she permitted him to look through the vast and ancient tome entitled "List of Fellows 17........" But he had to use white gloves, under the dragon's supervision, to turn the ancient pages very slowly. And there it was: 'Henry Cecil Cloudesly, elected Fellow 14 Nov 1937.

"Is he still a Fellow?

'Oh yes. Professor Cloudesly is well known to us."

"Do you have his current address please?"

She took away the ancient volume, and the gloves, and returned with a big ring-binder which she opened at the appropriate page before putting it on the counter before him:

'Professor H.C. Cloudesly,
School of Oriental and African Studies (S.O.A.S),
University of London,
10 Thombaugh St.,
Bloomsbury,
London W.C. 1

"Cripes" Morgan couldn't help exclaiming with delight "He's just round the corner from my computer centre. Yippee! Have you got a telephone directory?"

"Well I ...."

"I've found my girl. Please. It's so important. Oh please! The A to C bit."

And there it was: her father's home address in Kew. He jotted it down. Then he reached over, pulled the startled dragon towards him and planted a firm kiss on her forehead:

"I'm so grateful. We'll name our third daughter after you. What's your name?"

"Well I....."

"Don't be shy."

"Its Elspeth."

"Elspeth!" he cried dancing out through the door and into the sunshine "It's little Elspeth."

Dozens of people making their way towards the Royal Academy turned to stare at him.

"It's little Elspeth I tell you!" he cried exultantly, leaping high in the air and punching the sky with both arms "It's darling little Elspeth!"

Then he ran out into Piccadilly in search of a post office. His telegram read:

"Darling lovely Cloudesly. I can't live without seeing you. Not a weekend longer. Have mercy on Morgan. Please do."

After the RAS meeting , which passed in a blur, he rushed home to Lancaster Gate and knocked up the concierge.

"Yes this came for you Mr Morgan. Not ten minutes back. What a coincidence!" She handed over the small yellow telegram envelope which he tore open:

"What on earth delayed you ? Noon Sunday lunch here plus tennis. Miss Merciful."

Noon Sunday found Morgan walking up the drive of a rather comfortable detached house overlooking a cricket match which was proceeding on Kew Green; 'Tunbridge Wells Style' he would have called the house, probably Edwardian. In his arms the finest bunch of roses that West London could provide, glowed in the sunshine.

A woman even more beautiful than Ann, with startling amethyst eyes and brilliant white hair, opened the door.

"Oh how gorgeous." she leaned forward and smelled a crimson rose. "You must be Mr. Morgan the astronomer."

"Tom."

"Tom Morgan then. Ann told us about you. But she didn't mention how enormous you were. Quite enormous. Well please come in. I'm Ann's mother Gwendolyn – as you probably guessed. I can't shake hands; as you can see I'm covered in flour from mixing the Yorkshire pudding. I do hope you like rare beef. Henry insists on it. Ann's out in the back garden marking the tennis lawn. Her father's just finished the mowing and is having his shower. Go through the conservatory."

The garden was deep and secluded from its neighbours by trees. Ann in tennis clothes was walking away from him, carefully pushing a small wheeled trolley which etched the new mown grass in a white line.

Keeping quiet he was almost upon her when she turned to retrace the line:

"Oh. You startled me." her hand flew up to cover her throat. Time stood still as they stared at one another. Then he put the roses on the ground and stepped up to her.

"I'm going to kiss you," he reached forward "I have to kiss you Cloudesly. I thought I'd be terrified; shy. But I can't wait."

He folded her in his arms, snuggled his nose into her hair, nibbled the top of one ear, kissed her first on both eyelids then full on the mouth.

"Oh Tom" she murmured, putting her arms round his neck and kissing him passionately back "You'll have to hold me tight. My knees are giving way. Really and truly." she laughed. And they did give way. Totally.

He lowered her gently onto the grass, kissed the insides of both knees, then the tip of her long nose before staring into her hazel green eyes from inches away.

"My God you're lovely."

"Lovely for you, and that shall be enough."

"Oh Ann my darling, my Cloudesly Ann."

"Drink to me only with thine eyes. Why have you taken so long Tom? I've been waiting for you since I was twelve years old."

"That's not what Adrian told me."

"I got confused and sort of mixed him up with you. I knew about you all along. Honestly Tom, I did. You were in my destiny. And then when I saw you outside your class that first night, looking so strong and so deep, a Greek wrestler with a poet's head, I just began to pine away. You can feel my tummy. No not now! Daddy'll be coming here any minute to see if I've finished."

Professor Cloudesly, wearing cricket flannels and a straw hat, had the complexion of a man used to excavating under a desert sun. Like Ann occasionally, his thoughts seemed to wander inwards, or many a thousand miles away. But he looked at Morgan acutely as they shook hands:

"Astronomy um? Very similar to my game I should think. Big theories resting on slender facts, with lots of room for ego and imagination. How's your tennis?"

"Haven't played since I was in the Army sir – must be seven years ago. And not well then."

The professor harrumphed, as if he wasn't best pleased; "Call me Henry."

"Daddy's a tennis-bore Tom."

"It's just the pairings my dear. Where will we fit him in?"

"He'll play with me of course. You'll just have to play with Mum for a change."

"You know we always argue."

More people drifted in. Ann put her roses in water while Morgan helped Henry pour drinks in the conservatory.

It was to be a magic afternoon. For Morgan it truly felt like the first day of the second half of his life. The two of them drank one another in across the luncheon table while the other guests, many of them archaeological, debated everything from Wittgenstein to Wimbledon. After lunch the two of them volunteered to do the washing up alone together whilst the rest snoozed off their claret in the garden. Gwendolyn laughed when she discovered them in a passionate embrace at the kitchen sink, Morgan with a saucepan in one hand and a tea towel in the other, Ann with her dripping hands in rubber gloves.

Then there was the tennis tournament, presided over by Henry, keenly played and jovially applauded. Ann, as it transpired, was very good indeed whilst Morgan, although out of practice, had at least a good eye and a strong arm. Although they comfortably lost their first set to an archaeological couple, Ann was confident they would improve. Before they took on her parents she coached him:

"The secret is to annoy Daddy and make Mummy laugh. Neither very difficult you'll find. Then they'll both go to pieces. We'll keep you up at the net and remember to play on Mummy's forehand. And to annoy Dad all you've got to do is pretend not to take tennis seriously. But mind you only pretend. We've got to try and beat them."

Things didn't go well until somebody remarked aloud that Morgan played tennis like a gorilla. From that moment he aped a gorilla: beating his chest when they scored a point; jumping up and down in a simulated rage when they lost one; staring over the net honking, with his mouth wide open; lurching grotesquely round with his knees bent and his fingers trailing in the grass. He soon had Gwendolyn helpless with laughter whilst Henry's face grew darker and darker. Ann's relentless ground strokes pierced the no-man's land between her parents, whilst Morgan's volleys and smashes were directed either straight at Henry's body, or as far away from Gwendolyn as possible. In this manner, and to the delight of the audience who thought it was hilarious, they managed to win back four games in a row. At this point Gwedolyn collapsed onto the ground, her head between her knees, convulsed with Morgan's antics Henry, too polite to attack Morgan with his tennis racket — which he transparently wanted to do, lost his temper with his wife instead. Ann had to vault over the net and pacify him by whispering something in his ear. Whatever she said, it had an electrifying effect. Henry turned to stare at Morgan in incredulous disbelief, pulled his wife to her feet and proceeded to demolish Morgan's thin game with a barrage of withering passing shots and teasing lobs. He even shook Morgan's hand at the end of the game.

"Whatever did you whisper in your dad's ear?" Morgan asked Ann afterwards.

"If you can't guess then I'm not going to tell you."

"I've never seen a man so galvanized."

"I simply adore a man who can make me laugh" Gwendolyn remarked later, rewarding Morgan with a large piece of fruit cake "And I haven't laughed so much in ages. Ann needs somebody like you. She adores her father, but he's inclined to make her too serious. All those crossword puzzles and cryptograms…."

After everybody else had left, Ann showed him photos of the family out on digs, mostly in the Middle East. Gwendolyn, it transpired, nearly always went with her husband, organised his camps, liaised with the locals, and arranged the local labour.

"They're a wonderful team together" Ann explained "He can concentrate on the archaeology while she does the logistics – which are often much the harder part out in the wilds."

"What's his interest?"

"Trade. He believes trade was and is the driving force towards civilisation. He looks for and interprets evidence of trade between cultures distant from one another in space. He looks for characteristic artefacts and tries to date them as precisely as possible."

"And who's this serious little girl looking at pottery fragments?"

"That's me, out in Crete I think, about eleven years old. We were looking for trade links between the Egyptians and the Aegean."

"Did you always go with them?"

"Oh yes. Daddy taught me how to catalogue things, and later draw up maps of the digs, precisely locating every find. That's important in the later analysis."

"And now?"

"I can't alas. Just the odd week. I'm a working girl now. I miss it terribly. They're off to Petra next month, working on the Nabatians."

"Petra?"

"Jordan; a civilisation hidden in an inaccessible gorge and lost to history for almost twelve hundred years. It's the poet's '…rose red city half as old as time.' "

"Why did you give up on archaeology?"

"There are even more fascinating things to do. But I haven't really. I still keep my eye in during spare time. Dad got me interested in decrypting ancient hieroglyphs; you know, Linear – B, the Rosetta Stone and so forth."

"Thomas Young and Champollion?"

"Yes. Wait here and I'll get something."

She came back with a terra cotta earthenware disc about eight inches across and covered with mysterious hieroglyphs forming a spiral pattern. He turned it round in his hand, admiring the enigmatic writing.

"It's a replica of the Phaestos disc" Ann explained "The original disc, of which this is a copy, was found in 1908 at the palace of Phaestos in Crete. Its probable date is close to eighteen hundred BC. That makes it by far the oldest written script anywhere in Europe. Moreover it's the first example of moveable-type printing in world history. It predates Guthenburg by three thousand years. But no one's deciphered it. Not convincingly. I'm having a go in my spare time, using computers and so forth. If we could crack it, what a story it might have to tell. But I'm not hopeful. The 241 symbols, of 45 different types are probably not enough. There are too many alternatives. But you never know. If only somebody could find some more such writing. It must be out there somewhere, hidden in the earth."

"Doesn't it have any predecessors or successors?"

"Not convincingly, though some have suggested Minoan Linear A, whereas others have proposed Homeric Greek, or even Atlantan from Atlantis – if it ever existed. We don't even know if it was Cretan originally. Look at that symbolic ship. There's nothing else like it in the entire record. We don't even know if it's a story, or a game board, or an obituary. It's a fascinating mystery. Wouldn't it be wonderful to break it?"

"It's code cracking." He looked at her directly, "That's what you do isn't it?"

"In my spare time, yes." Her tone was opaque.

At Morgan's insistence they spun out their courtship:

"I want to woo you."

"Consider me well and truly wooed."

"No, there's more to come; much more. I can only woo you once, and I don't want to miss a single, delicious tiny phase of that experience. I want to serenade you with poetry, charm you with flowers, beguile you with laughter, enchant you with music and kiss a new tiny naked place on your body every single day. Let's pretend we're eighteen, not twenty-eight."

"Romeo and Juliette."

And so it was. They canoodled in the Park, stood with the other young things in the well of the Albert Hall listening to the Proms, dressed up for the opera, danced the night away in Chelsea, dined by candlelight on exotic foods, and explored one another's tastes and bodies tiny bit by tiny bit. Ann confessed to being a virgin:

"I was too young to begin with. Then, by the time I wasn't, Adrian and I were more like brother and sister."

"I wouldn't care whether you'd slept with a a dozen men. Not before. But if any man so much as looks at you from now on I'll beat him to a bloody pulp."

"My Tarzan."

But that was how he felt: childishly, ferociously protective. He couldn't bear for anyone to knock into Ann, even on the Tube, where it was inevitable. He was a young boy, ridiculously in love for the first time. All his sexual liaisons of the previous year meant nothing, absolutely nothing beside the oceanic experience which engulfed him now. He phoned her constantly, though he didn't have a phone in his flat. Just to hear her say 'Ann Cloudesly' on her office phone gave him a thrill. Indeed of all the things he loved about her he loved her soft feminine voice the best of all. He would make her lie on his bed, stark naked, and read to him whilst he caressed the most sensitive parts of her body until she was too helpless to continue.

"I'll explode." she groaned.

"I'm just about to press the detonator."

As they explored one another's bodies so they embarked on the even more fascinating voyage into one another's minds, souls and pasts. He told her about Malaya, something he'd told nobody else. She told him about the two years she'd spent studying abroad, one in Paris and one in Leningrad. He told her about his research, she told him about hieroglyphics. They were both addicted to mathematics, but to quite different parts of it, and for quite different reasons. He loved it as a magic casement onto the physical world, she loved it for its ability to unweave otherwise hidden patterns.

"Do you know" she said, lying beside him on his bed one day, and pointing at the wall "There can be only seventeen basically different wallpaper patterns? Whatever the motif the repetitive plan must belong to one of that exclusive group. No other patterns can repeat themselves both along the roll, and from side to side."

"I don't believe a word of it" he teased her "How could one ever find out?"

"By using Group Theory. It's a classical proof. I'll show you if you like." And she did. Morgan spent his life thereafter trying to fit everybody's wallpaper into the correct mathematical category.

She was smarter than he was. Her mind sometimes leapt ahead with lightening speed. He didn't resent this in the least: it simply made him prouder of her than ever, and proud that she loved him.

He especially delighted to hear her speaking of Stone Age life. Every day, like a child, he demanded a new story from that time, of which Ann seemed to know hundreds. The ingenuity of the Old Men and Women, which was all they had to resist their harsh surroundings, never ceased to astound him. She told him how an Eskimo could kill a giant polar bear simply by using his brain, or how an aboriginal could find honey in the deepest forest by catching a bee, attaching a hair to its tail with a lick, and following it back to its nest in the trees.

"But how on earth does he get the honey out?"

"He sends up his wife you chump."

"I'll remember that my girl, when we're short of honey one day."

Unfortunately there was a huge area of Ann's life, and of her past, which was closed off to him – her work, which evidently fascinated her. She wouldn't argue but was absolutely firm.

"I wish I could share it with you Tom, I so wish I could. I'd love to. It's not natural, but I can't. I've signed the Official Secrets Act and that's that. It's absolute, it's eternal, and believe me it has to be so."

"I'll beat it out of you."

"I'm trained to resist torture."

"Damn."

Then there was money. As opposed to Morgan's student grant Ann had a very good salary, with little to spend it on, living at home. But he refused, absolutely refused to let her pay for a thing. Neither of them cared about money but Ann thought he was ridiculous and impractical. And it certainly did cramp their style. She wanted to buy a ticket for him to come to New York whilst she was there, but he pig-headedly refused.

"You're my girl Miss Cloudesly Ann," he explained "And I hope you always will be. Protecting you, and looking after you in every conceivable way, is my pride and joy. You cannot imagine the pleasure I get from providing for you, even in the silliest little ways. You can buy me presents – but that's it."

"But it is a present. Not just to you but to me also."

"It's too much, and you know it is. I'd feel a kept man."

"Some lover you, turning down a honeymoon in Manhattan."

She wanted to sleep with him properly. But she wouldn't spend the night at his flat, and on those terms Morgan adamantly refused:

"There's going to be no hole-in-the-corner stuff here – if that's the appropriate phrase. When we go all the way for the first time you're going to wake up in the morning in my arms." But she wouldn't stay.

He gradually realised the problem – though Ann would never admit to it. Henry Cloudesly was insanely jealous, something against which she seemed powerless to act. She was his only daughter, his only child, and as close to him as any human could be. They'd lived together for nearly all of Ann's twenty seven years and he couldn't face the prospect of ever giving her up. They shared his interests: archaeology, tennis, hieroglyphics, crossword-puzzles, ancient music......He was used to spending several hours with her every day and resented it when he could not. Poor Adrian, Morgan realised, had never stood a chance. Cloudesly had probably withered any thought of sex for her long before it ever ripened on the vine.

The second time Morgan went round to Kew they lunched en quartette when Henry Cloudesly made no attempt to conceal his antagonism. He interrupted Morgan's stories, poured sarcasm on his opinions, spoiled his jokes, and found petty excuses to draw Ann away whenever the two of them got together alone. Ann grew increasingly distressed, Morgan increasingly angry and Gwendolyn increasingly stone-faced. Cloudesly even tried, on some transparent pretext, to prevent Ann from coming to the station to see Morgan off. She came, but she was almost in tears.

For once in his life Morgan had the good sense to button up his lip, although he was seething inside. Things were far too serious for a single wrong move.

He could see that Ann was, in more than one sense, Henry Cloudesly's creation; his Trilby. He had taken a brilliant child and moulded her into a female edition of himself. She adored him, emulated him, basked in the sun of his praise, shrunk in the shadow of his disapproval. He loved her unconditionally and without limit as he loved a reflection of himself, but he had turned her into a puppet. She was powerless to really act unless he was manipulating her strings. Why else was she still living at home? Why else was she still a virgin? Why else had she suffered a platonic engagement to drag on for years and years?

She talked of her father to Morgan all the time. She boasted of his achievements, shared most of his values, laughed at his foibles and tantrums, admired even his autocratic ways:

"But I like being bossed about Tom. I know it's not fashionable to say so, but it makes me feel womanly and it's no use pretending. You know how indecisive I can be."

"You'd never order anything in a restaurant if I wasn't there."

"Exactly. If I ever find a husband I'll need one who'll order me around. I know it sounds selfish but I want to relax entirely into his arms and love him, leaving the crises of the world, and the big decisions, entirely to him."

"Another big Daddy in fact?"

"You can laugh Tom Morgan but you had better listen."

"I am. Nobody ever accused me of being meek, or indecisive. I'm as bossy as they come,"

"You're bossier than Daddy."

Morgan realised that the longer he postponed, the more difficult things would become for Ann at home. Henry Cloudesly would never relent – short of facing a fait accompli. Perhaps not even then. And there was a frisson of fear in Morgan's mind. What had he got to show beside the great Professor Cloudesly's achievements? It might be all too easy for her father, drip by corrosive drip, to undermine Morgan in Ann's eyes. He would certainly be trying.

"How long does it take to arrange for a week off work?" he asked her.

"There's nothing much on at the moment" Ann replied "I could probably leave on Monday. Why?"

"Because I want to take you with me to Belgium. To Liege. It may not be Manhattan, or Mandalay, but it's all I can afford at present. There's a big international astronomical conference there, my very first, and I want you to come with me and find out what it might be like being an astronomer's wife. In every sense of the word."

"In every sense of the word?"

"In every sense of the word my little Cloudesly Ann. Without let or inhibition. From cock crow to cock crow. From night fall to day break. In ropey hotels and second class trains. In my bed and at my command. For better or worse; wife for a week."

"Golly, how could a girl refuse? This girl anyway. It sounds like an initiative test."

They went, though Ann didn't tell her father. They did stay in a ropey little hotel, but to both of them it seemed like heaven. There they consummated their love and there, the next morning, as she lay in his arms, Morgan placed the engagement ring on Ann's finger. It was an antique gold ring, found in a street market, decorated with amber coloured stones. She burst into tears and never left Morgan's side for the entire week, even sitting beside him clutching his arm through hour after hour of technical lectures on 'Star Formation'.

When they parted at Victoria Station Ann clung to him:

"I don't want to go. You're my home now. I want to come with you."

"You can my love, but you've got to tell your parents first."

"I know."

"Do you want me to come? It would be expected."

"No, don't do that. Daddy might be horrible and I don't want him to say things to you that he could never retract and that you could never forgive."

"Nor I to him. But don't let him bully you. And don't spare his blushes. Tell him you're sleeping with me, and will do so from now on. The sooner he faces up to the truth the better for him, and for all concerned. But I hate to see you do this on your own. Now promise me."

"I promise."

"And don't unpack your case. If things get too nasty pop it in a taxi and come straight round to Lancaster Gate. I'll be at home waiting. Whatever happens I'll ring you at ten. Keep calm but be firm."

"I promise darling."

"He'll come round eventually. He's got to; otherwise he'll never see his grandchildren."

When he rang at ten she replied in whispers:

"The worst is over now I think. So don't worry. When I told them, Daddy slapped my face and called me a slut. Mummy really went for him then, like a wild cat. Told him he was unnatural and needed to see a doctor. She told me to pack my bags and come to you. Then Daddy broke into tears. It was awful. He's never done that before. But then he kissed us both, apologised, and burst into tears again. He said he couldn't bear to lose me. We both told him he certainly would unless he sorted himself out and made it up with you. Then he lost his temper again and threatened to go out to Petra next week. Mummy said she'd pack his bag at once, and good riddance. Now he's locked himself in his study."

"Do you want to come to Lancaster Gate?"

"Of course I do darling. But if I did so now it would be tantamount to running away. And that, as I realise, is just what I've been doing for years. Seeing Daddy cry sort of broke the spell. It was awful at first, I couldn't bear it. But it was also liberating. He's just a little human being underneath – like me and you. And in some ways, under that masterful exterior, a rather pathetic one. It' harder for Mum to see him crack like that. I've got you; she's just got him. That's why I have to stay, at least tonight. For her."

"Are you sure you don't want me to come over?"

"It would only humiliate him further darling. He's got to be able to look you in the eye. If he knows you know he hit me, I don't know what he'd do."

"No, and I don't know what I'd do. Don't let him touch you again."

"It's long past that I think. We've all grown ten years older tonight. No twenty."

"God I hope you're not all wrinkly."

She laughed: "I can just feel my first hot flush coming on."

Ann wasn't the only one aged by the Liege experience. For Morgan it was a turning point too. First because he was now responsible for the happiness of another human being. Hitherto he'd made his decisions on selfish, emotional grounds, lurching from want to want. Now he would have to, would want to, look more coolly into the future, assess the possibilities and appraise the odds.

Secondly, at Liege, he'd met for the first time a fair sample of his future colleagues and competitors from far and wide: observers from California, Australia and South Africa; space astronomers from NASA and Russia building and launching satellite telescopes to see the universe through entirely new windows of the spectrum; theoretical astrophysicists from Princeton, Pisa, Yale, Paris, Vienna, Brazil, Moscow.......spinning their equations with effortless aplomb; computer simulators like himself creating artificial universes to compare with the real one; even physicists subjecting matter to cosmic conditions in their laboratories and measuring its vital properties. At Liege such men had talked familiarly of concepts he'd never heard of before: magneto-hydrodynamics; supersonic turbulence; cosmic-ray heating; linearised perturbation analysis; interstellar cooling; thermal instability; dust opacity.....the list went on and on and on. And these weren't just academic niceties; according to their various proponents such concepts might entirely control the whole process of star formation, a process Morgan had been attempting to model without being aware of them at all. In particular he met a school of vocal Greeks and Russians who were sure stars were the children of enormous currents and magnetic fields flowing through interstellar space. What Morgan had been doing was, to them, entirely irrelevant. Their magnetic universe was controlled by equations entirely unlike his own.

Then there were observations, so much more vivid as coloured slides on the screen than the mostly dry black-and-white graphs he had come across in the journals. Observations of young clusters of stars glittering amongst the remnants of their cocoon; of dark opaque clouds entirely impenetrable to light, and made manifest only because of the dark breaches they created in the tapestry of star-clouds beyond; of supernovae blasting billions of trillions of tons of chemically enriched, incandescent gas into space, there to seed future generations of stars; of spiral galaxies picked out in necklaces of light, each bead the product of not one but a hundred thousand nascent stars. And there wasn't just one universe to see but a dozen. The new infra-red pictures looked nothing like the familiar optical pictures of the very same region of sky. It was like comparing the X-ray image of a man with his portrait in oils. And if that wasn't mystifying enough there would soon be pictures in radio, in ultraviolet, in X-ray and in the sub-millimetre spectrum. Space research was about to turn observational astronomy inside out and upside down.

Finally were the men and women he'd met and talked to, future co-workers in the human quest to unravel the universe. Some were fakers and showmen he felt sure, and some were fools, but most were honest hard-working enthusiasts dedicated passionately to their profession. And many were dauntingly brilliant. There were men there no older than he, who were already full professors in big universities, with dozens of published papers behind them. Supremely confident in their knowledge and achievements, they made Morgan feel very small indeed. They were launching satellites, or controlling giant telescopes, while he was fiddling with his computer program. He'd talked about his work, to little evident effect. Nobody had bothered to ask a question afterwards though one young man approached him over coffee and asked him why he hadn't included cosmic-ray heating. Morgan could only admit that he'd never heard of it before, and asked for a reference. More galling was a conversation, overheard at the official dinner, about Bellfounder and Tinker's brilliant new work on his very own subject. They, apparently, were doing great pioneering things, and their new theory of protostars was expected any day.

Morgan realised that he'd been inhabiting a comfortable little world of his own choosing. It contained himself, his giant computer programme Ethel, Hood his very occasional supervisor, and Bellfounder as the villain to provide the necessary drama. From time to time papers with new results intruded on its periphery, but for the most part his world ticked quietly away, ignorant of and ignored by the thundering clamour of world astronomy. In other words he was a rank amateur, a weekend water-colourist in a world which the Impressionists had long since taken over.

For an egoist like Morgan, the perpetual hero of his own fantasy world, the Liege conference came as a devastating tsunami. He nearly drowned amidst the flotsam of his own dreams. Without his new found love and responsibility for Cloudesly Ann, he might have been swept away altogether. Also there was his revivifying hatred of Bellfounder.

To: Frank Cotteridge   From Jack Cockle
Mount Wilson and Palomar Observatories,   London Observatory.
Santa Barbara Street,
Pasadena,
California.

Dear Frank

Since you're going to be away in California for another three months I thought I'd keep you up to date on the Tom front.

He's in love at last, head over heels in love. You'd never think, listening to him, that anyone had been in love before. He certainly hasn't. It's rather touching really in one who, only last year, was up to his waist in tarts. He's even engaged to be married would you believe.

And the lady? We met her last week at somebody's garden party and I have to say we were all impressed, mightily impressed, even the ladies who can be relied on to be catty on such occasions. She's truly lovely, with a strong nose, hazel green eyes, and a smashing figure. She's called Ann, she's quietly spoken, aged 27, and clearly as besotted with Morgan as he with her. And she's very intelligent – that much was evident from the first moments of our conversation. Intellectually I'd say old Morgan has met his match at last – and that may be part of the attraction. Apparently she's something very hush-hush in Whitehall – which she can't divulge even to Morgan. I can see he's more than a bit peeved and jealous about that.

The one worry I have about this paragon is I cannot see her as the ambitious astronomer's wife. Will she bring up his babies almost single-handed while he looks through some telescope at the far ends of the Earth? Will she cook his meals and mend his clothes while he obsesses about the cosmos? And can she live on next to nothing while submerging her own ambitions totally beneath his? Only time will tell. I don't think either of them has any idea of what their lives will be like. And, surprise upon surprise, Tom is getting broody. He spent most of the party on his hands and knees playing lions with other peoples infants while Ann looked on indulgently. Good luck to them both; they'll certainly need it. Both are childishly unworldly and hopelessly romantic. It were better that one of them had a dash of homely common sense.

On the subject of Tom again, he was torn to bits by Bellfounder's gang at The Royal Astronomical Society. They held an all-day meeting on "The Advanced Stages of Stellar Evolution" with Bellfounder's Red Giant theory much to the fore. Eventually Tom, who was sitting next to me, couldn't bear it any more. He got to his feet and launched an attack on Bellfounder's work. To begin with, I have to say, Tom was calm, cogent and convincing. But then Bellfounder's terriers began interrupting, and the chairman let them get away with it. Finally some little pipsqueak asked Tom if his work had been refereed. Tom then exploded and mayhem ensued. Finally the chairman forced Tom to sit down like a naughty boy, before he had finished, leaving Bellfounder, who never had to speak, in complete command of the field.

Tom lost the battle ignominiously and was humiliated. All the same it left a very nasty taste. It clearly wasn't science and there were some in the audience who must have wondered what was going on; why Tom wasn't being heard out as he should have been, right or wrong. There were some mutterings along those lines over tea afterwards. In the long run Bellfounder's victory might prove hollow. If Tom is right, and I for one am convinced that he is, the truth must come out sooner or later. And when it does Bellfounder will be condemned for dastardly tactics.

If only Tom could learn to keep his temper. Perhaps the beautiful Ann
will tame him, a Delilah cutting Sampson's hair.
Mussels.

On top of Liege the R.A.S. fiasco made up Morgan's mind. Theories were all very well but in
astronomy it was the observations that mattered, overwhelmingly so. He was going to become an
observational astronomer, and that meant leaving Britain and going to America. High in the
mountains of the South West from Texas through Arizona and up into California, lay the best
observing sites on Earth. Once telescopes had been erected there, from 1910 onwards, European
astronomy, which had led the world for four hundred years, passed into eclipse. And street
lighting in an overpopulated continent had only made things far worse. He'd have to go to
America, and that was that.

He found himself reluctant to tell Ann about this until he had secured an American job. And
that wouldn't be easy. Why should any proper observatory employ a man trained only in writing
computer programmes?

He prepared his campaign systematically. He sat in the library for ages, compiling lists of all
the reputable American observers, ranking them all by their field of interest and the excitement
of their discoveries. Having picked his top dozen he traced their work back through the years in
the journals. Then to each he composed a long letter, spelling out his ambitions, the way that he
might fit in with their interests, and the range of his experience, such as it was. He described his
work on Ethel as dispassionately as he could, his continuing fight over Red Giants, and his real
desire to work on Quasars – like Frank.

Rejections followed from Berkeley, from Lick, from Palomar and Santa Cruz, from Kitt Peak,
from the University of Texas and so on. But then he got a brief letter from a Professor Wagoner
at the University of Arizona in Tucson:

> Dear Mr Morgan
> I heard your talk at Liege and I feel your skills in astrophysical
> programming might mesh with my own interest in investigating the fate of
> gas in Elliptical Galaxies. We are prepared to offer you a post-doctoral
> fellowship for one year, normally extendable to two, at an annual salary of
> $8,000. The post to commence immediately you receive your PhD. Please
> reply as soon as possible.
> Yours sincerely ....
> PS I enclose some literature about this institution.

Morgan immediately recalled Wagoner, a big formidable man of German-American
extraction. And Tucson, or Tuxon as he supposed it must be pronounced, appeared to lie in a
mountainous area close to the Mexican border. The University of Arizona operated a modest
sized telescope up on Kitt Peak and a smaller one down on the university campus. More
excitingly Tucson was rapidly becoming the world centre of optical astronomy with the
headquarters there of the US National Observatory at Kitt Peak; of the Cerro Tololo
Interamerican Observatory in Chile; of the Lunar and Planetary Laboratory with its finger in
many satellite and balloon telescopes, and of The Optical Sciences Centre of the university,
which specialised in building big telescope mirrors and sensitive astronomical instruments. In
Tucson he'd be right in the thick of observational astronomy. Without consulting Ann he
immediately cabled back accepting. He would get his PhD, they would marry immediately
afterwards, and go straight out to Arizona.

Morgan was exultant but Ann was not.

"You should have consulted me." she said quietly.

"But it's the only offer I've got! If I'm to become a proper astronomer I have to take it. I'm sorry darling but there was no choice. I thought you'd be delighted."

"Delighted for you Tom yes of course. But for me it will be difficult – perhaps impossible. Washington would have been fine, I could get secondment. New York maybe. But Arizona! I don't even know where it is on the map. The Admiralty will be underwhelmed to say the least of it."

Morgan felt like a rotter, even a fool. He'd never realised that Ann was so determined to carry on with her secret work, even after they were married.

Ann said no more and retreated into her shell. Henry Cloudesly had gone off in a dudgeon to dig in Petra, leaving his family behind.

Morgan set out to get his PhD, hoping things would blow over. He had three months to write, present and defend a book about his research, his so called 'Thesis'. Within 250 pages or so he had to critically review all the important papers on Star Formation, put his own work in context, describe his investigations in detail, argue his conclusions – such as they were, and suggest a plan for future research.

He set to work with ruthless determination, planning every moment of every day, setting milestones for the completion of each chapter along the way. The truth was he really only had two months if he was to leave a month for contingencies, for getting married and for planning their voyage at the end. It was, as he quickly found out, a nearly but not quite impossible schedule. The good thing was that it left no time for havering.

Ann, who was still worried about her own career, at least got on famously with Blodwen, though Morgan would have been happier if his mother had divulged rather less of his colourful past.

"But darling she's got to know."

"No she hasn't Mam. And thank God you don't know the half of it. I'm never going to tell you now."

"Ann's very intelligent."

"Of course she is, but I haven't behaved very intelligently at times Mam, and you know it."

"I'm sure she'll forgive you."

"But her father won't. You've only met Gwendolyn. Henry Cloudesly is a jealous sod, just waiting for something to queer my pitch. I want no unnecessary hostages to fortune mother, not a single one. He's already withered her first engagement. Anyway it's not even certain that Ann's going to come now."

And that was the truth of it. Morgan might have to choose between his love and his astronomy.

From Frank Cotteridge   To Tom Morgan
Pasadena, California   London Observatory.

Dear Tom
        I'm so happy for you. First Ann – who Mussels says is absolutely
stunning in every important way – and far too good for you. And then the
University of Arizona. I checked up on them with the boys here and the
scuttlebutt is that they are the coming place. Did you know they will be
completing the third largest telescope in the world shortly after your arrival?
You'll be right in the thick of it and taking your rightful place in world
astronomy at last – in the forefront. And about time too.

I'm coming to the wedding even if I have to row over. So don't you forget it.

You don't know how happy I am for you. I enclose a sealed note for Ann, which you're not to read, telling her what a great chap you really are. Just in case she hasn't noticed. It's easy to miss!
Love Frank.

PS Do you realise we'll only be a hard day's drive away from one another out here. I've been to Tucson (the 'c' isn't pronounced by the way) and the scenery around there is breathtaking. Culture though is somewhat lacking, unless you fancy rodeos or 'varmint calling'.

PSS. Guy Tinker came over from Los Alamos to give us a seminar on his work on star formation with Bellfounder. According to Tinker they've cracked the problem, and the cognoscenti here were mightily impressed. But after what you told me about boundary conditions, I'm not so sure. Their numerics, as anticipated, are far far better than yours, but numerics are not astrophysics and they may be fooling themselves. You have had the great advantage of doing it all yourself – you know the whole thing inside out, warts and all — whereas Bellfounder knows no computing and Tinker no astrophysics. So there are huge opportunities for misunderstandings between them, especially as they are working 4000 miles apart. So hang in there Tom and good luck.
Frank

Ann came round eventually:

"It was Frank's letter that did it. I'm not showing it to you, partly to spare your blushes and partly because Frank asked me not to. What a lovely friend he is Tom. I can't wait to meet him."

"What did he say – if it isn't confidential?"

"The burden of it is that you're not quite as bad a lot as you seem at first – and oh yes you are an incipient genius. That given enough love and support something might be made of you. And that is all I'm going to say."

"I owe Frank then."

"No you don't. Frank wasn't urging your case. He was simply trying to be honest. He also said you've got a huge capacity for messing things up, to say nothing of making unnecessary enemies. You know you have. You can be absolutely thoughtless at times, like accepting Arizona without consulting me."

"I'm sorry about that now darling. I never thought.`'

"Well there you are! It's partly my fault too, or the fault of my profession. You can't understand how important it is, and I can never tell you. So naturally you discounted it."

Morgan hung his head.

"I can come to Arizona for a year, two at the absolute outside. But there are conditions. My bosses have been very reasonable. They'll keep my position at the Admiralty open – provided I keep in regular touch. They'll pay for me to fly to our Washington office once a month, more often if there is an emergency. And every six months I must spend a fortnight back here in London. While we are away I won't get a salary but they'll pay my pension contributions, and all expenses, and I won't lose any seniority."

Ann's secret profession was like an invisible, unmentionable eight-hundred-pound gorilla in the room of their relationship. He'd promised not to bring it up but he couldn't help speculating all the time, until the urge to try out his guesses on her became almost irresistible.

It was, of all people, Henry Cloudesly, back from Petra for a few days, who came to his help. Morgan got a curt note from him through Ann:

> Dear Morgan
> I believe I owe you an apology. If we could discuss matters over lunch in my club at one on Friday, I'd be obliged,
> Henry Cloudesly.

Morgan went of course, though he felt none too charitable. He arrived at The Athenaeum and was shown to a secluded table where Cloudesly was drinking claret and reading an archaeology paper. His face was burned even redder than usual. He stood and greeted Morgan stiffly, but the handshake seemed genuine:

"I shan't pretend I'm happy about Ann marrying. That would be hypocrisy. At the same time I want you to know that it has nothing to do with you personally. Nothing. I shan't attempt to explain because if I did you wouldn't understand. But one day, if you father an exceptional little girl like Ann, one so wondrous to behold, so wondrous to listen to, so wondrous to feel clutching at your sleeve and calling you Daddy, then you won't need an explanation. Do you take my point?"

"I think so."

Cloudesly raised his glass:

"I wish that you should be so lucky one day."

Morgan raised his too and they clinked.

There was a pause while they ordered. Then Cloudesly leaned forward and spoke quietly:

"Have you wondered about Ann's profession?"

"Of course. It's driving me potty. Not knowing I mean."

"I thought it might. Perhaps I can help. Of course I know nothing for certain. She can't discuss it with me any more than she can with you. But it's obvious if you've followed her through the years as I have, if you know her exceptional abilities and if you've met some of her senior colleagues. She must be a cipher breaker working on Russian ciphers."

"I was getting warm then. I thought 'codebreaking'."

"Much the same thing. Do you know how it's done?"

Morgan shook his head.

"Well there's a lot of clever stuff with mathematics and computers which Ann has mastered. But the real basis is guesswork. Do you know what a 'crib' is?"

Morgan shook his head again.

"If you can guess, from the context of a message, a sufficiently long string of the original Russian characters it contains, then you can have a computer work backwards and break the cipher of the day. I taught her to do that when she was a little girl playing with hieroglyphics. She was a wonder. Quite incredible. It was uncanny, even disturbing until I understood her secret. Do you know what I mean?"

Morgan, his mouth open, shook his head yet again.

"It's her memory boy, her memory. It's supernatural. She didn't recognise it herself; how should she? We all think other people must be just like us inside. And mostly that's true. But not in Ann's case. She remembers, she has always remembered, almost everything she's ever read or heard, or seen. And more to the point she makes connections between present and past."

"I don't follow." Morgan exclaimed.

"Shhh! Suppose she's given a cipher which, from its context, probably comes from a particular Russian submarine. She will recall instantly every broken cipher she has seen from that vessel before. She'll know the captain's name and personal writing style, she'll know the idiosyncrasies of its radio operator, the previous failures it has reported in its machinery.

Knowing all these details, together with a huge background of knowledge about the Russian submarine fleet, she could quickly generate half a dozen plausible cribs, or messages from that particular submarine. Any one of them, all tried out on a superfast computer, could break into the Soviet naval command cipher of the day. Ann might do it where nobody else I've ever encountered could. Do you see?"

"So taking Ann to Arizona could weaken naval security?"

"Put like that, yes I suppose it could. But that's not my point. I merely want to warn you that were there to be another big emergency, like the recent Cuban missile crisis, they'd probably come banging on Ann's door, wherever she is. And you'd have to let her go while it lasts. I thought I'd tell you this, because she cannot. Despite my initial feelings I do now want you both to be happy together. I presume you know that the Russians have commissioned six hundred nuclear submarines to strangle our sea lanes?"

Once briefed it was easy for Morgan to clandestinely check Ann's supernatural memory. Her father was right. She didn't use an address book; she remembered everyone's telephone number. She didn't need time-tables; she knew the departure and arrival time of every bus or train she was likely to use. She was so untidy because she didn't need to remember where things were. She knew exactly. Unfortunately the awesome memory was selective and didn't extend to mundane things such as shopping lists, recipes, menstrual cycles and bank statements so that Morgan found himself constantly rescuing Ann from confusions of her own making. Sometimes endearing, it could also be intensely irritating.

Waking beside her and looking down on her dear face breathing quietly on the pillow he found it impossible to take in that this girl, so precious to him, might hold in her head the safety of Western Civilisation. In fact it was ridiculous. If he was ever to think of her like that their relationship would freeze completely. Her unnatural memory was a trick of genetics, a freak neither to be admired nor wished for. She wanted to be loved not worshipped, to be bossed around, so she said, not deferred to.

"Wake up Miss Snuggles" he said, flicking a loose pillow feather under her nose which twitched in response "Your turn to get the breakfast."

Once embarked on it he found the writing of his thesis most enjoyable. It meant getting to the bottom of all the new things he had learned, especially at Liege. It meant explaining how Ethel worked, and what he had learned from her: basically that the whole computational approach, plausible though it sounded, had been doomed from the start. That you could get out of it only what you put in, ground down to exquisite but irrelevant detail. Since man was at least a generation away from observing pre-stellar material in sufficient detail, it was pointless to compute what would become of it. And clever though they were Tinker and Bellfounder could never side-step the same trap-fall. Giant computer or no, they were bound to tumble into it and find themselves painfully impaled, just as he had been. The thought of Bellfounder writhing in agony, cheered Morgan up.

And there was another practical difficulty that everyone had conveniently ignored. Cosmic material swirled about and spun, so it would never collapse into a neat sphere as he, and everyone else had supposed – not because they thought it was realistic to suppose so, but because the computers of today were far too slow, far too lacking in memory, to calculate anything better. Whereas it was all very well to simplify, indeed scientific progress depended on simplification, no good would come of throwing the baby out with the bath water

In his final chapter therefore he tried to estimate, on the basis of forecasts in computer technology, how long it would be before a realistic protostar calculation would be feasible. Thirty to forty years he estimated. And that meshed rather neatly with expected improvements in observational techniques. By then infra-red telescopes on satellites would be sending back detailed images of interstellar gas so that computer modellers would know exactly where to start from.

He finished typing and gave the first draft to Hood his supervisor. Hood was disappointed but fair:

"I can't see what else you could have done Tom. It's all news to me. I thought it was feasible. You've convinced me that it is not. And that is progress of a sort. No one needs to go down this blind alley again. Are you disappointed?"

"Yes I am, I'm disappointed with myself. If I'd thought about it hard enough at the beginning, before throwing myself into Ethel's arms....."

"Ethel?"

"Oh sorry. My computer programme. If I hadn't been so quickly seduced by Ethel's charms, I might have thought a lot harder, and reached the same conclusions in one year instead of three."

"Umm." Hood was sceptical. "It's easy to be wise after the event. We wouldn't have got the money to do this if some pretty smart people hadn't been convinced it was worth trying. So you can't reproach yourself for that. Anyway you were wet behind the years then."

"Have I got anything I can publish in an astronomical journal, that's the question.?"

Hood avoided the issue:

"You've got a PhD thesis, that's for certain. And a job to go to afterwards. You can't ask for more."

"What about an astronomical discovery?" Morgan was stubborn.

"That would have been nice, but of course nobody is guaranteed one of those. Just nobody."

Morgan was disappointed but Hood was irritatingly right. It did gall to think however of all those other young astronomers, like Frank, with real discoveries under their belts. He swallowed his pride, made the revisions suggested by Hood and spent a whole night, assisted by Mussels and Ann, all of them smudged in purple printers' ink, running off four copies for the binder on the observatory's primitive Roneo machine.

The following morning, down in the main corridor of the College in Bloomsbury, he received a body blow. He ran into Dick Widdowes, a tall carefree graduate student who worked in the Atomic Physics group and who had helped him with some of Ethel's cooling calculations, routine technical stuff, but in which Morgan had no expertise.

" Ah there you are Tom. I wrote to you yesterday. You remember those cooling cross-sections you borrowed off me? They're all too high by a factor of thousands. We forgot about collisional de-excitation. Sorry about that. The new figures are in my letter. They should be reliable." And he passed on, chatting to his companion.

Morgan stood rooted to the spot. The repercussions were appalling. Six weeks to the day, they were sailing for New York. Two days before that he and Ann were getting married. The Registry Office had been booked, the invitations sent out, the marquees ordered and the menu decided upon. A day previous to that he was summoned to defend his thesis before the External and Internal Examiners of the University of London. Ann's long leave from the Admiralty had been arranged after tortuous negotiations, her trousseau ordered. Their American visas had been obtained, after much trouble, through the University of Arizona, and dated precisely. He'd given up the lease on his flat. Gwendolyn and Blodwen were buzzing about ordering hats and flowers; Herry Cloudesly had finally reconciled himself to the inevitable. And yet everything, absolutely everything, depended on Morgan getting his PhD , and getting it on time. And now this idiot Widdowes had blithely announced, just as it was about to be bound in leather, that his thesis was wrong. Even his comforting conclusion that Tinker and Bellfounder were barking up the same wrong tree, was now scattered in the whirlwind.

He faced three choices, and he gave himself twenty minutes only to choose between them. He could commit suicide –it had been done in similar circumstances before. He could bluff his way through his thesis, knowing it to be a lie. Or he could redo three years work, and write it up, in three weeks only. The first choice seemed attractive – but who would look after Ann? The second was totally unacceptable. He could either be a scientist or a liar, but not both. The third seemed impossible, wholly impossible, but he would have to try it anyway.

He marched round to the binders and retracted his blemished thesis, all four copies of it. They were amazed, but he was too preoccupied to notice.

Then he went round to his flat, packed an air mattress, a sleeping bag, an alarm clock, his shaving things, and went out to the observatory on the bus, his mind racing over the possibilities.

On the positive side, almost half his thesis was secure: the introductory review and the concluding chapter on future technologies. What was at risk was everything to do with Ethel, and the conclusions he had so confidently based on her. Ethel computed her cooling laws on the basis of Widdowes' faulty atomic physics. And all the rest of the dynamics followed from the loss of temperature, and hence pressure, brought about by that very cooling.

Another mercy was the way Morgan had constructed Ethel out of a number of completely autonomous routines or packages. He could change just the cooling routine, which could be done in a matter of hours, and expect the rest of Ethel to function perfectly. Then again he could take a risk, based on experience. Instead of running Ethel again, time after time consecutively, modifying the initial conditions for each run after the previous ones had come back and been analysed, he could create a dozen copies of Ethel, each modified from the others in appropriate ways, and run them simultaneously. That would squeeze at least a dozen weeks' work into one. But he couldn't risk a single tiny error, a single wasted effort, a single blind pathway, a single short cut that didn't march straight home, or a single frivolous conversation. He phoned Ann once, not revealing how serious things were, and nobody else whatsoever.

He slept on the floor beside his desk for three hours every night. And not a minute more. He never felt tired. He ate and drank only whatever Mussels and his other friends cared to bring him. and he ate it and drank while working. Once a day, and sometimes twice, Mussels raced all the way down to the computer centre on his motorbike to submit or collect Tom's latest efforts.

It took but a week to establish that Widdowes' latest cooling cross-sections made surprisingly little difference to Ethel. The atomic cooling was already so fast compared to the other timescales, which crawled along at an elephantine cosmic pace, that slowing it down by a thousand made no effective difference. A collective sigh of relief went up from the observatory. Morgan showered and shaved for the first time in a week and phoned to Ann with both the bad news and the good.

Then the trouble really began. Morgan made , or thought he had made, a really important discovery. In amending the short section on cooling and heating rates in his Introduction he decided to plot out graphs of the interstellar temperature and the interstellar pressure as a function of density in the interstellar gas. To his surprise the pressure-graph looked like an S on its side.

Morgan had never seen such a thing plotted before and wondered idly what it could mean. You'd expect the pressure to go steadily up, or steadily down, not to wriggle about in such a sideways S. He would remember the next moment of inspiration, and everything connected with it, for ever afterwards. It was Sunday morning, the early August sun streaming through the window onto his desk, the observatory was completely deserted. His bedclothes were an untidy heap beside him on the floor. He looked up and noticed a jolly summer cloudlet sailing into sight.

Of course! Inspiration struck him. Interstellar clouds: the birth places of stars and star-clusters. The dark pearls which strung between the bright ones along the braceleted arms of any spiral galaxy. The spores of the Milky Way. No photograph could miss them. No astronomer could explain them or, so far as he knew, had even puzzled as to their origin. And yet they *were* a wonder. Some mysterious process had squeezed them into shape, giving them the hard edges that were seen whenever there was a cosmic glow behind. And no one doubted that that they were the pristine beginnings, the dark nurseries of all the action which flourished out there in the spaces between the stars.

Now it was clear to him. They had to be the children of his fallen S. He slashed a horizontal straight line through the graph, representing the interstellar pressure, which must be everywhere the same. The line intersected the fallen S in three places, each place representing a different phase in the interstellar gas. The cold phase on the right obviously represented the dark clouds, the hot rarefied phase on the left the interstellar medium in between. The phase in the middle was a puzzle, but it looked unstable to him. Any gas there, like a pencil balanced on its point, would presumable fall away to either left or right, leaving in practice only the two phases observed.

The manifold implications of the S shaped curve astounded him. It could explain the spiral arms of galaxies, and the barren spaces in between, Elliptical galaxies which never produce young stars , and so on and so on. He had to tell someone.

"Mussels' he said when Jack Cockle blearily answered the phone "Get yourself round here at once I'm going to show you something really beautiful."

"But I've got something beautiful. I've got Jenny in bed beside me."

"Let the poor girl sleep. After what you did to her last night I dare says she needs it. It's Sunday morning you twit."

"Exactly!. And I don't go to work on Sundays. Not even for you."

"But this isn't work Jack, I swear it isn't. This is pure unadulterated, sparkling beauty; Truth unearthed from the bowels of Time."

"Bugger you Morgan. You're as mad as a hatter. The strain of the last few days has been too much for you."

"All right. Come and revive me then. If you call yourself a bloody friend!"

"I'll bring a strait jacket."

But Mussels was impressed when he eventually came; "By God you've done it Tom!"

Hood his supervisor, on the other hand was not. Definitely not:

"It sounds to me like the ravings of an overstretched mind. Not what I expect of my graduate students at all."

"But what's wrong?"

"What's wrong? It's barely the sketch of an idea is what's wrong. You haven't done the high temperature phase calculation for a start."

"One can guess that."

"Guess! This is science not guesswork. You haven't established the instability of the intermediate phase. And what about the timescales? You've got nothing to say about those, absolutely nothing. And they're crucial. If they're not as short, or shorter than the other governing processes in the interstellar medium, it will be all fine and dandy – but of no real significance whatsoever."

"I could tackle all those things in a few days."

"I'm not having you put any of this stuff in your thesis. Not a line of it. Not even a footnote. You could make a complete fool of yourself. And out of me."

"But it's a discovery."

"Discovery my eye. Even if it's right, which I very much doubt, there's years of work to be done first. Years of it."

"Well I'm putting it in, as a self-contained chapter on its own."

"No you're not."

"Yes Dr Hood I am. I know in my bones that this is right, and I'm sticking to it."

This was only the preliminary to a real row that lasted all day in Hood's office. Hood had eventually brought in a colleague of his called Summerson, an owlish looking expert on the interstellar medium recently back from a three year stint in the States.

All day long they raised one criticism after another. And all day long Morgan tried to rebut their points one by one. They showed him observations; he showed them observations back. They appealed to journal papers; he appealed to other papers with different conclusions. They resorted to mathematics ; he replied in kind.

As Morgan put it finally:

"I didn't invent the heating and cooling processes in the interstellar medium. They're reasonably well known and generally accepted. All I did was to look at them from a different point of view. Lots of people plotted the temperature; I happened to look at the pressure, which for a dynamicist like me is the natural thing to do. The S shaped curve is the consequence. You're not arguing with that are you? You can't."

They grudgingly conceded the fallen S shaped curve.

"Well then, any physicist faced with an odd shape like that is going to get excited. It means that at least two kinds of stuff can exist at the same pressure, but at different temperatures and densities. It's like ice floating in cold water. Or clouds in our atmosphere. All I'm saying is that that the same kind of thing must be going on in Space. The interstellar clouds correspond to icebergs while the rarefied medium in between corresponds to the sea in which the icebergs float. And even the third intersection of the S has an analogy; it's the equivalent to the water vapour in our atmosphere. It hangs above the sea and around the icebergs like sea fog. It's so simple!"

"It's not simple at all" Summerson snapped. As the day wore on he had become the main antagonist, with Hood slipping stone-facedly into the background.

"It just shows your ignorance Mr. Morgan. Argument by analogy, which you are employing now, is seductive but treacherous. Analogies can be pushed only so far. The solid-liquid-vapour phases of water, which itself is an anomalous substance, do not mirror the wholly gaseous phases of the interstellar medium."

"OK I concede that but……"

"No, let me finish pray. The interstellar medium is a complex and interesting phenomenon. Everybody knows it is the seat of star formation, just as it is the graveyard of stars dissolving themselves, one way or another, at the end of their lives. As such it has been the focus of intense interest by astrophysicists for over fifty years. Do you know there are over 300 professional astrophysicists in IAU Commission Number 34 dealing with The Interstellar Medium? Did you know that?"

"No, but I don't see……."

"Did you realise that those people , of which I am one, together with their assistants and students, spend their entire lives researching the The Interstellar Medium? Did you?"

"No I didn't."

"Do you think it likely therefore that someone so entirely new to the business, someone who is only interested in it from a peripheral point of view anyway, moreover someone who is an inexperienced student to boot, do you think it likely that that someone would stumble into something so fundamental that it must govern the whole subject – and its applications which seem to stretch far and wide into galaxy astronomy? Do you think it likely?"

"Likely or not Dr Summerson, that is just what I *have* done."

"It's what you *think* you have done. Whether you are right is a different matter, a very different matter altogether."

Morgan repeatedly tried to return to the science, but it gradually dawned on him that his two antagonists were preoccupied with an entirely different concern. As Summerson put it finally:

"If this was right Professor George Field and his team at Berkeley would be sure to have seen the truth of it long ago. I've just spent three years out there in his group, and believe me it's packed with brilliant people – theoreticians, observers, laboratory physicists, balloon flyers and satellite builders. I cannot believe, even for a moment, that they would have missed what you claim to have found in half a morning's work. I cannot believe it."

"But that's not a scientific argument!" Morgan protested.

Hood stepped in:

"I am your supervisor Morgan, and part of my responsibility is to see that you don't make a fool of yourself, which you are in danger of doing now. This is no part of your thesis, which is satisfactory as it is. So, as your Internal Examiner, I order you to take it out. It may, after two or three years of work, turn out to be sound. But if it's in the submitted version of your thesis then I will have no alternative but to see that you are failed. And I don't want this stuff talked about around the department either. I see you are proposing to give a seminar on it next week in Main College. Don't! It will make a fool out of you and, even more importantly, a bigger fool out of me. Professor Devon would have a fit if he was to think that this nonsense was general currency around his department. If you persist in talking about it in your PhD seminar I shall have to warn the entire academic staff to keep away. I don't want to be responsible for wasting their time."

Morgan gasped, his blood up at last.

"Well I am going to put it in my thesis. I've written the chapter, and it stays. It's my thesis after all. Fail me if you will, but at least have the decency to fail me on scientific grounds. So far I haven't heard a single scientific argument that will stand up. Dr Summerson's arguments, if I may say so, are of a sociological nature which I cannot rebut, and which I don't need to. One can summarise them by saying that 'Students at University College London are not permitted to make important discoveries.' That will be news to many people ; if it is true it ought to be more widely circulated. Apparently our PhD students are all working under a delusion; they should be informed explicitly so that they could, as they certainly would, move elsewhere. I am also sorry you feel as you do Dr Hood, but I quite understand that you have to protect your reputation. Accordingly, when I talk about the Three Stage Model of the interstellar medium, as I shall certainly do in my PhD seminar, I shall make it crystal clear that you had nothing to do with it, and indeed do not approve. Likewise, in my thesis, in the very Abstract itself if you like, I shall absolve you from any blame, making clear your heartfelt disagreement. But don't you see I have to put it in? I've just spent three years working my guts out on Ethel – with what amounts to a null result. Not a promising start to a career in which I am determined, absolutely determined to succeed. Now I've made a real discovery, possibly a major discovery. It has to go in; and it will."

"I cannot help feeling" Summerson added waspishly as Morgan was rising to leave, "I cannot help feeling that you've got the main topic of your thesis wrong as well. I understand that a Dr. Tinker from Cambridge (he heavily underlined 'Cambridge') has got entirely different, and much more exciting results than yours."

" Indeed he has; but they are catastrophically wrong." Morgan retorted, trying to close the door behind him as gently as his anger would allow. In the days before Ann he would have wrenched it from its hinges.

Morgan went back to his desk and finished an exciting version of his thesis, only two and a half hours before the absolute deadline for submission. He couldn't believe just how hard he could push his brain. Elaborate calculations, calculations that would normally have taken weeks, spun effortlessly and fluently off his pen in hours. The Three Stage Model was sound! The timescales were right. Thermal instability would work to condense the clouds out of the chaotic interstellar gas, just as he had suspected.

His PhD seminar was however a disaster. True to his threat Hood had warned the entire department and observatory to keep away, and was absent himself. Instead of the typical audience of two dozen Morgan had to go through the shame of lecturing to only two student friends of his from the observatory, to Mussels, and to Ann. And as they all knew about his work already, it was a total farce. After ten minutes of hoping against hope that someone else, anyone else, would turn up, he ground to a halt:

"Bugger this for a lark. I thank you all for your friendship and loyalty. As we used to say in the army 'Nil illegitima carborundum'. Let's adjourn to the pub."

He sounded jaunty but inside he was anything but. If Hood went through with his threat to fail, which it looked now as if he would, Morgan faced catastrophe: no PhD, no astronomical career, no job in America, indeed no job at all to support Ann. And in those circumstances how could he go through with the marriage, which would have to be called off with only days, in fact hours to spare? Between his PhD viva, if it ever went ahead, and the wedding, only forty-eight hours were scheduled.

He went home to Worcestershire to stay with his mother, where he virtually collapsed. Six weeks of intense mental effort and emotional strain, all on three hours sleep a day, came home to roost. The adrenaline fizzled out, the body slumped, the morale broke down. He was only glad Ann wasn't there to see his collapse. He was supposed to be getting ready for the wedding, for the viva – if it ever took place; for the trip to America, and for married life in Arizona afterwards. There were so many things to do, and people to see, and yet he could barely struggle out of bed.

He even concussed himself by banging his skull violently against the low beams of his mother's cottage He was alone and must have slept all day when the phone rang. Believing it might be Hood ringing up to say he'd failed, he ran along the darkened landing towards the phone and woke up on the floor with a splitting headache and a lump on his skull the size of a plum, a lump which bled profusely.

Hood remained silent so Morgan was eventually forced to ring him. Hood was cold:

"I've received your thesis, and I've read it. As you probably know it is the External Examiner who carries the weight in a PhD examination. I've decided to go ahead and let Professor Reddish read it too. If he doesn't complain to me in advance then the viva will go ahead in my office as scheduled and you must defend yourself and your ideas as best you can. But if he does so complain then you'll have to withdraw. That's the most I can do for you."

Morgan was relieved. Reddish was a sound man from Scotland, with no connection to Bellfounder, and a wide reputation in both Star Formation *and* the Interstellar Medium, which was more than could be said for Hood. If Reddish approved then he was home and dry.

Morgan was storing his books away in the attic, books which stretched far back into his childhood, including Rupert books, when the size of the step he was about to take dawned on him for the first time. If all went according to plan he might never live in Britain again, never see his mother except for brief holidays. His cat Sooty might be dead by the time he returned, the dog Goch (the Second) certainly would. These books he had treasured and was so lovingly storing away, could finish on an Oxfam stall, unseen by him ever again. To his annoyance his mother had already disposed of his army sword and the blue and scarlet ceremonial uniform with its regimental badges – to a passing tramp. His cricket bat, a Gunn and Moore Cannon, had dried out. His sea fishing rods from Pembrokeshire days were warped, the rings and reels rusted. His climbing ropes, to which he had entrusted his life so many times, couldn't be trusted any more. He boxed up his his pitons and karabiners, his ice-axe and his crampons and sent them to Steve who was now a mountain guide in New Zealand, climbing regularly in the Himalayas. His walking stick, a memory from his causalgia days, he hesitated to throw away. That climbing accident had, in the long run, changed his life for the better; for much the better. Mountaineering had been all very well, but it simply wasn't as exciting as astrophysics. A climber's battles lasted for hours, or for days at most. An astronomer might have to fight for a lifetime with men like

Bellfounder and Hood, and other foemen undoubtedly waiting for him out there in America. A climber could only lose his life; a scientist could lose his mind.

Feeling a profound sense of impending loss, Morgan hugged his mother far more than usual; she seemed to understand. He took Goch for long walks, cherished the Worcestershire hedgerows and spinneys and slept with Sooty purring down inside his bedclothes, his whiskers tickling his ankles and toes. He went to see Bob and Ernie Salt to tell them all his news and keep up with theirs. He held a stag party in the pub for old friends from school, from Army days, from days in the hills, knowing that some of them he was never likely to see again. Alas there was no time to say goodbye to his beloved Wales; to Swallowtree Cove, to Monkstone Beach, to the prospect of yellow mustard fields across St Bride's Bay or the rolling hills above Amroth. The feeling that he might never see Pembrokeshire again brought tears to his heart. He'd thoughtlessly decided to abandon all this for the arid deserts of Arizona. Now was his time to wonder why.

The day of the PhD viva dawned in Worcestershire, sunny and fair. He donned the Savile Row suit which Ann had bought him as a wedding present, and in which, all being well, he was to be married. He shared a hearty Welsh breakfast with his stepfather and Blodwen, which included ham, eggs, Pen Clawdd cockles, Lava bread, home made pork sausages and home made Seville marmalade. A 'fighting breakfast' Mam called it, and fight he would. He looked at his father's photograph in major's uniform, taken just before he went out to Normandy, looking cheerful in his regimental beret, with a swagger stick under one arm. What were Hoods and Bellfounders to a fighting man like that? He said a last tearful farewell to Goch and Sooty, and climbed into his mother's tiny car which he was borrowing until the wedding.

He started the engine, reversed the vehicle in the driveway when Blodwen opened the door to give him a last valedictory hug. Then she slammed the door again.

On his right thumb.

It was agony. The sound alone was sickening. Blood spurted out from under the nail. He staggered out of the car moaning. Blodwen was distraught. His stepfather rushed inside to fetch a torniquet.

"We've got to get you to a hospital Twm. We've got to."

"There's no time Mam. No time. No time at all. Get me a gin. Oh God it's agony. And a bucket of ice to deaden the pain. And painkillers, as many as you've got".

He drove the one hundred and fifty miles down the M1 motorway to London using his left hand alone, his right hand in a large plastic bucket of ice which rested on his lap, freezing his thighs. His thumb, torniqued with a pencil, but numbed by the melting ice, throbbed blood spasmodically into the swathe of bandages which encased his arm up to the elbow.

He must have looked a sight when he staggered into Hood's office over four hours later. Both of the men in it looked up and gasped.

"Good heavens what's happened to you man?" Hood stood in alarm.

The bandage, and indeed the arm of his white shirt up to the shoulder, was soaked in blood diluted with melting ice. His jacket, removed to preserve it for the wedding, hung from his left shoulder. His tie, also spattered with blood, as was the shirtfront, had had to be discarded.

"I'm all right really. I'll hold the arm over the bucket to stop getting blood on your carpet. Let's go ahead. Though I wouldn't mind a cup of that tea."

Professor Reddish, a small man with friendly eyes, introduced himself:

"Well one thing Dr. Morgan, this shouldn't take very long. I was particularly fascinated by your new theory of interstellar clouds. It's completely original and very important. And if you don't mind Hood, we'll start the discussion with that."

A small wedding in the registrar's office was followed by a large reception on the tennis lawn at Kew. Ann looked radiant in her white silk wedding gown with train. She received the guests on the arm of Henry Cloudesly, dressed in his morning coat and grey top hat, who gave his daughter as proudly away as if he'd never suffered a single curmudgeonly doubt. Blodwen had too many gins on an empty stomach, lost the plot, and insisted on saying goodbye to some of the astonished guests even before they'd had time to sample the resplendent wedding breakfast to be served later in the marquee. Morgan's friends who had never met her before were introduced to Ann. Ann in turn was delighted by Ernie, who Bob and Valerie Salt were pushing in a wheel chair, and by Frank, joint best man with Mussels, who had come over specially from California. Two of Morgan's mates from the Army were there, adding colour in their scarlet and grey regimentals with swords in gleaming silver scabbards. But even they didn't outshine some of Ann's colleagues from the Admiralty in ceremonial Royal Navy blue and gold. The tennis club was out in force as was Henry and Gwendolyn's ancient music ensemble which played renaissance gavottes and quadrilles on the lawn during the breakfast. Morgan's climbing friends, as scruffy and uncomplimentary as usual, sneered at the formalities, though not at some of the stunning girls:

"By Hell Tom you look like a bloody pox doctor dressed up in that flummery. You're not expecting us to drink this fizzy rubbish are you? Haven't you got some decent ale stashed away somewhere?" Anticipating their reaction, he had.

Frank added to his sense of well being by remarking confidentially:

"You look bloody awful Tom. It's not cancer is it? You look as if you could do with a blood transfusion. But if you do pop off I'll look after Ann. Honest. She's far too good for you anyway."

Then he gave Morgan a large cheque made out in dollars:

"You'll need this mate, when you get to Arizona. They don't like paupers in the States. I'm telling you from bitter experience."

Mussels, proudly clutching his fiancée Jenny, and wearing a morning suit from Moss Bros. which didn't fit at all, gave Morgan a present of an entirely different kind. It was an envelope.

"I hope you don't mind Tom. It came to the observatory a couple of days ago addressed to you. So we steamed it open."

Morgan stared at the envelope, as if it were a snake poised to strike. He'd spotted the logo on the outside: 'The Astrophysical Journal, University of Chicago.'

"Dear Dr Morgan,
We are happy to inform you that, subject to minor modifications, your paper entitled "The causes of Red Giantness in stars" has been accepted for publication in the December issue of this journal….."

Morgan whooped for joy, performed a war dance on the lawn, and swore aloud to drink Bellfounder's blood before the year was done. Then he rushed over to Dr Martin Johnson, who was chatting with Henry Cloudesly, and threw him, like a tiny child, bodily into the air.

CHAPTER 8
CACTUS AND STARS
1968

When Morgan staggered onto the campus at the University of Arizona he seemed to have walked for miles in the blinding desert sun. Having brought neither sun hat nor sun glasses his eyeballs felt like splintering under the glare. His British clothes felt like furnace-lagging six feet thick. Grateful for a respite from the incandescent sword above, he rested in the shade of one of the date palms which lined the avenue leading towards the main university buildings. How the immaculate lawns survived a temperature well in excess of a hundred degrees he couldn't imagine. It was noon and some kind of student demonstration appeared to be going on in front of the 'Old Main' building. Under a banner reading 'STOP THE DRAFT' a man with a megaphone was addressing a motley collection of bearded hippies and flower people. Around them, in uniform, an even larger number of campus police and heavily armed state troopers stood ready to intervene. As he approached, Morgan could hear the speaker being heckled by a phalanx of crew-cut cadets in army uniform. But before he could get close enough to hear he was halted by a campus policeman and redirected around the ugly scrummage:

"Keep away Mister. There's going to be trouble here. Big trouble."

Moving behind some oleander bushes towards another patch of shade Morgan was deafened by the thunder of a pair of Phantom fighter-bombers on final approach, their undercarriages down, their wings loaded with sinister ordnance. The high pitched screaming thunder of their four jet engines was barely endurable.

But they were as nothing. As he approached the Astronomy building he turned, and bearing down on him came a nightmare black shape cutting off half the sky. A colossal B 52 bomber with eight screaming turbojets thundered overhead, its shadow racing across the lawns, its black tail like the fin of an enormous predatory shark.

Inside the building it was cool and absolutely silent. He gulped down almost frozen water from the fountain while his eyes re-accustomed themselves to the relatively dim light.

"The faculty is at lunch" the receptionist announced "But Professor Bok will be back at two. He was expecting you this morning."

Directed to the student refectory Morgan stood in the queue behind the most colossal young man he'd ever seen . Big himself, his head barely reached the giant's enormous shoulders. Wondering if he was suffering from sunstroke Morgan turned behind him to check for normality. He was confronted by a giant bigger still, a colossus with a tiny head perched on a pillar of tapering muscle. He'd heard that Americans were big, but this was ludicrous.

Bewildered now he turned back to find the first colossus helping himself to six T-bone steaks piled on top of one another like a layered cake; a bucket, quite literally a cardboard bucket of fries, another of salad, and a whole tub of chocolate-chip mint-ice-cream which barely fitted onto his oversized tray. When the giant reached the cash desk the checkout lady ran through his Brobdignagian lunch:

"That'll be fifteen hundert, three thousand, four thousand five hundert, six thousand, seven thousand five hundert, nine thousand. The fries is another two thousand five hundert. The salad ain't nuthin' 'cept for the Blue Cheese dressing – which is four fifty. And the ice cream is another two thousand seven hundert.'

She bashed her machine:

"That'll be fourteen thousand eight hundert and fifty calories son."
She gave him a check, but he moved off without paying.
Morgan shamefacedly pushed forward his meagre tuna-salad roll.
The lady looked at it incredulously, then up at Morgan. She was suspicious:
"You ain't on the football team mister. I aint fooled. This is the athletes' queue.
You git over there and pay like the rest of 'em."

Bok turned out to be an irascible elderly Dutchman with a turnip shaped head and
stentorian lungs. He never talked, only shouted with exclamation marks:
"Tvelve Munce!" he roared incredulously "Tvelve Munce? No No No! Your
contract is vor nine munce like everbody else! Ve don't pay people to lie about
shlacking in der zommer! Dey gotter find their own zommer salaries – if dey can!
Even you Briddish! Hev you vound an apartment yet? Try Sixth and Country Club!
Den komm to my party! And bring your vife! At five thirdy! And don't be late! Ve
don't like late peoples here! Nossir! Not in America!"
Four hours later they were in Bok's capacious kidney-shaped swimming pool,
surrounded by dozens of astronomers and their partners. Grapefruit trees hung right
over the water so that Morgan could reach up to touch the pendulous yellow globes –
which were indeed real. Bart Bok, in an Hawian hula, was floating trays of cocktails
across the pool, roaring with laughter and flirting with half a dozen young women at
once. As Morgan helped himself to a margharita, a tequila cocktail with frosted salt
around the rim, he toasted Ann bobbing on the far side of the pool surrounded by
young men. It felt like a Hollywood film set with the two of them playing starring
roles.
A B58 supersonic Hustler bomber came screaming through the treetops. Bok
danced with rage, shaking his fist at it:
"Dem bastards! Dey does it deliberate! Deliberate! Right over der campus! To
remind the stoodents dere's a war on in Vietnam! As if ve didn't all know! Bastards!"
He pirouetted like an enraged King Lear.
Later on, incandescent with overmuch sherry, he turned his guns on another pet
hatred:
"Astrology! Vitchcraft it is! No bedder! And dere ain't no God neither! Ve are all
going to die. See dot bulding over there?" he pointed dramatically "Dot's Tucson
Medical Centre. Ven ve die, Priscilla and me" he hugged his surprisingly gentle and
elderly wife "Ve go up there to the mortuary! Yessir! And dey cut us oop chop chop
chop like in der butchers shop. Cut out de eyeballs, de kidneys and anything else dey
can use. Den der rest goes down the chute into the furnace! Astrology! Destiny! All
my eye and Beddy Martin! You youngsters enjoy life vile you can. Der aint a
tomorrow, not for me, not for you, not for nobody! Here's to life!" and he downed
another bumper of Tio Pepe on the rocks.
Ann found herself in a circle of women discussing childbirth. A precious young
man butted in:
"Oh it must feel so wonderful. So creative!"
A silence greeted this sally. Then Ruby, a leathery veteran of many confinements,
retorted:
"If you really want to know son, it's like shitting a pineapple."

Ann found them an apartment in the foothills, several miles to the North of the
campus. The jagged twelve thousand foot Catalina Mountains rearing above them

meant that no aircraft came anywhere near. Half built into the earth for coolness the quadruplex melded into the cactus forest of the mis-named Sonora desert. Giant thirty foot high Sonora cacti, like vegetable dinosaurs, loomed over their heads when they slept under the stars on the roof. Gila woodpeckers, nesting in among the cactus thorns, woke them with their chatter in the morning. And at night the only sounds that lulled them to sleep were the tinkle of the fountains and the imaginary rumble of the universe overhead. If they walked twenty yards in any direction the low building was lost to sight among the green-barked Palo Verde trees, the ocotillos with their flailing thorns, and the jumping chollas. The only path out there, beside the coyote tracks, was the arroyo or dried up river bed, which was rumoured to flash flood but once or twice a year.

Like Ann herself the apartment was beautiful but impractical. To be woken in the morning by inquisitive ruby-throated humming birds buzzing inches above their heads was unforgettable. To walk miles home in the echoing afternoon heat, because there were no buses, not even a tarmac road, was unforgettable in a different way. There was a small swimming pool in the central courtyard, which they shared with the other three apartments, but it was far too hot to sit out there after breakfast, or much before dusk.

The neighbour they first made contact with was Don, a large gentle bachelor who showed them how to make 'Sun Tea'. He took a jar of water with a couple of teabags screwed under the lid, and left it out in the sun for a day or so. When the sunlight had worked its magic he threw the bags away, added sliced lemons and sugar then put it in the fridge to cool. They found it a delicious way to soak up all the extra fluid the arid climate demanded.

Don worked way out in the desert for a Los Angeles contractor building missile silos underground. In each silo stood a Titan missile as tall as a cathedral, primed with liquid fuels, tipped with a megaton thermonuclear warhead and ready, at a few minutes notice, to launch itself twelve thousand miles to destroy Leningrad or Vladivostok. The silos were hardened against atomic attack so that if the Russians were mad enough to risk a first strike, their subsequent destruction was inevitable. It was eerie to think that the peaceful cactus forest around them was actually the front line in the Cold War.

While Bok was the observatory director Morgan's real boss was Wagoner a flinty eyed athlete of a man, as large as he was and not much older. Wagoner, as director-designate when Bok officially retired in a years time, was the power behind the throne as well as a brilliant product of some of the best schools on the East and West coasts. His unashamed mission was to transform a sleepy desert department into one of the foremost observatories on Earth.

When first talking to Wagoner Morgan felt as if he was being interrogated as a prisoner of war. Wagoner wanted to know everything; about Ethel, about Red Giants, about Hood, about the 3-stage model, about Morgan's views on pulsars and quasars, and about his astronomical ambitions, both short term and long. He took Morgan's thesis, and returned it to him, fully digested, within twenty-four hours.

"Write up your Three-Stage Model immediately " Wagoner advised. "Could be right, and if so interesting. OK you've got your Red Giant stuff in press but nobody will read that. It's negative. They'll listen only when you come up with a positive alternative. So find one. You've probably got two years start on any competition there. Don't waste it."

"What about Ethel… I mean the protostar stuff I spent most of my time on?"

"You'll have another battle there with Bellfounder. He's highly respected over here – almost deified. He's the arrogant kind of Brit most Americans expect and admire."

"And you?" Morgan wanted to know.

Wagoner smiled grimly:

"My family are Germans. They hate all Brits as a matter of principle."

"That's hardly an answer."

"No. You're right. Well I don't respect scientists, I respect their latest arguments. Or otherwise. We'll invite this Tinker guy over to give a seminar. Then the two of you can slug it out in public. Should be interesting."

Wagoner then tore three sheets off from his yellow note-pad and handed them to Morgan. They were covered with hand written equations.

"Take a look at that stuff, and give me your opinion. If you are interested we could work on it together."

The trouble was that Morgan, after his PhD fiasco wasn't interested in anything. He was mentally and emotionally drained. He would stare at papers for days without taking anything in. He barely heard the first word of a lecture before wandering off into a reverie. He would sit for a whole morning in his office looking at the walls and wondering what on earth he was doing in Arizona. Almost anything sufficed to distract him from astronomy. When the bell rang for the end of a lecture he would stand on his desk to look out of the high window at the undergraduates crossing the lawns from building to building. He was especially intrigued by the hoards of female undergraduates, or 'co-eds, who were majoring in "Physical Movement". At 8 am there would be a hundred and fifty nubile young Amazons with bows and arrows practicing toxophily under his window. At 9 am they would be replaced by a hundred and fifty differently attired young ladies improving their golf shots with equal seriousness.

And then there was the bitter war going on, both in Vietnam and on the campus.———————————————— Every night the television news presented a nightmare vision of burning Vietnamese villages, of Asian children scarred for life by napalm and worse, of body bags containing young Americans coming home to their families for the last time. Many of the male students belonged to 'Rotsee' the Officer Training Corps and marched about the campus in military uniform with their hair shaved in regimental crew-cuts. They paraded in platoons, saluted their officers and glared belligerently at their opponents the war protestors, who naturally wore their hair as long as possible. All the hubbub provided Morgan with another convenient distraction from astronomy.

Then there were his new colleagues on 'the faculty', as different from his lecturers back in London as it was possible to imagine. They mostly wore lumberjack shirts and jeans with all manner of paraphernalia dangling from thick leather belts, including key chains, voltmeters, even 'soddering irons' as they called them. All were either 'just going up the mountain' or had 'just come down'; that is to say they were just going observing for the night at some telescope, or had just returned. Their offices were packed with Cathode Ray Oscilloscopes, optical benches, electronic gadgetry, drawing boards, welding equipment, tape decks and computer accessories. Morgan went round introducing himself. They were amiable enough but mostly far too busy with their own research, or student enquiries, to spend much time talking to him. They were 'real astronomers' he felt, unlike he was. Instead of resenting them he was envious of their preoccupation. He admired the photos of telescopes or balloon-platforms on their walls. He could see they were struggling with real problems such as collecting enough light, or finding the right galaxies, or interpreting their observations in statistically significant ways. And with years at 'graduate school' after university they knew so much more than British PhDs like himself. As well as all the hardware they handled like toys, they could, when they had the time, talk knowledgeably about abstruse theoretical subjects such as 'synchrotron radiation' or 'non LTE' – whatever that was. Morgan wondered how on earth he was going to make his mark among these pundits in the nine short months which was all Bok had promised him. He grew depressed as well as exhausted. And yet this was supposed to be his 'great opportunity'.

When he could finally get down to it he found Wagoner's problem interesting. Wagoner had posed the question 'What has become of the gas in Elliptical galaxies?" Unlike Spiral galaxies such as the Milky Way Elliptical galaxies, the other main sort, were very red. They were red because they had no young blue stars in them. And there were no young stars because they apparently contained no gas out of which young stars could form.

But why not? As Wagoner pointed out, old stars in dying gave off copious amounts of gas. And as Ellipticals were full of old stars they couldn't avoid filling up with gas. But there was none to see! Why not? What was going on?

There were three possibilities that Wagoner could see. The gas was blown out into space by supernovae explosions. The gas collapsed into the nuclei of galaxies and mysteriously 'disappeared'. Or the gas remained in situ but was too hot either to see, or to form young stars.

All three possibilities seemed plausible to Morgan, and all were consequential in themselves. He was particularly intrigued by the idea that the gas could fall into the nucleus. If enough accumulated there it would eventually create a Giant Black Hole of the very kind postulated by those trying to explain quasars.

Wagoner claimed that deciding between these three alternatives would require a detailed computer calculation – which he was proposing that Morgan should carry out. They would need to simulate in the computer an imaginary Elliptical galaxy accumulating gas through the deaths one by one of its billions of individual stars. The fate of the gas would be followed by means of equations which governed each of the physical processes involved, including heating by supernovae and cooling by radiative loss.

Wary of wedding himself to another even more demanding Ethel, a weary and pessimistic Morgan stalled for time. Was the problem consequential? Yes definitely. Were the necessary starting conditions known unequivocally through observation, or were they, as in the protostar situation, too indefinite to be useful? As far as Morgan could see, the observations were well defined. That left the harder-to –answer question of whether a computer simulation would be decisive enough to repay the enormous effort, his effort, to write and to run it. It would be a question of opportunities, other opportunities such as observing, being lost. He hesitated because a wrong decision could easily wreck his precarious astronomical career.

Morgan badly wanted to share his difficulties with Ann. At the same time he realised that no new bride wanted to feel that she'd hitched her wagon to a faltering star. But he was no at good keeping secrets, at least not from her.

"You silly billy;" she chided him "Of course you've been walking round like a zombie since your PhD. And no wonder. Three years work in three weeks, the row with Hood, and now a sexually demanding wife to satisfy. I shall have to cut back on your sex."

She hugged him.

"Anyway" she added looking seriously into his eyes, "I know all about burn out in my game. Intense mental concentration, under pressure, for weeks on end can lead to break down. It's quite normal. Apparently the brain needs to recruit depleted chemicals. You'll be all right in a few weeks. I'm certain. Forget astronomy for now. Just tuck into a good novel or two. I've got just the one."

She had: 'The Magus' by John Fowles. He couldn't put it down. Then she moved him on to the Hornblower novels by C.S. Forrester that were, if anything, more addictive. They sometimes read them in bed together, under the stars, by torchlight, first she reading a few pages, then him, often for hours.

"Isn't married life wonderful darling?" she said one such night, gripping his arm fiercely inside their double sleeping bag. "Could anyone have imagined that?" she gestured at the northern Milky Way sinking behind the jagged summits of the Catalina Mountains which made a black cut-out in the firmament of star fields. "Aren't we lucky?"

"I am. But I've got my astronomy. All you've got is a swimming pool. And cacti. It's not like the Admiralty."

"But it won't be for long." she laughed "It's only a sort of extended holiday."

Ann's attitude began to worry Morgan. She seemed to assume that they would be returning 'home' in nine to twelve months time whereas he would need at least two years to make his mark. At least. There was so very much for him to learn.

Morgan took America seriously. Ann apparently did not. She hooted with laughter at appalling American TV, and read him snippets from the local newspaper the "Tucson Daily Star':

"Can you believe it darling? Here we are close to Armageddon, and all they can think about is the mayor's floozy. Headlines for the fourth day in a row. Took her to Las Vegas apparently. And his crime? To put her paltry airfare on the city accounts. He says she's his secretary. Really! How can we take them seriously? They're children."

She was equally dismissive of the ladies they encountered in the supermarket. And it wasn't too hard to see why. They wore slip-slops, Bermuda shorts displaying usually unappetising bums, and hair, seen through a plastic chiffon beehive, which was permanently crimped in pink plastic hair curlers.

"Ugh!" Ann shuddered "How can their husbands bear them? And yet they've all got six kids."

Which seemed to be true.

Ann, he realised, marooned at home, was seeing only the down sides of America. They began to argue about it.

"Don't you realise" he said "That nobody intelligent here watches the godawful television, except for the news. Most academics won't even have a set in the house, in case it contaminates their kids. And certainly none of them would read the Tucson Daily Star. If they read a paper at all it will be The Washington Post or The New York Times – both better than anything we've got in Britain."

"It's the only newspaper one sees on sale" she retorted. Which was true.

"You are judging America by its hill billies."

"They're all I meet!"

"If you spent your days in Deritend or Walsall you'd feel exactly the same about England."

"Oh no I wouldn't. At least I could watch and listen to the BBC."

"These people are holding back the Russians. Nobody else could. And they're going to the Moon. They can't all be hill billies."

"They seem so in Arizona."

The problem was that Ann was marooned at home. Without a car, which they couldn't yet afford, she wasn't meeting intelligent people. She spent her days reading, teaching herself to cook – with meagre results, talking with the neighbours' children and playing with a black kitten who'd boldly walked in through their door one night – to be named Scurvy.

Morgan felt awful about this. He'd taken her from the Admiralty, where in all likelihood she was a star in the Cold War, and cast her away in a physical and intellectual desert. That she never complained only made the situation worse. How she must be regretting her exile, the exile he had imposed upon her.

Their Arizona bank wouldn't lend them a cent, while at home he was borrowed to the hilt. So he cabled his stepfather, who cabled the money back. The following day he drove home in a battered Volkswagen Beetle and handed the keys to Ann:

"There you are sweetheart. It's your passport to America."

'But......I can't drive."

"What?"

"I can't drive, and I don't want to. I tried in London....but I was so hopeless."

They had their first row. And a big one. Morgan, predictably, lost his temper:

"Either you drive or we move out of this goddamned apartment into town, and we move tomorrow. You can't stay here all day living like an anchorite. There's only so much conversation you can hold with a Saguaro cactus."

"I'm not driving, so don't bully me. I was frightened in London. I'd be terrified here. Absolutely. Terrified!"

Morgan took advice from a colleague. A couple of days later, while they were having breakfast, a tough looking young woman arrived, dressed in a police cadet's uniform. Ann was shocked.

"This is Marilyn. She's the daughter of Bill Vogel at work. We're paying her fifty dollars a day to teach you to drive Beetle. And she's not leaving until you've got your Arizona driving licence. Isn' t that so Marilyn?"

"Yes sir. Sure thing. I've got my contract." She took it out of her shirt pocket and showed it to Ann.

"I'm NOT going to drive. I'm NOT!" Ann literally stamped her foot. Morgan picked up his rucksack and left.

A couple of days later Ann walked into his office triumphantly and threw onto his desk a plastic card with a hideous photo of her on it.

"It was easy! I don't know why there was all that fuss."

"I can't imagine." Morgan smiled, kissing her. "And pray why the tennis shorts?"

"I've joined the Faculty Wives Tennis Club. Marilyn's mum enrolled me."

From then on things improved rapidly. Most morning she'd drive him to work then go to the Mathematics department where she was temporarily allowed to 'sit in' on graduate level courses.

"They're really tough going" she conceded, and complained no more about hillbillies. Eventually the Admiralty paid for her to study courses in statistics and computing.

The first American couple they made friends with were Willard and Claire who they met quite by chance round the motel swimming pool while they were looking for an apartment. Morgan was amazed to find that Willard was an astronomer too, and like him was just about to start at the University observatory, but in a rather more senior position as a junior lecturer – or an 'assistant professor' as they were called in America. Like Morgan he was a theoretician with no knowledge of observing. And like Morgan he wanted to learn. Naturally they began to talk astronomy and to look for ways to collaborate.

Willard, who had a deep southern drawl you could cut with a knife, looked and sounded like Clark Gable playing Rett Butler in 'Gone with the Wind'. His background was Einstein's Theory of General Relativity, the highly mathematical field which had first attracted Morgan when he was at school. By now though the field had moved on and was attracting many brilliant young physicists. In particular they were looking for its applications to extreme situations in astronomy – such as the hypothetical creation and possible detection of Black Holes. The discovery, three years earlier, of Quasars, had recharged the whole field, while the announcement of pulsars the year before had electrified it.

"Ah'm interested in dense stahs" Willard confessed "It's the one area where ah kin see Ahnstein's general theory beein' tested. And that's important. Raht now it's no more than an elegant mathematical construction. From mah point of view it'd be real neat if pulsars turned out to be nootron stahs."

"I don't follow."

"Well the nootron stah should be a mere step away from a Black Hole." It turned out that Willard had been supervised in his PhD by John Wheeler, the brilliant physicist who, among other accomplishments, had first coined the term 'black hole'.

"Jahn believes nootron stahs might exhibit Relativistic effects. Frame dragging for instance. So it'd be real fundamental to prove out one of those babies." Willard had spent two years on a Fullbright Fellowship in Paris studying Differential Forms, an arcane branch of mathematics expected to be useful in analysing the four dimensional curved Space-Time around a Black Hole:

"But it's all too damned theeretical for mah taste."

"And mine" Morgan agreed. "Right now I can't face another equation."

"Me neither."

Both being stalled in their everyday research, and having no one to talk to at the observatory, Willard and Morgan spent a great deal of time in one another's offices talking about pulsars and discussing ways of getting into the new field observationally.

The whole field was buzzing with excitement, with crucial new papers appearing in the top journals 'Nature' and 'Science' every week. If Neutron Stars could be proven to exist they would represent an entirely new state of matter: Gases, Liquids and Solids were known on Earth, while "Degenerate Electronic Material" a million times denser than iron, must exist in the cores of White Dwarf stars. But neutron star stuff, were it proven to exist, would be a thousand million times denser still. One teaspoon of a neutron star would weigh as much as two hundred thousand ocean liners. No wonder scientists, even the general public, were so excited.

The trouble was that Pulsars were purely radio objects. No one had seen one optically, though all the big observatories had tried. And as Steward was not a radio observatory that didn't give them any scope for action. The one possibility, and it wasn't a very inspired one, was to look at White Dwarfs. If White Dwarfs could pulsate as fast as pulsars did, they and not neutron stars could be the basis of the new phenomenon. It turned out that very little was known about the pulsational properties of White Dwarfs though one had accidentally been found to vary on a timescale of twenty seconds.

"Not too far off one second" Morgan observed. "Why don't we compile a list of known White Dwarfs and find out how many would be visible from here."

Willard agreed. Even if it wasn't a very exciting program it would give them both the opportunity to experience observing for the first time.

To record the incoming signals with the extreme timing precision necessary would require a great deal of complex electronics. They decided to approach Don Tallon, the observatories electronic wizard. They found Don's boyish figure almost hidden amidst the thicket of wires and gadgetry in his lab. Seated on a high stool and intense with concentration he was using his soddering iron and cathode ray oscilloscope to carry out a delicate brain operation on one of his home-made computers.

When he did find time to look up through his thick owl like glasses to listen his face became amused and sceptical by turns:

"Don't you guys realise that the very best brains, on the biggest telescopes, have been searching high and low for optical pulsars for a whole goddamn year? You'd just be wasting your time, and mine. Anyway this baby is way behind schedule and I've made promises."

They pleaded, explaining that what they were proposing was slightly different. Don grew impatient:

"Look you guys have never observed before. The stars you want to observe are too faint to see with our telescope – so you'd need to use blind offsetting. And that's tough. The timing precision you're asking for is way outside my range. You'd need a ten thousand dollar Frequency Synthesiser with a crystal oven, and even then you'd need to toon the crystal every few minutes using broadcast time signals…." He went on and on listing a host of other practical difficulties they were too naïve to have appreciated for themselves. "You guys should stick to your equations and your computers. All this stuff' and he waved his hand around his lab " All this stuff took me years and years to learn. It's an entirely different ball game."

They must have looked crestfallen because he relented a little at the end:

"Tell you what I'll do. You guys find me that Frequency Synthesiser and maybe I'll help you to set it up. They got one of those babies over at Kitt Peak National Observatory. I'd sure like to play with it." And he went back to his brain operation.

Willard went over to the headquarters of the massive National Observatory which lay immediately across the street from the university astronomy department. He must have used his southern charm to good effect because they were soon back at Don Tallon's door with the magic Frequency Synthesiser held gingerly between them.

Don Tallon was both fascinated and trapped. Anyway he turned out to be far too decent a fellow to go back on his word. No he wouldn't come observing with them, believing it was all a hare-brained waste of time, but he would set up a complete electronic system in his lab and show them how to use it. His eyes twinkled behind his specs with a mixture of laughter and anticipation.

Ann and Morgan were intrigued by Willard and Claire. They were not like their idea of archetypal Americans at all. Their old adobe house was more like a shrine than a dwelling. Claire drifted about it like an Earth Mother, stirring her cauldrons of weird 'macrobiotic stoo'. Both were into Eastern mysticism and belonged to an Ashram. Willard had donated his almost new car to a passing Papago Indian in the street.

When Morgan expressed his astonishment Willard giggled: "It was only a goddamned corr. Ah kin live without one. This fellah sounded lahk he really needed one."

Not only did the Coxes not have a car they didn't have a TV either. Nor a radio. Claire, a Noo Yoiker, took the Sunday edition of the New York Times and that was it. They despised most icons of American life, were francophile pacifists and meditated a great deal. The shack at the bottom of their wild garden usually housed some colourful character down on either his or her luck.

"They're real Christians – if you know what I mean." Ann announced in shock "I've never met any before; certainly not in my church. I don't think there are any left in Britain. How nice!"

With the electronics on the way they were granted three dark nights on the observatory's 36-inch telescope out at Kitt Peak, a seven thousand foot mountain lying in the Papago Indian reservation. In the meantime Morgan's brain gradually recovered and he agreed to work on Wagoner's project. On the face of it it was quite different from anything he'd done before. In practice it employed the self-same skills in mathematics and computing he'd learned in London. But what had taken years there, he could, through familiarity, now do in months. He found a small mistake in Wagoner's maths, which impressed Wagoner more than it should have done. Then he began writing an immense computer program, like Ethel, to simulate the behaviour of an Elliptical Galaxy. He called it 'Cynthia'. This time however he copied Tinker, and used a coordinate mesh that could move inward or outward with the gas. And, thank God, paper-tape was now a thing of the computer's past. He typed his program onto cards, which could be altered in a matter of minutes rather than hours. And instead of having to go all the way to central London to get them to a computer, he could reach the one in Arizona by strolling across the campus. He did have to learn a new American computer language called FORTRAN, but it was so similar to his old British one that learning it didn't take long. Wagoner was impressed by his progress while Morgan himself felt much better now that he was actually doing some science. But he still couldn't face writing up his Three Stage Model.

With summer fading into fall, and fall into winter, the temperature mercifully dropped. The sky was still a blue savannah overhead but at two thousand feet – Tucson's height above sea level – the air was dry, crisp and comfortable, It was a delight to walk around the campus in shorts, listen to the mourning doves cooing in the date-palms, smell the scent of oranges freshly crushed under the tyres of passing cars, and watch the scarlet cardinal birds hopping about in search of scraps left by scholars lunching out in groups on the grass.

They had a tent and spent the weekends exploring the spectacular scenery of Arizona in Beetle. Regardless of expense the Americans built magnificent roads into the wildest of territory. They camped out in deserts and mountains, in canyons and forests, in national parks and designated Wilderness Areas. They stared in wonder into the Grand Canyon, watching it change colour in the dusking light; they hiked down the Bright Angel Trail under the crimson cliffs, marvelling at the sweep of geological time. They chuckled at the road signs: 'Sanitised Comfort Stations'; 'Earl and Dot's Eats', 'Air cooled, foot long hot dogs' ;….They white-water-rafted down a tributary of the Colorado River; watched the rising sun paint the sandstone mesas of Monument Valley rose and gold; swam in the high dams; climbed a snow peak in the San Franciscos; hiked into Cochise's Last Stronghold; cooked their steaks on many a log fire under the stars; got lost; ran out of water; met Mountain Lions; were shot at for trespassing; encountered rattlesnakes; fished for trout and met Red Indians.

"Sometimes I can't believe I'm here." Ann announced as she left him one Monday morning at the Mathematics department door : "This time yesterday we were in a log cabin on the Mogollon Rim, looking down over thousands of square miles of uninhabited territory. In five minutes I'll be studying Advanced Probability Theory. Where are we Tom? Really I mean."

"I guess we are slowly getting to America."

Morgan was hopeless with money. Ann hadn't a clue. Both of them resented every single minute wasted thinking about it. Consequently they got into debt. Morgan had blithely assumed that his new salary, eight thousand dollars, being on paper about six times what he'd received in London, would comfortably see them through. Petrol was dirt cheap, food was inexpensive, the rent wasn't exorbitant; they could even afford to eat out at times. It was the other unexpected things that hurt. Really hurt. He had a tooth out. Beetle needed servicing. Ann had to visit a doctor. There was expensive but inadequate insurance. They had to consult an immigration lawyer. Ann could cut his hair but of course he couldn't cut hers. The university salaries office made large, unforeseen deductions. There was Federal Tax, State Tax and far more infuriating bureaucracy than they were used to in Britain. And then there was their bank, the 'Bank of Arizona' whose mission it seemed was to betray and cheat them out of every cent they were foolish enough to deposit in its keeping.

Twelve days before Christmas Morgan got a furious letter from the Bank demanding more funds. How could that be? He paid them a visit. He found that the bank had self-righteously stolen nearly all the money they had left to last them into the New Year. At the end of a month a small cheque for a few dollars at a food store had bounced. Thirteen times. As it rattled back and forth from store to bank to store to bank to store... the bank, not informing Morgan once, had deducted fifteen dollars from their account every time. The original $7 cheque had thus cost them $202, $195 for the Bank. The Morgans had exactly nineteen dollars left to last them through Christmas and into the New Year. And the bank seemed to think it was entirely his fault, not theirs. He was outraged. They were scathing – and pitiless. No they wouldn't return his money, or give him a small loan. And he couldn't change banks because he didn't have the necessary initial deposit.

Ann took the bad news cheerfully though she was sorry to hear they wouldn't now be going to Colorado over Christmas skiing with Willard and Claire.

"Never mind darling. We'll make do with each other."

"No bloody alcohol for Christmas." Morgan was appalled.

"I can make Ginger Beer. Mummy taught me. It's pretty strong stuff."

They couldn't even afford a Christmas tree – to remind them of home. They were driving back from the university one evening when they passed a man trimming the casuarina tree in his front 'yard', as gardens were called in America.

"Oh look" Ann pointed "Why don't you ask if we could have a branch for our tree."

They stopped. The man was obliging:

"Sure thing. Borrow mah saw. Cut one you fancy."

Morgan did. The saw slipped and cut deeply into the flap of flesh between thumb and forefinger. Ann staunched the copious flow of blood with her handkerchief.

"When you last had a tetanus booster?" The man demanded.

Morgan couldn't remember.

"The soil an' stuff round here is alive with tetanus. Yew git straight round to the hospital and git a booster mah friend. Straight rahnd. And some stitches."

Ann drove him round to Accident and Emergency. Above the door, in very large letters, was spelled:

"NO TREATMENT IN THIS UNIT WITHOUT PRIOR PAYMENT OF $15. CASH"

"Damn!" Morgan swore. "That leaves us only four bloody dollars for Christmas. Barely enough to get petrol."

Worse was to come. On Christmas morning they drove the car-less Coxs out to the airport to catch their plane for Colorado. When they arrived home there were fire engines, police cars with their lights flashing, and a goodly number of spectators gathered around their apartment. Two fire fighters, dressed like divers in safety suits, emerged from inside it accompanied by the very angry landlord. When he saw them he rushed over:

"You clear that goddamned mess up you hear? Or I'll sue you for every goddamned red cent you got."

The carnage, when indeed they stepped over the threshold, was appalling. Ann's large flagon of ginger beer, just coming to perfection, and resting on top of a cupboard, had exploded violently. It had blown a hole in the ceiling and left the entire room dripping with foaming liquid. Shards of glass were embedded in the furniture and upholstery.

That was the last straw. Morgan broke into howls of hysterical laughter. They blew another rubber cheque and cooked a proper Christmas dinner with wine and Turkey.

That Christmas day was memorable in more ways than one. Since their phone had been cut off, through inability to pay the bill, they planned to sneak into Morgan's office and use the line there to ring their families. To their horror, at least half the faculty offices were occupied. On Christmas day! They looked at one another appalled.

"What kind of country is this? ' Morgan demanded fiercely "What about the kids? What about their families? Are they so insecure they daren't take Christmas Day off?"

"We couldn't live here Tom" Ann replied unsteadily. "We couldn't could we?"

Morgan and Willard Cox were increasingly preoccupied with the approaching observing run on the telescope. Don was assembling the complex timing electronics in his lab, shadowed by Willard who would have to run it at the telescope. Morgan spent his days combing through lists of White Dwarf stars, looking for candidates which would be bright enough to measure, and wandering between the various observatories in Tucson, talking to experts who might, or sometimes might not, offer them advice. Both grew nervous and excited as the dark of the moon, the only period when faint objects can be observed, approached.

The whole astronomical world was a-buzz with pulsars, which had superseded both quasars and the Big Bang as the main focus for excitement and speculation. Were pulsars Little Green Men – or at least radio beacons launched into space by alien, and now perhaps extinct, civilisations? That theory appeared increasingly unlikely as more, and more various pulsars were being found with radio telescopes all over the world. If they weren't artificial then what made them pulse with such regularity that they kept better time than the finest Swiss chronometer? Some thought they were stars panting like exhausted dogs. Others, in a growing majority, that they were rapidly spinning stars flinging lighthouse beams of radio radiation into space. To focus that radiation, enormous magnetic fields were invoked, fields a billion times stronger than anything seen on the Sun. In such fields atoms would behave in extraordinary quantum ways never observed, and perhaps never observable, in terrestrial laboratories. And how could a star, spinning as fast as a pulsar was supposed to do, stop itself flying apart? If the Sun were to rotate once a second, like a typical pulsar, its equator would be moving at an impossible ten times faster than the speed of light. Everything about pulsars seemed to be extreme, exotic and fascinating. But nobody really knew what they were. The radio observations were more tantalising than explanatory for they connected with nothing that astronomers had ever seen before. So many new papers on pulsars were coming out every week, so many new ones were being found, so many wild speculations were being launched, that Morgan and Cox had to share the papers out, and read a half each in order to keep one another up to date.

Just before Christmas Willard went off to the Texas Symposium on Relativistic Astrophysics in Dallas. While he was there Morgan came across a paper which caused his heart to miss a beat. Michael Large and his collaborators at Sydney University had discovered by far the fastest pulsar to date – one that pulsed eleven times a second! A White Dwarf spinning at that speed would simply burst apart. Their whole observing strategy was now redundant, In addition Mike Large had found something even more fascinating; his fast pulsar sat in the sky not so very far from the Vela Supernova remnant – a cloud of radio radiation left in the aftermath of a titanic Supernova explosion which had probably taken place fifty thousand years ago. At last a connection between pulsars and something else in astronomy, and a tell-tale connection at that. Weren't neutron stars supposed to be the tombstones of ancient Supernova explosions? It was all beginning to add up: pulsars weren't White Dwarfs. They must be, after all, the long sought after and far more exotic Neutron Stars.

As soon as Willard Cox got back from Dallas Morgan went to give him the bad news. Willard however had a big smile on his face:

"Some guys from MIT were there. They just found a pulsar beating thirty times a second, three times faster still. And you know what? The signals are coming from somewhere near the Crab Nebula. That's the grand daddy of all Supernova explosions. Wha' don't we look in there?"

The Crab Supernova was indeed the most titanic cosmic explosion of all. Back in 1054 AD a star had blown itself to smithereens, emitting so much light for a while that it was seen in broad daylight by Chinese astrologers. And by great good fortune the Crab was just now in the night sky right overhead. It had to be the place for them to look. It had to be.

There was now an almighty rush to change everything and get ready in time. Willard, who would be responsible for the timing, faced challenges he had never expected to meet. A pulsar beating at thirty times a second would quickly drift out of synch with their timing gear, unless that gear was retuned every few minutes to take account of the Earth's rotation about its axis, as well as its annual procession around the Sun. It all looked very tricky and challenging.

Morgan, who was going to navigate the telescope in the sky, urgently needed a photo of the Crab Nebula region, taken with the self-same telescope they were going to use. Fortunately a colleague obliged and he was able to mount the fragile glass plate in a microscope and measure exact positions for dozens of stars in the field.

Bur where exactly were they going to look? Their apparatus would allow them to examine only minute portions of the sky at a time. The radio observations were far too vague to be of any help. They went to the library and sifted through a vast catalogue of Crab observations searching for clues. Right in the middle of the nebula – that is to say the visible explosion – they could see two faint stars lying very close together: the "South Preceding Star' and the 'North Following Star'. From its spectrum the latter was an ordinary star probably passing in front of the explosion, and nothing to do with it at all. On the other hand the South Preceding Star appeared to be very odd in that Walter Baade's spectrum of it showed no normal stellar features at all. That made it a strong suspect.

But there were other suspects too, all rather close to the centre of the explosion debris. After all everybody had searched in there over the years – long before the pulsar was discovered — looking for the cause of the titanic explosion. There was, for instance, a very small radio source and a point-like X-Ray source with a vaguely determined position, but probably near the core.

But the pulsar didn't have to be in the core at all. The violence of the detonation had been such that the remnant neutron star might have shot outwards like a fragment of shrapnel from an exploding grenade. They would have to keep at least a dozen stars under suspicion.

On the day of the observing run Morgan and Cox drove out to Kitt Peak early. They wanted to savour the experience and get themselves ready in time. Don would come out later with the electronics.

Kitt Peak lay fifty miles South West of Tucson in the remote Papago Indian reservation. They left the ugly paraphernalia of American civilisation behind: the gas stations, the water towers, the burger drive-ins, the hoardings advertising Gatorade and the overgrazed desert. Once inside the reservation the native cactus forest of Sonora re-asserted itself. Named by the Spanish conquistadores, Sonora stretched far down through southern Arizona, across the Mexican border to the Sea of Cortez. The road drove through a wilderness of dried up arroyos, of giant Saguaro cacti, of spiky Palo-Verde trees, of mesquite bushes, of flailing ocotillo thorns, of sage brush, chaparral and tumbleweed. Purple jagged mountains shimmered in the noonday distance. It was an empty place where only the wheeling eagle and the dust devil stirred.

Ahead of them Kitt Peak loomed a mile above the desert. As they drove up the mountainside by a magnificent switchback road the vegetation changed with altitude, as did the temperature. The cacti first made way for agave bushes with their spear like leaves, then to juniper bushes, then to scrub oaks and finally, where there was shade and water, to pinyon pines.

The pink granitic rock beside and above the road formed pinnacles, overhangs and spires. The views on all sides were breathtaking: they could see at least a hundred miles across the desert to more mountain ranges in all directions. To the South, towards Mexico, rose the stark volcanic plug of Baba Quiveri where, the Papagos said, their gods dwelt.

At one point they stopped the car and got out to survey the scene. An uneasy feeling stole upon Morgan as he stood, neck craned, staring up at the stark white building of their telescope perched on the very lip of a dizzy precipice far above. But it wasn't the height which bothered him, it was more indefinable than that. He paused and listened. Nothing, except the occasional breath of cool wind catching the ear. He heard the cheep of a tiny bird half a mile away. Then he understood. For the first time in nearly thirty years of life he was hearing total and complete silence; he found it uncanny, almost disturbing.

At close quarters the bone-white telescope building, topped with a silver hemispherical dome, resembled a temple left behind by extraterrestrial beings who had once visited the Earth.

Inside the building it was cold and dark, as if something of the night had been captured within its curved walls. Breathless in the thin air they clambered aloft, their foot falls echoing on the steel ladderings which circled up the sides , then across and under the arching dome above. From the apex they peered nervously down into the open barrel of the telescope which, like a giant mortar, was aimed at the stars. Far from looking upward, as Morgan had imagined they would, they would be looking downward into the barrel, there to see the heavens reflected in the mirror at the bottom, like stars reflected in a well.

The guardian of the telescope, a towering but quietly spoken Viking of a man called Bob McAllister, appeared:

"You don't want to fall off this sucker. It's a long way to the floor."

He showed them how to mount the sensitive photometer on the very muzzle of the telescope, then cool it down with liquid Nitrogen. Don arrived with electronics which had to be lugged up the stairs and assembled on a tiny platform hanging over space. They spent the afternoon connecting it up and checking to see if it would work properly in total darkness.

"You can't afford to have any light up here." Don warned. "You have to dim your flashlights way way down with red filters. Otherwise you'll lose your night vision. You'll need all of that to see the dimmer stars. All of that. And for God's sake don't step over the edge in the darkness. Your wives are too young to become widows."

By the time they emerged from the dome the sky was turning gold and orange in the West while the mountain was casting purple shadows into the darkening pool of desert far below. They went to the living quarters, a mobile home wedged among the rocks, heated their 'TV dinners' and dressed warmly against the cold of the approaching night. In Morgan's case that meant donning pyjamas under his usual clothes.

He and Willard were both excited and nervous. Excited because this was their dream come true – to become real astronomers at last – with the opportunity to make vast discoveries. And nervous because there were so many new skills they would have to practice for the first time, so many things they could get wrong. There was the telescope itself which had to be navigated and steered to precisely the right pinpoint amidst an ocean of stars. There were all the complex electronics to be controlled and kept working in virtually absolute darkness. Then there was the timing which had to be continuously synchronised with the pulsar. By the dimmest of torchlight he and Willard, for Don was leaving before midnight, would have to carry out elaborate calculations, and get them exactly right first time, every time. Morgan felt like a young bullfighter, a novillero, facing his first 'moment of truth'. He also knew there was no other place in the universe that he would rather be at that moment.

When they stepped outside, and their eyes acclimatised to darkness, there were stars blazing not only above them, but seemingly below as well, so high was their eyrie perched in the sky. Only the night breeze brushing his cheek reminded Morgan that he was still on Earth. He looked up at their constellation of Taurus . Somewhere up there, somewhere out there six thousand light years away, far beyond the orange star Aldebaran, their quarry the Crab Nebula lay. The others disappeared into the dome but Morgan lingered for a moment, listening on the air like a hunter. The pale arch of the Milky Way vaulted overhead, plain in the moonless dark. He fancied he could hear the distant rumble of the cosmos.

Up in the dome it was dark as the proverbial pit. The roseate glimmer of his dimmed torch was useless for illuminating anything beyond a few centimetres away. He groped up the ladder and platform, partly by sound, partly by feel, partly by memory. He was grateful for his miner's hat when his head clanged into the sharp steelwork.

Inside the steel dome sounds echoed and reverberated. The telescope motors whirred faintly; relays clicked in the darkness, the static on Willard's radio hissed below the incoming timing pips; every footstep on the steel ladders clanged like a sledge hammer.

He climbed past Bob, Don and Willard to the uppermost platform from where he could look either out of the dome through the open slit, or back down into the open muzzle of the telescope.

"Lean over the eyepiece" Bob reminded him' "Whatever you do don't step forward. There ain't no protecting rail, and the telescope is moving away from you all the time. Remember that. It's always moving away from you, widening the gap into which you can fall. We've had one near fatal accident up here; we don't want another."

It was a warning to remember. But would he forget it just once, in the long hours of darkness ahead?

As his eyes gradually adapted, and he'd been told that it would take more than an hour for them to fully sensitise to the dark, he began to pick out more and more. A slit six feet across had opened in the dome just above his head. Through it he could feel the night air and see the stars blazing as he had never seen them blazing before. On the other platform below he could just pick out Don's and Dillard's faces dimly illuminated by the filtered light emanating from the electronics. Bob was huddled beside them. The circular rim of the telescope barrel stood level with his waist, pointing straight up into the sky.

Morgan groped for the red torch hanging round his neck, by whose glimmer he could just pick out the figures in his notebook. He found the coordinates of the Crab Nebula, rather like Latitude and Longitude in the heavens, but called Declination and Right Ascension. The latter had to be adjusted for the local time. Hanging from the side of the telescope by a thick cable was a ping-pong-bat shaped control known as the 'paddle'. By pressing the correct buttons on the paddle he could steer the telescope, and the dome, which had to follow it, to any part of the celestial sky. He pressed; the telescope whined while the dome rumbled like a heavy locomotive crossing a steel bridge. Looking upwards he saw the stars moving past in a dizzy whirl.

The silence when he stopped was deafening. Like a great gun the tube of the telescope was tilted forty degrees away from the zenith, pointing towards the southern sky. Looking out along its axis he could see Aldebaran the orange star that was to be their marker, centred in the slit of the dome. Good. He could now lean out of the bottom of the slit and look down thousands of feet to the desert below. All that broke the darkness was a handful of dim green lights, each one marking the silo of an intercontinental ballistic missile in full readiness for launch.

When he looked down through the eyepiece all Morgan could see in the blackness were a few faint pinpricks of light, fireflies in the distant night. The great explosion of the Crab Nebula, which he had expected to see, simply wasn't there. He checked the telescope coordinates against those in his notebook; OK; no problem there. He pressed the button to drift the telescope slowly over to the East and a different pattern of faint stars swam into view. Still no Crab. Then to the North. Then back to the West, and so on in a box search for their famous prey.

Since nothing turned up he looked at his finder-chart, a photocopy of this area of sky which clearly showed the Crab Nebula amidst its surrounding pattern of stars. All he had to do was identify that pattern in the eyepiece and he would know where he was in the sky.

Easier said than done because, as he soon discovered, and as he should have known in advance, the mirror on his telescope, which was of a peculiar design, inverted the pattern on the sky so that Right was Left but North was still up, whilst clockwise was anticlockwise.

Hours seemed to tick away while he struggled to invert in his mind's eye the pattern he could see in the eyepiece in order to match it with anything he might recognise on the chart; and to do that without falling into the gulf between his observing platform and the telescope, a gulf which was continually widening as the telescope automatically followed the star field down to the horizon.

Although the others must have felt impatient, particularly the experienced Don, they were good enough to remain silent. Which was as well because he had to remain unnaturally calm.

Having searched all directions in vain, and in the process become completely lost, Morgan used the telescope dials to move back to the original position. But this time, as the familiar star-field drifted back into the eyepiece he spotted the faintest wraith of milky white light drifting along with it. If he stared at the wraith directly it disappeared. But if he glanced out of the corner of his eye he could see what appeared to be a diaphanous jellyfish suspended in the ocean of night. Sometimes it was there, sometimes not. It took him all of twenty minutes to convince himself that it was real and not some figment of the over-excited imagination, and another twenty to be sure that what he could barely see was indeed the famous Crab Nebula.

That moment of recognition changed his understanding of astronomy forever. All the astrophysical theories, all the equations which had been his previous window into the universe, were as nothing compared to this faint whisper of light. He was staggered to realise that Man's whole understanding of the cosmos would depend on images as faint and nebulous as this jelly-fish coming and going in his eyepiece. He knew that by astronomical standards the Crab Nebula was relatively bright and that some men worked with images a million times fainter still. Their audacity and skill, which he had previously taken for granted, now seemed overwhelming. He felt like a scholar who, having spent a lifetime studying Africa from maps , had just been parachuted into the jungle.

'What in Hell's goin' on up there?" Willard's voice reminded Morgan that this was no time for philosophising.

His next job was to navigate a tiny aperture about inside the nebula, an aperture designed to exclude all the light except that from a very particular piece of the sky. There was no possibility of doing that by naked eye so he had to use the dreaded 'Offset Guider'. It's function was to move the telescope, by exactly calculated amounts, from the brighter stars that he could just see, to the precise target in black space that he could not. Like a ship's navigator he had to locate his vessel precisely over the sunken treasure by taking bearings from landmarks on the shore, in his case starmarks in the sky.

The minutes and quarter hours ticked away as he peered, measured, calculated with his slide-rule, and peered again. As the World turned so the stars sank towards their setting in the West, and so the telescope followed them down the sky, continually opening up the black pit into which he could fall.

Finally having checked and rechecked, he clambered down the steps to the electronics platform below.

"We're all set on the South Preceding Star – that is Baade's Star, bang in the centre of the nebula. I can't see it though so I've set by offset guider, which despite the warnings, actually seems to work. We're using the smallest aperture 45   arc seconds across, and the Blue filter is in."

"Mah Gahd." Willard was enigmatic. It didn't sound like admiration.

Morgan's eyes were by now so sensitive that Willard's face, and the others', were brightly lit in the roseate glow of their electronics – all carefully screened behind red plastic filters.

Now it was Willard's turn to sweat. His task, if anything, was even trickier than Morgan's. From the radio observations they knew that the pulsar was pulsing exactly 30........? times a second. Or it would seem to be pulsing so from a fixed point in space. But from their turning orbiting Earth the period would apparently change all the time because of the finite speed of light. When they were moving towards the pulsar its period would appear to shorten, when moving away, to lengthen. To compensate for all their continually changing motions Willard had to use Spherical Trigonometry and make continual adjustments to the computer clock otherwise the electronics would drift out of synchrony with any incoming pulsar light. That meant the telltale signal they were looking for would be washed out. Morgan was happy to sit back and watch Willard crouch over his slide rule, his notebook and his dials. Don was keeping a supervisory eye to see that they weren't mis-using his circuitry.

The minutes ticked away as Willard calculated, checked, recalculated and adjusted his dials. The large blond frame of Bob McAllister, more like a lumberjack than a telescope technician, fiddled with the tape recorder. His job, when they were actually running, would be to record their voices, the incoming timing signal from Willard's computer, and all the electronic pulses from their photoelectric eye – which actually detected the light. Bob's tapes, replayed down at the university later on, would allow them to reconstruct the observations and re-analyse them if necessary. It was a safety back-up.

"Beep-beep-beep......."   the timing signal from WWB radio was crackling through amongst the static on Willard's radio. Morgan and Tallon watched as Willard tuned his oscillator into precise frequency alignment with WWB, which was used as the nationwide standard:

"OK guys, ready to run." Willard giggled nervously.

Morgan climbed back up the curved stairway again and peered into the eyepiece. The telescope had drifted slightly out of position. He brought the tiny guide-star back into opposition on the dimly illuminated cross-hairs. He felt like a sniper. Then he glanced up and out of the telescope dome. With the passing hours the Crab Nebula had sunk down in the sky as the Earth turned, and instead of pointing straight up they were now looking out over the lip of the precipice towards California. Cold breaths of wind blew in through the slit, bearing scents of desert vegetation. The stars blazed above him, around him, even below. It was if Morgan was lost in space himself. He was startled to find Aldebaran, indeed all the stars, had lost their colour. His eyes had thoroughly adapted themselves to the dark. The supersensitive rod cells in his retina had taken over from the colour-sensitive cone-cells used during the day. Like the owl and the panther, like a hundred thousand generations of his ancestors stretching back to the dawn of Man, Morgan could see in the dark.

"How long we got?" Bob's shout echoed up from the blackness below.

"Only about half an hour" Morgan estimated guiltily, yelling back.

"Let's get going" Willard joined in "Before this goddamned crystal drifts out of synch."

They crowded excitedly together on the electronics platform. Bob switched the signal from the photo-sensitive eye into the loudspeaker. They could literally hear the light-particles from the Crab Nebula cascading into their apparatus like radio-active particles clicking into a Geiger-counter. Willard switched on his timing signal, which they heard as a perfectly steady series of clicks. They were listening to the Universe.

Bob spoke into the microphone attached to the tape-recorder:

"This is run number one on South Preceding Star in centre of Crab. Period is 33........ milliseconds. Ok let's go."

Willard switched on Don's computer and they all stared at its small circular screen. Five hundred faint dots swarmed up the screen like sperms in a race. Each dot marked the accumulating number of light particles detected from a particular phase of the pulsar's cycle. If a pulsar was there they expected several neighbouring dots to race out ahead of the others and form a vertical pulse on the screen.

No pulse. They waited in suspense, quietly watching and listening to the signals coming from six thousand light years away; signals that started out before The Pyramids or Stonehenge had been constructed. They were listening to ancient light. They knew that most of the particles would be coming from the Nebula itself, or from the foreground sky, and so wouldn't be pulsed. To begin with such particles could easily swamp the much fainter signals expected from the pulsar. But if the pulsar was there it should show up eventually. Five minutes passed in tense silence. Bob opened another pack of gum. Morgan climbed up to check on the telescope, half hoping that it had drifted out of position. But no. Then back down to the platform to stare at the climbing sperms.

No sign of a pulse.

"How long we going to go on?" Bob wanted to know. Dillard and Morgan had estimated that if they were going to see the pulsar at all they would see it in a minute or two. They'd been running for ten minutes with no hint of success. It was time to call quits and move on: to search the nebula bit by bit because there was no knowing exactly where inside it the pulsar might be lurking. They weren't finished yet, not by a long chalk. All the same, a certain excited expectancy ebbed away. The South Preceding Star, the very odd star at the heart of the nebula had always seemed much their best chance of success. And it didn't pulse!

Over the next two nights they searched every nook and cranny of the nebula without success. With practice they learned to do all the observing almost blindfold. They relaxed, enjoying the experience of being 'real' astronomers for the first time. Don had gone home half way through the first night and left them to it. Isolated on their mountaintop, perched among the stars, they felt half like priests, half like astronauts.

Morgan's imagination was deeply touched by its first true contact with scientific reality. Instead of reading about photons in a textbook he could hear them arriving one by one from outer space. And that they were not just particles but waves as well, was demonstrated by their interaction with the telescope. They reflected off the mirror and were focussed as waves, and yet were detected by the photometer as discrete particles. How could that be? Here was the central mystery of quantum physics made manifest before his eyes. Optics and Electronics, never exciting before, suddenly came to life for him. One didn't need a great accelerator to see into the heart of modern physics; a modest telescope would do. Astronomy was first and last observation – not speculation. Without making a discovery he'd undergone a profound, almost religious conversion.

Waking in the afternoon Morgan found the peace outside absolute; the only sound the faint hush of wind around the domes and rock pinnacles. He used to lie with binoculars and look out across the vast emptiness of cactus and mountain, watch the dust-devils wander through the mesquite, watch the towering cumulo-nimbus clouds develop in the afternoon and dissolve in the evening. He was puzzled by flashes of light down in the cactus, as if a distant army was on the march. He asked Bob:

"Wetbacks." was Bob's laconic reply.

"What are they?"

"Illegal Mexican immigrants comin' North to work the cotton in Texas, the fruit farms in California. Some have walked all two thousand miles from Mexico City."

They were about to pack up the electronics and go home when they got a call from the university. They were to have three more nights because their successor astronomer was ill.

What were they to do? They'd searched every corner of the nebula already. They decided to check all their calculations.

Morgan re-checked his, and was cooking the dinner when Dillard emitted a loud North Carolinan:

"Oh Mah Gahd!"

"What's up?"

"Ah've divided by two pi unnecessarily. All our timing has been out from the start."

"You mean we've not really searched at all so far?"

"Looks lahk it. Gotta start in all over again."

Morgan felt a small shiver of excitement. They had a fresh chance. He looked out at the evening sky: five-eighths cumulus cloud, but with clear blue streets in between.

As darkness fell the three of them climbed back up into the dome and opened the shutters on the half cloudy constellation of Taurus. They were practiced enough by now to work almost automatically.

"OK" Morgan yelled down. "Set on South Preceding Star. But hurry up. We've only got ten minutes of clear sky."

"Timing set." Replied Dillard crouching in front of his screen.

Bob McAllister set his tape recorder going and murmured into the microphone:

"The next observation will be observation number eighteen, on South Preceding SP Star."

He switched on the telescope signal: they could hear the sound of photons coming in like grasshoppers on a summer's day. Almost immediately, and incredulously, Morgan saw it:

"We've got a bleeding pulse here."

"Hey" said Willard, even more disbelieving than Morgan.

A long pause ensued whilst they watched and listened:

WC "Waow. You don't suppose that's really it do you? Cain't be."

TM "It really looks like something from here at the moment."

WC "Hmm!"

TM "It's growing too. It's growing up here too."

WC "Gahd it is isn't it. Son of a bitch."

TM "It's growing Willard!"

WC " So it is. Christ on a crutch. Who'd have thought."

TM "It's growing more! That's a bleeding pulse! By God we've got it! Shall I ring Don?"

WC "Naow naow. Ah kin hardly believe it raht naow."

TM "Nor me. In fact I won't believe it until we repeat the whole damn thing."

WC "It worries me that the pulse is raht in the middle of the screen. No reason for that. Seems too much of a coincidence."

They believed, and yet they didn't believe. It was too sudden, too easy, too momentous to be true. They were so inexperienced, knew so little of all the things that could go wrong. It was far too big a discovery for two novices to make at their first attempt.

In silence they stopped the run, recorded the data, re-set the telescope, switched the electronics off, then switched them on again.

WC "OK let's go. Ah want to see that pulse move somewhere else on the screen."

They all watched tensely as the little dots began their upward ascent like bubbles rising from the ocean floor.

TM "My God it's still there! It's as good as it was, or better than it was last time."

WC "But it's still in the middle of the screen."

TM "No it isn't Willard It's moved a little to the right. See. Look."

There was a long pause, waiting for the signal to accumulate

TM: in disbelief "It's growing!"

Laughter

TM "Yes, that's it. By God we've got it!" He was triumphant.

WC "It disturbs me that it's still near the middle of the screen. I hope to Gahd it's not some kind of artefact of the electronics. Let's move off the position, move the telescope somewhere else, and see if we get the same thing. If we do then it's an artefact."

Morgan climbed back up, noted that sky immediately round Taurus was still clear, and adjusted the offset guider to move the aperture off the South Preceding Star."

"OK" he yelled, tumbling down the stairs to watch the new data coming in.

Their hearts sank when the pulse began to appear again, somewhat attenuated, but still in the middle of the screen. Nothing was said as they concluded the run. It was now looking like interference. It had to be. But Morgan was thinking.

Leaving the telescope exactly where it was, they reset the clock completely out of synch with the pulsar. If the pulsar appeared now then it was definitely interference of some kind; it couldn't be coming from the pulsar.

No pulse appeared. Their confidence began to trickle back.

"I've been thinking. Maybe I didn't steer the telescope off far enough last time. Maybe atmospheric seeing was allowing some of the pulsar light to leak round the edge of the aperture. I'll move the telescope way off Willard, and you reset the period correctly. Then let's see what happens."

This time there was no pulse at all. Their confidence grew further. Had interference been responsible the pulse should have reappeared.

Finally came the acid test; a repeat of the first discovery run, aimed at the South Preceding Star and with the timing right:

BMcA "This is observation number twenty three. On SP star. Period......secs. Go."

TM "Here she comes!"

WC "Mah Gahd."

TM "It's growing!"
WC "Son of a bitch. So it is. Jesus Christ!"
TM "My God! It couldn't be more definite than that."
WC "Ah'll be damned." A hysterical giggle.
TM "Any room for the American national anthem on the tape? "
Just then the clouds rolled in for the night.

Morgan felt a mixture of hysterical elation and regret. After having done so much towards making the big discovery Don Tallon had missed the magic moment. He ran downstairs and rang Don at home in Tucson. Don was very guarded, very noncommittal. He made them swear to tell nobody what they'd found. Morgan could hear him thinking 'What on earth have those theoretical clowns done wrong?' But he promised to come up on the morrow to look through his gadgetry for a gremlin.

But the three on the mountain were utterly convinced and happy. Morgan rang Ann who screamed with excitement on the phone .Willard rang Claire and both wives were sworn to secrecy, though they were allowed to chat with one another.

But there was no doubt in Willard's mind or Morgan's that they had found the first optical pulsar. And they had found it bang in the middle of the most spectacular supernova explosion. From now on no one could doubt that pulsars were the fabled Neutron Stars, and as such matter in an entirely new state.

Bubbling with excitement they drank most of a flagon of cheap California red wine, before going to bed dreaming of fame.

The following evening Don arrived from Tucson. He was stone faced and non-commital as he checked through all his electronics – but it wasn't hard to guess what he thought.

The night was absolutely clear. By twilight the dome was open and Morgan was setting the telescope confidently back on The South Preceding Star. Willard set the newly adjusted period into the Frequency Synthesiser, and they were off. None of the mountain team said anything.

"Hey" Don sounded amazed "That baby looks like something."

"OK cut." Willard was curt

"I'm offsetting the aperture three aperture widths East." Morgan called down from above "OK. Go."

They went smoothly and professionally through all the routines of the previous night. The pulsar behaved perfectly. Don became wildly excited. His amazement was plain:

"You fellers have done it! With this itty bitty telescope. The guys down at the university won't believe it. Nobody will. Not till I tell 'em. Boy what a discovery! And I thought you'd screwed up. I really did."

They used the rest of the clear night to measure the pulsar's colour. It turned out to be, by comparison with a normal star, abnormally blue. And they confirmed that there were two pulses in each cycle, one sharp and the other, half a period away, broader and shallower. In some utterly mysterious way the neutron star was acting like a spinning lighthouse, emitting twin beams of intense radiation from its opposite poles. When those beams flashed briefly into their telescope they appeared as two pulses, one from either pole. The ultra blue colour of the pulsar light meant it was not ordinary radiation from a hot star, but some strange emanation from a bizarre kind of body that nobody had ever seen before.

Impressive as it had appeared to Morgan their 36 inch telescope was, by professional standards, small, and certainly very old fashioned. Hence the weird and dangerous observing platform up in the air at the 'wrong' end of the tube. Hence the mirror – the oldest one ground in America. And hence especially, the ancient guidance system which was far too crude for them to distinguish which of the two invisible stars in the centre of the nebula, the South Preceding or the North Following, was for certain the pulsar. Because the guidance was so crude they had been forced to work with a large aperture, one ten times larger in diameter than the separation of those two stars in the sky. Thus the light from both stars, and indeed from a wide swath of the nebula itself, was getting into their apparatus. In consequence the pulsed light was much diluted, and all the harder to see. Through a large modern telescope they would actually be able to see both faint stars by eye, not using blind offsets as Morgan had been forced to do, and then put a tiny aperture over each one individually and measure them by turn. Moreover such a tiny aperture, perhaps a hundred times less in area, would exclude ninty-nine percent of the unwanted, un-pulsed nebula light. As a result the pulsar light beam ought to shine through like an undiluted beacon, as they could never see it in the thirty-six inch.

A few hundred yards along the mountain–top from Steward lay the Kitt Peak National Observatory, with its new 84-inch, one of the most powerful and certainly the most up-to-date optical telescopes in the world. If only they could fix their apparatus to that for half an hour all their observing problems would be over. So the following afternoon Willard Cox and Tom Morgan decided to scout along to the 84 inch and ask for help.

They made their way into the immense white dome which, after the brilliant afternoon light, was almost black inside. Standing talking underneath the telescope structure were, by the most amazing coincidence, America's two foremost pulsar hunters: Roger Beverly the ace observer at the National Observatory and Jerry Christoffel from Mount Palomar in California, both of whom had been racing one another for over a year to find the first optical pulsar.

Morgan had never realised that the phrase "their faces fell' could be a literal description of men faced with a bitter disappointment. But that is exactly what happened when Cox handed them a paper trace of the Crab pulse. Their faces fell with such a thud that they almost hit the floor. For a year they'd been scheming, working, planning, racing against one another to make the big discovery, and now some unknown greenhorns had beaten them to the prize. Briefly Morgan felt sorry for these two older much more respected men. Science could be arbitrarily cruel.

They asked Beverly, who looked like a Chinese mandarin in jeans, if they might bolt their apparatus to his telescope, for just 30 minutes, explaining the reasons why.

Beverly's refusal was immediate and adamant.

"Oh go on Roger." Christoffel pleaded with him.

"I can't. I've been assigned this observing time by the director. You can't change the rules."

Disappointed, and not a little surprised at Beverly' reaction, they made their way back along the mountain top to Steward. The cat was now well and truly out of the bag. News of their discovery would race around the astronomical world. Telescopes all over the globe would be pointed at the Crab Nebula tonight.

To stay in the race they had one desperate alternative. They had to replace their present aperture with a much smaller one. It would have to be a perfectly square - shaped hole one tenth of a millimetre exactly along each side. And they had two hours before dark to make one.

But how to make it? Willard found some kitchen tinfoil to pierce it in. Morgan located a scalpel in the observatory First Aid kit to cut it with; Don Tallon found a microscope, usually employed for measuring plates, to magnify the fiddling operation. They all held their breaths while Cox, who turned out to have the steadiest hands, carried out the brain surgery. And it worked. By dusk they had a scarcely visible piece of tinfoil with an invisible pinprick of a square hole in it, installed in the photometer atop the telescope.

By now the big news had leaked out. Telephone calls were coming in from all over; calls for information and calls of congratulation. But one of the calls was a warning. Beverly had called down to the National Observatory headquarters in Tucson with the result that a truckload of electronics and engineers was even now roaring up the mountain to the 84 inch hoping to scoop them. The unsporting race was on.

Before night had properly come Morgan had the old telescope set on the familiar star field. But the tiny aperture was so small that he could see nothing through it. Instead Don Tallon proposed a brilliant piece of extemporization. Instead of looking for stars through the tiny hole they would listen for them. He turned up the volume of the loud speaker so that they could hear distinctly the clicks of the incoming photons, very few in number now that their aperture was so small. But when they actually managed to get a faint star aligned with the hole the click rate should audibly rise. Then they'd look at the computer screen to see if the star was pulsing.

Using Don's ingenious technique they quickly eliminated the North Following star out of the only two possible candidates. But when the invisible South Preceding star clicked into the aperture, now undiluted by un-pulsed light, a pulse positively shot up the screen producing a wonderful clear shape which caused them to break out in cheers. They felt like a team of mountaineers who had come up the North Face and were now placing their flag on the un-trodden summit. They had, despite the odds, got there first.

And just in time too; the clouds rolled in and blotted out the stars.

Feeling elated and not a little self satisfied they trooped along the dark mountain to to the cafeteria of the National Observatory to see what the opposition had to say.

There were a dozen of them seated round a table drinking coffee. Roger Beverly was there, as was Steve Sugarman, an aggressive New Yorker who seemed to be in charge of the pulsar operation. When they arrived and sat down an uneasy silence gripped the table. A bombshell was about to drop. And it was aimed straight at them.

The two teams swapped pulses. As expected, given the relative size of the two telescopes, the Kitt Peak pulse was much stronger and sharper, a wonder of potential scientific information to behold. Morgan couldn't help admiring it, wondering what secrets of astrophysics it might encode.

But that wasn't the bombshell.

Sugarman handed them a telegram he was just about to send to the International Astronomical Union, the body to which astronomers sent news of urgent astronomical discoveries, so that they could be confirmed elsewhere.

When Morgan read the telegram he couldn't believe it. Sugarman was claiming the entire pulsar discovery for his team. There was no mention of themselves. No mention that Kitt Peak was merely confirming what they had found several nights before. Morgan was dumbfounded. It was blatant, barefaced theft.

"You cain't send that." Willard Cox spluttered.

Sugarman was totally unabashed, even hectoring as he launched forth in his Noo Yoik accent:

"Yoo goys, your photo toob is non linear. Yoo cain't claim nuthin….." and he went on in a farrago of bare faced lies. His team looked uncomfortably into their coffee. Even Beverly argued with him – just a little.

Beside Morgan Willard Cox was swelling up with fury. Morgan couldn't say a thing. He simply couldn't believe what he was hearing. Such behaviour as Sugarman's was entirely outside his experience. He gripped Willard's thigh under the table and whispered in his ear:

"Shh! Don't forget our discovery telegram went out this afternoon. He's too late. Let the little sod hang himself."

They retreated angrily into the darkness. Morgan realised that being an astronomer involved making enemies as well as friends. So be it. If they wanted to fight then, so far as he was concerned, let them!

The following night Ann and Claire brought a celebration banquet up to the dome where everyone toasted the stars, toasted their forthcoming fame, damned the opposition as scoundrels, and sang into their wine. How no one fell headfirst into the telescope was a wonder.

Such was public interest in pulsars that indeed they became small time celebrities overnight. They had their photographs in 'Time' magazine – the great American accolade. An entire BBC production crew was flown out from London to re-enact the discovery. Their colleagues at the observatory, who had been amiably contemptuous beforehand, now avoided them altogether. Morgan and Dillard found themselves lunching alone. Don, the oldest hand, who took the full brunt of the hostility, retreated entirely to his laboratory. They were learning that big discoveries are not supposed to be made in small institutes. The small laboratories don't like it, and the big ones hate it.

But they were invited to give an especial seminar at the university. The big auditorium was packed out with astronomers and journalists who buzzed with anticipation. Since they had a tape recording of the pulse coming in, they thought to mount it on Don's computer and replay it so the audience could see the discovery pulse growing on the screen. However, just before the performance, a flustered looking Don came and called them into his lab.

"You guys better listen to this. What do you want to do about it?"

He switched on the tape. They heard the incoming photons singing like grasshoppers. Then, to their complete astonishment, they heard their voices clearly overlaid. All the excitement, the blasphemy, the doubts and the ultimate triumph were there too. Unknown to them, unknown indeed to himself, Bob McAllister had recorded the whole discovery.

They played a short excerpt of the tape at the seminar. It brought the house down. But it was to prove a serious mistake, and an expensive one in the long run.

As to their clash with the National Observatory, that was settled when Bart Bok got back from a long observing trip in Chile. Unlike other American astronomers – who seemed to think that Sugarman's behaviour was only to be expected – Bok went berserk. Morgan found himself relieved about that because it meant that his future profession would not be entirely bereft of morality. Amidst rumours that he'd been ignominiously fired, Sugarman shortly afterwards disappeared from Tucson.

By some miracle their pulsar paper appeared in that most prestigious scientific journal 'Nature' within a week of being faxed from Arizona. Morgan proudly showed the journal to Ann:

"Well done darling. I think you deserve a holiday. And so do I. We've never had a proper honeymoon yet. I was sick all the time on that horrible boat to New York, while you've been running round like a headless chicken since we got here. Let's go to Mexico. If we camp it needn't cost much.

Though nothing had been said, Morgan presumed that his future at the university was now assured for at least twelve months and probably twenty four. So they went.

The border town of Nogales was squalid in the extreme, but continuing south they found themselves in empty, unspoiled Sonoran desert. Although the natural landscape was unchanged the philosophical transition from north to south of the border was unforgettable, even disturbing. Where Americans had tamed and colonised the landscape the Mexicans ignored it. The American bulldozed a road onto his 'property', towed in an enormous silver mobile home, erected a Television aerial, drilled a bore-hole to fill the water tower, got the generator going and filled the prefabricated pool. The yellow school bus would call and the Stars and Stripes would fly at full mast. And, in a land where not so long ago the Apache roamed, Hereford cattle turned cactus into beef burgers.

South of the border the same landscape was empty, pristine. Instead they found the Mexicans teeming together in ramshackle townships of haunting poverty. They were both shocked by the hovels of tin and board which crowded round the old white Spanish missions. Women carried water on their heads. Jeeps gave way to donkeys. There were frightening numbers of children.

The contrast was so stark that it begged for an explanation. Ann supposed it lay in exterior circumstances:

"You need capital to build roads, drill bore holes, buy cattle and even buy contraceptives. They don't have it and the rich wouldn't lend it to them."

"Why not?" Morgan objected "They have exactly the same natural resources as the Americans north of the border, and much lower labour costs. On the face of it they should therefore be an investor's dream."

"It's ignorance then. They wouldn't know how to build good roads, or drill bore holes."

"Technical advice must be dead cheap to buy. One good road engineer could train dozens of Mexicans every year. And drilling bore-holes is not exactly rocket science. Nor is purchasing cows. No, it must be something else. Investors won't lend these people money because they know they won't get it back. It must be the corruption and dishonesty."

"How do you know that?" Ann was indignant.

The argument continued as the road deteriorated into dirt, and potholes large enough to threaten their car, Huge oncoming trucks hurled stones against their windscreen. Slowing down however only encouraged the truck behind to pull out, overtake and blind them with its dust – and its stones. Driving became hot, dirty and dangerous.

Towards evening they reached the ancient Spanish port of Guaymas where they turned off for Bocochibampo Bay. In the darkness they found a very ancient hotel that smelled as if it was somewhere near the sea. But they were too exhausted to do more than crawl into bed.

They were woken in the morning by palm fronds rattling against the wooden shutters. When he pushed them open Morgan found they were on an ancient balcony overlooking the sea. Perched on the stone balustrade, staring at them rather like a sleepy clown, was a pelican who flapped off in disgust when Ann laughed at him. They leaned on the balustrade which was entwined with trumpet flowers:

"Oh look darling!" Ann was ecstatic.

They were staring down into the bluest water either of them had ever seen; The Sea of Cortez.

"We're going to love this place Tom. Come on, let's go and find a lonely beach."

It was easier said than done. A hot, horrible day later they'd learned their lesson. Perhaps because of the burning sun Mexicans never build a road unless they really need one. And having built a road they all want to live on it. Thus they discovered there were only two types of beach in Mexico; beaches that were wholly inaccessible because there was no track to them, and beaches that were crowded with shacks, people, donkeys, garbage and flies.

By mid afternoon they were desperate. The temperature inside the car was over one hundred and twenty degrees; its metalwork was far too hot to touch. Beetle was being jolted over the most abominable stone tracks; the map was useless and their Spanish worse. The ruts were so large that he had constantly to get out and check under the car to see that it wasn't vitally damaged.

Morgan swore as they reached yet another dead end in the cactus. Ann, who was suffering from car sickness, got out to look for herself. He turned off the engine, which ticked in the heat. Ann disappeared into the cactus. His bum was stuck to the seat with sweat. He gulped down some water that was almost hot enough to shave in.

"I'll swear I can smell the sea" Ann said when she returned. 'Come on. Start Beetle and follow me."

By now he was willing to try anything, however mad, as long as it wasn't another Mexican road.

So he drove off into the cactus while Ann lead the way prospecting on foot. They struggled between cacti, around trees and in out of dried arroyos. It was madness really because at any time the car could have become irretrievably stuck. But they could definitely smell the sea and after a mile reached a promising grove of palms with a tall white sand dune on the far side. He parked the car on the pristine shell-white sand and the two of them struggled up the enormous dune hand in hand.

They'd arrived. Below them curved the most delicious white sand bay with no sign that humans had ever set foot on it. The arms curved round a mile or more on either side of it, finishing in two rocky islets almost directly out to sea. They slid down the dune, threw off their clothes and plunged into the refreshingly cold water.

They pitched camp on the landward side of the dune under an organ-pipe cactus, a vegetable monster thirty feet high, bigger even than a saghuaro. Its dozens of pipes were home to a family of gila woodpeckers. Around them, at a safe distance, flourished every variety of spiked and thorny plant. The aptly named barrel-cacti protected their watery green pulp with close-knit hooked spines fully an inch and half long. Only when they had learned to outwit these spikes had the early pioneers been able to assuage their thirst and cross the western deserts. Behind and above them towered pinnacles of sandstone turning blood red in the evening sun.

Morgan took his spear gun and goggles in search of supper. The colour had gone from the depths by now, apart from an incandescent orange goldfish. Morgan was pretty useless with a spear-gun, more likely to shoot himself than anything edible. But here the fish were tame, even curious. A fat black grouper with swivelling button eyes followed him around like a dog. More than half ashamed, he put the spear-gun to its gills , pulled the trigger and despoiled paradise.

The desert night was unforgettable. A trillion stars burned right down to the cactus. The heat of the day radiated off into space leaving a coolth that caressed the skin. A hint of dew stole in off the Sea of Cortez. Their fire crackled and popped, orange sparks climbing to die among the blue stars. The grouper sizzled in tinfoil while Ann turned the potatoes over in the embers. They were sipping from their demi-john of wine when a coyote howled from a hundred paces away. They had slipped back half a million years.

At the first paling of dawn they dragged their sleeping bags out of the tent and made a nest for themselves among the succulent ice-plants at the summit of the dune. They watched the stars fade, first the Milky Way then the bright constellations. The sun rising from behind the inland mountains burnished their spires first with crimson, then with gold, finally silver, projecting their shadows out across the bay. Purples and greens stole out upon the sea's cold lapping surface with a night breath from the land. The tips of the organ-pipe cactus were the first to catch the sunlight and cast their shadows upon the mesquite below. The gila woodpeckers stirred from their holes in the organ-pipe and announced the coming of the day.

As the sun rose above the mountains, driving the colour out of the desert, the sea turned into a bowl of liquid cerulean blue. There were so many fish in it they could smell them. Fishing turned out to be no sport, for the fish impaled themselves as soon as the bait was in the water. The Morgans however were more interested in sea mammals than fish. Sea-lions were rumoured to live off this shore while grey whales came to give birth to their young in this sea. Snuggled in his sleeping bag Morgan kept watch through binoculars. Skeins of cormorants passed far out to sea while frigate birds with pointed wings and crescent tails were lords of the high air. But the pelicans, so ungainly on the ground, excited their greatest admiration. A line of perhaps a dozen would pass across the deep, barely millimetres above the surface. The odd syncopated flap seemed to suffice them for a hundred meter glide.

They saw no whales that that first morning, though they were to see them later. They were intrigued however by a loud smacking from across the bay. `Through the glasses they discovered a huge manta-ray hurling itself out of the water again and again to belly flop back into the sea with a crash.

Then Ann gasped and grasped Morgan's arm. Three feet above, hovering perfectly still, his tiny head turning inquisitively from side to side was a ruby throated humming bird. Suddenly the dunes were alive with them, sipping nectar from purple flowers opening in the sun. They could hear the whirring before seeing them flash by. There was nothing delicate about their behaviour. They chased one another exuberantly and noisily about the sky. Arrowing upward like projectiles they would scream down again to pull out but inches from the ground. Seeing them Morgan could understand how these same mites were capable of crossing two thousand kilometres of open Caribbean in a single flight. At times there were half a dozen hovering about their heads, intrigued apparently by the red tartan patchwork of the sleeping-bags. Then, as suddenly as they came, they were gone .

"You know Morgan" Ann raised on her elbow sounded serious "This is the place where we ought to conceive a baby."

He looked up at her, hanging over his head:

"You know Cloudesly, I think you are right."

The humming birds returned to visit every morning. And every morning, after they had gone, Ann always said exactly the same thing.

During the night coyotes visited their camp leaving footprints everywhere. Nothing however was damaged and nothing stolen. To protect it against just such a

visitation Morgan had left the uneaten half of the grouper on top of the car roof.
Despite paw marks on the sides of the car where they must have stood up to sniff, it
remained there unharmed. Unwrapped from its charred foil the remains looked wholly
uneatable, but Ann flaked it from the bone, whipped together some mayonnaise a la
desert, and they feasted on a delicious breakfast.

Having packed some lunch, they secured camp and set off along the margin of
the bay to explore. The seaward side of the dune was now bright with purple sea figs,
succulents whose flowers opened only when the sun was in his zenith. Ann, who
collected shells, was pleased with the twisted black-and-purple horn shells found in
the shallows, but more delighted with the pentagonal sand-dollars.

From the top of the islet at the arm of the bay, to which they swam, they had a fine
view back over their domain. Protected by the most rugged mountains, their beach
was surrounded by a pristine cactus forest. It was hard to see how they could ever
have found their way into such a hidden land. There was no sign of man, Even the
sea, far out beyond their bay, was empty.

When he cast a line from the rocks, an immediate tug denoted success. The fish
wasn't large but had a parrot's beak, and a formidable array of spines. While he
worked out how to remove the hook, it began to swell up alarmingly into a globe.
And if that wasn't enough to put them off he grunted piteously until they threw him
back in the water. On their way back to camp something happened which neither of
them were really able to believe afterwards. There had been a great deal of aerial
activity far out to sea. Lines of pelicans, cormorants and other sea birds seemed to be
milling about in the air over a shoal of fish. Through the glasses they could just see
the pelicans diving into the melee from the air. The morning wore on and the shoal
moved in towards them as the flocks of accompanying birds increased. The pelicans
appeared to be working in well-regulated squadrons, driving the shoal into the bay
and towards the beach where they stood. About a hundred of them filled the air with
the frenzied beating of wings. Climbing to about sixty feet, each bird would take aim,
close its wings into a perfect arrow and plummet seaward like a harpoon. The instant
before hitting the surface – and they could hear the 'whomp' as they did so – their
wings would fold completely and the whole bird would be gone deep in a flurry of
spray. Seconds later they'd be on the surface again manoeuvring to get a struggling
fish out of their beaks and into their mouths. They could see the prey still writhing in
their pouches and then in their crops. After a final shake the pelican would thrash its
way into the air again for another climb, another dive and another meal.

They came closer and closer. The air was filled with the beating of wings and the
cries of gulls and other sea-birds involved in the feeding frenzy. The water in front of
them became a seething mass of crashing pelicans and frantic fish. They came right
into the shallows almost at their feet. Suddenly the sand was alive with a million
silvery shapes leaping and flashing in the sun. The pelicans had literally driven the
shoal ashore. All around them, within yards, the birds gorged and the fish died. The
gulls screamed and fought over the gleaming harvest until they could swallow no
more. The Morgans too joined in that primal feast, collecting enough of the
shimmering bodies, turning mauve and green in death, to cook for dinner that night.

Apart from the total lack of fresh water, Humming Bird Dunes remained their
paradise for ten days. Morgan's home-made still proved unsuccessful and as they had
with them only a single five gallon jerry can, they had to retreat to the nearest village
for replenishments, for local oranges and for giant watermelons which somehow
remained cool and fresh in the shade. During their stay they had only one visit, but a
very strange one. A troupe of Indians dressed in gaudy clothes passed along the beach

one morning and disappeared as mysteriously as they had come. The men carried heavy packs, the women bore children on their hips. They stared at the Morgans without recognition or greeting, then passed on their way. They were afterwards told the Indians were exiles from the island of Tiburon which lay just over the horizon. Some years before, the police had been called in to investigate the frequent disappearance of citizens from the mainland shore. It was concluded the cannibals from Tiburon were responsible. The army was sent out, the waterholes were poisoned and the people exiled to the mainland where they still roamed the beaches in hope of one day being allowed to return.

When they had packed the tent on the final morning they climbed to the top of the dune for the last time to bid farewell to their kingdom. They christened it 'Humming Bird Dunes'. Ann said:

"Promise me Twm, you'll never ever tell anyone about this place. Ever. We'll just tell our baby when he's born. And then again when he's twenty-one. And perhaps he'll want to come and find the place where he was conceived, for himself."

The Crab Pulsar was definitely a neutron star, but was it really spinning, as everybody seemed to think? The way to find out for certain was to look at the polarisation of its light.

Up to now Morgan had only the vaguest idea what polarised light was – something to do with expensive sun-glasses. So he read about it. Light is a transverse wave – like a wave travelling along a rope held at both ends. If you shake one end up and down a vertical wave propagates along the rope to the other end. But if you shake it from side to side a horizontal wave propagates instead. This plane of directionality of a wave was called its 'polarisation' , which could be vertical, horizontal, or anywhere in between. Every wave-packet of light, every 'photon' as it was called, would be one hundred per cent polarised in one direction or another. The light from most sources however consisted of a stream of photons, millions of them perhaps, and usually they have such a mix of polarizations distributed at random angles that the net polarisation averages out to zero. Others, particularly sources of reflected light, are highly polarised, with nearly all the photons vibrating in a particular plane. So the degree and direction of polarisation of a light source could be a strong clue as to its physical origin. The *radio* radiation of the Crab Pulsar was strongly polarised, but the direction of its polarisation remained fixed right across the pulse, not at all what one would expect from a rotating source. Did that mean that the spinning theory of neutron stars was wrong?

They had discovered that the optical pulses from the Crab Pulsar contained hundreds of times more energy than the radio pulses – which might be caused by some uninteresting peripheral phenomenon. It was therefore vital to measure the polarisation of the *optical* signal as a test of the spinning theory, and so that is what they set out to do next. But to measure the polarisation they needed a larger telescope than the 36 inch and a highly specialised instrument called a 'polarimeter'. As luck would have it one of the world experts on cosmic polarisation, Tom De Kok, operated out of The Lunar and Planetary Laboratory of the University of Arizona just across the campus. He agreed to join forces with them and booked observing time on the 61 –inch Kuiper Telescope up in the very Catalina Mountains which hung over the Morgans' apartment.

While they were getting ready for the run Frank Cotteridge came over from California to stay. He was full of praise and congratulations for Tom:

"You can't imagine what a shock it was to the Californians, and to Palomar in particular. Talk about David and Goliath! Here you are with your tiny, old fashioned 36-inch, a peashooter really, beating the pants off a mirror fifty times the area. They are humiliated – and very angry. They can't make up their minds whether it was plain genius or sheer good luck"

"Sheer genius" Ann pronounced. "Twm and Willard were planning it round the motel swimming pool the first week they both arrived here in Tucson. But it's awful; most of their colleagues at the observatory are so jealous that they pretend to believe it was all luck; that they are clowns who fell with their noses in the butter. And they use that wretched tape, out of context, as evidence."

"The real experts at my place don't believe it was luck. They say pulsar observing is far trickier than any other observing techniques we use today. So it can't have been luck. Not at all. Tom I'm envious. In four nights you've surpassed my own efforts over four years."

"Ann's right about the jealousy. We never expected it. The only way to show them they're wrong is for us to go on and do better things. We're going to have a crack at the polarisation."

"You'd better be quick then. Our boys have just been given fourteen dark nights on the 200-inch to beat you to that. They're throwing everything and everybody at it in an effort to redeem our reputation."

Frank was also able to talk to Ann tête-à-tête about Morgan:

"He's amazing Ann, he really is. I'm smart but Tom's driven. He never stops thinking. He can't."

"Don't I know."

"It's like a great turbine going on inside him, day and night. It goes on and on turning until he finds the right answer – or one that satisfies him. Otherwise he can't stop – until he runs completely out of fuel."

"Like he did over his PhD?"

"He can get really down you know. When he was seventeen Ann he hardly said a word for six months. We never found out why. Any sign of that?"

"No, but he's been frightfully short tempered. Not with me, but with silly inanimate things. A few weeks ago, before we went to Mexico, we were driving across the desert and stopped off at this café for a cold drink. They hadn't got any orange juice, which he'd been looking forward to. Do you know what he did when we got back to the car? He ripped the door off its hinges. I couldn't believe it. I don't think he could either. We *had* to get away. We had to. Mexico was good for him."

Frank wanted to see the 36 inch so Morgan drove him up to Kitt Peak.:

"What are your long term plans Tom?"

"I can't afford to think far ahead. London eventually. It's Ann's job. She wants us to go back this year."

"And you?"

"I'm learning so much here Frank. Every bloody week. And there's so much to learn. You know our education in Britain, our technical education, is just shit by comparison."

"I know what you mean."

Morgan wanted to know about Bellfounder.

"Oh he's very chipper at present. He's convinced that he and Tinker have solved the proto-star problem"

"What?" Morgan was astonished. "What have they discovered?"

"Their computer models show collapse down to a tiny core, one thousandth of the mass, followed by accretion on to that. It looks pretty convincing. Bellfounder calls it 'Solving the last great problem in stellar astronomy'. "

"My God the silly fools." Morgan laughed harshly.

"What do you mean?"

"That collapse is not real – it's a numerical artefact. I showed that in my thesis."

"Have you published it yet?"

"No. But I'm going to."

"Shall I tell Bellfounder?"

"No, please don't. I'll tell Tinker when he comes over here to give a seminar next month."

"Do you know Tinker is the hot favourite to get the chair at Yale – on the strength of it? With BF's influence of course."

"Chair or not, it's still rubbish."

"You and Bellfounder Tom; you seem star-crossed enemies. You could do without that. He's so powerful, even over here."

"Especially over here," Morgan was bitter. "The Yanks fall for that snooty British superiority of his. God knows why."

"What about your Red Giant stuff?"

"It came out a couple of weeks ago. Your Bellfounder will have to look to his laurels now."

"He's not 'my Bellfounder' Tom. I'm growing to distrust him. I rather hope you'll bring him down a peg."

"I will. And more than one."

"But why do you always pick such powerful enemies? It's Schweinhundt all over again. And we know what he did to you. BF could do far worse. Far worse. He could even have you drummed out of astronomy. I'm told he's a vindictive man with tentacles everywhere."

"I blame you Frank. Entirely. It was you gave me his wretched book. Remember?"

On their last night Ann served dinner on the roof under the stars. For once they had some decent wine – which Frank had brought from California. After two bottles Morgan grew expansive:

"You know Frank the more I do science the less I understand it. Where's the underlying theme? What is the so called Scientific Method? Look at me for instance. I thought I was doing science back in Worcestershire, entirely using deductive mathematics. Then in London I'm writing and running computer simulations. And here I'm observing. I'm damned if I can see any connection between them. Can you?"

"I know what you mean. As you say nobody seems to know what 'The Scientific Method" is. I read this wonderful quote from Peter Medawar the immunologist . It's so good I think I can even remember it: 'Ask a scientist what he considers the scientific method to be and he will adopt an expression that is at once solemn and shift-eyed; solemn, because he feels he ought to declare an opinion; shifty eyed, because he is wondering how to conceal the fact that he has no opinion to declare."

Morgan nearly choked with laughter, and so did Ann.

"I just love it Frank. I love it."

"Please say it again Frank" Ann added. And he did.

"But surely somebody must have got some idea." Morgan protested.

"Well of course there are the philosophers."

Morgan groaned: "Why on earth should we ask them? You remember why I got into science in the first place?"

"Go on."

"I was fascinated by Philosophy when I was twelve to fifteen – as you know. I read all the great men. And do you know what they were saying? They said 'You can't understand philosophy unless you understand Einstein's 'Theory of Space and Time' – in capital letters of course. So I struggled like mad to master Einstein. And eventually I did. And what had it got to do with philosophy? Damn bloody all! Either the shysters didn't understand Relativity, or they didn't understand philosophy. Either way they weren't worth reading."

"Well you did ask me. Medawar is an advocate of a philosopher called Karl Popper. Popper calls science a process of 'Conjecture and Refutation'. He says you can't prove any scientific hypothesis – you can only refute it."

Morgan thought about that:

"Well that's nonsense for a start. We've proved that the Earth is round – and that was once no more than a scientific hypothesis."

"It does seem amazing," Ann interjected "That you scientists, who are so successful, don't seem to know what science is."

"Yes": Frank agreed "And you never hear scientists discussing it. Or giving their students lectures on 'The Scientific Method'. I've never had one. Not one. Have you Tom?"

"Nope. But if we could get to the bottom of it perhaps we'd both be much better scientists. Perhaps we should try; as a sort of back burner project."

It was Ann who ran Frank out to the airport next evening because Morgan was going observing. Frank wanted to talk about Morgan:

"I know you want to get Tom back to London Ann. It's understandable. But Tom's career prospects are bloody precarious. He's old for a start. That's never good. And he seems to have made an enemy of Bellfounder. I can hardly imagine anything worse – not in British astronomy. If he goes back to Britain now – even supposing he can find a temporary job of some kind – which is fiendishly difficult – he could be out on the street in two years. He's got to establish his reputation over here; get his Three-Stage-Model published, and his proto-star computer stuff. And become an ace observer. Then he can go back to a permanent job, a university lectureship somewhere, where Bellfounder won't be able to 'get' him."

Ann didn't say anything.

The Catalinas were rugged, heavily forested mountains over twelve thousand feet high. Half way up it began to snow heavily so that the big Chevrolet station wagon, loaded down with four men and a ton of equipment, began to lose traction. Darkness fell as, under Tom De Kok's instruction, they fitted chains. As they resumed their switchback climb the headlights caught the tall Douglas firs loaded down with snow like the trees in fairy tales.

The higher they climbed the deeper the snow became. There were no tracks because no one had come up or down for hours, possibly days. Several times they had to get out and dig their way through a snowdrift. The fainter hearts were for turning back but Tom De Kok, the driver, was made of sterner stuff. Eventually however even he couldn't force the vehicle any further. The snow was two or three deep and falling steadily.

They turned off the lights, got out and put on their warmest observing clothes. In Morgan's case that meant pyjamas; Dillard had his skiing gear, Don Tallon a deer-hunter's suit and Tom De Kok a B52 rear-gunner's flak suit which could be electrically heated.

"You guys" he said in his Dutch-American accent " Get the equipment ready. I go oop to the observatory and bring back a sledge." And with that he walked up into the tall trees until his torch light disappeared among the tall trunks and the falling snow.

They sledged the delicate electronics the last half mile up through the forest to the observatory. Beside the big dome of the Kuiper telescope stood the log cabin which was the observers quarters. As de Kok kicked the snow away from the front door he announced gleefully:

"Ve could be snowed in here several days. Veeks even."

"What about food?" Morgan wanted to know.

"First we eat the foreigners. Then we draw lots." He roared with laughter."Vait you see freezer. Ve can last vinter."

He was right. A reassuringly gigantic freezer occupied one wall. In no time they had a log fire roaring away in the grate while De Kok superintended the brewing of glauwein. They supped the warm alcohol like antifreeze while toasting their frozen toes by the fire. They looked at one another with delight like boy-scouts on their first camping expedition.

When Morgan woke in the morning the snow was up to the windowsill but the sky was burnished blue. He put on snow-shoes and went for walk. The high altitude desert light reflecting off the pristine snow was dazzling. The dry cold air sparkled like champagne .The boughs of the great fir trees were bent under their fresh burden of snow. All sound was muffled out by the white blanket. He seemed to be on the summit ridge because he could look down on either side, between the treetops, and see the brown heat of the desert far far below. He felt like a character in Jack London's Klondyke. Although he seemed to be alone animal tracks in the fresh snow told another story. He followed them through the drifts and between the trees, trying to guess what had made them. Was this a snow-rabbit? Was that overlying trail the track of a coyote in pursuit? And surely those were the pugs of a Bob-Cat or a Lynx – even a Mountain Lion. An avalanche of snow slumping down out of a tree nearby startled him into wondering about hungry grizzlies. He didn't think there were any left in Arizona; but he wasn't sure. And what was this amazing trail made by a large animal with long claws but with puzzling brush marks all around it? He followed it far into the trees until it terminated against the bole of a giant fir. He stepped back to look up. Near the very top, feeding noisily on the pine branches, he was astonished to see a large porcupine.

They were well and truly snowed in. Morgan relished it all: the log fires, the silent forests, the camaraderie, the sense of a period stolen out of time The uncertainty about how long they might be there – perhaps weeks, added to the holiday air.

And Tom De Kok was a fascinating companion. As a boy of fifteen he, with his brother, had literally walked out of occupied Holland, across Belgium, across France, across the Pyrenees, across Spain, and knocked at the door of the British embassy in in Portugal. Lying about his age he'd been accepted into the British paratroops and, when trained, dropped behind enemy lines in Holland to act in that most dangerous role of Resistance wireless operator.

After the war was over in the European theatre De Kok was off to the Far East as a frogman fighting against the Japanese.

Later on, at Leiden University, he fell in love with astronomy and somehow, while still a student, worked his way across the Atlantic as a waiter, then hitched his way across America to Mount Wilson Observatory in California. There he met the famous astronomer Walter Baade, who was so impressed by Tom's saga, that he recommended him for graduate training at Yerkes observatory in Wisconsin.

De Kok loved observing, whether it was from a balloon platform, or high in the Catalina Mountains. The tougher, the colder, the darker the harder it was, the more he seemed to relish it. And it was bloody cold up there on a clear night at twelve thousand feet. Once, observing on his own, Morgan reached for a steel guard-rail and found his flesh irretrievably frozen to the icy metal. To get it off quickly, before frostbite set in, he had to urinate on the rail.

Every clear night they observed the Crab pulsar – which was now bright enough to see in this much bigger telescope. But something was going hopelessly wrong with their electronics. Tallon and de Kok eventually traced the problem to a commercial television transmitter perched nearby on the summit. Its powerful transmissions interfered with their circuitry. Before they could get going they had to build a shielding cage out of chicken wire that de Kok found in the workshop. Though not completely effective it seemed to work most of the time, but not during commercials.

Unfortunately, after the Faraday Cage was completed, they were left with only a couple of clear hours before the snow clouds rolled in. They retreated to the log fire with their measurements and sat round it with slide-rules, becoming ever more excited. It appeared that the pulsar had a huge, an unprecedented polarisation. That is to say all of the measurements, bar one, fitted perfectly on a double-sine curve of high amplitude. Unfortunately there was one rogue measurement which didn't fit. Its reading was minus 0.75 whereas it should have been, to agree with all the other readings, plus 0.75 exactly. They argued passionately. Had de Kok made a slip in the dark calling the numbers out to Morgan at the electronics? Or had Morgan misheard, or mis-recorded it in his notebook? Had TV interference raised its ugly face again? Could they ignore that measurement as suspect, and simply accept the other seven as true? Or was that slipshod? Or even dishonest? They wrangled over the choice for several nights, waiting for the skies to clear again – which they never did. They were forced to return to Tucson with tantalising evidence of a very strong polarisation but, this was the important point, no rotation!

They knew that that the proper thing to do was book time on another telescope, one free of interference, and repeat their measurements. At the same time they realised that all the big observatories, including Palomar and Lick, would be racing them to get the polarisation out first. They wrote a paper for 'Nature' but then fought over whether to send it or not. It was a choice between cautious failure and bold risk. In the end, against the better judgement of some, they faxed it off to London, where it was published within the month. They were first – but were they right?

Fortunately Steward's new 90-inch telescope, third largest in the world, was just coming into operation on Kitt Peak – which was free of television interference and they were amongst the first to be granted observing time on it – to repeat the Crab polarisation. Unfortunately the weather closed in again and they got only a total of ninety minutes worth of data, not enough to do a good job, but sufficient to prove that the Catalina results were nonsense. The polarisation wasn't high at all. Over-competitiveness had betrayed them into making a false claim and publishing their foolishness in the most prominent possible place – 'Nature' magazine. The wiseacres in the observatory, when they found out, would nod their heads to one another and say 'I told you so.'

It knocked the stuffing out of Morgan and Willard Cox. Morgan threw the data into a desk drawer and tried to forget about the whole fiasco. But he couldn't for long because the spokesman from the big Palomar group came over to give a seminar on their polarisation results.

It was a very odd performance, very odd indeed. He boasted at great length about the size of their telescope, the vastness of their data resources, the clarity of their weather, and the excellence of their technique. At the same time he was extremely vague about what they'd discovered. Afterwards he came to Morgan's office and was very dismissive of their 90-inch data:

"We've got seven full clear nights of data on a telescope with four times your collecting area. Altogether that's a factor of thirty in our favour."

They were forced to agree with him, but after he left, Morgan and Cox held a council of war.

"Somethin' mahty pecooliar's going on heah. Wha' come all this way and then conceal theyah real results?"

"Exactly. It seems more like playing for time than science. It's as if they're trying to put a shot across our bows."

"If their data is so darned good wha' don't they just publish?"

"Maybe they've cocked up? As we know, that's all too easy to do. They've only got a single polarimeter, not a double-channel one like Tom de Kok's. Tom reckons that makes a huge difference. They have to rely on perfect weather conditions for hours at a time whereas we can observe through practically anything."

"That's so" Willard Cox agreed "A little bit of hah cirrus cloud could screw them totally."

"There's something fishy going on. It doesn't small right."

"Ah reckon either they fucked up, or their data is lousy. But it can hardly be worse than ours."

"No" Morgan agreed in disgust. "Anyway we'll know soon enough. They've promised to send us a proper pre-print. To be honest I'm sick of this polarisation lark. I just wish now we hadn't made such fools of ourselves over the Catalina data."

"Me too" Willard giggled" It was god-damned Murphy's Law."

Several months later while Morgan was in the library he stumbled upon the California preprint. He snatched it up and devoured it in his office. To his amazement he realised that their data, far from being better, was probably worse than the 90-inch stuff. Perhaps through overconfidence in the size of their huge telescope, they'd made their observations through far too large an aperture. Instead of the tiny aperture that they had cut out of tinfoil the Californians had observed the pulsar through a hole so large that most of the light coming through it wasn't from the pulsar at all, but unpulsed light from the surrounding nebula. In other words their pulsar signal was seriously and unnecessarily contaminated by nebular noise. Moreover, as Tom De Kok had maintained from the start, his two-channel machine was inherently much more sensitive to polarisation than theirs.

What to do next? They held a council of war in Morgan's office. The best polarisation data, together with the astrophysical secrets hidden in it, were probably lying in the magnetic tapes at the bottom of Morgan's drawer. Moreover there was a point of honour at stake. They all felt they'd been conned. But it wasn't too late. If they worked like lightening, and could get a paper into a rapid-publication journal such as 'Nature' they could still win the race and beat the Californians into print.

As the 'computer jockey' in the team it was Morgan's job to sort out the mess. Thanks to the fiasco over his PhD thesis he was used to this kind of emergency by now. He got the computer to print the data off the original tape onto paper and did the crucial calculations using his slide-rule and graph paper.

The results were fascinating. They could see the beams swinging smoothly through each pulse. The neutron star *was* rotating after all! Here was the direct evidence. And the two pulses were obviously searchlight beams emerging from the opposite poles of the star. It's spin axis was fortunately at right angles to the Earth, in the plane of the sky, otherwise the narrow beams would have missed the Earth entirely. And perhaps the most interesting result, which the Californians had missed altogether, was that the spin axis, which they could measure but the Californians could not, was perfectly aligned with the magnetic field of the whole giant Crab Nebula. The neutron star, which had given rise to the explosive nebula in the first place, must presently be energising its powerful, and previously inexplicable, magnetic field. It was thrilling to decipher such an excitingly clear picture, as it emerged, bit by piece, off those dry and enigmatic tapes. 'Nature ' must have been pleased too for, despite their Catalinas blunder, the journal rushed it into print so that they also won the race for publication. Moreover, having corrected their own work, they were saved the embarrassment of. having it publicly corrected for them by somebody else. Morgan, exhausted by his efforts with data analysis, was yet immensely satisfied.

Indeed his astronomical cup was running over. He received a letter from Hood, his supervisor in London, not only congratulating him on the pulsar but apologising handsomely over Morgan's Three Stage Model of the Interstellar Medium. They, that is to say he and Somerford, had thought over the matter some more, made enquiries in the States, and realised that Morgan had been right all along. Hood concluded by urging him to publish as soon as possible, as it was very important stuff.

Then again there was so much astronomical activity for him to share in. At one observatory or another in Tucson, all within walking distance of his office, there would be a seminar almost every day. In a single week he could attend talks by experts on topics as diverse as telescope design, rocket-born X-Ray astronomy, Moon dust, infra-red detectors, and the finiteness, or otherwise, of the Universe. The whole Space Science fraternity was in a turmoil as NASA gathered its strength behind the Apollo project to hurl the first men to the Moon. Ann and he watched the television in amazement as titanic Saturn rockets climbed from Cape Canaveral towards the stars.

Then the observatory itself ran a very complete course of advanced lectures for its PhD students, covering a range of topics which Morgan felt he needed to learn. He would often observe all night at Kitt Peak, then, as the stars began to pale, jump in the car and drive back home across the desert. This, he discovered, could be surprisingly dangerous. Far ahead, weaving towards him through the cactus, he would pick out the lights of an oncoming truck. On closer approach it would seem to be lurching drunkenly from side to side of the road. The Indians had banned alcohol on their reservation. The addicts therefore drove into Tucson and caroused all night. Morgan learned to pull his car right off the road into the cactus while the drunken Papagos lurched by. That they often crashed was attested by sad little clusters of white plastic crosses and bouquets along the desert road.

Safely at home he could breakfast with Ann, attend the first lecture at eight, sleep from one until five, and be at Kitt Peak in time to open the dome at dusk. It was a punishing schedule, but exhilarating. He had a long way to catch up; spectroscopy, optics, electronics, stellar atmospheres, radiative transfer, Space instrumentation…..he gorged on them all.

There was a magic interlude when, all expenses paid, they went to Italy via New York and Britain. They felt the snow falling between the skyscrapers in Greenwich Village; had a postponed Christmas dinner in Kew and another with Blodwen in Worcestershire. Morgan spent a day with Bob and Ernie Salt who were working on the entirely new Mark V, the Mark IV having proved a disappointment. Then Morgan flew on to a pulsar conference in Rome while Ann caught up at the Admiralty.

Never having visited the city of which he had read so much, Morgan was staggered by Rome, which was locked in winter. He spent days walking about, reflecting on the ruins, staring at the beautiful women in their fur coats, sampling the Cozze a la Marinera, listening to shepherds from the Abruzzi mountains playing pipes in the Piazza d'Espagna, and shuddering at the Castel San Angelo where the Pope had played with his concubines while the city below was raped by the Vandals. It all made Tucson seem so brash, so superficial, so hollow. Rome made him realise that he was, and would always remain, a European.

He and Ann met up at Kennedy airport and flew back to Tucson holding hands all the way:

"Oh Tom I wish I could share my work with you. It's not fair! I know yours is fascinating, and I love to hear you talking about it. But if you only knew, mine is more fascinating still. I'd almost forgotten just how exciting it can be. I made a break through you know, and everybody at the Admiralty were so grateful, so complimentary."

The following morning, a Sunday, they had to shop at their supermarket for food. Muzak played; fat young women in slip-slops, with enormous bums bulging through Bermuda shorts, pushed infants in shopping trollies between the aisles. Their hair was in pink plastic curlers, which could be seen through a beehive of nylon chiffon. The muzak stopped to announce:

"Tomado ketchup is on special today folks – but only till midday. We're practically giving it away at one dollar ninety-nine for a large family sized boddle. An' if you buy two boddles we'll be giving you a free can of Gatorade for the kids."

Morgan groaned:

"How could we live here?"

"How could we?" Ann agreed.

But then Morgan found a delightful little girl seated by herself on the floor next to the candy stand. She was trying to get the cellophane off her lolly.

"Do you think I could help?" he asked, squatting on the floor beside her.

She looked at him. She looked at her lolly. She looked at him again. Then she shyly held out the lolly. He unwrapped and handed it back.

"Fank you." she murmured, staring at him wonderingly. She slowly transferred the lolly via her cheek, then her nose, to her mouth.

"Oh Tom, I wish you could see yourself now. You look so happy."

"I just love young kids. Especially American kids. They're so open."

"I was going to keep it from you. Until I was certain. But now seems to be the right moment. I think I'm pregnant."

He leapt to his feet and crushed her in his arms:

"Oh you clever clever girl Annie. I love you so."

"And I love you too Morgan. But I believe you had something to do with it too."

CHAPTER 9
QUESTION MARKS IN THE SKY
1969

One morning Morgan woke up early, prepared to leap out of bed as usual, when he realised that for once there was no need. Ann was sleeping quietly beside him with her bum pressed into his side. The fountain was hushing away while their mocking bird was in full-throated ecstasy out in the chinaberry tree.

Morgan relaxed. There was no lecture to go to; no papers to be rushed to completion; no observing runs to prepare for; no computer output to be analysed and turned round in a hurry; no race to be lost or won; no urgency; no emergencies.

He sank back into the pillow and hugged his wife.

How wonderful. He could lie here all day and read a book if he wanted to, as he often used to do in London. London. The thought transported him back to his Lancaster Gate flat with the morning sun streaming in through the open window from across Kensington Gardens, accompanied by the sound of double-decker buses passing along the Bayswater Road on their way to Marble Arch or Notting Hill.

Great days those were, he remembered. Freedom. Freedom from rush and obligation: time to think: time to choose: time to plan. Lying here, sniffing Ann's delicious smell and enjoying the mocking bird, Morgan realised what an unnatural rush the last year had been. Ever since the discovery of the mistake in his PhD thesis, Time had seized him in its jaws and raced away. The re-write, the Three Stage Model, the row with Hood, his visa, their wedding, packing up, the voyage across on that awful boat the Aurelia; poverty in Arizona; the Crab pulsar; pressure, pressure, pressure. Things had happened to him, mostly good things it was true, but they had happened largely outside his volition, and he didn't like that. 'Take pulsars' he thought. A casual conversation with Dillard Cox by the swimming pool – and they'd taken over his life completely. Yes they were exciting to work on, very exciting – but not what he would have chosen to work on if the choice had been open. And they'd pushed all his other work aside: the Three Stage Model, Protostars, Red Giants – ideas about which he cared very dearly – had been totally neglected for a whole year.

Then there were the new things he'd been learning, some of them fascinating and to which he would have loved to devote more time. Take stellar spectroscopy as an example. He'd attended a wonderful course of lectures on the subject by Helmut Abt from Kitt Peak National Observatory. Abt had made it all seem like an exciting detective story and invited Morgan out to observe with him on the 84-inch there.

They'd driven out in Abt's Stingray sports car and spent the afternoon installing his stereo system in the Coude' Laboratory, deep underneath the dome of the great telescope. The Coude' focus was used during bright phases of the Moon when the sky was too bright for ordinary astronomy. Astronomers like Abt then worked on brightish stars using the big Coude' spectrograph to analyse the starlight in the minutest detail.

By comparison with pulsar research it was all very leisurely. Abt tuned his stereo then put on Schubert's C-major quintet, which echoed deliciously round the confined laboratory as if inside a cave. Abt's graduate student, a tiny fellow called Jim O'Leary, who wore high-heeled cowboy boots and gun holsters, called up a star. They felt the rumble of the vast dome rotating overhead. When it stopped there was the image of a brilliant white star shimmering and wobbling on the mirror of the spectrograph. Abt focussed the light then directed it into a slit in the mirror which led it further underground to the analysing instrument.

Then switching off all the lights he loaded a plate into the camera of the spectrograph before switching them on again.

"That's it?" Morgan was amazed.

"That's it. We can leave Jim to guide the star for half an hour."

They stepped into the measuring room next door where Abt showed him the spectrum of a star which he had taken the previous month. Under the microscope Morgan could see a thick black line broken by hundreds of thin pale gaps.

"This is a negative of course. Zo the black is the light and the pale lines are absorption lines, narrow gaps in the spectrum where no light is coming through. Each such gap or line is the mark of a particular type of atom or molecule in the atmosphere of the star."

"What are you looking for?"

"Movement. Look!"

He now mounted two spectrograph plates, one above the other, in the Blink Comparator. By turning a wheel first one then the other came into view in the identical place in the microscope eyepiece."

"Vot do you zee?"

"The two spectra are identical. Except…….."

"Except what?"

"Well one or two, maybe a dozen of the faint pale lines move back and forwards."

"Exactly zo. It is not one star but two, and they are orbiting one another. Zose spectra were taken a night apart, during vich time their velocities in our direction have changed. Hence the relative positions of their absorption lines have moved very slightly due to the Doppler effect. One star is much fainter than the other, but its spectrum is slightly different so you can see its changing relative motion in this Blink Comparator. Otherwise ve would never know it wass a double-star, or as ve call it, a 'binary'."

"What's your basic research program here?"

"Ve are trying to find what proportion of all stars are multiple. Is it one per cent, or ninety-nine per cent, or somewhere in between? You need a big spectrograph like this to separate the lines, and a big telescope to feed it enough light. Ve need to look at hundreds of stars, maybe a dozen times each. Ve can then measure the changing relative speeds and zo reconstruct their orbits: and how far apart they are from each other, how mazzive, how far away from us, how luminous, and zo on and zo on."

"Each spectrum is like a finger print?"

"Exactly zo. And I am your Sherlock Holmes. Our Zun is a single star. One day I vill be able to tell you if it is normal zo, or if zingle stars are a rarity."

"All from a few spectra of each star?"

"Ah but that is only the beginning. Sherlock Holmes could never tell as much from a man's appearance as ve can from a star's spectrum. Look I show you."

As he manoeuvred the spectrum so as to bring a particular part of it into view for Morgan's inspection Abt lectured away:

"First of all a quick glance at the spectrum tells us the star's temperature. This spectrum is yellow-white. It is an F-star with a surface temperature close to 6,500 Degrees. That's easy because I can zee lines of neutral Iron. Now look at these." He moved away to let Morgan use the eyepiece.

"You zee the strong line to the left of the cross-wire?"

"Yes."

"That is a Luminosity-sensitive Calcium line. From experience I can tell it is strong. Zo this is not a Supergiant F-star, it is a dwarf. And knowing the temperature I can read off the luminosity for zutch a dwarf from this Herzprung-Russel correlation."

He pointed to a big chart on the wall:

"Here along the bottom is the temperature 6,500 degrees. Zen I go upwards until I hit the dwarf line zo, and looking sideways from there I read off the Luminosity zo. What do you read?"

Morgan traced with his finger: "About nine solar luminosities. It's nine times as luminous as the Sun"

"Egzactly zo. Not bad eh – from just one line? But now alzo we know the distance of the star. Why zo? If we know how luminous it is, and we measure how bright it looks in our spectrograph, which ve have done, then we infer it must be 44 light years away."

"Of course."

"And you want to know how big it is? I tell you. Because we know the zurface temperature ve know immediately how much radiation it gives from each square meder of the surface. But we just calculated how much luminosity it has in total. And because it must be a sphere like the Zun we immediately get the surface area, and zo the radius."

Abt, as enthusiastic as a schoolboy, used his slide rule to calculate:

"Ach zo. It has a diameter of 3.3 million kilometres . It is 2.4 times bigger than the Zun or 250 Earth diameters. You want to know more?"

Abt didn't wait for an answer as he moved the spectrum further along in the eyepiece:

"Now look at these two weak lines on either side of the cross-hair."

Morgan found two rather insignificant lines of equal strength.

"I see them."

"Zose lines are pressure zensiive. From their relative strengths I can measure the atmospheric pressure on the zurface. And vot causes the pressure?"

"The gravity there I suppose."

"Exactly. Zo I can calculate the gravity, and from the gravity the weight of the whole star."

"It's damned ingenious, the whole process of inference; to get so much truth from so little information.

"Ah but ve only just begun. Other lines give us the chemical composition of the star; how much hydrogen, helium, oxygen, carbon and zo on. From zose chemical abundances one can estimate the age of the star. I can estimate how fast it rotates, what its' magnetic field, and zo on and zo on and zo on. You see Tom what a fascinating game stellar spectroscopists play? Every night, every star, it is a new story for us to read. You keep your pulzars. These are my babies."

"Helmut's a mad bastard," Jim O'Leary complained as he and Morgan drove back across the desert to Tucson at midnight. "But I love him. He's the kind of fellah that makes astronomy seem more important than anything else a guy could do. When I get back from 'Nam I'm doing my PhD with him."

"You going to Vietnam?"

"You bet baby. I wanna zap some of them 'Cong before they all git wasted by our B 52s."

Morgan had heard from some of the other graduate students, who because of their education easily avoided the draft, that Jim O'Leary was variously 'eccentric' or 'plain fucking mad'. Apparently he had a whole arsenal of live weapons hanging from his office wall. Looking back at his own eagerness to fight in Malaya, an eagerness incomprehensible to him now, Morgan wondered what worm was driving O'Leary's ambition to fight. Was it his bantam-cock size? He was scarcely five feet tall even in his high heeled cowboy boots.

But before he could ask he was flung forward as O'Leary stamped on the brakes, bringing the big Ford Galaxy to a skidding halt. A hapless looking Papago Indian in a straw hat was caught in the headlights. He seemed to be gesturing for help. As he came round to the driver's window O'Leary reached in the glove pocket before rolling down the window. As the Indian bent down to speak O'Leary cocked the Luger pistol and thrust it into his face:

"One move from you motherfucker an' I'll blow your brains clean out your goddamned asshole."

Morgan thought: "Eccentric? No. Plain fucking mad? Yes."

Having been bent over the car bonnet and aggressively body-searched the Papago was allowed to stand up and try to explain himself. O'Leary, who was from Texas, interrogated the man in pidgin Spanish. Apparently it was something to do with the water in the radiator of his truck.

Morgan moved down the moonlit highway to try and gather his thoughts. The Saguaro cacti were silver up against the stars, the mountains in the background black. Something moving on the roadway caught his eye. Switching on his torch he found an enormous spider trundling towards a locust that had been half run over by their wheels. Its thick legs, eight inches across, were covered with red hairs, as was its segmented body, the rear part of which alone was the size of a tennis-ball. Its mandibles reached out and gripped the locust's head. Morgan, who had been petrified by spiders ever since a large one had fallen on his face when he was three years old, stood there mesmerised. The monster was awful; beyond anything he'd imagined in a nightmare. And it wasn't a nightmare. It was real. He could hear its jaws working on the carapace of the locust.

Unable to look a moment longer he turned back to the car only to see another monster marching towards the feast. He ran, leapt into the car, and slammed the door behind him. He could almost feel hairy spiders crawling all over his skin.

Although these monster spiders were called 'Tarantulas' they were, with their abdomens larger than golf balls, and their bodies covered all over with long red and black hairs, actually members of the 'bird eating' family, the largest spiders on Earth. They were most common in the desert and at certain seasons the Morgans would see hoards of them out on the roadway devouring locusts killed by passing cars. Sometimes one couldn't avoid running over them, an event accompanied by a perceptible 'thunk'. The monsters apparently were plentiful even inside Tucson, which caused Morgan – something of an arachnophobe – to take a good look between the sheets before getting in to bed.

Their worst encounter occurred when they were invited out for dinner by a lady friend of Ann's who lived way out in the desert. She had a bumptious husband who wore high heeled boots and who preceded every sentence with "Hell shit" :

"Hell shit, why don't we go eat dinner."

"Hell shit honey, you done them beans real good."

"Hell shit, I 'member when we was livin' out Fort Collins way…"

Morgan found the greatest difficulty not replying in kind.

During the course of dinner a thunderstorm burst overhead, lashing the aluminium roof of the mobile home with rain. When it was time to leave their host ushered them out onto the deck, turning on the powerful outside lights.

"Hell Sheet!" This time he really meant it. "Jes' look at them spahders. Orl over our godamned yord."

To the Morgans' horror he was absolutely right. Presumably to escape the flash flood, literally hundreds of the monsters were swarming all over the asphalt between them and their car, some standing tiptoe to avoid the ground water. Nothing would have induced either Ann or Tom to move among them; nothing on Earth. But Hell-Shit had his methods:

"Ah'll git mah shot gun. A few rounds of buckshot 'll shift them mother-fuckers."

He was wrong, although the buckshot whanged and whined round poor Beetle. Eventually he managed to blast an avenue through them using the high pressure hose he used for washing his truck. They literally ran for Beetle and then found themselves driving away across a moving carpet of giant spiders, both Ann and Tom gagging all the way.

Abt's demonstration impressed Morgan so much that he determined to take up spectroscopy himself – after all it was most of astrophysics. But how? He was walking to work one morning when he looked up and noticed, really noticed for the first time, the large cream dome of the twenty-one inch telescope atop the observatory building. Why not use that?"

He made enquiries.

"Sure you can use it. It's meant for the graduate stoodents – but I never heard of one using it."

"The sky's too bright see. The campus lights have killed it. The students use Kitt Peak nowadays."

"Stellar spectroscopy? I guess you could. But I believe the spectrograph is broke."

"We tried several times, but the spectrograph camera won't focus."

Morgan got the keys and found a powerful modern telescope, dwarfed by the dome which had originally housed their 36-inch, now atop Kitt Peak.

He switched on, opened and rotated the dome, slewed the telescope about in both Right Ascension and Declination. It all worked smoothly.

Below the dome he found a small darkroom, and another with tools, instruments and a wooden crate. Opening the crate he found what was evidently a Cassegrain spectrograph, too heavy for him to move on his own. With the help of Jim O'Leary and a technician he mounted the spectrograph on the bottom of the telescope tube.

"That sucker don't work." averred the technician.

"You bet." O'Leary agreed.

Undaunted, Morgan equipped the dark room with chemicals and glass photographic plates which he cut to size to fit the spectrograph camera.

That night he opened the dome and focussed the telescope on a very bright star. Then, as Abt had showed him, he diverted the light through the slit jaws into the big spectrograph.

Nothing emerged – not a peep of light.

It took a while to work out that the grating must be missing. The grating, the modern equivalent of a prism, was the vital component which split up the light into its constituent colours.

Eventually he found the precious grating – a block of silvered glass ruled with thousands of microscopic furrows, packed in cotton-wool in a draw of the tool room.

There was no manual for the spectrograph but, with the aid of Allen keys and a torch, he was able to bolt the grating into its mounting deep inside the instrument.

Now when he looked through the spectrograph camera he saw the most gorgeous spectrum of starlight ranging from pigeon's blood red, through ruby, orange, gold , emerald, sapphire, ultramarine, purple to ultraviolet. But in its brilliance and purity, the stellar spectrum was more sensual than anything crafted by earthly jeweller or cunning painter. Morgan was lost in wonder at so much beauty, potentially containing so much information. He turned to another bright star and found a quite different cocktail of colours to assault his senses.

He searched in vain for the absorption lines, the narrow breaks in the spectrum which had told Abt so much. Probably, he reasoned, that was because the spectrograph itself couldn't focus properly.

To focus the camera the spectrograph contained its own light-source, which gave only sharply defined colours – essentially single lines in the spectrum. With the aid of these lines Morgan adjusted the focus until they were maximally sharp. Now, when he looked at the stellar spectrum again, he could see patterns previously concealed from view. Satisfied, he loaded one of his cut photographic plates into the spectrograph camera and exposed it to starlight.

Guessing that an exposure of two minutes on such a bright star would be enough, Morgan closed the light-tight plate-holder, switched off the telescope, and carried the plate-holder to the darkroom. He closed the door, pulled the black curtains and checked the chemicals as Jim O'Leary had taught him. By the dim red-light he measured the temperature of the developer and noted the strong hypochlorite smell coming from the fixer bath. He set the electric clock with its luminous dial, turned off the red-light and in total darkness pulled the slide on the plate-holder and tipped out the plate, about the size of a stick of chewing-gum, into the palm of his hand. Using the tip of his tongue he checked to see that the black-and -white emulsion was on the upper, the right side. There were too many grizzly stories of astronomers who'd wasted a week's starlight by putting a plate in back to front.

Satisfied, he noted the time and lowered the plate into the developer bath where he left it for exactly three minutes, rocking the liquid gently back and forth by hand.

The he turned on the red-light ,by which he could immediately see a narrow black spectrum, it was a negative, etched on the otherwise clear plate.

It had worked! Sort of. He felt both surprised and satisfied. Perhaps those rumours about defocusing were wrong.

The plate had to be washed in distilled water, fixed in the hypo bath, washed again and then dried with a hair drier before it could be mounted in the microscope.

Looking through the eye-piece he could see the sharp comparison lines from the spectrograph's light source both above and below the almost continuous stellar spectrum. They were satisfyingly sharp, so they at least were in focus.

But the stellar spectrum itself was not. Yes he could see the absorption features, but they were all unnaturally fuzzy, not at all like those Abt had shown him up on Kitt Peak.

Morgan was bitterly disappointed; so near and yet so very far. Being no optical expert he had no idea how to put things right. He took the spectra of several more stars but didn't develop them before closing the dome and going home to bed.

When he developed the spectra the following afternoon he was surprised to find that, although most were fuzzy, one was very sharp – as sharp as Abt's.

That could only mean one thing. Something in the spectrograph must be loose. He stripped it down and poked about inside, feeling each element in the optical train by turn: the slit assembly, the internal light source, the collimator, the grating turret, the camera and the plate-holder. All felt reassuringly rigid, as they had to be whenever the telescope tilted about in the sky following a star. However one small flat mirror, whose purpose seemed to be to divert the collimated light on to the grating, rattled a little in its mounting when he poked it with a pencil. That, he surmised, could be the problem. He cemented it into place with a piece of chewing gum and reassembled the instrument.

That night he took many spectra and every one was perfect. Some exhibited hundreds of sharp absorption lines, promising a cornucopia of information.

From then on Morgan became a collector of starlight. It was a leisurely hobby and no part of his professional ambition. Like a Victorian beetle collector, or an ornithologist in search of new birds, he searched for and added new specimens to his private hoard. And when he found them it was his pleasure to analyse and dissect their stories under the microscope: Blue Supergiants, Mira Variables, Delta Scuti stars, Cepheid pulsators, Eclipsing Binaries, Horizontal Branch stars, Planetary Nebulae, RR Lyraes, Novae, Red Dwarfs,,,,,,there was inexhaustible variety. He took Ann along one night and she caught the bug too. He taught her to guide the telescope, take spectra and develop them in the dark room. She found the idea of decoding a star's entire life story from the minute details in its spectrum as fascinating as he did.

One dark night Morgan tried to get a spectrum of the nearest galaxy, the giant Spiral, Messier 31 in the constellation of Andromeda. In the eye-piece he couldn't see it against the campus lighting reflected in the sky but he knew he must have got it on the slit of the spectrograph because it was a giant object, several times larger than the disc of the full Moon. But despite collecting the light for several hours there was nothing of the nebula on the eventual spectrum, which was a mess of atmospheric and man-made lines.

Through his work with Wagoner, Morgan was becoming interested in galaxies anyway. One clear moonless night when he was up on Kitt Peak alone using the 36-inch, he decided to take time off from pulsars and take a picture of a nearby spiral galaxy, which ought to be easy, so far was he away from the city lights.

He'd taken up to the mountain with him de Vaucouleurs' 'Atlas of Galaxies', the bible on the subject for serious observers. Picking out from the thousands of candidates what he thought would be a suitable specimen, nearly overhead, he set the telescope on the right celestial coordinates and looked through the eye-piece. At first, although his eyes were perfectly dark-adapted, there was nothing to be seen. But then, out of the corner of his eye, he saw the merest phantom of light, a wraith which conjured itself in and out of existence against the background panoply of pin-prick stars. When he stared at it it fled away. When he looked off centre it sneaked back into the very periphery of his conscious sight. He marvelled that men with primitive telescopes had ever noticed such poltergeists. And yet he knew, from de Vaucouleurs' atlas, that he was looking at a monster a hundred thousand light years across containing hundreds of billions of stars. Only its immense depth out in space could account for its elusive, its diaphanous appearance.

A long exposure would be needed – something like an hour. So he set up the auto-guider, an electronic eye which locked on a star in the field, set the alarm clock for fifty minutes, and opened the dark-slide.

Now there was nothing for him to do but wait while the incoming galaxy photons slowly accumulated on the photographic plate. He put Berlioz's Symphonie Fantastique on the stereo, attached one end of a climbing rope to a stanchion, the other round his waist, and climbed up the ladder from the Newtonian observing platform out onto the roof of the dome.

What a sight! Nothing but stars above him, around him and even below. He'd literally climbed into the heavens, for the curved dome concealed the entire mountain-scape below him from view. Only the blackness of the far desert distinguished his eyrie from the very depths of space. Lying on his back, staring up at the shivering star fields, he felt tiny, disoriented, giddy. Vertigo gripped him, as it sometimes had in his mountaineering days, so that he had to squeeze his eyes shut and cling desperately to the wind vane, the only flimsy hold he had on that slippery precipitous surface. Belioz's 'March to The Execution' clanged and tolled in the egg-shell thin metallic dome beneath his ribs; a gentle wind, seven thousand foot high, cooled his cheek.

When his heart had slowed he opened his eyelids millimetre by millimetre. And there they were in their myriads and millions, tumbling away into the blackness: clouds of them, clusters of them, filaments of them, oceans of them, aeons of them – worlds upon worlds upon worlds: unplumbed, undiscovered, unnamed and unknown. They eluded all comprehension, and all emotion. He shivered as he crawled like a snail back down into the comforting blackness and music of the dome

When Morgan switched on the red-light in the dark-room there was his galaxy staring up at him from the developer bath. Fixing and washing it he mounted it on top of the light-box and switched on.

He could scarcely believe that this spiral whirlpool, glittering with star clusters, could be that same, scarcely visible wraith of light he had struggled to glimpse with his naked eye. By accumulating for fifty minutes what the eye must be able to see in a tenth of a second, or not at all, the photographic emulsion had captured an entirely unsuspected world. It was beautiful, it was substantial, it was obviously immense; it must be a vast distance away and, for a moment, it was entirely his. Probably no human had taken a better picture of it than he had now. He marvelled at the spiral necklaces of stars that it flung off into space as it spun; at the bright nucleus; at the clouds of smoke and dust which obscured large parts of the inner disc; at the brilliant nebulae where new stars were obviously being born; at the tiny dwarf satellite galaxies which attended it in space. He stared and stared, questions forming a growing queue in his mind.

How far was it away – and how could you possibly measure such a vast distance; why did it spin – and how fast; how were the spiral arms formed and why didn't they wind up; where did the satellite galaxies come from and why weren't they sucked into the whirlpool; what was hidden beneath all that smoke; what made the nucleus so brilliant; was the galaxy as big as the Milky Way, or even bigger; how old was it and what had it formed out of; was it receding away from the Earth due to the expansion of the Universe; did it contain other solar systems like our own, other intelligences like our own; was there another astronomer out there at this very moment looking at his own picture of the Milky Way and asking the self-same questions? That first galaxy bewitched Morgan, casting a spell upon him that he would never be able to, would never want to throw off. He framed a large print of it which would hang over the fire place at home.

As time passed their lives, both jointly and separately, filled up with interests and people. Where Morgan had his astronomy Ann was "onto something really big at work" which necessitated fairly frequent, if short trips to Washington. She sang in the thriving local Gilbert and Sullivan society, swam to replace tennis, started some research with a professor of statistics and enrolled them both in the University film club. As it happened the club was running a cycle of Kurosawa's masterpieces which bowled them both completely over. Ann's favourite was 'Rashoman' while Morgan couldn't decide between 'Ikiru" and 'The Seven Samurai.'
But Ann's main interest, aside from work, centred on the local Indians:
"What a fool I was reading about Stone-age peoples when here we are surrounded by tribes who were hunter-gatherers, and irrigation farmers, a mere generation or two ago."
Through the university department of Anthropology she became involved in Indian Affairs, particularly the tribal history and archaeology of the local Papagos, Yaquis, Apaches and Navajos.
Their history, or rather what the invading European Americans had done to them, outraged her:
"Perhaps one can understand their Victorian greed and their sense of superiority. What I can never forgive, never, is our continuing dishonesty about it all today. Look at Hollywood turning cowboys into heroes and Indians into villains. The truth is the very reverse of that; cowboys used every low-down, cowardly, treacherous trick to defraud the Indians out of their land. By comparison the Indians were brave, honourable and trusting."
"For instance?" Morgan wanted to know.
"Just take this area for example. The Papagos inhabited it but they had Apache overlords who'd defeated them in battle. There was no love lost. So what do the ranchers do? They convene a pow-wow, ostensibly to make peace between the two tribes. But secretly they've armed the weaker Papago with rifles. The Apache chiefs turn up in good faith and the Papagos murder all of them round the fireside. And who gets the Apache land?"
"I can guess."
" But that's nothing compared to 'The Missionary Trick'."
"Go on."
"White people, masquerading as missionaries, would go out to the villages and make the people gifts of blankets and clothing. The Indians of course were puzzled but grateful. What they didn't know was that those blankets had been deliberately infected with measles and small pox, European diseases to which they had almost no resistance. Soon they would all be dead and dying, men, wives and little children. And who got their land?"
"But that's sickening. Awful……. Are you sure it's true?"
"Oh yes. No question. The perpetrators even boasted about it, sometimes in writing."
"I find it hard to believe." Morgan was dubious.

"So do the Americans" Ann was indignant. "They've re-written their own history from start to finish, to cover up the truth. All that bunk about heroic pioneers in their wagon trains. All that propaganda about 'The Boston Tea Party' and 'No taxation without representation'".

"And the truth?"

"The British government had signed treaties of peace with the Indian Nations – in return for their support against the French. But after the French were defeated the poorer American settlers coveted the rich Indian territories of the Mid West. But to steal them they had first to repudiate British agreements and therefore British governance. It wasn't a glorious 'War of Independence' so much as a greedy and treacherous land-grab."

Ann, normally a gentle soul, became a firebrand on mythical American 'propaganistory' as she dubbed it. She was likely to quote Orwell to their shocked American friends: 'He who controls the past controls the future.'

When the lease on their desert apartment came up they decided not to renew it because it would be far too remote when the baby came. Instead they rented a small old-style house just outside the campus. Built for coolness it had shaded balconies, a small 'yard' or garden and a 'haybox' on the roof, a primitive but effective form of cooling. While by day they had to put up with McDonnell Phantoms and Boeing B52s constantly screaming in on final approach, Morgan could now walk home from the observatory in only eight minutes while Ann could keep most of her social engagements without having to drive Beetle. There was a spare room in which Scurvy immediately gave birth to five delightful kittens and, more importantly, a room for the baby when it came. They quickly acclimatised to the jet noise while the resident mockingbird in their chinaberry tree sang every bit as sweetly as his cousin out in the desert. They could eat lunch together at home now and, when they felt like it, walk to the observatory after dark and use their private 21-inch telescope together.

"I love it here now" Ann admitted "At least for a while. It's not London of course and I couldn't bear to think of settling here permanently. But I shall miss it when we go back."

"What especially?"

"Oh, I don't know. It's never easy to say is it? I'll miss the freshness in the mornings, with the sunbeams coming through the shutters. And the mocking bird singing. And the red Cardinal birds hopping about in the garden. And the smell of oranges. And camping in the wilderness."

"I'll miss the snow up in the mountains, with the sun glinting off it. " Morgan replied "And walking through the campus gardens to work. And the Saguaro cactuses."

"And the ruby throated humming birds?"

"Yes. And being married to Ann Cloudesly."

"And Domino's pizza." Ann laughed.

"Yes that's even better. And the race to get to the Moon. Even the Vietnam war, horrible as it is, is exciting."

"And watching the sunrise on the red rock pillars of Monument Valley."

"And Cochise's Last Stronghold. And white water rafting in the Grand Canyon."

"I was terrified" Ann admitted "But it was certainly unforgettable. Do you remember that poor man's head floating by? And you laughed at him you beast. I wonder where he is now."

"Humming Bird Dunes. Wasn't that something? Just knowing it's there. That we could go again any time we want."

"Oh Tom let's go again before Tadpole is born."

"Yes let's"

Morgan was out at Kitt Peak observing when Ann had her miscarriage. He rushed back to find her lying in hospital, very white and distressed.

"I'm so sorry darling." she burst into tears.

"She'll be very depressed" the doctor warned "Don't leave her alone too much."

"Will she be able to conceive again?"

"Oh yes. I've told her that – though it is rather puzzlingly late in her term."

Without being asked Gwendolyn Cloudesly arrived from London and took charge. Morgan was rather calmed by his mother-in law's presence. She confided in him:

"I did rather worry about this Tom. It may run in the female side of our family. I had four miscarriages before Ann was born. And my mother likewise – though she managed three healthy children in the end. So don't worry too much. Ann's weepy right now but her body will recover quickly. I've come mainly to reassure her, and you. Now you get on with your astronomy."

But now there was violent turmoil at the observatory. Bok had retired precipitately – none too soon some said because he had become increasingly irate and erratic. Wagoner, the heir-apparent, immediately called a meeting of all the academic staff, which really set the fox among the chickens. He began the meeting with the grimmest possible news:

"As you know the Ninety-Inch telescope has run into a series of serious cost-overruns. Now we have the final straw. A design fault has been discovered in the declination bearings, which will have to be replaced. The President can't find any more university funds – which have already been drained by such a hugely ambitious project. He can see no resort but to raid the observatory's future budget. The money has to come out of our hides."

The audience looked at one another, wondering what this portended. Wagoner continued:

"As you know the University is determined to have a world class astronomical staff to go along with such a world class telescope. Provision had therefore been made to hire six, and later ten tenured professors, to exploit the telescope to the full. Hiring negotiations have already begun with key people out on both the East and West coasts, as well as in Europe. Now that hiring process is in jeopardy. The Regents have decided it must go ahead – at a slightly decelerated rate. You can see the implications I hope?"

People looked puzzled:

"It means we are going to have to get rid of a significant number of the existing astronomy staff to make way for the incomers."

The awful truth dawned.

"Professor Bok did all he could to prevent this happening – indeed he refused to participate in this 'butchery' as he calls it. So it falls on my head instead."

There was a long pause before he continued:

"It means that almost all of you here who do not have tenure already will have to leave when your existing contract is up. That is to say all assistant professors and post-docs."

There were gasps and execrations around the room. Well over half of them had just been given notice.

"But it doesn't end there I'm afraid. While the university cannot legally get rid of tenured Associate Professors and Full Professors they could, if they wanted to, and they might want to now, make life so very unpleasant for us that it would be better to find posts, while there is time, elsewhere."

"What do you mean? Spell it out." An angry professor with a beard stood up.

Wagoner thought for a minute:

"They could remove a man's observing privileges. No telescope time, no research."

"They couldn't!"

"Oh yes they could. It's been done before. Think of Handorff. They could so load us down with teaching duties, or administration, as to make research impossible anyway. And sabbaticals could go – remember they are a privilege not a right. This university can be pretty goddamned ruthless; it's a private institution, like a corporation. To survive the Depression it sacked half the faculty remember; over half. This isn't Harvard with its huge Endowment, nor yet California which is beholden to state law."

There was uproar, People like Willard Cox and Don Tallon, who had imagined themselves settled in Arizona for life, would now have to find jobs elsewhere, while most of the professors from the sleepy old days, when Steward was just a provincial observatory, could see unemployment looming. When Wagoner managed to establish some kind of order he continued:

"The worst hasn't happened yet. Not yet. But my advice is this. If you think you are on schedule to get into the National Acadamy of Sciences then try to hang on here. If not then you should start looking elsewhere. That's just how serious the Regents are. They've risked their asses building this Ninety-Inch telescope. But they want Arizona astronomy to get into the really big league; alongside Palomar, Caltech, Harvard, and Berkeley. If you and I can play in that league fine. If not then they're happy to fire us – one way or another."

Since Wagoner was already in the prestigious National Acadamy, this infuriated the other senior professors and the meeting broke up in fury and recrimination.

"I reckon Wagoner is just using the excuse to get rid of those of us he don't like, so as to bring in his own cronies." said one.

"He's enjoying being a hatchet man." another agreed.

"No he isn't." others demurred "He's doing Bok's dirty work. I feel sorry for the poor bastard. If it wasn't for the cost overruns we wouldn't be here now."

"And whose fault were they?"

"Not ours. Nor Wagoner's. Wishful thinking I'd say."

The impending blood-bath changed the whole atmosphere at Steward: astrophysics gave way to politics, seminars to meetings, papers to petitions, conversations to conniptions, collaborations to cabals, contemplation to paranoia, optimism to depression. Any chance of the Morgans staying on at Steward vanished, but it was the plight of their friends such as Don Tallon and Willard Cox, who really wanted to, and who had counted on staying on, which aroused their compassion. Such 'tenure-track' faculty usually had young children and huge mortgages, while the wives had given up well paid careers to come to Tucson where employment was very limited. Now they would be 'on the road ' again, as most of them had been for many years previously, moving like refugees from one temporary post to another. And even if they could find another astronomical job – which was always doubtful – most would have to move thousands of miles away, leaving behind friends, networks, research projects, gardens and schools in a way few Europeans would tolerate.

"They're scarcely better off than the Okies in 'The Grapes of Wrath' " Morgan remarked. "All their belongings will have to go in a rental van, with Pop driving, while Mom will be following in the family car with the pets and the kids."

"It's barbarous," Ann agreed. "Most of them will never see their friends again – except at some grisly 'Thanksgiving Reunion'."

"Don is really depressed. He told me he's given up on Steward already. He's even refusing to finish the scanner he's been building for three years. Marion wants to move back to California where she can take up her former career again. But Don will be lucky to get a job there. Too much competition already."

"Claire is incandescent. She's pregnant and she believes they were lured here under false pretences. She and some of the others are consulting lawyers. Thank God we were never hoping or expecting to stay. But I must say it's very sad – coming on top of everything else." 'Everything else' being poor 'Tadpole' their dead baby.

"One can see now just how precarious astronomy is — as a career." Morgan mused ruefully, recalling Bellfounder's remarks about astronomers being like first-division footballers, or prima ballerinas. Many were called, but few were chosen.

The low point of every week now became the 'internal seminar' instituted by Wagoner. The idea was that each member of staff, by turn, should explain to his colleagues the research he was doing and the research he intended to do in future – particularly using the 90-inch. Wagoner sat on his own in the front row with a spiral notebook on his knee, jotting down notes and asking nasty questions.

Morgan discovered a grisly fascination in these public trials which sometimes ended in summary execution. Men were forced to justify their scientific philosophies, expose their ambitions, or lack of them, and defend any hypotheses upon which their research depended. Wagoner, as the chief prosecutor, was ruthless. He left no place for an easy assumption, or a threadbare imagination to hide. He forced men to confront themselves, as much as one another:

"OK suppose you do get the Colour-Magnitude diagrams of six more Globular Clusters. What's that going to do for astrophysics when we've got fifty already?"

"Probing the Galactic centre sounds exciting, but if you don't know the wavelength dependence of the absorption in interstellar space, and you don't, then it could turn out to be a complete waste of telescope time. That's why nobody else has bothered."

"That's an argument in a circle. First you assume LTE, then you use a consequence of LTE to justify your original assumption. I don't buy that, and you shouldn't either."

The weaker members of the staff grew to hate Wagoner's probings and to loathe the man behind them. Morgan however gradually began to understand and admire him. What possible benefit could any scientist derive from a muddled hypothesis or a threadbare research program? Wagoner came from a hard school at Princeton where men were not encouraged to waste their lives in complacency, but to admit their failures, and so to move on. As Wagoner continually reminded them, most scientific endeavours ended in failure. There was no crime in that. The crime lay in failing to acknowledge failure, in clinging on to comforting ideas when their time was past.

But Wagoner didn't get it all his own way. One elderly European astronomer who'd devoted a life to studying eclipsing binary stars, a fashionable topic in the late nineteenth century, turned on Wagoner:

"Vot you think Darwin spent most of his time doing?"

Wagoner shrugged his shoulders: "Studying Evolution I imagine."

"Vrong! Vrong, vrong, vrong, His real fascination vos in collecting beedles. He said Gott must have been inordinately fond of beedles because he made so many different varieties. And you know the largest study he made in his life? Ja – not on 'The Origin of Species', not even beedles. Nossir. He spent seven years studying the life cycle of the barnacle."

He wagged his finger angrily at Wagoner:

"Now professor. What questions you ask Charles Darwin if he attend your research seminar? Vy waste your time on beedles? Who cares about silly barnacles? You can't tell him to conzentrate on the Theory of Evolution. Vy not? I tell you vy not. Because he hasn't invented it yet. It komms to him vile he is collecting beedles."

The old man was becoming more incoherent as he got angrier:

"Dot is vot I find so zilly about these internal seminars. They azzume that someone in this room, perhaps your good zelf, is vise enough to know the future, and vot will become important and vot vill not. But dat of course is der whole fallacy. I don't know, and not even you do know the future. Zum presently unconsidered trifle, zum astronomical barnacle or beedle, might lead to the great discovery of the future. Dot is the nature of zience chentlemen." And he sat down to applause from some of the audience.

Wagoner was unfazed:

"All very true Gotthardt; who can deny it. But that can be no defence of sloppy thinking. Yes we can't guess the future. But we've got to try. If we don't, the whole subject would descend into anarchy, become entirely wasteful and idiosyncratic – like literary criticism, or French philosophy. We scientists gamble with our time and other peoples' resources. But we shouldn't gamble before considering and calculating most carefully. Someone said 'An unexamined life is scarcely worth leading.' Likewise an unexamined research program is scarcely worth pursuing. I'm not throwing away my research career, no more should any of you, just because Darwin had the hots for beetles. It could have been all pure luck in his case, and no poker player, unless he's a fool, relies entirely on luck. One can only hope for luck. In the mean time we've all got to play the odds."

Morgan realised that his growing fascination with the internal seminars derived entirely from his own uncertainties. What would he say if and when it was his turn to step up on such a dais? Did he have a research philosophy? So far his brief career derived from pure chance. Frank had given him Bellfounder's book. Jack had photocopied for him the early papers on quasars. If he hadn't discovered the mistake in his thesis he would never have stumbled upon the Three Stage Model. If he hadn't gone to the RAS that day he wouldn't be so interested in pulsars. And if by chance he had never met Willard Cox by the motel swimming pool they'd probably neither of them have finished up working on the Crab Nebula. What could he say in his defence? That he was no better than an opportunist? He didn't even know if he was by temperament an observer, a theoretician or a computer modeller.

Wagoner could be verbally brutal. Like a training officer readying men for battle he saw no point in protecting them from the truth, however bitter. If they were going to survive out there they had first to be hard and true. And some of them weren't.

To one poor devil, who shortly afterwards resigned, Wagoner said:

"It seems to me you're still doing your PhD thesis ten years later. And your thesis, like most theses, was based on your supervisor's ideas. But even he doesn't believe in them any more."

The signs of strain in the observatory were everywhere: gaunt faces, bitchy remarks, uncalled for aggression, silence when a new face appeared, obvious people missing from a party. Graduate students, often men in their late twenties and early thirties, hated the professors who were constantly examining them and marking them down. One young man blew his brains all over the ceiling.

Morgan found this turning of his beloved astronomy into a competitive business thoroughly abhorrent. But he also recognised it had to be so. The only one there who had worked on a factory production-line, he knew how drab and futile so many men's and women's lives were. Oscar Wilde had said 'All of us are lying in the gutter, but some of us are looking at the stars.' So this was a competition for the very highest stakes, far beyond money; the right to look at the stars, both literally and figuratively. As a young student working in Catalonia Morgan had watched the 'novillos', the young bullfighters coming out to face the bulls for the first time. Now he saw it again; the chalk faces; the trembling hands; the horn, in the form of a devastating question, hooking up under the ribs and deflating the lungs. He saw his friend Art destroyed like that in a matter of minutes. Called up to talk about his research Art spent thirty minutes going into all the technical details. Wagoner eventually broke in coldly: "Does this kind of work have any wider significance?" Instead of having an answer prepared for such an obvious question, Art reacted aggressively, blustered on with ever more technicalities. Morgan watched with growing embarrassment and dismay, his fingernails digging into his hands. He knew Art had a good defence, but in his terror he had thrown it away. They were all forced to watch ten years of blood and sweat pulse out onto the sand, a young life's ambition lie still in the ring.

The reality of an astronomical career, its insecurity, its dependence on luck and connections, settled like a chill round Morgan's heart. He began looking in the job columns of journals like 'Nature' and 'Science' for astronomical posts, anywhere, which might suit him. There simply weren't any. He was reduced to writing letters of enquiry to the heads of various university departments back in Britain where he knew some astronomy went on. He would have liked particularly to work at Imperial College, just across the park from his old flat in Bayswater. If they lived in Kensington both he and Ann could walk to work.

Wagoner's seminars made Morgan think. He began with pulsar research – which was developing in a direction he didn't like. First of all it was very hard work. No further optical pulsars had been found since the Crab. And if more were to be found they would most likely turn up in the Southertn Hemisphere where most of the Milky Way was situated, including the Galactic Centre. Second, the physics of pulsars, so far as it could be understood, looked very complex; people talked about 'relativistic beaming' and 'magneto-hydrodynamic turbulence' about which Morgan knew nothing. That in itself was not the obstacle for him: no doubt he could learn – with an effort. But it all sounded so esoteric, so unconnected with anything else that interested him in astronomy. It seemed likely to finish up as a highly specialised branch of physics – not astronomy at all. And then there was a personal problem. Willard Cox, perhaps because of his newly discovered job insecurity, was becoming increasingly propriety about optical pulsars, as if he'd invented the whole endeavour himself. For instance Morgan found observing runs being organised about which he'd not been consulted at all. Amused at first he became increasingly irritated. It was sad that after working so well together, and becoming friends, or so he had thought, they should end up distrusting one another.

He tried to explain Willard Cox's behaviour to Ann:

"He's fighting for his astronomical life. He and Claire have invested absolutely everything in this move. They really expected to stay in Arizona whereas we didn't."

"But it's so ….petty."

"Pettiness is the very least thing at the observatory right now. There's paranoia and sheer bloody funk. All of them feel betrayed and some are indeed ruined. The others live in fear."

"How beastly it all is. Do you remember how happy they all seemed?"

"Only on the surface. I'm coming to believe that America runs on fear. Do you remember how many of them came to work on Christmas day? They can sense the knives whirling not far below. And who can blame them? There's no welfare state here. Despite all the brave bullshit about 'The New Deal' only the Second World War ended the US depression."

"Perhaps we shouldn't worry about them Tom. We should worry about ourselves. At least Willard's got a three-year contract. You've only got twelve months. You can't afford to let him steal pulsars away from you."

"I suppose not, but I'm going to need another arrow in my quarrel."

"You'll have to write up your Three Stage Model Tom. That'll make you famous. Even Wagoner said so. You've been promising to for ages. You can't leave it any longer."

Ever since leaving London Morgan had had two entirely contradictory attitudes towards his Three Stage Model. On the one hand he'd recoiled from the whole unpleasant episode associated with his PhD. On the other he hugged the theory to himself, like a child's comforter. It was simple, it was beautiful, potentially it could explain so much, and it was all his own work. When it was published astronomers would say 'Yes of course, that's how it has to be. That fellow Morgan must be bright.' And then one thing ought to lead to another. Once he was acknowledged as a good scientist people wouldn't write off the Crab Pulsar as luck, or fight so hard against his ideas on Red Giants. And who knows, a decent job might then turn up.

To begin with he found it extremely hard to backtrack almost a year and pick up the reins of his thesis work. But once started the pleasure of it flooded in again. With more leisure, far more than he'd had in those last frantic London weeks, he could think through the problem again from a more leisurely, a more fundamental point of view. He read into the history of thermal instability theory, followed up George Field's elegant work and, to his surprise, even ran into a paper on the subject by Wagoner – who had never mentioned it. Morgan had discovered that while Wagoner might be hard on everyone else he was even harder on himself, belittling his own work as 'of minor interest'.

The great excitement for Morgan lay in following up the applications and implications of his theory. They seemed endless: the seeding of star formation; the appearance and disappearance of spiral arms in disc galaxies; the formation of interstellar smoke....... His imagination spun new ideas and new equations by the day.

One noon he stepped into the university library to check on a reference. And as he usually did when he left he scanned the rack for newly arrived journals. 'Astrophysical Journal Letters', which often contained current work on pulsars, had just come in so he picked up the grey journal to scan the cover for interesting titles. And there it was: *"Cosmic-Ray Heating Of The Interstellar Gas"* by G.B.Field, D.W. Goldsmith and H.J.Habing The Abstract began 'We present a model of the Interstellar Medium.....

His heart missed several beats.

He tore open the thin journal and there, on the third page of the paper, was his diagram of the pressure in the interstellar medium, a replica of his S fallen on its side, perfect in almost every detail.

He howled, an animal cry of pain, of rage, and of vengeance. Flipping back to the title page he read the date the paper had originally been submitted: 'Dec 19 1968' exactly 4 months after Morgan had presented his thesis and six after his row with Hood and Somerson.

"You bloody thieves!" he screamed at the empty library. It was obvious what had happened. That fool Somerson must have checked with Field, his old boss, to see if he'd worked on Morgan's theory. And thus tipped off Field, with two post-docs, had stolen Morgan's idea and published it in Astrophysical Journal Letters, a fast publishing journal. It had to be so. Any other explanation involved far too much coincidence, far, far too much coincidence.

"I'll get you you bloody thief." Morgan vowed, recalling with satisfaction the fate of Sugarman at Kitt Peak. Field was a full professor at Berkeley, quite impossible to sack. But the higher his status the worse the degradation when his theft of an idea from a student was uncovered.

Morgan wrung the journal in his hands like a wet cloth, imagining himself standing up in a huge audience of astronomers and pointing his finger at Field. The traitor. He'd be finished, done for, disgraced, divested of students and assistants, shunned by collaborators, distrusted by funding agencies, a pariah who could never show his face in public again, a member of the walking dead. What more heinous crime could an academic commit? A Full Professor at one of the most prestigious universities on Earth, a man already blessed with fame and fortune had used a well meaning if foolish enquiry from a colleague to steal away the idea of, the one idea of a poor graduate student who would need it desperately to find even a lowly toe hold in his chosen profession.

Morgan growled again at his loss, a hungry lion deprived of its kill by a slinking, slimy sneaky hyena. Never in his life had he so wanted to tear someone apart, limb from socket, ball from eye, throat from neck.

"The fucking thieving treacherous swine!" he cried aloud at the sunlit books and the empty chairs. It wasn't right and it wasn't fair. First Bellfounder, then Sugarman , now Field.

His first instinct was to rush home to Ann, to pour out his story and his rage, and have her lick his wounds.

But he couldn't, not yet. Since the miscarriage Ann had been in a weepy, fragile state. Pale, depressed, inactive, she had clung to her mother like a child until Gwendolyn had had to fly back to Kew. Gwendolyn's last words to Morgan had been:

"Make light of it. Make her laugh. Be the clown you can so be when you want to. She's badly down – worse than one can see superficially. She hides her hurt does little Ann. She so wanted her baby – as much for you as for herself."

No he couldn't ask Ann for comfort. How could he even tell her about his loss when she had lost so much more? How could he convince her that the loss of her baby wasn't irretrievable, when he felt that the loss of his own, certainly was?

So Morgan licked his wounds in solitude, the pain made worse, far worse, by the growing realisation that he had no hope of justice, of retribution. What evidence had he, apart from the obvious coincidence, to substantiate a charge of plagiarism Who was going to believe a humble post-doc when the eminent professor, moreover one with a substantial reputation and past record in that very field, denied everything? As Hood and Somerson had argued at the time, it was the very discovery they would have expected Field, of all people, to make first. Even if Somerson owned up to having contacted Field about Morgan's thesis, as he must have done, Field could always claim that the idea had been in his own mind beforehand. An accusation against Field could only turn back with redoubled force on his accuser, particularly on an unknown like Morgan, barely out of graduate school.

Morgan had to grind his teeth, swallow his bile, and try, for Ann's sake, to carry on as if nothing had happened. But inside he was bitter with unrequited, unrequiteable revenge. His baby had been stolen out of his brain and was being paraded in public by the thief, a man far above the law.

As he had promised to do, Wagoner invited Guy Tinker, Bellfounder's collaborator and former assistant, over from Los Alamos to talk about their work together on star formation.

The title alone of his talk "The Star Formation Problem Solved at last." was enough to make Morgan's hackles rise. Nor did Tinker's appearance help. He was a very tall thin man, not much older than Morgan, with eyes hidden behind thick, horn-rimmed glasses. His whole appearance, his unsuitably thick tweed sports jacket, his college tie, and his studiously tousled shock of hair, made claim to membership of an exclusive club: the club of the brilliant Brits who circulated only between Oxbridge, and one or two select Ivy League American universities. Morgan loathed Tinker instinctively on sight, and loathed him even more when Bok , who was to be chairman, concluded his introduction to the seminar by announcing that "…..and he tells me that he's just been appointed to the prestigious Guggenheim Chair at Yale."

Guy Tinker spoke in an exaggerated, braying BBC accent:

"Sir Adrian Bellfounder and I decided to tackle the classical Star formation problem several months ago……" implying first some kind of equality between himself and Bellfounder; second that they could have chosen any one of a number of hard problems to demolish first; and third that it had taken them a mere few months to succeed. Tinker's whole manner, very well rehearsed and articulate, was designed to impress and intimidate. The 'Sir Adrians' came thick and fast, interspersed with the odd 'Adrian' here and there. There were in-jokes, indicated with a hee-haw upper class laugh, that no American could be expected to, or was intended to understand. There were the usual obscure Cambridgey allusions to "Alice in Wonderland" and "The Hunting of the Snark'. There were enormous equations bristling with Greek symbols, which were "…intuitively obvious and easily solved" while a raft of intimidating graphs succeeded one another in such rapid succession as to bewilder even the smartest people in the audience. Here was a man, he was trying to say, more brilliant than the rest of you; a man who found hard science easy, a man who belonged with the immortals.

Morgan listened with a growing mixture of admiration, anger and disbelief. They had attempted the same problem as he had with Hood, but they had used numerical techniques light-years in advance of his own. He'd had to make up the mathematical approximations, needed by any computer, as he went along. Tinker had purloined, presumably with their consent, the techniques developed by a whole generation of brilliant émigrés working at Los Alamos, such as Stanislav Ulam and Richard Courant, to compute the explosive effects of the Atomic Bomb. 'How ingenious' Morgan was forced to admit time and again. He even whistled involuntarily when Tinker sketched the implicit time-forwarding algorithm they had used.

Having dazzled the cognoscenti with his numerics Tinker came to the astronomical results, the nub of the project:

"As you can see " he indicated with a long pointer "The centre of the cloud collapses inwards, in a wholly non-intuitive way, to form a dense central core. Even Sir Adrian was amazed when I demonstrated it to him first. This tiny core then goes opaque, heats up and halts. The remaining evolution consists of the outer envelope raining in on this hydrostatic core, dumping its energy in a shock, which subsequently re-radiates in the thermal infra-red. During this stage the protostar will appear as a luminous source far to the right of the Main Sequence."

As he flicked through more and more slides, bumptiously predicting this, and conclusively proving that, Morgan's brain was racing back to London. Tinker and Bellfounder had fallen into the very same trap as he once had. He too had found this self same core-collapse but, because it was so surprising, he had looked, and with great difficulty found, the explanation. It was a pure computer artefact arising from a subtle conspiracy between the initial and boundary conditions. In a computer, but not in the real universe, the calculation had to start at some sharp instant in time, and the outer part of the computation had to end at an artificially abrupt outer boundary; after all it couldn't go on for ever like the real universe. If the starting cloud was close to equilibrium, which Tinker's cloud deliberately was, then the core would appear to collapse as this artificial boundary-condition propagated inwards at the local speed of sound.

Morgan waited for the end of the talk with glee, punching his thigh in anticipation. This was his chance to wreak some long anticipated retribution.

When Tinker finished amidst a flurry of equations and applause, Bok stood up as chairman, looking more florid, more irascible than ever.

"Vell ladies and gentlemen, it is not often ve are privileged to hear the solution to a classical problem described by the very man who has found it, hot out of the computer as it were. Now Dr Tinker, or should I call him Professor Tinker in the British tradition, has agreed to take questions."

Morgan shot to his feet:

"I would first like to say, as one who has very recently worked in the same field, how much I admire Dr Tinker's numerics. They represent a real advance in the computing within this particular field. On the other hand, I am sorry to say, your astrophysical conclusions " and he faced Tinker "Are completely wrong. You haven't solved the star formation problem at all. What you have done, indeed all you have done, is encounter the self-same numerical instability that I did, over a year ago in London, and mistaken it for astrophysics. You admit to being surprised, as one should be, that an initially uniform cloud could so dramatically turn into a centrally condensed one. Intuition argues that it must be a numerical artefact, and experiments showed me, beyond doubt, that indeed it is. You have made the same mistake as I did initially, and anchored your outer boundary. If you allow it to drift then the whole phenomenon of central core-collapse vanishes completely. It's an easy mistake to make, and I certainly made it initially myself, but reflection and experiment will convince you that it is an artefact nonetheless, and a fatal one. All you are seeing......

"You must be Tom Morgan," Tinker interrupted impatiently "One of Cecil Hood's students at London ?"

"Yes." Morgan admitted

"Well Hood sent your thesis to Sir Adrian who in turn gave it to me to read. So I know exactly what you're talking about. Exactly. But who would believe anything computed in such a primitive way? I mean Eulerian coordinates?" and he haw-hawed at the audience as if it was an enormous joke they could all share "I mean explicit time-differencing?" and he haw hawed even louder "I mean really – that's undergraduate stuff."

"That has nothing to do with the point at issue here." Morgan thundered back "My computer methods, crude as they may appear to you, nevertheless agree with yours almost exactly. So they can't be far out can they? It is the interpretation of them which counts. What you…."

"I can't agree! Your numerics were so crude. Respectable hydrodynamicists abandoned such methods in the nineteen forties. I wouldn't believe a thing, not a single solitary thing that came out of them."

"Numerics have got nothing to do with it." Morgan shouted over-loudly back.

"My dear fellow I think you must be confused. One moment you claim that our results are all faulty numerics, the next moment you contradict yourself by saying they have nothing to do with it."

"That's not what I said at all." Morgan was infuriated by Tinker's sophistry. "What I said was….."

"Really Mr Chairman I think you have a duty to protect me from such hectoring, I really do. In any case I refuse to respond any further to such ill informed, and I have to say it, personal bile. Sir Adrian warned me…"

"Damn your 'Sir Adrian'." Morgan lost his temper completely. " And damn your ad hominem response. I'm trying to talk science and you are merely covering up. I can assure the audience that you are wrong."

"Sit down Tom" Bok roared, purple with fury "I'll have no discourtesy to one of our invited seminar speakers."

"But he's spouting rubbish."

"Sit down d'ye hear! How dare you use such language."

"But surely this is supposed to be a scientific discussion, not a sales pitch? "

"Vun more such vord from you Tom Morgan and you're out! I'll have you banned from seminars, all seminars in future."

Morgan glared at Tinker, who looked triumphant. He was damned if he would lower his colours. He made as if to start again when Wagoner interrupted quietly from behind:

"You've made your point Tom. I think this audience is smart enough to get it."

There was something in Wagoner's manner which disarmed Morgan. It suggested, rather subtly, that the audience actually knew that he had won. So he sat down reluctantly.

"Now perhaps ve can have a civilised discussion." Bok was still infuriated.

Her miscarriage had definitely knocked the stuffing out of Ann. She would still be in bed when he left for work in the morning, and was sometimes still there, desultorily reading a novel, when he got back for lunch. She'd lost interest in America, lost interest in his work, and even lost interest in her own. She ate very little and if he woke in the night and reached out for her, she was quite likely awake, her heart hammering wildly. Oftentimes her pillow was damp with tears. When he tried to talk she would sometimes turn her back to him. His hand, resting on her hip, found unaccustomed bone, for she had lost weight dramatically.

Sometimes she would put on a brave performance and he would return home to find her bright and breezy. On one such occasion she put on a good lunch and pushed a letter towards him. It was one of those pale blue air-mail letters, post marked California, and addressed to him in the most appalling, almost indecipherable handwriting:

> 'Dear Tom
> This is from your long lost Aunty Patti and Uncle Walter

158

Gilkey in Long Beach California.

"I remember her." Morgan said "She used to send us food-parcels in the war. And better still she sent us packages of 'Colliers Magazines', and 'Saturday Evening Posts'. We loved them. Everybody in the village wanted to read them."
"Read on then." Ann sounded impatient

> 'You may not recall me but I was related to your
> father's side of the family, and when I saw your ugly mug in
> 'Time' magazine I recognised your father in you immediately.
> You had to be Evan's son, and I just loved that man. So I said
> to Walter 'It might be fun to have those kids visit us while
> they're over here.'
> We have a beach house on the ocean front at Alamitos
> Bay and we're off on a cruise to Alaska in July. The house is
> yours if you'd care borrow it then. Come and see us anyway.
> Pat Gilkey.

"Oh let's go." Ann sounded eager for once "I'd love to live beside the Pacific Ocean. I'm fed up with Arizona. And Frank could come over couldn't he?"
They looked at their school atlas and confirmed that Long Beach was conveniently close to Los Angles and San Diego.
"Good idea. I can tell Wagoner that Frank and I are collaborating, then the time needn't come out of my vacation."
"Goodee! I'll start packing the suitcase."

It was an all-day drive across the desert and over the coastal ranges.
"I can smell the sea." Ann asserted when they reached San Diego, but Morgan was too preoccupied with driving on the Freeway, at one point being overtaken by five 18-wheeler trucks at once, to notice.
The Gilkeys' house was perched on a narrow sand-spit which separated the Pacific Ocean from Alamitos Bay, which was largely an anchorage for luxury sailing yachts.
Walter Gilkey, a quiet elderly man with a grey moustache, took them upstairs to the sun deck to meet his wife Pat.
They were both taken aback. A skeletal figure in her late seventies, she wore a bright red toupee ridiculously askew on her head, and lipstick lavishly daubed on at an angle of thirty degrees to her lips. Sitting cross-legged on some cushions, wearing a pink kaftan, she appeared to be smoking half a cigarette, which she transferred to her carmine lips on the end of a long hat-pin.
"Walter!" she had the foghorn voice of a deaf person "Where is that wretched man?" She peered about, evidently able to see very little through her mauve-tinted spectacles; "Walter are you keeping those good people away from me?"
"No my darling" Walter had to shout back "Here is Tom – and his good wife Ann."
"Let me see you boy. Let me see you."
She let the glasses fall from her nose and picked up a lorgnette to examine him.
"Well I'll be damned. The spitting image of his father. But bigger. Much bigger. Come here boy, give your Aunty Patti a kiss." and she picked up two scrawny arms to embrace him. Then she turned to Ann:
"My my, what a pretty gel! His father had an eye for the ladies too." She embraced Ann warmly. "And you keep an eye on this man m'dear. You can't trust those Morgan men. I should

know – I was married to one. That Gwilym Morgan he two-timed me before the ink was even dry on the wedding certificate. And I was a pretty gel too – wasn't I Walter?"

"The prettiest I ever saw."

"Go on with you you old sweetheart."

"But I love that Man" she turned to Tom "Pure gold right through. Not a dashing rogue like that Gwilym Morgan of yours. Come and sit down my dears and talk to an old lady. Walter will rustle us up some fruit cake and tea. You young Briddish still drink tea? Well I should hope so. And Walter, my goddamned cigarette's gone out. I need another one. Where the hell are they?"

Pat talked all the time, pausing only to light yet another menthol cigarette -- which she conveyed to her mouth by means of a jewelled hat-pin with which she harpooned it just above the tip. Walter was a courteous gentleman of the old school who followed about in Pat's wake, putting out fires, and generally obeying a string of stentorian orders from his commander in chief:

"Walter1 Where's my godamned ear trumpet. Can't hear a thing without it."

"Walter! Ring up those boring people who invited us for dinner. Tell 'em we're not coming. Got better things to do than talk about money and golf. What dear? No, you think of an excuse. You're better than me."

"Walter! Who wrote that history of Aegean civilisation I was reading last year? I want Tom to read it. Walter never forgets anything you know. Amazing memory."

That evening the Gilkeys took them out to a lucullan restaurant in LA The prices on the menu made Morgan feel ill. Pat, dressed like a grand dame in bright incandescent green, with gold shoes and a veil, and equipped with her lorgnette and ear-trumpet, somehow contrived to smoke through the purple veil without setting herself alight. Having commanded the attention of the entire restaurant she ordered an imperial banquet, sending the head waiter, and a dozen minions, scurrying in all directions. Ann and Morgan watched agape as trolleys of hors d' oeuvres, flaming braziers of lobster, jeroboams of champagne, enormous bouquets of orchids, were wheeled forward for their delectation. Pat behaved as if she owned the establishment. She ordered and reordered dishes, misheard then bullied the waiters, insisted on seeing the proprietor to complain furiously about being served the wrong dish – when in fact it was her fault; shouted loudly enough to irritate nearby diners, spilled cigarette ash all over the tablecloth and finally summoned the head chef into her presence.

When that dignitary arrived, unaccustomed to such summonses and accordingly resentful, she laid into him like a naughty boy:

"I wanna know why I can't order corned beef and cabbage. I don't want to eat all these goddamned shellfish and foll-de-rolls. Can't stand 'em, can't digest 'em can I Walter? I want something plain and I'm prepared to pay for it. You've got a goddamned kitchen full of cooks and sommeliers, surely to God one of 'em can take five minutes off to cook something decent, something plain, not all these goddamned French fricassees or whatever they are! "

"Madam" the head chef was outraged "May I remind you that this is principally a fish restaurant specialising in French cuisine. We are the best such in Southern California. You will notice that none of our tables are unoccupied. Our clientele......"

"What in hell's he saying Walter?"

Pat had her ear trumpet pointed entirely in the wrong direction, though whether this was a deliberate ploy, like Nelson at Copenhagen, they couldn't tell. The whole restaurant had come to a standstill in order to hear the battle of the titans. The Morgans wished they could have slipped out of sight beneath the table.

"Now listen here my man" Pat roared at the chef, who was literally hopping with fury "I'm not used to back chat from the kitchen staff. When we stay with the Governor General of

Hong Kong, and I want something different, I get it. Don't I Walter?" Pat swung her ear trumpet back again like a battleship gun turret.

"You hear?" she turned back on her victim:

"And if you can't cook the goddamned cabbage yourself then you can send out for it and charge me the taxi fare. Now get off to your pots and pans instead of hovering round our table like a wretched mute at a funeral."

The chef was only prevented from falling upon her by the intervention of the proprietor, assisted by several waiters. Only Pat, in the entire restaurant, did not hear the execrations he called down upon her head.

The food, when it did turn up, was quite wonderful. There was even a portion of corn-beef and cabbage for Pat who spurned it on the grounds that she was no longer hungry; indeed she contemptuously stubbed out her cigarette in it. On her fourth vodka martini and smoking a menthol cigarette, specially cut in half by Walter and poised on her hat pin, she was well launched upon an anecdote about a female Russian sea captain who decided to do something about the sex starvation of her male crew.

Concentrated on his lobster Morgan was only half listening when the old lady lost the thread and started a second rather good story about Winston Churchill. This in turn reminded her of Lloyd George and some of the mistresses he kept down on the farm, which in turn lead to a very funny story about the sexual powers of eunuchs. In fact he laughed so much he nearly choked, and Ann had to thump him heavily on the back. But Pat wasn't finished. She completed the Lloyd George story, which was even funnier, then the Churchill one, and finally the Russian sailoress one, by which time Morgan was so helpless with laughter that he literally couldn't touch either his food or his wine. Both he and Ann had to retreat to the bathroom to recover:

"I thought I'd die of embarrassment." Ann said "But she's so funny."

"I think she's a genius" Morgan agreed "You know she's a better raconteur than Peter Ustinov. Far better. And what a mimic!"

"I thought she really was Churchill. She's a modern Scheherazade."

Nothing about Pat Gilkey was life sized; not her opinions, not her manners, not her appetites and certainly not her influence. They found out from the Gilkeys' friends that Pat was renowned throughout the Los Angeles area, not only for her sometimes outrageous stories, but for her wisdom. She had once been an influential journalist whose opinions mattered to famous people. She had, for instance, fought hard to get America into the Second World War, and fought equally hard against Macarthyism. She seemed to know, or to have known, everybody important, and to have an original but considered opinion about virtually everything. She was an outrageous snob, had crossed China on horseback with Walter in the nineteen thirties, stayed with Nehru, interviewed Mussolini, and been a war correspondent in France and Germany.

"Do you know she's got two thousand pairs of shoes?" Ann reported "And she adores children. What a tragedy she couldn't have any. I think she's hoping you're going to be a sort of adopted grandson. How's she related to you?"

"I don't quite know, but I'm sure we'll find out."

When tackled Pat was only too ready to tell:

"Well darlings, there I was, a sweet innocent gel of eighteen, raised in Chicago, when this Briddish war-hero turns up, Gwilym Morgan. My Gahd the women were mad for him. He only had to look at me at this dance and I went weak at the knees. From that moment I chased him, shamelessly. Poor man didn't have a chance – I can see that now. What happened was probably more my fault than his. When it comes to us women, good men are mostly weak creatures. Well Gwilym married me and took me back to Wales to see his folks, a big family they were, spread across the South West area, from Pembrokeshire through Llanelli and Cardigan. And I loved 'em, they were such a rumbustuous lot . Why........." Pat painted cameos of several colourful Morgans.

However when they got back to Chicago, where Gwilym had a job in finance, she was standing on a crowded railway station one day when she noticed Gwilym on the opposite platform with a woman.

"I knew it at once, it was instinct, that that woman was his wife. Don't ask me how. It was the way they stood together, the way he was carrying her shopping bags. I felt I'd been stabbed with a knife. I went straight home to my mother. She spoke to a judge friend of hers. He hired a detective. And sure enough Gwilym turned out to be a bigamist, married two women in two years, she first. So he wasn't rightly married to me at all. I never saw him again, not once. But I kept in touch with his folks in Wales and they kept in touch with me. They were embarrassed about him – the black sheep of the family. You know when he got out of prison he went to Hollywood and became an actor – not a bad one either. A natural impostor if you ask me. Married little Patti for the hell of it, to see how long he could get away with it."

"I'd have thought you would have hated us Morgans."

"Not a bit of it. They took me in and comforted me. They thought I was their responsibility. Why I was only a slip of a gel with no father. My mother didn't believe in 'em – husbands I mean. I stayed with your grandfather's family near Saundersfoot for months after the annulment. Your father Evan , when he was only six years old, God bless him, taught me to catch razor fish at low tide. He was always the apple of my eye was Evan, and I dearly wanted to steal him away. Cried all the way to Swansea on the train when I had to leave him behind in Britain. So you see your family was kind of mine too."

"So that's why you sent us all those food parcels and Colliers magazines?"

"That's why. I couldn't bear to think of Evan's family starving. It nearly broke my heart when he was killed in Normandy."

"I wish we'd kept in touch more."

"I tried. But your mother Blodwen didn't trust me. Woman's instinct you see. And she was partly right. I coveted her Evan, and I coveted you. And I only saw you but the once, back in 1948 when you were ten and off at boarding school. Blodwen could see the way the land lay and I wasn't welcome any more. You must remember that – when you tell her about me."

"But what an amazing coincidence that we should meet again, like this."

"Tell me. I don't usually read that cheapskate 'Time' magazine. But that pesky Walter keeps forgetting to cancel our subscription. I recognised your face at once – it was your father staring out at me when he was a young man. Walter and I went over on the Queen Mary for your parents wedding. When I looked for your name on the caption there it was, Morgan. Divine providence I thought. Then I recalled that I'm a respectable atheist."

They saw Pat in her pomp at a dinner party in a vast mansion over at Pacific Palisades. The movie mogul owner had assembled a glittering array of Hollywood talent and beauty, but Pat was quite obviously the guest-of-honour, seated on the mogul's right. Discreetly amplified, her stories, her political opinions and her quips kept the table of twenty uproariously entertained.

"She's a female Oscar Wilde." Ann remarked in wonder to Walter who was seated next to her at the opposite side of the table from his wife.

"Isn't she a darling?" Walter replied "Why she married a dull fellow like me I shall never understand."

"She's the court jester isn't she, and the Lord Chancellor, all rolled into one. They just love her."

"The secret is my dear that Patti's very smart. She's way smarter than the rest of them here. By agreeing to talk to them as equals, by entertaining them, why, for an hour or two she makes them feel just as smart as she is. And they love it. She turns down at least a dozen invitations for each one she agrees to attend. If people know Patti's going to be there they fight over an invitation. She's made her life, her acquaintance, and a great deal of money with her tongue. Very few are willing to gainsay anyone with a wit like Pat's."

"I know it's a rude question Walter" Ann blushed "But do they pay her to attend?"

"You'll have to ask Patti yourself my dear. She won't mind. She and I never talk money. She thinks I'm a fool about it – and she's right. But I believe she does it for tips. Tips on the stock exchange I mean, and she bets on films, invests in them during production. Here she gets tips on the right films to back. And she gives them advice in return. They used to say she was the best informed woman in California."

Morgan was seated between two overdressed ladies who had seen better days. They were excited because the famous sexual therapists Masters and Johson were also attending the dinner party. They craned forward talking eagerly across Morgan about their husbands sexual inadequacies.

"Now mah Elmer – he 'jaculates premachoorley. Ah cain't have an orgasm nohow."

"Huh, you're lucky I'd say honey. Earl, he jus' goes on and on like a god-damned outboard motor. Somethin's goin' to wear out soon if he don't stop."

They were hoping, it seemed, to have their husbands 'serviced', rather like faulty exhaust pipes. Morgan was embarrassed and infuriated because he was missing the half of Pat's stories. It amazed him that she never repeated herself, not once.

Once the Gilkeys had departed on their cruise the Morgans found themselves in possession of the most eccentric and endearing house built of sea-worn timber. It looked more like the flying bridge of a Misissipi steamboat than a conventional dwelling. On every floor and corner there were rickety outside stair-cases, balconies and crows-nests to espy the sea. Its inspired design was in fact the result of catastrophic evolution. Three times since they had bought it as a beach house in the 1920s, earthquakes had knocked it over, allowing Pat and Walter to reconstruct it to their ever more eccentric design. Never was there a house so inhabited with the sound, the smell and the light of the sea. Every room seemed to have windows on at least three sides, every deck had its bar, even its kitchen, so that, depending on the state of sun and wind, you could enjoy the best vista of sea and sky.

"I think it's a fairy story house, like Hansel and Gretel's." said Ann "I feel like eating it. I love the pelicans, and the smell of the sea. Can't we stay here for ever?"

"I dare say Pat and Walter would love that. You know they live in London for half the year? They've got a flat in Chelsea. We could house-sit, and I could become a yacht-bum."

"What's a yacht bum?"

"Some guy was telling me that all those fabulous yachts out on the bay belong to big firms who use them for 'corporate hospitality' and charge them against their taxes. You notice they hardly ever go out to sea. The yacht-bums are the muscular young fellows who look after them, while their girlfriends open the champagne when the guests come to party."

"I could manage that. But I'd want to live in this gorgeous house. Couldn't you get a job in California – like Frank?"

"Even if I could my salary wouldn't even cover the cost of mowing the lawn. According to Pat, Long Beach has the highest per capita income in the world. It's the oil field underneath. I estimate that every time one of those oil pumps in their gardens goes up and down they earn another twenty-five dollars or so for the owner. That's getting on for a hundred thousand dollars a day."

The extravagant houses along the margin of the bay, and the artificial sea-water canals which debouched into it, all had their own oil pumps nodding away in their gardens.

"Do you know why it's called the Encyclopaedia Brittanica Oil Field Tom? Apparently some real estate dealer bought this whole area as a speculation in the nineteen twenties when it was little more than salt marsh and scrub. His plan was to sell it in lots to ignorant Iowa farmers who could build winter homes here when their own land was buried under ten feet of snow. But he had difficulty selling it to them. So he offered a free encyclopaedia with every lot. And it worked. He'd just sold the very last plot when oil was discovered underneath. He never kept a lot for himself either. Most of these owners today are descendants of the original Iowa farmers."

"They don't know what to do with their money. Who would? Do you know they even have 'sexual therapists?'"

"And 'tree surgeons'."

"And 'personal decorators'."

"And 'body consultants'."

Before she left, Pat arranged for a roster of her friends and neighbours to entertain the Morgans. The first phone call invited them for dinner at a house 'just along the beach.'

When they rang at a modest porch a tirade of hysterical barking emerged, as well as an electronic order to 'step inside'.

The door opened automatically to disclose a poodle with its head in a plastic bucket, used as a collar.

"What on earth……."

All was explained when they made their way down the grand stairway into a room virtually built on the beach. Their host and hostess, as if dressed for a ball, were standing waiting for them beside an absolutely enormous white grand piano:

"Don't take no notice of Rooseveldt." their host explained "He's had eight hundred dollars worth of therapy – and he still bites his ass. Now he can't. No sir, not with that bucket round his head."

After 'cacktails' an elevator with gold handles whisked them into an underground garage. The owner, a purple faced gynaecologist in a mauve corduroy suit and mustard coloured shoes, twirled his keys:

"Ah got eighteen corrs in here. What's your pleesure? A Rolls Royce Phantom? A Bently Continental? A bullet proof Packard that belonged to Al Capone? A Mercedes Benz coupe' like Hitler had?……."

The Morgans enjoyed themselves in Long Beach. Ann began to sleep and eat again while Morgan took up fishing from the mole that guarded the entrance to Alamitos Bay. Watched by pelicans he cast a spinner with his trout rod into the oily blue waters and eventually got a tremendous bite which bent the slender rod double. For twenty minutes the fish fought, testing the line, the rod, the reel and indeed Morgan's nerves to the very limit. He couldn't see what he had hooked, just occasional flashes of silver and white before the fish rushed again, ripping line from the screaming reel. When he eventually netted the creature, a royal blue, streamlined member of the tuna family, Morgan was panting almost as heavily as the exhausted fish. Unfortunately, before he could extract the hook from between the bonito's jaws the creature expired in a shivering rigor, its corpse turning through the colours of the rainbow. When he proudly took it to show Ann she said they would have to eat the poor thing, otherwise it would have lived and died in vain.

Frank Cotteridge, who was staying only fifty miles away in Pasadena, drove over most evenings for dinner and stayed at weekends. He was amazed by the house and in particular by the antique furniture which Pat had brought back from her travels in China. He and Morgan went fishing together and they spent hours every night on the top deck talking about their astronomical lives and ambitions.

Frank was becoming fascinated by the absorption lines turning up in his quasar spectra. As he explained it to Ann, who enjoyed listening in to theirs discussions:

"These absorption lines don't belong to the quasar itself but to some object, some mysterious thing, lying between us and the quasar. When the quasar light passes through this object the hydrogen gas in it leaches out the light at the redshift of the object, leaving a dark gap, or 'line' as it is called. And sometimes there are several lines in a single quasar spectrum, indicating that the light has passed through several such objects located at different redshifts, that is to say at different distances along the line of sight."

"Couldn't they be intervening galaxies?" Morgan asked.

"They could be in principle. That is the natural hypothesis: after all what else do we know that's floating out there in the vast realms of extragalactic space? The trouble is there are too many, a hundred times too many absorption lines to be accounted for by the population of galaxies we know about."

"That's ridiculous." Morgan retorted.

"I know" Frank beamed "That's what is so damned fascinating."

"What about intergalactic gas clouds then, gas left behind after the galaxies condensed out of it?"

"Ah well, that leads to an even more intriguing problem. If cool gas was distributed all the way along the line of sight to a quasar it would cut out all, and I mean all, of the ultraviolet light in the quasar's spectrum. But it does not, Far from it. Those lines cut into the spectrum only here and there, at very precise redshifts, The rest of the ultraviolet spectrum is entirely unobscured. It means that most of the gas you would have expected to remain behind in intergalactic space, after the galaxies condensed out, has disappeared."

"So there are far too many of your quasar absorption lines to be accounted for by galaxies along the line of sight, and far too few to be accounted for by the primeval gas?"

"Exactly Tom, exactly. Quasars are telling us something unexpected, something we cannot comprehend at present, about the early evolution of the universe."

"Of course this all assumes that the redshifts are cosmological, caused by the expansion of the universe."

"But why not? Nobody's come up with a satisfactory alternative explanation."

Morgan nodded, ruefully recalling his Superstars.

"I've no idea what's going on." Frank continued. "I think I'm going to devote the rest of my astronomical career to it."

"You lucky sod!" Morgan sounded envious.

"How come?"

"Knowing exactly where your astronomical future, your astronomical life lies. I mean I've no idea about mine. Optical pulsars have petered out. Some one's stolen my Three-Stage-Model."

Ann, listening in, was horrified to hear this for the first time. He had to explain the whole grisly episode to them.

"It has to be theft." Ann argued. "Field and his collaborators submitted their paper on Dec 5 1968 you say, whereas you presented your thesis on Sept 3rd 1968. If Somerson got in touch with his old boss Field when he was arguing with you in late August, that just gave them time to write the paper. I think it's horrible, and criminal, and you should accuse them."

"What do you think Frank?" Morgan was grim.

"It does seem a hell of a coincidence if it's not theft." Frank admitted. "Ann's right there. Whether that would suffice for a legal case is another matter. If you accused them, and couldn't prove it conclusively, you'd be ruined."

"I think that's awful!" Ann was furious.

"Try and look at it from an unbiased point of view." Frank responded. "I know that's difficult for us three, but impartial astronomers would have to decide the truth or otherwise of Tom's accusation in the end. First of all Field and company will be assumed innocent until proven guilty. Then Field is a very nice chap, at least he seemed so when I met him. Very distinguished too. Why should he bother to steal Tom's idea? He's just going to Harvard as the boss. Then again, this sort of thing happens all the time in science, as we know. Two groups, or two individuals, exposed to the same stimuli, reading the same papers if you like, quite literally leap to the same conclusions at the same time. What could be more natural? Look at Wallace and Darwin. Look at Newton and Leibniz; they nearly ruined one another's lives by accusing each other of plagiarising their invention of calculus. In retrospect we can see that the idea of calculus was 'in the air', waiting to be snatched. Almost certainly they invented calculus independently. Or take Adams and Leverrier and the discovery of Neptune. Although it seems most unlikely in the circumstances, I think it quite possible that Field and Co. are innocent. So our colleagues would naturally give them, in public at least, the benefit of the doubt."

"But look what happened over the Crab Pulsar." Ann was outraged. "That horrible little man Sugarman tried to steal the discovery away."

" Ah yes." Frank responded "But there there was evidence; the telegram he sent. He was caught red – handed and paid the price. What evidence could you hope for here?"

"Well Somerson might testify that he spoke to Field about Tom's idea." Ann maintained.

"He might I suppose. But I doubt it. People hate testifying against their colleagues and peers. And even if he did, I doubt that it would be conclusive. Field could always maintain he'd had the idea previously, from elsewhere. Doesn't he work closely in that sort of area?"

"Yes he does." Morgan admitted.

"Well, if you ask for my advice, Tom is going to have to bite his lip and forget all about it. I know that's hard in the circumstances, but if Tom goes about accusing a man of Field's stature, without conclusive evidence, astronomers will turn on him. He'll be finished in astronomy before he's started."

"I bloody blame myself now." Morgan admitted bitterly "Wagoner warned me to write it up at once but, for one reason and another, I hesitated. To be honest I couldn't face it – going into the unpleasantness of my thesis all over again."

"Well I shall tell everyone – even if Tom won't." Ann was adamant..

"No don't do that Cariad. It's my battle not yours. And if you fought it for me I'd seem like a weakling."

"I wouldn't Ann." Frank was serious "Not if you want to help Tom's career. Think of it this way. Ever since I've known Tom he's been bubbling over with original ideas. He's got a supernatural imagination, and he's going to have lots more great ideas. And no doubt some of them will be pinched by lesser mortals with none of their own. The temptation is too great sometimes. But think of it this way. Which would you rather be? A rare genius like Tom, brimming over with original ideas – who has some of them pinched – or a poor sod with none of his own, who steals others' ?.Who will feel better about himself when he wakes up in the middle of the night, or on his death -bed? The thief – or Tom?"

"A thief can usually convince himself he's innocent." Ann retorted "Gaols are full of innocent people."

"Perhaps, but I bet it's only a blustering, phony conviction most of the time. I'm quite positive Tom should put this behind him, even if, as is possible, he really has been robbed. And bitterness can be worse than robbery in the end."

"Yes." Morgan nodded "It's more or less what I'd decided. To begin with I can't take much credit for the idea. It's a beautiful one no doubt – but it fell on me by accident – when I was correcting my thesis. The loss of it won't matter – unless I never get another job in astronomy as a result. Having that on my CV would have helped enormously."

"Well you *have* got it on your CV." Frank retorted "Hood knows you were first, and so does Wagoner. Those two will provide your main references presumably, to say nothing of your external examiner. So far as jobs are concerned you *did* invent the Three Stage Model."

"I hadn't thought about that darling." Ann smiled. "Frank's right. As always." She got up and hugged both men.

At that moment a helicopter flew low overhead with a tremendous clatter and hovered over the beach. They stood up in the gale of its downwash to see what was going on.

In the beam of the helicopter's powerful searchlight they could see a dozen people standing individually, and quite still, in the light surf. Some had buckets. Occasionally one would stoop down and scoop something out of the surf with their bucket.

"THIS IS THE LONG BEACH POLOCE DEPARTMENET" the helicopter megaphone crackled out "HEAR THIS. HEAR THIS. IT IS A MUNICIPAL OFFENCE TO CONSUME ALCOHOL BETWEEN THE TIDELINES AT ANY TIME OF NIGHT OR DAY. IT IS A STATE OFFENCE FOR MINORS UNDER THE AGE OF EIGHTEEN TO BE IN POSESSION OF ALCOHOL OF ANY KIND. THIS IS A POLICE WARNING."

The searchlight beam flicked up and down the surf looking for transgressors before the helicopter moved two hundred yards down the coast to recommence its performance.

"Look" Ann cried, "There are people lining the beach all the way. All standing still. There must be hundreds altogether."

Something stirred deep in Morgan's memory:

"I know. I read about it in Steinbeck. The grunion must be running. Come on, lets get a torch and see what's going on."

They stood silently with the others, ankle deep in the gentle surf. Most of the shore-side houses had turned off their lights so that the night was pitch dark.

"What's going to happen?" Ann whispered.

"Sssh. Not a sound. They could hear us."

They stood for five to ten minutes, their eyes gradually adapting to the dark. There were no stars even and the air was still. None of the watchers moved or spoke.

Then suddenly a wave broke in front of them, alive with thousand upon thousand of sardine-sized silver fish all writhing and leaping, struggling against the receding water to get up the beach.

"Look! Look! Look!"

Morgan focussed the torch on a silver fish wriggling frantically to bury herself tail first in the wet sand. Her large black eyes look frightened in the torch beam. But she wriggled on as the next breaker carried in another wave of frantic fish. One of them wrapped itself around her, as if in protection. Then the two tiny creatures shuddered their ecstasy together.

"They're mating." Frank cried.

"She's burying her eggs in the sand. " Morgan corrected him "And he's trying to fertilize them."

Another larger wave came in and swept the silver lovers away. As suddenly as they had come all the grunion were gone.

"It makes me want to cry" Ann whispered, clinging to Morgan's arm. "It's so brave. Tiny little creatures trying to save their eggs and their children for posterity; against all those savage predators in the ocean. And did you see the people – some of them – scooping them into their buckets. As if they haven't got enough to eat already."

Morgan was equally moved. Twice more the grunion washed in and did their dance of life, their brief defiance of death and oblivion.

They sat on the roof deck afterwards drinking Scotch in the darkness.

"It makes you bloody think" Morgan remarked. "Those poor little devils. They'll be gone in a few days. The bonito are waiting out there to tear them to pieces. Most of their eggs will fail, or be eaten by worms. There'll be nothing left of them – only the atoms which briefly consorted to make them. Nothing left but the darkness, and the voids between the stars. And we are no different. We'll go the same bloody way too. My own great grandchildren, if I have any, won't even know my name, or care. We live like grunion; a brief dash out onto the beach and then we're gone, dissolved into the darkness forever. Doesn't that thought terrify you? It terrifies me."

He was greeted by a long silence. They could hear the hushing of the surf.

"I never knew you felt like that darling." Ann sounded sad. "I don't."

"Ann's religious." Morgan explained "Not an atheist like me and you."

Frank sipped his MacAlan in the darkness before replying:

"I agree with Ann."

"What?" Morgan sounded shocked. "Surely not you too Frank? What changed your mind? Not all those creepy crawlies at Cambridge?"

"It was Mum and Dad's death. When I saw Mum's dead face, just before they put her in her coffin, I suddenly realised they were both gone for ever. There was nothing of their family, of their dreams or their laughter left behind. Nothing. Even their house didn't belong to them – it was a council house you know. Everything inside, and it wasn't much, had to go. They didn't even have many photographs – they couldn't afford a camera. It seemed as if all they were, or ever had been, were unskilled car workers. There was only me to remember them. And they'd always been so cheerful, so optimistic, so encouraging. They looked forward to retiring one day. They were scrimping and saving towards a caravan on a site somewhere near Rhyl. But they never got there. Dad went suddenly, leaving Mum alone. She went to pieces. If it hadn't been cancer something else would have taken her away. I wanted desperately to find something that would remind me of them both before they vanished into oblivion. And the awful thing was that there was hardly anything to find. You remember those awful flights of plaster ducks Tom, the ones she had on the wall?"

"Yes I think I do."

"Well I took one of those and put it up in my rooms at Trinity. If anyone sniggers at Mum's ducks, and they do, they're never asked again. That's all that's left of her. Do you know I couldn't even get burial plots? Apparently you have to order them years in advance. So it was down to the council crem. for them both."

"Poor Frank." Ann reached out a hand.

"Mum had Dad's ashes scattered on his allotment two miles away. Of course that belonged to the Council too. I had to sneak in at night with her ashes and scatter them in between someone else's sprouts, hoping they'd mingle with Dad. And all I had left of him were the tools from his motorcycle sidecar. Do you remember that old Aerial Tom? Somehow the three of us all used to get on it together when we went on our summer holiday."

"Did you keep it?"

"No, it went for scrap after Dad died. But I kept his 'Gripper' – you know, one of those adjustable spanner things. I use it all the time. I even call it 'Dad'."

"Cripes Frank I wish you'd told me."

"You might recall Morgan that you'd been giving me the brush-off for years. And I didn't have any other really close friends at Cambridge. We all had to work too hard. I'm sorry for all this maudlin nonsense Ann. I've never told anyone else before. It must be this whisky. I'm not used to it. And the grunion."

"Don't apologise Frank. That's what friends are for, aren't they Tom?"

"I'll go down and get us some more ice and some more Scotch. We all need it. I know I do."

Frank and Ann sat silently, holding hands in the darkness, until Morgan got back:

"But you haven't explained Frank" he said, pouring them all another tot "You haven't explained where religion came in."

"No. Well it was very odd. Mum wanted a church funeral. She used to go to Evensong because she and Dad invariably worked at the car factory on Sunday mornings, like everyone else. They got triple-time you see. Anyway I arranged for the service there. It was a horrible clammy winter morning, with smog in the air. And there was her coffin covered in flowers. The service began. Mum had chosen the hymns – she'd told the vicar apparently. We were singing her favourite one 'All Things bright and Beautiful' – you know?"

"*All things bright and beautiful"* Ann crooned
"*All creatures great and small*
All things wise and wonderful
The good Lord made them all."

"Yes, well we were singing that when the strangest thing happened. First of all a totally unexpected shaft of sunlight burst through the stained glass window of the church and illuminated Mum's coffin. Just the coffin and nothing else. But then, and you've got to remember this was February, a butterfly flew out of her flowers and ascended, as we were singing, up through the sunlight until it disappeared into the glooms of the church tower. It was as if Mum's soul was leaving her body and returning to her God."

"How extraordinary Frank." Ann was moved.

"It was wasn't it. For a moment I thought it was some kind of cheap trick arranged by the funeral director. But when I turned round to look at him his mouth was agape with astonishment. So I turned back and watched Mum disappear into the belfry. And I felt this warm oceanic feeling as if me, and Mum, and Dad, and all their friends and fellow workers in the audience belonged to some great company, on its way towards a welcoming eternity."

"Those flowers were probably frozen" Morgan interrupted "From the tropics. And the butterfly was naturally there and moribund in the cold. But when the sun warmed its wings it took to flight."

" Don't be so materialistic Tom." Ann sounded cross.

" No. Tom's right to speculate. The same thought crossed my mind later on, outside the church. But the funeral director – who came up to express his own astonishment – told me the flowers all came from Holland, where they were grown in greenhouses. There's no chance a butterfly would survive until February in a sterile place like that. They're sprayed practically every day apparently, to kill all possible pests, especially caterpillars."

"OK" Morgan conceded, "Very unlikely I agree. But there has to be a chance, one in a thousand say, that the odd butterfly will get through."

"And the sunlight?" Frank asked.

"OK one in a hundred for that say. Multiply that by one in a thousand and you get one in a hundred thousand. But, let me see, there are roughly sixty million people in Britain and they live for sixty years on average. That means a million funerals a year. If you multiply one in a hundred thousand by a million you are going to get roughly ten butterfly-funerals a year. So what happened to you Frank, though admittedly improbable, is no good reason to believe in God."

"I disagree" Frank retorted "Even if I accept your figures the chance against a butterfly turning up at Mum's *particular* funeral by accident are a hundred thousand to one. But one did turn up! So, if you ask me, the odds are a hundred thousand to one against a natural explanation in this instance. Goodness me Tom I've thought about it every day since Mum died , and that's five years ago. What do you think Ann? You're studying statistics aren't you?"

" I am, yes. And I find Probability Theory, which is what we are using here, very very hard. I'd have to think about it. But on the face of it I suspect you must be right. If I'd been there, and it had been my mother, I know, I absolutely know, I'd have felt just like you."

"That would just be the natural susceptibility of the moment." Morgan objected. "We could all feel like that – temporarily. But that's not an argument to believe in God, and to act on that belief, for the rest of your life."

"I might have guessed what you'd say Tom. But what about Ann? Why do you believe in God too Ann?"

"Well it sort of grew on me. No sudden epiphany like yours. My parents are archaeologists and through them I grew up with a strong interest in the subject. And the more I learned about it the clearer it became to me that Man is, in the broadest sense, a religious maniac. Almost no people, no tribe on Earth has been driven primarily by rational considerations or natural necessities. They all have demons and gods and taboos and superstitions. So you don't really have to explain religion. It's there; it's everywhere. It would be more sensible to wonder why some people, some rare people if you take the large sweep of time and space, don't believe in a God – of some kind. Surely they are the rare exceptions who need explaining. It's not you who has to justify your belief to Tom, it's Tom who has to justify his disbelief to you."

"But your Dad's not a believer is he." Tom retorted "And he's the professional archaeologist in the family."

The argument raged on far into the night and resumed between Tom and Ann in bed next morning.

"I'm sure there's a fallacy in Frank's calculation." Morgan maintained.

"It was your calculation if you remember – not Frank's."

"I only put it into numbers. Frank's faith rests on his unstated conviction that a natural explanation for the butterfly is too improbable to be taken seriously. Right?"

"Right."

"But his calculation of that improbability, and the calculation has to be made somewhere, stated or not, is quite simply spurious."

"Why?"

"I'm groping a bit, but think of an analogy. One day three carroty haired men get into a bus, at separate stops, and sit themselves, one by one, on the seat behind you. You'd be surprised wouldn't you?"

"I'd be amazed."

"Why?"

"Well I suppose because the probability of that happening, by chance, would be very tiny indeed. If only one man in twenty say, is carroty haired, then the chance of three, one after another, and quite independently, sitting behind you, would be one in twenty, multiplied by one in twenty, multiplied by one in twenty again. Or one in eight thousand. So I'd be justified in my amazement."

"Are you quite sure about that?"

"Yes I think I am. I'm sure I am."

"OK" Morgan smiled "Then you've fallen into the same logical trap as poor Frank. How many bus journeys does one make in a lifetime?"

"Say two a day, five days a week, that's ten a week, or five hundred a year. Multiply by say sixty years and that comes to thirty thousand bus trips in a lifetime."

"Exactly!' Morgan was triumphant "You've got to multiply your odds of one in eight thousand by thirty thousand. That comes to about four. In other words there will probably be four occasions in your life when three carroty haired men will get onto the bus seat behind you. So you shouldn't be in the least surprised when it happens once."

There was a long pause while Ann thought.

"I'm confused now" she admitted eventually. "Both calculations seem right – but they're contradictory."

"I know." Morgan agreed "I've been lying here for hours, while you were asleep, trying to reconcile things in my mind. And I think I've got it now. It all hinges on the particularity of the day on which the carroty haired men appeared on your bus. Suppose it was June 27 1964. If you'd asked yourself the question in *advance* 'What are the chances of this happening on just this coming day?' then your first calculation would have been correct. But that's not the question at issue. You don't really care about the bloody date. What has really amazed you is that the men are there at all, irrespective of the date. Then you have to do the lifetime calculation, and then it all seems probable."

"I think I understand what you're getting at now." Ann conceded. "Indeed I remember a lecturer at Arizona referring to it as the well known fallacy of *'a posteriori statistics'*. In other words 'calculating the probability of a rare event *after* it has already occurred', can only lead to false conclusions."

"Poor old bloody Frank. His comforting belief in God is based on a false statistical premise. And he's a bloody ace mathematician for heavens sake."

"Ah!" Ann sat up excited "That is precisely where you're wrong. Or rather your analogy of the carroty haired men is invalid. I may be going to get onto a bus thirty thousand times in my life but Frank is never going to bury thirty thousand parents. He buried his mum once, and the butterfly appeared exactly at the magic moment. So there Tom Morgan. You atheists are too clever by half."

"That's nonsense."

"Oh is it? Then you tell me exactly why."

But Morgan couldn't. All the same he was fairly convinced, immutably convinced, that buried somewhere there must lie a fallacy in Frank's unstated argument for the existence of God.

The two men went fishing next morning, taking it in turns with Morgan's rod. Frank was thrilled when he hooked into a big bonito, squealing like a little boy when the fish made a big run.

Morgan watched his friend fondly. Tall and languid as ever, Frank cultivated a short dark silky beard like that of an Elizabethan grandee or a Spanish conquistador. His large globular head was topped by a white straw hat with a black ribbon round it, a 'Vicar's garden party hat' as Morgan called it, and this, together with his dark sensitive eyes, made him look like a missionary, or a colonial administrator. Tom realised how much he loved Frank, regretting how long he'd left him to face the world alone. Frank might be a Fellow of Trinity College Cambridge, but he was still a lonely human being.

"What do I do Tom?" Frank sounded panicky. "There's only ten yards of line left."

"Pray to your God." Morgan laughed.

"I couldn't bear to lose it now." Frank reeled in some slack, never taking his eye off the line.

"If you catch it Ann will make you eat it; every darn scrap of it. And they're vile. Absolutely vile!"

Frank was panting when he finally landed the fish:

"Gosh that was exciting. I'm all shaky. It was like a playing a Bach Toccata on the college organ, or scoring a century at school. Do you remember Tom when we beat Manchester Grammar together, you and I?"

Morgan, who'd suddenly seen the fallacy in Frank's argument for the existence of God, put an arm round his friend, fearing for his vulnerability:

"As I recall you did most of the beating."

"But you skittled them out. Do you know who ought to be here now?"

"Jack Cockle of course."

"If he'd been here I'm sure he'd have helped me eat this damned fish. Every time I look at it it seems to grow larger. I don't suppose you'd help Morgan?"

"Bloody right I won't Frank Cotteridge. They're absolutely revolting. You'll have every scrap of cartilage and bone and gristle and skin and scales to yourself. Come on I'm dying to see you eat it."

"I'm feeling queasy already."

"There's no going back now Cotteridge. Having taken the poor creature's life you can hardly refuse, as a Christian, to accept its sacrifice."

The stars were out when they sat on the top deck again that night.

"I wonder where our little grunion is now?" Ann was looking out over the ocean.

"Probably in Frank's stomach" Morgan laughed. "That bonito of his could easily have eaten her."

"You've married a swine Ann."

"I know. It's a pity he's not a Christian. Perhaps you should convert him."

"Huh!" Morgan snorted "I'm rational. I need evidence."

"All right." Frank took up the challenge "Then explain my mother's butterfly."

"I don't need to. Nor should you ascribe its appearance to the existence of God."

"It's too improbable otherwise Tom, far too improbable, flying up as it did just when we were singing her favourite hymn. Surely you can see that. Without going into detail the odds must be a million to one against that happening just as it did, just where it did and just when it did. Nobody will convince me otherwise."

"Ah but you see there's a fallacy in your argument."

"Leave Frank alone Tom."

"It's all right Ann. I can defend myself against Tom. We've never held back before have we?"

"Not likely. Don't worry darling I'm only helping Frank out. It's better for him to see through this God-stuff while he's young, than for him to wake up disillusioned and suicidal in middle age."

"You cocky devil Morgan!" Frank laughed "Let's hear your argument."

"OK, but it's not my argument, it's the fallacy in yours."

"Go on."

"You were impressed by, and are now convinced by the improbability of the butterfly ascending. I can understand that, and one could likely work out the probability of it occurring by chance – and indeed find out that it would be vanishingly small. But you've forgotten something. You are implicitly assuming that no other occurrence, happening at that precise moment, would have convinced you of the existence of God. Suppose for instance that the church bells had suddenly started ringing, apparently of their own accord? Or that a white dove had flown down the aisle and perched on the pulpit? Or that your father's voice had come to you, bringing words of comfort. And so on and so on. All highly improbable in themselves I grant you. But the chance of *any one* of them happening, taken in their uncountable variety, is probably high, even certain if you were in a susceptible frame of mind. If you really wanted to believe in God at the time, because of your loneliness and grief, you could easily have found a sign, some sign, that would confirm you in your hope. And since it is not possible to enumerate all the possible occurrences that you might have accepted as a sign, then an improbability argument, like the one you are using, is simply not valid in this context."

Frank scratched his head:

"To be honest I hadn't thought of that. And it's a good point – at least in a formal sense. And I cannot deny it. But it doesn't worry me either. Only I can know what was in my mind at the time. And I can categorically deny that I was looking for a comforting sign. Categorically. No, I was absolutely pole-axed by it at the time, and sceptical immediately afterwards. What your argument denies is the sheer appositeness, the sheer closeness of the analogy of the ascending butterfly and the ascension of Mum's spirit. Your white dove, or the church bells spontaneously ringing, wouldn't have shaken me in the same way at all. Sorry Tom but you'll have to think again. Indeed if you were honest about it you ought to be disturbed in your own atheism. I can't explain what happened in material terms, and neither apparently can you. Either I'm lying about the butterfly, and you know I am not, or else you ought to be calling your own scepticism into question."

"Well said Frank!"

"Well I'm not going to." Morgan retorted "Nor need I. There are roughly one million funerals a year in Britain. So even if the odds were a million to one against a butterfly appearing at any one funeral, such a butterfly would nevertheless appear on average somewhere in Britain every year. The fact that it happened in my friends particular family is, so far as the argument about God is concerned, neither here nor there. Improbable events happen all the time – simply because there are almost infinite opportunities for them to occur to somebody, sometime, somewhere."

But Ann had her tail up now:

"What I can't understand Tom is how you can live with yourself, and without God. Aren't you very lonely? Doesn't it frighten you that you are going to die, to be forgotten entirely, to be dissolved again into your individual atoms, as if you'd never existed?"

"Of course it does. I was terrified when I was a boy. I went to Confirmation classes at school for a while. I even went to the actual Confirmation to see if the bishop's laying on of hands would, as claimed, make a difference, would confer a revelation. But it didn't. Worse still one could see it was just a cheap way of tricking young and ignorant peasants into the church. Ugh! God, those ghastly old churchmen are so transparent."

Frank laughed: "You see Tom Morgan you can't even mock the church without referring to the deity. God is in your blood somewhere, like it or not."

"I don't see how you can live with the emptiness darling. How can you behave morally if there are no morals and you are just a grunion? Why don't you just snatch things for yourself, and live for the moment? You don't you know. You are a very moral, non materialistic man."

"I can't answer such questions Cariad. But suppose you were a soldier, like my grandfather at Cambrai, shaking in your trench, waiting to go 'over the top' and face the machine guns and the barbed wire. Would you snatch your best mate's last cigarette – just because you are not a Christian? I think not. There's a lot more to us men than your simple priests allow. We are the only creatures on Earth, in the Cosmos perhaps, who have to face the certainty of their own oblivion. And our glory is that we can – some of us, sometimes – without resorting to childish fables about God and resurrection. Man is, he can be at his best, a heroic creature. He has to make some sense out of the cruelty, the sheer hazard of his life, and in doing so inspire and comfort his fellows. I imagine he's been facing the truth for a hundred thousand years, huddling round his fire, listening for the wolves crying out their hunger, and his own hunger, while the blizzard rages just outside his cave."

"What else could he do?" Frank demanded.

"He could have given in. He could have said 'Bugger this for a lark.' and opted for extinction. Many probably did, the Neanderthals for example – they had bigger brains than us, and perhaps more sense. But some of us clung on, and here we are aiming at the Moon. I'll settle for that. It may be bleak darling but it's brave, and it's true and it's honest."

"You're a humanist." Ann said.

"That's all very well" Frank countered "And rather brave I grant you. But so bloody abstract. How is it going to help you lead your own personal day-to-day life, face your own certain mortality, your own Gethsemane? You are not going to the Moon are you?"

"No I'm not. And I get pretty depressed at times. I believe it's in the nature of thinking man to get so. It's not so much death, which after all you cannot feel after you are gone, it's the whole senselessness of being alive that hurts so much sometimes. For instance Frank, what you told us about your mum and dad resonated with me. You two have never worked in a car factory; I have. To see all those poor decent men and women working six and a half days a week, like machines, just to make cars most of them will never be able to afford – it used to haunt me when I was there, and it haunts me now. And a car factory with its mindless, soulless turning lathes is just a microcosm for the modern world in general. Like religion it's another transparent lie. 'Get a car' it says, 'And your life will become worth while'. Do you know there was a chap at the Austin who realised that, no matter how long he worked, he'd never be able to afford a car. So he started smuggling components, one by one, out of the factory, and assembling them in his garden shed. One day he started the engine, packed his family on board, and drove off into the sunset".

"Apocryphal surely." Frank remarked.

"Many believed it. That's the important point."

"I don't see that you've answered Frank's point; how is the bleak destiny of the godless man, however brave, going to help him face the trials of life?"

Morgan didn't reply at once. He got up out of his deck chair, turning his back on them, and stared out over the moonless Pacific. When he spoke he spoke almost inaudibly:

"It's ridiculous I know. You don't have to tell me and you must never tell anybody else. But it's the only star I can find to which I can hitch my wagon."

He paused for a time, rattling the ice in his glass, looking down at it before looking up into the darkness again:

"I'm going to make, or rather I'm going to try to make, I have to make, a great scientific discovery, one that reverberates down the centuries; like Galileo, like Kepler, like Clerk-Maxwell, like Einstein, like Columbus, like Darwin. You can laugh, but it is the only form of immortality to be had. A thousand years from now even Shakespeare and Mozart will be forgotten, as languages and tastes change. Churchill will be swallowed up in the turbulence of history to come. But Ernest Rutherford? Only one man could discover the nucleus of the atom, and he did. Even thirty thousand years from now children will be taught, will know about, Ernest Rutherford. That's the only immortality on offer, and that's what I aim for."

Getting no response from the other two he went on:

"I used to think that some great first ascent, like Edward Whymper on the Matterhorn, or Heinrich Harrer on the North face of the Eiger, or Joe Brown on Cenotaph Corner, I used to think that that would be enough. That's why I was happy to risk my neck mountaineering. Now I can't do that any more. And anyway science is far more exciting, more consequential. No mountaineer will be remembered thirty thousand years from now. What do you think?" Morgan swallowed the ice in his glass before continuing:

"Dylan understood, Dylan Thomas I mean. Do you know he came from the next village along the coast from me? 'No Good Boyoh'."

"Do you mean" Ann asked "His poem about the dying of the light? How does it go? Yes I remember now: 'Do not go gentle into that good night. Rage, rage against the dying of the light.'"

Morgan nodded, barely visible in the starlight:

"It's not much is it? But it's all I've got."

The following morning Frank refused to go fishing with Morgan:

"The mere thought of eating another bonito makes me heave."

He and Ann breakfasted on the top deck, from where they could see Morgan fishing off the mole half a mile away.

"What do you think Frank, about what Tom said last night?"

"About immortality you mean?"

She nodded. Frank groped for the right words:

"Well in one sense it's touching; poetry in an atheist. It's all he has. But in another sense it's ridiculous, pathetic even. You can't set out to make an immortal discovery. Take Rutherford – the very example he quoted. When he planned, in a dingy little cellar at Manchester University, to bombard gold foil with alpha-particles he could have had no idea, no conception that he was going to stumble across the atomic nucleus. Great discoveries usually come partly by accident –

when you're trying to do something else. They are great precisely because they were totally unanticipated. Tom knows that as well as I do. Look at Columbus – discovering America when he was looking for Asia. So he can't build the prospect of immortality into his research program. He simply can't. Not even Tom."

"Why do you say 'Even Tom' ?"

Frank looked up at Ann; "Well Tom's different. He always has been. He marches to the beat of a different drum."

"How do you mean?"

"It's hard to explain. It's not just a matter of brains, though God knows he's got scads of those, far more than me."

"Surely not? Tom says you were top of 'Part Three' or something. The equivalent, he says, of being 'The Senior Wrangler', whatever that is. Real genius stuff anyway."

"Oh that; not terribly relevant really. If you look back some very few Senior Wranglers, men like Clerk-Maxwell and Rayleigh, turned out to be geniuses. Some others, like Bellfounder, became distinguished. But most passed into decent obscurity – as schoolmasters or clergymen. No Tom's different. Did he ever tell you about his exploits in the army out in Malaya?"

"A little."

"I only heard the saga from a school friend of Tom's who was also there. Tom never mentioned them to me. But it's all of a part. There's always been something of 'The Man of Destiny' about Tom. People at school could sense it. You couldn't be neutral about Tom. Either you loved him as I did, still do, or you resented him like billy-oh, as did some of the masters and boys."

"Can you be 'a man of destiny ' in science?"

"I don't know. We shall see won't we. The one thing about Tom that resembles Ruthereford, is that he 'never stops thinking'. Once he's got his teeth into a problem the bulldog jaws clamp shut. The great brain worries away on it day and night, week after week."

"Don't I know." Ann laughed.

"That's not normal you realise? Then there's his scientific nerve. Nothing daunts him. Do you know, when he was fifteen, he taught himself Tensor Calculus, so that he could read Einstein's papers on General Relativity in the original. When I told Bellfounder that he wouldn't believe it. But it is so. I was there. I don't know anyone else in Britain who would have had the bloody cheek to do that. Not at his age."

"Isn't there a ..a . danger in that?"

"Yes there is. Oh look!"

Frank picked up the binoculars:

"Tom's into a big fish; a really big one by the look of it. He's dashing up and down the mole after it. I must go and help." He stood up.

"What danger?" Ann wouldn't give up. Frank looked lost for a moment, picking up the threads:

"A scientist has to pick his problems sensibly. Medawar called science 'The Art of the Soluble'. Tom's character could lead him to tackle the impossible, to fail heroically. In fact that's just what I feel he's going to do."

"And then?"

"Then he'll finish up a bitter old man – despising the rest of us, like Bellfounder."

"Go on. You'd better go and help him. And if it's too big to eat tell him to put it back."

Before the Gilkeys got back Frank had to leave, first for an observing run on Mount Palomar, then back off to Cambridge for the summer. He offered to take Morgan up to Palomar. Morgan accepted eagerly, but then changed his mind:

"I suppose I'd be jealous if I saw your gigantic 200-inch. But I don't think that's what stopping me. It's more a sense of inverted snobbery. I wouldn't get much satisfaction out of making a discovery with the largest telescope in the world. Anyone could do that. It would be to the credit of the instrument, not the astronomer."

"My God Tom, you are an egoist."

Morgan reflected on that before replying:

"Yes, in a way. But it's more like us fishing for bonito. If we use a fly rod it's a titanic and exciting battle. But if we used a Big Game rod we could yank them out like minnows. No fun at all. No room for ingenuity, for imagination, for patience stamina or skill."

"But that's ridiculous!" Frank was indignant "Astronomy isn't a sport. We're trying to understand the universe, using every tool to hand. Anyway you may be trying to catch a bonito on your fly rod, but what about a thousand pound Blue-Fin Tuna. That's what I'm after with the 200-inch."

Morgan couldn't be persuaded, but he did spend a lot of time talking to Frank about quasars. Unlike optical pulsars, dozens of higher and higher redshift quasars were being found every month.

"And it's becoming queerer Tom. Some chaps at MIT are rumoured to have found quasar radio sources expanding faster than the speed of light."

"But that's impossible." Morgan gasped.

"I know. But the rumour is pretty substantial. Somebody at CalTech. saw their reprint. But there's something even worse – if less spectacular. If you look at the spectrum of a quasar – I mean across its whole range from the radio to the ultraviolet, there's something damned funny going on. Look."

He whipped out a graph from his brief case:

"You see it's low in the ultraviolet, higher in the optical, higher still at microwave, ludicrously high in the radio. Almost all the energy of these beasts is coming out at radio frequencies. That's not like anything physical we know of. The more intense the energy output of a normal object , and these things are bloody intense, the hotter they tend to look, the more high frequency energy they produce, and the less radio energy by comparison. You'd be surprised wouldn't you to feel a very hot fire that looked very dim, as if it was going out. But that's what we have here. Bellfounder calls it 'A major crisis for physics' and is madly trying to solve it. And of course these faster-than-light observations, if substantiated, put the whole question of quasar distances on trial. We desperately need some proof that quasars really are as distant as their redshifts imply. Desperately. But the higher the redshifts are the harder it's going to be to tell. This whole area's becoming hysterical. It's screaming out for a fundamental breakthrough. It drives me almost potty at times."

"Why?"

"Because you feel the solution ought to be staring you in the face. If only we could keep calm enough, and think straight, the answer would come like a revelation."

They were all sad when it was time for Frank to leave. Frank said to Morgan privately:

"Where does one find another girl like Ann? How on earth did you find her?"

"I stole her from another chap."

"I don't blame you. I'd steal her myself – if I thought I had a chance."

"Oh she likes you well enough Frank – but your telescope is far too big."

"Huh! I'd say yours is far too small to satisfy a full blooded woman."

They picked up Pat and Walter from the Matson Line berth at Los Angeles. Never having met a gigolo before, or not to their knowledge, the Morgans were astonished to see a flock of these colourful creatures descending from the luxury liner, some in possession of their elderly prey, others alone and disgruntedly out of pocket.

Ann was persuaded to stay on at Long Beach while Morgan drove back to Tucson for an observing run. Pat obviously saw her as a proxy daughter-in-law while Ann, who had perked up no end in California, was fond of the two Gilkeys and found California society bizarrely entertaining:

"I hope you don't mind darling. I feel like an anthropologist making her first encounter with a new tribe – The Super Rich. And in a way that has to be interesting – not because of the individuals, who are mostly banal – but because their money releases them to do whatever they please. This is, if you like, a laboratory for the study of 'Human Free Will' – of what we become when nothing material restrains our choices."

When Morgan demurred at Ann travelling back to Tucson later on a Greyhound bus Pat insisted:

"She flies home first class at our expense. I know you scholars are poor. For Walter and I the fare will be a trifle; less than I spend on a pair of shoes, and God knows darlin' I've got plenty of those."

Back in Tucson Morgan missed Ann, missed the smell of the sea and missed his fishing, but it was an opportunity for some unremitting research.

'Cynthia', that is to say his program with Wagoner to study the fate of gas in Elliptical galaxies, was beginning to bear rich fruit. According to his computer program, the fate of gas ejected by the dying stars in them appeared to depend on where that gas was. In the outskirts of such galaxies it was too hot to be restrained by the galaxy's gravitational field and streamed out into intergalactic space. But in the inner regions the gas cooled rapidly and collapsed towards the centre. But what happened when it got there? The computer program wasn't able to tell him this so he tried to analyse the situation mathematically.

It wasn't unlike the Star Formation problem he'd attempted to tackle in London – but with one big difference. The centres of Elliptical galaxies were packed with stars, especially towards their nuclei, where their density would be very high. And these stars, acting in concert, generated a strong gravitational field which would affect the fate of Morgan's infalling gas. In fact, according to his calculations, a remarkable thing would happen. As it fell inward the collapsing gas would be subjected to a stronger and stronger gravitational field which would exert a sort of tidal effect, pulling the inward edge of the gas away from the outward, completely preventing the gas from collapsing upon itself and fragmenting into stars.

But if it couldn't fragment what would become of the infalling gas? After all, huge amounts of it would accumulate. It struck Morgan like a blinding light, that here could be the origin of quasars. Quasars often had huge double radio sources, that is to say two huge lobes of radio emission situated a million light-years to either side beyond their visible extents. But so did giant Radio Galaxies – which were invariably Ellipticals. Perhaps quasars were simply Elliptical Radio Galaxies of monstrous proportions seen very far out in space, and powered ultimately by the gas infalling from the Elliptical's dying stars. The mechanism for generating the radio emission in its weird double-lobed configuration might be a complete mystery, but the ultimate source of the energy powering it could now be dimly perceived. Provided, and it was a big proviso, that there was a massive Black Hole at the centre of a Radio Galaxy or Quasar then Morgan's infalling gas would, according to his calculation, provide just the right amount of power. And as it accumulated it would build up the Black Hole, indeed be responsible for its existence in the first place.

Morgan was so excited that he had to tell someone, apart from Ann on the phone, about his new insight. But he was learning prudence; he'd made too much of a fool of himself over quasars before. And then, in retrospect, the idea seemed so obvious that he could hardly imagine that it was original to himself. The proper person to talk to was obviously Wagoner who, after all, had originated the whole project.

Morgan had always been puzzled as to why Wagoner, whose main astronomical preoccupations lay quite elsewhere, should be so interested in the fate of gas in Elliptical galaxies. In explaining the problem to Morgan Wagoner had never mentioned Quasars or Black Holes. Now Morgan understood why. Wagoner had suspected all along that the gas might accumulate in their nuclei but he had been too canny to tell Morgan ,in case it influenced his conclusions. He had obviously worried that, as an inexperienced and over-enthusiastic research worker, Morgan might look too hard for a particular result, and so find it when, in truth, it wasn't there. Cunning Wagoner. Morgan's respect for the man, already considerable, grew even further.

So Morgan decided to play Wagoner's game. Instead of rushing in where such a wise man feared to tread, he would subject his every result to the most scrupulous examination. He would check and double check until he was sure, was aware of every pitfall, assumption, alternative and caveat. Only then would he mention to Wagoner, almost casually in passing, that he had some possibly interesting results. Not only would it be the best way to impress Wagoner – it was the best way to do science. Passion, obsession he had in abundance; now he must and would learn dispassion, to turn a searching and sceptical eye on his most exciting ideas. It was an almost inhumanly impossible double-act, but it was surely what distinguished the scientist from the fanatic.

As he thought about the matter more deeply Morgan realised that Cynthia was whispering a profound truth in his ear. If she was right then *every* Elliptical galaxy, even the Milky Way's apparently quiescent Elliptical neighbours, must harbour a Black Hole in its core because the gaseous in-fall process appeared to be inevitable and must therefore be universal. Quasars and Radio Galaxies might represent rare and transient outbursts from the dark monsters lurking in their cores. Just because an Elliptical galaxy looked peaceful didn't mean that it didn't have a dark heart fed by the gentle but inevitable rain of in-falling gas. And this was, as he was able to establish by checking the literature, a truly original and unsuspected truth. Out of the gentle evolution of their stars Elliptical Galaxies must, indeed couldn't avoid, growing monstrous super-massive cores packed with explosive amounts of gravitational energy arising from the in-fall. It would be like rain falling into a large catchment area and accumulating behind a dam wall. Unless there was a gentle way out, and he could see no possibility of one deep in the core of an Elliptical, the rain would build up and up until it burst the dam wall and flooded out with explosive force. Precisely how and where it flowed was less important than the fact that it must eventually do so.

Morgan hugged this truth to himself. He found it delicious to know something profound that, for the moment, no other man on Earth suspected. He felt like Vasco de Balboa, at the top of his tree on the Isthmus of Panama, the very first European to look out upon the vastness of the Pacific Ocean. He didn't tell Wagoner, he didn't even tell Ann. It was childish he knew but the pleasure was so delicious, so oceanic, that he wanted it to last. He pinched himself at the glory of it, smiled idiotically into the sky, punched his pillow, skipped with delight. Why shouldn't he savour and relish it? Very likely he would never again in his entire life enjoy such an orgasmic revelation. Why should he speak it out loud, have others begrime it with their scepticism or jealousy? It was his for a moment, a melody of such transcendental beauty that there was a part of him that wanted to die there and then, like a lark ascending, while the glory anthemned in his ears.

On the one hand there was ecstasy, on the other there was doubt. Hadn't he been here before, back in Worcestershire when he first stumbled over his ill fated Superstar Theory? He'd missed something, been ignorant, only to fall out of the sky at Bellfounder's malicious feet.

So he checked and he delved and he worried. He lived an entirely schizophrenic existence, varying between ecstasy in the morning, scepticism at night. He went over the program, he went over the equations behind it, and he re-examined all the physical assumptions behind the equations themselves. He altered the parameters, he altered the initial and boundary conditions, and he checked that Cynthia was obeying all the relevant Conservation Laws. He experienced awful moments when something seemed to be seriously awry, but time and again he was able to re-assure himself that actually all was well. And in a general sense he had reasons for confidence. Whereas his Superstar Theory had relied on complex General Relativity, Cynthia was nothing more that an amalgam of well understood hydrodynamics and gravity. Yes there was simplification. He'd ignored angular momentum. He'd assumed a chemical composition for the gas which was probably reasonable, but couldn't be justified in detail. Fortunately, unlike Emily, his Star Formation program in London, the initial and boundary conditions were not critical.

When he met Ann at Tucson airport they threw themselves into one another's embrace Then they stood back, arms on each other's shoulders, staring into one another's brimming eyes:

"You look like my little Cariad again, sparkling, almost plump."

"And you Morgan. I can sense something different. What have you been up to while I've been in California? You look like that cat that found the cream."

"It's embarrassing really. I'm pregnant."

"You ass!" she hugged him again. "Oh I've missed you so, especially your jokes. But seriously?"

He told her about Cynthia's whispered secret.

The following morning, while they were lying in each others' arms, having made love four times during the night, she asked him what he was going to do next.

"Well, I've been thinking. The obvious thing would be to tell Wagoner and then publish a big paper together, perhaps in 'Nature'. But what would you do darling if you were the only person in the world to possess a really valuable piece of information?"

"Use it."

"Exactly. Why don't I use Cynthia's secret to go out and observe Elliptical galaxies and actually prove that indeed they do contain dark monsters. I might even be able to solve the quasar distance problem. You remember Frank said that that was currently the most important question in astrophysics?"

"But how are you going to see Dark Monsters?"

"Good question. Do you remember that when we were in New York I went to the American Astronomical Society meeting? Well, almost by accident, I heard a talk by a radio astronomer called Dave Heeschen. I didn't pay much attention to it at the time, but he's found that some nearby Elliptical galaxies appear to have compact radio sources in their cores. Now, if I'm right, these ubiquitous Dark Monsters must be mostly dark, bursting into violent life only now and again, when they produce quasars. They are probably like volcanoes, dormant most of the time, then erupting spectacularly. But volcanoes rarely go entirely dead. In between eruptions they can emit plumes of fiery smoke or occasional gobbets of lava. I suspect Heeschen's compact radio sources are sleeping monsters emitting occasional snorts of fire. Anyway I'm, planning to look into them with our new 90-inch telescope."

"If you succeed will that make you immortal?"

"Hardly" he laughed embarrassedly. "But some one might offer me a decent job in astronomy. We might even go to work with Frank at Palomar."

"Well I shall pray for you Tom Morgan – even if you are an incorrigible heathen."

Morgan wrote up the case to observe Heeschen's Radio Elliptical galaxies, scarcely mentioning Cynthia, and submitted it to the observatory telescope-time allocation committee. They must have been impressed because he was one of the first astronomers to be awarded dark-of-the-moon time on the brand new 90-inch. Then, almost casually, he told Wagoner Cynthia's secret as if it was obvious and scarcely worth getting excited about. Wagoner wanted to see the computer output as well as Morgan's algebra. As if it was a competition between the two of them to see who could play cool the most convincingly Wagoner returned the papers with the comment that he 'couldn't find anything wrong with it.' But he had kept the stuff for over a week, which suggested to Morgan that he must have become pretty interested. He did however suggest:

"You ought to work with Rich Ironsides on observing those Radio Ellipticals."

"Oh, why?" Morgan had been looking forward to observing alone.

"For a start you're not a spectroscopist."

Morgan described his apprenticeship on the 21-inch. Wagoner was impressed for once but he maintained:

"You're going to need to use an image intensifier on those things. Otherwise the cores will be too faint."

And so it was arranged. Rich Ironsides, a genial chap with such a wry sense of humour that Morgan couldn't tell when he was joking, and when not, turned out to be a good companion:

"You take care of the universe Morgue, I'll look after my baby." He patted his electronic eye.

"How does it work?"

"Developed by the military for seeing the Viet Cong at night. It can spot a gook taking a crap five miles away."

"Then what?"

"K-Boom."

"How nasty."

"Yep it is Morgue. You'd think they'd have the decency not to shit in Uncle Sam's back yard."

The 90-inch was a squat beast of a telescope that looked like a giant mortar. The Boller and Chivens spectrograph, about the size of a large motor-cycle, was bolted to its bottom end, and Rich bolted his image-intensifier under that.

"This baby'll pick up ten per cent of the photons falling on it."

"Doesn't sound much." Morgan was disappointed.

"That's still ten times as many as your unaided photographic emulsion. An'
then it juices 'em up a million times, amplifies 'em so every little one makes a mark on your photographic plate. With this sucker Morgue you'll be faster than the 200-inch."

Now Morgan was impressed.

Rich, who'd already used the 90-inch, showed him how to use the big spectrograph, how to load its tiny plate, how to rotate the grating, how to focus the camera, how to get the galaxy onto the slit, how to switch on the comparison lamp, how to use the 'moonlight eliminator' and how to operate the shutter.

Morgan was slightly nervous at the thought of operating the world's third largest telescope. He practiced with his eyes shut so that later on he would be able to operate in total darkness.

When night fell Rich tactfully retreated to the control room, allowing Morgan to make his own mistakes.

Morgan climbed up onto the observing platform, a large flat-topped trolley that could be moved about or jacked upward so that the observer could always look through the eye-piece wherever the telescope was pointing in the sky. At least it was far safer than the 36-inch, having a low safety-railing around it.

Using his walkie-talkie Morgan ordered the night assistant to set on the first galaxy. The immense dome rumbled round, the 90-inch tilted like a giant howitzer against the stars. When the telescope settled he pressed on the paddle button and the platform began to whine upward into the darkness. Then he manoeuvred it about until he was close to the spectrograph, which was now canted over at a crazy angle. Inch by inch he manoeuvred himself upwards and sideways until his face was opposite the big eyepiece. Hanging the paddle on the railing of his platform, now probably a dozen feet in the air – though he could see nothing in the blackness, he groped gingerly forward until he could feel his eye-lashes touching the convex swell of glass. And there, sitting almost in the centre of the field of view, was a bright elliptical swarm of light. It was his first galaxy clearly seen – NGC 5077 by name. He stared at it, trying to think what else it reminded him of. Apparently greenish white in colour, bright in the centre, its smooth diffuseness tailed off so gradually into the surrounding darkness that there was no telling where it ended, or if it ended at all. He knew it was swarming with hundreds of billions of stars, most of them extremely ancient Red Giants, but at the colossal distance of the galaxy, one hundred and twenty million light years, they were far too faint to be seen individually. The brightest of them would still be a thousand times too faint to be seen even through this giant telescope. He could infer the galaxy's distance only because someone had measured its spectrum back in the nineteen thirties, taking all night on the world's then biggest telescope, and found that it had a redshift of 2,500 kilometres a second. that is to say it was being hurried away from the Earth, and from the Solar System, and from the Milky Way to which the Solar System belonged, by the expansion of the entire Universe. He stared at it in wonder. The photons he was seeing it by had been on their way to his eye, through the voids of intergalactic space, for one hundred and twenty million years. They were far older than Mankind, older than the apes, older than the oldest monkeys, older than the mammals. In fact they came from the age of the dinosaurs, the last of which had gone extinct sixty five million years ago, in the Cretaceous.

"You OK Morgue?" Rich's voice came up from the darkness below.

"I'm lost in wonder. Do you realise just how old these photons are?"

"Nope, but I do know they cost a cent each and you've just blown a year's salary."

"Huh!" Morgan snorted "If Congress ever finds out that your image-intensifier throws away ninety per cent of the light, they'll draft you to Vietnam."

Rich retreated to the warmth of the control room.

Morgan stared into the very heart, the nucleus of NGC 5077, knowing that it contained a compact radio source and therefore, quite probably, a Dark Monster, a quiescent quasar. But he could see no discontinuity, nothing that marked the nucleus sharply out from the rest of the surrounding galaxy. It was time to take a spectrum, which ought to be more revealing

He tweaked a knob until a ghostly pair of cross-hairs could just be seen, illuminated by the palest orange light, in the centre of the field of view. Using the paddle he guided the telescope until the galaxy was exactly centred on the cross hairs. Then he slid the eyepiece mirror sideways until the galaxy disappeared down though a dark hole in it down into the spectrograph. Transferring his eye to the much smaller spectrograph eye-piece he could now see a magnified image of the galaxy reflected back off the spectrograph mirror. That mirror was divided in two by a long thin black crack which was the entrance aperture to the spectrograph itself. He manoeuvred the telescope until the nucleus, and just the nucleus, disappeared down into the crack. Then he transferred back to the big eyepiece and manoeuvred the cross-hairs until they lay exactly over a faint but clearly visible star in the foreground Milky Way. So long as he maintained the guide-star on the cross hairs, so long the nucleus of the galaxy would be shining its light down through the crack into the spectrograph where it would be minutely split into its various colours before being focussed into the camera. As the Earth turned on its axis so the galaxy would move across the sky, and the telescope would have to follow it. Its hundred ton frame was supported on a thin film of oil so that it could rotate oppositely to the Earth's rotation and so follow the target across the sky. But this guidance mechanism could never be perfect, especially on a new telescope with teething troubles like the 90-inch, so he would have to check the guidance by eye every minute or so by looking at the guide-star relative to the cross hairs.

With the telescope aimed he felt in his pocket and pulled out a steel box the size of a cigarette packet, which contained the precious photographic plate which would store the light. Feeling by hand in the darkness he bolted it to the bottom of Rich's image intensifier then opened its dark slide so as to expose the plate to the light.

"OK Bob" he called down to the night assistant through the walkie-talkie "We are set on then nucleus of NGC 5077. Count me down for a forty-five minute exposure."

"'Kay Tom. Fahve, Fower, Three, Two, One, Go."

Morgan opened the spectrograph shutter and checked the eye-piece to see the guide-star on the cross hairs. He was excited. This would be his first serious spectroscopic observation, the first observing program initiated and directed by himself and his first attempt to observe the extra-galactic universe – the vast universe beyond the Milky Way.

He jumped in the darkness when Rich's voice broke through on the intercom:

"Morgue, you remembered to open *both* dark slides?"

"Yes thanks."

"An' you checked the galaxy on the slit jaws?"

"Yep."

"Then you're goin' baby. Want some music to keep you company?"

A few moments later Beethoven's Pastoral Symphony was echoing and clanging round the dome, and seemingly around the cosmos beyond.

He sat back on a stool in the darkness. The telescope was so huge above him that only by craning far out to one side of the platform could he look through the slit in the dome and see the stars. Cold high altitude air blew inside his sports jacket making him shiver. There'd been so much to do that afternoon that he'd forgotten to don his pyjamas underneath his shirt. But he was more than contented. Four years ago he'd stormed out of Bellfounder's office a broken man. And here he was in command of the world's most modern large telescope, investigating a galaxy which might well contain the closest known Black Hole.

That reminded him. He reached out in the darkness and found that the telescope had already moved a significant distance away, too far for him to look through the eye-piece any longer. Using the paddle he moved the high platform on which he stood, in pursuit. With little jerks and lifts he manoeuvred his eyeball back up to the eye-piece and re-aligned the guide star.

Beethoven's romantic accompaniment, rolling and thundering about his ears, made the alignment of a prick of light with dim crosshairs even more banal than it already was. He needed the cosmos to be romantic too. He transferred his gaze to the spectrograph eye-piece where he could stare at his galaxy reflecting off the slit jaws like moonlight off a calm sea. His imagination squeezed through the eyepiece, launched off the giant telescope mirror and leapt across a hundred and twenty million light years of intergalactic space. He imagined himself floating between the billion Red Giant stars which made up that galaxy, imagined himself at the eye-piece of a twin telescope looking backward towards the Milky Way, towards the Sun, towards the Earth, towards himself in the Arizona mountains. It was entirely possible, given the billion stars out there, and the ten billion possible planets, that on one of them a creature, not entirely unlike himself, was that very night staring back.

What would he wonder? What would he see?

To begin with the Milky Way was a Spiral galaxy, far more spread out, far dimmer than an Elliptical. Even in a 90-inch telescope it would be difficult to pick up by eye. And his twin out there would face a far larger problem All those Red Giants around him would illuminate his own sky like a dozen full Moons. The consequent glare of his atmosphere would hide the Milky Way from all possibility of detection. Indeed it would impossible for such an alien astronomer to know of the existence of *any* spiral galaxy. He would be building up a distorted picture of the universe bereft of all spiral galaxies, indeed of any galaxies much dimmer than his own. He would be like a man in a lighted room looking out through his window at the darkened world. He would see other lighted windows – but not the buildings to which they belonged. He would see the street lamps, but not the trees, and certainly not the hilltops beyond. He would be a prisoner in his local cell of light.

This thought arrested Morgan. He felt sorry for his poor twin creature who would be forever blind to most of the wonders of the universe. And he would never know his own blindness. He would no doubt, if he were like a Man, build up a world picture of the cosmos, a narrative, missing its most essential ingredients. And if it didn't fit together he would no doubt conjure up plausible imaginary features, until it possessed the coherence he craved for. It would be a fairy story partly composed of fact, partly inhabited by imaginary genies who could supply the services of spiral galaxies which, in his prison of light, he would never ever see.

'Poor Blind Creature' Morgan thought, 'doomed forever to dwell in a distorted, impoverished world, a world of theoretical, nonsensical fabrications. Telescopes would not be enough, nor curiosity, nor the most scrupulous honesty. Blinded by light, an Elliptical-galaxy - astronomer is condemned to live in a Phantasmagoria of his own imaginings.'

"Forty-fahve coming up Tom." Morgan was jolted from his astronomical revery by the abrupt cessation of Beethoven. ".....Fahve, Fower, Three, Two, One, Zeero."

Morgan closed the two slides that cut off the galaxy light, unclipped the plate-holder from the image-tube and put it in his pocket and lowered the platform down fifteen or more feet to the dome floor. From there his dark-adapted eyes could see star fields blazing through the dome slit. The silence, after the rip-roaring Pastorale, was deafening. The telescope was a scaffolding of blackness against the much brighter heaven

"You want me to take over?" Rich was an unseen shadow in the blackness.

"Would you? I need to develop this plate and look at it. Go for 45 minutes on NGC 4374. Bob's got the position."

The small dark-room was off to one side of the dome. He switched on the dim red-light which wouldn't ruin his dark adaptation. He checked around for scorpions, well known denizens of this corner, and placed the metallic plate holder – which was now very cold to the touch – on the bench. The trays of chemicals he had prepared that afternoon. He dipped the thermometer into the developer and found it be one degree below the specified nineteen. He popped the heating coil in and counted ten seconds aloud. Good. The temperature came within range. Next he set the big photographer's timer to three minutes before switching off the red-light.

In total darkness he picked up the plate-holder, pulled back the slide and tipped the thin glass plate, not much bigger than a postage stamp, into the palm of his right hand, being careful not to touch the precious emulsion-side. Putting down the holder and using touch alone he transferred the plate, emulsion side up, into the warm smelly developer. His right hand reached up and set the clock, with its dim luminous dial, ticking. His left switched on the tray rocker which would ensure that the emulsion was smoothly developed.

All he could do now was wait. This was the Moment of Truth. If he was right the spectrum would show faint traces of quasar light superposed on the majority of ordinary starlight. Stars had dark bands in their spectra whereas quasars had bright bands corresponding especially to ionised Oxygen, and Hydrogen.

The clock buzzed three minutes. Groping gently into the developer he lifted the plate by its edges, washed it briefly in the wash tray and transferred it to the fixer tray. He counted fifteen seconds aloud and impatiently turned on the red-light,

Peering into the fixer he could see that the plate was at least exposed. In the centre of the postage stamp was a thin band of darkness – it was a negative – two centimetres long but less than half a millimetre wide.

He washed the plate thoroughly and dried it with the hair-drier. Then he placed it on the light-tray, turned up the light source just enough, and swung the microscope into place above it.

The spectrum was almost perfectly exposed – which was pure luck. He picked out at once, down the violet end of the spectrum, the famous twin H and K absorption lines of Calcium that were apparent in nearly every galaxy spectrum and which Slipher and Hubble had used to discover the expansion of the Universe. Being present in all Red Giant stars they were naturally present in all Elliptical galaxies, whose spectra were dominated by Red Giant light. To the red of them he picked up the G-band – due to the iron in starlight. Then well to the red again the Sodium D line due not to stars but to the smoky gas between them.

But he was looking eagerly not for dark lines but bright ones. And there they were, tiny little black smudges on his negative. There was one down in the ultraviolet near the Calcium doublet – that must be Oxygen Two at 3727 Angstroms wavelength. Then much stronger, near 5000 Angstroms, the 4959 – 5007 doublet of doubly ionised Oxygen. And finally out in the very red the triplet of Hydrogen alpha 6563 flanked by Nitrogen 6548 and 6584.

Morgan breathed for the first time in a minute, the oxygen suffusing through his blood with a little flood of exaltation. A long chain of reasoning had led to a theoretical prediction. And here was the evidence that he was probably thinking along the right lines; tiny little smudges, barely containing a dozen photographic grains each, betraying the presence of quasar- like light in the heart of this galaxy where, according to his theory, it ought to be. Just as he had surmised, NGC 5077 probably contained a miniature quasar, or perhaps a true Dark Monster, but one asleep for now. Moreover, as he could see at once, the quasar-like emission lines were redshifted by the same amount as the ordinary stellar absorption lines. In other words quasar redshifts were presumably cosmological after all, a consequence of the expansion of the Universe at large, and not of some exotic physics associated with quasars themselves, as he had supposed back in Worcestershire. The high redshift quasars had therefore to be immense distances away, and consequently ultra luminous.

He stood up, feeling a real glow of satisfaction, recalling the long train of reasoning, coincidence, interaction and plain luck that had led to this evidence: first Jack Cockle photocopying on to him, in Worcestershire, the early quasar papers. Then his Superstar Theory, dashed by Bellfounder. Then Wagoner and his stellar mass-loss idea which had led to the construction of the Cynthia program by Morgan. Then his attempt to teach himself spectroscopy on the 21-inch with Ann. Next his visit to New York and his unplanned attendance at Dave Heeschen's talk on Radio Elliptical galaxies. Then his discussions in Long Beach with Frank on quasar distances. And finally, after seeing the output from Cynthia, came his 'proof' that the gas collapsing in Elliptical galaxies could never fragment into stars and so must aggregate to form a single coherent nuclear monster.

In fact it was almost too good to be true. He pinched himself mentally, searching for the flaw which he had learned to expect in almost every facile scientific argument. The obvious one here was that he had looked only at a single galaxy – and one swallow never made a summer. Moreover he'd never looked at Elliptical galaxy spectra before. Perhaps they all contained, for whatever reason, very weak emission lines like this. Hot young stars, or dying Planetary Nebulae might mimic the same effect. Fortunately he had more substantial tests. At that moment Rich was looking at a second Radio Elliptical, but one which, according to Heeschen, did not contain a compact quasar-like radio source in its nucleus. If that too exhibited emission lines then Morgan's whole theory would fall to ground, or at least look implausible.

He hung up the plate to dry properly, switched off the red light, and returned to consult the Universe. Groping through two light-tight doors he found himself out on the floor of the dome again staring up at the frame of the huge telescope picked out against the stars. Beethoven had given way to Bob Dylan singing 'Like a Rolling Stone'. He could make out the black silhouette of Rich Ironsides high above his head, huddled up to the spectrograph eye-piece. Out of the warm darkroom Morgan shivered in the air. The stars, which had twinkled visibly when they first entered the dome at nightfall, were now steady as a rock. The whole rationale for coming out into the desert, for perching telescopes high up mountains, and then, as with the 90-inch, constructing them atop very tall towers, was to reach this steady air, free of turbulence, through which the Universe could be studied with maximum clarity. Up here they were almost in Space. Morgan realised that the 'Seeing', as astronomers called it, must now be close to perfect.

Groping through two sets of curtains Morgan entered the control room where, in a very dim light, the night-assistant Bob McAllister was sitting at the control desk admiring a girl's buttocks, or rather a photograph of a girl's buttocks in 'Penthouse' magazine.

"Not bad" Morgan commented, looking over Bob's shoulder "But not as beautiful as my wife's."

"Jeeze Tom, you lucky bastard. Yes Ann is a looker. What you wastin ' your time up here for?"

"Man cannot live by buttocks alone Bob – it's in the Bible, didn't you know?"

Morgan switched off the music and spoke to Ironsides, out in the darkness, by telecom:

"That was a perfect exposure Rich. So stick to forty-five minutes for this one too. And what do you think? It's got emission lines!"

"Wowee!"

"If you'd like to finish this one and develop it, I'll load another plate-holder and do the next galaxy."

" 'Kay Morgue. But switch my music back on. It's lonely out here baby."

Back in the dark-room Morgan took the box of unexposed plates out of the fridge. It had cost him painstaking hours that afternoon to cut the tiny plates from a much larger glass plate with a diamond glass-cutter in total darkness. Switching off the red-light he opened the box, felt about for a plate and lifted it to his lips. Using the tip of his tongue as a probe he licked a spot near the edge, looking for the side with the active emulsion. Unlike the glass side it was slightly tacky to the tongue. Every astronomer's nightmare was to load a plate backwards and so throw away all of the light.

During the course of the night the temperature plummeted as the desert radiated away its heat into space, unhindered by the dry mountain air. Morgan shivered fiercely, and dreamt about his warm pyjamas back in the dormitory. He also had time to sober up. One galaxy with emission lines didn't prove anything much. He remembered from his reading that one galaxy in five had emission lines anyway. Only the statistics, over a fair number of galaxies, would be convincing. All, or almost all of the ones with compact radio sources would have to have emission lines, whereas all, or almost all of the ones without such sources, would have to lack emission.

And so it turned out. Over the course of six clear moonless nights spread over two months, he and Rich observed a dozen Elliptical galaxies. None of the three normal ones showed any sign of emission whilst seven out of the eight compact ones did. And the anomalous one, which caused Morgan some puzzlement, turned out to have a red core, suggesting that its emission might very well be cloaked by smoke, smoke which tended to give a characteristic red colour, as it did to the setting sun.

So it all fitted together. Almost. Unfortunately the emission lines they found were similar but not identical to the emission lines found in quasars, which were usually extremely broad, suggesting that they had been emitted or scattered by gas exploding outwards at tens of thousands of kilometres a second. In the Ellipticals however, they were only hundreds of kilometres a second wide. Worried by this huge discrepancy Morgan went to talk to experts. They pointed out that his mini-quasars would never have the power to accelerate gas to such high speeds. So it was consistent after all.

They wrote up their results and submitted them in a brief paper to the prestigious Astrophysical Journal, which published it immediately. And the even more prestigious 'Nature' magazine paid them the extraordinary complement of reviewing it for the general scientific reader. Frank rung up from Cambridge to congratulate Morgan:

"Your result is so clear cut, but so beautifully understated. It's not conclusive mind you, and I can tell you it doesn't convert the sceptics. All the same it is good evidence in favour of the Cosmological interpretation of quasar redshifts, evidence which no one can ignore. And the implication that most, perhaps all Elliptical galaxies, contain slumbering Black Holes, is obviously fascinating. Well done. Now you've published three pieces of absolutely first rate observational research: the Crab, the polarisation of pulsars, now this. You're on your way Tom, you're leaving me behind. What are you going to do next?"

"Find another job – if I can. This one runs out in six months."

"Surely they'll offer you one at Arizona?"

"Huh; they're sacking most of the existing staff. Anyway I don't think I'd want to stay."

"Why not?"

"It's the atmosphere here right now Frank, with so many careers on the line, so much rivalry, so much desperation, so much disappointment, and so much hatred. It reminds me of the time I worked as an undergraduate in a bar in Catalonia. I got to know some novillos, young toreadors going out to face their first bulls; the Moment of Truth and all that. Now I see it again during our weekly internal seminars: the yellow-white faces, the trembling hands; the horn, in the form of a devastating question, ready to hook up under the ribs. Last week I watched a friend of mine hooked into the air."

With scarcely a thousand professional astronomers on Earth, and twice that number of aspirants jostling to seize any vacancy left by death or retirement, jobs in astronomy, especially good ones, were the very devil to find. Often posts weren't advertised, having been promised to someone waiting in the wings. And when they were they often drew two hundred or more serious applications.

In one respect Morgan was lucky. If astronomy was going to be a high adrenalin sport then he knew he was definitely suited to it. He had always lived most intensely when the fast bowler flung down the opening ball at him, when the boxing bell rang for the first round. He hadn't expected it, but astronomy looked like climbing without a rope. He'd done it before – and enjoyed it. But hadn't he also fallen off?

But enjoyment wouldn't be enough. Nor could he depend on luck. To stay in the game, as Morgan was absolutely determined to do, he would need some philosophy, some strategy that would guide him through the fray. Academic brains, he was relieved to find, obviously weren't enough. The college star who could reel off Quantum Electrodynamics didn't necessarily have the judgement, the curiosity, the imagination or the stamina to succeed as an explorer. As far as he could see successful astronomers were a very mixed lot. Like the variety of creatures in a tidal pool that had each discovered a personal ecological niche, an individual survival strategy to see them through. But what was his own strategy to be?

Some younger astronomers became obsessed with job hunting. They listened to every rumour-mill, applied for every vacancy, endlessly rewrote their CVs. Instinctively Morgan knew that was both undignified and wrong. If you became obsessed with your career then how could you be obsessed with the Universe – which surely every successful astronomer had to be? He wanted to be an explorer, not a businessman. He wanted to enjoy astronomy, not just earn a living from it.

One way to locate a successful personal strategy was to identify what he liked most about astronomy and could do best. And that wasn't hard. He liked thinking about the Universe. He loved to lie in bed in the morning, while Ann was till sound asleep, reading papers about galaxies, doing calculations about quasars, evaluating the evidence for and against cosmological hypotheses. He liked computing, and he enjoyed observing, but he loved thinking and calculating by far the best of all. He was, he knew, endlessly curious, and nothing made him happier than following up a paper trail of clues in the library. And yet, now that his career was fairly launched, there seemed all too little leisure left for thinking. Observing time had to be applied for;

equipment organised; people persuaded; data reduced; papers written; referees convinced; travel planned; money obtained; expenses accounted for….. Thus a whole frantic week could pass without a moment's thought for the cosmos. This began to worry him so much that he quizzed his colleagues. Yes they too lived in the same frantic state, filling in expense claims over lunch, answering referees comments in the airport lounge….The average successful astronomer guessed that he could spend no more than one percent of his time seriously thinking. The more senior ones, the ones with enviable permanent jobs, had correspondingly burdensome responsibilities. They had students to teach, exams to grade, money to raise, committees to attend, assistants to supervise, and so on and so on. It was doubtful if they had any time to think at all. Some of them confessed that they had no opportunity to read a serious scientific paper from one month to the next. They relied on coffee time scuttlebutt, on seminars and conferences, and above all on their own assistants and graduate students to keep them up to date. Morgan realised that the one thing that astronomers were supposed to do, and to do well on behalf of mankind, was to think hard about the Universe; and yet it was the one activity that most of them had no time left for. Such thinking as was done was mostly done by PhD students of limited knowledge and experience. What a paradox; what a scandal; what an opportunity! He resolved that, come hell or high water, he would spend at least ten per cent of *every* day thinking. And he would do it first, before anything else. He was a short sleeper and an early waker, whereas Ann was the reverse. He would take his books, his papers, and his slide-rule to bed at night, ready to think quietly for at least two and possibly three hours every morning. And two of those seven mornings would be devoted to astronomy beyond his own immediate interests; to advances made by other workers in entirely different fields. Morgan knew he was good at thinking, being both imaginative and dogged. And if he could devote ten times as much time to thinking as most of his colleagues then it might give him a decisive edge. But other things would have to give.

And what kind of an astronomer did Morgan want to become? There appeared to be broadly three kinds. There were Theoreticians who spun theories to explain the Universe and worked with equations and computers. There were Instrumentalists who worked in labs where they devised, built and tested the equipment needed to observe the cosmos, ranging from spectrographs to light detectors. Finally came the Observers who spent their nights up in the mountains observing the skies.

In many respects the Instrumentalists were the most important. If they built innovative or more sensitive equipment, then discoveries seemed to inevitably follow. Quasars and Pulsars for instance, were the direct result of innovative radio instrumentation. Theirs however was a precarious and highly time consuming craft. A new technology could render their skills obsolete overnight. Even worse, a sophisticated new instrument might take several years to develop, years when they would have no time to think about the Universe at all, years when no new scientific papers were likely to emerge. Thus Instrumentalists could fall hopelessly behind in the brutal race for tenure.

At the other extreme Theorists could run off papers by the dozen. But that in itself devalued their currency. Very few such papers, or their authors, turned out to be of lasting worth. Theorists were the most numerous, the most vocal, but also the most expendable members of the profession. However those few who did survive into the tenured ranks enjoyed, Morgan thought, an influence out of all proportion to their contribution to the science. Because only they had the time to attend all the conferences, to write popular books, appear on the media, and meddle in politics, they frequently finished on top of the astronomical heap. For instance the astronomers known to the public, men like Hoyle and Bellfounder, were Theorists to a man.

But the men who made the discoveries, the men whose names were handed down through history, men like Herschel, Hubble and Galileo, were the observers – the glamour boys of the profession. So why didn't he, why didn't everyone become an observer? The answer was simple. A single telescope could support the ambitions of no more than a dozen observers. And as there were less than a dozen competitive telescopes on Earth – telescopes of sufficient size, sited on cloudless mountain sites, there were posts for scarcely more than a hundred observers on Earth. Each telescope had its own privileged team of observers and if you weren't on that team you were 'out'. And how you got on such a team wasn't clear to Morgan. Most of the observers he knew, were the lucky protégées or apprentices of famous predecessors, as Frank was of Bellfounder.

All these reflections on his 'career prospects' didn't come naturally to Morgan. He was above all an emotional creature who reached important decisions on intuitive, not rational grounds. He could no more drive himself to become a particular sort of astronomer than he could drive himself to marry a girl with whom he was not hopelessly in love. Calculating about the Universe was one thing, calculating about himself and his life was quite another. In any case he was so innocent, so unformed as an astronomer. The day to day winds still blew him hither and thither. An exciting talk, an interesting paper, a new insight or an unfamiliar idea could set him sailing off in an entirely new direction. There were so many fascinating fields, so much to learn, that it seemed foolish to wed himself so soon to this particular field or that.

Take galaxies. Of course he'd known about them before and given superficial lectures on them to his evening-class students back in London. But it was only through the accident of Wagoner putting him onto the problem of collapsing gas in Ellipticals that he'd gotten seriously, professionally interested in galaxies. And the more he read and thought about them, the more fascinating they became. Their beautiful shapes, their momentous connections with every branch of astrophysics, their sheer elusiveness when seen through the telescope eyepiece, all these contributed to their romance for him. Even through the giant 90-inch they could be seen only during the darkest phases of the Moon. Monsters tens of thousands of light-years across, these creatures of darkness vanished beneath the slightest hint of moonlight.

Who can say what excites illogical passion? For Morgan it was probably galaxies' sheer mysteriousness. These islands in space containing billions of stars each, were the fundamental building blocks, the primal cells of the Universe. And yet, because they were so hard to see, and were such vast distances away, astronomers knew next to nothing about them. As late as 1886 a distinguished astronomer called Robert Ball was reflecting on deciphering the distances to the 'nebulae' as they were known then, nebulae' being the Latin for 'clouds'. He said "….but the difficulties are apparently insurmountable in the case of nebulae and no method has been devised which will enable us to solve this mighty problem….It is believed that some of these nebulae are sunk in space to such an appalling distance that the light takes centuries before it reaches the Earth……We have reached a point where man's intellect begins to fail to yield him any more light."

How much more appalled Ball would have been if he'd lived another fifty years. Thanks to the development of astrophotography, and to the construction of monster telescopes in the mountains of California, the very largest nebula, the Andromeda nebula, which can just be seen in perfect conditions with the naked eye as four times larger than the Moon, was found to contain some few variable stars which waxed and waned in a regular pulsating fashion from night to night. Using the newly opened 100-inch on Mount Wilson near Los Angeles Edwin Hubble took dozens of plates of the monster over a number of years. He found a perfect correspondence between the periods of these variable stars, which ranged from days to months, and their apparent brightnesses, with the longest period ones being the brightest. This was the vital clue because a similar correspondence had previously been found among variable stars in our own Milky Way and in the neighbouring Magellanic Clouds. Hubble's variables in Andromeda were presumably of the same kind as the Cepheid variables in the Milky Way, rare monster stars with luminosities thousands of times greater than the Sun's. But Hubble's variables in Andromeda were incredibly faint, at the very limit of detection with his giant telescope in perfect conditions. It followed that the Andromeda Nebula, to which they belonged, must be at an enormous distance away, not a hundred light years as Robert Ball had incredulously supposed, but ten thousand times further still – at a million. And as Andromeda looked far bigger than a myriad spiral nebulae, photographed or barely seen by man, it was presumably much closer. The smallest appearing nebulae must then be billions of light years, that is to say thousands of millions of light years away. And ten years later still, using the same telescope, but in the 1940s, during the war when the lights of Los Angeles were blacked out leaving Mount Wilson dramatically darker, Walter Baade showed that Hubble's distances were still far too small. The nebulae, the 'galaxies' as they were to become known, were ten times further away still.

The consequent shock to astronomy was akin to the shock felt by geologists around 1910 when radio-activity forced them to accept that the Earth was not thousands, but billions of years old. The credo of a generation brought up to believe in the literal interpretation of the Bible was crushed in an earthquake. Many couldn't bring themselves to believe in the new truths. And yet the discoveries of Deep Time by the geophysicists and of Deep Space by the astronomers were intimately related. Light certainly travelled at a finite speed so that Hubble's nebulae, billions of light years away, could not have been seen without billions of years for their light to reach the Earth.

Morgan was transfixed by his first sight of galaxies in the 90-inch. He suffered a coupe de foudre as the French would say. He was in love. His searches in the library quickly revealed how little men knew about the galaxies. Men knew they were titanic islands of stars in Space, containing up to a million million stars each , though, because of the distances, their individual stars would be seen only in the case our closest companion galaxies, such as Andromeda. Each island was huge – about a hundred thousand light years across. Because its volume was so immense its light was very thinly stretched out across the sky, rendering it extremely difficult to see. In other words its contrast to the surrounding night sky was very low.

Some galaxies, like the Milky Way, were spinning discs called 'Spirals'. The others, called 'Ellipticals' looked, as he knew, more like giant swarms of radiating bees. Whereas the Spirals contained cold gas and smoke, out of which further generations of stars could and did form, the Ellipticals appeared bereft of such cold gas, and looked very ancient. Some galaxies were blue, some were red. Some were tiny 'dwarfs' a ten thousandth of the luminosity of a giant like the Milky Way. Some were isolated while the others, Ellipticals especially, congregated together in giant Clusters of a thousand or more. Each galaxy was typically separated from its nearest neighbours by a few million light years, a distance equivalent to a hundred of its own diameters.

But the questions about galaxies far outnumbered the answers. How old were they and how had they been formed? Why were they so massive – and yet so diffuse? Were the stars in them just like the ones in our Milky Way – or were they different? Were they made out of the same chemical elements as our Solar System – and in the same proportions? Were they evolving or were they eternal? Why did some of them emit copious radio emission – whilst most did not? Did they fortuitously radiate all their energy in the few narrow bands which penetrated the earth's atmosphere, such as the optical band, or was there a lot more of their radiation to see from Space? Why did some spin, and some apparently not? What happened when they collided with one another? Were there invisible ones whose stars had either all burned out – or radiated their energy in bands still undetectable through the atmosphere? Morgan worked out that there were five tons of air in the atmospheric column through which the 90-inch had to look, a veritable ocean of it. The wonder was that any radiation from the cosmos got through it at all. The tiny trickle that did leak through was far surpassed by all the gamma radiation, the X-radiation, the Ultra-violet radiation, the Infra-red radiation and the microwave radiation that did not. Galaxies might appear as quite different beasts in such unseen radiations.

Expecting to find dozens of books on galaxies in the library Morgan was disconcerted to find a mere handful. And indeed beyond Hubble's classic "The Realm of the Nebulae" there was almost nothing for the professional like himself. It gradually dawned on him that only five men, Vesto Slipher, Edwin Hubble, Fritz Zwicky, Erik Holmberg and Gerard de Vaucouleurs had ever done any significant research on galaxies. Slipher discovered the redshifts, Hubble the relation between redshifts and brightness – which others had interpreted as the Expansion of the Universe; Zwicky the clustering; Holmberg had measured the sizes and de Vaucouleurs had compiled a bird-watchers catalogue of all that was known about a couple of thousand of the largest and therefore presumably the nearest of the galaxies. With great difficulty, like Marco Polo returning from China with fabulous but scarcely credible tales, they had assembled a tiny but intriguing caucus of knowledge. Fritz Zwicky had shown that for a Cluster of Galaxies to hold itself together, every galaxy within it would have to weigh hundreds of times more than could be inferred from its visible population of stars. What could that possibly mean? It was bizarre – literally beyond belief.

This meagre accumulation of knowledge was all that could be expected, seeing how difficult galaxies were to observe. A handful of men working on a handful of telescopes, all in the South Western corner of the United States, and only during the darkest of cloudless nights when the Moon was down, had been able to see anything of galaxies at all. For now galaxies were little more than tantalising question marks in the sky, as puzzling to modern man as the movement of the constellations must have been to the ancient Sumerians.

The more he read about them, the more he thought about them, the more Morgan fell in love with galaxies. So little was known, so much was to be learned. Here was a Pacific Ocean of ignorance upon which he could launch his tiny barque of curiosity and set out for the Blessed Isles. Surely, during his lifetime, men would launch telescopes above the bars of the imprisoning Earth, see the dimmest structures from the total blackness of Space, and receive whispers at other wavelengths, from continents out there waiting to be discovered.

CHAPTER 10
WILDGOOSE
1970

Morgan now had three fascinating careers. In the daytime he worked with the computer on Cynthia. On dark nights he was up on the mountain tops searching for pulsars or nuclei. And in every spare moment in between he was in the lecture hall or the library trying to learn more, particularly about his beloved galaxies. Sometimes he'd close up the telescope dome out at Kitt Peak at five a.m, then drive the seventy miles back to Tucson through the serried ranks of Saguaro cacti standing black against the orange dawn, snatch breakfast with Ann, and be in a lecture hall by eight. He'd sleep in the afternoon and be back up at Kitt Peak for dinner and another night with the stars. Someone so in love with his profession needed very little sleep.

One morning he was lying in bed doing calculations on galaxies when Ann, who he'd thought was asleep, interrupted:
"I'm jealous."
"What?' She'd spoken more sharply than usual.
"I'm jealous. You look so incredibly absorbed, so happy. Even when you're making love to me you don't look like that. I feel cast aside, like an old wife for a new mistress. Who is she Morgan?"
"She" he said, putting aside pen and notebook and kissing the tip of Ann's nose "Is more ravishing than any houri, more demanding than any duchess, more satisfying than any wife, even gorgeous mine. She is the Extragalactic Universe and I shall lie with, and conceive many brilliant children upon her, on every morning of the rest of my life."
"Until your real wife wakes up."
"Just so my Cloudesly."
Ann sat up with her arms round her knees, looking at the wall:
"I used to be like that – back in London. Almost every morning I'd wake up and immediately my mind would slip into the problem I was working on at the Admiralty. Everything else would be forgotten. It was so fascinating......."
"Isn't it the same now?"
"No it isn't. Yes it's the same kind of work but here I'm working on long range stuff. There there was an urgency, a race against time. There was instant feedback; colleagues to argue with; daily success and daily failure. I needed that, just as you need your telescopes and your galaxies. When I see you now Tom I'm envious, conscious of what I'm missing. You're so lucky!"
"I know" he said "Don't think I don't know. I can't believe that just four years ago I was a production car worker in Birmingham: bored out of my mind , de-humanised by my surroundings, a tiny almost worthless cog in a vast almost worthless machine. I keep on pinching myself and saying 'When is all this going to stop?' And if I don't get another decent job soon it *could* stop. Forever. Right now my career hangs by a thread."
He started applying for jobs as they appeared, advertised in 'Nature' or the Bulletin of the American Astronomical Society. Decent ones were rare while jobs suited to both his ambitions and Ann's constraints were non-existent. He wanted a post in extragalactic astronomy while she had to be sited where she

could keep in close contact with the Admiralty, much closer contact than she enjoyed in Arizona. Ideally she had to be sited close to either London or Washington.

The more he lived with her the more he realised just how bright Ann actually was. She would say things out of the blue, surprising unpredictable things, which sometimes made him think for days. Her mind was far less imaginative than his, but at the same time far more analytical and deductive. She could tear a weak mathematical argument to shreds in a moment, and when he asked for help with statistics – which he found extremely hard – she could often see to the heart of the problem within minutes.

"I'll still love you when you're an old bat." He announced one day.

"Thank you kindly Sir. You're so so romantic. Pray may I ask why? Not that I have any intention of becoming an old bat."

, "It's your brain. You'll never be dull or boring. Never. I never realised how entertaining one's partner's brain can be. How could a man ever live with a dumb blond?"

'Or a woman with a dull Tarzan?"

Ann was, he knew, making big sacrifices for him. Quite by accident he'd come across a letter, addressed to her, from the National Security Agency in Washington. They were trying to attract her away from the Admiralty with an enormous salary, a staggering salary by academic standards. But she would have to live within 25 miles of the NSA headquarters in Maryland. He waited to see if she would say anything to him, but she did not. Morgan inferred that she must be putting his career before her own.

He was short-listed for a tenure-track Assistant Professorship at the University of British Columbia in Vancouver. Ever since reading, as a boy, Negly Farson's 'Story of a Lake', he'd dreamed of British Columbia, of its forests, of its salmon, its islands and its Pacific fjords. He didn't tell Ann about the job he simply said he'd been invited to give a seminar there – which was true, but nevertheless dishonest. Vancouver wasn't on Ann's list of possible locations. She was bound to resist initially, but she might come round to it, he imagined, if she really liked Vancouver, and was given time to decide. He asked her to come, suggesting a short holiday on Vancouver Island afterwards.

They took an Air West DC9 to Los Angeles and changed there onto a Western Airlines Boeing 720. It was a superb flight in perfect weather giving them wonderful views of San Francisco, the Golden Gate bridge and later the Olympic Mountains sparkling with snow. They could even see individual fir trees sticking out of the snowfields.

"Gosh, theres's so much of America!" Ann exclaimed. "I want to see it all."

She was even more excited when the plane let down over the sea and scraped over innumerable wooded islets in the Strait of Georgia.

Their room in the faculty club at the University of British Columbia had the most spectacular view of any room they had ever occupied. The university lay on a headland and the club stood above a cliff with flowering lawns falling away beneath their window to the edge. Beyond, and across a great strait of blue water the wooded fjords and snow capped peaks of the North Shore glittered in the bright sun.

"Gosh I could live here darling." Ann sounded awestruck. "It's like 'The Alps on Sea'. Let's go outside." They found themselves in a Japanese water-garden where immense coloured carp glided lazily through lily ponds.

In the evening the Head of Astronomy, a very courteous Englishman, and his wife, took them back to their house for drinks. From their high apartment the views were breathtaking. The snow on the North Shore mountains glowed pink in the westering sun while to the right, up the Straits, the skyscrapers of down-town Vancouver were a blaze of light curving round the shore.

After drinks they drove through Vancouver, across the Lions Gate Bridge to the North Shore, then up a deep timbered valley beside the darkened Frazer River. From there they took a cable-car which climbed four thousand feet to the top of Grouse Mountain – the most prominent of the snow-clad peaks leaning over the city. The large car swayed between the tops of Douglas Firs like the gondola of an ascending balloon, opening a view of the city below with its myriad twinkling lights strung round all the bays and inlets of the shore. They could see individual skyscrapers and bridges, ships alight in the harbour, the university ablaze on its distant headland – and out across the Georgia Strait, lighthouses winking on darkened islands.

At the summit they debouched into The Grouse's Nest, a restaurant perched on stilts overhanging space, with vertiginous views down the ski slopes towards the sea and the city. Ann began to wonder why they were being so royally entertained, why her dinner of black cod, roast turkey and mushrooms, all served with excellent local wines, was so very good. Surely not all seminar speakers, and their wives, were treated like this?

They were woken in the morning by brilliant sunshine reflecting off the sea. Mrs Director came to pick up Ann and show her the sights while Morgan was closeted with the faculty and later delivered his seminar on 'The Formation of Stars in Interstellar Space'

When he got back to their room Ann was waiting:

"I've always trusted you Tom. Always. Without ever thinking. How could you do this to me?"

" Mrs ----- told you?"

"She didn't have to. She assumed I knew. It was so very embarrassing. But that's the least of it. The very least. You stupid stupid idiot!" She began crying.

He sat down on the bed beside her; put an arm round her shoulder, which she shook off.

"Look darling I had to. If I told you in Tucson you'd never have come. Now you've seen the place we can decide together. Anyway I had no idea they'd offer me the job – until this afternoon. How could I have decided, how could we decide, if you'd never seen the place? What do you think?"

"It's beautiful." Ann cried even harder. He's never seen her cry like this and found it awful. "You should never have put me in this position. Never, never, never!"

"If you don't want to come sweetheart, of course we won't. Of course we won't"

"But I do want to come. It's so lovely." She threw her arms round Morgan's neck. "We went round Stanley Park – and I've never seen such a beautiful place. And we saw a sea otter in the aquarium floating on her back giving birth to her baby. Mrs. ... couldn't tear me away. Not for hours and hours. But you've put me in a terrible position."

She got out her handkerchief and blew her nose, which had turned bright red:

"It's such a wonderful place, and such a perfect job for you. Do you know there were two hundred and thirty six applicants from all over the world? Mrs O told me. But as soon as they saw your references they wanted you Tom, and you alone, although you're not Canadian. If I say 'No' now it could ruin your whole career. But what about mine?" She stared at him, expecting an answer that he had no way of giving. It was a miserable night, the first bad night of their marriage.

The following morning they packed their bag and caught the ferry from Nanaimo to Vancouver Island. The sea of the Georgia Strait sparkled in the sunshine as the ferry wound its way through the sounds between the many islands, calling at tiny harbours to deposit and pick up passengers and vehicles. There was so much to see out on the strait: huge log rafts being hauled down from the North by tugs; salmon fishing vessels; huge container ships ploughing in from the Pacific; float -planes taking off and landing; sailing yachts and sea-going kayaks; skeins of water-birds and wild geese; distant views of Mount Baker an enormous snow-cone in the Olympic Peninsuula of Washington State. There being almost no rise or fall of tide the islands looked like lake islands, Chinese Willow-Pattern islands with the branches of their big fir trees hanging out over the sea and reflected in the calm water. After the aridness of Arizona the sheer smell of the sea drove Morgan almost mad with nostalgia. When they got to Saltspring Island with its apple orchards, its green lawns coming down to the water's edge, he couldn't help himself:

"You know I could live here for ever."

"It's idyllic isn't it? What a place to bring up children."

At the quay in Sidney there was a car waiting to take them up to the Dominion Astrophysical Observatory, where the telescopes that Morgan would use, were sited. There was a 74-inch up there, almost as big as the 90-inch at Steward. When it was commissioned, back in 1918, it had briefly been the largest telescope in the world, a monster built by Grubb-Parsons back in England. One glance at it was enough to make Morgan's heart fall. It was in completely the wrong place for a start; too far North, in a cloudy area, and on a low hilltop; not thousands of feet up in the clear dry air of the desert.

And the spectrograph on it was the original three-prism photographic instrument that may have been cutting-edge in 1918, but fifty years later was now completely obsolete. Were his astronomical career to depend on that he'd be opting for mediocrity and scientific oblivion. There was a sickening feeling in the pit of his stomach.

Outside the dome Ann put her arms round his waist and looked earnestly up at him:

"It's all right darling. I've decided. I think it was Saltspring Island that did it. If you want to come I'll come too. I'm sure I can arrange something."

"Thank God you feel like that Cloudesly." He put his arms round her shoulders and kissed her. "Isn't it beautiful. Couldn't we just live here darling? Did you see those wooden cottages round the lake at the bottom of the hill?"

He could feel her nodding her head silently against his neck.

"But we're not coming. I didn't join this profession just to become a professor. I want to be an astronomer and explore the universe. And I could never do that properly from here."

Ann looked up at him searchingly:

"You're not just saying this to please me Tom, are you?"

"I wish I could say 'Yes' darling. But it's an entirely selfish decision. We'd have withered away here – like two comfortable old biddies. I'd take up growing marrows and you'd be quilting in no time. No thanks. But I'm sorry. We've got far bigger adventures ahead of us than all this – beautiful as it may be."

When they arrived home in Arizona, after a few regretful days on the lush coast of Vancouver Island, bad news was waiting. Really bad news.

"Look" Ann said "Here's a letter from Ernie."

But it wasn't from Ernie Salt, it was from his father Bob:

Dear Tom

You'll be very sad to learn as our Ernie died last week. We knowed as you would have wanted to come to the funeral, but all on us, specially Ernie, decided not to tell you till now as you couldn't have afforded to come. Anyway there was more than 500 people at the reception at the Model Aero Club at Castle Bromwich where his mates gave a flying exhibition of some of his most famous models You'd have been lost in the crowd – like me and Valerie. I knew he was respected and that, but we never realised how many people across the world, some on them there, used his designs and were touched by his life. It was, as they said, a celebration of our Ernie's life, which we tried to enjoy with everybody else.

Ernie didn't go sudden, nor did he last a long time. Three month ago he started falling asleep in the middle of his work, or at meals, and he was very difficult to wake. We took him to Mr Small who said he was afeared the original diagnosis were right, and the tumour was growing down towards the brain stem. There was nowt more he could do.

The fits of unconsciousness grew more frequent, and longer. Sometimes we weren't sure he'd wake in the morning. And one morning he dain't. His Mum went in as usual with a mug of tea and there was our Ernie, his light on, plans for the mark VI on his lap, specs on his nose, asleep for ever.

We all knew it was a'coming, including Ernie. He were never sad and he tried to cheer us up believe it or no. He said as one way or another he'd had a better life than what he'd have done if he'd grown up healthy and been swallered in a factory. And I think he was right, though his Mum dain't. His one regret, he said, was that he'd never see his nephew and niece grow up. And of course he never broke the world endurance record – not flying it hisself. But his Mark V did. When his mates heard as he couldn't fly any more they got together and one of them flew it in Ernie's place. Ernie were sitting in his wheelchair, proud as Punch, when the V smashed the old German record by more'n two hour, and she might have gone on for an hour more if the International Officials hadn't stopped the flight because it were getting dark.

Ernie were worried about you Tom. He said as you'd done so much you'd be upset as you weren't there to see the record broke, or come to the funeral. But he was determined to see as we helped you, like you helped us, and the best we could think on was to see as you stayed in Arizona and made a success of astronomy, as he was sure you would. Anyway he rung up your Mum hisself and told her not to tell you about him. And he's written a letter to you as you'll get in few days. I've no idea as what's in it.

It's lonely here without him I can tell you. Dead lonely.

Best wishes

Bob Salt

PS. You remember that proposal what we wrote to NASA with your help, about building a super-long-range drone? Seems as they really liked it. Ernie got a big letter from them just before he died. Seems the Yanks are really interested in putting half a million dollars into a project to fly a really small drone across the Atlantic, like you suggested. Ernie was really chuffed about that. He'd already sketched a design of it. The Yanks would provide a navigation system based on satellites. Pity because it would have been a great project."

Ernie's letter arrived a couple of days later:
Dear Tom:

I wished as you'd seen the Mark V coming home. She done us all proud, including you. She'd have beat the record anyroad but your extra aspect-ratio helped her clean out of sight. If I had time to build a Mark VI, which I ain't, I'd push the wingtips out even further, though we might need inboard stiffening near the wing roots, and that would add some weight.

But this letter ain't about aircraft its about our Dad. He's devoted his entire life to me, over twenty-five year. Now what's he a'going to do?

You tell me 'cos I daint know. He aint sixty yet. All I do know is this; he talks about you like you was his other son. He's always talking about you, reading your letters over and over again, finding out about astronomy for 'isself, getting excited about your research, worrying about your career and your bleeding temper which, he says, could be your ruination if you daint look out.

So, instead of getting jealous, which I might 'a done, I'm leaving him to you. He is, as you know, an argumentative and opinionated old sod, but he's great father to have, and a great man.

So I'm leaving him entirely to you. You deserve each other.

Love

Ernie

PS Dain't forget to do Wild Goose. I'll never forgive you else.

"What are you going to do?" Ann asked.

"We'll have to ask Bob out here. I mean I want to. It's what Ernie would have expected. You wouldn't mind would you?"

"Of course not darling. Though I only met him the once, at the wedding. Do you think he'll come? What about his work?"

"We can only ask. I'll ring Mam and get her to go round and see them. Valerie might want to come too."

"I dare say we could fit them in. In the Nursery….."

Ann's voice trailed off. She was still far from over the loss of Tadpole.

Bob Salt arrived in Tucson by the same nine pm flight from New York as the Morgans had come by eighteen months earlier. The short stocky figure in his Sunday best suit and workman's flat cap looked completely out of place among the prosperous 'snowbirds' arriving for a vacation in Arizona. But he was jauntier than Morgan had feared:

"Ar Tom" he said in a Birmingham accent you could cut with a knife "I got stook on the steps of that erryplane joost a lookin' oop at the stars. Can yow believe 'em? I couldn't. I joost stared and stared oop at 'em. The stewardess'ad to come oop and fetch me down."

Settled back at home with a cup of tea and a snack, Bob was eager to talk:

"Yow cook a mean sausage-role Missis."

"You're not to call me 'Missis' Bob. I'm Ann."

"I'll try, but it won't be easy. Yow'm such a lady."

Morgan laughed: "She's not a lady Bob. She's my wife – and that's an infinitely higher status in life."

Bob explained how he'd managed to come:

"It were foonie really. Two weeks after our Ernie died I got this letter from The Norwich Union – that big insurance company. They said me insurance policy had matured – what I've been paying for since I were an apprentice at Rolls Royce back in 1929. An' they sent a bloody great cheque – and they said there'd be cheques every month on me life. Yow could've knocked me over with a feather. I'd thought as I wouldn't get anything 'til I were sixty-five; years and years away. I'd forgot all about the details ages ago. But it matures after forty years, irrespective of me age."

"What a pleasant surprise." Morgan clapped Bob on the back.

" Ar it were an' all. I were dumbfounded. Not as there were anyone to speak to. Valerie were over at our Jacquie's. I just stood there, all alone, wonderin' what I was agoin to do with me life. An' then the strangest bloody thing happenend. Yow'll never believe this Tom. Nor yow Missis."

"Ann!"

"Ann. I'm sorry."

"Go on Bob."

'Well it was Ernie. Bright as a pin. There 'e was a'sittin'at the kitchen table, joost loike he'd allus done at breakfast. 'Yow silly sod' he says, joost as he used to do when he were alive. 'Yow silly sod. Now's yer chance. Go oop the Austin and 'and in yer notice. Then gow out and see our Tom. An' I'll coom with yer an' all. So I did, an' 'ere I am 'an all. An' Ernie. Yow must think I'm daft. Valerie does. I think so meself sometimes."

The Morgans looked at one another.

"Daft or not" Bob continued pugnaciously "That's 'ow it is. I can't explain it. I don't need to. Ee's just there and it's nice. I can feel him all the time, joost a couple a rooms away. Ee's 'ere now somewhere Tom, all the way from Brum. I know he is. Now I better go to bed a'fore yow fetch in a psychiatrist."

Rather to the Morgans' surprise Bob Salt turned out to be excellent company. He loved the stars, he loved the cacti, he loved the mountains; he marvelled at every new thing like a garrulous schoolboy, so that it became a pleasure for both of them to show him around. Ann took him out to her Indian reservation and left him for a whole day at Davis-Monthan airbase to admire the largest collection of warplanes on the globe.

Morgan took him up to Kitt Peak for a two night observing run on the 90-inch. Bob was entranced and finished up guiding the telescope while Morgan developed the plates. Being an expert on bearings he was interested in the problem with the telescope which was exercising the observatory's brains, and preventing the telescope being used to its design specifications down towards the Southern horizon:

"It's allus' dangerous to use cylindrical bearings." He told Morgan. "An' I made soom suggestions as they're looking into. Might 'elp, might not.

Ann grew quite fond of the older man; after all they both shared a passionate interest in Tom. She took him out to J.C.Penny's department store and made him buy two lumberjack shirts and a suit of jeans in place of his Sunday best.

"What yow think Tom?" he asked, turning uneasily before Morgan's gaze. "It was our Ann made me gettem."

" 'Our Ann' is it now? You've really been promoted darling. I think Bob that you look like......look like a........."

"Gow on gerrit out. I can allus take 'em back. The man said so, dain't he Ann?"

"Well if you want to know" Morgan continued "They transform you. I've always seen you dressed either like a toolroom foreman, or in that bloody undertaker's suit. You were always in an anonymous uniform. Now you look like an individual, like the real Bob Salt. Seriously. Instead of fifty seven you looked sixty seven. Now you look forty-seven."

"Not like a Yank?"

"There's nothing wrong with that. At least its classless – not like all that British shit. You look like a new man Bob."

"I suppose I am in a way" he paused, lost in thought "I kin do what I like with the next twenty year on me life. Anything I like – provided it don't cost too much. Not as we'll be badly off mind. An' when Valerie retires an' collects 'er old age pension too, we shall be in clover. It's a great feelin' to think as you can do what yow want – within reason. I've never had it before.. We allus 'ad to work – since we was nippers. And grateful for that, what with the Depression. Now I wake oop of a morning and say to meself 'What yow a goin' to do today Bob? What you going to do next week? Or next year?' I tell yer its like bein let out of yer cage for the first time. Frightenin'. But wonderful. 'Ood swop it? Not me."

"What *are* you going to do Bob?" Morgan asked.

"I dain't rightly know. I want to talk it over wi yow and wi' our Ernie. Oh ar, he wants to know too."

"The more I see of Bob" Ann said "The more I like him. He's extremely intelligent….oh I know that sounds patronising. But with that awful accent you somehow don't expect it do you? I hope it's not contagious."

Morgan told her Ernie's story of Bob's invention of asymmetric gear wheels –and its possibly winning the war."

Ann looked thoughtful:

"I could look that up you know. Or have someone at the War Office do so. They're very good at that sort of Intelligence. They have to be. Shall I try?"

"Why not."

One day Bob announced; 'I daint tell yer but Uncle Sam's paying for most of this trip. At least the US Air Force is. There's a 'ole lot of people over 'ere what wants to see our Bob about that contract what I told you about Tom. I've gotter see a colonel in Dayton Ohio, an' another chap in Washington. I'll drive, and see a bit of the coontry. An' I'll 'av Ernie for company an'all. But me and you Tom we've got to discuss this contract. An' I may need yore 'elp in Dayton an' all. The US Air Force is payin', daint worry."

"Why don't you drive up with him?" Ann suggested in bed that night. "You'll see a bit of each other, and the country."

"We bloody would. Do you realise Dayton is fifteen hundred miles from here? But I've go to get this Ernie lunacy out of his head first."

"What on Earth for?"

"Because it's a delusion. It's batty. It's dishonest."

"I think it's charming. And helpful."

"No it isn't. It's a lie. The sooner Bob faces up to the fact that Ernie has gone for ever, the sooner he can recover and get on with his life."

"But he's happy."

"Of course he's not. At a certain level he knows, as well as I do, that it's all clap-trap. He wouldn't be making it up if he was happy."

"How can you know that?" Ann sounded furious "It's a circular argument. How do you know what's going on in that wise old man's head? You don't even understand religion. Frank believes in it and he's no fool."

"What the heck has religion got to do with it?"

"Everything of course. Everything. The existence of the soul outside and beyond the body. Bob is experiencing that now. Ernie's soul is travelling with him."

"Rubbish." Morgan was contemptuous "There's no such thing."

"What you mean" Ann was angry now "Is that *you* don't know there is a soul. By the same token you do not know, and cannot ever prove, that there is not. What possible proof, or even argument could you offer? You have no idea. How then have you got the nerve to try and talk poor old Bob out of his beliefs? If it makes him happy – and it might be true – leave him in peace."

"I can't do that. I know Bob far better than you. Honesty is his touchstone, his religion. And Ernie'd never forgive me."

"Ernie!" Ann sounded astounded. "But you just said Ernie's dead – so what has he to do with it?"

"You know what I mean."

"No I certainly do not. And nor evidently do you Tom Morgan. All that schoolboy rationality ought to hang its head in a case like this."

"Well it won't."

They had a terrible row which flared up again and again over several days. It wasn't, as they both realised, merely a clash over Bob, but the unbarring of irreconcilable religious differences, somehow mixed up with the loss of Tadpole. Ann couldn't move Morgan, anymore than he could convince her. Bob only made matters infinitely worse by bringing his living Ernie into every tripartite conversation: "Ernie thinks......."

"No he doesn't!" Morgan finally snapped. "Ernie's dead. He's gone Bob. Ernie's no more here than Napoleon Bonaparte. You know that as well as I do."

"Oh but 'ee is Tom." Bob looked shocked.

Ann got up, walked out and banged dishes in the kitchen.

Morgan found no pleasure in being at home after that, and agreed to drive with Bob up to Dayton Ohio. Driving though Colorado, Kansas, Missouri and Illinois… they talked about almost nothing else but Ernie for six days and five evenings. Bob went back over Ernie's childhood, and the bravery of the young boy when he was first faced with his mortal illness.

"I joost daint believe it Tom. Why should a young shaver like 'im cheer *us* oop? He had no warning, no training, no faith, no example to give him strength. But he had it. Where it coom from I daint know. Not from me. I were cursing destiny, cursing God – if there were one – which I doubted and still do, cursing luck and cursing meself. But 'ee dain't. Ee never complained once, never cried, never behaved except with grace – yes 'grace', that's the word. He inspired every one on us to lead a better life. I know 'ee inspired me and Valerie. An' look at all them friends an' people as come to 'is funeral. Hundreds an' hundreds on 'em."

"He inspired me too, in hospital."

"Did he?" Bob pulled the car to the side of the highway and stopped. The tears were coming from him too thick and fast to drive safely.

The meeting with the Air Force people in Dayton amazed Morgan. It was held under tight security in a research establishment housed within a huge airbase. Since he wasn't expected, Morgan had to undergo a security clearance interrogation lasting several hours. And when he did meet up with Bob again he found him confronting more than a dozen scientists, air-force officers and government personnel seated round a large table, chaired by a general.

"Cripes Tom I'm glad yow'm 'ere." Bob whispered " They want to know everything. Joost everything. They want to know about you an' all. Mind you they'm friendly enough; inquisitive loike, but not aggressive."

Morgan kept quiet and listened. It became evident that the Americans were very interested in the Wild Goose Project, but none too keen to divulge why. And they were insistent on absolute secrecy:

"If one word of this gets to the Soveets" a fierce looking colonel announced "The deal is off and we pull out our money; every goddamned red cent. You're going to need a cover story. And it better be a good one."

"We could help with that." announced one of the civilian 'suits' who looked both lachrymose and menacing – like a gangster attending his kid brothers funeral.

The meetings were still in full swing when Morgan had to leave for Tucson.

"I'm that sorry yow'm going Tom. Yow kin deal with these fellers better'n me.

"I'd love to stay Bob. But I'm missing Ann – we had that terrible row over Ernie. And anyway I've got a run on the 61-inch in the Catalinas."

"Yow'm like a son to me Tom. But yow go back and make it oop with your missis. Yow'm wrong about Ernie, and yow can tell 'er so from me; but I understand as why you tried. Yow might be a great astronomer but you ain't got a clue sometimes. When I fly back to Tuxon from Washington I'm a going to sort you out. I promised our Ann. An' Ernie an' all." He laughed.

"Christ I give up. If I could afford to I'd have a psychiatrist waiting."

"Well you can't. An' a good thing."

"Don't sign anything Bob. Not a single thing. You're going to need a good business lawyer, an American one, and you're going to make them pay for him. God knows why but they seem desperately to want Wild Goose. And their pockets are bottomless – after all its not their money they'll be giving away. So why not get plenty of it? The Yanks stole us rotten in two world wars. Just take antibiotics and jet engines. If you don't take their money they'll only give it away to some less worthy engineers. You should put Valerie on the payroll for a start."

"Valerie?" Bob was astounded.

"Yes. She's a qualified bookkeeper isn't she ? You'll need one with all that money passing through your hands."

"I dain't know. I'm outer me depth."

"No you aren't Bob Salt. I watched you. Maybe it's all unfamiliar, but you were asking all the right questions. Take your time. Play canny – which you are anyway. Above all try to find out why they really want Wild Goose."

"Ar, that's a poozle an' all."

"What about Ernie?"

"Ar, he's poozled too. An' ee's a coomin' to Washington with me and yow ain't. Proper son 'ee is."

They hugged one another, the small man's head barely reaching up to Morgan's collar bone:

"An' yow make it up to our Ann. She's that oopset by losing her babby. Yow'm going to 'ave trouble there; bad trouble."

When Morgan got home husband and wife, made miserable by their differences and their separation, avoided the subject of Ernie and talked about Bob Salt.

" I could have killed myself trying not to laugh Ann. They hardly understood a word of his Brummy accent. They kept looking at each other for clarification – then shaking their heads. If such existed they'd have sent for a professional translator of Brummidgem, but they had to do with me. How they hated it when I left. But they really seem to want the Wild Goose Project."

"Why, do you think? Or rather what for? Remind me."

"Well it was something we dreamed up between the three of us. Ernie wanted to know what the absolute extreme range might be of a model aircraft – what to do next after his Mark V endurance record. He called it the Mark VI then. He was interested in range in miles, not endurance in hours. How far could a model aircraft fly? So I spent a lot of time calculating the aerodynamic s. And this amazing formula dropped out of it. None of us could believe it at first."

"Why not darling?"

"Well first of all it implied that an aircraft could be made to fly right round the Earth without ever refuelling."

"Gosh."

"But that's not the half of it. There was no size in this formula. The weight and the wingspan had dropped out somewhere in the algebra – that's why I couldn't believe it. I must have made a mistake."

"Why?"

"Don't you see the implication?"

"No."

"It meant that a model aircraft, even a tiny one a few centimetres across, could, in principle, girdle the Earth in a single flight."

"Golly that does sound impossible."

"Doesn't it just. That's why we were all so incredulous. But eventually I convinced myself, and then the other two. That's when Ernie dubbed it the Wild Goose Equation, because wild geese , and indeed much smaller birds, occasionally do fly the Atlantic. And that's the project he dreamed up: to make a model aircraft that would fly the Atlantic. And to be first. The trouble was that it would need some expensive components, particularly a guidance system. Ernie suggested we write to NASA and ask for financial support. I helped them write the proposal – frankly never expecting it would come to anything. But apparently it has. They're mad for it. Bob and I have been wondering, if the Yanks are so keen on it, if we shouldn't have offered it to the British first."

"You said you offered it to NASA – but Bob's talking to the US Air Force isn't he?"

"That's another of the odd things which don't add up. NASA passed it on – though NASA are interested too – they're the people Bob's going to see in Washington."

"What else doesn't add up?"

"The Yanks are better at this stuff than we are. If they want to do it they could do it without us. They've got this genius over in California – Paul Macready. And another thing – they want us to build it out of wood, like all of Ernie's models – instead of high-tech. materials.

"My God" Ann exclaimed "I know what it's for."

"What?"

"Surely you remember the U2, the US spy-plane that was shot down over Russia with Gary Powers in it, spying for America?"

"Of course."

"Well the West desperately needs to keep an eye on the Soviet Union – in case they're preparing for a pre-emptive attack on us. But after the Powers incident America can never use piloted spy aircraft again."

"What about satellites?"

"Exactly. What about satellites? They can't see a thing when it's cloudy. And much of Northern Russia is almost perpetually under cloud. Wild Goose could solve all of that. Especially if she were made of wood."

"I don't follow."

"No radar signature don't you see? She could fly in completely undetected, like the wooden Mosquitoes did during the war. Better still she could fly low, just under the cloud, with miniature cameras and get all the details we want. And if she did crash, balsa wood can't be traced. The Russians would find it impossible to pin anything on America. It's perfect don't you see. No wonder the US Air Force wants Wild Goose!"

"But why us?"

"It's obvious."

"Not to me."

"Because you and Bob, as you presently are, are a ghastly security risk. You've only got to blab in public and Russia might get wind of it; find some kind of antidote; radio jamming for instance. They might even build a Wildgoose of their own to use against us. The US military must be desperate to sign you both up to the deepest possible secrecy. The implications are extraordinary. Have you told anybody about Wild Goose?"

"Not me. Why should I? I don't know about Ernie and Bob though."

"You've got to get on to Bob at once,"

"I can't. Not until he rings."

"Meanwhile I'm going to ring round some friends in Whitehall. And don't you dare show that Wild Goose Equation to anyone."

"Why not?

"Never you mind. Just don't. Think of it as the patriotic thing to do."

"I suppose" he grumbled "This is what becomes of being married to a spy."

When Bob flew back in from Washington he looked tired, thin and thoughtful.

"What's wrong Bob?" Morgan asked immediately.

"It's Ernie. Ee's gorn. I woke oop in this motel in West Virginia and he'd gorn. I could feel it at once Tom. He was there the night before, jist round the corner somewhere, like allus, but when I woke oop in the morning, afore driving down to Washington, he was gorn. I knowed immediately. Clean gorn. I drove off thinkin' ee'd coom back. But he dain't. `Ee's gorn completely and I'm afeared ee wont nivver coom back."

There were tears in the old man's eyes. Morgan didn't know what to say.

"I'll feel that lonely in our 'ouse back in Westheath. Ernie's everywhere there. His ghost is. I'm dreadin' goin'."

"You're going to have to move house Bob."

"Ar I think yow'm right; we will. It's what Valerie 'as been sayin' ever since the funeral. She want's us to goo into the country. That's why she's livin' round our Jacquie's."

"How about the US Air Force?"

"That Ann of yourn she's got 'er head screwed on straight. Dead right she were. It's a long range reconnaissance drone as they want, with a miniscule radar signature. They dain't say what it's for but it ain't hard to guess is it? A good idea I'd say. I'm all for it. And money's no object."

"So you're going to do it?"

"I dain't say that. I want to think on it. If only Ern were back ee'd know what to do."

"But surely Ernie would love to think of Wild Goose taking to the air, crossing the Atlantic, realising his dream – and even contributing to Western security? Surely Bob that's a 'no-brainer' as the Americans say."

" Ar it sounds right. But I can't get over Ernie leaving me like that – just afore I was going to talk to NASA. Mebbe he thinks I should offer it to the British Government instead."

"You'd be mad Bob, absolutely mad! How d you think a bunch of Oxbridge clubmen would react if you went to talk to them? With your accent they'd laugh you out of court. And if by some mischance they did take you seriously what then? They'd steal your idea, give it away to their Oxbridge pals in the right firm, in return for a KBE or a CBE – not for you but for themselves! Look what they did to Frank Whittle. After he'd been working brilliantly and loyally on the jet engine for twenty years they gave his invention to Rolls Royce, his bitter rivals, who'd done all they could to suppress jet-engine technology, and then, worse still, they sold the patents on the Jet Engine to America for 800,000 dollars. Then the swine collected their KBE's for "Fostering Anglo- American relations". It was the greatest act of betrayal, and financial folly, in British history. And poor old Whittle, a great British patriot, finished up exiled in Florida. Come off it Bob. Ernie'd never forgive you – and neither would I. Worse still Wild Goose would never fly across Whitehall – let alone the Atlantic. The Americans may be ruthless bastards – but at least they've got some imagination. Can you see the British ever going to the Moon? They might try of course. They'd send a party of Royal Navy volunteers to man-haul themselves along a moonbeam!"

Bob Salt was now a confirmed and depressed insomniac. Ann blamed Morgan for Bob's loss of Ernie. Morgan was inclined to think it was an encouraging sign of a father finally acknowledging the passing on of his beloved son. Bob spent a lot of time talking to both of them; separately but not together, in case bitter husband-and wife arguments broke out again. He didn't want to talk about Wild Goose much:

"It ain't joost the issue of loyalty," he told Morgan "I'm not sure as I could do it on me own. Ernie was allus the aerodynamicist and chief designer. One or two of 'is mates are pretty good mind. If they could devote full time to it, like our Ernie done, they might come good. An' Ernie's already done the outline design – which is the 'ardest bit."

"Well then."

"An' then there's the obligation. Up to now we done it all for fun. But with a million dollars or more in the kitty – and that's what they're budgeting on – oi'd 'ave to deliver. Simply 'ave to. Is that an obligation I want to take on at my age? Is it? Would yow?"

"It'd be the making of you Bob." Morgan was certain "You can't spend the next twenty years sitting on your arse moping."

"Mebbe not. But mebbe I've got summat better in moind."

"What?"

"Yow'd only laff if I told yer."

"Try me."

But Bob clammed up completely at that point, changing the subject:

"It's yore career as I coom back to Tuxon to talk about Tom, not mine." Bob stubbornly refused to pronounce 'Tucson' correctly.

He separately, and in some depth, quizzed Tom and Ann about their disparate career ambitions and constraints. He then asked to be left alone in the Astronomy library for several days, keeping very close about what he was up to. However he confessed to Ann:

"This freedom thing seemed wonderful when it first coom. I felt like a bird let out on me cage. Still does. But it's 'ard aint it? Real 'ard. An' I never 'ad any practice before loike. First I joost 'ad to work – for the money. Then when our

Ernie fell sick I 'ad to do me best to keep 'im 'appy. Now I gotter choose. I find it easy to choose *for* something. But a choice for one thing usually means a choice against summat else – which yow'd like almost as well. On the Toosday I think I'll go fer Wild Goose; its obvious. Then I wek oop Wednesday night thinking 'But I dain't want to miss out on that other. Having one dream means giving oop another. Or that's 'ow it seems to me. What yow think Ann?"

Like Morgan Ann tried to get out of Bob this secret ambition which he evidently felt he might miss out on if he ran Wild Goose. But Bob wasn't forthcoming.

One evening after dinner Bob, looking pleased with himself, drew a large piece of paper out of his pocket and folded it out on the table:

"This is the world map what I've been drawing oop in the library. I've marked all the main observatories and astronomical sites, and I've marked all the places as Ann thinks she can happily work from. What yow think?"

Morgan looked at in bemusement. It was almost ridiculously methodical.

"What a good idea." Ann wanted to be diplomatic.

"I thought on it as a good place to start loike. Narrow things down – which it 'as. There's only foive places left. Tom dain't want to be in England."

"That's the first I've heard." Ann was sharp.

"Not from preference darling. If I have to for your sake I will. But we don't have any decent optical telescopes."

"Then" said Bob, breaking in hurriedly "I went to see Tom's boss to see what 'ee thought of these foive possibilities. And 'ee ruled out three straightaway. Said there'd not be enough research scope for our Tom. That left only two, and I studied oop on them, and talked to some of Tom's colleagues. Both on 'em sound very promising. Yow want to hear?"

"Go on." Morgan said, dreading what might be coming.

"Well the fust one is in Maryland, not far from Washington. It's Goddard Space Flight Centre. Heard on it Tom?"

"Vaguely."

"It's where they've started building the satellite telescopes to go into Space an'see the Universe in new wavelength winders; the ultra-violet, the infra-red and such-loike."

"That sounds exciting Bob." Ann was keen on Washington. "What do you think Tom?"

"On the face of it it sounds like a promising idea Bob. I'd never have thought of it. But I'd have to look into it properly. There might be all kinds of snags."

"Er course. It's run by NASA."

"An' the other one?" Ann was impatient.

"That's a different coop of tea. It's in Australia: The Mount Stromlo Observatory. Heard on it Tom?"

"Can't say I have."

"It's in Canberra, the capital. So that'll suit our Ann. The Aussies 'ave all the 'eadquarters of their defence forces there, including their navy. The British Admiralty is sure to be represented."

"It is." Ann leapt in eagerly.

"An' the British High Commission is there. You know, the Ambassador 'an such."

"What about telescopes?" Morgan broke in.

"That's where yow'm in luck Tom. Mount Stromlo 'as the biggest telescope in the Southern hemisphere. A 74-inch. An' it's equipped with a Boller and Chivens spectrograph with an RCA Image intensifier, joost like yore 90-inch."

"Are you sure?" Morgan was doubtful.

"Ar I am. Your mate Willard found the Observatory's annual report for me. I've got it in me brief case. An' I got the annual report from Goddard Space Flight Centre an'all. Read 'em."

"Interfering old bat!" Morgan sounded furious in the conjugal bed that night. "What the hell does he know about astronomical careers?"

"Quite a lot if you ask me."

"Huh!"

"You're angry Tom because Bob has done what you should have done yourself."

"I don't think like that – in that cold blooded business-like way."

"Perhaps it's about time you did."

"What do you mean?"

"You very well know how difficult it will be to find you a position in astronomy which suits us both. And what do you do? Go to Vancouver because of some boyhood romance you'd read, not thinking about me at all. I didn't say much at the time but I was furious. And now today, through Bob, I find out you're not going back to England – which I had more or less counted on, as you well know. Bob's thinking for both of us — which is more than you've done. As far as I can see you're being utterly selfish about your career. What have you got against Bob's two suggestions?"

"Well nothing – so far."

"Then look into them properly. I'm not going to be dragged off to some God forsaken place where I have to give up my career – just because you're too lazy to do things properly. Now I'm going to sleep." And she turned off her light, not kissing him goodnight for the first time since their wedding.

Morgan had had his eye on Australia earlier in the year. It would be ideal from two points of view. It was in the Southern hemisphere, where most of the radio pulsars were found. And John Bolton worked there, the man who had done more than anyone to find quasars and radio-galaxies – galaxies that might contain miniature quasars. Indeed he'd written to Bolton expressing his interest in working with him but Bolton had written back saying there were no posts available, or in prospect, at the Parkes Radio Observatory where he worked.

But if Bob was right about the 74-inch, and if he could find a post at Mount Stromlo, then he might be able to collaborate with John Bolton after all. Having only the haziest notion of Australian geography he crept out of bed and looked in their school atlas. Parkes, it turned out, was a mere two hundred miles from Canberra. Instead of going back to bed with Ann, Morgan spent most of the night in his pyjamas reading Bob's Annual report from Mount Stromlo Observatory. The more he read the more promising it sounded. It formed part of the Institute for Advanced Studies at the Australian National University, a prestige university specially constructed in the new capital city to keep Australia at the cutting edge of scientific research.

Morgan ought to have been grateful to Bob Salt, and to Ann for that matter, but he was not. He was fiercely, illogically resentful of anyone, however well intentioned, interfering in his career. It was his career, his life, his destiny and he was damned if anyone else was going to interfere in it. He might just survive the buggeration of his astronomical career if it came about through a mistake of his own. But, if he were brought down through somebody else's cock-up then he felt he would never survive. So while he attentively read the Mount Stromlo report, also the one from Goddard Space Flight Centre, he resolved never to discuss his future career moves with Bob. Not even with Ann. He knew this last was deeply wrong, but he couldn't help himself. Nothing and nobody would, from now on, stand between him and his chosen career in astronomy.

The negotiation over Wild Goose with the US Air Force dragged on, and Bob arranged to move into a motel:

"Tain't fair on yow young things 'avin an old codger like me around this long."

But they wouldn't hear of it. Apart from anything else Bob's presence helped to smooth out some of the tensions that were beginning to develop in their marriage.

As Morgan had insisted, Bob had hired a lawyer recommended to them by Bart Bok. The lawyer in turn had insisted on bringing in a business accountant. There were all kinds of complications that Bob and he had never foreseen: patent rights, tax, precisely written and mutually agreed get-out clauses for both sides, a project time-table, provisions for extra funding in the event of unforeseen difficulties, penalty clauses, profits, and so on and so on. Bob was dismayed, seeing himself chained to a desk for the rest of his days. The Air Force were however very obliging. They sent down their negotiator, a Colonel Siedelmayer from Dayton, who agreed to stay on in Tucson for as long as it took. His concern seemed to be not money at all, but security; security of ideas ,or what he referred to as 'IPR' or Intellectual Property Rights, and security of personnel. The Air Force insisted on themselves vetting anyone who came to work on the Wild Goose project, and having total control over any kind of information release. None of their requirements, as Morgan quickly realised, was insurmountable. The real problem was Bob Salt. For reasons unspecified he simply wasn't prepared to commit himself. Just as negotiations would seemingly be coming to a conclusion, he would raise completely new, and often unreasonable objections. Morgan, who attended every meeting as Bob's adviser, grew exasperated.

After three weeks of inconclusive wrangling the dark-of -the-moon returned and with it a five day run on the 36-inch at Kitt Peak for Morgan. Bob Salt begged to come. Morgan, who had rather been looking forward to a relief from Bob's vacillations, finally, under duress from his combined family, agreed to let Bob come. There was one concession he exacted though: there was to be absolutely no mention of Wild Goose whilst they were 'on the mountain'.

To begin with the run went well. Morgan was using an image tube at the prime focus to image directly the radio elliptical galaxies whose spectra he was taking with the 90-inch. Bob was entranced with the 36-inch whose old fashioned drive, with its falling weights and exposed cog wheels, appealed to his engineering mind.. He did their house-keeping, cooked their TV dinners and guided some of their exposures from the airy and non-too-safe Newtonian platform at the very top of the telescope.

"Yow'm in amongst the stars oop 'ere; " he announced in wonder "Yow can't see the Earth at all. Yow'm floating in Space, like a jellyfish in the ocean."

But after three clear nights the clouds rolled in. They couldn't go to sleep in case the weather cleared up so they sat in the dorm drinking Bob's whisky.

"This Glen Morangie is good stuff " said a pleasantly inebriated Morgan, who'd never been able to afford decent Scotch.

"Ar it is an all." agreed Bob who'd been able to afford it only because it was duty-free; "I could fly without wings I could."

"You could fall off the Newtonian platform more like, and never feel a thing."

Not being accustomed to spirits drunk at high altitude, they both became expansive and garrulous. Morgan decided to confront Bob about his mysterious alternative ambition. Bob shied off immediately. Morgan persisted. Bob set a condition:

"I know as yow'll only laff. I'll tell you what though. First yow tell me your greatest ambition, yow wildest dream, then oi'll tell yer moine. That's fair ain't it? Coom on ,'ave some more Morangejuice – or whatever it is" He giggled "Oi reckon as we'm getting drunk."

"Well it's quite easy in my case Bob. I want to make the greatest possible scientific discovery."

"Ter make yer famous – like Newton?"

"Well that'd be nice – after I'm dead. But no, it's not that. I want to have a …have a ….revelation. That's it: a revelation. I want to be the first man ever to see a Great Truth, and to see it naked. I want to be knocked backward by it, scarcely believing that such an incredible thing could be true, but knowing in a deeper layer of my mind that it must be so. That it has an inevitability, an elegance, a beauty to it that makes it impossible to disbelieve. And it must not be a discovery that anyone could have made – if they were lucky enough to be in he the right place using the right telescope at the right time. No this must be a discovery that could have been made centuries ago – but wasn't made because no man had had the imagination to look at the world in this precise and original way. Do you see ? It's a discovery of the imagination, not a discovery by accident, not a discovery of the deliberate and purposeful mind. And more than that it's a discovery I can hoard to myself like a miser, knowing that no one else will ever know it – until I choose to tell them."

"Blimey, yer dain't want much do yer?"

"Well you did ask."

" Has anyone been in that position before?"

" Well, let's see; Charles Darwin I suppose. They say he discovered the Theory of Evolution by Natural Selection back in 1839 when he was voyaging round the Galapagos Islands as naturalist aboard the Beagle. But he never published a word of it for nineteen years, and only then because Alfred Russel Wallace was about to publish his own identical theory. Imagine that, knowing where all the plants and the animals and the birds – even the humans, came from. And telling no one, not even his wife, especially not his wife. And more shocking still, far more shocking, realising there was no God."

"Ow do yer mean?"

"We forget. In former times there simply had to be a Creator. How else came there to be the tiger, the dolphin, the albatross and the humming bird?"

"All things bright and beautiful?"

"Exactly. But now Darwin could see a perfectly rational way to create species – with no need of a Creator: Evolution by Natural Selection; the Survival of the Fittest. What a shocking revelation. He couldn't even tell his wife; she was a devout Christian. Some say that is why he didn't publish for twenty years, and if it hadn't been for Wallace independently coming to the same conclusion while collecting butterflies in Indonesia, Darwin might never have published at all – not while his wife was alive anyhow."

"D' yow think it made him happy."

"I don't know Bob. But I don't think that's the point. It was the sheer wonderment; it was like a blind born man seeing the world for the first time. It was a feast of discovery, a celestial light that illuminated all he knew about or could imagine."

"D'yow think as there's room for more revelations of that kind?"

"Of course there is. Especially in astronomy."

"But I thought as you astrophysicists had got it all wrapped up – with the Big Bang an' all."

Morgan laughed:

"You know Bob the most surprising thing I've learned about astronomy – and it's probably true of all sciences—is a universal failure to concede our ignorance. We're like children frightened of the dark. We'd rather swallow some childish just-so story, based on the flimsiest evidence, than admit that it's dark, its cold and it's possibly frightening out here. Astronomers snatch at clues to comfort themselves against the dread and awful dark. Take those galaxies you've been staring at. The story is that their light is red-shifted because the entire Universe in which we live is expanding. But how do we know that? Because the galaxies have red shifted light! It's nothing more than a circular argument. It's scarcely better than Jack and the Beanstalk. I want to be Jack and climb that beanstalk, and see what's really up there in the clouds."

"It might be an ogre."

"I don't care. I want to see. I want to know. And I want to think about it – all on my own. That's my dream."

Bob wanted to speak, but Morgan interrupted him excitedly:

"And do you know Bob, I didn't realize that was my dream, not until this very moment. It's been there, underneath, since I was a boy, bursting to get out. I must have known it on an unconscious level, but now it has spoken for itself – in words. Gosh!" he got up and paced about ;

"Do you realize, I know who I am for the first time."

The two of them were both so excited by Morgan's self-discovery that they entirely forgot about the real cosmos until Bob had to go outside for a pee. He came back, short of breath from the altitude:

"Coom on Tom, there's a million bleedin' stars out there. We gotter go oop the dome."

It wasn't until they were eating bacon and eggs in the dorm, with sunlight streaming through the window, that Morgan remembered:

"Come on Bob, I told you my dream. Now it's your turn."

" I ain't got no Glen Morangie."

"You don't need it now. You can't make more of an exhibition of yourself than I did."

"Oh ar I could. An' I will." He poured out more coffee for Morgan, more tea for himself Then he went out to feed the scraps to the coatamundi waiting patiently outside, their tall furry ringed tails standing straight up towards the sky.

"Yow promise not to laff ? Yow do an' I'm straight in that car an' down the mountain. Yow can find yer own way home."

"I promise Bob. Boy Scout's honour."

Bob sat down heavily, and supped his tea;

" Well it's loike yours in one way. It's allus been there – under me skin. I knowed it in me heart – but not in me mind. Anyroad there was no opportunity. First I 'ad to work, then there was Ernie. So perhaps it was a mercy I dain't recognise it before. Might 'ave drove me crackers. But then it slipped out loike, after the funeral, when I got this letter from the insurance. It was if it'd been biding there hidden, a'waiting for its chance. And now that chance has coom. That's why I'm all confused about Wild Goose. I wanna do Wild Goose desperate. 'Course I do. But there's this other thing that's been a waiting patiently for years. It don't seem right to deny it now. It'd be giving me hearts blood away. 'Ow would yow feel if yow 'ad to abandon your dream completely? For a good reason moind, like lookin after a sick wife say?"

"I couldn't!" Morgan was fiercely certain "I wouldn't. If I didn't die right away, I'd wither away within a year or two. I know I just couldn't. My dream is who I am. No dream, no Twm Morgan."

Salt supped his tea again, looking miserably into his mug.

"Out with it Bob. You promised."

"All right then. Yow ain't going to believe me."

"Try me"

"It's history."

"What do you mean?"

"British history. I want to write the first proper history of Britain – from a practical man's point of view. Not all that crap about kings, not all that Marxist propaganda neither, what some on them unionists spout. Not all that condescending roobish from university dons about 'the working class'. There ain't sich a thing as a 'working class'. Yow know that Tom, yow been there with us, down in the galleys. There's just people see, people what finish oop there on the factory floor by accident, by lack of opportunity, 'cos their parents couldn't think of 'owt better, or because they 'ad a babby at the wrong time. There ain't a man in Britain 'oo really thinks 'ee's 'working class'. They all got their dreams, same as me and you. They're all dukes when it comes down to it. They'd know exactly what to do on a grouse moor, on a sailing yacht, or with a French mistress."

"I bet." Morgan's brain was still racing.

"But it won't be a 'istory of the down-trodden, full of socialist indignation. It's been done, it's been overdone, and to tell the truth it's dull, and not very enlightening."

"OK, so you've told me what it is not. But what will it be Bob? How will 'Salt's History of Britain' differ from all the rest of them?"

"Ar' Bob's eyes lit up "Now we'm talking. Well to begin with it will concentrate on what is *distinct* in our history, compared to other's. We've 'ad an amazing history Tom. Look what we done. Developed Representative Democracy; invented The Industrial Revolution; evolved the Middle Class; built the word's greatest empire – then give it back again. We won three World wars."

"Three?"

"Including the Napoleonic one. Then there's the Royal Navy, Pax Britannica, the Abolition of Slavery, the sewerage system and clean water and the 'uge increase in world population what resulted; steamships and railways and world trade; leisure, photography, radio, broadcasting, football, computers, the jet engine, antibiotics….the bleeding list goos on and on and on. Nobody in world history, not the Romans, not even the Greeks 'ave had anything like the effect what the Brits 'ave done."

"Don't you think it all sounds a bit jingoistic, nationalistic, almost fascist if you like?"

"Ar" Salt grinned "That's where yow'm wrong. O' course that's the fashionable attitude these days. It suits a lot of people to say that. But it's oop to me to show it's roobish – which it is."

"And how do you intend to do that?"

"By comparison. Oi'm going to compare Britain with half a dozen countries which might a' done what we done – but dain't. I 'aint decided yet exactly which ones, but probably France, Spain, Germany, Holland, Sweden and Switzerland."

"By God it sounds like a gigantic undertaking, and a gigantic book, far too thick for anybody to read."

"Ar' " Bob responded delightedly "That's where yow'm wrong. Since Oi'm interested only in what is *distinctive* about British history, I can leave out most of what passes for British history nowadays, as it's more or less universal, at least in Europe: kings and queens, dynastic and religious wars and persecutions, plague, trade, economic imperatives and so on. I reckon as 'ow that will coot out ninety per cent of what's in a typical history book today. An I'm not going far back into the past neither. What'appenend in 400AD, or even 1400 AD 'ad little effect on the specifics of Britain today, as opposed to Europe as a whole. Yes the Black Death killed off thirty per cent of the population, and so changed the balance of class power – but so it did across most of Europe. So my book might be quite short."

"Quite Salty in fact."

"Ar. " Bob laughed, happy his secret was finally out.

"But what would you put in it that other books don't have? I don't understand."

"Now we'm a'getting at it. This is the interesting bit. I believe as history, interesting history that is, is largely made up of a small number of crucial advances, usually practical ones."

"Examples please, in the British context."

"OK then. What about tides?"

"Tides? " Morgan was incredulous.

"Ar, tides. 'Ow do you think the majority of the trade was possible that started off the Industrial Revolution? 'Ow did they carry hundreds of thousands of tons of coal and iron ore and limestone and bricks about the country? An', before that, in earlier times, the building stone, the lime and the timber? Do you know 'ow much yow can carry on a horse and cart, and 'ow far it can go in a day? It were pathetic. Half a ton, and then only ten mile a day. An' what about feed for the horse and shelter for the driver? So 'ow did they transport all the heavy trade?'

"I don't know. Sailing ships I suppose."

"Well yow'd suppose wrong. 'Ow the 'ell are sailing ships to get up the Thames estuary to the Port of London, by far the biggest port in the world till recent, against the prevailing wind from the West, and against the flow of the river? 'Ow in 'ell?"

"I've never thought."

"Ar yow dain't. An neither 'ave all those historians. An' why not? Cos they ain't practical men – and I am. Britain 'as the second largest tidal range on Earth. Twice a day the sea floods along our coasts and up and down our estuaries, tidal rivers and firths, providing free and regular transport for one and all. That's 'ow it were done. That's 'ow wealth and industry started in Britain. All them coastal trading vessels used their sails mainly to get 'em in and out of tidal streams. An' when the tidal stream was against them they dropped their 'ook and went to sleep for a few hours until the tide turned. Do you know that them Thames sailing barges could carry two hundred ton of cargo all round the Southern and Eastern coasts with a crew of two men and a boy? The poor sods on the continent were mostly stuck with 'orses and carts. London were built where it is, and became the greatest trading city on Earth, 'cos of its tides, and only because of its tides. Historians dain't look down at the muddy current an' see the gold lying there. But that's where it is. London is a tidewater city. An' it's the same story for Bristol and Gloucester and Cardiff and Glasgow and Southampton. Nobody's wrote the effects of tides on British history. But I'm going ter."

"I'm beginning to see what you're getting at". Morgan, who'd read a fair amount of history himself, was impressed.

"There's lots of examples loike that. Yow take timber. D'you know it took three thousand mature oaks to build a ship-o-the line – the ramparts of the Royal Navy, the 'wooden walls' of Britain. Three thousand big oaks. That's almost a bleedin' forest for one ship. An' who 'as got oak forests like that? Almost no one I tell you. Not in Europe. We 'ad 'em, so we built the Royal Navy and ruled the trade routes of the world – from Shanghai to Pernambucco. But then the oaks ran out, dain't they? Imported oak wouldn't do. Ship-worm got into it and the bottoms dropped out in a few year. There was summat special about British Oak. But beein' short sighted and stoopid we cut 'em all down. It got so bad in the seventeen 'undreds as people couldn't even find enough firewood to cook their food, or warm their 'ouses. We 'ad the world's first firewood crisis. An' it were dire. An' so what did we have to do? Dig for coal, invent the steam engine to pump out the mines, and so start the Industrial Revolution. Tides and British oak trees did far more to dictate the course of our history than all the kings and tyrants since William the Conk"

"It sounds plausible."

"An' I'll tell yer another thing. Why was the coal there joost waiting to save us from our own greed? And the iron ore too, and the limestone needed to reduce it? Why was it here Tom? There ain't any coal in Ireland, an' not much in Spain. And where there is coal there mainly isn't iron, or limestone. But in Britain they was all there; right on top of one another – in a magic, providential mix. Why was they there Tom?"

"I don't know, come to think of it. I supposed it was natural. Then why?"

"For the same reason most on the geological epochs are named after the parts and peoples of Britain. 'Cambrian', that's after Wales; Silurian and Ordovician – Roman names for Welsh tribes; Devonian ,and so on. It's 'cos

Britain is joost about the most complex piece of geological jigsaw on this planet. Joost by chance. It's all down there, joost underneath us: coal, anthracite – an' that were vital; iron ore, tin in Cornwall, copper in Swansea, salt-domes in Cheshire, lead in the Pennines, potash in Yorkshire – and now they'm finding oil and gas under the North Sea. Never mind the Middle East; the Creator blessed Britain with geological wealth beyond fable. Did yer know as in the nineteenth century three quarters of all the steel in the world were coming out of one tiny Welsh valley – Merthyr. An' for why? 'Cos they had great heaps of iron ore, coal *and* limestone all right beside each other. No place on Earth were like it. So there's three of the things as is going into Bob Salt's History of the Brits' : tides, trees and mineralogy. But there's a lot more, one 'ell of a lot more An' it aint been done I tell yer Tom. It'aint been done. I been reading history since I left school as a nipper; mostly British history. And it ain't there. That's why I'm hesitatin' about Wild Goose Tom. This 'Practical Man's History of the Brits' could be much more satisfying to me – and ultimately more significant. Now they got the idea the Yanks can do Wild Goose on their own. Ann's right; they only want us so as to shut our traps. I dain't blame 'em moind yow. But that's the truth on it."

"Tell me Bob; do you think the historical effect of asymmetrical gears in aero-engineering might get into your book?"

"Ar," Bob smiled, then winked at Tom "Ar , it might an' all."

Once Bob had started talking about his 'Brits', as he called it, he couldn't stop.

"What did Ernie think about it, and Valerie?" Morgan wanted to know.

Bob looked crestfallen:

"Valerie's not interested o' course. She thinks it's an ' 'obby like growin' marrers: 'armless and keeps me from getting' under 'er feet. But Ernie were different. 'Ee thought it were daft. 'An amateur historian' ee said 'Were as ridiculous as an amateur aerodynamicist.' Pull yer finger out' 'ee says 'And gerron wi' what you know'. We 'ad some good old rows about it. I said to 'im 'The first person in any new enterprise is bound to be an amateur; there can't be any professionals at the beginning'. But 'ee dain't buy it. Said the world must be full o' historians. 'Ow else did all them history books I was readin' get writ?' Ar, we ad' some fine old arguments we did. Ernie liked arguing – same as me. You heard us at it. What yow think Tom?"

"I'm not sure. As you know I used to read a fair amount of history myself. And to me your basic idea sounds fresh, though there are some 'Histories of Technology' out there. But they don't, so far as I am aware, deal with the driving effect of technology on a specific nation's history, as yours will do. So you've probably got a fresh idea to start from. And that's bloody important. On the other hand I'm sceptical you can actually carry it through."

"Why?"

" First of all you simply haven't put the time into it to know what you're really talking about. You can't have done. What with work, the war, compulsory overtime and Ernie you simply can't have done. Yes I know you hardly sleep Bob, Ernie told me. But I imagine that by the time a professional historian actually starts to write a history he'll be in his early to mid thirties. Starting from his A-levels at age sixteen at school he'll have at least fifteen years of full time history behind him – and in the company of professionals.

And he'll have professional assistants, graduate students probably. You've got a hell of a lot of catching up to do – and you're isolated. Isolated scientists, as a comparison, contribute very little to real science. The isolated genius is a myth nowadays – with honourable examples; Einstein for instance. But he didn't work in a car factory. And there must be all sorts of professional historical skills that you will need – and which you probably cannot learn outside a university: archival skill for instance, and tracing primary sources. You might write an entertaining, even influential essay on your subject – but the professionals would never take it seriously. Never."

"Yow'm bloody encouraging." Bob sounded crestfallen.

"I just don't want you to waste your life Bob. It's too valuable. I think Valerie may have got it right. You should do Wild Goose – where you are a professional, and remain an amateur historian for fun. So what do you think about my dream? And spare me no blushes."

"Ar," Salt sounded reluctant to change the topic. "O' course I thought a lot on it since yow told me. Yow want a revelation about the Universe. I dain't blame yer. Sounds incredible. Oy can imagine it. Our Tom sittin' there, knocked clean sideways by the wonder on it all; recognizing the 'ole Universe is quite different to all what his predecessors and colleagues think, an' all what he thought hisself jist the minute before. What an amazin' bleedin' fantasy. It's like Billy Liar – remember 'im? An' its jist possible I suppose. Trouble is yow can't jist order oop a revelation can yer? Either it cooms or it dain't. There's nothing yow can do to bring it about – 'less yow go out into the wilderness an' lives on locusts and honey. At least I kin try with me own ambition, daft as it may seem to you. Yow can't. Yow kin only stand there in the bleedin' wilderness and wait to be struck by lightening."

"I know what you mean Bob. But it's not quite as bad as that. They say revelation only comes to the prepared mind; that genius is ninety percent perspiration and ten per cent inspiration. If I soak myself, day and night, every day and night I mean, in galaxies, in cosmology, in star formation and stellar dynamics, until it's all part of my living flesh and mind – after all that's what 'going out into the wilderness' meant, total immersion in the problem, then maybe lightening will strike me one day. If I spend more time thinking about galaxies than any man who has ever lived then I will deserve, even if I do not earn, the great revelation that might come stealing in from the darkness of the night."

"All very poetic. An' I wish yow well Tom – o'course I do. But dain't yer turn into an 'oly man, and neglect our Ann, or yer daily bread. Yow can't live on revelations – 'less you want to get crucified."

After the run was over they drove back down the mountain, stopping at the most spectacular view-points for Bob to get some last nostalgic prospects far out across the mountains and the desert.:

"I shan't never be the same again Tom. Never. Even when it's a pissin' with rain in Brum, an' dark afore tea-time, I shall see Babaquiveri in me minds eye, know the mountain is out here in the desert , an' I'll look oop in the black clouds an' I'll know that above 'em are a million stars and galaxies, like what I've seen here in Arizona, stretchin' to eternity. An' I'll look at the poor blind creatures around me, like moles a'workin in the earth, an' I'll feel sorry for 'em, cos I'll know what they dain't."

At the bottom, when they reached the saguaro forest and the Papago reservation, he went on:

"We 'ave coom to earth again ain't we. I only wish as we hadn't landed with quite sich a bump. Oop there it were all dream-stuff and ambition. Down 'ere it's all bleak reality. I ain't goin' to write immortal history and yow ain't going to 'ave a revelation."

"My God!" Morgan gasped as he swerved the big Ford Galaxy to avoid a Road-runner which had dashed across their path like an insane but very fit chicken. He pulled off into the cactus and doused the engine, which ticked in the desert heat.

"You know Bob I think you are going to write that history after all. If you had two mustard keen full-time assistants, two young PhDs trained in historical research techniques, you could do it, and do it well in five to ten years."

"Ar" Salt looked bewildered. 'I reckon as I could. But oo's going to pay for 'em?"

"Ernie is, or rather Wild Goose is. Or rather the US Air Force is going to. In your proposal you haven't asked for a salary for yourself have you?"

"No. I got me pension."

"Well you are going to ask for one now: a great big fat salary suitable to the boss of a company which is vital to Uncle Sam's security interests. The Americans would naturally expect that, and so should you. And one managing director's salary would very comfortably support at least two keen young scholars of history."

"S'trewth – it might an' all." Bob leaned over and gripped Morgan's arm; " I reckon Tom, as yow've jist had a revelation. Yow'm getting into practice loike – for the big 'un."

After Morgan's 'revelation' things moved swiftly on the Wild Goose front. Knowing now what he wanted, Bob Salt and his lawyer completely rewrote their proposal with a much increased budget for 'management and consulting fees'. The Air Force responded by insisting on much stricter conditions on secrecy. Bob baulked at first but Morgan urged him to accept:

"These fellows you're negotiating with are basically underlings. They can't afford to tell their real grey boss up there that they've conceded everything for nothing. Let them have their little triumph – while you bank the crown jewels. The engine contract is the really tricky item. You should sign up on a 'best effort' clause and leave ultimate responsibility for delivering an efficient power plant to them." Morgan was worried that the ultra efficient engines required might require the development of either new materials or new fuels, both immensely costly undertakings.

"Ow' d' yer know all these things?" Salt was sceptical "Yow can't even service yer car."

"True" Morgan agreed "But that's the great thing about mathematics; its principles override mere details. It controls the Saturn moon-rocket's main engines as it controls the wing-feathers on a humming bird."

"Wisht I could bleeding understand it."

"So should all humans. It's the magic carpet which can carry a man's imagination as easily into the nucleus of the atom as it can beyond the furthest star. Without it men are blind and crippled. With it they can complete almost any voyage they can imagine. Wild Goose flies on mathematics. Mathematics –

Tsilkovski's equation in particular – took astronauts to the Moon. Even history is dominated by mathematics."

"G'arn. That's roobish."

"I bet you Bob Salt that when 'The Brits' is published there'll be a whole lot of stuff on mathematics in it."

"Gi' us an example then."

"OK. Let's see. What about the origin of the First World War. Hundreds of books have been written about it; none of them convincing. Then in 1921 Lewis Fry Richardson wrote a paper about it in Calculus, which of course none of the historians could understand. But those of us who can, have little doubt that Richardson was right. It came about from a mathematical instability in the business of threat and response, in other words the arms race. The war was accidental, but inevitable – like a drunkard driving a high powered car. Ask Ann, she agrees with me. Better still get her to teach you Calculus. You'd be three goals up on ordinary historians then."

The Wild Goose contact went through with surprising, almost suspicious speed. Bob got his Managing Director's salary, Valerie went on the payroll as bookkeeper, on the sensible ground that she could surely be trusted as a security risk, while Morgan had to sign away all rights to his equation and take an oath of secrecy.

'Old Salt' as Morgan was beginning to call Bob, was more than ready to leave. He was dreading going home to face Ernie's ghost but reluctant to postpone the encounter any longer

" Our Valerie's house-hunting already. If I dain't get back there soon Jacquie and her will 'ave us marooned in some bleedin' palace. But it's not me as I'm worried on Tom, its you. Yow gotter find a proper job , one as'll suit our Ann too. An' yow ain't got much toime."

Shortly after Bob departed Ann left for her six-monthly sojourn at The Admiralty. She thought she was pregnant again, but wasn't sure, and much on tenterhooks in consequence.

Deprived of all company Morgan felt sorry for himself, with more than enough time to worry about his job prospects. The first blow came from Canada when it was announced that the Canadians and French were jointly to build a 3.6 meter in Hawaii. To be situated at no less than fifteen thousand feet up on the summit of Mona Kea it would be by far the most powerful telescope on Earth. If only he'd taken the Vancouver job. If only! He rang Professor ---- to see if were too late to change his mind. Of course it was; they'd offered the job to the man second in line and he'd accepted immediately. The professor was apologetic about keeping Morgan in ignorance of the Canada-France-Hawaii-Telescope, as it was to be called but, for political reasons, he'd been sworn to absolute secrecy. Morgan felt very bitter. He'd won the perfect job in front of 236 rivals, and been forced to turn it down for political reasons. Now he had nothing, and time was running out fast. Goddard Space Flight Centre, Bob's first suggestion, was a great place by the sound of it, but was entirely out of the question so far as Morgan was concerned because he found it would entail applying for US citizenship, while the second, Mount Stromlo in Australia, hadn't even bothered to reply to his enquiry. The only thing on the horizon was a wretched twelve-month British fellowship designed, not to get him a proper job in astronomy, but merely to reverse the 'brain-drain' which, periodically and far too erratically, worried a UK government which had presided over the loss of most of its best young engineers to the States. Anyway the prospect of finishing up in British Industry simply appalled Morgan; to have flown so high, only to crash so low; he'd kill himself first, wife or no wife, baby or no baby. He even began to think of feasible ways of doing so: poison, drowning, a car crash, or organising a fall while climbing alone on Babaquivari – to make it look like an accident. Anything was better than another British factory. Anything.

Morgan was prone to such occasional suicidal fits. He'd had them ever since he was an adolescent. They came without warning, usually in the summertime as now. Part of his obsessional drive to succeed, first as a mountaineer, then as an astronomer, stemmed from his need to escape from 'Black Dog', as Churchill, a fellow sufferer, had called it. If he was frantically busy such attacks rarely seemed to intrude. But in periods of enforced idleness, or solitude as now, they crept in from the shadows. They painted every thing in a gloomy shade; made failure seem certain, and worse than that, success seem futile.

He realised he had no real friends in Tucson, merely colleagues, no one he could share a drink with or confide in. All around him other astronomers were squirming, impaled on their own thorns of misery, searching for non-existent jobs to stave off imminent unemployment. And in his jaundiced mood Morgan began to feel that much of professional astronomy was no more than bullshit and careerism. Seminars were often no more than elaborate advertising shams erected to disguise a total lack of imagination, or a result so insubstantial as to defy interpretation. More often than not mathematics was used as a smoke-screen designed to conceal a totally implausible assumption. Talks had to be given as part of one's career development – even if one had nothing interesting to say. Shabby little minds, and even littler ambitions, had to be cloaked in solemn respectability. For the audience it was like listening to a preacher who had lost his faith, but didn't dare to admit it.

And what did his own ambitions and achievements amount to? His Red Giant stuff was out in the literature but no one, so far as he could tell, was reading it. His thesis had led to nothing but frustration – and the Three Stage Model of the Interstellar Medium – which had been stolen. The Crab Pulsar had turned out to be a one-off dead end, all the remaining radio pulsars they'd looked at proving to be light-less. The Elliptical Radio galaxy observations had been very promising – but lacked the statistics to be absolutely convincing – and there were no more candidates to look at in the Northern hemisphere. Radio astronomers like Heeschen would have to carry out huge radio campaigns before significantly more quasar-like sources could be found nearby. The one ace he had up his sleeve was his theoretical proof that all Elliptical galaxies ought to generate Back Holes in their nuclei. It was a fascinating and provocative idea – but he could see no way to exploit it observationally – at least not with the tools available in 1970. It was becoming clearer and clearer that radio-emission from galactic nuclei was very much the exception rather than the rule: optical astronomers like Frank and Sandage were now finding large numbers of quasars with no radio signature. So even if he was right about Black Holes being universal in Elliptical galaxy nuclei, the vast majority would never give themselves away through detectable radio emission. And to find them solely by optical means would require optical observations of far greater precision than could be made from below the Earth's deep ocean of air. Atmospheric turbulence produced 'seeing' which wiped out all the finer detail. Indeed it was a wonder that ground-based astronomy had advanced as far as it had done. Looking for tiny nuclei through tens of tons of bubbling air was bound to be frustrating – and probably impossible. Through the 90-inch he'd never been able to actually *see* a single nucleus in an Elliptical galaxy, although the radio suggested that they must be there, and the spectroscopy supported that suggestion, without proving it definitely; after all there were other mechanisms beside Black Holes, such as star-formation, which might account for the emission lines.

All these difficulties were however as nothing compared to the black heart at the core of his own inadequacies. He didn't have an astronomical philosophy, a key idea, or a wide ranging astronomical program to guide and spur him on. He was, as he realised now, nothing more than an opportunist, and a parasitical one at that. He'd come into astronomy in the first place not through vision but through the accident of having fallen off a rock climb. He'd dived into quasars only through Jack Cockle's encouragement, and the feeding to him of other men's papers. Red Giants were the consequence of Frank's gift of Bellfounder's book. His now stolen Three Stage Model had grown out of not his, but Cecil Hood's ambition to understand star-formation. Pulsars were out there, an accidental discovery of radio astronomy, and fair game for any optical astronomer with a telescope. It was Wagoner, not he, who had originated the Elliptical gas-loss investigation, whilst it was Heeschen's radio work, not his own, which had motivated the galaxy nuclear program. He had been, and still was, nothing more than a parasite upon other mens' work, on other mens' ideas, upon other mens philosophies. He was, he realised with some disgust, no more than a smart alec, a gunslinger slightly quicker on the draw, so far, than his contemporaries. It was a way to survive of course, and many astronomers aspired to nothing more. But for Morgan it was a deeply dissatisfying, and ultimately futile way to live. If he could succeed in astronomy only by pulling off obvious coups slightly quicker than dozens, nay hundreds of his contemporaries, what was the point of it all? He felt like a hollow man with a hollow heart So far it had proved exciting, very exciting, but the novelty would soon wear off. His craving for a revelation, which he had confessed to Old Salt, was really nothing more than the pathetic self-doubt of a man with no faith or philosophy of his own. And why should such a hollow, faithless man deserve a career in astronomy? Surely the very few astronomical jobs that society would support should go to men who knew where they were going, men with scientific programs of their own to spur them on, men with imagination and vision, and not to failed rock-climbers. He remembered Karl Popper's remark: " I think there is only one way to science, or to philosophy for that matter: to meet a problem, to see its beauty, and to fall in love with it; to get married to it, to live happily with it till death do ye part – unless you should meet another and even more fascinating problem, or unless, indeed, you should obtain a solution. But even if you should obtain a solution, you may then discover to your delight, the existence of a whole family of enchanting though perhaps difficult problem children for whose welfare you may work, with a purpose, to the end of your days."

The terrible truth was that Twn Morgan hadn't found a Scientific Problem to fall in love with. Like he had been before he met Ann he was, in scientific terms, nothing more than a greedy sexual predator.

All this self-analysis made him desperately depressed, undermined his determination to look for a job – he didn't deserve one – and fed an increasing but futile need to talk to the handful of people who might understand his predicament: Frank, Mussels, Ann, Old Salt and Pat Gilkey. But all of them were enjoying summertime seven thousand miles away on that fortunate Atlantic isle which he had abandoned so insouciantly. He looked out of the window and saw a Prickly Pear bush, stark and thorny in the burning glare of Arizona. It looked like a creature from an alien world that might creep in and murder him.

As the weeks of Ann's absence grew into a month – she'd rung to say that she was onto something really big at work – Morgan slipped into a depression such as he had suffered only once before – at school when he was seventeen. That had lasted a year and made him suicidal. Now he couldn't sleep and so was chronically fatigued all the time. Actually he could go to sleep, but then would wake up after an hour or so with his heart pounding for no obvious reason, his body covered with sweat. Then he'd be tossing all night, his mind wandering gloomily and ineffectually over his past and his increasingly bleak future. Then he'd nod off just before dawn to wake up exhausted and depressed.

Worst of all came a gradually increasing sense of indecisiveness and paralysis. He knew he had to do something quickly about a job – but then sat in his office all day unable to make a sensible move. And that made him even more depressed. In fact he couldn't think why he was at the observatory at all. He was merely showing up to prevent anybody realising what a hollow shell he had become. He suffered continually from diarrhoea so that the weight dropped off him at almost a pound a day. It never occurred to him that he was suffering from a disease, in his case brought on through mental exhaustion – the result of slave driving his nervous system without let-up for the six years since his climbing accident. His brain had completely run out of some essential chemical and was spiralling into a fatal spin, from which it had no idea how to pull out. And the worse he felt the more ashamed he became. He was haunted by what Henry Cloudesly might say now when he found out that his daughter had been stolen away from him by a pathetic mental ineffective.

He desperately wanted to summon Ann back to his side. But he didn't dare. What would she think if she saw him as pitiable as he was now? Her compassion might survive – but her love certainly would not. And it was love he wanted above all. To lose it would be the final fatal straw.

But he had to do something. He had already taken in three notches in his belt and was sleeping scarcely at all while suicide, which he knew at some level to be utterly ridiculous, came to seem increasingly desirable. Ann would never have to see him in his shame, and would look back on him proudly, even as she married another man – which she certainly must do.

Morgan never thought of climbing Babaquivari as an explicit attempt at suicide. He felt that taking on something as physically and emotionally demanding might get him to sleep soundly – what he craved most desperately of all. Also it was a childish reversion to the only activity that had called to him almost as much as astronomy. He'd heard at third hand that the climb wasn't so technically demanding, providing one could find the one feasible way up, which was apparently by a ramp on the West Face. But he didn't have any map or guide. At least it didn't sound as if his still half-paralysed foot would completely disqualify him. But apparently it was dramatically steep, with the 7,700 foot pinnacle tower leaning out beyond the vertical from some directions. No small part of the challenge, apart from route finding, would lie in carrying enough water. The approach through the foothills was rumoured to be long, demanding and completely dry. However, at some seasons of the year, there was a pool, fed by a waterfall, at the foot of the savage tower. But his information was all very vague and, had he been in a sane frame of mind, he would never have relied on it, especially climbing alone, which he had solemnly promised never to do again. But he was a big strong man who could carry a great deal of water.

Setting off at midnight, telling no one where he was going, he drove the car far out into the desert along a track in the Papago reservation. Eventually the track became impossible for Beetle so he parked close to a clump of large saguaro cacti that might provide some shade in the daytime, and waited for the dawn.

When the sun finally did come up there was no sign of Babaquivari, only steep brown hills in that general direction. There was no path, he had no map, but he knew it must be up there somewhere above and beyond the foreground hills. He changed into his boots, put on a sunhat, loaded onto his back a ruck-sack heavy with plastic water-bottles and set out.

That first attempt turned out to be hopeless .He panted up one roasting, boulder-covered mountainside after another, then down the reverse slope, with the sweat dripping off his nose, guzzling water whenever he could deny his thirst no longer. He ran completely out of water without ever catching a glimpse of Babaquivari and stumbled back to the car suffering badly from dehydration. But at least he did sleep soundly that night – for the first time in weeks.

For the second attempt he set out in early afternoon carrying far more water. Stopping at the saguaros as before he set out in early evening and took out as much water as he could carry and cached it at nightfall by a cairn he built on a hilltop. Then he returned to the car by moonlight, ate, drank as much as he could, and dozed on an air mattress.

Setting out at midnight with another hefty load he climbed slowly uphill again with the last of the moon and the aid of a torch to reach his cairn just before dawn. He halted and drank until he could drink no more, left water behind for the return trip, and set out under a staggering load while the air was still cool.

This time he did get within sight of the awe inspiring tower, one like no other he had seen before. Babaquivari was an ancient volcano whose outer slopes had gradually eroded away over aeons of time. But the core of the old volcano, the ancient plug of frozen magma, was far harder than its outer mantle of loose rock. Thus the mantle had eroded leaving a vertical, and more than vertical tower of igneous rock spiring far up into the burnished blue. It was both beautiful and terrifying to look up at. Surely no one could climb that. Surely. He got out his binoculars to search for a possible route up. Nothing obvious could be seen on its awesome precipices. He would need to get closer. Mountains nearly always looked more impregnable from a distance.

The approach hills grew steeper all the time, forcing him to climb with his hands at times. On one such climb he received a shock. Using his hands to pull over a ledge he heard a rattle and found his face confronting a Diamond Backed Rattlesnake from all of eighteen inches away. The big snake, as surprised as he was, reared up from its coil, its jaws wide open to display its venomous fangs. Nearly falling off in fright Morgan lowered himself down again out of sight, expecting the fangs to strike into his still clinging fingers at any moment. Finding a secure foothold he slowly withdrew his fingers to safety.

After recovering from the shakes he set off again, by a slightly different route. The altitude was increasing all the time and the vegetation changing. The valleys were now thick with long dried grass, sometimes above his waist, in which any number of snakes might have been hidden. More dangerous though was the prospect of a broken ankle. Even a moderate sprain up here would mean almost certain death from thirst.

He had some water left, but not much, when he reached the last summit before the main tower. The view was staggering. The awesome cliffs soaring above his head, reached outward beyond the vertical. But the first priority was water. And there it was clearly visible in the glasses below him, a reflecting pool of perfectly blue sky. He drank the last of his water and scrambled down the scree towards it.

But the pool was guarded. As he approached Morgan was surprised to see, skipping just above the surface, and sometimes sipping in to it, swarms of large insects. Not realising the danger he was in he approached eagerly, taking off his rucksack as he did so, to bathe his face in the azure water. Flinging off his hat he got down on his knees to immerse his skin in the surprisingly cold lake. As he did so he received an agonising sting in the scalp and, before he could stand up, another and another. Dozens of huge yellow and black hornets were swarming round his head buzzing angrily. He got another sting in the scalp, two in the neck, one in his hand as he tried to beat them off, another on his lower lip. He ran for his life, snatching up the rucksack but leaving his hat. The hornets stung him several more times before he was free of them.

The stings were agonising, particularly the four in his scalp, each of which formed a hard throbbing lump. He'd once been stung in the hand by a venomous Bark Scorpion but each of his dozen hornet stings was considerably more painful. And there was no gin, no ice cubes and no painkillers to provider relief this time. Moreover the noonday sun beating down on his naked scalp only made the agony far worse. There was no question of climbing Babaquivari now, and without water there was some doubt whether he'd get back to his cache before thirst and dehydration got him. Suddenly it was all very serious. At least it had the effect of sobering him up. He knew he wasn't going to get back now without the soundest judgement and the clearest purpose.

It proved to be a nightmare journey back. He lost his bearings once, finding the water cache as much by good luck as by good navigation. His lip swole up like a balloon while there were no anti-histamines or decent painkillers in the only Indian store he could find on the way back to Tucson. At home half a bottle of Mexican gin was needed to make the hornet stings bearable.

A couple of days later, when the swellings had gone down, he went to a boring seminar in the department. Afterwards he found himself in the urinal with the speaker, an Australian who turned to look at him keenly`;

``You must be Tom Morgan, the fellah whose coming out to join us at Mount Stromlo?"

"It's the first I've heard of it."

"S'Truth. Stone the bleeding crows! It's that bloody personnel department again". He gave his peter a last shake, stood back, zipped, and held out a hand:

"Pleased to meet you mate. Bill Lawson. We've offered you a three year fellowship, extendable to five. Haven't accepted anywhere else have you?'

"Not yet."

"Well don't!" I'll go straight to the office here and put a rocket up their bleeding backsides in Canberra. You should get a cable back tomorrow, at the very latest. But take it from me mate, we want you."

CHAPTER 11
SOUTHERN CROSS
1970

As the great white ship began to move away from Fisherman's Wharf a negro band on a fire engine broke into New Orleans jazz, tugs whooped, the ship's basso profundo siren echoed back off the sky scrapers down town, the paper streamers from ship to shore began to stretch out and snap. Passengers, some in tears, ran frantically up and down the rail to catch a last glimpse on the dockside of the friends and relations who had come to see them off on the long voyage across the Pacific.

Ann and Tom Morgan stood, clinging to each other, on the fantail, a vast open deck at the stern which commanded a magnificent view of the city, the Golden Gate bridge, the San Quentin island penitentiary, and San Francisco Bay sparkling in the morning sun. As the screws began to turn, throwing a huge welter of wake out from under the stern, the P and O liner Oriana swung its bows for the Golden Gate, Vancouver, Hawaii, Fiji, New Zealand and Australia.

"What a wonderful adventure it's been" Ann wiped a tear from her eye; "Thank you darling. And thank you America! It's been tough but I wouldn't have missed a thing. Would you?"

He hugged her, remembering Tadpole who would have been six months old now: "I've learned so much here; so darned much. I'm not the same person who left London. We owe America so much. At least I do."

Ann looked up at Morgan's face, still gaunt from his recent depression:

"Do you think we'll ever come back?"

"I'd hate to think not. Who can tell? To work probably. To live? It's in the lap of the stars, literally. If I make discoveries we can go anywhere in the world. But if not then it's back into the welcoming jaws of Bellfounder."

"Of course you will. You're my discoverer." She squeezed him so hard that his ribs ached. "I love you so much......." She was going to add 'more' because, now that she'd seen her giant beaten to his knees, she could love him as a man, not merely as a hero. Arriving back in Tucson, jubilant in her new pregnancy, she'd been shocked to find the state he was in: gaunt, hollow-eyed from lack of sleep, unsmiling, listless, indecisive, his scalp still blistered from sunburn. The laughing giant she'd married, the hero who brushed all difficulties aside, had become a shell, a child stumbling around in a wilderness of fears. He couldn't even make up his mind about the Australian job – which to her mind seemed idyllic for him.

Lost herself, unsure what to do, she rang Old Salt:

"If yow ask me ee's exhausted – like a sodjer what's been in too many battles. Ever since we've knowed him ee's been fighting. First 'is leg. Then that Bellfounder. Then 'is thesis. Then the Crab. I reckon losing that Vancouver job were the final straw. Yow take charge Ann. Our Tom will recover, dain't 'ee worry. Ee's a warrior and no mistake. Ee'll go down fightin' will Tom – if ee goes down at all. Jist yow give 'im a little rest. Make the decisions yerself. A week's fishin' would probably see 'im right."

Pat Gilkey, when consulted, was more forthright. Ann had to hold the receiver even further away from her ear than usual:

"That boy's a dreamer honey, and he lives in a bubble. I should know – been married to one for fifty years myself. Walter's the sweetest damned man – but if he has to think about jobs or money why he goes plain underground like a mole. He doesn't come up again until the coast's clear. And I bet Tom Morgan is even worse. Why he looks like Byron, he behaves like Byron, and if you don't hold his pants up sometimes, he'll die like Byron. Imagine a poet like him working in a car factory."

When Ann protested that she was even less practical than Tom, Pat Gilkey was impatient:

"You're different honey. You're a woman. We women can do anything. We have to. Why me and Walter would have plum starved to death if I hadn't taken him in hand – inexperienced as I was, and much younger'n you sweetheart. You just put him in a boat and take him off to Australia. And if you need any help just ring Patti."

Ann concluded that both of them were right. Tom was exhausted, he should go to Canberra, and she would find them a berth on a ship – which she managed only through Pat's influence:

"I know the chairman of P and O honey. Walter and I have travelled first class many times with them. He'll do anything for Patti." And he did.

They'd had only five short weeks between cabling off their acceptance and taking ship, weeks when Tom had to clear up his work and write two papers, when Ann had to sell up everything including Beetle, when they had to give a big Thank-you-and-goodbye party for all their friends, weeks when they had to organise their visas and clear up Morgan's income-tax affairs, for he wouldn't be allowed to leave the USA without a complex quittance from the Revenue authorities. He wrote the papers and did the heavy lifting, all in something of a daze, while Ann did everything else. Having been passive for so much of her life she found the effort intimidating at first but exciting once she'd started. Tom didn't seem to mind her taking charge, in fact he was grateful. Indeed the experience completed their union. She looked up to him as her master, met him eye to eye as a lover, and now looked fondly down at him as her child.

They hired a big U-Haul truck and, with ten days to go, threw everything in the back, including a double mattress to sleep on, and set off across the desert on a star-spangled night. They called in at Long Beach to say goodbye to Pat and Walter, lived in a log cabin in a redwood park, strolled in wonder through the great sequoia groves, and finally camped on the Monterey Peninsula which was, according to Robert Louis Stevenson "the finest meeting place of land and sea and sky."

"I know" said Ann as the Oriana sped under the red span of the Golden Gate "Let's have a last wish. Have you got a penny?" He gave her a newly minted red cent. It flashed copper highlights as she threw it into the ship's boiling wake. She closed her eyes, wishing devoutly as it disappeared from sight.

"Penny for your wish" said Morgan

"You're not supposed to tell silly."

He felt in his pocket, took out all the remaining coins and, in his first spontaneous gesture for a month, flung them extravagantly as far astern as he could:

"I'm not shy about mine." he said kissing her passionately.

"Oh?"

"I'm wishing the next fifty years of our marriage will be as happy as the last two."

"Then you shouldn't have told me." Ann, always superstitious, looked pained.

Three weeks later Ann and Tom stood forrard with most of the ship's company as the Oriana raced towards the cliffs of New South Wales at her full twenty seven knots.

Even with the morning sun behind them there was no sign of a breach in the rugged limestone cliffs, indeed no sign of the great city right ahead. Ann looked around her at the expectant faces, some apprehensive, some delighted, some merely relieved: immigrants from Britain and America, young 'Aussies' returning from their three years in Earl's Court, oldies secretly happy to be back after the trip of a lifetime "home"; all waited to catch their first glimpse of Sydney.

The engines throttled down, the tall slabby cliffs rose around and above them until suddenly they were into the long low fjord of Sydney Harbour, its blue waters sparkling in the Saturday morning sun, busy with ferries and sailing yachts.

"Look there's the Opera House" Tom, now back to his old self, shouted with excitement.

"And Sydney Harbour Bridge" Ann pointed

" Look there's Manley......Cremorne........Balmoral ......Vaucluse.....Kirribilli.....Point Piper..... Rushcutter's Bay...." the locals shouted as their favourite suburbs hove into sight.

"Gosh look at that." Tom pointed "It's a Sydney Harbour Eighteen Footer – the fastest sailing craft afloat."

The crew of three young men, leaning far out on trapezes to balance the huge press of sail, waved up at them as they raced under the Oriana's bow.

"It all looks so English." Tom remarked, pointing at the higgledy piggledy suburbs of red roofed bungalows.

"But look at the palm trees and the bougainvillaea darling – and the poinsettias. You don't get them in Kew."

They docked at Circular Quay, right next to the Opera House, the Harbour Bridge, and the skyscrapers of Wooloomaloo. Morgan was intrigued by the heavy traffic of green ferries and hydrofoils making off or returning from places with names such as Dee Why, Curl Curl, Avalon, Balmain, Parramatta, Darling Harbour and Bondi while Ann was impressed by the botanical garden. They strolled ashore, admired the ivory sails of the Opera House, which Morgan declared to be the most beautiful building he'd ever seen, and finished up sitting in the shade of an impressive Morton Bay Fig looking across the Botanic Gardens and far down the bay to the 'Heads' through which the ship had come.

"Look, look,look!" Ann cried with delight as a troop of Sulphur Crested White Cockatoos settled on a branch above their heads to look down at them with frank curiosity.

"They know we're Poms" Morgan said "They're going to take the Mickey out of us."

While there was something tropical and raffish about Sydney, Canberra was respectable, and planned down to the very last detail. They were met at the station by a lady with a clip board from the university who took them to their furnished house, showed them their dinner warming in the oven, counted out the linen and spoons with Ann, showed Morgan a box of logs for the stove and, before she left, turned on the television to demonstrate that it worked. The ABC news was just starting. The headline was an item about a well backed horse that had just been scratched from the Melbourne Cup because of 'coughing'.

Morgan, used in America to watching harrowing bulletins from the war in Vietnam, howled with derision. But Ann stopped him:

"Wouldn't you rather be in a country obsessed with triviality rather than tragedy Tom? I know I would."

Like everything else in Canberra, the university estate on which they lived, known to its inhabitants as 'Nappy Valley' had been thoughtfully planned. It was a circle of brick semi-detached houses built round a central green where the innumerable children could play, safe from any traffic. Each house had a small private garden on the outside with an open garage to shade the car from the Australian sun. Their suburb of 'Hughes' was soul-less but efficient: there was one mini-market; one nursery school; one surgery; one bus-stop; no pub but three gas-barbeques, the only sign that the inhabitants were expected to enjoy themselves.

"It's a council estate." Morgan said in disgust. "You can just see the architects sitting round a table, counting the number of inhabitants and saying 'A hundred a fifty families, at the specified rate of one gas barbeque per fifty families, that's three barbeques in all'."

"But you've got to admit the house is nice, and ideal for young children." They had picture windows looking Northward into their private garden and towards the sun. Canberra, at a height of nearly two thousand feet was surprisingly cold at night, so the log stove made a pleasant and hypnotic focus for family life. The open plan kitchen-dining room was full of sun while upstairs there were three bedrooms and a bathroom. And they didn't have to buy a single fork or spoon. Even a saw and axe were provided by the university for chopping up logs.

The city itself, of less than two hundred thousand, was built round artificial Lake Burly Griffin and broken up into self-contained suburbs, all named after Australian prime ministers, concealed from sight of one another by low hills covered in black bush. Away from the modest civic centre, and the government buildings and embassies situated around the lake, it was possible to imagine oneself living in a small out-back town.

The day after arriving, since there was nothing else to be done, Ann made Morgan's sandwiches, and at 8.30 he caught the observatory bus which trundled out of town, along the Cotter valley, up the steep side of Mount Stromlo, to the government observatory on the summit. There were three serious telescopes, an impressive house for the Director, a large workshop, and modern offices for the astronomers. Morgan was assigned an office which peeped out, between the trees, across the valley of the Murrumbidgee river, towards the tall forested Brindabella Mountains about five miles away. He was sitting at his desk taking in the view when a crimson and ultramarine parrot strolled into view. Its colours, by contrast to the dark green pines, were outrageous. Indeed it was several seconds before he could convince himself that it wasn't some mirage.

The astronomers, met over sandwich lunch, were a low-key bunch who talked about anything but astronomy: sport, television and politics for preference. The director, Professor Oliver Bacon from America, showed no signs of wanting to meet him. One astronomer explained:

"Bacon's a bachelor. He works nightime hours, so we scarcely ever see him. If you need anything see Duggie, he's the Administrator."

The motto of the observatory, almost the antithesis of Steward, was 'Get on with your work, but for Christ sake don't talk about it.' There were no lectures, while the seminars, which Bacon never attended, were few and far between. After all, apart from a handful in Sydney, the nearest astronomers lived on the far side of the Pacific in California. Morgan suddenly realised just how isolated he was going to be. He might have been over stimulated in Arizona. Here he'd be lucky to find any stimulation whatsoever.

Ann was rather proud of her new house; it would be the ideal place to bring up her baby. She sat in the garden in one of the provided deck-chairs, soaking up the sun – something you couldn't do in Arizona, sipping her coffee and planning the little improvements which would turn the house into a home. Then she called briefly on the neighbours. There was a Russian family on one side, the Olegonskys who had somehow escaped with their young children from Siberia. And on the other side, in the other half of their semi, lived an odd couple who worked with the Department of Aboriginal Affairs. Only the wife Karen was at home, a tall dreamy beautiful girl of Australian-Italian extraction, who was writing a PhD on the social problems of the aboriginal people in Arnhemland in the far North of Australia. With their common interest in Stone Age peoples Ann thought they might become friends. Karen's husband Roy, who was scarcely ever there, turned out later to be a small, shy balding man quite old enough to be Karen's father.

Although the house had been thoroughly cleaned it had been empty for several weeks so Ann decided it needed a good airing, and that all the pots and pans should be thoroughly scrubbed. Making the mistake of leaving the door wide open for them the Canberra flies swarmed in and buzzed about the kitchen whilst she climbed on a chair to take down the saucepans from a higher shelf. To her surprise something black launched itself off the shelf past her face and landed with an audible clunk on the fly screen over the sink window behind her. There was a frantic but short-lived buzz as the large black spider closed in and murdered a fly that had been resting on the screen. An arachnophobe since childhood Ann teetered on the chair with a saucepan in either hand, watching in absolute horror as the beast sucked the paralysed fly dry, rotating the body in its mandibles. Not as large as the bird-eating Tarantulas of Arizona, it was nevertheless larger than the span of her hand, and very active. The thought of a spider that could jump eight feet onto its prey paralysed Ann's breathing mechanism so that she that she began to faint. Fortunately she realised in time, dropped the pans onto the floor with a crash, and tottered down onto the ground herself. When she'd gulped a few breaths and looked up, the beast had disappeared.

Knowing there was a giant black spider in her house, one that was crouching hidden somewhere, waiting to leap out and swarm up her body, was more than Ann could bear. She ran out into the garden and collapsed into the deck chair.

When Morgan returned at five he was astonished when his wife threw herself into his arms and burst into hysterical tears. He had no conception of the nightmare ordeal she'd been through over the past few hours while he'd been peacefully catching up with the astronomical journals in the observatory library. Unwilling to ring him up, or bother the neighbours, she'd several times screwed up her courage to confront the hidden monster in her house. Armed with a garden broom she'd tottered back into the kitchen, expecting at any moment that the beast would leap out and sting her to death. But it wasn't in the kitchen, at least not anywhere that she could see, though it could easily have been concealed behind the fridge or in the darkness underneath the sink. She tried the living room, her heart palpitating as she shook the curtains, fearing that 'the thing' might fall down upon her. She moved the sofa and the arm chairs, but it wasn't under any of those. The large wood-box piled with eucalypt logs seemed a likely hiding place. Donning rubber washing up gloves and gritting her teeth with horror she lifted the logs out one by one and put them on the grate. Suddenly the spider ran out from among the logs, leaped onto the floor and swarmed up the wall where it stood, sinister and still, just within reach of her broom.

It needed all the courage she could summon, to approach the monster. If it fell she would be right underneath. She didn't really have a plan. All she could think of was to hit it with the stiff bristles of her brush, immobilising it by transfixion. She held her breath, drew back the brush with her one trembling arm, she had the dustbin lid in the other as a shield, and hit the spider with all her might and main. The beast fell onto the floor with a thunk, obviously stunned at least. She threw the dustbin lid over it and ran into the garden to wait for Tom. Nothing in the world would have induced her to lift the lid and confront the creature waiting underneath.

Morgan, who had a strong distaste for spiders himself, was disturbed by Ann's agitated, almost hysterical state when he got home. Having calmed his wife as best he could he went into the house to confront the monster himself. It was about fifteen minutes before he emerged, feeling pretty shaky himself, with the corpse, which had been crushed under his shoe, in a paper bag. Ann was wild eyed with adrenalin shock.

They went round to the Mini market hand in hand and explained their problem to the little Italian behind the counter. He sold them a large yellow can of poison spray guaranteed to instantly kill the largest spider that ever lived. Before nightfall Morgan had sprayed every nook and cranny of their of the house three times over, more to give his wife the reassurance she so clearly needed.

She clung to him all night long. And in the morning she had her second miscarriage.

Ann, who looked d like a ghost when she came out of hospital, had to cope with this miscarriage without maternal support. Australia was too far away from Britain, and far too expensive a journey for Gwendolyn to undertake. Quantas and British Airways had sown up some kind of crooked monopoly which meant in effect that only the rich could travel casually in and out of Australia. Morgan stayed at home as much as he could, while Karen from next door was continually in and out of their home. She reassured Ann that Huntsman spiders, grisly though they looked, were in fact quite harmless to humans. Indeed she and Roy prized theirs as a form of free pest control:

"They're nocturnal hunters" she explained. "So even if you have one in the house you'll rarely see it. That one must have been extra hungry because the house has been vacant for so long. The only sort of spider you really have to worry about in Australia, the one with the fatal bite, is the Funnel-web, and we don't have those anywhere near Canberra. So there's no need to worry."

Phobias are not logical however and in her debilitated and disappointed state Ann wasn't capable of logic anyway. She looked upon the new house, and Canberra in general, with gloomy distaste. She didn't say much against their new home but was continually nostalgic for London.

Morgan decided that what she really needed was excitement and a change of scenery. What had reconciled her to Tucson was camping out in the wildernesses of Arizona.

A Polish astronomer in Tucson had explained to Morgan that there was an anomaly in the US tax system which would enable him, once he'd left the country, to claim all his considerable US income tax back, provided he could show that his research had been self-motivated, that he hadn't come to America solely to work on some large corporate project. This was easy to do and three weeks after they reached Canberra he received an enormous cheque in the post. Keeping it as a surprise from Ann he went round to the Volkswagen dealers and bought a brand spanking new white Volkswagen bus.

Ann didn't notice it standing in the garage at first, so he lured her into the garden on the pretence of having a drink.

"Golly" she said "Whose is that?"

"It's a present from the United States Revenue. It's ours darling. And in it we're really going to see Australia. Let's take it for a test drive."

The VW Kombi, or 'Bus' as they unoriginally christened it, was the iconic vehicle for exploring the outback. With massive ground clearance and a powerful air cooled engine set over the rear driving wheels it could thrash along all day on the roughest of Australian dirt roads. Rugged and reliable, with a high driving position, it could easily carry half a ton of camping equipment, jerry cans of fuel and water and, if necessary, half a dozen spare tyres on the enormous roof-rack. Morgan had had a kangaroo-bar or 'roo-bar' fitted across the front equipped with a spare wheel, so as to absorb the impact of any kangaroo foolish enough to leap out onto the road in front of them.

After Beetle 'Bus' was a capacious luxury which they kept permanently fitted out for camping. Though its sliding side door they placed a double mattress on the floor for sleeping aboard. On the platform over the rear engine they kept the big orange tent which they'd bought as their wedding present, a table and chairs, the big camping stove, a Tilly lamp, jerrycans, tucker-box, entrenching tool, medicine chest, a saw and axe for firewood, tools, spares and torches. The tent was something of an unnecessary luxury for they could sleep inside with the side-door wide open but protected from rain by a 'tarp' which was attached to the roof rack above and boomed out on two tent poles. It would take all of five minutes to make camp in the evening, and rather less to strike in the morning.

"She's our land yacht." Ann boasted. "We can go anywhere."

"Yes you can" Karen was envious. 'You could do the Olgas in the Red centre, or go right across the top of Australia and visit Kakadoo."

"I want to see Tasmania." Morgan asserted.

"Well where shall we go first?" Ann wanted to know.

Karen didn't know, being new to Canberra, so Morgan asked around at the observatory

Discouragement was universal:

"The moskeeters out there in the bush'll eat yer alive mate."

"Yeah they even drive some of those big buck 'roos barmy."

"And what about snikes?" Christ they're bloody teeming in the bush. There's Browns, and King Browns...."

"Tiger snikes......"

"Red bellied Blacks......."

"Yeh they're bloody vicious."

"And Taipans."

"One bite of a Taipan's got enough venom to kill two hundred and thirty six sheep. They tested it mate.

"Then there's leeches that drop from the trees."

"It's the kangaroo ticks I'd worry about. They drop from the gum trees too and bury their 'eads in your flesh. Try to pull 'em out and the 'ead comes orf and goes sceptic in yer body."

"An'that's not the worst. Some of the buggers carry brain-fever – parasites that cause incurable encephalitis."

"You must be joking." Morgan protested. But apparently they weren't. Aussies huddled into their cities because their hinterland was so inhospitable. His heart sank:

"Well we'll stay on the beach."

They were equally scornful:

"What yer gonner do? Go in the sea? What about the blue-bottles?"

"And the sea wasps."

"And the blue-ringed octopus."

"And the White-pointer sharks."

"And the hammerheads."

"And the barracudas"

"You could step on a stone fish. They say the sting is such agony that guys have put their foot in a bucket of boiling water to relieve the pain."

"I think you're having me on" Morgan laughed "Taking the mick out of a Pom."

"Nah really." They were earnest, elaborating further on the dangers:

"The CIA has tested the venom of the Box Jelly-fish. It's the strongest poison known to science; leads to paralysis and death. They're trying to turn it into a weapon for use in Vietnam."

"Yeah the lifeguards up in Queensland have to wear body-stockings made out of a sheila's underwear to protect themselves against the stings. The jellyfish tentacles are yards long and totally invisible."

"I'd rather one of them than a seawater croc. They measured one off Darwin more than thirty five foot long."

"Jesus – you're kidding."

"No bluff mate. They showed it on a newsreel taken from a fishing boat that went alongside. The crock stuck out both ends."

Morgan was dismayed by all these evidently sincere warnings – which he certainly didn't relay to Ann. The only reassurance he received was from a taciturn Pom in the workshop who curled his lip:

"Ask if any of them have tried bush camping for themselves."

It turned out that none of them had:

"Why would I mate? Why would anyone? We stay in a motel. And if my kids go in the surf there's got to be a life-guard on duty with safety flags flying."

They decided to make their first weekend foray down to the South Coast of New South Wales which was about eighty miles from Canberra as the crow flies. Looking on the map they decided to avoid the main road via Bateman's Bay and follow a bush track down the Araluen Valley.

As soon as they struck off the main road the emptiness of Australia became apparent. Miles and miles would pass without the sign of a single dwelling. Tarmac gave way to stones and red dust which flew up in a plume behind them. Even the sheep paddocks gave way to millions upon millions of gum trees, grey gums, white gums, red gums, ghost gums…..gums gums gums. Their grey-green leaves and loose stringy bark seemed to have crowded every other form of vegetation out. To clear the bush farmers 'ring - barked' the gums which turned into desolate ranks of white skeletons that stood for generations before collapsing.

"And everything looks black" Ann noticed.

"I believe it must be fire" Morgan grunted, struggling with the wheel as they powered across a shallow ford and climbed the far bank.

They later learned that the Eucalypts or 'gums' encouraged bush fires which they could withstand, but which the competition could not. Their superficial bark burned black, protecting the live tree underneath. Indeed some gums couldn't even germinate without fire to crack open their seeds.

The endless gums were to Morgan depressing, to Ann dismaying, but neither said much. Then the track fell away beneath their wheels and they found themselves plunging down the Great Divide, a steep wooded precipice almost two thousand feet from top to bottom. The dirt road switched-backed wildly round and round with Morgan spinning the wheel, the tyres skidding, the forest bushes dragging tinnily along Bus's flanks. Clouds overhead gave way to brilliant sunlight which fell in darks and lights across the track. The gums gave way to other eucalypts, far taller and more jungle like, and beneath them Black-boys, spiny aguave like plants with black upright cores, tree-ferns, mosses, creepers and lawyer-vines.

"It's a different world." Ann gasped.

Morgan, concentrating to make sure a wheel didn't slip over the edge, barely noticed, but in their two thousand foot descent they moved as many miles nearer the equator. He was worried that they hadn't seen a single vehicle in two hours. Who would rescue them if there was an accident? Perhaps the way ahead was blocked off by a tree-fall or a landslide? Bus was bucking and rearing, their camping gear slamming about inside. Was a Volkswagen designed for a precipitous track like this?

"No wonder" Ann yelled at him "No wonder the pioneers took a century to climb the Great Divide. I shouldn't think even a mule could have climbed this without a road.

Suddenly though they were at the bottom and out of the trees. Bus crunched through the Araluen River up to her hubcaps and stopped in a meadow on the far side. When they silenced the engine and leaped out the silence was hypnotic. The river ran clear, babbling over its pebbled bed. From the depths of the forest they could hear an unearthly 'Pink', 'Pink', 'Pink'

"Bellbirds" exclaimed Ann. "They must be Bellbirds. How beautiful."

There wasn't a sign of human life; not a telegraph pole, not a strand of barbed wire; not even a fence post. Even the tyre marks on the track looked ancient.

"Tom, if anything comes along here once a week I'd be surprised."

"Can you blame them. Who the hell would want to risk a vehicle up that bloody incline. There were times I thought we were coming off."

"I don't believe it." Ann whispered dramatically. A troupe of half a dozen parakeets had swooped into a bush on the far bank. Their colours were beyond description or belief: orange, crimson, ultramarine , emerald and powder blue.

Morgan reached quietly into the bus and drew out the binoculars:

"You'll never believe what they're eating." he whispered

"What then?"

"Grapes; plump white grapes. For God's sake who planted those here? Lets go and look."

Once the Rainbow Lorikeets, for such they were established to be in Ann's bird book, had vanished, they waded across the river with a machete and hacked their way into the bush towards the vine. To their astonishment they discovered an ancient wooden dwelling entirely tangled in brambles and undergrowth. Morgan hacked his way up the rotten verandah and burst open the door with his shoulder, half expecting to find a skeleton in bed.

There was a bed with a rotten mattress, but no skeleton. The tin roof had rusted through and light was entering , along with creepers. There were pots and pans, vary ancient in style, a brick fire-place, two plates and a mug on the table.

From outside Ann cried out:

"There's an apple tree here. Several. This must once have been an orchard."

In amongst the undergrowth, or rather overgrowth, they found rusted and rotted implements; a pick, two shovels, the skeleton of a home-made wheel-barrow, an axe-head.

"My God, I know what this is," Morgan exclaimed "It's a riddle for washing gold. This must have been a gold miner's shack. They must have been panning alluvial gold from the Araluen River. I read about it somewhere. That was a hundred years ago or more. They probably left in a hurry when the big gold fields near Bendigo and Baliarat were discovered down in Victoria."

"Leaving their vine behind, and their apple trees. Are you sure there aren't any bones in there Tom?"

"We could look for graves."

"I wouldn't mind dying here. It's so peaceful. What a heavenly spot. Couldn't we camp here tonight?"

"Why not?"

Morgan hacked down some dry brush and lit a fire. Ann erected the tarp, put a billy of tea on to boil and sorted the bedding. The first mosquito whined round their ears as the stars came out.

"We'd better spray ourselves thoroughly." Morgan worried, apprehensive about how vicious they would become.

The gum wood snapped and crackled, giving off an excellent heat and a pleasant eucalypt aroma. Spuds in foil baked in the fire's edge, chops sizzled in the pan. Above the babbling of the river, from far far away in the forest, they heard the howling of a wolf.

"They don't have wolves in Australia do they?"

"I don't think so," Morgan replied 'But dingos are much the same thing. Could be a farm dog though from some lonely property way out in the bush."

"It's funny to think isn't it" Ann said, leaning back in her canvas chair, her face lit by the fire, and by the Tilly lamp hanging from the branch overhead "It's funny to think that the last person to camp here was an old gold-miner from a century ago. I wonder what became of him."

"He got on his horse and rode down the valley to the coast carrying his alluvial gold in a secret pouch next to his skin. There he got roaring drunk in a pub and lost the lot playing Two-Up with a couple of desperate rogues who stole his horse. So he took ship for Melbourne, walked up to the diggings at Ballarat and staked a claim which turned out to be almost solid gold. So he took a passage on a wool clipper bound for London where he turned all respectable and built a handsome house in Kew."

"Liar!"

"On my honour, hope to die."

"Then what?"

"He had elocution lessons, learned to play the piano, went to church twice every Sunday and changed his name by deed-poll."

"Why would he do that?"

"To snare a respectable woman of course."

"And did he?"

"Naturally. What passionate young lady could resist his enormous whiskers, the wicked gleam in his eye, not to mention the chink of gold in his pocket."

"Go on with you."

"Against the wishes of her entire clan, who could see the shameless rogue hiding behind those whiskers, and the obviously stolen gold, she eloped in the night."

"Hussy."

"She raced with him in a coach and eight to Gretna Green, where she lost her virginity and duly became Mrs Arabella Cloudesly."

"You devil." Ann smacked him fondly on the arm.

"And they fornicated madly, bringing forth a tribe of villainous boys and oversexed girls who took up respectable occupations, such as archaeology, to cover up the rotten gold-miner's blood coursing in their veins."

"Yo ,Welsh Morgan, are the most shameless story teller."

"If you don't believe me you can go back actually see the old house. It's called 43 Kew Gardens Walk now. But if you look carefully at the big iron gate you will see, painted over now, but still legible because it was heavily embossed, the original name 'Araluen'."

Ann giggled as she turned over the chops.

"But you haven't heard the worst." Morgan continued, pouring red wine into two tin mugs:

"Do you know what our rogue was called before he changed his name?"

"Crippen."

"No"

"Mussolini."

"You're getting closer."

"Hitler then."

"No. It was Morgan. So you're actually my second cousin, thrice removed. That's how I know the story."

Morgan had bought an enormous piece of mosquito netting which he draped over the entire bus, pegged to the roof-rack with tent pegs, and sealed with stones from the river bed. After Ann had climbed into bed he lit a hurricane lamp and went off in to the bushes for a pee.

As he peed he tried to pick out the unfamiliar Southern constellations. The Southern Cross was obvious, as was the bright star Canopus. To the North Orion looked upside down. He was looking for the Omega-Centauri cluster when something unexpected caught his eye. Surely not. He buttoned his fly and held the lantern above his head. He froze as the light picked out the most enormous spider's web. It was set between two trees and the ground with its perfect spiral pattern spanning well over twenty feet. He backed away, scarcely daring to imagine the monstrous spider to which it belonged. When he crawled under the blankets with Ann their giant mosquito net provided a comforting thought. But could a monster like that bite its way through?

Actually the net was no good. Somehow mosquitoes got through and whined about their ears. Both were bitten half a dozen times before Morgan turned on the light and squashed their blood bloated corpses against the walls of the van.

But the morning was glorious. The sun made shafts through the river mist; the Bell-birds pinked, the currawongs cried out like ghost-babies in the bush; a troupe of wallabies grazed the natural meadow, some with joeys in their pouches, heads out; parakeets, budgerigars and pink cockatoos came to visit their camp. They took off their clothes and washed one another in the river. There was only one leech, which got Morgan in the private parts. Ann was more amused than horrified, but quite a bit of both. Morgan nervously revisited his spider's web – just to check that it was more than a nightmare. Sure enough it was still there, vaster than ever and sparkling with droplets of sunlit dew.

The bush went right down to the sea's edge, which was still largely wild. The difficulty lay in finding a way down to the sea which didn't end in the odd private property. Rivers flowing down from the divide formed lagoons behind sandbars which also made access difficult. Ann, who'd more or less memorised the bird book, cried out with delight at ibis, egrets, terns, all manner of unfamiliar gulls, black swans gliding among the reeds, even a pair of huge sea eagles which used their V-shaped wings to glide along the beach, using sea breeze deflected upward by the bush to remain aloft.

After several aborted attempts off the coast road they used their senses of smell and sound to slowly guide Bus between fern trees to a white sand beach heaped with driftwood and therefore obviously pristine. They parked the van under the shade of a bottle-bush tree and ran into the heavy Pacific surf, throwing off their clothes like children.

"We've got it all to ourselves!" cried Ann with delight, as she was knocked over by a big green wave.

And so they had, apart from the tiny sandpipers who ran in and out of the surf, and the black oystercatchers with red eyes.

That night they built a giant bonfire from driftwood on the beach and ate baked fish which Morgan caught but couldn't identify, but which tasted well enough.

When the fire burned low, and the moon had set, they wandered in the surf hand in hand, admiring the Magellanic Clouds, apparently two chunks of the Milky way which had drifted off into space.

"Actually they're two galaxies in their own right," Morgan explained "Smaller satellites of our own. They're the only two galaxies one can easily see with the naked eye – because they're so close."

"How far are they?"

"About two hundred thousand light-years."

Ann stopped, looking up, the surf pounding in her ears, the breeze blowing out her hair against the stars.

"Do you mean to say that the light I'm looking at actually comes from the Stone Age?"

"That's the story."

"Do you believe it?"

"I suppose so. But that's what I'm aiming to find out for sure. Galaxies are going to be my life…."

"Oh are they Tom Morgan? Don't forget about your wife."

They slept that night with the sliding door wide open to listen to the surf roaring not twenty meters away. The sea breeze blew through the van keeping mosquitoes away.

In the morning they went body-surfing and five dolphins joined them for the sheer hell of it, flipping high backward somersaults in and out of the water whenever it became too shallow for them to swim.

"I swear they're laughing at us." Morgan yelled above the thunder.

"With us you mean" Ann yelled back.

"I'm glad you dragged me here darling."

"So am I." she replied before diving head first into the front of a wave that was rearing above her head.

The two astronomical ideas fixed in Morgan's head before he came to Australia were to read all he could about galaxies and to visit John Bolton at the radio observatory at Parkes

All that he knew of Bolton was that he was an ex-Royal Navy radar officer who'd settled in Sydney after the war where he'd pioneered the early work on quasars. He'd stolen a march on his rivals in Britain and America, including Bellfounder, by sheer ingenuity. As the radar officer on a ship he'd noticed that the radar return from an incoming aircraft sometimes went haywire. The explanation was that the sea's surface was acting as a reflector, a sort of mirror for radio waves. The ship's radar antenna would thus pick up two returning waves, one direct from the aircraft, the other reflected off the sea. The two waves, having travelled along different paths, would thus interfere with one another at the antenna. Sometimes the two wave-crests would meet at the antenna – to produce a doubly strong signal. Sometimes the crest of one wave would meet the trough of the other, leading to net cancellation and zero signal.

When he went to work in radio astronomy at Sydney it occurred to Bolton that the interference off the sea surface could be put to good effect. In those days the existence of powerful sources of cosmic radio signals had been established by numerous radar stations during the war. But the positions of those sources were far too inexact to identify them with particular stars or other astronomical objects in the sky.

So Bolton and his colleagues used a war surplus radar receiver on the cliff top at Sydney looking eastwards across the Pacific. When a cosmic radio source rose above the horizon the receiver would pick up two signals from it, one direct and one reflected off the ocean. At certain times, depending on the exact angle of the source above the horizon, the two signals would reinforce one another. Later, as the Earth turned, the two signals would cancel each other. By this following the waxing and waning of the combined signal in his antenna Bolton was able to pinpoint the exact positions of two powerful cosmic sources, Taurus A and Centaurus A. Comparing his positions with existing optical maps of the sky Bolton was able to conclude that Taurus A coincided with an exploding star, or supernova, called The Crab nebula. Apart from the Sun this was the very first identification of a cosmic radio-source, and so very exciting. Even more surprising was Centaurus A; it coincided with an Elliptical galaxy ten million light years away, a thousand times further than the Crab. No one had any idea what could generate such a colossal outburst of radio energy. Thanks to John Bolton the subject of quasar physics was born.

Since then the ingenious radio engineer had continued to pioneer the field. The Americans had hired him to build their first radio interferometer – in California. Instead of using the sea as a second source of cosmic waves, he used a second radio antenna, and interfered the signals from the two antennae together. With two big antennae, separated several hundred feet apart from each other on the ground, Bolton had been able to measure very accurate radio positions for weak, and therefore probably very distant radio sources

The people at Manchester and Cambridge had quickly caught up with Bolton, and even surpassed him in several respects: the Manchester people by using highly separated antennae; the Cambridge team by a mathematically sophisticated technique called 'Aperture Synthesis'. Where Bolton had kept his lead was by working at higher and higher radio frequencies. While technically challenging this had proved crucial, for quasars turned out to be predominantly high-frequency radio sources. That is to say they emitted far more energy at high frequencies than the low frequencies detectable at Cambridge. Frank Cotteridge and Bellfounder were having a low success in identifying quasars because the Cambridge radio telescope was working at the wrong frequency, for quasars at least.

In visiting Bolton Morgan didn't expect to prise out of him the positions of newly found radio quasars. Bolton had his own optical team, mostly at Mount Palomar in California, working on those in direct competition with Frank. What he did hope to prise out of him were the positions of high frequency radio galaxies which apparently Bolton wasn't interested in. Morgan hoped that among these particular radio galaxies he might find the crucial clue as to the true distances to quasars – for the moment the predominant problem in astrophysics.

Parkes being inland, two hundred miles North-North-West of Canberra, Morgan decided to drive up via quiet country roads, camping leisurely along the way.

The countryside was farmed, the farmsteads with their universally red corrugated – iron rooves standing well back from the road. Fortunes must have been made during the war when wool prices were sky high for often he saw swimming pools, floodlit tennis courts and even airstrips with a hangar for the farmer's private aircraft. But those days were evidently long gone; the pools were dry, the tennis courts cracked, the air strips overgrown.

He passed through pleasant little country towns like Yass, Booroowra, Cowra, Coonawindra, Eugowra, Mudgincoble. Each had two or three 'hotels', for which read 'pubs', its RSL (Returned Serviceman's League club) – another pub, one or two bookie's shops, an open air Memorial Swimming Pool (usually of full Olympic size), a Bowling Club, a golf course, an Anglican and a Catholic church, a public library, a country race-track, a water tower, a market for stock, one school, a cricket ground, and some sleepy old businesses selling farm machinery and sheep dip, mostly all laid out along or just off a main road wide enough to turn a bullock cart with eight oxen.

It was the custom of the pubs to give away free 'counter lunches' usually consisting of meat, gravy and two veg, This wasn't a charity, as Morgan had at first supposed. The food was so heavily salted that the diner found himself compelled to buy several extra 'midis' of the very expensive beer. Sitting at the counter, surrounded by sunburned farmers with forearms thick from lifting sheep, and wearing broad brimmed bush hats, he would listen to them discussing wool prices, or horse racing bets.

Part of the way lead along a 'drovers trail' through the Lachlan Valley. These trails, designed for moving large 'mobs' of sheep, had wide tracts of common land to either side for grazing the flock. Several times he was halted for a quarter of an hour as the 'woolies' flowed round him, occasionally leaping high into the air and landing on one another's backs. The drovers, on horseback and accompanied by their collie dogs, usually consisted of a man and his family, with the wife following, towing their caravan behind a heavily loaded 'ute'. Apart from the 'ute' Constable would have been at home painting such a pastoral scene. At dark Morgan would drive Bus off the road, through the grazing which was now thick with blue flowers. On a river bank, overhung with English Willows, he'd set up camp, light a fire and watch the stars come out while the steak and onions sizzled in the pan. The nearest man-mad light, beyond a farmhouse window, might be thirty mikes away. Here was a solitude and a freedom which he'd never enjoyed before – even in the wilderness areas of the American West.

The farther North he drove the flatter and more fertile the land became, the more distant the nearest clump of trees. Indeed so open did the country become that he caught his first glimpse of the radio telescope from fifteen miles away, a giant sunflower of steel filigree pointing at the heavens.

From close by it dwarfed the trees; the cockatoos that swirled about its aerial cabin looking scarcely larger than swallows . Built on the lines of a windmill its circular dish, more than two hundred feet across, sprouted out of the top of a circular control tower with small windows.

Parking the bus half a mile away in case it caused interference he approached the monster, camera in hand, awed by the majesty and symmetry of the steel-work. Every strut and rivet had to balance strength against weight. Chagrined to realise how very little he knew about radio astronomy Morgan did at least understand that to focus the incoming waves accurately up into the aerial cabin the whole steel dish would have to remain stiff to a fraction of the length of the waves it was detecting, which was about ten centimetres. So as it tilted about the sky the immense structure, which must weigh several hundred tons, couldn't deform under the forces of gravity and wind by more than a centimetre altogether. Such rigidity could only be attained by the most exquisite marvel of design and calculation. Sheer brute reinforcement wouldn't do because extra girders would also add their own weight and bending moment. Staring up at the intricate steel Morgan longed to know how its designers back in Britain had gone about the task. After all there were no precedents. Radio astronomers were the first beings on

Earth, perhaps in the cosmos, with the requirement for such a precision moving structure. Had the designer started from a sketch, or by using mathematics, or through pure intuition? How had he reassured himself that it could ever be done?

He was staring up wondering, when the dish began to move, tilting itself slowly towards him as if curious to see what he was like. Fully tilted and with its rim almost touching the ground, he had an excellent view of its inner reflecting surface, which was painted brilliant titanium white, presumably to prevent it overheating in the Australian sun.

So hypnotised was he by the big dish that he almost failed to notice a second sixty foot dish on rails a hundred meters to the east. That must be the interferometric dish that played the part of the ocean surface in Bolton's sea-interferometer. The combined signals from the two dishes would presumably yield radio positions on the sky far more precisely than the signals from either dish separately. He would love to have asked, but when he tried the door of the control tower it was locked, and there was nobody about except an old gardener in the distance mowing the grass beside the only building, a wooden hut that looked like an abandoned woolshed.

Lacking any other option Morgan strolled over towards the gardener, who totally ignored him. Only when the bin of his mower was full of grass did he dowse the clattering motor.

"Excuse me I wonder if you could tell me where I'd find John Bolton?"

The stringy old man glared at him, took a tin out of his khaki shorts and proceeded to roll a fag. He licked the paper, cupped his gnarled workman's hands about the fag to ward off a non-existent wind, never taking his eyes off Morgan's face, and set the incendiary on fire:

"What do you want to see John Bolton for?" he demanded truculently, spitting out a leaf.

Taken aback, Morgan was about to riposte "What business is it of yours?" when he realised that without this workman he had no idea of how to find the great man. Rather reluctantly he explained who he was. The man finished his revolting fag, some of which stuck to his lip, and ground the stub of it into the dirt.

"I am John Bolton." he said, the Yorkshire accent evident at last.

Morgan was so astounded he didn't know what to say. It was Bolton who eventually broke the embarrassing silence:

"D'you play cricket?"

"Y-y-yes." Morgan stuttered.

"Bat or bowl?"

"Bit of both."

"Any good?"

"Not bad. Once upon a time."

"What standard?"

"Played for the Army." Morgan replied, picking up the laconic tone.

"All right then. You can give me a net. I've got a big match tomorrow." And with that the great man walked over to an old ute' and hopped in, evidently expecting Morgan to follow.

Thus for the next two days John Bolton kept Morgan at arms length. He arranged for him to be put up at the observers' quarters about a mile from the dish, but otherwise refused to discuss astronomy. He was however invited over to the Bolton's for supper where Mrs Letty Bolton looked him over. The results must have been satisfactory because the following morning Morgan was invited into the old woolshed – which turned out to be Bolton's office.

"What did you come to see me for lad?" – the great man was at last willing to talk about science – or rather to listen, for he had little to say for himself.

Morgan explained at some length his ideas about the quasar distance problem: "If I could find just one radio source with all the characteristics of a quasar, but which looks to be lying in a galaxy, I might be able to settle the distance problem once and for all. I'm assuming there will be a weak quasar in the nucleus – from which I will measure an optical spectrum, with a certain redshift. Then I'll move the slit of the spectrograph out to the faint outer halo of the galaxy, presumably consisting of normal stars, and attempt to get a spectrum from that. If I succeed, and if the redshift of the quasar light is the same as the redshift of the starlight, then both redshifts must be attributed to the expansion of the universe – from which we will get the distance. But if the two redshifts are different then we'll know that some kind of exotic physics is involved, and we won't be able to say anything about either quasar distances or luminosities."

Bolton was silent for some time after this outburst, licking the paper on yet another of his disgusting home-made fags. He lit it, inhaling deeply, and spitting out odd bits of tobacco that had escaped from the crude paper tube. His eyes, black and piercing, apprised Morgan coldly through the smoke. It was hard to believe he was a Cambridge graduate.

"So what do you want of me lad? If its quasars you want then I can't help. I'm already committed to Palomar, and to some chap in Chile."

"No, no" Morgan explained hastily, "I don't want quasars. I want the sources you've classified , on the basis of their optical appearance, as radio galaxies."

"There's plenty of those. I can't see how they're going to help."

"It's my guess" Morgan responded "that some few of those actually are quasars, weak quasars it's true, but quasars nonetheless. They're so weak that their light hasn't overwhelmed the starlight from the galaxy inside which they live, and of which they form the nucleus."

"And how are you going to select those few?"

"By looking at their radio spectra. As you've already shown, quasars have much flatter radio spectra than normal radio galaxies."

"Aye that's true."

"And with your high frequency telescope you'll be the only one to come across galaxies with weak radio quasars in their nuclei – if they exist. The Cambridge people, searching at much lower frequencies, will miss them."

"Aye that's true too. But how will you prove they're quasars, not just some new species of radio galaxy?"

"By showing they're optically variable" Morgan concluded triumphantly. "I'll measure the brightness's of their cores every month. If they vary from month to month they have to be quasars. They just have to be."

Bolton stared at him speculatively, through a haze of blue smoke.

"Might just work lad. Ah've never paid much attention to radio galaxies. But as I recall there are soom with flat spectra."

He stood up, went to one of his filing cabinets, bent and opened a drawer:
\   "There y'are; my radio galaxies. They're all yours. See what you can do with them."

At the time Morgan didn't realize what a precious gift John Bolton had given him, what a complement he had been so laconically paid. For thousands of hours the great dish had been scouring the sky making the first map of the radio Universe seen from the Southern Hemisphere, and indeed the first high frequency map from anywhere. Sources had first to be found, then located precisely in position using the interferometer, then identified with something plausible on optical photographs of the sky, then re-measured at a second frequency if possible, in order to measure the radio spectrum. Most of the sources thus found turned out to be radio-galaxies, and Tom Morgan had been given first option to search through them all, hundreds and hundreds of them. Bolton gave him a corner of his big table to work on, showed him how to use the Polaroid camera, the light table and the microscope, and left him to get on with it.

Bolton's data consisted of filing cards, one for each radio source, designated by its name. The name consisted of a code such as PKS 2048-57. The PKS stood for Parkes, 2048 stood for its celestial longitude on the sky, in hours and minutes, and the minus 57 stood for it's latitude, in this case 57 degrees South of the equator, projected onto the sky. Under the name would be scrawled the accurate position in Bolton's untidy hand, and under that the signal-strength at various frequencies. Finally there would be a Polaroid print of the best available photo of that bit of sky – with the likely responsible galaxy indicated in ink. Occasionally Morgan found a brief comment from Bolton such as 'Looks like a 17th magnitude elliptical'. Unlike the galaxies Morgan had worked on at Steward , these were typically a hundred times fainter, ten times smaller, and therefore presumably ten times further away. The power of the Parkes dish meant that it could find such distant sources. For Morgan though the worry was that they looked so optically faint that he wouldn't be able to measure their optical properties at all. That explained why nobody had bothered so far. His heart sank. Nothing worthwhile was ever easy in science it seemed.

The first thing Morgan did was calculate the radio spectral index of every galaxy using his slide rule. That would enable him to winnow out those with 'flat' spectra, i.e. high-frequency emitters that looked like quasars. He was left with less than two dozen. Next he examined the optical image of each such galaxy very carefully under the microscope. Fortunately Bolton had glass copies of the Southern optical sky survey. Morgan looked into the core of each tiny galaxy for a distinct point-like nucleus, something he'd never seen in the Steward Ellipticals. However these beasts were a hundred times more powerful in the radio, and so might be correspondingly bright in the optical. He was hoping to actually see a starlike mini-quasar in the core. In most cases he was disappointed; most resembled common or garden Ellipticals, of which he could see thousands, even millions, swarming like germs on the photographic plates. But in one case at least – PKS 1514-24 by name – there was the exact signature he was looking for, a sharp star-like nucleus containing about half the total light. And what was exciting was that 1514-24 had the flattest, most quasar-like radio spectrum of them all. He stared greedily at the minute image seen through the microscope, wondering if this was the Rosetta Stone needed to decode quasar astrophysics.

There were one or two other 'possibles' with some but not all of the characteristics he was looking for, but PKS 1514-24 was by far the most convincing candidate. This was disappointing, he'd been thinking in terms of dozens. But then he did a calculation. Judging from their redshifts quasars were probably very far from the Earth, and therefore from each other, and therefore very rare in space. He was therefore able to calculate the chance of finding just one quasar within sight of the Milky Way close enough for its halo of stars, if it had one, to be seen, to be visible from the Earth – as was the apparent case in PKS 1514-24. He was shocked to find that the answer came to be much less than one. In other words there shouldn't be a single Rosetta Stone, of the kind he was looking for, in sight of his telescopes. He was stunned. No wonder no one else has bothered to look. They'd been more intelligent than he had been – and realised the quest was impossible.

Then he reflected some more. Full blooded quasars, thousands of times brighter than Elliptical galaxies were certainly very rare. But they were not what he was looking for.

A quasar as bright as that would swamp its parent galaxy, making it impossible for any astronomer to detect its underlying stars – which is what he was aiming to do. No, he wanted a relatively faint quasar, one no brighter than its parent galaxy, in order to do his work. And on the general grounds that here were usually far more faint specimens of any astronomical object than bright ones, far more sand grains than boulders, such relatively faint quasars might be relatively common, making it likely that there was at last one in the neighbourhood on which he could work. He looked again at PKS 1514-24 with a sigh of relief. This could well be the one and only Rosetta Stone in the entire sky. And in one sense that was comforting. If there had been similar beasts all over the sky then quite likely somebody else, probably in America, would decode the big answer first.

He took Polaroid prints of PKS 1514-24 and about two dozen others, mounted them on filing cards with all their other details, and showed them to Bolton. John Bolton, deeply preoccupied with his own research as usual, merely grunted and wished him a gruff goodbye.

At coffee, when he got back to Mount Stromlo, people wanted to know where he'd been. When he said "Parkes, to see John Bolton" they literally drew back as if he had the plague.

"Why, what's wrong?" he asked, feeling uneasy.

"Does Ollie Bacon know?"

"Why no, not yet. He's never bothered to see me. I shouldn't think he'd care."

"Jeez!" somebody said aloud as the astronomers looked knowingly at one another.

"Well , what have I done wrong?"

"Wrong? Brucie Doolan, Bacon's second-in command, said "You're wet behind the flaming ears mate. Don't youse know that Bacon hates Bolton? Won't let him on the observatory grounds. And Bolton hates him back. They're like a pair of fighting cocks. If you're mates with Bolton, Bacon's going to hate your bleeding guts."

"How the hell was I to know? "

"It's the first, second and third law of Australian astronomy mate. Either you're on Bacon's side , or you're on Bolton's. There are no go-betweens. Christ you really put your foot in it, both feet in fact. Ollie's certainly going to want to see you now. If I was you Morgan I'd start looking round for another job. Right now fellah. Strewth, what a balls up!"

Now that the cat was well and truly out of the bag everyone was eager to tell Morgan how grievously he had sinned, and the awful punishments he must expect. It reminded him of his first week at boarding school,when he was nine.

There were, it appeared, only three astronomical establishments in Austraia, all of which loathed one another. Sydney University hated CSIRO Radiophysics – which controlled Parkes; CSIRO hated the university back, and both detested Mount Stromlo because it had a monopoly of all Australian optical telescopes and was, in any case, far more lavishly funded by the government. Since he'd come to Australia from America as Director, Bacon had done all he could to exclude radio astronomers, who composed the vast majority at both CSIRO and Sydney University, from any access to the optical telescopes under his command.

"But why?' Morgan was pained. "They desperately need one another."

"You tell that to Bacon fellah. He despises radio astronomy. Says it's not proper astronomy at all."

"How ridiculous." Morgan couldn't help himself "Why it's more than half of all exciting astronomy just now: quasars, pulsars, Big Bang radiation.... The list is endless."

The Australian astronomers shook their heads sadly.

"Well what the hell am I doing here?" Morgan wanted to know "I spelt out in my job application precisely what I intended to do here, and who I wanted to work with; very largely radio astronomers – including John Bolton. And next month I've arranged to go down and meet the radio people at Sydney University"

The other astronomers looked meaningfully at one another again. Some of them rolled up their eyes. Bruce Doolan, a bony, red faced man with a prominent adam's apple took him aside:

"Listen fellah, Ollie didn't want you here at all. But he was over-ruled down at the university. Your's was much the best application – so they said. He did everything he could to hold things up."

"So that's why I didn't hear for so long." Morgan exclaimed.

"I don't know about that." Doolan snapped "But Ollie' got enemies down there...."

"Like everywhere else it seems."

".....and they shafted him good and proper. Since you weren't his birthday-boy beforehand, now he'll have your guts for garters. You just wait and see."

Morgan didn't have to wait long. There was a curt note from the secretary ; 'Professor Bacon wants to see you at once.'

Bacon turned out to be a grossly fat man with tiny hands and feet, and glasses so thick that he must have been clinically blind. They shrunk his eyes into tiny inscrutable dots.

"What's this?" he barked, flicking a paper towards Morgan across his enormous desk.

Morgan had to step forward to see what it was.

"It's the application for my travel expenses to go to Parkes."

"Can't pay it."

"Why not?"

Bacon didn't even bother to look up: "You didn't request written permission from the director in advance."

"But I didn't know...."

"Ignorance of the law is no defense." Bacon continued writing obliviously.

"But surely in this first instance...." Morgan tailed off limply. Probably he should have asked.

"Read your contract."

"I did. In a general sort of way."

"General's not good enough here." Bacon snapped , as if Mount Stromlo was a superior kind of place. Morgan thought he looked like a pork butcher – or a Dickensian washer-woman dressed in male attire.

"So you're not going to pay anything?" Morgan was shocked. He could ill afford to pay five days and nights accommodation at the Parkes observers lodge.

"I thought I made myself clear." Bacon pushed the form back towards Morgan in dismissal. "If you've got any complaints put them in writing. But not to me. Mrs Watts, my secretary, will forward them to the appropriate authority."

Morgan stepped out, almost as furious at his own feebleness as he was at Bacon's malignance.

Bacon was a legend who dominated the observatory by his sheer absence. He could be seen only in the late afternoons or evenings, waddling over to the library where he spoke to no one. He never came to coffee or lunch and rarely made an appearance at colloquia, where he sat at the back and never spoke. The lights in his office were on all night and he was said to sleep in his enormous house, where nobody was ever invited, only between dawn and midday. He was rumoured to be divorced, had no family or students, and gave no talks. He was often absent abroad, spending the observatory's entire foreign travel budget on himself. He was rumoured to work fantastically hard, and didn't approve of holidays. The Australian astronomers slunk off on their vacations, if they dared to take them at all, only when Bacon was in America. He had one observing assistant, who kept to himself almost as much as Bacon did. How observatory business was conducted Morgan couldn't imagine. Apparently Bacon delegated everything to a few sycophantic cronies, principally Bruce Doolan. He was hardly spoken of around the coffee table, except in hushed tones:

"Professor Bacon thinks this….."

"Bacon said that……..

"Ollie feels we ought to……"

To Morgan it semed inconceivable that anyone so pathologically reclusive could be accorded such respect. But, as he quickly realised, it wasn't respect but fear. There were so few permanent jobs in optical astronomy in Australia, and Bacon had one hundred per cent control over all of them. Get on the wrong side of him and you were either out of astronomy, or out of Australia. Either you sucked up to his dictatorial ways, or you shipped out.

Morgan wondered if the awe in which Bacon was held had something to do with the research which went on all night in his office. Though he'd never heard of Bacon's name in America he supposed there must be something going on beneath all that quivering flesh. Certainly Bacon published a vast number of papers, as many as a dozen in a single year. But when Morgan scanned them in the library he found nothing of any significance; periods measured for delta Scuti stars; colours for stars in clusters; proper motions for groups of stars. It was all terribly obscure, unimaginative and insignificant. No big questions were being addressed. It was publishing for publishing's sake, the kind of thing you expected of an amateur, or of a student lacking in self confidence. Moreover Bacon used only one observational technique, photo –electric photometry. He'd learned it for his thesis, and he'd stuck to it ever since. Morgan found it pathetic, and being Morgan, didn't hesitate to say so in the coffee room:

"I see Fatso's latest masterpiece has just come out in Astrophysical Journal; 'Photometry of Sothern variables XIV' can you believe it? Can anyone explain to me what its about? What the hell does he do in his office all night then? Eat? I don't know how they find anybody to referee such junk, let alone read it." Or:

"Why didn't Fatso turn up at the seminar yesterday? He might have learned something about modern astronomy."

Such remarks clearly unsettled some of Morgan's Australian colleagues, who looked over their shoulders, or moved hastily away. One of them warned him not to upset Doolan – who could prove a dangerous enemy.

Bacon had his spies and Brucie Doolan, second in command, was obviously one of them. A scrawny Irish-Australian astronomer, fond of making snide remarks about 'the Poms', he acted as Bacon's oracle, coming out with statements like 'Ollie thinks we ought to put a lot more money into the Coude spectrograph…..' or 'Ollie's dead against wasting money collaborating with the Poms….."

Morgan, who liked nothing better than a good verbal scrap, learned that the best way to get Pommie-bashers like Doolan riled up was to criticise Australia for the very things patriotic Australians believed made their 'Lucky Country' so great:

"God" he'd say, just to get up Doolan's nose "I don't know how you chaps can stand this awful climate. It's either too bloody hot and dry, or too bloody cold and wet. If you're not being drowned in floods, you're getting skin cancer on the beach."

"So why do so many of you flaming Poms emigrate out here?" Brucie Doolan riposted.

"They don't" Morgan blithely assured him. "It's only the inferior ones – who can't make it at home. We find it's a good way to get rid of them. A sort of humane form of transportation. And they fit in out here."

Morgan found himself getting on well with most Aussies, who seemed very hospitable. But he couldn't stand the third or fourth generation Irish like Doolan, who were far more anti-British than the Irish themselves. Their views of the Potato Famine, or the 1916 Easter 'Uprising' were twisted and romanticized, almost to the point of self-parody, especially in some of the low Sydney dailies.

Since the others went in fear of Doolan, not only because of his spying for Bacon, but because of some indefinable political influence he was supposed to have down in the University, Doolan had been allowed to get away with murder – until Morgan arrived. Doolan wanted to get rid of the British Monarchy; he hated the idea of singing 'God save the Queen'. He scoffed at the Poms for not fighting alongside the Aussies and the Americans in Vietnam. He used Anzac day to belittle the Poms' part in Gallipoli, and more generally in two world wars.

"I didn't realise" said Morgan innocently, sipping his tea "I didn't realise that Australia was much in the Second World War. I was told they pulled out of North Africa after Pearl Harbour and skedaddled off home. Not like the Kiwis who stayed on to help us fight it out."

"Whatcher mean?" Doolan sounded furious.

"Well where were they fighting then?"

"In New Guinea of course."

"New Guinea? I thought the war in the Pacific was against the Japanese."

It wasn't hard to route Doolan over history – he adhered to such a selective and self-serving version of it. For instance when he went on, as he was inclined to do, about the sixteen men the British shot after the Easter rebellion of 1916, Morgan calmly asked if he knew how many Irish volunteers were fighting and dying in France on the British side at the same time. Doolan of course had no idea.

"One hundred and forty thousand, of whom thirty thousand were killed."

"Then they were bloody fools." was all Doolan could say, unused to being contradicted.

"No they weren't" Morgan continued remorselessly "They knew that loyalty to the crown would earn Irish independence – which it did in 1919, not backstabbing – like those fools in Dublin. Do you really believe that we Brits would have given in to a pin-prick like that? The trouble is that some poor saps, particularly the Sydney ghetto press, believe, or at least pretend to believe, all that propaganda put out retrospectively by the IRA and their friends, dishonestly trying to claim the credit for independence, when in truth they had little or no role in it. It's like the communists claiming credit for the 1917 revolution in Russia, when in truth they were just come-after gangsters who exploited and betrayed it."

After less than six weeks in Australia Morgan had thus made bitter enemies of the two most senior men in the observatory.

Enemy or not Morgan was granted a fair allocation of observing time on the observatory's telescopes, and he was impatient to take a first look at Bolton's radio galaxies with the spectrograph on the 74-inch. Built in Britain back in the 1950s the telescope had been kept thoroughly up to date and was equipped with a Boller and Chivens spectrograph identical to the one he'd been using on the 90-inch.

Observing on the 74 was in one respect quite different from Arizona. He could get the telescope ready in the afternoon, drive down to Canberra to have a civilized dinner with Ann, then drive back up to the mountain in time for astronomical twilight. The down side was that the sky was brighter than it should have been, thanks to the lights of Canberra, who's city centre was only a dozen miles North from the telescope.

From the saddle where the dome was situated he couldn't see Canberra at all. Looking out towards the dying glow in the West, across the Murrumbidgee valley to the rugged black Brindabellas, outliers of the Snowy Range, it was easy to imagine they were in the middle of nowhere. He could see only two pinprick lights from farmsteads down in the river valley. Overhead the Milky Way, so much more prominent than it was in the North, was past its zenith and rolling away to leave half the universe entirely to him. And that wasn't fanciful. In 1970 there was no other telescope in the entire Southern hemisphere as powerful the one he was about to use. Almost every object he looked at would never have been studied optically by mankind before. All manner of unexpected discoveries were out there, just waiting for the prepared and imaginative mind. As he donned his parka, and stared upwards, he gave a deep shuddering sigh of delight. He'd come so far already, in such a short time. In his heart he believed that he had a lot further to go.

The night assistant Jim Mckinley, an ex-RN submariner, had everything running smoothly inside the dome and was soothing his soul, as he usually did, by gloating upon the simpering tarts in 'Playboy' magazine. The Australians referred to this hobby as "perving" and some of the astronomers, Bruce Doolan in particular, contributed to the subscription for several such titillating publications. When he thought he could get away with it Morgan delighted in inking in moustaches, or tangled beards of pubic hair, in the hope of enraging Doolan.

Morgan ordered the light down, handed Jim the night's observing list, checked the dark-room with his dim red torch, and climbed on to the observing platform. It was vital to get his eyes perfectly adapted to the dark because Bolton's galaxies would be extremely distant and dim. Indeed he wasn't sure he'd be able to see them at all. With the slit open and the Moon set, the only light in the dome came from starlight. Morgan, feeling excited, pressed the intercom button:

"OK Jim, find us a focus star at about fifteen hours Right Ascenesion, and not too bright please. I need to get dark adapted."

The telescope, a long thin tube of thin struts, allegedly designed by Barnes Wallace, tilted silently over. Morgan steered his platform up to follow it . He found McKinley's focus star in the middle of the eye-piece and turned the knob which directed it down onto the mirror of the spectrograph. Amplified by the six foot diameter mirror the star was brilliant, with sharp diffraction spikes of light pointing outward. He moved the secondary mirror, at he top of the tube, back and forth until the spikes were as sharp as possible, indicating that the telescope was in focus. He used his right eye exclusively for this, protecting his left and more sensitive eye for the serious business of finding dim galaxies.

"OK Jim, record that focus position please."

He moved the stellar image until most of the light was disappearing between the jaws of the slit in the mirror and into the spectrograph.

"OK Jim, record that offset. And remind me of the slit-width please."

"One and a half seconds of arc."

"OK. Well at least ninety percent of the light has disappeared down the slit. I don't know what that means in terms of seeing here?"

"About one arc second."

"OK, record it as such. I'm just going to refocus the main eyepiece." He shivered. It was much colder than expected. "OK done. All set. Let's go to the first object."

He lowered the platform, allowing the telescope to swing onto its first proper target. The dome rumbled round and fell silent. The telescope drive relays whined and clicked.

"OK" Jim's voice came through. "Set on object Parkes 1514 minus 24.". PKS 1515-24 was Morgan's prime target. If he couldn't see it he was sunk. This was his moment of truth.

Morgan glided his platform up in some trepidation and manoeuvred it into perfect position, with his left eyelash brushing the eyepiece, Morgan switched on his exceedingly dim red torch and inspected the finding-chart he had prepared at Parkes. He would have to find the galaxy with reference to the pattern of slightly brighter stars in its vicinity. Trying to memorise that pattern he applied his dark-protected eye to the eye-piece. A dozen pin-pricks of starlight swam in to view. Nothing immediately recognizable. He drove the telescope East. Nothing there either. He drove West. Ah yes. There was the distinctive little triangle he was looking for. The galaxy ought to be further West still, in line with the top two stars.

"My God there it is Jim. It's brighter than I thought. Good optics!"

"We do our best."

Morgan inspected his galaxy. It was indeed very very dim and small but, out of the sensitive corner of his eye he could see the distinct stellar nucleus – which he was hoping was a miniature quasar. With far more difficulty he could just see, or thought he could see, the dim envelope of galaxy light surrounding it. The question was 'Would the specrograph be sensitive enough to get a decent spectrum?' He patiently guided the nucleus onto the cross hairs, then switched the light down onto the spectrograph jaws.

Switching his eye to the spectrograph eyepiece he could see almost nothing, though the slit congealed into a slightly darker blackness than the blackness about it. He nudged the telescope a second of arc out of position and picked out, but only just, the dim glow of the galaxy on the edge of the slit jaws. Another nudge and the nucleus came into view. Perfect. He nudged them back down into the slit and, going to the main eyepiece, offset the crosshairs onto a dim guide –star.

"OK Jim, I'm all set. How long we got?"

"Fifty four minutes till she sets."

It wasn't long enough, but it was all he had.

"OK. I'm pulling the dark slide out. Now! Plate exposed. We're going. Give me an alarm with fifteen minutes to go, with five minutes and with two."

"Wilco."

The 74-inch guided itself pretty well. All he had to do was occasionally glance at the guide star, and more occasionally still, nudge it back onto the cross hairs. And keep warm. It was perishing cold, as he now realized. Far colder than it ever was at Kitt Peak; almost as cold as it had been up in the Catalinas at twelve thousand feet. They said Canberra had a hundred and seventy frosty nights a year. Why was that? Something to do with the Great Divide? He rubbed his nose with a glove, pumped his arms like a boxer to keep warm.

He didn't know what to make of the spectrum when he saw it in the dark room. At least there was plenty of light. The set up was, if anything, faster than at Steward. But there were no features on it, none at all. No emission lines as from a quasar or nebula, no absorption lines as from a star or normal galaxy, just a bluish continuous glow. He cast back in his memory, trying to recall some report of a similar featureless spectrum – but he could not. He concluded tentatively that something in the system must be at fault. He'd carefully tuned it the afternoon but some idiot, one of the engineers perhaps, had readjusted it later. He'd only know for sure when he looked at the second galaxy – which Jim ,up on the observers platform, was guiding.

Morgan was jubilant when he saw the second galaxy's spectrum , and the third's. They had perfectly focussed, immensely strong emission lines such as had never seen before. In one case the lines were sharply tilted, implying that the source was rotating rapidly. They weren't precisely quasar spectra, being too narrow, but they weren't boring radio-galaxy spectra either – such as Frank had shown him. They were of some intermediate type that needed puzzling over. Whatever else they were they could never have been generated by normal starlight; there had to be abnormal, and powerful sources of ultraviolet radiation buried in the heart of Bolton's flat-spectrum radio galaxies. And ultra-violet radiation was what quasars radiated in abundance. It occurred to Morgan that if a quasar was embedded in enough hot gas the gas would absorb the ultraviolet light and re-emit it in the form of emission lines – of the kind he was looking at now. So perhaps, just perhaps, Bolton's galaxies were embedded quasars.

These later spectra though made the first spectrum of PKS 1514-24 all the more anomalous, all the more puzzling. The spectrograph was evidently in perfect focus – so why the complete absence of features? The spectra of galaxies ,and quasars for that matter, always had features of some kind. Always. As he pushed into bed beside Ann's back, she rolled over, half asleep:

"How did it go darling?"

"Puzzling, but damned fascinating."

Ann had never recovered psychologically from her second miscarriage. She became obsessed with matters obstetric and found out that Canberra had the most distorted sex ratio among new-born babies known to science:

"Do you realise there are a hundred and thirty girls born here per hundred boys? Isn't that suspicious?"

"I don't know Annie. It does sound suspicious."

"It's very odd indeed. Male foetuses are known to be more vulnerable to the environment than females. It suggests there something poisonous here. Very poisonous." She couldn't get that suspicion out of her head.

Though she went in to the British High Commission every day or two, and they gave her a desk, she was very dismissive:

"Patronising lot! They must send the dregs out here. London doesn't trust them with anything juicy. And I don't blame London. All they can think about are cocktail parties and tennis. Can you imagine spending a whole quarter of an hour discussing whether the canapés at the French embassy are better than the ones at the Italian? My golly it's pathetic. I'll go mad here if they don't give me something better to do."

 She did enjoy the camping though – even if she did seem to run into an unfair share of the legendary Australian creep-crawlies. For instance they went up in to the Brindabella valley one weekend, as close a spot to Paradise as Morgan ever expected to enter. He was standing up to his thighs in the river, casting a spinner into a pool which he was certain, from the occasional rise, contained a fat trout, while Ann in a deck chair was watching both him and a pair of nesting blue wrens through her binoculars, when suddenly she let out a squawk. He turned in alarm. Slithering out of the grass beside her and down the bank into the river was a Red bellied Black snake about six feet long. With its head held high and its tongue flickering it swayed rapidly through the stream straight towards him. Before her could make up his mind whether to try and hit it with his rod, or leave it alone, it swept past him down stream and slithered up the opposite bank and into to the long grass.

"Oh my Golly" Ann gasped "I thought it was coming to bite you darling. My legs are all wobbly." She sat abruptly down again.

"No worries" Morgan said, aping the Australians. "Didn't appear to notice me. Snakes aren't interested in any thing bigger than they can swallow. Tiny brains. I told you."

"It looked so determined."

"It did didn't it. But not about us. Think of it this way. There are fifty million sheep in Australia grazing all day long, and all night, with their noses in the grass. If the snakes were lethal there wouldn't be a woolie left alive."

"I suppose not. But the Aussies do go on about 'snikes' so."

"They do don't they. I imagine it's their ghastly newspapers. If it wasn't for the tits, the gossip and the scare stories, there'd be nothing to read in them. They've literally scared themselves out of their own country. I'm glad. All the more for us mad Poms. Isn't this all ruddy beautiful? Back in Britain I'd have to pay a thousand a day to fish in a trout stream like this."

"I agree. Just look at those Eastern Rosellas."

Life in Canberra was pleasant enough, if not very exciting. Most couples in Nappy Valley were too busy raising their families to be very sociable. There were hoards of children about for whom Ann kept open house, baked biscuits, told stories and organised games. She dug, or rather got Morgan to dig, a sand-pit in the garden as a child attraction. She watched birds a lot, particularly the local magpies which were indeed characters. They dived down and stole locks of womens' hair out of their scalps to make their nests with. They terrorized the local cats and dogs by dive-bombing them from several directions at once. They warbled unearthly and improbable songs in the morning sun, imitated outrageously and were fearless of everything and everybody. Morgan wanted one as a pet but was put off at the thought of getting it to Britain:

"It would probably follow the plane." Ann suggested.

They played a lot of chess, but they had to stop playing one another when Ann became far too good for him. She entered them instead in the Chess Club where Morgan found a convivial opponent called Amory who was a perfect match for him. Their keenly fought weekly games lasted for hours and hours. Amory was a self made millionaire who admitted to doing only one hour's work a month:

"Most people" he declared "Work far too hard to think, and therefore far too hard to earn a fortune, or indeed several fortunes like me."

Amory had been one of those scrambling workers himself until he was forty. Unable to pay the bills for his large and turbulent family he'd found himself one day in one of the new outer suburbs of Melbourne looking for a cheaper house to buy in place of the one he owned. Running short of petrol, he couldn't find a garage. No one had thought to build one yet. So instead of a house he bought a plot at a likely intersection and installed a petrol pump and an attendant. Two years later, by then the owner of half a dozen such 'garages', he auctioned the first site to Shell for three million dollars.

"It got too easy" Amory commented, moving a pawn "So we came to Canberra to look around."

His first venture in Canberra, providing stone for local buildings and gardens, had proved a roaring success. His second, providing mature shrubs and trees for all the new gardens, a miserable failure. He'd bought a hillside outside the city and seeded it with the necessary plants, before realizing that the hillside formed part of the territory of a tribe of Sulphur Crested Cockatoos. The large white cockatoos loved juicy young shrubs and there was nothing Amory could do to stop them eating his investment. The cockatoos employed not one hour of his thinking every month, but twelve hours a day. He became obsessed with them. And over the weekly chess match Morgan had to hear every blow and counterblow in the awful campaign. Amory installed scare crows. The cockatoos perched on them. He bought a shot-gun and roamed the plantation. At the end of a month he'd shot precisely one of them. After the first they followed him around, just out of range, emitting deafening screeches until he couldn't stand it any moré. He tried bird lime. One young bird got entangled in it and warned the others completely off. He installed loudspeakers which automatically broadcast cockatoo distress calls. The birds found them hugely amusing. And all the time they were eating the young shrubs and Amory's future profits. Eventually he installed land mines set off by trip wires. He killed three domestic cats, dozens of wallabies, a Cairn terrier, a Sealyham puppy, any number of song birds and three protected Echidnas. But not a single Sulphur Crested Cockatoo.

"Bloody intelligent creatures" Amory conceded. "I've a good mind to write a book about them. . Do you know they've solved the birth control problem? That's more than we have." Whether Amory was referring to he and his wife – they had six children – or to mankind in general, Morgan wasn't sure.

"What they do" Amory continued gloomily, calculating his next move "Is designate a fixed number of nest sites within their territory. Nobody is allowed to nest anywhere else. If a couple don't bag one of those sites they don't breed that year. Simple. But bloody effective. Check."

Mount Stromlo formed part of a gigantic Government conifer plantation. On his way home Morgan would sometimes fill the back of their kombi with fallen timber, which provided a cosy fire every night. One night Ann was putting a log on the stove when she drew back:

"What's that?"

It was a slowly moving, shiny black spider with a red spot on its back:

"Isn't it a Redback?"

"I rather think it is." Morgan agreed, glad for Ann's sake that the Australians had chosen a typically unimaginative name for the very poisonous 'Black Widow'. He used the tongs to throw it in the flames.

"Don't worry sweetheart. I'll spray the logs in future before bringing them into the house."

But it was one more creepy-crawly for Ann – of which there were all too many. One afternoon she'd gone to sleep in her deckchair in the garden and woken up with the stars out. She could vaguely feel there was something wrong with her bare legs – which felt very cold considering it was summer. She felt down to find, in absolute horror, that both legs were encrusted in dozens of slimy snails which had reached her knees and were starting up her thighs.

"I hate this bloody country Tom." she railed at Morgan later. "Sometimes I loathe it. No wonder the Australians barricade themselves up in their houses. I want to go home." And she burst in to tears.

Ann's one consolation was Karen from next door. Both were fascinated by Aborigines, Karen professionally, and Ann from her stone-age point of view. So far she'd never actually met one. The two women were planning to take the minibus together far up into the Atherton Tablelands in Queensland to meet some of Aborigines still living in their natural state. Ann was very excited about the prospect. The aboriginal culture, at least fifty thousand years old, and probably much older, was disappearing so fast that it would have gone before anyone realised, Karen and Roy were fanatical about it:

"Their culture" Karen said "Is a unique window into our past. Humans came of age in the Mesolithic and Neolithic. As such their culture is far more valuable than the Louvre, Chartres Cathedral and the Parthenon combined. For God's sake it's *alive,* it's still here, but not for long. We Europeans, in our ignorance, judge aboriginals by our own parochial standards. How pathetic – that's like criticising tigers because they don't drive cars. Aboriginals don't look like us – which is a black mark against them, and they don't behave like us – which is worse still. And the poor devils – and this is a tragedy for most non-Europeans, can't metabolise alcohol. It's a powerfully addictive drug which poisons them to death – and it's wiping them out right now. But why not? Because they never drank filthy European city water contaminated by sewage, there was no need to add alcohol to the their drinking water, no evolutionary advantage in breeding a tolerance for the poison."

"All right," Morgan never liked to be preached at "Tell us what's so bloody wonderful about their culture, apart from the Didgery bloody doo."

Karen's eyes lit at the challenge:

"You are a man, so let's start with their hunting weapons. Think of the boomerang and the woomerah. Nobody else, certainly not the Europeans, was clever enough to think of those."

"What's a woomerah?"

"It's a spear thrower – which increases the effective length of man's throwing arm, enormously increasing the range and force of his spear throw."

"Sounds clever."

"It is. Very clever. But it doesn't impress Europeans because it's not a bloody great pile of stones like St Peter's. But it's much smarter. Aboriginals didn't leave monuments because they are – or were – nomads. They had to be. This bloody country was far too dry to support anyone else. So if you couldn't carry it, either in your hands or in your head, you didn't need it. And that's also why the aboriginals didn't breed like rabbits. They couldn't carry too many babies from waterhole to waterhole. And yet, indirectly, we despise them for that. If there'd been millions of them here when we arrived they'd have thrown us out – like the North American Indians threw out the Vikings. We had so overbred in the stews of Europe, Britain in particular, that we looked upon Australia as a dumping ground for our unwated excess. That's exactly what it was – whether you call them convicts or not. So where does that place us in comparison with them?"

"Tell us more about their ingenuity. That *does* impress me."

"Adaptability." Karen responded "That is the key to human beings. I'll tell you two aboriginal stories: about bark-sandals and mothers-in-law."

"Ann laughed; " I know what's coming. You tell him Karen."

" The thing about Australia, most of Australia, apart from it's aridity, is the heat. You can't go out in the midday sun – neither men nor animals. Apart from anything else the stony ground gets too hot to walk on. Just try it some time in your bare feet. It blisters the feet even of kangaroos. So they rest up during the day under a shade tree. Some clever aboriginal hunter thought of a way to exploit that. He cut the bark off a paperbark tree and made himself a pair of heat-proof sandals. They can make a pair in ten minutes. I've sen it done. Then he picked up[his club and marched off towards the nearest big shade-tree. The roos there were naturally reluctant to move – but they had to. So they hopped out onto the burning landscape, and sizzled their tootsies. You can bet they ran to the nearest bloody shade-tree, and stayed there."

"What next?"

"Off our hunter sets again, to that very tree where they've taken refuge and are licking their badly blistered paws. This time, when he arrives, they're determined not to move. So he lifts his club and bonks one on the head, drums on the tree-trunk with his club to tell his troup where dinner is, then lies down to sleep until nightfall. Bark sandals: they'll leave no permanent record behind – like Aristotle's manuscripts, almost all of which we have lost. But don't you think they were the product of genius?"

" I have to concede." Morgan smiled "But what about mothers-in-law?"

" The landscape is mostly so barren, supports such a low population density, that bands have to stay together. Individuals can't simply move to a neighbouring village if they are failing to get on with others of their troupe. And that is bound to produce personal tensions. So the aboriginal rule is that when a man marries he is never thereafter allowed to speak to his mother-in-law, not even in the direst necessity, nor she to him."

"Gosh that's clever." Morgan was impressed at last."We *have* got things to learn from them."

"Too right!" Karen stood up because she couldn't contain her enthusiasm. "But we are *not* learning. And very soon, in ten years perhaps, it will be too late. For ever. Did you know there are only one hundred pure blood Aborigines alive in the whole of New South Wales, which is bigger than France?"

"That's tragic." Ann was shocked.

"But those tangible things – which impress Tom – are the least of it. What about their poetry, their imagination, their huge fund of stories, their spirit world, their Dream Time? That is probably the greatest part of them – and it's all fading, fading, fading……..Listen to their language, or their languages, for there are literally dozens – Roy is the expert there. Listen to the music of the few names they have ;eft behind – and which we have adopted. Aren't they poetry in themselves?" And she stood above them, declaiming lie an actress in a soliloquy:

"Barenjoey, Gilgandra, Billabong, Mooloolahbah, Goondiwindi, Jindabyne, Cootamundra, Tuggeranong, Dandenong, Maroochydore, Googong, Bungle Bungle, Tallaganda, Wyong, Oudnadatta, Coolabarragundy, Mollymook,…….."

Karen was quite some woman but Morgan wasn't quite sure about her. She was amusing, intelligent, well read and friendly. But there was something disturbing about her too. Occasionally, when Ann wasn't looking, she'd give him a knowing glance, as if in assignation. It was subliminal, but nevertheless it was there. Then she had the habit of sunbathing in her garden practically naked, showing off her undoubtedly magnificent figure, like a female cat in oestrus. Or coming into their house wearing a thong which covered absolutely nothing of her buttocks. Morgan used to fantasise about them when when he was guiding a star in the darkness. It wasn't fair on a man. Where was the husband she was supposed to have – who was rarely mentioned, and even more rarely present. Since her second miscarriage Ann had practically lost interest in sex, except as a medical phenomenon.

They were delighted to get their first letter from Bob Salt, though it was odd to get a communication from him written almost in tthe King's English. After the preliminaries he went on:

"......and Valerie has found us an old farm near Hopwood, out in the country and not far from Tom's Mum's, but down in the valley bottom. I've rented out all but one on the fields to neighbouring farmers, the other being our airfield, while I'm converting the farm buildings for Wild Goose. I bought two caravans second hand for a song, and set them up inside the big barn. One contains Valerie's office, a tea room, and my work shop, while the two lads I've hired, both mates of Ernie's, work in the other. We are building a sound-proof cubicle so as to run the engines without driving ourselves mad. Our only neighbours are Friesian cows. And in another hay-barn we've built a large wind-tunnel, much more accurate than the old one, though it does use a lot of power. There are plenty more work-benches and storage areas and, especially at weekends when some of Ernie's other mates come out to help, we are quite a busy family. The story they all believe is that we are preparing a hush-hush drone which the RAF can use for testing out its coastal anti-aircraft defences. Only the two permanent lads, one working on airframes, one on guidance, have been approved by the You-Know-Whos[YKWs].

I've bought over fifty four-stroke diesel engines between 25 and 2 cc capacity and I'm impressed with their fuel economy. It's possible that among them we will find what we want, provided they turn out to be sufficiently reliable, which ain't guaranteed since they was never designed for the endurance we have in mind. The one problem we run into so far on the engine side is coking up – which we hope to cure by modifying the fuel. I may have to consult a fuel chemist on that.

The biggest challenge looks like guidance – ultimately the responsibility of YKW. But we can't wait for them, otherwise we won't be able to carry out vital test flights, which we need to start soon. Last week we run the prototype down the M1 Motorway from Brum towards London with me driving the mini and Ron guiding WG using radio control from the passenger seat. WG ran fine, we could hardly keep up, but Ron was absolutely knackered after 90 minutes and we had to bring her down in a field next to the motorway. We are going to have to think of something quite different – like a miniature Turn and Slip Indicator, to take most on the strain, so as the pilot only has to intervene every minute or so.

On the History front I've done what you said Tom and went to see the professor at Birmingham university. He contacted his mates elsewhere and I've hired a young lass working out of Manchester called Beth, and an ex Oxford type, working out of London, called Adrian. Both on them have PhDs and come highly recommended. Beth's a little dynamo though Val turns up her nose and says she'm a 'Lesbian' – whatever that is – V won't tell me. Adrian I ain't sure about. He looks down his nose at me, obviously thinks he should be in charge of the project, not Bob Salt. Anyroad

we all get together once a fortnight, and I'm really enjoying it – so
far. And we'm going along at a cracking pace. Thanks Tom.

You won't neither on you believe this but Beth has persuaded
me to take elocution lessons. She says no one will take me seriously
in the history world so long as I talk 'Unreconstructed
Brummagem'. So me and Val go to see a Mrs Fortesque in
Edgbaston twice a week and practice on each other. Old Salt will
never speak BBC – but he's learning to do a fair imitation of the
accent, like an actor, which he can only keep up for ten minutes. But
I can't change me vocal grammar, not at my age, and I don't know
as a BBC accent grafted onto Balsall Heath grammar will sound
better than the original. Beth is also trying to correct my prose-style,
of which there is more hope, and I have to send her an essay for
correction every week. That I will definitely need if I am going to
write most of the final text, which I want to. Poor Old Bob. Anyroad
you may encounter the sorry results sooner than expected. I have to
visit California in connection with WG and a ticket via Australia
ain't all that much extra.

"Oh I hope I don't miss him" said Ann , who herself was preparing for a month's
visit back to the Admiralty.

Mount Stromlo Observatory was dying. As Canberra expanded and the city lights
moved out towards the site, so the night sky was becoming too bright for really
competitive astronomy. For instance if there was slightest bit of mist about, or high
cirrus, Morgan couldn't find his prey. The university had planned for this and opened a
remote site in the Warrumbungle ranges several hundred miles to the North West.
Morgan applied for time to do imaging and photometry there, and flew North.

Morgan found the two hour flight exciting. He and the pilot took off from Canberra
airport in a light plane with one propeller at the front, and another reassuringly behind.
The pilot was quite happy to let Morgan take control as they flew at about four thousand
feet over inland New South Wales. It was a vast country of sheep paddocks, cloud
shadows, winding river valleys picked out by willow trees, lonely red roofed farmsteads,
low forested hills and emptiness. Seen from the ground, when he'd been driving to
Parkes, the same country had looked grey-green, but from the air it was yellow brown.
He supposed that looking downwards on it he could see between the grass stalks.

The Warrumbungles, when they eventually appeared ahead, came as a surprise.
Australia was an old worn-down continent lacking in brave mountains, but the
Warrumbungles, of geologically recent origin, were sharp volcanic peaks coated in dark
sclerophyll forest. The pilot took over and brought them down onto a hairy strip just
outside the little town of Coonabarabran.

Siding Springs Observatory, as it was known, twenty miles out in the range, operated
four small working telescopes, with two much larger ones under construction. Morgan
walked straight over to the 40-inch, the largest of the working instruments, to prepare
for the first of his seven assigned nights of observation. The first three nights were to be
used taking deep photographs of his Bolton galaxies, the last four making brightness
measurements. All he had to do was prepare the darkroom and familiarise himself with
the telescope and dome controls, for he'd be working entirely on his own. As soon as
he'd done that he climbed out on to the roof to look around.

The telescope was situated on the lip of a precipice looking out towards the West where he could just see tall mountains a hundred miles away across the barren pilliga, miles and miles of bloody Australia, or the MMBA, as some one had named it, baking and empty in the afternoon sun. Only the Williwaws moved, and the cloud shadows. Man-made lights would never bother him here. He was staring out across the pilliga when two Wedge Tailed Eagles shot up past him, being carried aloft by the West wind which was being deflected upwards by the cliff below. A thousand foot above him one of them closed its wings and powered into a vertical dive. The other hurtled down after it and in midair plunge they met for a few seconds and made eagle love. As they plummeted down into the blue gulf below him Morgan worried that in their ecstasy they would forget to open their wings. But he needn't have bothered because, a few seconds later, they shot up past him again to give a second exhilarating performance, another demonstration of the superiority of birds over men.

An astronomical source can only be seen in the night-time sky during certain seasons. As the sun moves through the constellations during the course of a year so it will bring any source into the daytime sky where it will remain unobservable for several months. So it was with Morgan's Rosetta galaxy PKS 1514-24, which was setting below the Western horizon two hours earlier every month. By the time he arrived at Siding Springs he had scarcely more than an hour after sunset to "get" it, an hour when there was still a half moon shining its interfering light from the East. If he started his photographic exposure too soon it would be contaminated by twilight, too late and it would be taken too low through a long path length of atmosphere which scattered moonlight. The first night he was too eager, the second too greedy, the third about right. The negative image on the thick glass plate showed a sharp stellar object centred perfectly at the heart of a dim, circular halo of light, almost certainly a Giant Elliptical galaxy very distant from the Earth. The image, on a far larger scale than anything available to Bolton, was exactly what Morgan had been dreaming of. The mini-quasar, if that was what the nucleus was, and the halo surrounding it, each appeared to emit roughly equal amounts of light, opening up the crucial possibility of obtaining a significant signal from each. On the fourth of his four photographic nights he repeated the exposure, but through a blue filter instead of a red. This time the nucleus leapt out by comparison with the halo. Either it had brightened in the intervening 24 hours, or more probably it was far bluer than the halo stars. He'd guessed this latter from the spectra he had taken with the 74-inch, which puzzled him more by the day. They were absolutely featureless, unlike anything seen by any of the Stromlo astronomers, or anything he could find by poring over journals day after day in the library. Oddly enough the only other object known to astronomical science with a featureless spectrum was his old friend the Crab pulsar. In that case the enormous pressure on the neutron star's surface had washed out any sign of discrete atomic emission or absorption. If PKS 1514-24 was a gigantic Black Hole the same effect might be expected. All the same, other quasars' spectra weren't so featureless. It seemed as if he had accidentally located an entirely new astronomical phenomenon.

Once PKS 1514-24 had set he photographed the other dozen or so in his collection. One source was clearly a pair of giant galaxies in collision, a Spiral with an Elliptical. Others were nucleated, though none so clearly as 1514. Two of them inhabited galaxies belonging to giant clusters of galaxies containing fifty visible members or more. And that gave him an exciting new idea. If his Bolton collection were quasars with redshifts, and if those redshifts corresponded with the redshifts of the other galaxies in the cluster then Bingo! He would have proved the Cosmological redshift hypothesis at a stroke. How obvious! Why hadn't people like Frank thought about it long ago? Because the quasars they were looking at were too far away for any cluster galaxies in their neighbourhood to be visible. So now Morgan had not one but two original ways to attack the greatest current problem in astrophysics. Potentially. First he had to prove that the sources he had selected were quasars, and second convince everybody else.

For the last three nights of his run Morgan removed the camera and put in place of it the photo-electric photometer. This was a simple but supersensitive photo-tube designed to measure the signal strength of any source focussed on it. Individual light photons striking the photosensitive surface liberated individual electrons. These electrons, being electrically charged, could be accelerated through an enormous voltage and slammed into another surface so hard that millions of electrons, enough to form a measurable electric signal, were liberated. It was light amplification with a vengeance. Since the photometer had no imaging capability all the astronomer could do was block off the sky, except for a tiny hole or aperture, and place the star he was interested in inside that aperture and measure it. The photometer had different sized apertures and different coloured filters. Morgan's plan was to use a tiny aperture to measure the brightness and colour of the nucleus of 1514-24, and a larger aperture to measure the whole thing. The first would yield the properties of the potential quasar, the second – after subtracting the quasar out – the properties of the surrounding galaxy. Simple in principle the technique was in practice exceedingly tricky. First the nucleus was so faint in the 40-inch as to be virtually invisible through the tiny photometer aperture. It took him twenty of the total forty minutes available before setting, to convince himself, or half convince himself, that it was there at all. He knew, from comparing what he could see with what other astronomers could, that he had great night vision, but all the same it lay at the very limit of what was humanly detectable through 40-inch telescope. Then he had to keep it there in the aperture using the offset guider – which took another ten minutes to set up. That left ten minutes only, with the object far too low in the sky for comfort, to make the measurements through three separate colour filters and two apertures before 1514 set altogether. Morgan was sweating with effort and concentration when the buzzer went warning him that the telescope would reach it's safety stop within sixty seconds. But he wasn't finished yet. Electrical signals meant nothing. They had to be 'calibrated' to turn them back into their equivalent in light. The traditional way to do that was turn the telescope upon well measured 'standard stars' in the sky, at approximately the same 'zenith distance', or height above the horizon i.e. observed through the same column of atmosphere, to allow for the same amount of atmospheric absorption. And he needed to find and observe not one such standard star but half a dozen in order to obtain an accurate result. And all the time he had to assume that the sky was 'photometric', that is to say steady. Even small amounts of high invisible cirrus cloud could ruin everything. Or the 'seeing' could change between looking at his object and looking at he standard stars. This atmospheric 'seeing' could scatter some of the starlight out of an aperture, particularly a tiny one like the one Morgan was using, and if different amounts were scattered from measurement to measurement, as could happen in unsteady seeing, the whole process would be a waste of time. Worst of all he wouldn't know about such a wasted night until he'd reduced all the data together by calculation. He found it very exciting work, especially working entirely on his own, but he'd be back in Canberra with his notebook and his slide-rule before he knew whether it all amounted to anything scientifically useable.

Thank God, Morgan thought, wives weren't allowed at Siding Springs because the observatory was literally crawling with spiders, both Huntsmen and Black Widows. The Widows were no problem – provided you glanced under the lavatory seat before sitting on it. But the Huntsmen were a plague because they hunted for moths in the telescope domes at night. You couldn't see them without turning on a light but astronomers couldn't afford to do that for fear of losing delicate night-vision. Morgan loathed the wretched things; there was for instance one monster which crouched over the red light illuminating the stairs down to the darkroom. As he warily moved beneath it carrying the plate-holder the bloody thing set itself for a leap every time. But if he was to do astronomy he had to put out of his mind any loathsome things which might lurk in the darkness around him. He'd taught himself the same discipline during ambushes in the Malayan jungle. If you'd worried about the creepy-crawlies out there communist terrorists would have been upon you.

Not everybody could be as phlegmatic. A few weeks earlier Jim, a hairy young American, had been using the 24-inch. One beautiful clear night the stars had suddenly gone out. No matter how hard he looked through the eye-piece there was nothing to see. Thinking that his long hair might have escaped from its bandanna and got in the way he reached up on top of his head and retied it. Still no stars. He leaned forward until his eye-lashes were brushing the eye-piece; blackness. Really puzzled now he reached out in the darkness with his hand. It closed over an enormous hairy struggling spider. An instant before his eyelashes must have been brushing its grisly carapace.

What happened next was never made clear, Th telescope dome was found still open in the morning but deserted. Jim had disappeared entirely. The police in Coonabarabran were alerted and Jim was located trying to catch a bus out of the area. Nothing and nobody could induce him to return to the observatory and he drifted out of astronomy.

Further along the mountain, half a mile from the 40-inch, two major telescopes were under construction, both with British involvement. The 'UK Schmidt' was a special kind of photographic telescope with a huge Field-of-View. It was designed to map the entire Southern Sky to as great a depth as the Palomar Schmidt had mapped the North. Almost complete, it was expected to commence operation within the year. Jack Cockle had written to say he'd applied for a job on it.

The other instrument, 'The Anglo Australian Telescope' or 'AAT' was to be a true monster. When the one hundred and sixty inch diameter mirror was installed it would be the most powerful optical telescope on Earth, not quite as big as the Palomar 200-inch, but much more modern in conception. As yet only the dome could be seen under construction for the telescope itself was being built in Britain and would be shipped out to Australia in a couple of years. But even the half finished dome was inspiring. The walls were three times as thick as a mediaeval castle, and at least twice as high. And above them towered girders arching high into the sky where workmen, no bigger than insects, were welding. The foremen allowed him to climb up onto the parapet in a hard hat from where the cream dome of the 40-inch looked no more than a paltry mushroom, far below. Not having visited the 200-inch with Frank Morgan had no conception of the breathtaking scale of such a colossus. Although the mirror would be only four times the diameter of the telescope he was using, its area would be four times four, or sixteen times as great. And just as a large oak must have far sturdier proportions than a small one so the AAT itself would have to weigh no less than two hundred and fifty six times as much. Were it less sturdy it would bend under its own weight as the astronomer slewed it about the sky, and a bent mirror would completely ruin its performance.

Shading his eyes against the Sun Morgan looked far upward to where a steeplejack, balanced on a narrow girder, was welding a joint that would one day support a moving cathedral-like dome big enough to enclose the monster. And it was going to be half British. That meant he could use it! A fierce ambition pierced him as he looked up, imagining the monster in operation. He, Twm Morgan was going to make the first major discovery with the AAT – if only to show those Pommie-bashing Aussies like Bruce Doolan.

In the middle of his run Ann rang up to say the Admiralty had called her up from London. Something very big was up and they needed her urgently. She'd have to leave at once, even before he got back home.

"But I'll be back in Canberra in three days." Morgan protested.

"I know sweetheart, but they want me at my desk by then."

"My God it must be Armageddon"

They warned us if you remember. It was always on the cards."

"How long?"

"Who can tell. It could be three days; it could be three weeks; it could be even longer."

"You seem rather pleased."

"I am in a way. I was beginning to worry they could do without me. And it's really exciting. I only wish I could tell you."

"So do bloody I!"

"But I've got some wonderful news too."

"Go on."

"I think I'm pregnant again."

"Really? It must be spontaneous creation."

" Don't be silly. You never leave a girl alone. Aren't you happy?"

"Of course I am darling. But I'm worried for you. Do you think such a long flight at this juncture is wise?"

"I wondered. Rang the gaeny. He said I'd need to lie flat on the plane most of the time. So I rang the Admiralty. They didn't hesitate; booked me First Class British Airways both ways."

"Your country needs you eh. God I'll miss you."

"Are you cross?"

"Yes. Very. But not with you Annie. Come back to me soon."

"I'll miss you to death Tom."

"So will I. Look after Tadpole Mark Three won't you."

The Moon at Siding Springs was turning out to be a real nuisance. He'd asked for 'Dark Time', near New Moon, but been allocated "Grey Time' instead. During 'Grey' time you could expect about half a Moon in the sky half of the time, either in the first part of the night setting in the West, or in the second part of the night rising in the East. Thanks to the uninhabited landscape the sky at Siding Springs was so dark, darker by far than either Kitt Peak or the Catalinas, that the slightest moonlight made a noticeable difference.

Wondering who at the observatory would need a darker sky than he did Morgan idly inspected the observing schedule hanging in the observers living quarters. He was amazed to see that every Dark-of -the Moon period was reserved for Bacon.

"What the Hell does Fatsow need it for?" he demanded furiously of Greg Anson the Australian astronomer on the 24-inch. "Fatsow works on bright bleeding stars. He doesn't need dark time. I do. And so, I dare say, do several others."

Looking furtively around to see if he was being overheard, Anson leaned forward:

"He's always taken it – ever since he became the director."

"But that's criminal" Morgan spluttered "Literally criminal."

"Ssh Tom! For Christ's sake keep your voice down. You don't want Mrs Bulstrode to hear."

"Mrs Bulstrode!" Morgan nearly exploded.

"Pipe down you idiot. Haven't you got a spark of flaming common sense? If you want this conversation to continue we'd better go outside."

They walked up the steep track through the bush towards the 16-inch telescope on the summit ridge. Morgan barely knew Anson, who was rarely about at Stromlo, and taciturn when he was. A shortish, barrel-chested man of about forty, he was remarkable for his violently red hair and spade beard, and for his long powerful arms. He looked more like a mountaineer, which indeed he was, than an astronomer. When they were well out of earshot of the quarters Anson resumed:

"Don't you realise Bacon's purblind? He can hardly find his stars in the dark-of-the-moon, never mind the grey. Even then, half the time, he's set on the wrong flaming object. Norm, his assistant, told me that over a couple of beers one cloudy night. Norm has to re-do many of Bacon's observations properly during the bright of the moon when nobody else wants the telescope."

"But that's even crazier. What with the Canberra lights the 40-inch is our only significant dark telescope. And it is dark here. It's completely wasted on Fat Sow."

"Don't we all know that sport? He's buggered us since he came out here. But what can we do? In a remote community like Australian astronomy he's an absolute dictator: like one of those old British Governor-Generals, like Bligh. Their word was life and death. He and Doolan have already driven our two best blokes out, out of Stromlo, and out of Australia. Bacon's a despot mate, and no mistake. He's not above the law, he *is* the law out here."

"But how on Earth did such a purblind incompetent get appointed?"

"You may well ask sport. We all have. There's a plausible conspiracy theory – which you can find out for yourself. I've said enough. And please don't quote me! I've got a wife and kids who all want to stay in Australia, It's our only home, and we like it. Everybody says you're flaming clever Tom. They say you can go right to the top in world astronomy. I never will. I'm just lucky to be an astronomer at all – and I want to keep it that way."

They stood on the summit of the mountain with a gentle afternoon breeze soughing in their ears . Between Mount Exmoor and the Flatiron the empty bush stretched in its silent emptiness all the way to nowhere.

"She's not a bad country is she Tom? You can say we took it from the poor flaming Abos. But not by force. They never owned it. They never stayed anywhere for long – they moved on. This country was tamed by poor bloody settlers – raw Poms many of them. A man would come out here with his missis, two or three kids and a small flock of jumbucks. Jeeze it must have been lonely. The missis might not see another woman in years. He felled the bush with his bleeding bare hands. She'd work in the sawpit with him to cut the logs to build their first bush home. God knows what they ate. The little girl milked the cow and tended the chooks while the boys were out in the bush hunting for roos and goannas."

"Goannas?"

"Flaming big lizards that can run on two legs like a man. How'd you fancy living on boiled lizard for twenty years?" When Anson smiled, his normally gloomy face radiated with humour.

"Sounds like Mrs. Bulstrode's cooking."

"Even worse chum. There was little choice. No veggies. The wife would try to grow 'em from seeds of course. Either they'd shrivel up in the sun, or the possums would eat them before the humans. And everything, literally everything, depended on the water running in the creek. They wouldn't know would they, that a crucifying drought comes here every dozen years or so. That their mob of sheep, now grown to hundreds, would mostly all die of thirst. That the well they dug was too shallow. That the boys would run off to the goldfields and never return. That the missis would die of loneliness. That the man, broken by disappointment and overwork, and his little girl, now grown into a wild uneducated woman, would sing hymns over her grave; hymns to a god who never cared a flamin' damn."

"You're quite a poet Greg."

"Nah. Wish I was. Just a realist. You should read Henry Lawson to find out what bush living was truly like. But my mum grew up in the Never Never. She told us, when we were kids, what it was like. Some of them endured; built little communities like Coonabarrabran. They might seem nothing to you Tom, coming from London, but to the people who live here they're like paradise after what they've been through out there in the pilliga. They built Australia by clinging on against the odds. And they're proud of it. We call them 'battlers'. Do you know that down in Coona they've formed an Early Music Society? Taught themselves to play crum-horns and sack butts. Not bad either: I heard them give a Corelli concert once. And over there, he pointed to the Southeast, there's a tiny settlement called Tooraweena; one pub and one store. Conceived the idea of setting up a gliding club would you believe. Built an airstrip, imported a two seater glider all the way from Poland, and an old crop sprayer to tow her up. You can look up and watch them soaring round the Warrumbungles at weekends. Australia may be a country of small dreams – but we do have them."

Greg Anson stopped, as if embarrassed:

"Why the hell I'm telling you all this Tom I dunno. Yes I do. I don't want you to think we're all like that skite Bruce Doolan. If we put up with Bacon it's because he's like the flies, and the heat, and the drought and the bloody wool prices. We'll get through in the end by enduring. If you take on Bacon yourself, and some of us hope you do, not an Aussie in the observatory will lift a finger to help you. Not even a little finger. But they'll be smirking behind their beers hoping you'll win."

"How bloody pusillanimous!"

"You'd think so, wouldn't you. And I don't blame you. But when Bacon and Doolan have pulled you down Tom – and they almost certainly will, the Aussies will still be here – enduring."

Beside the spiders the other horror observers at Siding Springs had to bear with was the food. It was legendary. Mrs. Bulstrode, the generalissimo of the Residence, prepared it herself. The meat, of unknown provenance, consisted mostly of gristle, scorched beyond recognition. The vegetables came entirely out of cans, carelessly warmed. The potatoes, reconstituted out of powder and served with an ice-cream scoop, were invariably cold in the centre. A deep brown 'gravy' of a smooth glutinous consistency, betokening its chemical origin, smothered all. Desserts however were her special pride. Her Lamingtons were prepared several weeks in advance – judging by the dust on them – and her Pavlovas were sugary rocks which broke the teeth and stuck in the gullet. Some astronomers, unable to endure the fare, brought a suitcase full of sandwiches from Canberra to last the whole week.

But it didn't do to question Mrs Bulstrode's sense of amour propre – founded on the delusion that she was a fine cook. She was the tyrant of the mountain, a despot known for extracting terrible revenge. One innocent American astronomer, maddened by a solid month of her cooking and utterly unable to face yet another petrified Lamington, sent the offending pink confection back to the kitchen to have gravy poured on it.

When he awoke from his sleep the following afternoon he reached out for the glass of water beside his bed in which he kept his contact lenses. The water was there but the lenses were not. A smug Mrs Bulstrode was pleased to explain:

"I ordered Jainiey the maid to tip toe in an' chinge yer water while you was sleepin'. S'not 'ealthy leavin' it all die long , what with the dust settlin'. Not as there's much dust in *my* rooms I'll 'ave you know. An 'ow was Jainey to know yer kept yer contacts in there? I ask yer! Snot the poor girls fault she flushed 'em down the dunny. They'll be deep in the cess pit by now. Ten foot under I wouldn't wonder. Pity you can't do yer astronomy without 'em. You'll 'ave to go 'ome now sonny wontcher?"

Mrs Bulstrode didn't tolerate astronomers who failed to eat her food or consume entirely the packets of midnight sandwiches prepared for them, known as 'Vegamite Perils'. The sense of terror she inspired, heightened by her very rare personal appearances, was such that astronomers surreptitiously disposed of the food they couldn't consume, in plastic bags which they brought with them to mealtimes and concealed under the table.

Morgan, who gagged on the food with the rest of them, hadn't been let into the full horror of Mrs Bulstrode. Even grown men with permanent jobs spoke of her in bated tones. Besides, the Aussies on the staff were looking forward to a full-blooded confrontation. And they weren't to be disappointed.

Exhausted, hungry because he hadn't been able to eat his Vegamite Perils, cross because of Ann's disappearance, and angry because he wasn't going to get any Dark Time in Australia, Morgan was in a foul mood when he came into dinner one evening.

"By Cripes" he said to the three other astronomers who were enjoying a pre-dinner beer, "Do I smell steak and onions – or have I gone loco?"

"Not loco mate. Bacon's flown up here with Doolan and a couple of high-ups from the Ministry. They're talking AAT business. They'll be in here in a tick."

"So the bloody food's going to improve is it? Just because Fatsow's here." Morgan was furious.

"Better have a beer Tom. You'll soon find out for yourself. Won't he fellahs?" Greg Anson winked at his compatriots.

Bacon waddled in, his shirt hanging out as usual, followed by two men in suits; bringing up the rear came Brucie Doolan. Talking loudly they helped themselves to sherry, completely ignoring the junior astronomers.

"The Minister's worried" one of the suits boomed out "He says he's being asked to pay a lot more towards running your Anglo Australian Telescope than was ever envisaged. And as he says, it's only for half the telescope. The British get the other half of the telescope time."

"That's what they think." Doolan sneered "But they haven't got a clue. The Poms will pay half but we'll get ninety percent of the use of it."

"I don't understand."

"They can't expect to get observing time just because they're paying for it. They've got to compete with the Aussies. That's the rule we made 'em sign up to. And what do the Poms know about optical astronomy? Under all them rain clouds they've probably never seen a fair dinkum star. And even if they did what do they know of the Southern hemisphere. Even in a fair competition they'd be no hopers."

"You mean it won't be fair?"

Doolan sniggered, then looked over his shoulder at Morgan, as if to rub it in:

"We keep a couple of tame Poms down at Stromlo don't we Ollie? Complete bloody drongos ! How are they going to raise half a competent Observing Time Allocation Committee between the lot of them? Even here in Oz more than three quarters of that committee will have to come form The Australian National Uni. And that means Stromlo. You can tell the Minister he'll be getting ninety per cent of a bonzer telescope for half the money. It'll be a straight subsidy from Pommieland to 'Strilia. Isn't that right Ollie?"

"That's the way we see it, yes."

"But surely" the other suit interjected "The British are far better at science than we are? Radar, penicillin, the jet engine – that sort of stuff?"

"Not any more mate." Doolan was confident "Since the Nips kicked the shit out of 'em at Singapore they've kept their heads down. Dad's Army all the way."

"What about the Atomic Bomb? I read recently that it was pretty well all conceived and designed in Britain before the Americans had ever heard of it? At Birmingham University I believe."

"Nah, that's typical pommy bullshit. Anyway the Yanks 'ave shafted 'em good and proper since. Look at Suez."

"I don't see what Suez has got to do with the Anglo Australian Telescope. The Minister would never wish to enforce a one-sidedly unfair agreement. Such things don't work in the long run."

"If he reneges on it now mate he'll have Mick Doolan to answer to."

"Ah yes. Senator Doolan. He's your uncle I understand ?"

"Too right sport."

"A very powerful man."

Morgan had so far been listening to these pleasantries with only half a ear. The rest of his being, led by his olfactory gland, was dreaming of steak and onions.

At that moment Jaynie, Mrs Bulstrode's half witted skivvy, entered with a huge T-bone steak which she placed in front of Professor Bacon. In the other hand was a bowl of chips.

All the conversation stopped while Bacon helped himself to chips and Janie served everyone else. When Morgan's turn came he found himself staring not at a T-bone steak, but two frozen fish cakes ,smothered in the usual glutinous brown gravy, tinned sweet corn, which he abominated at the best of times, and two scoops of reconstituted mash.

After all his expectation it was too too much; or rather too too little.

"Janie" he called after the girl as she was vanishing back into the kitchen "You can take this stuff back to Mrs Bulstrode and tell her I'll have steak and chips like Professor Bacon."

There was an awful Oliver-Twist -like silence as Janie stumbled back and took the offensive plate back to her mistress. Bacon froze, with the first forkful of steak and onions poised under his nose. The other diners, whether out of embarrassment or dismay, looked down at their own portions of fish cakes.

A terrified looking Janie returned and put the offending plate back in front of Morgan:

"Mrs Bulstrode says as it's all the tucker yer gonner get. So you better eat it."

Morgan picked up an elbow and plunged a thumb down through the gravy into a fishcake:

"As I thought gentlemen. It's still partially frozen inside." He picked up the plate and thrust it back at Janie. "Tell Mrs Bulstrode it's unfit for human consumption. Tell her that Professor Bacon wouldn't like to poison his guests, not even his junior staff, with frozen fishcakes he doesn't deign to eat himself. He isn't going to take even one bite of his own delicious looking steak until we've all been furnished likewise. Isn't that true professor? It would be the greatest discourtesy."

"But there ain't any more stike " Janie wailed, wringing her hands "Ony a bit for Mrs B. And me."

"Ah, I thought there might be. A rather big bit I should imagine?" Janie looked at her shoes. "I tell you what. You take these fishcakes back to Mrs B and tell her to cook up that big steak instead, with lots of onions and extra chips, and bring it out to me. Then I'll share it with these gentlemen. Naturally they all hope to get back alive to their wives and children. They know, as Professor Bacon so evidently does, that partially unfrozen fishcakes are a serious danger to health. Ptomaine poisoning. The authorities would be horrified."

As Janie fled back to the kitchen with Morgan's plate the rest of the tableau remained frozen:

"Well go on, stick your fingers in the bloody things; see if I'm lying."

One of the Civil Servants obliged:

"I must say professor, it is still half frozen."

The kitchen door swung open, as if a gunslinger were about to storm the saloon. And out of it waddled one of the fattest women Morgan had ever seen. So big were her belly and her dugs that, to balance them, she had to lean noticeably backwards. Her eyes were tiny currants of hatred as her massive arms slammed the fishcakes back down in front of Morgan:

"Youse eat these my fine fellah. If youse don't yer'l starve. Yer'll get nothin' else to eat yere. Not tonight. Not tommorer. Not ever. Yer'll bleedin' starve and it serves yer."

Morgan drew himself up to his full height:

"What's wrong with you my good woman is that you are too fat to bend over and use the oven. You must cook that gristle, which you pass off as meat, with a blow torch."

"Ollie" she screamed "You fire this this this…impudent whingeing pup before I 'it 'im." She lifted up an enormous arm. Instinctively Morgan moved out of reach.

"It's not just me Mrs Bulstrode. Apparently none of these gentlemen is willing to touch your frozen fishcakes. Perhaps you didn't realise they're supposed to be heated up to kill the bacteria? Look around you."

Mrs Bulkstrode screamed an imprecation.

"But perhaps Docter Doolan will set us an example? He's always telling us how tough fair dinkum Aussies are."

"You leave me out of this you bleedin' larrikin. It's not Ollie's fault – he's on a diet. Can't yer see?"

"Oh I can see all right. Look at the shape of him. Look at the size of his meal. He's been eating all the observatory's rations for years – that is to say any that Mrs Bulstrode hasn't consumed herself. Just like he steals all the Dark Observing Time – and the observatory's entire foreign travel budget. Just look at him gentlemen. Ready to shamelessly engulf not only his own steak and chips, but yours and mine also."

"You shut 'im up Ollie" Mrs Bulstrode shrieked like a cockatoo.

" He doesn't need to" Doolan snarled, standing up himself "Ollie'll sack him as soon as he get's back to Canberra. You better look for another job sport."

"Another profession you mean" Bacon intervened at last . "I'll see he never gets another job in astronomy. Never."

"Never!" Mrs. Bulstrode screeched in triumph "Never. Never. Never!"

"I wonder" Morgan picked up his plate and held it on high:

"Here's the evidence. I'm going to freeze this, such of it as isn't frozen already, and take it back to Canberra. As I've already frozen the Dinosaur Gristle Pie you served us up yesterday dear lady. When the Canberra Times gets to taste that gristle, even Senator Mickie Doolan won't be able to save Professor Bacon's skin, or should I say rind. I can just see the headline: 'Coona poisoner strikes again'."

And that was only the beginning of 'The Great Blue' as it came to be known around the observatory, and later throughout Australian astronomy. With each telling the story grew until it reached legendary proportions. St George and the Dragon wasn't in it. Morgan became either the villain, or the hero, depending on one's point of view.

Later Rod Anson came round to Morgan's room, threw his arms round Tom and burst into laughter:

"Jeeze I wouldn't have missed that cobber. Not for all the flamin' tea in China. I'll never forget it, not all me bleedin' days." And he burst into another fit of hysterics.

"You see the thing is…" and he was taken by another paroxysm . "The thing is mate they can't touch you."

"Why not?" Morgan was resigned to dismissal.

"Why not? Because you just happened to hit exactly the right issue. Didn't you realize Bacon is sleeping with Mrs Bulstrode?"

"God how repellent!" Morgan was genuinely disgusted "It must be like two of those giant Galapagos tortoises drooling and grinding on top of one another."

"That's why he comes up here every month. To get his end away. He hired her. And everybody knew – 'cept you sport." A fit of incapacitating giggles racked him again.

CHAPTER 12
TIDBINBILLA
1972

Back in Canberra Morgan was lonely. He and Ann had become such good friends that they hadn't needed any other. Now he made friends with Anson, who never seemed to be much around at Mount Stromlo:

"Nah, the astronomers don't like me, and I don't like most of them."

"Is that why you never come to sandwich lunch?"

"Partly. I'd rather go home anyway. We live just down there in the Murrumbidgee valley. Why don't you bring your sandwich and come down with me."

Greg's old ute bumped them along a dirt road, forded a creek, and ground over a steep brow before plunging down to a farm gate with three large horses on the far side, their heads over the top bar in welcome.

"They're waiting for me. They know when I'm coming. God knows how. Come and meet them."

Greg jumped out and nuzzled the giants, who towered above him

"They're Shires aren't they?" Morgan asked.

"Too right. This is Cyclops – he's twenty. This is Vanessa, she's eighteen. And this big old fellow is Cromwell. We don't know how old he is."

"I haven't seen a Shire since I was a boy in Birmingham. They used to pull the Co-op milk carts, and the brewers drays."

"They're the last descendents of the great warhorses that carried knights in full armour into battle. But they're a dying breed now. At a ton each they cost a fortune to feed."

"What do you do? Breed them?"

"Nope. We – that is my wife Penny – looks after them in their old age, when nobody else wants them. Right now we've got two dozen old Shires spread around the paddocks. Come on, make friends with them. They're soppy things really, gentle giants."

The single story farmhouse lay right beside the river, its rickety verandas betokening a fine old age for Australia. There was a cluster of outbuildings, a large shade tree and several hay-ricks, obviously set apart from the buildings for safety. The name 'Tidbinbilla' was carved above the doorway.

"She used to be a sheep-station before we bought her. But the falling price of wool killed her off."

The Murrumbidgee, about fifty paces wide here, slid swiftly past the property, gurgling among its rocks. On the far side, beyond the willows and casuarinas, a forest climbed steeply into the Brindabella Range.

"What a place Greg!"

"She's not bad is she. And we own the bank for almost a mile on this side. Great for fishing. There are Murray Cod in there weighing more than a hundred pounds. The boys saw one the other day, and they're trying to catch it. But the soil hereabouts is stony and infertile. It's great for bringing up kids though."

"How many have you got?"

"There's Kylie. She's fourteen. Then there's Sean nine and Kevin six. All at school right now."

"Do you grow anything on the farm?"

" Grass and hay. How else would we feed all those great beasts?"

To eat lunch they sat on the veranda overlooking the river, shaded by the ubiquitous tin roof. Two more old horses came up to join them, snuffling and flicking away the all too plentiful flies with their fore-locks, eyelashes and ears.

"They've seen your bleeding carrot." Greg laughed "You're going to have to sacrifice it now Tom. You don't want two tons of hungry warhorse breathing down your neck; and I mean breathing."

" This is a world away from the trim suburb where we live." Morgan said, letting the warriors lip the divided carrot out of the palm of his hand by turn.

"Thank God." Greg replied. "We don't want our kids to grow up like house-pets. The two boys spend half their time out in the bush – even across the river. They often sleep wild in their several dens. Yesterday they were out past midnight catching yabbies."

While Greg went out to the barn to see to a sick horse Morgan, who liked nothing better, prowled round the bookshelves in Greg's study. They were all on glaciology, geology, climatology, even oceanography; scarcely a mention of astronomy. When Greg returned Morgan challenged him.

"Nope. I'm not an astronomer really. That's why they don't like me up at Stromlo – even if I do do more observing than any of them – which I do."

"How come? What's your interest?"

"Ice ages. I did my PhD in glaciology – looking for signs of recent ice ages in Australia. Nobody'd bothered much before."

"I didn't know you'd had an ice age here."

"Yes, that was the big question. Did we or didn't we? And that could have a significant bearing on what the cause of Ice Ages might be – for now a total mystery."

"I thought it was something to do with changes in the Earth's orbit, changes brought about by interactions with the planet Jupiter?"

"That's one theory – quite popular just now. It may have something to do with it – but in my opinion it doesn't explain much. For a start it implies ice ages more in one hemisphere than the other. That's one reason I wanted to see if the Australian climate had oscillated in sympathy with the Northern one."

"And did it?"

"Seems very likely, though dating palaeoclimates is notoriously tricky. It's all about Carbon 14, cosmic rays and tree rings. But it does now seem that there was a Large Glacial Maximum here, and in New Zealand, about twenty thousand years ago, at the same time as in Europe and America."

"So where do your stars come in?"

"Ah well, that's a really wild idea. Everybody pretty much assumes that it is the Earth which is to blame. But what if the sun should vary? A few per cent drop in solar output would plunge us deep into an ice age – no question. And there's some evidence that the Sun *has* changed in recorded history. Did you know there were virtually no sunspots between 1650 and 1720? It's called "The Maunder Minimum". And it coincided with the 'Little Ice Age' when winters in Europe were perishing cold."

"No I didn't. But surely we can measure the output of the Sun very precisely?"

"Not as easily as you might think It's so overwhelming; what do you compare it with? Then there's the variability of the atmosphere, and pollution. And anyway it's the long term variability we need, over centuries, millennia, and even longer. The records simply don't exist, though some heroes are trying tree-rings."

"So where do you fit in?"

"The Sun is a very common type of star, a G-Dwarf. And there are millions of G-Dwarfs out there. Literally. I'm monitoring as many of them as I can, on an annual basis. If I can measure enough of them, and measure them extremely accurately, we should find out whether Sun-like stars vary, by how much, and over what periods."

"What a clever idea Greg."

"It is isn't it. Not mine though. A fellow called Olin Wilson came up with it first in the 1960s, though he is more interested in sunspots. Sunspots can't be seen on other stars because they're too far away, but the spots do produce Calcium lines in their spectra, which can be monitored from here. So that's what he and others have been doing since; monitoring spectra. Unfortunately by themselves sunspots don't necessarily prove that there is an accompanying change in luminosity – which is what we climatologists really need to know, and you need to measure luminosities from the Southern Hemisphere where most of the brighter G-Dwafs are to be found, simply because we are facing the centre of the Milky Way. The astronomers here refused to do it – I can't blame them. So Muggins here volunteered."

"Why Muggins?"

"Just think about it. I have to monitor the same bloody thousand stars, with the minutest painstaking exactitude, year after year, decade after decade, probably for the rest of my life. It's like a life sentence in the salt mines. Would you do it?"

"No." Morgan was adamant. "But surely other people can help you?"

"Eventually perhaps. If any one will pay them. But I'm working to such fine precision that the variances from one observer to another could be significant. I've locked myself in and thrown away the key."

"But dammit Greg your project is so important! There's probably no more important project than yours – so far as the future of the human race is concerned, what with Carbon Dioxide and climate modification – in the whole of astronomy!"

"Are you telling me mate? Why the hell do you think I stick it? But it's gradually driving me barmy, and I've told my boss in Sydney Uni so. I need to do my other science. Believe it or not I'm a red hot glaciologist, if there is such a thing. I'll stick it so long as I can have two full-time assistants, one of us up at Siding Springs observing, one resting or doing something else, and one reducing and publishing the data. And all of us trained to do the measurements in exactly, and I mean exactly, the same way. But who is going to pay for them – indeed for me? The Climate people at CSIRO, the ones with the clout, say that Stromlo should employ three of their permanent astronomers to do the job. The astronomers here absolutely loathe that idea. That's why they pretend I'm not here. It would mean three less jobs for them. Bacon only keeps me on because of an undertaking by his predecessor Bok – which he will repudiate if I give him half a chance. Just half a chance. Sometimes I'd like to pinch little piggy on the snout – then I could become a proper glaciologist again, visit Antarctica and New Zealand like I used to do before."

"But you can't do that Greg!" Morgan was passionate. "What about World Climate?"

Greg sighed heavily: "You don't have to tell me. We can't leave Tidbinbilla anyway – not while the kids are still growing. They'd never fit in a city now. And what about the poor old horses? They'd all have to go to the knackers. Then Penny'd never forgive me. And talk of the devil, here she is."

A battered old station-wagon drew into the farmyard. The horses immediately left to welcome it. Penny was a sturdy lady with lots of energy and freckles, frizzy hair and wise eyes:

"Greg's told me all about you Tom. I nearly died laughing when he described your big blue with La Bulstrode. This is Kylie."

Kylie was a Downs kid of about fourteen who came forward and gave Morgan an extravagant hug. She looked too old to be Penny's biological daughter, and perhaps she wasn't.

 Penny wanted to know about Ann:

"You must come over to dinner, as soon as she gets back."

"He can come over before." Greg said.

"Of course he can." Penny laughed "Give me some warning and I'll put on frozen fishcakes with brown gravy."

Despite his new friendship with the Ansons out at Tidbinbilla Morgan still pined continually for Ann. It was far too expensive to ring up Britain, while airmails took five to seven days. There were so many things to discuss: the Big Blue for a start. Evidently he had no future, and probably very little present in Australian astronomy. The noose was already knotted tightly round his neck. And, despite Greg Anson's reassurance, he couldn't imagine that Bacon and Doolan would fail to open the trap door. Should he be looking for another job already? And where? Ann was so sensible; he so impulsive. Part of him wanted to get out; another to make his going as bloody-minded as possible. If he was going to be drummed out of astronomy he'd take Bacon, Doolan and La Bulstrode with him. For a start he wrote to every influential British astronomer, except Bellfounder, exposing the Bacon-Doolan plan to steal the Anglo Australian telescope for Stromlo.

But he didn't want to leave astronomy. He desperately didn't want to. It had become his love, his obsession. He couldn't imagine living without astronomy. Why? It was sometimes hard to explain – even to himself. He sometimes thought that it was, above all, because astronomy whispered such fascinating questions in his ear. Every week, almost every day there was a new one. He woke up thinking about these new questions, ideas, arguments and calculations. And he went to bed at night still wrestling with them. Take the week at Siding Springs. Seeing the skeleton of the AAT, the colossus rising from the earth, had whispered, not only an inspiration, but a new question in his ear. With its mirror exactly four times the diameter of the 40-inch's' its area sixteen times, and its weight two hundred and fifty six times as great, how much more powerful would the colossus actually be from an astronomical point of view? It was not a question he had asked himself, or heard discussed before. He presumed the astronomical power would rise with the mirror area, and thus be sixteen times as great. He set out to calculate, using as example the astronomical quest he knew most about – searching for pulsars.

Finding a pulsar meant picking out a faint signal against a loud 'noise'. And the noise came from the foreground and background sky. You placed the smallest posible aperture over the pulsar position, that you could afford, in order to block off that noise, a noise of photons streaming in from the atmosphere, from the dust of interplanetary space which scattered sunlight, from Milky Way stars too faint to be seen as individuals, and from faint galaxies at the end of the universe. Even in the dark of the moon, at a site completely remote from civilisation, this background noise of light would always limit what the astronomer could see. And here was the rub. A bigger telescope would pick up more signal, but it would also pick up more of that noise too. At the end of his calculation Morgan was shocked to find that the AAT, despite its colossal weight and area, would pick up pulsars only four times fainter than the 40-inch. Something had to be wrong. He went over the calculation again and again and again. The performance of an optical telescope improved only with the diameter of its mirror, not even its area. Yet another question had come down out of the cosmos to torment and intrigue his mind. Then there was the radio galaxy data he'd gathered at Siding Springs. After struggling over it for a fortnight the data was beginning to look good – the Rosetta galaxy PKS 1514-24 in particular. Most of the nights had turned out to be 'photometric' and he was particularly encouraged by the colours he had measured for its halo light, which were exactly as they should be for an Elliptical galaxy. Bacon or no Bacon he desperately wanted to stay in the South for several years. Cracking the quasar problem was in distant sight of solution. He scarcely dared to look in his pigeon-hole, for fear of finding a letter of dismissal.

But as the days and week passed he began to hope. Bacon had gone off on one of his long trips to California – some said to keep his position there 'warm;. As a consequence the whole observatory relaxed a little. The junior staff nicknamed Morgan 'T-bone' while the attitude of the seniors toward him became slightly less aloof. Doolan, preoccupied with running the observatory in Bacon's absence, hardly appeared in the tea room any more. Mrs Bulstrode though, like a harpooned whale, was wreaking vengeance on all and sundry at Siding Springs:

"S'trewth T-bone you better not show your 'ed out there again. She'd probably shit in yer soup."

Morgan wondered whether he'd ever be awarded any more observing time at Siding Springs – or even at Mount Stromlo. Shutting him off from the cosmos would be a slow and painful death – the ideal revenge for Bacon.

He asked about. One of the senior astronomers, a Kiwi called Ben Pees, who'd been more friendly than the rest, took Morgan aside:

"The written observing proposals which you and others submit are sent out to referees, many abroad, and marked anonymously. The custom is for the highest marked proposals to be given observing time automatically. There's no discussion of them round the table. Only the lower ranked proposals are a matter of debate. Bacon can't easily change the procedure – though he's tried. Too many enemies. So provided Tom that your proposals get the very highest marks, which they have so far, neither Bacon, nor Brucie Doolan, who is also on the committee, can stop you getting observing time. But if you drop down in ranking then they could sabotage you – and probably would. So your salvation lies in your own hands Tom."

"Phew! You don't know what a relief that it is. But couldn't they sack me instead?"

"Not easy. You've got a three to five year contract, and the unions over here are very strong. So long as you're doing great astronomy even Senator Mickey Doolan couldn't sack you. After all he's a union official himself."

Morgan's sense of relief was considerable. He wanted to fly. Or better still talk to Annie. So he blew several days salary on a brief and unsatisfactory phone-call, unsatisfactory because most of it was wasted catching Ann up with the Big Blue. Ann though was very happy. Her pregnancy was confirmed while the project she'd been called home for was going very well.

"How long will you be then Annie? I'm missing you dreadfully."

"Me too. I'll do what I can Tom – but it could be several weeks. We can't possibly stop now."

Morgan was appalled and resentful. The whole secrecy and unpredictability of Admiralty business irritated him beyond endurance. It wouldn't have been so bad if Ann had been able to confide in him. As it was he felt excluded, as if he'd married a priestess whose loyalty belonged first to some church. After he put down the phone he flew into a rage. He kicked one of the logs on the hearth so hard that he had to limp to the doctor to get some really strong pain killers.

Even they didn't assuage his temper. He took his big axe into the garden and set about a eucalypt log until chips were flying everywhere:

"Fuck you! Fuck you! Fuck you!....."

"My word Tom you do sound cross. If you go on like that you'll chop off your ankle."

It was Karen from next door, in her skimpy bathing costume as usual.

Morgan, panting with exertion and temper tried to explain.

"Sounds to me as if you need a bit of feminine consolation. You'd better come round for supper, about six. And bring a bottle of wine."

When she turned away her buttocks were entirely naked.

They were still naked when she let him in through the back door, though she was wearing a short apron.

"Open the wine" she said, returning to her stove. "I hope you like sea-food. I'm doing an abalone risotto. It's a Melbourne – Italian dish my granny taught me."

Morgan poured two glasses of Zinfandel and tried not to stare at Karen's buttocks, now perfectly displayed thanks to her high heeled shoes. He tried to think of a way of handing the glass to her without disclosing a rampant erection. He had to hope she was too busy adding herbs to notice.

"How's Ann?"

"She's pregnant again."

"Oh how wonderful!" Karen turned, a spatula in hand, evidently delighted. "We must drink to that Tom. We must."

In fact they drank two bottles to 'that'. After the risotto came a King Island blue cheese with grapes. And after that passion-fruit ice cream. Karen prided herself on her cooking.

"I'll wash up." Morgan offered.

"No you wont. Men are hopeless. You can dry."

The trouble was that, bending over the sink, Karen's buttocks became literally irresistible. He couldn't help his hand reaching out to one of them:

"My God they're beautiful. Your skin's so silky."

Karen stopped rummaging in the sink: "I didn't think you noticed such things; not with your head in the stars."

He put down the drying-up cloth and began massaging both buttocks. She clung to the sink with her rubber gloves, involuntarily pushing out her bottom."

His finger slid under the thong and down between her legs. She moaned.

"You're a naughty girl Karen. You really are. I'm going to have to take this right off."

He bent her over the dining room table, still in her apron and gloves, stripped off the thong, picked up her knees, and slid into her vagina as far as it was physically possible. The sugar bowl fell off onto the floor spilling its contents. Then he fucked her until she screamed and he burst.

"I ought to feel ashamed." he said afterwards, lying contentedly beside her on the coach.

"I ought to be you mean! Ann's my friend. Would she be very angry?"

"I dunno. People are different. She's not a jealous person. And it was only a fuck after all."

"It was wasn't it. But it was a lovely one. One of the nicest I've ever had."

"I may have to give you another one. I certainly will if you go on showing off that lovely bum as you do."

"Oh goodee."

Karen's bottom got a good deal more attention while Ann was away. Morgan would never have been unfaithful to Ann, not for a second, if he'd thought he was endangering his marriage. But he didn't. So far as he was concerned love was love and lust was lust. He loved his wife dearly, and missed her dozens and dozens of times every day: to talk to, to laugh with, to simply be with side by side. It never occurred to him to kiss Karen on the mouth, to whisper endearments, to spend the night in her bed. Such deeper things belonged, and belonged exclusively, to Annie his wife. And on her side Karen wasn't the least sentimental. She made Morgan feel they were participating in a therapeutic activity, although she obviously enjoyed it tremendously.

They had to be careful because Carroll Street was a typical village in the sense that it entertained itself with prying and gossip. So they organised a signalling system based on the rotary clothes-lines to be found in every Australian garden. If Karen fancied some therapy she'd hang out her red panties; if he did he hung his blue swimming shorts out to dry. When both were out it meant an assignation after dark in Karen's house. Always in hers. For Ann's sake Tom would never have arranged an assignation at The Morgans.

The centre of the Milky Way isn't visible from Europe. From Australia it was an immense cloud of stars, both bright and feint, crossed by dark lanes of smoke, centred in the constellations of Scorpio and Centaurus. And because pulsars belonged to the Milky Way, far more of them were being found in the Southern hemisphere than in the North. One of Morgan's reasons for travelling to Stromlo was his hope to find the optical counterparts to some of the most promising radio pulsars in the South. To do that he needed two things: precise radio positions and an electronic set-up to match the one the team had built in Arizona.

The ace pulsar hunter in the South was Mike Viggers an ex-British radio astronomer based at the University of Sydney. In fact Large had discovered half of all the pulsars known. Morgan arranged to meet Viggersand drove down to Molonglo in New South Wales where Vigger's radio telescope, The Molonglo Cross, was situated. Viggers turned out to be a tall friendly fellow who Morgan trusted and liked immediately. The Molonglo Cross was an extraordinary sight, not at all like the radio dish at Parkes. Two lines of wire aerials, in the form of a cross, each line a mile long, met at a central hut. The aerials, which looked more like clothes lines than anything else, could crudely be steered to follow a source in the sky. It was all very Heath-Robinson, being controlled by a tangled spaghetti of wires which emerged from the hut. Mike Viggers took Morgan round and explained the logic of the device. Although it looked extremely crude it was, so far as positions were concerned, far more precise than Parkes, simply because of it's extent. The Cross was an interferometer in which the signals from each separate aerial were brought together in the hut where they were interfered with one another in a deliberate way. From the patterns of that interference one could infer the accurate position of a source in the sky. It made up in ingenuity for what it so obviously lacked in funding. Mike explained:

"Bernie Mills, who designed this, was the real pioneer of interferometry in radio astronomy. Unfortunately the CSIRO and Stromlo got all the government funds for astronomy while we have to scrape by on a shoestring."

Morgan detected a current of understandable resentment. It might account for the hatred which existed between the three establishments. Although Sydney University, and the CSIRO which controlled Parkes, were based within miles of one another in Sydney, neither group cooperated with, or indeed acknowledged the presence of, the other. Viggers listened attentively while Morgan explained to him what he's seen and done at Parkes. He sighed:

"They do with brute force and money what we have to do with brains. And of course they've got a professional publicity machine. That's their real secret. They got all the credit for discovering quasars – because it was done using their fully steerable dish. But it was all Cyril Hazard's idea and he was at Sydney University."

"What happened?"

"Cyril noticed that a powerful radio source called 3C-273, was about to be occulted by the Moon, that's to say blocked out when the Moon passed in front of it. Unfortunately we couldn't reach quite that far North with the Cross. So Cyril went over to Parkes to do it. But when the paper came out with the accurate position in 'Nature' magazine, and the spectrum showing it to be the first quasar, there was no mention of our University. It was as if it was all Parkes's idea."

"Gosh, how shitty."

"Wasn't it? Still, it's no good being bitter. There lies madness. We're lucky to be professional astronomers at all aren't we? Come on let's go and collect the morning's mushrooms. That's one thing they don't have at Parkes."

The Molonglo Cross was erected in lush grassy farmland now sprouting all over with mushrooms, some so gigantic that one of them would have provided a meal for three. As they walked around the sprawling antenna filling their sacks Morgan explained what he was hoping to do.

"I'd love to help of course" Mike was enthusiastic "But how accurate do you need your radio positions to be?"

"As accurate as possible. The greater the accuracy the smaller the aperture I can use, and hence the deeper I can go. If the inaccuracy is say twenty arc seconds then I have to use an aperture on the sky of at least forty arc seconds across in order to include the pulsar. But the sky noise coming through an aperture that size would be so large that it would probably swamp the pulsar signal, unless it was very bright, which seems unlikely from past experience. So there wouldn't be much point."

"I see". Mike was thoughtful as he cut the stem of a giant with his penknife: "These big ones don't eat well, but they make great mushroom soup. My wife freezes it for the winter.". He popped it into a sack. "The positional accuracy we can get with the Cross rather depends on the effort we put into it. Its basic resolution is about one hundred and fifty arc seconds."

"Oh no! "Morgan was dismayed.

"But wait on. We can easily measure positions to a tenth of that. So you'd need an aperture twice that, say thirty seconds of arc across. Would that do?"

"No. We'd need ten arc seconds at worst."

"We could do that too. But it would need a campaign – that means a graduate student and a year or two of messy calibration.."

"What about the Vela pulsar?"

"I thought you'd ask about that. It's the obvious one for you optical chaps isn't it? After all, at eleven pulses a second it's the fastest one after the Crab pulsar. We're working on it of course."

"I know you discovered it Mike. In fact it was your paper in 'Nature' which caused us to change our attention to supernovae like the Crab."

"Well eventually we could get a position for you accurate to a second or two."

"Perfect."

"There's a natty trick do you see. As the Earth orbits the sun during the course of a year, the pulsar period appears to change a bit – depending on its position in the sky. We intend to work backwards from the measured changes of period to a very accurate position."

"Bloody ingenious! " Morgan was lost in admiration.

"I've got a student, Alan Maugham, working on it for his thesis. If you can take him under your wing Tom and teach him the optical side, the two of you could go and find Vela together in the optical. But we'd need to keep mum. We don't want those wretched people at Parkes to steal our thunder again. Which they could."

It was an extremely generous offer and the two of them shook hands on it out in the mushroom field. Mike Viggers's student Alan would supply the best radio position he could, whilst Morgan would build an optical search system and train him to use it. As they put the mushrooms into their respective cars Mike added:

"Do what you can for Alan Tom. It's a wretched business for young Australians to find astronomical jobs out here. Most of them either have to migrate or drop out."

Morgan offered to do his very best.

To his cost Morgan had learned just how nearly impossible it was for an astronomer to learn electronics. The problem was that the field was advancing so fast that even a full-time insider could barely keep up. Valves, then transistors, then integrated circuits, then digitisation, then chips.....it was all too much. He had resigned himself to learning only what electronics could do – not how it did it. He could explain what he wanted to a skilled digital engineer but the engineer would have to put the circuits together using his own arcane wizardry. The problem was that the top digital engineer at Stromlo had just drowned in a swimming accident and Doolan had to find a replacement.

Wayne McGarrity was by all accounts a prodigy. Doolan was ecstatic. He said, during one of his rare appearances at morning coffee:

"We got ourselves a flamin' magician. You should see his refs from the uni. His prof said he's the most brilliant digital engineer they've ever seen. Designed and built a superquick computer for his undergraduate project. Can you believe it? I reckon he'll shake this place up. You fellers better find him something challenging to do. Otherwise he'll be off to California."

For an engineer Wayne McGarrity had the oddest style. He was very young, he wore bell bottomed corduroy suits, expensive shirts and a different floral tie every day. His blond hair and moustache were beautifully coiffured, his Sydney accent heavily repressed, his turquoise Mercedes sports car the envy of most of the younger staff.

The Butterfly, as he became know to the other engineers, was certainly a new broom. Within a week he'd decreed that all of the observatory's computer systems would have to be replaced. When Doolan demurred at the cost McGarrity threatened to resign. Then he went off for a grand tour of the States and came back with a digital television camera system costing quarter of a million dollars which, so he said, would replace photography in astronomy. Morgan was intrigued by this, never having imagined before that television might be the astronomical future. But why not? It was obvious. He began reading technical reports, which he found very hard going, about the subject.

There was no doubt that McGarrity mesmerised everybody else on the staff. He was indeed an exotic butterfly who'd landed in their midst. They didn't know where he'd settle next. Morgan went to see him about his proposed pulsar electronics, proffering a system design based on the Arizona set-up, but with several refinements.

McGarrity glanced briefly at the plan:

"It won't work Tom." He was certain. Morgan was non-plussed.

"Why not?"

"Well for a start you'd get feedback between the oscillator and the A to D converter. Then there's the timing clock in the computer itself. Have you thought about that?"

"Well no."

"Electronics is obviously not your strong suit."

"No it isn't."

McGarrity screwed the plan up into a tight ball and threw it into his wastepaper basket:

"We'll have to start from scratch and redesign completely. I can't promise anything right away mind. I've got our new computer system and the digital TV on my plate right now. But send me the specs Tom, and I'll see what I can do."

Morgan left the elegantly remodelled office feeling confused. Why wouldn't his system work? It had in Arizona. And what about the delay? He had obligations to Mike Viggers and Alan Maugham. By the sound of it McGarrity was talking years rather than months.

After a troubled week thinking things through he went back to the Chief Engineer:

"I don't have years here Wayne. I need this pretty quickly, within three months. We put our system together in Tucson in a couple of weeks. After all the components are all standard. Why can't we reproduce it at Stromlo? I'm only asking for minor improvements – mainly in flexibility and accuracy. And obviously we want the data to go straight into the computer, not into a tape recorder."

"Ah but that's the problem don't you see. You'll get electronic hysteresis in the bus-boards."

McGarrity patiently tried to explain the esoteric difficulties. Apparently it was hopeless. Morgan retreated from the Butterfly's office, disappointed yet again.

This fruitless advance and retreat was repeated several times over the next few weeks until Morgan was utterly frustrated. To whatever scheme he proposed McGarrity raised cogent objections. Morgan grew increasingly angry and suspicious – but what did he know compared to this brilliant digital engineer. He realised how much they'd depended on Don Tallon back in Tucson. Without another Don he wasn't going to get anywhere with pulsar research in the Southern hemisphere. But surely electronics couldn't be as esoteric as Wayne McGarrity made it out to be? He was puzzled.

The one thing he *was* learning about, thanks to McGarrity's initial stimulus, was astronomical television. He couldn't have repaired an ordinary television-set for the life of him, but he did now understand, at a profound level, what a television set could and could not be expected to do for astronomy. And apparently McGarrity was doing great things in the dome of the 74-inch. Doolan was so excited by his protégé's progress that he invited any astronomer who cared, to come along one night for a demonstration.

Morgan went, with several others. The camera was bolted to the spectrograph in the Coude laboratory under the floor of the telescope dome. It was connected by a host of wires to several electronic racks, each one the size of a grandfather clock.. McGarrity, in charge of a squad of minions, was controlling things from the ultra modern computer console. Doolan, astronomer for the night, looked on complacently.

"OK Brucie" McGarrity announced "I'm ready to run."

"Right you are sport. Here comes your first star. I'll take out the dark slide."

The screen of the computer console filled up with a wobbly stellar image, far brighter than any star Morgan had seen before. Several other astronomers 'wowed' at the apparition.

"Bloody marvellous quantum efficiency" Doolan boasted "Twenty times what you'd get with a photographic plate. Thanks to Wayne here we'll be way out in front of everybody.

Morgan, drawing from his reading, asked several technical questions. McGarrity and Doolan between them provided numbers which he scribbled down in his diary. Then they all went home, wondering at the exciting future of optical astronomy. Photography's time was over.

Morgan couldn't sleep that night, wondering at what he'd seen. All branches of optical astronomy were about to be revolutionised. Even galaxies, those elusive question-marks which haunted his dreams, might now come into focus. If he were to put television and galaxies together then perhaps, just perhaps, he might break into Tuten Kahmoun's tomb. And yet there was something about McGarrity's TV system that wasn't quite right, that niggled at the back of his mind. Turning and turning in bed, unable to locate what it was, he went downstairs, poked the fire into life, got out his notebook and began to think.

When Morgan entered the coffee room next morning an unusually animated discussion was in progress concerning the previous night's demonstration. Astronomers were all enthusiasm about what could now be done with television in their own particular fields. Morgan stirred his tea and dipped a biscuit in it:

"It won't work." He announced categorically.

There was silence.

"What do you mean?" somebody ended it. "We saw it."

"It won't work. I've calculated it."

\ "Explain yourself."

"OK. What makes the photographic plate superior to the human eye for astronomy? It isn't sensitivity is it?"

Several astronomers shook their heads in agreement with him.

"No it isn't." Morgan continued. "The eye's at least ten times more sensitive than the photographic emulsion. So where does photography win out?"

"Long exposures." Somebody said.

"Exactly." The eye can store data for no more than a tenth of a second. But a plate can go on accumulating and storing light for hours, building up a faint signal into a deep image."

"So?"

"McGarrity's TV system can't do that. He's using an SEC vidicon target with damn all dynamic range. They were designed to look at fairly uniformly illuminated scenes, not at the stark contrast between bright starlight and inky darkness. It's just another eyeball: a quarter of a million dollar eyeball."

"But...but....but...." there were lots of buts around the table. Thanks to his recent reading Morgan was able to deal with them all convincingly.

"Look," he summarised the situation. "If it was so damn good why didn't the Yanks use it for astronomy? After all they built it didn't they. Are they so bloody stupid?"

Nobody was prepared to argue that they were.

"So if they're not being stupid" Morgan wanted to know "Who is?"

As if on queue Brucie Doolan walked in and helped himself to coffee.

There was a long silence while Doolan stirred in his milk and added sugar. Finally he sensed that something was amiss:

"Come on you jokers, what's up? Have I barfed or something?"

Morgan wasn't going to say anything. He didn't need to. Someone from the far side of the room broke in:

"Tom's been explaining to us why your television system won't work."

Doolan looked astonished:

"Him? What the hell does T-bone know about television?"

Quite a lot it seemed. Or at least considerably more than Brucie Doolan, who was reduced to silence, not by anything Morgan had to say, but by the evident anger of his senior colleagues who'd been deprived of funds to pay for Doolan's folly.

Morgan though had another grenade to lob into Doolan's trench:

"But that's not the end of it, not by a long chalk. How much has it cost us to replace all our computer systems?"

"Two million." somebody said.

"And who ordered that?" They all looked at Doolan.

"It wasn't me fellers. It was Wayne McGarrity."

"The very same genius" Morgan continued "The very same genius who bought the digital television with all its associated electronics, over in the States. Are you all beginning to smell a rat?"

Several of the senior engineers, who'd been uneasy all along, now looked at one another.

"I've had my suspicions for some time" Morgan continued "He kept fobbing me off about the electronics for my pulsar system. Used a whole lot of intimidating jargon I'd never heard of before, for instance 'digital hysteresis'. Anyone familiar with that?"

Silence.

"No, because it doesn't exist. I rang up Mike Viggers this morning to check. He assured me there's no such thing as 'digital hysteresis'. Nor do a whole list of friend McGarrity's other fancy inventions. We've all been fooled chaps. McGarrity is an imposter. And his mate Brucie here has encouraged him to blow two entire years of the observatory's equipment budget on crap."

Uproar followed with half a dozen people yelling at Doolan. Doolan retreated to the door in a fury. Then he turned:

"I knew this observatory should never have hired a whinging bloody Pom."

McGarrity disappeared, leaving the observatory finances in ruins. There was no enquiry, as might have been expected, The rumour was that he'd forged his references. Everybody said there should have been a prosecution – after all millions of dollars had gone down the drain, with Mcgarrity quite likely siphoning off huge kickbacks from the firms concerned. But there was not. Doolan refused to take any of the blame, claiming that it was the responsibility of the university personnel department to check all references.The angry and defrauded astronomers felt differently. But nobody was prosecuted, or even reprimanded. A prosecution would have shown Doolan and Bacon up as dupes.

Morgan now found himself the victim of the two most senior people in the observatory. Bacon ignored him altogether – probably having put the word about that he was unemployable. Since Bacon was on the Council of The International Astronomical Union, the most senior body in world astronomy, his word would certainly count. Doolan, on the other hand, now actively hated Morgan. He'd somehow convinced himself that Morgan was entirely responsible for the McGarrity debacle. Apart form snarling and sneering at him over coffee, there were many crueller ways for Doolan to, make Morfgan's life a misery.

Not long after The Debacle Morgan received a letter from Professor Martin Schwarzchild at Princeton University in America. Even more than Bellfounder, Schwarzchild was the doyenne of the Stellar Evolution world. His computer calculations his papers, and his book on the subject, were regarded by experts as the final word

> "   Dear Dr Morgan
>
>   your paper on Red Giantness was recently brought
> to my attention. I must say I was sceptical at first. After all Sir
> Adrian's theory is so elegant. But after a careful reading, and long
> discussions with several colleagues, I find your paper convincing. It is
> a real contribution to the field.
>
>   As it happens we are holding an IAU symposium here on 'The
> Advanced Stages of Stellar Evolution' in January. Sir Adrian has
> already been invited to review the Red Giant problem. However the
> Scientific Organising Committee, of which I am the chair, now feel it
> would be seriously remiss not to offer you an audience for your

provocative ideas. We therefore invite you to give a 45 minute presentation: the same length as Sir Adrian's.

I'm sorry this is so very late in the day. Had we known of your seminal work earlier we would unquestionably have invited you as a key speaker at the outset. It is most important that you should come.
Congratulations once again
Martin Schwarzchild.

Morgan walked on air. He was so excited he couldn't sit down in his office for hours. After so many rebuffs, after six years of thinking, dreaming and fighting, now to get the seal of approval from the pope himself! He so wanted to tell Ann, to tell Frank, to tell Martin Johnson, to tell Jack Cockle, but above all to tell Annie who he missed so much. His spirit cried out for her to share in the sweetness with him. Such moments may come but once in a lifetime. But she wasn't there. She was probably fast asleep in Kew, with his baby warm inside her.

Instead he rang up Quantas to find the cheapest possible seat to New York. The price, at such short notice, was steeper even than he'd feared. But surely the observatory would cover it – after all it was an invited talk at an IAU Symposium, a blue ribbon event in astronomy, and therefore a major feather in the observatory's cap. There was nothing for it but to plead with Bruce Doolan, still acting Director in Bacon's absence.

Doolan looked astonished when Morgan turned up in his office. But he did read Schwarzchild's letter. His nose actually turned white with jealousy: observational stellar evolution was his own field.

"So waddyer want sport?" he flicked the letter back contemptuously across his desk "Another bloody T-bone steak?"

"I thought the observatory might pay, or at least contribute to the travel costs. It would be the normal thing to expect."

"Expect!" Doolan rose to his feet in indignation. He was outraged at the very idea. White foam actually appeared on his lower lip.

"Expect! Who the hell do you think you are? No don't tell me! I'll tell you. You sport are a temporary, bloody temporary in your case, Research Fellow. The lowest of the bleeding low, scarcely higher than a worm. Why the hell we invited you here in the first place I dunno. We're certainly not wasting a red cent flying a joker like you across the Pacific. Not unless you want to go permanently? Now that'd be different. I'd sign the cheque this minute. Now geddout of my office." He pushed the letter off his desk onto the floor. "Oliver bleeding Twist they ought to call youse. Where do you Poms get the flamin' nerve?"

How Morgan would have loved to go to Princeton. It would have been the ideal opportunity to put Bellfounder in his place. Better still he might there have made the impression and made the contacts which would lead to a decent permanent job. But he couldn't afford to go, not out of his own salary for, on top of the flights would come the subsistence and accommodation costs, as well as a hefty registration fee. Not only were he and Ann hopeless with money but the Australian dollar was very weak. He wrote back to Schwarzchild thanking him for the invitation, sincerely regretting his inability to come. Doolan was uncharacteristically cheerful for a couple of weeks after that, while Morgan couldn't even look forward to therapy next door. Karen's husband Roy had shown up at last, a quiet little fellow never seen without his sports jacket, his tie and his briefcase. What Karen could see in him Morgan couldn't imagine, but for now there'd be no red knickers on the washing line.

On the good side Mussels had just arrived in Australia for three years. He'd got one of the astronomers' jobs on the UK Schmidt Telescope now completing at Siding Springs. The next time Morgan went up to observe there he stayed with Mussels, his wife Jenny, and their two little girls Natasha and Lara. Jenny fed him, so he didn't have to encounter Mrs Bulstrode. She was apparently suffering from 'veins' and was even more tyrannical than ever. Morgan had picked up a second-hand copy of '*Basic Principles for the Novice Cook*" and posted it to her along with an old medical manual entitled '*Handling the Extremely Obese.*'

It was great to be with Mussels again, though it was hard to take his wild enthusiasm for Australia. Better that way he thought than the alternative. Mussel's colleagues were all ex-pats who had a vitally important task to do since much of the sky below minus forty-five degrees had never been explored in any depth. Mussels had been entrusted with the task of exploiting the very latest photographic techniques to try and go even deeper than the Americans had been able to go from their identical Schmidt-telescope survey of the North from California. Houses being very cheap in Coonbarrabran he and Jenny had bought a big house with a swimming pool. The two men had great fun trying to teach the two little girls how to swim.

They sat in deckchairs beside the pool afterwards, drinking a cool spaetlese:

"You can't imagine Tom how wonderful all this is for us. While you were hogging all the sun and the stars and the fame we were living on a council estate in Tottenham. Rain, strikes, sad immigrants everywhere, bolshie bus drivers, union bullies hogging the television….if you've got any gripes about Australia I don't want to hear them just now. Cheers cobber! I don't think we'll ever go back. What's up in astronomy?"

Biting off all his problems with Bacon and Doolan Morgan spoke of his ambitions one day to work on the staff of the AAT:

"Do you know Jack no one seems to have actually carried out a complete mathematical analysis of telescope performance in terms of size. Everyone assumes the bigger the better. And superficially, very superficially, that's true. But I'm thinking another way. If one had a fixed amount of money to spend should one spend it on one big 'un or on several smaller telescopes? The point is, which combination would make the most astronomical discoveries? Nobody has actually analysed that."

That got them into the kind of passionate argument which he, Jack and Frank had always engaged in and which Morgan had so completely missed in Australia where passion was too often mistaken for 'skiting' or boasting. Since they were both observing at nights they had the afternoons to argue. During one such afternoon beside the pool Morgan said:

"Of course the obvious way to build a giant telescope is to build an array of smaller ones, then add their signals afterwards. That way' you'd collect far more light for your money."

There was a silence afterwards. Cockle was thinking of the implications of Morgan's idea. Morgan was wondering where in heaven the idea, the thunderbolt idea had come from. It had rolled off his tongue and out of his mouth without it ever touching his conscious brain. It was as if someone else had conceived it. He was more the listener than the proposer. He wondered , like Jack, whether the idea of such an optical array of telescopes was sound.

"Why do you say that Tom?"

It took Morgan some time to collect himself and turn the unconscious thought in to some kind of rational argument:

"I suppose it's all got to do with trees really."

Mussels looked startled.

"What I mean is Jack that a big telescope is much more stoutly proportioned than a little telescope, just as a big oak is far sturdier than a little one. Right?"

"Check"

"And for the same reasons. The longer a branch the greater the leverage of its weight. So you have to make it thicker to stop in drooping. But if you make it thicker it gets heavier and droops more. And so you have to make it thicker still. Thus young oaks are slender, old oaks are sturdy. Thus small telescopes are slender, big ones are sturdy."

"So what?"

"Weight in engineering costs money. Roughly speaking the cost of a car or an aeroplane goes up with its weight. Likewise I presume a telescope. Thus the cost of a large telescope is out of all proportion to the area of its mirror. Worse still it's not the area that matters but in many cases it's the diameter only. Remember big telescopes collect more sky noise as well as more signal. The AAT will have a mirror four times the diameter of my 1 meter, but it will weigh four to the power of four, or two hundred and fifty six times as much. For the price of one AAT we could buy two hundred and fifty one-meter telescopes. The real question is 'Would an array of two hundred and fifty six one-meter telescopes make more discoveries than a single four-meter?'."

"I see what you mean now. The 256 one-meters would collect four times four, or sixteen times as much light as the single four-meter."

"Exactly Mussels. And if you could efficiently add all that light together you'd have an array telescope of awesome power."

"I'd never thought of it that way."

" To be honest, neither had I. Not until this very moment. It was a bolt from the blue. But I have been worrying about telescope performance for several weeks – in fact ever since I saw the enormous scale of the AAT."

"The 'Morgan Optical Array'. Hey I'll drink to that. Have some more Aussie plonk."

Morgan was dazed. He'd read that the unconscious mind was often the source of inspiration – but never experienced it himself. The great French mathematician Henri Poincare had been so convinced that the unconscious brain did all the great work that he used to read over his latest research problem before putting out the light at night. Often the solution had appeared in his conscious brain by the morning.

"It won't work." Mussels sounded disappointed

"Why not?"

"Reciprocity Failure."

"What the hell is that?"

"I've been learning about it for my new job. I presume that you intend to collect the light from a single weak source using a photographic plate in each of your array telescopes, and then add the plates afterwards in the lab to make the final signal?"

"Yes."

"Reciprocity failure means it can't be done Tom. It's a fifty quid phrase simply meaning that the photographic process has a threshold problem. Below a certain light threshold it won't record anything at all. So the signal from a very faint star might fall above that threshold for the AAT, but below the threshold for each of your 256 array telescopes. And 256 times nothing is still nothing."

"Shit!" Morgan was disappointed. "Are you sure Jack?"

"It's what I'm supposed to be doing for a living nowadays. There are papers on it going back fifty years. I'm afraid that's why no nobody has built – or even proposed, an optical array telescope; Reciprocity Failure. Didn't somebody say, Huxley I think it was, that 'The tragedy of science is a beautiful idea killed by an ugly fact.?"

Morgan was so excited when he heard that Ann was coming back that he drove down to Sydney and met her at Kingsford-Smith airport. Looking radiant, as she always did when she was pregnant, she threw herself into his arms, while Morgan actually cried with joy:

"Oh I've missed you Annie. I've missed you so much. Come on I've got a lovely surprise."

The surprise turned out to be an apartment on Potts Point with marvellous views up and down the harbour. They scarcely went to sleep for the two days and nights, which was all they could afford, catching up with one another's news."

"I can smell the sea from here." Ann said, while they were breakfasting on the balcony.

"I can throw a coin into it." Morgan said, and did.

"That earns you a wish darling."

"Am I allowed to tell?"

"On this special occasion yes."

"OK. I'm wishing that Tadpole will grow into a little girl called Cariad."

"But I want a little boy."

"I don't care really – as long as it's just like you Annie."

"And you."

Ann couldn't tell him about her work, but she'd seen a lot of Frank:

"He's sitting on some important committee looking into the future of British astronomy. And he's got a season ticket for the Royal Opera. And you know how I hate going out on my own."

Morgan experienced an unaccustomed twinge of jealousy.

"And guess who else turned up."

"Tell me."

"Old Salt!"

"How is he?"

"He turned up at Kew, beautifully dressed, and talking like an Oxford professor. Fooled the parents completely. Then he turned all Brummagen again and Daddy nearly had a fit. Bob puts it all down to his elocution teacher. But it's only an act, he says, and he can keep it up for only so long. But it's astonishing Tom, really astonishing. You'll hear it. He's given me a tape for you, with all his news. It's exciting apparently."

From Sydney they drove the Vee-Dub up through the Blue Mountains, over which Ann was ecstatic, to Parkes. He had his first run on the radio telescope – which he wanted Ann to share with him. They'd been assigned a self-contained flat which looked down a long avenue of firs towards the great dish.

"It's beautiful darling, in a way more beautiful than the Opera House. It's like a giant white sunflower."

Ken Eckersly who was going to be Morgan's mentor and collaborator, was one of John Bolton's closest associates. A bearded 'sand-groper', that is to say a Western Australian, with clever grey eyes, he had acquired his boss's no-nonsense manner. Having left their bags they went down to the telescope with him. The dish was pointed vertically upwards while the engineers installed the high frequency receiver that Morgan had specified.

Up in the control tower Ken asked:

"How are your heads for heights?"

"Tom used to be a mountaineer weren't you darling? I'm hopeless."

"This is your chance to see the aerial cabin. But I warn you it's airy."

"Can Ann turn back if it's too much?"

"Of course" Ken reassured them.

They all put on hard hats and walked out onto the balcony.

"I'm dizzy already" Ann said .You can see for miles and miles and miles."

Morgan was looking up at the web of silver steelwork that stretched far out into space supporting the gigantic upside down umbrella from beneath.

"We've got to out along that catwalk" Ken said "And climb up through the surface of the dish."

"I'm not going on that." Ann declared.

"Very sensible cariad." Morgan took her back to the control room, where she sat down with relief:

"I'd like to go really, but with Tadpole…."

Even Morgan found the catwalk giddy-making. While the guardrails made it perfectly safe, there was absolutely nothing below the wire grating on which they stood but empty space.

Near the edge of the great dish they climbed up through the hatch to find themselves in a gigantic bowl of white steel plates with an aerial cabin, apparently a tiny box, far far above them perched on a tripod of girders which rose up from edges of the dish.

"I feel like Jack in the Beanstalk." Morgan said in wonder. They were in a completely new world of steel and sky because the Earth was now completely hidden from sight by the raised rim of the dish.

"This is where the fun begins" Ken mutterd. 'Follow me. Hold on tight and whatever you do don't look down."

Half way up the steep ladder running up one of the tripod legs Morgan, being Morgan, did look down. And wished he hadn't. The dish had shrunk, become a transparent web of steel with a round saucer of white solidity in the centre. Beyond the rim of the dish the ground looked as far below as he remembered when looking down the core of the Eiffel Tower. Up here the wind plucked at his sleeves, even threatened to pull him from his perch. He knew it was only vertigo. Only. He switched his focus to Eckersly's backside, now well above him, and continued up the ladder to the trapdoor underneath the aerial cabin. Once he'd crawled inside he didn't look down again.

"He's an Old South Welshman." Eckersly explained to the two be-shorted engineers bending over the receiver. They grunted.

"Did you know Tom that this dish was designed and built by another Welshman called Taffy Bowen? From Swansea."

"Never heard of him."

"Shame on you. He built the word's first airborne radar back in the 1930s.Then he took the cavity magnetron over to America. Rooseveldt called it 'The most precious cargo ever to land on these shores'. Then he showed the Yanks how to build radar. After the war he came out here as director of CSIRO Radiophysics. Smashing bloke apparently. The Americans gave him the money for this dish – more or less out of gratitude."

"How does it work?"

"The radio waves hitting the dish are all focussed back up onto this thing," he pointed to a metal fixture looking much like a miniature television aerial. "This is the feed. From the feed the radio waves are piped down this gold-lined pipe into this cryogenically cooled receiver here. What it does is combine the incoming waves with a steady train of waves we generate ourselves, and mix them down to a much lower frequency."

"Why do that?"

"Because such intermediate frequency waves are far easier to handle, We can use wires for instance, not gold-lined pipes. The wires carry the amplified signal down to the control room where it is detected by another more conventional receiver."

"Why is it all cooled?"

"You've heard the background hiss on a radio I'm sure. That's 'receiver noise'. If you don't reduce that to a minimum by cooling you'd never pick up weak cosmic signals. Radio astronomy is dominated by receiver noise. It's caused by odd electrons whizzing about in the circuitry. The colder the receiver, the less the whizzing."

What Morgan was hoping to do at Parkes was find close-by Elliptical galaxies with miniature quasars in the cores. The idea sprang from the calculation he'd made back in Tucson of the fate of gas given off by the ancient stars which predominated in such galaxies. That gas, according to him, would sink into the galaxy core but could never fragment. Therefore it would pile up as a single massive lump which would eventually collapse under the force of its own gravity, to become a Massive Black Hole – the probable driving engine of a quasar. Quasars gave off predominantly high frequency radiation, and it so happened that Parkes was the most sensitive antenna in the world to high frequency radio radiation. No astronomer on Earth had a better opportunity than he now had, of finding the closest mini-quasars. And of course the closer they were the more precisely they could be investigated. If he found any they would be ten times closer than the sample given to him by Bolton, though intrinsically far less powerful.

He'd selected as his sample to look at, the two hundred brightest Elliptical galaxies discovered by optical astronomers in the Southern hemisphere. Nobody knew how far most of them were away, but he aimed to find out by pointing the spectrograph of the 74-inch at them. The spectra would yield their redshifts, and hence their distances, from the expansion rate of the Universe.

Once the engineers had tested the receiver the serious observing could begin. From the control room in the supporting tower underneath the dish Morgan typed the position of his Elliptical galaxy into the control computer. Immediately they could hear the rumble as the eight hundred tons of dish and superstructure above them turned towards that position on the sky. Through the many windows they could see the dish tipping down towards the ground. When it stopped, and the console announced that it was on position, Morgan, under Ken's direction, pressed another button and the dish proceeded to nod up and down every minute or so.

"Why is it doing that?" Morgan wanted to know.

"To take out the receiver noise." Eckersly explained."When we are on-source we got a lot of noise plus the tiny cosmic signal. When we are off-source we get the noise only. Subtract the two and you get the signal you're after."

"Simple really."

"Provided the noise is steady."

"And isn't it?"

"Depends on many factors, including the time of day, and where we are focussed. The receiver doesn't like the sun focussed on it."

"What do we do if it's extra noisy?"

"Just go on observing for longer. Eventually one hopes to cancel out the noise and pick up the signal. After all the signal is steady while the noise is varying up and down. But I wouldn't go on for much above thirty minutes per galaxy. If you haven't detected it by then, you're not going to find it."

It appeared all rather straightforward compared to optical astronomy. No darkness, no clouds, no high platforms to fall from, no starfields to navigate, no cold and no Huntsmen spiders. In fact after a few hours it became dull, particularly so as none of the first dozen Ellipticals showed any radio signal whatsoever. Morgan began to worry about his whole plan of attack, his calculation, everything.

"I bet I could do that." Said Ann, who had been sitting behind watching him."Why don't you train me and then I can help. Would that be OK Ken?"

"As long as Tom doesn't leave the control room, or go to sleep.. Once I leave he will be entirely responsible. For instance if the wind gets up he'll have to park the dish in the 'safe' position. But let's see what you can do."

Ann moved into Tom's seat and typed in the twelve-figure position for the next galaxy.

"Wait a moment. What the heck's going on?" Eckersly sounded astonished. "Where did you get that position from? Tom's left his list over there."

"Oh I memorised them all while I was watching."

Eckersly was incredulous:

"But surely not. Nobody could memorise two hundred twelve-digit numbers accurately. That's ridiculous."

"Oh Annie can. That's nothing."

"Goddamnit Tom!" Ken Eckersly was amazed. "Just think what she could do with a brain like that."

"I believe she's doing it already. For the British Admiralty. Unfortunately it's all so hush-hush she can't even tell her poor bloody husband."

"Stone the bleeding crows. What a waste."

"Oh I'm not wasted entirely." Ann smiled as if she knew things her husband did not.

That was how Ann Morgan became something of a legend throughout world astronomy.

"Tom!" Ann was excited" I think I've got a signal."

The two men looked at the cathode ray screen, then down at the graph plot that was slowly coming out of the plotter:

"You certainly have." Ken said. "Quite strong too. Two hundred or so millijanskys. Your first galaxy and it's a radio source. I think we can dispense with Tom."

After that, to Morgan's immense relief, about one galaxy in ten came up with a signal. He would expect the signal to vary as more or less gas fell into the Black Hole, so that, art any one time, not all galaxies would be detectable sources.

Being able to manage with very little sleep Morgan spent as much time as he could with Eckersly during Ken's shifts in the control tower; he wanted to thoroughly pick the radio astronomer's brains. But it wasn't as easy as he'd hoped. Radio astronomers used a vocabulary as different from his own as French was from English. And that difference wasn't accidental. Radio astronomers thought of their subject in terms of receiving and handling waves. The five Gigahertz waves they were looking for now actually had a wavelength of six centimetres – about the width of a man's hand. They used 'antennae' not 'mirrors', they spoke of 'diffraction' rather than 'reflection', of 'receivers' rather than 'detectors', of 'Fourier components' rather than 'photons' and so on and so on. Above all they interfered their waves which was something almost impossible for optical astronomers to do. On top of that they had their own jargon derived from radio engineering: 'spectral indices' instead of 'colours', 'Janskys' instead of 'magnitudes', 'receiver temperature' instead of 'detector noise' – the differences seemed endless. Morgan was mystified but fascinated. How could radio astronomy be so very different from the optical variety? After all they were both doing identical physics. Identical physics! A wave was a light particle or a 'photon', while a photon was a wave. He supposed it was all to do with the central mystery of quantum physics; the wavelike nature of particles and the particle-like nature of waves. He'd been taught this in a theoretical sort of way at university, but here the mystery was made manifest by the differences between a radio antenna and a reflecting mirror. He was greatly puzzled – and so was Eckersly. Both men could do astrophysics in their different ways, but at a truly fundamental level neither of them really understood it. Morgan was to be haunted by this mystery to the end of his life.

Ken Eckersly was an intelligent man. He'd started in philosophy, switched to physics, done a PhD in radio astronomy and recently returned from three years in California. He could talk mathematical statistics with Ann, Roman history with Morgan. Radio astronomers appeared to be far brighter than the optical variety. It was what they knew not who they knew which mattered. It was hard for Morgan to imagine that Ken Eckersly and Brucie Doolan came from the same continent. Morgan could see now why Bacon and Doolan were so terrified of letting radio astronomers loose in their observatory. Like shipyard workers or doctors they were clinging on to their petty monopoly for fear of ending up on the street. It was understandable but despicable nonetheless, and ultimately futile. No wonder they hated Morgan at Mount Stromlo. He was, so they must believe, the very thin end of a very thick wedge. The enmity between the optical and the radio fraternities in Australia was partly explicable.

But what about the equally rabid enmity between Sydney University and Parkes, both of them radio observatories? He decided to tackle Eckersly.

"I agree it's totally unfair" Ken said. "We get all the money while they live on scraps. But what can anyone do? The Yanks generously paid for this super dish – it's better than anything they've got themselves. The least we can do is operate it properly. Indeed that was part of the agreement with them. And of course that costs Australia a fortune. That cryogenic receiver up in the aerial cabin cost a bomb. It's not the hardware so much as all the top engineers we need to employ, to design, to build and to maintain it. The government doesn't care a damn about the universe. What government does? They have fantasies about turning Australia into a hub of high technology. You can't blame them can you? It's what the people would like to see: Silicon Valley here in

Sydney. Nobody wants their sons herding a mob of jumbucks out in the never never. So the government trickles a little money into the CSIRO in hope that we'll lay some silicon egg for them. They'd much prefer me to perfect a blind-landing radar system than discover the central mystery of the Universe. That's why I'm going to have to spend my life abroad. You too presumably. There just aren't the jobs – and there never will be. Not here, not in Britain, not even in America. All we can do is cling on or move on. We're scholar gypsies. When the locals get fed up, or find out what we're trying to do, they'll chuck us out. Who wants to spend a dollar on the gypsies? Who ever did?"

"You've thought about it a lot. More than I have."

"Yes I wake up nights sometimes. My wife doesn't want to leave Australia again, and neither do I. But what's the choice? Work in some dreary lab in Oz testing equipment – or get on the road and try to cling to astronomy. Luckily my wife knows I'd die a dusty death in that lab and so she's willing to support my dream, with all the inconvenience and heart-ache its going to cost her – and her children. Successful astronomers are the ones with exceptionally brave and unselfish wives. We'll shoot through — go abroad I mean. Our kids will grow up as Yanks or whatever – and then she'll never be able to return. Her parents will die here alone, her friends will be lost to her for ever."

"You make it sound bleak."

"It is bleak Tom, for the partners. Believe me. Australia is still a remote bloody place. It's not big enough yet to retain its brightest people. They must go into exile. And if a decent vacancy does arise who will get the job? A second rate Pom probably, or a third rate Yank."

"Like Bacon."

"You said it. You have to forgive us Tom if we sometimes sound bitter or we brown-nose the boss. I hear there's a lot of that at Stromlo."

"I'll say."

Morgan also tackled Eckersly about Mike Viggers's accusation that Parkes had stolen the quasar discovery.

"That's a complete mystery to us. John Bolton actually risked the dish, and his career, even his life, to make Cyril Hazard's lunar occultation possible. He sheered off the safety bolts with a power saw so he could take the lip of the dish right down to the ground – where it was never designed to go. Yet John never put his name to the paper. We do know that when the paper left Australia it had the "The University of Sydney" on it after Cyril Hazard's name – and he was the first author. Who knows what happened later in the editor's office in London? Who knows? The University people don't believe us – and who can blame them? But it's sad sad sad. Do you know Tom you are the only go-between amongst the three observatories?"

"Can I do anything to smooth things out?"

"It's probably a forlorn hope. But you can try."

"They regard me as a traitor over in Stromlo."

"I bet they do. You make one slip and they'll have you out. Unless you can get rid of Bacon first. And that awful side-kick of his. What's his name?"

"Brucie Doolan."

"Come on Tom we've got to make a big discovery. It might be the only way to save our hides – both yours and mine."

By the end of the week they'd looked at a hundred and ten Elliptical galaxies and found radio signals from twelve of them. Morgan was jubilant and his head was full by the time he and Ann got back to Canberra. Quite apart from Ellipticals and quasars and pulsars and Red Giants and Protostars and television systems and radio astronomy he was also thinking about his latest mad idea of 'Optical Arrays'. They were such an obvious winner that there had to be a way, there just had to be a way round Mussels' Reciprocity Failure'. And over and beyond all these preoccupations was his overriding fascination with galaxies in general. By now he'd read everything on the subject there was to read – which to tell the truth, wasn't much. There was plenty of data but very little understanding. Even coherent questions about them, which might have formed the basis of a decent research program, had yet to be formulated. Moreover the easiest things in the Southern hemisphere had been done already. He'd been surprised to learn that Gerard de Vaucouleurs, one of the giants of galaxy astronomy, had been stationed at Stromlo for several years. He'd moved to a bigger telescope in Texas when the lights of Canberra began to threaten the Stromlo sky.

And that was the great problem for Morgan. He'd hoped to work on galaxies, but the Stromlo sky was gradually becoming too bright, whilst the Sidings Springs sky, which was truly dark, was blocked to him, and to everybody else, by Bacon's selfishness. But there was more to it than that. To make a breakthrough in galaxy research you were either going to have to have new equipment unavailable to the pioneers, or a totally new idea. And, for now, Morgan had neither. All he could think of was returning to Australia one day to work on them when the AAT had been fitted with electronic marvels. Fortunately he was working on Elliptical galaxies whose surface brightness's were high, and exceeded that of the sky. He'd tried Spirals too, but they were buried in light pollution. Of course he had one or two tantalisingly beautiful images of spirals from Siding Springs, but they were far too few to provide for any sort of research program. He would have to put off doing fundamental galaxy research yet again. It was maddening, but unavoidable.

When they got home Ann went straight round to see Karen to tell her all the news.

"Do you realize Tom" she said as she kissed him goodbye "Out at Parkes I didn't see a single woman to have a chat with. Not a single solitary woman."

When she came back she was all excited:

"I've met Roy and they've asked us round for supper. He's a funny little man isn't he? Not at all Karen's type I would have thought. But isn't it exciting?"

"What's exciting?"

"Karen's baby of course!. She's going to have it just after I am. Didn't you know? It's super. We'll be able to share everything. Absolutely everything."

Two days later, up at Stromlo, Morgan got a phone call from Karen. She sounded frightened:

"Ann's bleeding badly Tom. What shall I do? She's in agony."

"Oh Christ! Oh no. Ring for an ambulance at once. Dial emergency. Get her to the hospital as quickly as you can. I'll ring the gaeny people there. Oh hell I haven't got the car today. But I'll get home somehow. For God'd sake don't waste a second. Not a second do you hear!"

Greg gave him a lift in his old Holden. They hurtled down the mountain at breakneck speed, skidded over the cattle grid onto the Cotter road and raced all the way into Canberra and through a red light at Hughes.

The back door was open when he ran in. But there was no sign of Ann, just bloody towels on the sofa. Karen wasn't next door either.

"The hospital!" Morgan yelled at Greg, who'd already lined up his car, and they set off, doors slamming, tyres screaming.

Karen, looking awful herself, was waiting for him outside the entrance to Accident and Emergency:

"She's gone down to Theatre just now."

"Can they save the baby?"

"How should I know? She's lost a bucket of blood. The ambulance guys had to give her a emergency transfusion."

"Poor little Annie!"

"How's it going mate?" Greg had just run in.

"We don't know. They've just rushed her down to theatre. But if she's lost another baby – this 'll be the third since we got to Australia – it'll kill her! She won't want to live."

He sat with his head in his hands:

"Poor little Annie. Poor little thing. She so wanted her baby. It's not so much to ask for is it ?"

Greg and Karen sat on either side of him, arms resting across his shoulders, all three with tears streaming down their cheeks.

Ann survived, at least her body did; the baby didn't. When eventually allowed home she was more like a ghost than a woman. She wanted a funeral for the baby but officialdom wouldn't allow it. This provoked a fit of hysterics. To assuage her grief Morgan and Greg arranged a private ceremony out in the bush near Greg and Penny's property Tidbinbilla. All of Greg's family came including Kylie with her horse Cyclops and her Kelpie dog Picton, together with Karen and Roy. Greg had dug a small grave over which Penny had erected a cross with 'Ann's baby' written across it. Ann lowered a little box of secret things into the grave which Morgan covered with soil. Kylie and all the children came forward with wild flowers to scatter on the grave. Roy said a long Aboriginal prayer half translated into English, after which Karen, backed by Penny on the recorder, led the mourners in a series of rousing hymns including 'Onward Christian Soldiers', 'All Things Bright and Beautiful,' and 'Bread of Heaven'. Kylie, completely out of tune, sang louder than anybody else except for Morgan, whose stentorian baritone cracked. The Kelpie Picton howled like a wolf and although everybody, except Ann, forgot some of the words, the bush around them rang.

The Ann Cloudesly who Morgan had married was gone. In her place appeared a haggard, restless creature, convinced that something about their home or their environment was responsible for her tragedy. If Morgan tried to reason with her Ann raged:

"Don't be stupid! I hate complacent men. Look at the odds: three miscarriages in twenty months. One as soon as we come here from America; another as soon as I get back from Britain – in both of which places I was perfectly fine. And the one in between, nurtured entirely here, scarcely lasted at all. Don't be so pathetic Tom. There's something toxic in this place and you know it."

"But nobody else has this problem....."

"How do you know?" she fumed. "Does everybody go about boasting of their miscarriages? If it's all so healthy here why does Canberra have the highest sex ratio in the world in favour of baby girls? Why? Why? Why? Why? That's a classic clue."

"Well I don't know darling."

"Of course you don't know. But it's your child we lost – just as much as mine."

"I agree sweetheart. But what c...."

"Well find out then ! You're supposed to be the scientist in the family. Find out!"

He pleaded total ignorance of medical science, which infuriated Ann even more:

"Forget your stupid universe for a while. What about your sons and daughters? How many do we have to bury before you wake up?' She slammed out of the room, crying yet again.

Their GP prescribed Valium. Ann threw the prescription in his face.

The woman who had once been so contented, now raged restlessly about. She couldn't read, she couldn't sit, she couldn't listen, she hated company, but couldn't be alone either, not for a moment. When he was at home she followed him from room to room blazing her misery. When he was asleep she woke him up to argue. When he went to work she rang him up every thirty minutes, endlessly repeating the same arguments and complaints. He couldn't be with her for too long in case he lost his temper. But if he went off to hide, which he did sometimes in order to work, he felt too guilty to concentrate. The children she had made friends with in the street she now couldn't stand.

Even Karen couldn't be tolerated. In fact Karen's manifestly healthy pregnancy added barbed insult to injury:

"I want to have a baby! I want to have your baby. I want, I want to, I want to!." She screamed, before bursting into sobs but pushing his consoling arms away:

"Don't be so pathetic! Find out what's wrong in this bloody house! Why can Karen have a baby while I can't?"

She was insanely jealous.

Morgan had no idea what to do. The doctor was an ignorant little pill pusher who, like so many of his profession, had joined up purely for the money. Morgan rang the university accommodation people to see if they could find them another house. All they could offer was a vacant bungalow up on Mount Stromlo, about fifty yards from Bacon's mansion; otherwise they would have to wait several months for a possible vacancy.

Morgan had a sweeping contempt for the medical profession. As far as he was concerned they were no more than leeches with a ruthless trade union, leeches who sucked enormous unearned salaries from society by claiming the credit for breakthroughs made, not by themselves, but by ill paid medical scientists.. They hadn't invented antibiotics but they'd ruined the miracle by inappropriate and over prescription. That was good for their business. He always referred to Ann's gynacologist as 'That woman-butcher' which did nothing for Ann's confidence.

But something had to be done. He found out that by paying a month's salary he could secure for Ann an appointment to see the professor of obstetrics and gynaecology privately. It would do no earthly good but at least Ann, when she saw the bill, would realise her husband was anxious to do his best

The professor gave them exactly fifty-five minutes of his time, most of which he wasted reading Ann's extensive notes. He gave her a perfunctory examination behind the screen, and frostily dismissed her argument about the anomalous sex-ratio:

"I assure you Mrs Morgan we've looked into it. It's just one of those things. It's not statistically significant."

He'd said the wrong thing. Entirely the wrong thing. Ann had more statistics in her little finger than the professor would have been able to understand in half a dozen lucrative careers. Their subsequent row ended when Ann snatched up her notes and walked towards the door. Before leaving she turned on him:

"Instead of lecturing everybody else why don't you attend a few elementary statistics lectures yourself. *Very* elementary ones. If nothing else they might reveal to you the cavernous extent of your own ignorance. In the mean time God help the women of Canberra. You won't!"

Ann's misery haunted every interstice of Morgan's time and space to an extent which, in the end, he couldn't tolerate. He still had to live, to get over his own grief, above all to think. She didn't understand, or she didn't care, that to deprive him of his daily reverie was to force his head under water and hold it there. To cut him off from day-dreaming, from thinking, was to steal the only way he had of annealing himself. He was miserable too, because the latest miscarriage probably meant they could never now have the children he wanted almost as much as Ann. Had he been able to think about astronomy he might have healed himself and so, eventually, have healed his wife. But she wouldn't let him. She followed him about like an avenging angel. If he sat with a piece of paper she took it as a personal insult. Where was her baby? That was all she could think of, or wanted to know.

They had rows, more and more rows, rows which escalated. She threw crockery, tipped up food, goaded him beyond endurance. He moved into the other room. She followed him. He locked the door. She banged on it all night long. with her fists, then with a frying pan. At three am he ran away in the Vee Dub and slept in the bush. She was suicidal when he got back next morning, demented with grief. Karen, who'd been called in by the other neighbours, told Morgan never to leave her in the same state again.

The whole miserable cycle restarted anew. They shouted and screamed. She tore at his hair. He snapped and gave her a jolly good hiding, after which she ran out of the house in the middle of night and disappeared. He couldn't have cared less; fell into a desperately needed sleep on the sofa.

Morgan was woken next morning by a loud rat tat on the door. It sounded like the police. Recalling last night he ran to open it in his pyjamas. But it wasn't the authorities it was Karen. She hit him so hard across the ear that he went deaf. Then she marched off revealing Ann trembling on the lawn, barefoot, still in her nightie.

There was a kind of reconciliation after that. Morgan, shocked by his own violence, offered his tenderness instead. Ann, shocked by her own, declined into helplessness and apathy. Penny Anson, pretending to an ailment of her own, begged Ann to come out to the farm to help with the children and the animals. Morgan packed Ann's suitcase and said goodbye to his wife with a guilty sense of relief.

Part of the frustration which had led to his violence was the sense that Ann was standing in his way, blocking off his approach to a great astronomical idea. Ever since it had come upon him during his discussion round the pool with Mussels the notion of an Optical Array, a family of small telescopes somehow linked together to form a telescope far more powerful than a single giant of the same cost, had been fermenting in the depths of his mind. While it was certain that Jack's 'Reciprocity Failure' would prevent it working photographically, what about television? It was true that the kind of television that McGarrity had purchased would never be of much use to astronomers. But were there other electro-optic devices in prospect that might one day work instead? If there were then his Optical Array concept might become feasible after all. He forgot almost entirely about Ann and started to calculate, from fundamental physics, the properties of the kind of electro-optic imaging detector that astronomy would need. According to his extensive reading nobody had done this before. Several ingenious engineers had tried to adapt the properties of existing TV cameras to suit astronomy, so far with little success. Morgan was approaching the problem from the diametrically opposite direction, using pure calculation. He had to pioneer his way through a thicket of entanglements including quantum efficiency, storage capacity, resolution, sky-noise, field of view, bandwidth, dynamic range, read-out noise and dark current. It was as hard as the hardest rock climb he'd ever attempted, demanding every particle of his concentration.

A week later Greg Anson turned up at the house to find out what was going on. Morgan hadn't been to the observatory; hadn't rung them at the farm, not once, while his own phone seemed to be out of order. As Anson described the situation to his wife later:

"You never seen such a mess darl, he hasn't washed up in a week. There was dirty dishes and pans all over the floor. The flies were buzzing round the bin – which was full of empty cans. It smelled like hell, and so does he. I reckon he hasn't changed his undies since we left. He certainly hasn't shaved; he had egg on his beard and ink stains all over his hands. He's taken the pictures down off the wall and stuck up dozens and dozens of large sheets of paper instead, all covered with bleeding equations.. And do' you know the first thing he asked me when I arrived?"

"Ann?"

"Oh no not Ann. 'Ah Greg' he says in his Pommy accent 'Do you happen to know how an echelle grating works?' I reckoned he'd gone barmy. But somehow he looked so flaming happy. Like he was in a trance. Like he'd glimpsed the promised land or something."

"Didn't he ask about her at all?"

"Eventually he did. After I'd had a good barney with him. It was like waking him from dream. I reckon he'd forgotten everything, including the miscarriage. He'd escaped into heaven – or rather the Universe."

"What about the phone?"

"Taken it off the hook, would you believe? Didn't want the distraction, he said."

"Is he coming over here?"

" 'Not yet' he says 'Not yet. I'm just getting to the tricky pitch' – whatever that means. He reckons he'll be through in ten to fourteen days."

Penny was incredulous. Her husband went on:

"He says he's on the verge of some colossal breakthrough."

"Do you think he's come unhinged?"

"I wondered. Made him clean himself up. We did the washing up together, and I went out for some shopping. But do you know what I felt? Envious. Tom may be half mad but I reckon he's the happiest man I know. Bloody ecstatic."

"Poor Ann."

"She'll be right. Anyway, even if he wanted to, I don't think Tom could help her now. He's off this planet."

Ten days later Greg went round again. The back door wasn't locked. The mess was even worse than before with open books and journals all over the surfaces, including the floor. There was a half eaten loaf green with mould.

"Tom" Anson called out. There was no reply. He ran up the stairs. Morgan was lying on the bed in the darkness, apparently dead. His heart in his mouth Greg crept forward and shook the big man's shoulders. Morgan opened his mouth in a yawn and grinned at Anson;

"I've done it Greg. I've finished it. I know how to build the telescope of the future. I finished the paper last night. How's Annie?"

"Annie's all right mate. She's far too good for you. You're a flamin' monster."

"I'll make it up to her. I promise. She always wanted to go to Queensland. Our friends the Gilkeys are coming over from California to join us. Now I can take her."

When he eventually did get out to Tidbinbilla to explain his triumph to Ann, she understood immediately:

"My baby's dead, but it looks as if yours has grown into a beautiful child. Congratulations darling."

The fact that she could speak in such terms was immensely relieving.

"It's all these lovely people and animals." she explained. "There's too much going on to think about yourself. A new horse has arrived who needs befriending. He's so old and he's been so lonely. Then Kylie's been teaching me how to ride. Haven't you love?" She squeezed the girl who was holding Ann's waist while looking up at Morgan quizzically.

"And Scamp has got new kittens." Kevin announced. "She's just brought them in from the bush and Mum says I can have the ginger one."

"And I've planted a garden, haven't I kids, with all sorts of things in it."

"Dad says the possums'll dig up up her bulbs 'less she puts wire over it."

"Shall we go and show Tom?"

"Yeah" the smaller ones chorused

Morgan looked at Penny. She winked.

"Ann can stay as long as she likes." Greg said to Morgan later as the two men sampled Greg's latest home-brew. "In fact we'd like to keep her. Raised the whole tone of this bucolic establishment she has. Annie's had a bad trot but she's a great sheila. The kids adore her. Penny's never had anyone to talk to like Annie. And me? Christ she's taught me so much. Paid for her tucker a thousand times over."

"How do you mean?"

"Maths mate. Mathematics. It's what's always held me back. Frightened to death of it. Annie's shown me what a beaut subject it really is. And common-sensical. A bloody revelation. I'm dancing. You just watch Greg Anson go from now on. I'll teach some of those snooty sods up at

Stromlo. They won't be able to understand my papers any more – not with all the Fourier Transforms in them. How long can you lend her? I'm going to learn statistics next."

During his grand obsession Morgan had succeeded in defining combinations of properties which would make an electro-optic camera valuable for astronomy. Current television cameras would be useless. They were designed to image more or less uniformly illuminated scenes, not light stars against an inky black night. But, using his new combinations, he had combed the literature and discovered 'Silicon Videcons' , then in a very primitive state of development. According to his mathematics these devices alone had the potential to revolutionise astronomy. Two American physicists, looking for novel computer memories, had discovered by accident that some of their silicon ships were sensitive to light. For them it was a nuisance, but for photographers and others it promised to be salvation. According to Morgan's calculations such Charge Coupled Devices' or 'CCDs' as they came to be known, would eventually revolutionise astronomy – and do away with Reciprocity Failure.

Having thus satisfied himself that an optical array would be feasible *in principle* Morgan faced the much greater challenge of showing it would be superior to a great telescope in practice. He'd had to analyse a wide range of observing modes, from imaging to spectroscopy. Since the largest telescopes were used almost exclusively for spectroscopy, an optical array, if it wasn't superior for spectroscopy, would be practically useless.

Analysing astronomical spectroscopy from a mathematical point of view cost him an immense mental effort. Surprisingly, it seemed never have been done before. But the outcome was thrilling. According to Morgan there was an upper limit to the size of a spectrograph, which meant that any telescope larger than the current Two-hundred-inch would be grossly inefficient for spectroscopy. The array was not just the most efficient way ahead – it was the *only* way to build an immensely powerful telescope. Game set and match! He wrote a long paper, which, he felt sure, would someday make him famous. Morgan had joined an illustrious company, including Galileo and Newton, who'd proposed fundamental improvements in telescope design.

Bacon, back from America, returned Morgan's written application for five weeks leave to go to Queensland with 'Refused' written across it. Morgan, who knew his rights by now, sent it back with;

"Going anyway Sport. Might help if you read the university's regulations."

Morgan's jauntiness was partly assumed but he couldn't afford to disappoint Ann. Whatever he did Bacon was bent on ruining him – and probably would – unless his array paper, quickly accepted by a prestigious journal, caused an international stir. To test the water he offered a seminar on it at the observatory. The reponse was discouraging. He gave what he thought was a brilliant talk, concluding with the dramatic claim that he could build an array with the power of a supergiant 400-inch, for only four percent of the cost of a conventional design.

Such a claim, spelt out aloud, sounded outrageous, even to Morgan

Finally one of the senior astronomers spoke up:

"Nobody'll go for it Tom."

"Why not?"

"Politics. If you get a poli to sign a cheque for a single four-hundred-inch he can't go back afterwards. But if you get him to sign up for thirty six cheap array units – as you propose – he, or his successors, can always dip out later on. They'd say ' OK fellows but we can't afford it right now. We'll give you six instead.' Then we'd be buggered."

"But that's not a scientific argument." Morgan protested. "It's political. Neither of us are in a position to give it any authority. Anyway politicians aren't all fools and liars, though some academics pretend to think so."

Howls of laughter greeted this sally. People began to file out of the room chatting as though Morgan's thesis had been an excellent joke. He stood there gaping until the auditorium was empty.

On their way to Queensland in Bus the Morgans stopped in Sydney to greet Pat and Walter Gilkey off their liner. Frailer and deafer than ever Pat was still in great form, bizarrely dressed and somehow smoking menthol cigarettes through a purple veil. Ensconced in a luxury hotel in Wooloomooloo she regaled them with a string of anecdotes about the passengers she'd encountered aboard ship.

"Well I'm famished." she barked eventually. "Tom, find us a restaurant for lunch. A simple restaurant mind you. None of those expensive foll-de rolls with sauce. Can't stand 'em can I Walter. Just a simple chop or something!"

Patti had generously offered to pay for them all to spend a holiday together on Dunk Island near The Barrier Reef. The Morgans, who couldn't afford to eat out anywhere on Tom's salary, were terrified of the auxiliary expenses which might arise in consequence. Patti, a self-proclaimed socialist, was notoriously extravagant. But Morgan had done his research and he took them to Doyle's fish restaurant which floated on Rose Bay.

What an inspired choice. The sunlight off the harbour reflected its moving dapples upon the ceiling. The menu was redolent of all the seafood for which Australia was famous: native oysters, crayfish, abalone; they had barramundi flown down from Queensland every morning – and all at reasonable prices. What was more Doyles was a BYO or 'Bring Your Own' establishment for it didn't possess a liquor licence.This would avoid the outrageous 'corkage 'fees they would have had to pay in a licensed restaurant. When they arrived Morgan gave the waitress some really good bottles of white wine which he'd purchased previously, to cool. After they'd ordered, and were admiring some of the yachts sailing by, Pat suddenly announced that she wasn't hungry after all:

"Can't stand restaurant food can I Walter? I like something simple like corned beef." She glared at the waitress as if it were the poor girl's fault . "I'll just have a vodka martini. But I want it just like they served it on the boat. Walter you tell that young woman" she pointed with her walking stick as if Walter couldn't see the waitress. " You tell her how I like it. None of that goddamned ice!" She foghorned in a voice that could be heard from one end of Doyles to the other. "And I want one of those small green Mexican olives in it. You tell her Walter!" She busied herself lighting yet another cigarette through her veil.

Morgan hurriedly explained to Walter about the lack of a liquor licence. Walter, looking uncomfortable, tried to pass the intelligence on to his wife. Patti turned purple with rage:

"Listen here young woman" she bellowed, banging her walking stick on the floor:

"When I order a vodka martini I expect to get one. And if you won't fetch me one then you fetch the manager. You hear! Not some underling. Now are you going to fetch me that vodka martini or aren't you?"

The waitress stuttered an explanation.

Pat was however beyond reach of reason or indeed rational conversation, literally quivering with indignation at being cheated out of her vodka martini.

The manager came to try and explain BYO. Pat railed insultingly at him, at his antecedents, at his clientele – who were all agog, at Australian law, and at Australia and Australians in general. The phrase 'rapscallion convicts' was mentioned.

"Now am I going to get my goddamned martini or am I not?'. She glared at the unfortunate man as if she might have him flogged.

Realizing finally that she wasn't going to get a martini of any kind she rose majestically to her feet, stick in one hand, cigarette holder in the other, and tottered out of the restaurant like a thwarted czarina.

Excruciatingly embarrassed, and furious at the thought of leaving his delicious lunch and wine behind, Morgan would cheerfully have thrown Patti over the side into the harbour for the sharks. Instead he had to follow her out into the road, scattering apologies to all sides while Walter tried to settle up with and pacify the manager.

"I'd like to bloody strangle her." Morgan muttered to Ann. "Oh hell now look what she's doing!"

He ran.

Pat was standing in the middle of the freeway, flagging vehicles down with her stick, unable to distinguish between private cars and taxis. Morgan manhandled her back onto the pavement while Ann rushed out into the traffic to calm some of the angry drivers.

Eventually she climbed into a taxi and rapped her orders at the driver:

"I want you to take us to the best goddamned restaurant in Sydney you hear? I want a restaurant where I can order exactly what I want, when I want, and how I want – including a vodka martini with a Mexican olive in it. You hear young man ?" She rattled her stick against the glass partition, making the sixty year old driver wince.

So of course they finished up in an appalling restaurant with appalling prices. Pat got her martini, she even got an olive in it which, so she was assured, had a Mexican provenance. The Morgans ordered for themselves the very cheapest items on the menu, Walter had his usual cottage –cheese salad, whilst Pat ordered half a dozen extravagant dishes only to stub her cigarette out in them as soon as they arrived. She boasted "I can't stand restaurant food, can I Walter?" After he'd paid the bill Morgan wondered what they'd be living on for the next six months. He wanted to cry.

Pat, who seemed to specialise in Governor Generals, flew off next day with Walter to stay with the Governor General of South Australia. The Morgans meanwhile were to drive and camp their way North and meet up with the Gilkeys again on Dunk Island.

Ann wasn't recovered yet but she was recovering, though whether she would ever again be the same soft, indecisive, over- forgiving girl he had married, Morgan doubted.

"I'm nor starting another child, not in Canberra. I'm going on the pill and staying on the pill."

She was adamant. She was also determined:

"When we get back I'm going to get to the bottom of this. Something is killing large numbers of babies in Canberra, something physical, and I'm going to find out exactly what it is. It's no use relying on those pathetic little medics. You saw."

Ann had rarely criticised anyone in such terms before.

Travelling North mostly by inland byways the Morgans found lonely camp sites to heal the noise and heat of a day out on the burning dirt roads, where a plume of white dust followed for a hundred yards behind the van, and where the occasional onrushing road trains blinded and bombarded them with hailstorms of pebbles. Ann did her fair share of driving, which was dehydrating and demanding. You didn't dare slow below fifty for fear of being shaken to pieces by the corrugations in the surface: they'd learned that the only way was to fly across them. Tyres blistered and burst in the heat. They lost a windshield to a flying stone and had to drive without one for several hours. Petrol stations were very few and far between, three hundred and seventy five miles on one occasion. Sometimes it was monotonous:

"I'll swear we've passed that bush " Ann said, her face plastered with dust, "Three million times already."

All the more delightful when they found themselves in their first tropical rainforest. They thought they were dreaming as they wandered the shady aisles between the enormous trees, seeing the occasional shaft of sunlight pierce the canopy above like a theatre spotlight to illuminate a single fern in brilliant emerald green; hearing the whip-birds cracking in the gloom, the parrots screaming from far overhead.. They could literally feel the struggle for existence between plants, climbing by any means to reach the life giving sun. Hopeful young trees sent impossibly slender trunks upward into the windless air. Epiphytic ferns, plants without roots, grew high among the branches, relying on rainwater gathered in the crooks between the boughs. Aptly named lawyer vines sent their strangling cables across the forest floor in search of trees to carry them aloft. Then there were the fallen giants, crumbling back to soil under the combined onslaught of rain, moss, fungus and ants.

"It feels like a cathedral in here." Ann whispered.

They became rain-forest fans, searching ahead for it on the map, camping either in or as close to it as possible. At night they were surrounded by a chorus of a million frogs. First one would start, then another, more would join in until, at its climax the clamour was literally deafening. They had to shout across the camp fire. Then, as if at some pre-arranged signal, the chorus would abruptly stop. They would whisper, or look around ,wondering what the silence foreboded. Was some panther stalking towards them in the night? Then the performance would start all over again, first one frog, then another, until the chorus was fully joined.

They discovered a mountainside covered in rain forest with a river cascading down it among giant white boulders worn pearl smooth by its passage. Swimming in the deep green pools they were startled by irridescent butterflies whose wings flashed with a blue-bottle fire brighter than a sultan's sapphires.

They saw flying foxes, giant fruit bats which hung upside down against the disc of the grape-fruit moon, screaming bad-temperedly at one another before they took off in flocks to feed in the cloud forest. Ann had a fright one night when she heard a crashing in the undergrowth close to where she was sitting beside the fire. Turning a tremulous torch in that direction she picked out a toad about the size of a Christmas Turkey.

"I can't believe it Tom" she clung to him. "It's like something out of a horror film."

"I think I know what it is." Morgan watched the nightmare creature breathing in and out. "It must be a Cane Toad. The Aussies imported them from Africa to control beetles in the sugar cane. Of course they've run wild. Quite harmless I should think. Unless one landed on you."

To see the Reef they'd booked passage on a boat out of Townsville which carried ten passengers, a skipper aged twenty, an anonymous engineer and a rascally looking Chinamen who gradually emerged as the power on board. Not only did he cook like a master but he organised the passengers into gangs to clean ship, to wash up and to generally do the chores. At night, when all was ship-shape in some lonely anchorage, he'd organise the entertainment. Morgan surmised that he probably owned the boat.

There were literally hundreds of islands inside the main reef, most uninhabited for lack of water. After breakfast the boat would weigh anchor and cruise through waters simply alive with fish. When the cook set his trolling line from a spring-loaded reel all hands would go aft confident of seeing him land a twenty pound fighting mackerel within minutes.

"Gotter get 'em in quick" he explained to the admiring passengers "Otherwise the shahks 'll get 'em". He had a perfect Oz accent, being in fact a third generation Australian whose grandfather had come out during the gold-rush. Sometimes he would cause the boat to drift over the coral heads so that they could watch fish twenty fathoms down through the limpid green water. When Morgan baited a heavy line and let it sink the odds were that it would be torn out of his hands when a big fish struck. The first one he landed was pink and silver with iridescent blue spots.

"Coral trout" the cook announced "We'll have him for lunch. See if you can get a Sweetlip. They're bloody delicious grilled over a driftwood fire."

At noon the anchor would rattle down into the coral sand of some desert island. Ann would be rowed ashore with the orchid hunters, the swimmers and the shell collectors while Morgan donned his snorkelling gear, to the derision of the skipper:

"Yer must be mad going down into that lot mite. There's nineteen foot 'ammerhead sharks waiting for yer down there. Tike off yer legs fer a snack."

Morgan was indeed nervous, for he'd never bargained on diving alone. But he could hardly come all this way out to the Barrier Reef without admiring the main attraction. Anyway he'd learned to be sceptical of anything the Australians had to say about their wild life, In fact the reefs were so spectacular that he instantly forgot all thought of giant sharks. Light flickering through the surface wavelets painted the stag-horns and the brain corals in a trembling pattern of colour. Shoals of brilliant tangs, damsels and angelfish nuzzled round him, eyes swivelling to inspect this strange intruder. The orange and white Clown Fish, sheltering amidst the tentacles of a giant anemone, made the gaudiest butterflies seem drab. What was the purpose, he wondered, of so much brilliance and colour.

Ann concentrated on bird-watching, particularly on the many species of sea-swallows or terns. They'd flap lazily over the clear shallows looking to spear-dive small fish swimming near the surface.

"They only work for an hour a day." she marvelled "They spend all day sitting out on a spit of sand, mostly surrounded by sea, communing with one another. I wonder what they talk about. Do you know they can fly from pole to pole if thy want to – and some of them do. They have no predators and they're absolutely free. They can live for fifty years too."

"That means five hundred in human terms." Morgan explained "Being ten times smaller than us their brains have to work ten times faster than ours: otherwise they'd crash into things or fall over. So in fifty years they must have five hundred years' worth of thoughts."

"Sounds like they are superior beings. They don't have to worry about bankruptcy, or finding a job. They must have solved their population problem too. Perhaps they are the most advanced form of life on Earth."

"That's a good point." Morgan stopped in his tracks to look at half a dozen terns standing on a sand-bar together, their black-capped heads pointing into the trade wind. "You know Enrico Fermi asked a profound question. 'Where is everybody?' he asked. Meaning that if the Universe is stuffed with life then surely some of the aliens would have slipped over to chat with us. But they haven't. However Fermi assumed, and so has everybody since, that the aliens would choose to chat with mankind. But if you are right they probably chatted with the terns instead. Perhaps that's what those buggers sitting out there on their sandbar are doing right now."

"Chatting with the Cosmos?"

"It sounds ridiculous doesn't it. But why not?" I can't see a rational objection."

"Small brains?"

"You can make up for size with speed. Computers do."

"I suppose all creatures would naturally imagine they are the superior species on Earth."

"I know I do."

"Oh I do love you Tom." Ann dropped her towel on the beach and threw her arms round his neck "You may be mad. And you certainly are. You may be obsessed with astronomy, absolutely obsessed. But you can't help it can you?. Any more than you can help rowing with everybody – all the people that matter anyway. Or being a brute and beating your wife. But you do keep a girl entertained. There's never never never a boring moment with Tom Morgan."

"Nor with Annie Morgan." he whirled her round in his arms like a child, her feet off the sand.

Their favourite part of the day was the evening. The boat would drop anchor close to a larger island, sometimes sparsely populated. The passengers would be rowed ashore to disperse in different directions. The sun would set over the mainland in a blaze of crimson and orange, backlighting plumes of dark smoke rising from bush fires burning hundreds of miles away in the outback. The water lapping inside the coral lagoons would turn into a cauldron of black and gold until, quite suddenly, the tropic night would fall, with bright stars such as Achernar, Fomalhaut, Diphda and Saiph casting their silver paths across the sea. Sitting alone, apparently the only spectators of Nature's incomparable pageant, they felt at home in it, knew that this had been waiting in their future all their lives.

Their reverie would only break when the cook rang his hand bell from far across the water. The passengers would reassemble on the beach, either whispering, or lost in silence, to be rowed back out to the boat.

After they'd done the after dinner washing-up to his satisfaction the cook would organise fiendishly intelligent games, or get the passengers to entertain one another. Morgan rather lost his credibility by the taking the company on deck to show them the stars. Jupiter being in his pomp he told the story of the Galilean Moons, remarking that no one could see them with the naked eye. Thereupon young Jennie, whose' cretinous intelligence and loud Melbourne whine had proved a trial to all, interjected:

"Oy kin see them. Yes oi kin. Orl four."

Morgan explained patronisingly that she must have a lash in her eye.

"Oy bleeding kin." She maintained defiantly, explaining where each moon was situated in relation to Jupiter. Appeal to binoculars revealed that she was exactly right. To some passengers Morgan had been caught out 'skiting' or shooting a line, a crime in Aussie eyes almost as vile as 'bludging'. He tried to explain that one person in a hundred thousand ,with the most exceptional eyes, could do what Jennie had done. In vain.

On its journey home the boat dropped them off at Dunk Island, an almost unspoiled paradise, and Australia's most expensive resort. Pat and Walter, who had flown in by seaplane, met the Morgans on the beach to conduct them to their private cabin under the cocoanut palms.

"It's like a dream" Ann exulted, once they were alone.

"I hope this won't ruin us." Morgan was worried about Patti's extravagance.

The cabin, not ten yards from the lagoon, was made out of palm leaves and cooled by the trade wind. There was a steep forested hill to climb from where they could see East across the Pacific to the Barrier Reef or West to the mango-swamps of the mainland, not three miles away. In a saga worthy of Robert Louis Stevenson the island had been settled by a man from Liverpool. Under sentence of death from TB he had sailed for the tropics in search of a paradise in which to end his days. He eventually found Dunk but instead of meeting death he had met an aboriginal lady, married her, founded a dynasty, and lived to a ripe old age. His descendents ran the resort.

The handful of guests met for meals in a communal dining hut under the trees. Pat had come to an accommodation with the chef who provided for her the tiny portions and simple dishes she could digest. They had even stocked a private bar for her in the Gilkeys' hut which was next to, but a discreet distance away, from the Morgans'. Thus Walter could manufacture cocktails exactly to Patti's specification and delight. Morgan loved the snorkelling, Ann loved the peace, Patti loved the audience and Walter loved Patti.

It was touching to be with two people eighty years of age who were so much in love. When they were alone with Pat she talked continuously of Walter, 'My Sweetie' as she referred to him. When they were with Walter he talked mostly about Pat:

" During the war " he explained to Morgan as they were walking along the shore-line of the lagoon, "During the war that woman was worth an armoured division to the British. Anthony Eden told me that. Ernest Bevin wanted to honour her afterwards, but she turned him down. Pat started the Spitfire Fund in California: raised I don't know how many millions. Then she ran the food parcels thing, and clothing for victims of the Blitz. But mainly she got after those pro-German anti-British politicians like Colonel McCormick in Chicago. My word Tom you should have seen them quail. In those days she could give a speech worthy of a Mark Twain – or Winston Churchill himself. She just idolised that man. Said he was standing up for Civilisation against The Forces of

Evil: that Americans ought to be ashamed of sitting back like cowards, making another fortune, after the fortune they'd made out of the First World War. The Irish-Americans, the German-Americans and the Italian-Americans hated her. But our Pat didn't care one damn. She swung her tongue at them like a shillelagh."

Patti was equally effusive to Ann about Walter:

"Do you know that man is a hero? Why he's only got twenty per cent of one lung left to live on. And where's the rest? Back in the Mayo Clinic in Cleveland Ohio. When he was a physician at the Mayo in the 1930's a fire broke out in the night. The blaze got into the store where they kept the X-ray films. Toxic fumes escaped into the wards, killing patients. Walter rushed into the blaze and dragged out dozens. But his own lungs were gone at the end. That's why we went to California. They told us he'd die without sea air. I just love that man Annie. D'ye know I still get a thrill when my sweetie walks into the room? That's how love should be darlin'."

"Pat's tragedy was that she couldn't have children." Walter confided in Morgan " Mine too. I guess that's why I took to paediatrics. Patti couldn't do that. But she just loves kids. So she sort of turned the whole world into her family. You know Tom when she was younger I didn't know who I'd find when I got home evenings. She brought them out of orphanages, out of police courts, out of homes….Lordy Lordy, God only knows how many stray kids she's rescued off the street and put through high-school – even college. They still bring their children and grand-children to see us. But she sure would have loved one of her own. If she mothers you son I hope you'll understand."

It was hard to reconcile the compassionate Aunty Patti with the raging tyrant of Doyle's Fish Restaurant.

"She's losing her freedom." Walter explained. "Pat used to be the freest creature alive. Now she can't hear, she can hardly see, and so she doesn't always know what's happening around her. She's no longer in charge of the situation. Or of herself. And my poor Patti can't abear that. I don't know what's going to happen when she gets older. The crisis will come when she can't read any more. Reading is her greatest solace now that she can't get about on her own." Pat read with a large magnifying glass supplemented by a powerful angle lamp that Walter carried for her from room to room.

"You seem to be getting on well with 'The Armoured Division'." Morgan commented to Ann.

"Why not. Most of the time we talk about you. Patti thinks of you as a mixture of Leonardo da Vinci and Clark Gable."

"How perceptive." Morgan laughed

"Don't worry darling, I'm putting her straight. Unfortunately, like most powerful women, she's got no time for her own sex. I find that irritating at times. But she's mostly an old dear. Because she knew your grandfather and your father so well, I think she feels that, in a spiritual sense, you are half her son. Anyway, in her eyes, you can do no wrong."

One day when he and Pat were alone Morgan asked her about her marriage. He had to shout in her ear because she'd lost her hearing-aid yet again:

"What's the secret Patti? Everybody warms themselves on your relationship with Walter. It glows like a blazing fire on a cold night."

"I dunno honey" she trumpeted back, "I guess it's magic. The only rule Walter and I have is honesty. Absolute honesty. If I don't like something about Walter, or more often about something he wants me to do, I tell him straight. And if Walter feels likewise about me, why he tells me straight too. And right away. Boy we've had some rows. Still do. Still do. But we go to sleep in one anothers' arms every night, and in the morning its all forgiven or forgot. Honesty. You might think it's easy Tom. It is not. It is the hardest goddamned thing in marriage, as it is in life. The French don't believe in it. But when the hell did the Frogs get anything right?"

Morgan, who was becoming more worried about Karen's baby, wanted to ask Patti what he should do. Should he tell Ann about his suspicions, and possibly wreck their marriage? Or should he keep his fingers crossed and his mouth shut, and hope that Ann would never find out. He wished now he'd never set eyes on Karen, particularly Karen's bottom. She was talking of going to Melbourne to have the baby, possibly his baby. Morgan hoped she'd go at once and never come back. He'd even thought of resigning, and taking Ann back to London before the bloody baby arrived. But she trusted him absolutely. That was the awful worm now keeping him awake at night. Should he tell Ann? Should he tell Patti? He could guess what Patti would recommend. He didn't have the stomach for that. Why should Ann find out anyway? Unless Karen told her. But why would she do that? And if Morgan ever saw the baby would he know if it was his own? Would Ann know? Would Karen? And what would they all feel and do then? The questions chased one another round and round in his mind, unresolved and unresolvable.

He might have made up his mind if Ann hadn't had her usual bad luck with creepie crawlies. She and Morgan were walking along the shore looking for shells when she espied an attractive cone-shell in a shallow pool. As she reached it to pick it up there was a sudden flurry of splashes and something bit her in the hand. She jumped back in fright,

"Are you all right darling?"

"I think I've been bitten Tom."

"What was it?" he was immediately alert. If it was a Stone Fish she'd soon be in agony. Ann looked shocked.

"You sit on the sand sweetheart. I'll go and have look." If Ann was to be treated with anti-venom it was vital to find the culprit.

He poked about in the pool with a stick. All that could be seen was a very small octopus, smaller than his hand. It looked pretty harmless.

He sat beside her on the sand to give her reassurance:

"I don't think it's much. How do you feel Annie?"

Her pupils were dilated;

"Sort of funny."

"Perhaps we ought to go back to the hotel" he lifted her to her feet. They hadn't walked far when she collapsed.

"I can't breathe properly Tom." She began to claw at her throat.

"Christ!" he picked her up and ran.

There was no doctor on the island, only an aboriginal nurse. By now Ann was going into paralysis, couldn't speak. Morgan, now terrified, stammered about the small octopus. The nurse took one look at Ann's hand, felt her chest and ran out of the room. She was back in a minute:

"Blue Ringed Octopus," she said "We have to get her to a hospital immediately. A helicopter is on its way. In the mean time mister we've got to give her breathing assistance. You know mouth to mouth?"

By now Ann looked dead She was lying on her back evidently paralysed, unblinking, pupils dilated, staring at the ceiling. Morgan looked at her in horror. He shook his head.

"OK. Out of the way. I 'll do it."

The black nurse leaned over Ann, opened her jaws with her fingers, put a spatula over the tongue, took a deep breath and blew it hard down Ann's throat. Morgan could see his wife's chest expand and contract.

The next few hours passed as a nightmare, one of those childhood nightmares where the monster is approaching but you cannot move your feet.

A tiny helicopter clattered in and whisked Ann away, the nurse keeping her alive by mouth to mouth resuscitation. There was no room on board for Morgan. Later on a floatplane landed in the lagoon to fly him up to Cairns where Ann was reputed to be still alive in the hospital.

When he reached her bedside she was in Intensive Care, breathing through a plastic tube cut into her trachea and connected to a respirator:

"I'm afraid there's no anti-venene for the blue ringed octopus bite." the young doctor in charge said. "But she's breathing well, that's the main thing. That abo nurse saved your wife's life you know. There's every chance she'll recover now. Go and talk to her. Calm her down. Although she can't respond right now her brain is probably working perfectly inside there somewhere."

"Is she in pain?"

"That's not usual."

"Will there be any long term effects?"

"Nope. If she pulls through the next few hours she'll be right."

Morgan burst into tears.

"The worst thing" Ann explained to them all back on the island afterwards "Was not being able to speak, or to move an eyelid even. I knew exactly what was going on. The only thing that worried me was that Letty might grow too tired to carry on, or have to go to the loo, or think I was dead. Then I'm sure I really would have died. You know I couldn't breathe for myself at all. I don't know how we can ever thank Lettie darling. Australia's got such poisonous creatures hasn't it?"

"Ollie Bacon and Brucie Doolan for a start."

Ann flew back to Canberra with the Gilkeys who were going to stay for a fortnight, while Morgan drove the bus two thousand miles back on his own. It was a bad trip, principally because he had so much time to reflect on how nearly he'd lost Ann, how much she meant to him, how he'd betrayed her with Karen, and how Karen's baby might blight all of their lives. Ann so much wanted to have his babies, and had lost them through no fault of her own. Could he wound and humiliate her any worse than by fathering a baby with her friend next door? The more he brooded on it the more certain he became that she would leave him – if she ever found out. Morgan hadn't lied since he was nine years old – and only then to avoid a flogging at boarding school. He hadn't lied because every lie a man tells diminishes him, and he knew that a man needed every inch of stature and pride to get him through life unconquered. Now he would be telling not just one lie but a new and dastardly lie every time he looked into Annie's face. It was almost better that she should find him out and run away. Almost. He longed to tell her; absolutely longed. But he dreaded to face the consequences. It seemed to him that the price of a casual fuck could be a lifetime of misery. If only……..

As soon as the Gilkeys left, Ann started to collect figures on births in Canberra and the surrounding ACT (Australian Capital Territory). It quickly became apparent that the sex-ratio, the ratio of girl-babies born to boys, varied drastically with the time of year. That confirmed beyond question that Ann's hunch about a poison in the environment must be right. Morgan urged her to publish the figures immediately. Ann hesitated. She didn't trust the medical profession to realise their significance, or even then to act promptly. She wanted to identify the poison herself.

Meanwhile Morgan got a long letter from Frank containing two items of welcome news:

....the preprints of your array paper have aroused a good deal of
interest and debate, both here and in America. Nobody disputes your
mathematical analysis, which is both original and brilliant. However
there are some who point out that in the long run it is the running costs
of a telescope, not its initial cost, which dominates the equation. I
think you ought to take this up, and immediately, otherwise you might
have the ground cut out from beneath you by enemies of the array

idea. And of course you will have enemies. Who and why? The observers with privileged positions on the largest telescopes (like me). The very last thing they want is a whole rabble of competitors using your arrays to steal their present monopoly of thunder. Some of the most powerful actively hate the idea – and are not afraid to say so. You do have a talent for making powerful enemies Tom!

Talking of which Bellfounder just got back from the Red Giants conference at Princeton. For once he didn't get his own way apparently. In particular Martin Schwarzchild strongly defended your point of view. Your darts have at last penetrated BF's hide and, from his temper, I would judge that the poison is gradually seeping into his soul. The man has become increasingly ego-maniacal. I could forgive him if he put science above self, but it is increasingly clear that he does not. He'd rather live a successful lie than a painful truth – and what could be more contemptible than that?

I think your idea of working on the AAT when it is finished is a great one. In fact I aim to join you in that. Wouldn't it be wonderful if we finished up in offices next to one another?......

Ann was summoned to the Admiralty again. She was very reluctant to go this time because she'd almost certainly pinned down the culprit poison. It was tap water. The clue came from the clear seasonal variation in the sex ratio. Her first thought was that a seasonal plant, a seasonal allergy was responsible. But that could be ruled out because in New South Wales, which surrounded the ACT, the sex ratio was normal. Then Ann discovered that Canberra's water supply came from two different reservoirs, between which the city switched on a seasonal basis. "And one of them" Ann announced in fury "Contains enough Mag. Sulph to be sold as a laxative. That's criminal. Do you know what Mg. Sulph is? Epsom salts: one of the strongest natural abortificants known to science. Those idiot idiot doctors! It was staring them in the face all the time. I lost my babies, our babies, because of those lazy, complacent swine. What am I going to do? The Admiralty needs me again desperately. Desperately."

She had to go and she went, leaving her findings in a scatter of private letters to various officials in the municipal health system. It was surely no coincidence that, several months later, the culprit water was denounced by the authorities and replaced. However Ann's name was never mentioned.

As soon as Morgan's Rosetta-Stone radio galaxy Parkes 1514-24 moved back in to the night sky he began observing it again. There were two crucial things he had to do: first prove that it really was a quasar; second measure its distance.

As to its quasar-like nature he had three pieces of positive evidence: it was a radio source with a flat spectrum; its nucleus had a star-like appearance; and it had rare ultraviolet-blue colours. Unfortunately its spectrum did not exhibit the strong emission lines so characteristic of a typical quasar. In fact the nucleus had no features in its optical spectrum at all – which made it weird and unique. Critics might argue that whatever else it was, it wasn't a quasar at all. Morgan was therefore on the hunt for one other crucial clue; variability in brightness. Of all extra-galactic objects only quasars were variable. Unfortunately his first set of observations, taken over the course of a week at Siding Springs, showed it to be as steady as a rock. Of itself that proved nothing because quasars tended to vary over timescales of weeks to months, even to years, and to be highly irregular. Ideally he would have to monitor the nucleus regularly over the course of several years, and Bacon would see he never had the opportunity to do that.

He was flummoxed too by the featureless nature of its spectrum – which seemed to be unique. And that in itself was unlikely. In a universe containing billions of beasts one expected to find, and invariably did find, many many specimens of any particular species. So Morgan kept going back to the library to look for analogues.

Then one day, to his great excitement, he came across exactly what he was looking for. Some Canadian astronomers had followed up a flat spectrum radio source in the North known as Vermillion River Observatory 42.22.01 or VRO 42.22.01. It too had a weird featureless spectrum exactly like PKS 1514-24. Moreover it was variable optically – in fact it coincided with a long catalogued variable star known as BL Lacertae or BL Lac for short. And this gave Morgan a fairly obvious idea: perhaps his PKS 1515-24 was a known variable star too? If so past observations of it might lie in the literature, absolving him from the need to monitor it for years himself. But where would he find those observations, the vital evidence he needed?

He knew that variable stars had always been of great interest to astronomers. Mira, the Demon Star, had been known since Antiquity. But the coming of the photographic plate had led to the discovery of fainter and fainter variables in their hundreds and thousands. Variable stars were vital to the subject because they could be used as beacons, or 'standard candles'. Henrietta Leavitt had discovered a perfect correlation between the periods of certain Cepheid Variable stars in the Magellanic Clouds and their brightness's. Thereafter it was only necessary to measure the period of such a Cepheid to infer its true Luminosity, and hence to infer its distance away. Thus Cepheid Variables had first unlocked the Third Dimension of astronomical space – distance away from us. But there were many other variable stars; eclipsing binaries, RR Lyraes, Alpha Virginis stars, Miras and so on, all with interesting stories to tell. Thus Variable-Star astronomy was a big subject with many practicioners both professional and amateur. Where did they store all their findings?

He consulted Greg Anson who measured the variability of stars for a living. Greg told him there was a thick catalogue containing the positions and properties of all known variable stars. Morgan took it out of the library and then, disastrously, forgot all about it. Or rather he didn't so much forget it as drop it down his ever growing list of urgent priorities; arrays, television systems, Elliptical galaxies, Red Giants, Pulsars, Bolton radio-galaxies – they were all clamouring for his attention. At least that was the excuse he made for himself months later when the blow hit him. The wound was almost as painful as the time back at Steward Observatory when, also in the library, he found that his Three Stage Model of the Intersteallar Medium had been pre-empted. This too was a paper in The Astrophysical Journal, from a Dr Howard E Bond of Louisiana State University Observatory entitled "The Optically variable Radio Source PKS 1514-24= AP Librae." Bond had noticed that the star AP Librae, discovered to be variable by M.D. Ashbrook at Harvard College Observatory back in 1942, coincided pretty convincingly in position with Morgan's source Parkes 1514-24. Moreover he'd collected together all known information about both AP Lib and PKS 1515-24. Morgan was mortified to read that both its featureless spectrum and its colours had been published previously. Moreover it was not the first variable star coincident with a radio position, but the third. Michael Penston, a friend of his back in Britain, had discovered the first, RW Tau. Then there was BL Lac – now AP Lib. He dashed back to his office, unearthed the Variable Star catalogue from beneath the heap of papers on his desk – and there it was: AP Lib's position coincided with 1514-24's.

Morgan was furious and upset. The one project, above all others, with which he hoped to make his name in Australia, and rescue his career from Bacon's jaws, was now out in the open for anyone to grab. The first person to get a redshift for AP Lib would receive all the glory for proving the cosmological nature of quasar redshifts – the hottest astrophysical question of the day. It was an obvious thing to do now and he could imagine astronomers all over the world would be adding AP Lib to their observing lists. At only minus 24 degrees of Declination it was gettable from the Northern hemisphere as well as from the South.

Morgan was in despair for a while, and with no Ann to give him consolation, or a proper sense of balance, in a rage as well. But who was he to rage at? Only himself. He'd been lazy, greedy and self-indulgent: self indulgent in imagining he could keep a good idea all to himself for long, especially in a hot field like quasars. There were so many clever astronomers out there, reading the same papers, thinking the same thoughts. To win first prize you had to single-mindedly sprint for the line. There were no second place prizes in science. None at all. And he hadn't been single minded because of greed – as usual trying to run after too many rabbits at once. And finally, and unforgivably, he'd been lazy. How could he have not followed up every clue in the literature? And why had he put off looking in the variable star catalogue lying on his desk? If he had spent just fifteen minutes doing that he might already have had the laurels in his grasp.

The fact was there was a defect in his personality, or so be began to think. He wanted astronomy to be a gentle, ivory tower thing where scholars debated the Universe at leisure, not the cut-throat, super-competitive business it actually was. He hadn't come into science to gouge or race or cheat his fellows, or to be gouged in turn. But that was the way it was, especially for young astronomers, like himself, with no permanent positions. Like eaglets in a nest the strongest was bound to push the others over the side – in order to survive.

Nor was his temper improved by another run-in with Brucie Doolan. Some one at tea had brought up the question of the observatory directorship. Apparently such appointments were made for only five years at a time, and had to be renewed. He found that Bacon's reappointment woujld be coming up soon and the staff would have some input into the matter:

"You mean we might actually be able to get rid of Fat Sow?" Morgan was astonished. An animated discussion followed. Then Doolan turned up and broke in:

"Ollie's a shoe-in, take it from me."

"I would have thought" Morgan replied mildly "That after the McGarrity fiasco the university would welcome the chance to get rid of Fat Sow – and his underlings."

"Don't you worry your little head about it T-bone. By the time this comes up you'll be out of astronomy for flamin' good. Probably back in that Pommy car factory you're always skiting about. Hope they kept your lathe warm Morgan."

"You know Doolan – we all know – what an idiot Bacon is. It's up to us to bring his incompetence and his unsuitability to the university's attention. And I intend to, whether I'm an astronomer or not, or whether I'm at Stromlo or not. And so should we all; unless you fancy Bulstrode's cooking, no Dark Time, no foreign travel – and television systems that don't work."

Doolan's turkey cock neck went red, his prominent Adam's apple jerked up and down:

"Anyone raising a finger against Ollie will get his head shaved off – at the neck!"

The threat was so crude and so self-serving as to be counter-productive. Astronomers openly murmured about a replacement director. But the old hands were confident that Bacon's reappointment was a formality. As one of them put it:

"Short of being committed for gross moral turpitude he's here for life – if he wants to stay."

And another: "Who ever heard of an academic being replaced for incompetence. That would mean wholesale slaughter. The Establishment would never stand for it."

Nevertheless Morgan openly went ahead with his plan to make the re-appointment as difficult as possible. He wrote to everyone he could think of, both in and out of Australia, including John Bolton, explaining the situation, and requesting them to intervene with the university authorities. After all, what had he got to lose?

He was surprised to learn that not everybody on the staff was as contemptuous of Bacon as he was. In fact several of the graduate students came to his office and begged him not to make life difficult for the man. Apparently Bacon was very supportive of students and gave them generous allowances of telescope time. One pointed out:

"Oliver never uses the 74-inch does he? And that's greatly to our benefit. He could have done couldn't he? Most directors would."

Morgan was surprised, but he wasn't persuaded.

On top of his disappointment over AP Lib – as he had now begun to call PKS 1514-24 – was the first letter he got back from Ann in London:

> "You'll never believe this Tom but who should I meet in the Admiralty
> canteen the other day but Frank Cotteridge. You could have knocked us
> both down with the proverbial feather. He had no idea I was temporarily
> back here again while I had no idea that the Admiralty had signed Frank
> up as an honorary consultant. They're always on the lookout for the best
> brains in academia and of course Frank's mathematics is legendary. My
> boss, who was also at Trinity, recruited him at some college dinner at
> Cambridge. And although he comes in only once a fortnight Frank's got
> the highest security clearance. What a relief: I can tell him everything
> I'm doing. Frank says…."

Blind insensate jealousy seized Morgan in its jaws and shook him like a rat. The one agony in his marriage, the one barrier that had separated him from Ann, the sore that rubbed, the flea that bit, Frank had casually sidestepped over wine during some cosy college dinner.

Too egotistical, too self-assured of his wife's affections ever to be jealous before, Morgan was eaten out with it now. He would rather that his former friend had sneaked into Ann's bed than into her private mind, the chamber from which Morgan was forbidden, by the Law of the Land. He sat up all night in an apoplexy, composing the letter which all of them would regret for the rest of their lives. Something deep inside him whispered to hesitate. But Morgan was in no mood to listen. He went out at four am to post all thirty-five raging pages to Frank at his college.

Days later, whilst he was up at Siding Springs, he went to Jack Cockle for solace. Mussels was appalled:

"You bloody fool Tom Morgan. We all knew you'd go over the edge one day, and now you really have. But why in your private life for Gods sake? Ann would never betray you, and nor would Frank. No, I stand corrected. They never *would* have betrayed you. Now they might."

Morgan protested but Mussels wouldn't listen:

"Don't you realise you idiot that you've despoiled them both, spattered them both with the foulness of your own ignoble suspicions. They'll naturally turn to each other now for comfort. Where else could they turn? If I were you I'd get on the first bloody plane to England. Try to catch up with that letter before Frank opens it. You might just be lucky. You know he's away a lot."

Morgan was furious. He'd come to Jack for support, not recrimination. The last thing he was ever going to do was beg Frank's forgiveness. But Cockle was angry too. He pushed Morgan backwards into his deck chair by the pool:

"Now you listen to me for once. I swore never to tell you this but now I'll have to. Several years ago Frank confessed to me that he was head over heels in love with Ann. Apparently he fell for her while the three of you were holidaying together in California. Remember? Poor Frank. He couldn't help himself. You know what a softy with women he is. He's never been able to think of another woman since. He was in tears. He didn't know who to talk to."

"There you are" Morgan struggled to his feet "What did I tell you? Frank's wormed his way into the Admiralty using those sodomite Oxbridge networks, to get at my Annie. What did I tell you?"

Mussels raged back:

"Frank is an honourable man. If you want to know Morgan I'd trust him before I ever trusted you. If Frank was after your wife why would he come and tell me? Why? He'd know I was bound to tell you – as I'm telling you right now. Don't be such an ass."

Morgan was an inferno inside. He loved and trusted Mussels. But the thought that Mussels might actually be right, and that he Morgan had demeaned himself as well as Ann and Frank, was itself intolerable. The two of them rowed all week until Jack's wife Jenny threatened to kick Morgan out, to find his food up at the observatory, and to place himself at the mercy of Mrs Bulstrode.

By the time he got back to Canberra Morgan's jealousy had subsided sufficiently for him to wonder if Mussels wasn't right. He was even prepared to pick up a phone and ring Ann or ring Frank, or ring both. But there was another long letter from Ann on the mat when he opened the door:

"And I got a telegram from Roy yesterday to say that Karen has had a little boy, and that both are doing well in the hospital in Melbourne. She expects to be back next door in two to three months.

I've seen quite a lot of Frank, not because he comes to the Admiralty much, but because he's on so many committees that meet either in London or Paris. Did you know his fellowship has recently been turned in to a permanent Lectureship – so that his astronomical future is assured for life? He's on some committee dealing with Britain's manning of the Anglo Australian Telescope. They are involved, along with some top Australians, in choosing its first director. I tried to pick his brains about that but, quite understandably, he clammed up. Then he's one of our main representatives to the European Space Agency, a European wide rival to NASA. They are planning all kinds of super-rockets and missions to outer Space which would interest you darling. Frank himself is heavily involved with something NASA is doing, called The Large Space Telescope, or LST, which Frank thinks will make ground based optical astronomy obsolete.

Anyway since he's around so much we decided to do the complete Ring Cycle at The Royal Opera together. I know how you hate Wagner so this is a wonderful, perhaps one-off, opportunity for me to see the whole Ring, because I can't go on my own. Frank just adores Wagner, like me, and is a paid up 'Friend of the Opera' which is why he's managed to get last minute tickets at Covent Garden for me. I was so grateful that I took him out to our favourite 'Laughing Cavalier' for an après theatre supper in Soho. Nothing has changed darling. The same old Hungarian lady was in the corner knitting and the Duck in Green Peppers was nearly as scrumptious as it was the night we got engaged (But of course I didn't tell Frank that). He seems to be very happy with life: his research is going extremely well, he gets as much observing time over in California as he can handle and he's now got a full-time post-doctoral research assistant as well as two graduate students who do all his donkey work. The one cloud on his horizon is hair loss. His hair is thinning dramatically. He's so self conscious about that I had to pretend that he looks even more distinguished, like a professor, which he undoubtedly will be one day. He sends his love and hopes you will survive the bites of all the poisonous creatures in Australia, particularly the two-legged variety. I told him not to worry because you can be pretty venomous yourself, and we drank to that.........."

The letter put Morgan into a second fit of temper, partly out of uxorious jealousy, but more this time at the outrageous unfairness of it all. He was the one who made the discoveries while Frank, as usual, pulled off all the glittering prizes. He had no job to go to, and quite likely no future whatsoever in astronomy. But Frank, bloody Frank, was the Golden Boy, the one with the perfect future. Frank was organising the AAT, Morgan's only hope of redemption. And Morgan ground his teeth at the thought of all that he was missing in Space Astronomy – there was none of that in Australia – while Frank glided effortlessly into all the plum projects, at the key moments. It was school and university all over again. Morgan felt like bursting into tears, or better still smashing someone, though it wasn't clear who.

      Morgan was so confused and upset that he decided to get away for a few days fishing. Greg, who was eager to try out his new boat on the sea, agreed to come, and so with the boat in tow they set out in Bus for the South Coast.

      They pitched camp on some deserted greensward, designated as a camping site because it had a rough earth dunny. They weren't thirty yards from the beach where the wind was driving a heavy surf on to the shore.

      "I don't like the look of that." Greg said "Lets wait until the morning."

      Morgan collected driftwood, Greg lit a fire, and they 'brewed up'.

      At this point, to their disgust, a shining new caravan drew into the field, which they had already come to think of as their own, and parked at the farther end. Out of the car stepped a middle aged husband and wife. The wife scuttled into the caravan while the husband donned smart green overalls. What was he going to do, they wondered as they drank their tea.

      Out of the back of his car the husband took a motor mower. The motor roared into life, rending the peace of their lovely evening. He mowed right round the caravan, out to a distance of thirty yards. That took half an hour. Then he mowed a broad pathway down to the beach, going right past their camp. Greg and Morgan's peaceful evening was quite ruined. Morgan was incensed when the man came back yet again, his motor clattering, to broaden the mown pathway even further. He got up and stopped the man:

      "What the hell are you doing?"

      "What?" the man was obviously deafened by his two-stroke engine. Morgan stepped forward and turned it off. In the silence Greg clapped ironically.

      "What?" the man repeated.

      "I said what the fuck are you doing? What do you mean shattering our peace with your mower. This is a camping site, not a bowling green."

      "It's me 'obby" the man replied in a thick Sydney whine "Oy loike mowing grass see. It's me 'obby."

      "Well you go and practice your silly little 'obby somewhere else. Not at our expense. We've come all the way from Canberra to get some peace."

      "Oy can't do that mite. It's me missis. She's frightened to death of snikes. Can't go to the toilet 'less the grass is mowed smooth."

      Morgan stood incredulous, agog, aghast, staring at the alien creature from Sydney:

      "Am I mad Greg – or is this a cretin?"

      "Hey, you watch your Pommy tongue. Oi've got as much of a right to this field as you 'ave."

      "For camping you have. Not for shattering the peace."

      An altercation, as they say, followed. Morgan refused to let the man restart his mower. The man threatened to go to Merimbula and fetch 'the perlice'. By that time the wind had dropped, the stars were out, the surf was quiet. Eventually the man slunk off into the gloaming complaining about his wife's phobia. Morgan called after him:

      "Get her a fucking potty."

      They had a very pleasant dinner after that, with a lot of beers. At the far end of the field the television inside the caravan flickered blue and white.

Next morning they were woken by the shattering roar of the motor mower bursting into life just outside their tent:

"Christ Almighty!" Morgan unzipped the flap and leapt out in his pyjamas. The man in overalls was making off towards the dunny behind his machine. Morgan, his feet soaked with dew, raced over, seized him by the arm and dowsed the engine.

"But we're leaving for Sydney in a hour" the man whined, obviously cowed by Morgan's size and ferocity. He couldn't have said anything worse.

"Do you mean to say" Morgan gasped "You mowed all this grass, made all this row, just for a single overnight stay? We thought you'd come for at least a month."

" Me wife's gotter go to the dunny. Look at 'er."

By the light of a sun just showing its fringe above the Pacific, he could see a woman standing in a white dressing gown in the open door of the caravan staring their way.

"I tell you what" Morgan said menacingly. "Either you carry your wife to the bog or I do. But if I do I'll leave her there to die. And while she's dying I'll drive your bloody mower straight into the Pacific Ocean."

Within thirty minutes they were gone. The woman, evidently able to hold her water longer than anticipated, screeched back at them from the car window"

"We're going strite ter the perlice station."

"They might and all." Greg laughed "I think we should put to sea before the rozzers arrive."

They found it a struggle to get the small aluminium boat out through the surf, and the outboard motor started. Despite the beautiful morning a big swell was running as they set out for the island a couple of miles away. The land disappeared from sight whenever the little cockleshell sank down into the troughs. Morgan trolled over one quarter with his stoutest rod while Greg, at the wheel, trolled over the other. As they closed the island, still bursting with spume, first Greg, then Morgan got a bite. When boated Morgan's fish turned out to be a lean barracuda-like brute with jaws bristling with needle sharp teeth. Its big bold eye never left Morgan as he held it firmly against the thwart to remove the hook. At the crucial moment it exploded from his grasp, biting his left thumb so effectively that blood spurted in the sunlight. Before Morgan could do anything about that Greg called out for help. He was trying to steer the plunging boat, fight his fish, and retch over the side at the same time. The big seas had got to his breakfast.

Morgan landed the second fish, identical to the first, but this time held on to it more determinedly than before. With the hook successfully removed he pointed out to Greg the needle-like teeth responsible for his own dripping wound. But before Greg could get his head back in over the gunwhale the second fish exploded, and bit Morgan quite deliberately on the other thumb, which bled as profusely as the first. And so the boat pitched and rolled, Greg heaved and groaned, Morgan bled and swore, while the two fish, no doubt planning a second attack on their toes, thrashed about in a mixture of seawater and blood among the bottom-boards.

In the same inept manner they boated a few more Tailor, as the fish were called, from a school that was holding its ground on the edge of the breaking island surf.

Morgan was having the time of his life but Greg was retching so horribly that he had to be shouted at to steer properly. He'd given up fishing long since.

Eventually though, even shouting at him didn't work. Greg was so far gone that they had to turn, very reluctantly on Morgan's part, back towards the beach, now three miles away. En route he put on his biggest lure and trolled over the stern. Half way home an enormous fish struck the line, almost pulling him overboard. The reel screamed, Morgan screamed at Greg to turn the boat, and they raced back out to sea in pursuit of the monster. His rod, designed for big Tuna, was bent almost double. The reel creaked alarmingly whenever he managed to win back a few yards of line. His forearms and wrists cracked with the strain. Greg, sicker than ever, begged Morgan to cut the fish loose. But Morgan's blood, or what was left of it, was now thoroughly aroused. Even if Greg died in the struggle, or he bled to death, they were going to boat this fish.

What was it? It didn't jump, so it wasn't a sail-fish or a marlin. It was far too vigorous, too energetic for any shark. First it would race out to sea, tearing the line off his reel although the boat was at full throttle in pursuit, until he was down to the last few yards of backing. Then it dashed sideways faster than the boat could turn. Then it would double straight back towards them, threatening to tangle the loose line in the boat's propeller. Since Greg was virtually hors-de-combat Morgan had to control both the boat and the fish.

The longer the fight went on the surer Morgan became that he was into a tuna, and that a life-long dream was within distance of becoming true. But when? The boat tore up and down the coast behind the big fish for what seemed ages – especially to Greg.

Finally Morgan got the monster close enough to the boat to see the fish silhouetted in the crest of a clear green wave. What an unforgettable sight: the steely blue back, the deep athletic body, the predator's eye, the characteristic lunate tail. He'd got into a tuna all right – if only he could boat him.

"Get the gaff ready." Morgan yelled at Greg who had by now reached the suicidal stage of mal-de-mer.

"I left it in the car." He croaked back feebly.

"You bloody fool, you……" Morgan shrieked imprecations upon him, and upon all his ancestors back to the beginnings of time. Without a gaff, a big hook on the end of a stout pole, there was no hope of heaving the heavy fish on board. The titanic battle had been a waste of time.

But there was no way Morgan was going to give in! If necessary he'd have Greg drive the boat ashore through the heavy surf then pounce on the fish with his bare hands.

Morgan cast about for a better scheme. He noticed a small boat anchored in the shelter of a promontory with four men in straw hats fishing over the side.

"Over there." he yelled "Work the boat over there – we'll borrow their gaff."

Another exciting quarter of an hour ensued as they worked the gradually tiring monster towards the other boat.

Quite apart from his seasickness Greg was totally ignorant about seamanship, this being his very first voyage at the helm. The four old men in the other boat could see what the approaching boat was up to, and in any case were the beneficiaries of a long stream of commands roared at them by Morgan. They stood up, holding up their gaff, ready for Greg to grab it.

The sea was still running heavily, tossing the two small vessels up and down so that one moment A was poised right above B, a moment right below. Even if Greg had been a skilled seaman it would have been an extremely tricky manoeuvre to execute. But he was not, and he made a complete hash. Greg's boat rammed the other amidships. The old men fell in a heap. The fish, seeing the new vessel for the first time, went berserk.

Pandemonium now broke loose. The old men, who'd mostly lost their straw hats in the sea, along with their equanimity, shook their fists. Greg, fearing for his new boat, as well as his life, tried to go full astern. The fish however had other ideas. It careered frantically round and round the old men's boat, while Morgan fought desperately to prevent it entangling itself in their anchor rope.

In vain. The line went slack. Morgan roared, threatening the lives of both Greg and the poor old men. Snatching the wheel he bore down on their boat again, ramming it with a second splintering crash. Abandoning the wheel and rod he grabbed their anchor rope and began to haul it in. The two tin hulls banged and slammed together. He could feel the fish, down there somewhere, entangled in the rope. The old men, furious now but fearful that they might be tipped out in to the wild sea, hurled their gaff across, almost harpooning the prostrate Greg.

Through a series of further miracles, the six of them somehow scrambled the beautiful tuna, now dying and entangled in both rope and line, into Greg's boat.

As Morgan gazed at the great fish, in a mixture of wonderment and love, the old men cut themselves free:

"Bugger off you bloody ignorant Pommy bastards!" they yelled. "Keep away from us!"

Arrived back at Canberra Morgan found the dreaded letter from Trinity College Cambridge lying on his mat. He needed two hours to summon the courage to open it:

> Morgan
> There is no way I could have entered Admiralty Intelligence of my own volition. For obvious security reasons you have to be invited. Then, if you are a patriot, you are bound to accede. That Ann and I encountered one another 'on the inside' could thus have had nothing to do with me. I suggest you check with your wife.
> Indeed Ann is the only reason for bothering to reply to your infantile but nevertheless wounding letter. Beside what Ann does at the Admiralty, your research, mine ,indeed that of astronomers at large, is a mere bagatelle. I am in a unique position to tell you that. She is irreplaceable and will remain so for at least 5 to 10 years. Until computers can replace her, Western security depends on the magic in Ann's head (burn this for her sake). What excuse have you then for dragging such a national treasure round all those hick places in pursuit of your own comparatively paltry, and apparently not successful, ambitions? Only your excusable ignorance – which I hereby dissolve.
> While I never doubted your brains Morgan, you are in the wrong profession. You were born to die on some forlorn hope or some unscaleable mountain face. Science these days is a communal, corporate effort – not a show-case for heroism, not a do-or-die dash for the Pole, not merely an opportunity for Tom Morgan to immortalise his name. You must be the last adult alive who actually believes in Jack and the Beanstalk – which by the way is a classic Freudian pathology.
> We've always been rivals, but friends too. Now you have made us enemies. Whilst I regret that in so many ways, at least it leaves me free to take the other hand from behind my back and fight with both fists: which I now intend to do.
> If you ever write to me again I'll return your letters unread.
> FC.

Morgan was crestfallen, not so much at the thought of losing Frank – they'd fallen out too often before, even physically in their youth, to imagine it would last – but at the clear evidence of his own stupidity. Yes Britain was enfeebled by creepy old-boy networks emanating from the main tumour at Oxbridge, but there had to be limits, particularly in Security, since the Maclean –Burgess-Philby affair. He was also disturbed by Mussel's revelation. At some unconscious level he'd been aware, since their holiday together in Long Beach, of an affinity between Frank and Ann. Though it had seemed more a matter of temperament than romance. The two were effortlessly clever – which he was not, and religious – which he could never be. They both' fitted in ' whereas he usually found himself, through no fault of his own – or so he assured himself – at odds with the hierarchy. He was a loner, they very definitely were not. Now Frank was threatening 'to take the other hand from behind my back and fight with both fists', by which he could only mean making a bid for Ann. In normal circumstances Morgan would never have worried about such a challenge. He and Ann were too well matched. Even the defects in each other's personality attracted husband and wife; his dominance, her indecision; his emotionality, her political detachment. But what if Karen's baby was his too – and Ann found out? For once Morgan had no idea how his wife would react. Having a baby with him had been her obsession for the last three years, an obsession stolen from her by

Australian medical incompetence. And what had he done, or probably done? Casually fathered a baby with the Australian girl next door – and Ann's best friend. Ann might be stricken. She might be jealous. She might forgive him. She might run away and leave him for ever, or even for Frank. He had less idea of what she would do than he had of whether the Universe was finite or not. At the same time he felt it would be a tragedy, a total ruination of both their lives, for them to split; especially over a casual, if enjoyable, fuck. But that was the trouble with religious people like Ann. You never knew when they were going to betray an eternal truth for some intellectual moral principle – and march off to a war until death. If Protestants and Catholics could murder one another in the name of Transubstantiation, anything could happen. Anything. He wasn't ashamed in the least of fucking Karen. It meant nothing. But he was furious with himself for jeopardising such a wonderful marriage as he had enjoyed so far with Ann.

He was still wondering what he should do, what he should say, when the telephone rang:
"Where do you think I am darling?"
"No idea. Heathrow?"
"I'm at Canberra airport."
"What?" he yelled "I'll be there before you get through Immigration."

She threw herself into his arms:
"Oh Tom I've missed you so much. I couldn't bear it any longer. 'Hang the Russian Fleet' I thought. 'Never mind the Ring Cycle, I need to see my husband!' Oh Morgan Morgan Morgan....' She bit his ear "Take me home and take me to bed." And she burst into tears.

Once she was at home again, banging pots, talking nineteen to the dozen, the whole Frank thing in London seemed childishly ridiculous. Several times he was on the verge of telling her but each time, at the last moment, something steered him off. It was probably his own shame; he deeply despised jealousy.

The one thing that rankled was the sting at the end of Frank's letter: the accusation that he was in astronomy only to make his name. It was, he felt, the very reverse of the truth. He was out to make his name simply to stay in astronomy. And it looked increasingly as if he would have to.

When he told Ann about the latest run-in with Doolan she wanted to scratch out Brucie's eyes:
"That was your great chance Tom! Going to Princeton would have made your name. Oh I wish you'd told me darling, we'd have raised the money somehow. You shouldn't have to depend on jealous little earwigs like that."

But when he told her about the approaching crisis over Bacon's reappointment, she warned him to keep out:
"It's not your business Tom. What do we care? We're not going to stay in Australia, let alone Canberra. You've got enough enemies already. Just do your research and get us back to England."

"But that's just it." Morgan complained "So long as he is the director he will have the power to ruin my future in astronomy; as much in Britain as anywhere else. He loathes my guts. If we could depose Fat Sow before my contract is up I might stand a chance."

" I think you're exaggerating as usual Tom. From what you've said Bacon is an astronomical dwarf. If you get references from giants like Bolton and Wagoner and Schwarzchild what will anyone care about Bacon's opinion?"

"It'so damned hard to get an astronomical job these days that even one negative reference can tip the balance. I should know."

"But Tom, Schweinhundt is a mere ghost from the past."

"Not to me he isn't."

CHAPT 13
KAREN
1972-3

When Karen arrived back from Melbourne with her baby Morgan scarcely recognised her. Where before she had looked the same age as Ann, now she looked ten years older. The statuesque figure had slumped, her hair was wild, her clothes slovenly. Her appearance was surely a reflection of an underlying change in her spirit. She looked beaten, down, distraught, depressed. Not that he saw her much for she kept to her house with the baby.

"Poor thing." Ann explained "She's had post-partum depression – still has. Roy's disappeared back up to Arnhem Land. Then she had mastitis – which is terrible when you're trying to breast-feed, which she is. And Kiralee screams all the time. It's not his fault. He's hungry. She's up half the night, every night. I've got to help her, poor thing."

"Sounds awful. Curly?"

"No, Kiralee. Apparently it means 'baby' in some aboriginal tongue."

"Is he black then?"

"Don't be silly! Those two were always going to choose an aboriginal name. He's lovely darling. I'll bring him round to show you."

Curly turned out to look pretty much like any other baby, though he did seem to have an extra lusty bellow.

Ann placed him on her lap, and put the bottle to his mouth. He fell silent at once and sucked greedily.

"There you are sweety. Isn't he lovely Tom? He's only hungry after all. Babies should cry when they're hungry. It's Kiralee's main job in life right now – getting enough to eat."

"I thought he was being breast fed."

"He is. This is Karen's milk She has to use a breast-pump because of all her problems. But she's not producing enough. And the less she makes, the hungrier he gets and the louder he screams. Then she gets frantically stressed, and produces even less milk."

"Well why doesn't she give him a bottle?"

"It's not good for him. It's not good for a baby of four months. Didn't you know? Mother's milk is far superior. It's full of antibodies for a start. I bet you were breast fed."

Curly finished his bottle and screamed for more.

Ann picked him up, put him over her shoulder, and rocked him back and forth. Despite the continuous bawling Morgan was touched by a blissful look on his wife's face that he'd never seen before.

But no amount of rocking would pacify Kiralee.

"He needs at least another half-bottle," Anne explained "I'll go round and see if Karen's produced any more. Here, you hold him while I'm gone."

Morgan was reluctant.

"Come on. He won't explode."

She stood up, placing Curly on Morgan's shoulder, before going next door.

Morgan walked round the room, trying out comforting noises dredged up from an unconscious store. Strangely Curly calmed down, first into a whimper, then total silence. Worrying that he might have choked or something, Morgan detached the baby very gently from his shoulder and laid him on his knee. Morgan inspected Curly, who seemed to be inspecting him back, though Ann said babies of four months couldn't focus properly. But Curly definitely seemed interested, and sucked contentedly when Morgan put the end of his little finger in the baby's mouth.

Morgan had been both dying and dreading to see Karen's baby, and here it was. Whoever it looked like it didn't look like Roy. Morgan had never looked closely at little babies before but this one seemed to have an abnormally large, abnormally round head, and a shock of black hair – both characteristics of the Morgan family. There was something odd about this baby – which brought his father to mind, a father he'd lost in 1944. Kiralee sucked contentedly at the finger end, pausing every so often, while Morgan tried to summon up a man he'd last seen and felt almost thirty years ago. He could still recall the bristles on dada's chin, the rough battle-dress, the smell of pipe-smoke.

"What have you done to him?" Ann was amazed when she returned to find them both in a silent trance.

Morgan guiltily slipped his finger out. Curly howled.

"Dropped him on his head of course."

From then onward Kirallee seemed to be round at their house almost as much as at Karen's. Morgan was highly uncomfortable about this, retreating into his work. Ann explained that it was the best way to help Karen, giving her a chance to sleep. Morgan however suspected that Ann simply loved mothering a child. A woman with a brain apparently capable of defeating the Russians, now talked of scarcely anything but feeds, wind, nappies and child devolvement. And why shouldn't she, he thought. The poor creature had had three of her own babies taken away from her. But did she have any suspicion of who the father was? And if she did – how would she react? The baby's birthday certainly tallied with his fling with Karen – but then, as he recalled, Roy had come back from Arnhem Land straight afterwards, so perhaps Karen herself didn't know. 'Thank God for that' he thought, as he buried himself in astronomy.

He'd got a pulsar system working in the Southern hemisphere at last. The observatory, being bankrupt thanks to the McGarrity fiasco, hadn't been able to purchase the expensive electronic items he'd been promised. A year had gone to waste before some Tasmanian radio astronomers generously lent him the vital components. Then he had to teach himself all the intricate timing mathematics which Willard Cox had struggled with in Arizona. There was so much Algebra, so much Spherical Trigonometry and so much specialised Astrometry that it would have been easy to go astray. Fortunately he could still see the Crab Pulsar from Mount Stromlo and use it to test out both his equipment and his calculations. Alan Maugham, Mike Vigger's graduate student from Sydney University, came up to help , as well as a very clever undergraduate from the ANU called Phil, who was assigned to Morgan for his Summer Project.

They only had a thirty inch telescope this time, smaller even than the one at Steward, but at least they could leave their equipment on it for a whole dark-of-the-moon and make up for lack of aperture with length of observing time. Since Bacon used photo-tubes himself the observatory had a lavish collection of spare devices, amongst which Morgan located one with twice the sensitivity of anything at Steward, so that, in effect, the 30-inch became, in light-collecting terms, the equivalent of a 42-inch. And of course they had a large menu of Southern radio pulsars to choose from. From amongst these they selected the fastest because it was becoming clearer and clearer that pulsars drew their luminous energy from the spin-down of their neutron stars. The faster the spinner the more luminous the source. And in that respect Vigger's Vela pulsar, spinning eleven times a second was by far the most promising candidate. Its position though was still not well enough defined for a deep search – and this was what Alan had been working on for his thesis. He timed it every month with great precision, looking for the annual period changes due to the Earth moving in it's orbit. Since those changes would depend on the pulsar's precise position in the sky Alan was hoping to invert the argument and refine that position. But then something extraordinary had occurred. Without warning, the spin rate, normally slowing down, had suddenly speeded up or 'glitched'. This was thought to be due to a 'star-quake', or a crack in the crystalline neutronic crust of the neutron star. The glitch, fascinating in itself, as a clue to the nature of that neutronic 'stuff', nevertheless interrupted Vaughan's work on the pulsar's position – which now wouldn't be know accurately before Morgan had left Australia – another blow to his job prospects.

Nevertheless the three of them had a lot of fun searching for, but failing to find, the optical counterparts of the fastest Southern radio pulsars. The other two young men learned to observe on their own eventually, while Morgan had the satisfaction of seeing the first piece of complex equipment he'd designed and built himself, working satisfactorily. Apart from the confidence that gave him he learned a far more important and general lesson: as an astronomer you didn't have to go into all the details – you could leave them to engineers, often brilliant men in their own right – who enjoyed the technical challenge. The astronomer's job was to lay down precisely the minimum specifications the equipment would need in order to answer the scientific question at hand. You could then leave the detailed design and construction of the equipment to specialists.

This was an enormously liberating and unexpected lesson for Morgan. It meant that he could design innovative astronomical instruments without having to learn electronics, or optics, or cryogenics – or whatever. As long as he could tell engineers precisely what he wanted, and as long as he could understand enough of what they said to understand their difficulties, then he could design pioneering telescopes, spectrographs, television systems, radio receivers, interferometers and satellites. Where before he'd walked in fear of all these alien technicalities, and regarded instrumental astronomers as superior beings, now he knew himself to be a master too. Not because he knew a lot: on the contrary. It was because he knew how little he needed to know – but he knew that little with unshakeable uncertainty. Like the pilot of an aircraft who'd just completed his first solo, he knew he could fly this, or indeed any other plane, without having to understand how the engines or the instruments functioned. It was a lesson in confidence acquired through struggle, a life-long and life-giving licence to fly amongst the other gods of his profession.

As like as not when he got home, be it dawn or dusk, Curly would be there, in his pram, not more than a few feet away from Ann. At nearly six months his diet was heavily supplemented with formula milk so that he was no longer utterly dependent on Karen, Not hungry any more he was as good as gold. And Morgan, although he felt guilty about it, increasingly enjoyed playing with Curly. He loved putting the teat in Curly's mouth and watching the little fellow sucking away contentedly, his eyes flicking about to see whatever was going on around him. He was fascinated by flies, of which Canberra could supply all too many.

"It's funny the way he relaxes when you're here." Ann remarked.

"He's a typical Australian male chauvinist pig, aren't you Curlikins? As far as he's concerned, you women are mere cooks and bottle-washers. With his genes he's destined for greater things."

"Like kicking pneumatic bladders about and getting drunk?"

"Exactly. Just look at him. In sixteen years he'll be perving the sheilas like Brucie Doolan."

"Perhaps we ought to strangle him now then."

"Good idea Annie. You oughtn't to get too attached to him anyway."

"You're a fine one to talk."

"How's his Mum?"

"Karen's a clockwork orange. I used to think it was just post-partum. That she'd get over it. But now I'm not so sure. The other day I caught her looking at Kiralee as if he were a ticking time-bomb, and she a bomb disposal officer. I nearly snatched him away from her."

"Poor little sod. What future has he got then? To grow up like Hitler? What a bitch she is."

"It's frightening isn't it. Well it frightens me. What if, when I have our baby, I don't bond with him – or her. It can happen. I'm sure Karen didn't want it to fall out this way. She told me. She desperately wanted a baby – and now it's all gone wrong. You can imagine how she feels."

"Let's adopt him then."

"No!" Ann's reaction was instantaneous.

"Why not?"

Ann turned away and looked out of the window:

"Don't think I haven't thought about it. Of course I have. Over and over again. You can see how I love him. But I don't want him."

There was a long silence. Ann turned to sit on the high kitchen stool facing her husband:

"I want *my* babies. I want babies that are mine and yours. If it's a boy I want him to be like you, and if it's a girl like me. They've got to have our genes. Kiralee's lovely – but he'll grow up to be like Roy and Karen. He's bound to."

"I suppose."

"But that's not the main reason. Though it is an important one, and it does explain why adoption so often doesn't work."

Morgan's heart had fallen. He realized that, deep inside, he'd been hoping that Curly, somehow or another, would be with them for ever. This recognition so stunned him that he didn't realise Ann was crying:

"……and so that's why we can't have him Tom. Give me your handkerchief."   He gave her some Kitchen Roll:

"Sorry, I was in a day dream. Say that again."

"I said…" and she broke down again "I said if we keep Kiralee I might not ever have a baby of my own."

"But that's ridiculous!"

"I know it is. But that's how I feel. I can't help it but I do Tom. I haven't thought about anything much else for years but having babies. My babies. Your babies. Our babies. And I've got this awful feeling about Kiralee. He'd be like a cuckoo, and stop us ever having babies of our own. No don't argue! I couldn't bear it. That's how I feel. I can't change my own mind. It's female intuition. But I can't change! I can't change! I can't." She was shouting now, her eyes wide and defensive.

He got up to comfort her – crying as she was like a little girl who'd seen a ghost in a dream.

"All right Annie," he hugged her, tears running down his own cheeks – for whom he wasn't sure. "All right Annie. All right girl. Of course you shall have your own babies. Of course you will. And Curly's nothing to do with you. Karen will look after him, I'm sure she will."

She took a long time to calm down. She felt guilty. But she couldn't change her mind, or rather her heart. For she realised, far better than Tom, how irrational her feelings were. And on his side he knew how much she'd been hurt by those three miscarriages, and how much she wanted a baby of her own. Any superstition, however unreasonable, was understandable in Annie's case.

"Come on." he held a new tissue to her nose "Blow." She blew. He licked the tears from the corner of either eye.

"Cheer up. Penny and Greg have asked us to stay over the weekend. Greg and I have bought half a lamb between us, and we're going to roast it on a spit by the river."

"But what about Kiralee?"

"If Karen doesn't want the little blighter I'm sure Kylie will. She loves babies apparently. We might have a job getting him away from her."

Often and often Morgan was to remember that last happy weekend at Tidbinbilla together. After the children had gone off to their various dens, tents and nests to sleep, the four gorged adults sat round the fire in the darkness, listening to the Murrumbidgee, not five paces away, gurgling among its rocks. The Brindabellas loomed into the stars on the opposite bank; Kylie crooned to Kiralee who was fast asleep in a makeshift cot on the picnic table. Morgan kicked the main gum log, which hissed and crackled back into life.

"When we get back to London we'll miss Tidbinbilla and all it's good people." Ann said.

"Yes" Morgan agreed, "We owe you two such a lot."

"Aw come off it." Greg objected

"Yes we do. And no mistake .You healed Annie."

"She can stay any time." Penny continued "When she'd gone it left a big hole at Tidbinbilla. All the kids noticed. And I've never had a better natter in my life. Maybe we'll never be able to afford a trip to Europe – but Annie made me half feel I'd been there."

"Yep, and look at me" Greg continued "She taught me Fourier Analysis."

Morgan laughed.

"You can laugh mate but that Fourier stuff has opened my eyes. No that's not what I mean. It's as if I can see colour in the world for the first time. I look everywhere for it now, everywhere."

"You can say that again" Penny added. "He goes on and on about it. I wish I could understand."

"Go on then Greg" Morgan challenged his friend "If you really understand it then you ought to be able to explain the main idea to Penny."

They could hear Kylie behind them humming to Curly.

"OK I'll give it a go." Greg assented, after a pause. "Imagine you're looking at the sea's surface darl. It's all rough and confused, with no pattern to it. Now look down on it from an aeroplane just as the Sun is setting. You'll often notice a perfect pattern of waves perpendicular to the direction of the Sun. The low sun picks out the wave shadows. Night falls earlier in the wave troughs if you like. I've seen it. Now what does that mean? It means that the sea's surface, although it looks confused, isn't confused at all. It's made up of lots of beautiful regular wave-trains coming from different directions – some from Cape Horn, some from Tassie, some from Fiji, and so on. It's just that when you're right in the middle of the ocean it seems like a messy confusion, because they're all interfering with one another. But this Fourier fellow found a beaut mathematical way of disentangling all that confusion, and seeing all the regular patterns underneath. And in seeing them, understanding what was really going on. You take us here now. There's sounds coming from everywhere; from the river, from the fire, from us talking. If I recorded all that mess on a tape, and then did a Fourier analysis of it, like Ann showed me, with my computer, I could pick out all sorts of regular beats in it, normally hidden in the noise. For instance look at Picton down there." He pointed to the Kelpie dog who was staring intelligently into the fire, jaw resting on his paws. He swivelled one ear at hearing his name mentioned.

"If I had a long enough recording I could pick up the faint sound of Picton's heart-beat, simply because it's fairly regular, and because it's faster than ours and it's slower than Curly's. It's a tiny tiny sound. You'd normally need a stethoscope to hear it. But because it's regular, Fourier Analysis could pick it up above the clutter. In my case it's like I have a mathematical stethoscope for listening to the deep heart of the stars. How about that?"

"I think I understand" Penny agreed. "It does seem like magic."

They were silent for a while, the fire painting their faces as orange masks.

"Well I've learned a thing or two from Greg " Morgan resumed "Apart from Strine."

"Garn!"

"No seriously. I've been watching him, and learning to be a father. You see I didn't have one, so I don't know. Greg seems a great father to me. He knows when to be hard, and when to be soft: when to intervene, and when to leave things alone."

"And Penny's the same." Ann interrupted.

"Exactly. That's why they've got such wonderful kids. And why their kids will have wonderful kids too. And so on and so on until the fifth generation. Whereas poor Curly over there is going to grow up into a right bloody mess."

They looked over at the picnic table where Kiralee was asleep in his tomato box. Kylie had gone to sleep too, one hand clutching the box, her head resting on her other elbow. Penny got up, put a blanket over her daughter's shoulders.

"When's that blighter his father going to get back from NT?" Greg wanted to know.

No one could tell him.

"What about bloody Karen then? I reckon she's taking the easy way out. If you blokes weren't next door she'd probably get on with it."

"I sometimes wonder whether we're doing the right thing." Ann agreed.

"Well I don't. That woman's crazy. If we hadn't helped out – or rather you hadn't helped out Annie, Curly might have snuffed it."

"More likely he'd have been taken away from her." Penny said, going round with the bottle "Who wants some more red?" A fullish moon was peeping over the Brindabellas.

"I reckon they should lock her away before she fathers any more brats." Greg kicked the log into a blaze from his side.

"Don't be too hard on her" Ann replied "She's been telling me – in bits and pieces. I haven't even told Tom some of it." She glanced at her husband and reached out a hand for his. "You see Karen and Roy were brought up, quite separately, inside some weird religious sect down in Victoria. The usual thing. They're waiting for the Second Coming, when all shall be consumed – except the Righteous – who will inherit he Earth of course. Naturally there's a charismatic leader in daily touch with the Almighty. The One True Prophet he calls himself. Among his duties, personally bestowed upon him by God, is deflowering all the young virgins in the flock. He is The Vessel of God's Seed. All the usual banal pathetic nonsense. Anyway Karen ran away when it was her turn to fulfil his lusts. She was only fifteen. The police picked her up half starved, and didn't know what to do with her. The sect, and her parents, wanted her back. She threatenend to kill herself. Then Roy turned up. He was part of some rescue group for runaways from the sect – being an older runaway himself. The authorities agreed to release Karen to him – provided he married her when she reached sixteen. Which he did."

"My God, how……how….sick!" Morgan sounded flabbergasted.

"So she's more in a refuge than a marriage." Penny concluded

"Exactly' Ann agreed "And what makes it worse is that they are now both committed Catholics. And you know what that means in Australia. No divorce. Absolutely not."

"It's a wonder they've conceived a child." Greg interrupted.

Morgan began to feel uneasy.

"I've been trying to get it out of her." Ann continued "Apparently they do sleep together but they don't have sex. Or at least not deliberately. But sometimes Karen wakes up and

Roy's inside her, still asleep himself. It's more of a shared sex-dream on both sides, than a sex reality."

"Nature will find a way." commented Penny.

"Roy doesn't want a child. He's absolutely against it. He's a badly scarred man himself apparently. Which is easy to believe when you know him. As a Catholic he doesn't subscribe to abortion. But he definitely wants the baby adopted. He's not coming back to Karen, he's told her, until Kiralee's gone. And he's not being selfish either. He reckons that with their background neither he nor Karen are fitted to rear a normal child. And goodness knows he might be right. He's insisting that Kiralee be adopted by Catholics, and brought up in the True Faith. And as the legal father he's got rights. He's contacted the Catholic Adoption Agency, and they come round to see Kiralee regularly. And she's got her priest coming to see her on a weekly basis, and is much under his thumb."

"Bloody Hell, what a mess!" Morgan stood up, not knowing how else to vent his feelings.

"So Kiralee could be gone any day now." Ann resumed, "Karen's only got to give her written consent. First he'd be fostered until they can find suitable Catholic parents to adopt him. Apparently there are plenty."

"Well perhaps that's the best thing." Greg offered, "There are lots of good would-be parents out there. Curly might have a beaut childhood."

"Or not!" Morgan turned back to the fire indignantly. "Greg do you remember those idiot people with their caravan and their motor mower down on the South Coast? I bet they're exactly the kind of couple that an Adoption Agency would think ideal. Perfect! God help Curly then – because nobody else could."

Immediately after the Tidbinbilla weekend the Morgans drove down to Sydney for a month's stay. Morgan was worried that Curly would be gone before they returned, but far more worried that Ann would find out who his father really was. If he was. Annie meant everything to Morgan. He felt sorry for Curly, very sorry, but he could never let anybody or anything jeopardise his marriage. He was conscious of a sneaky, shameful part of him which hoped the problem would somehow vanish before they got back to Canberra. Ann was worried too but she said:

"Let's try not to think about Kiralee while we're in Sydney. Penny's probably right – as usual. We've got to give Karen the chance to sort out her own affairs."

The trip to Sydney had been organised so that Morgan and Ron Eckersly could write their paper on Elliptical galaxies together. Ron had arranged for them to have a room in the observers quarters on the Radiophysics research establishment in North Sydney. It was small, it wasn't luxurious, but it was free. They shared a kitchen, they could use the canteen, Ron's office was just across the lawn while Ann could walk to Epping station and catch the excellent train service down to central Sydney. They planned to catch up on all the cosmopolitan delights which they'd missed since leaving London, including concerts, the opera, art galleries, restaurants and pubs. Morgan was dying to see the Test Match between England and Australia at the Sydney Cricket Ground while Ann wanted to explore Sydney harbour and its historical environs by foot and ferry.

In return for his free accommodation Ron asked Morgan to give a course to the radio astronomers on "Galaxies'. Morgan was delighted to comply: it gave him a chance to clarify and consolidate in his own mind all the reading he'd done on the subject over the previous four years. He found the act of preparing a lecture, and afterwards responding to the comments and criticisms of the audience, a wonderfully stimulating way to really learn for himself. He'd never lectured professionals systematically before and he enjoyed the experience as much as anything he'd ever done in astronomy. Ann said, as she marched off to Epping station, that he was becoming a 'Galaxy Bore'. To Morgan she sounded not a little envious of his complete preoccupation. He had to promise that at least three days a week would be devoted to her, or rather to Sydney.

Morgan decided to skip quickly over those aspects of galaxies that were relatively well know or straightforward and concentrate on what he considered to be the greatest puzzles. In that manner he hoped to provoke his audience whilst challenging himself the most. The act of actually formulating a question in the clearest possible way was, he found, the perfect stimulant to his own research. To voice a question or an idea before a learned audience was to rummage about in the deepest recesses of his own curiosity. He learned how and why teaching and research can feed off one another.

His audience was ideal. It consisted of mostly young, mostly bright radio astronomers with a knowledge of galaxies largely confined to their radio properties – which were interesting, but peripheral to the subject at large. After all only a handful of galaxies were significant radio sources and their radio emission was probably transitory, arising in the nucleus, and unconnected to the stars – which made up the great outer mass of the galaxy and which generated virtually all of its light. But, as Morgan quickly discovered, radio astronomers were a cocky, irreverent lot. And why not? Within the last few years it was they who had made the big discoveries which had set the whole of science abuzz; first Quasars, then the Big Bang radiation, thirdly Pulsars. So they wouldn't let a lecturer get away with anything. They interrupted, scorned any weak argument, questioned assumptions, provided alternative hypotheses, and were generally sceptical of the most hallowed ideas. Morgan had to fight his way furiously over every inch of the battle ground. More than once he was driven backward in headlong retreat. As like as not when Annie got back from Sydney she'd find him surrounded by papers, deep in a calculation designed to rescue his latest argument from total defeat. He'd hug her absent-mindedly before returning to the affray.

Ron Eckersly was his most furious, his most penetrating critic of all. Ron would leap to the blackboard, the light of battle in his eyes, and attack, attack, attack. To get an argument past Eckersly it had to survive the fiercest barrage of shot and shell. The battles between the two of them raged long after the seminars were officially over, and revived, if not in the pub over dinner, then first thing next day in Ron's office. Both young scientists were having the time of their lives.

"You two" Ann said, as she sat between them in the grill at the Epping Hotel " Should always work together. Think of what you could achieve, and how much fun you would have."

"We could actually." Ron agreed. "Did you know the AAT Headquarters is coming to our place?"

"No!" Morgan was astonished. He'd assumed it would go to Canberra, probably Stromlo.

"Announced yesterday. So if you got a job on the British side, and I got one on the Australian – and why not, we could have offices next door to one another."

"And we could live in Sydney!" Ann crowed. "I'd love that. It's such an exciting city."

"What about the Admiralty?" Morgan worried.

"Oh I'd sort them out." Ann was insouciant. "These new optical fibres will make all the difference."

The three of them were delighted with their plan.

"I think this calls for a round of drinks." Morgan said, getting to his feet "What's it going to be? It's my shout. We'll drink to 'All together in Sydney'."

"I'll be in that mate. Make it a schooner."

"Me too." Ann clapped her hands with delight.

Now that they had a plan Sydney became a delight to them both – for a start it would be their first home, since they were married, which would suit both their careers. They pored over maps, spent the weekends exploring by foot and ferry, and argued passionately, careless of the costs, about which suburb they would live in. Ann would be working on the South Shore, somewhere close to the Australian Naval HQ, and was determined to commute every morning by ferry from the North Shore and argued passionately for Cremorne or Kirribilli, or Seaforth or Neutral Bay or Manly. She was even prepared to catch the hydrofoil from one of the Northern beach resorts such as Dee Why, Curl Curl or Avalon. Morgan, who would be working up in the Northern suburbs also wanted to commute by ferry, but in the opposite direction, from the South Shore and argued for one of the Southern Suburbs close to the sea, Watson's Bay, Coogee or Vaucluse for preference. No compromise could be reached, unless they moved up-harbour towards Lane Cove or even Paramatta. But that was too far from the ocean. Morgan had never known Ann argue so passionately for her own interests before. Inwardly, he was prepared to give in, having dragged her all over the globe to places she would never have chosen to live in for herself; outwardly it was fun to put up a fight. Every weekend was spent catching ferries, trudging round suburbs with views of the sea, looking in estate agents' windows, and finding Sydney more and more attractive. It would be the ideal place for them both to live for five years before returning to Britain permanently. For Morgan it would be the stepping-stone to a Senior Lectureship, or even a professor's chair at a British university, for Ann the perfect place to raise her babies while keeping in touch with the Admiralty in London. In terms of life, colour, people and civilisation there was no comparison with either Canberra or Tucson. True the climate wasn't very pleasant, with high humidity, blistering summer temperatures, and sixty inches of rain a year. And commuting, unless you were rich enough to live round the harbour, was apparently a nightmare. Mike Large told Morgan that some Sydney University lecturers left for work as early as 3am in order to miss the rush. But if he was appointed to a senior position on the AAT and Ann got paid again – which now seemed likely, they could afford to live wherever they wanted.

And what a lovely city Sydney was, almost a country in itself. Morgan had forgotten how much he enjoyed the opera, and to see Monteverdi's 'Coronation of Poppea' in the inimitable Opera House came close to paradise for them both. And by amazing good fortune Morgan was at the famous Sydney Crickey Ground to see Ray Illingworth's English team take the Ashes from Australia – an ambition he'd had for over twenty years. Meanwhile Ann was gorging in second-hand bookshops and the city's art galleries. She dragged him to see the National Gallery of New South Wales, and in particular to see a small gem of a painting, a study of a man's head, made by Van Gogh in preparation for his 'Potato Eaters'. Morgan, who'd been something of a painter in his youth, was arrested by it too.

"I so wish I could own that." Ann said, her eyes moist with emotion,

"I promise you shall. Within six months."

Ann stared at him in astonishment.

"No really Annie. I'm going to steal it."

She laughed, punching his arm.

"Cross my heart and hope to die." He sounded serious. "I've just worked out how to do it. Here's the deal. If I get it for you, can we live in a house on the South Shore – either Watson's Bay, or round the corner in Coogee? "

Ann, never quite sure when her husband was kidding, dragged him away from the Van Gogh:

"If you do I won't be able to live with you anywhere. You'll be in Paramatta gaol, or somewhere, for about thirty-five years."

"Betcha. When a clever scientist like me sets his mind to it, the police don't stand a chance .When did you ever hear of a scientist going to prison? Oh I'm going to steal that painting all right. It'll be on your bedroom wall within six months. You'll see."

As soon as they stepped out of the car in Canberra Ann went round to see Karen. Morgan was still carrying suitcases into the house when the telephone rang. It was Ann:

"Tom come round here at once. Karen is frantic."

Curly was in his high chair ,screaming his head off. He smelled. The kitchen looked as if it had been hit by a mortar. Ann was staring at Karen who was sitting on the sofa, her hands covering her ears, elbows on her lap, eyes closed, rocking back and forth slightly, chanting over and over:

"I goddago, I goddago, I goddago............"

"She says she's going to New Guinea."

"What?"

"And leaving Kiralee behind with us. For three months. I think she's hit him."

Morgan lifted Curly out of his chair. Curly was hysterical, his face purple, tears flying off into space:

"God he pongs. Poor little mite. His nappies can't have been changed for days. There, there little fellow, come to Tommy."

Curly's screams abated, but only slightly, as Morgan held him over his shoulder, patting his back.

"I goddago, I goddago, I goddago......."

"I think she's snapped Tom." Ann looked aghast. "What are we going to do?"

"Well she can't just bloody leave. What about Curly?"

Karen must have heard that because she took her hands from her ears and screamed up at him:

"I AM going! It's my life. Nobody can stop me. Nobody do you hear? It's MY life!" her face was red from tears and anger.

"But you can't leave Kiralee love." Ann tried to calm her "He's your baby."

"He's not just my baby" Karen shouted defiantly "What about his father. Why doesn't he help?"

"But Roy's in Arnhemland."

"Not Roy. Roy's not his father. I mean Tom!"

Ann turned and stared at Morgan, her mouth open. Morgan couldn't look at her, staring at the floor. Curly nearly choked on his saliva, before screaming louder than ever.

Ann was gone from the room. Morgan saw her passing quickly across the window as she traversed the garden on the way back to her own house.

"Aow Jeeze...." Karen moaned   "I never meant to say that Tom. I never never..." then she began crying.

"Where are his bloody nappies?" Morgan snapped. "You can't have cleaned them for ages you dirty bitch."

"I'm not a bitch." Karen roared back at him. "Clean him yourself. We haven't got any more clean nappies...."

"Come on Curl." Morgan ran out of the house with Curly over his shoulder, and up the road to the pharmacy. When he got Curly back to their house there was no sign of Ann. He carried Curly up to the bathroom, stripped him off, cleaned him up, ran a bath and got into it with him. The warm water calmed Curly down at last. He floated on his back, whimpering quietly, trying to lift his head and look at his father.

"There's a boy. there's a good little fellow. It's all right now. My God what's Mummy been doing to you?" He'd noticed some bruising on the baby's upper arms as if he'd been squeezed or shaken. There was a bump on his forehead and one eye was definitely swollen.

Ann came into the bathroom, staring at the two of them in the bath:

"Is he all right?"

Morgan shrugged, looking straight up into her face:

"I didn't know Annie. Not until that moment, I promise you. I wondered but......"

"How could you Tom? How could you? When you knew I was trying to have your baby? Our baby?" She began crying quietly and left the room. He heard the key turning in their bedroom door.

After Kiralee had had his bottle he went to sleep. Morgan wrapped him in a blanket and left him tucked up on the sofa. Then he went upstairs to try and explain things to his wife.

She wouldn't let him in. From the landing he spoke to her through the door, through the keyhole.

He told her how it happened. About his jealousy at Frank seeing so much of her, about Karen's naked bottom. That he'd never kissed Karen; never spent a night in her bed; never allowed Karen in theirs. That there was no love in it from end to beginning. It was just fucking. That he loved Ann more than ever. That even if she never had a baby she would be his wife and his love for ever. That his love had grown with every year, every month, every week, every day they'd been married. That beside his Annie, Curly and Karen were nothing. That he'd naturally supposed Karen was on the pill – because she'd had no children with Roy. That he'd been glad that their liason had been so quickly over. That he and Karen really had nothing to say to one another. That it was lust on both sides, and that lust and love weren't the same thing at all. He said all the things that other guilty husbands had said since the beginning of time. But he really meant them.

Ann didn't let him in. She didn't say a word back: not of reproach, not of anger, not of misery. Not a word.

He pleaded, he wept, he banged on the door. But no Annie. All night long, first standing, then sitting, then lying on the floor he begged for understanding. But he didn't beg for forgiveness because he didn't feel he'd done anything so very wrong. Yes he regretted it bitterly now, realising how it might have hurt her. Yes he'd been a fool for not understanding that at the time. But it was only lust, which beside love was nothing.

He went on and on and on until Curly cried out in the middle of the night for attention. Morgan fed his son, lit the fire to warm the room and to give Curly something to look at. Then he returned to the landing to plead with Ann all over again.

Just after dawn, physically and emotionally exhausted, he fell into a catatonic sleep. He didn't wake when Ann stealthily unlocked the door and stepped over his body. He didn't notice that she was smartly dressed, had a small suitcase in one hand, a pair of shoes in the other. He never heard her open the back door or leave by the garden path. He didn't see her enter the phone box opposite to call for a taxi. He had no idea that his marriage was over. Nor did he see the second taxi arrive to whisk Karen away.

CHAPTER 14
KIRALEE
1973-4

Ron Eckersly watched Morgan clean the food off Curly's face, take his bib off, lift him out of the high chair and place him sitting up on a blanket in the playpen beside his toys.

"How long since Ann left?"

"Four months and eleven days."

"How on earth do you cope?"

"With difficulty. We live from day to day don't we Curl?"

"I mean what about work?"

" I drop him off with his little friend Kylie most mornings. Kylie's Curly's best mate. Kylie lives on a farm not far from the observatory. Then I nip down at lunchtime, give him his midday feed and get him off to sleep, then race back up the mountain again. It's a tight squeeze but so far nobody up there has found out that I'm a single parent. And I don't want them to. That would be giving a hostage to fortune."

"What about observing?"

"Yes that's super tricky. Kylie's only sixteen, and she's a Downs kid. So Curly comes with me. I have to leave him sleeping in the van – just outside the telescope dome. I'm sure it's illegal – but what else can I do? I've even had to leave him down on the farm for an hour with only the dog to keep an eye on him."

"Jeez."

"I'm not so worried about Curly as about a stranger turning up. If Curly was crying and the stranger went up to his cot to help, Picton would have his leg off in a second. He's Kylie's Kelpie sheepdog."

"Can you do any astronomy?"

"You'd be surprised. The little bugger sleeps a lot – he's not a year old yet – and I hardly sleep at all."

"And Siding Springs?"

"Obviously I can't take Curly up by plane so we drive up, and by great good fortune my mate Jack Cockle and his wife Jenny have come out to Coonabarabran from England, so Curly stays with them over nights."

"And how's Ann?"

"Not a peep. I write to her every day. I'm sure she'll come round in the end. All I know is she's back at the Admiralty full time."

"I'd have sworn you two were the perfectly matched couple. Me and Kay find it impossible to believe that you've split."

"I don't think we have." Morgan said, washing up. "I think about her all the time – she must think about me. If Curly was a shock to me – which he bloody was – think of the shock to Ann's system. Right, the little sod is looking sleepy; let's get his head down and do some work."

Ron had come up from Sydney to help Morgan finish off the paper on Elliptical Galaxies. They'd found some interesting if not spectacular results. About twenty percent of the two hundred galaxies turned out to be radio sources. The interesting question was 'Why this twenty per cent, and not the rest?' To try and answer this question they were carrying out a "Correlation Analysis". This was a classical statistical technique to see what other characteristics of the galaxies corresponded with radio activity, and which did not. This was more complicated than it sounded because they had to eliminate secondary correlations. For instance it might seem, from the raw numbers, that radio activity was correlated with a galaxy's colour. But it might turn out, on further analysis, that colour corresponded closely with a galaxy's luminosity. So the real correspondence, the one which might give a hint as to the physics going on, might be the one between radio-activity and luminosity, with colour merely being a secondary intermediate characteristic, not a causative agent. And with a dozen measured properties for each of their two hundred galaxies there were many such secondary correlations to be discovered and discounted.

They both found the analysis fascinating. There was always the hope that vital clues, invisible to the naked eye as it were, might pop out of the statistics. Thus it was that the link between smoking and lung-cancer had been established.

What they found, in between attending to Curly, was that radio active galaxies were more luminous, were rounder, were redder, and were friendlier, that is to say closer to other companions, than the rest. And all these correlations were independent of one another and 'statistically significant' i.e. could hardly have arisen by chance.

All this made sense to Morgan, if not to Eckersly, because it seemed to confirm his theoretical work in Arizona on the fate of gas in Elliptical galaxies. He had discovered there that the gas from dying stars was most likely to collapse inwards and form a massive nucleus in galaxies which were massive (luminous), and not spinning (round). Since the gas would carry smoke in with it they ought to be redder too. And having close companions would deepen the gravitational well in which they were captive, making it harder for gas to escape.

"That's bloody ingenious" Eckersly said, helping to fill Curly's paddling pool on the lawn. "How did you think of all that?"

"It came out of this computer model Ray Wagoner and I made in Arizona. When I saw what was coming out of the model I worked back and found the physical justification for it using maths. Not very clever really."

"Why haven't you written it up?"

"Partly funk I think. It's all theory, and theoretical papers face such horrible refereeing battles. Whereas observational papers largely speak for themselves, theoretical papers can be kicked about by any shit, big or little, whose either jealous or got it in for you. They wouldn't publish my Red Giant stuff in Britain because Bellfounder has so many toadies over there under his thumb."

Morgan stripped off and sat in the paddling pool:

"Hand me the little grub will you."

Ron Eckersly expertly removed Curly's nappy and handed him naked to Morgan:

"Oh he's going to enjoy this. Aren't you Curly Whirly? You know he's just started walking." Morgan dunked the baby's feet in and out of the water before lowering him in up to the waist. Kiralee squealed with evident delight, splashing everyone with his hands.

"You really ought to write it up and publish," Ron admonished "It seems pretty fundamental to me. After all, powerful radio galaxies are all bright Ellipticals – and it seems to me you've produced a very natural explanation – which might account for quasars too."

"Well to begin with," he threw Curly high up into the air "It was more Wagoner's idea – at least he started it – than mine. And then you're not allowed to make important theoretical discoveries in a place like this."

"What do you mean?"

"Didn't you know? Up you go monster! All important theoretical discoveries are reserved for a handful of places like Cambridge or Berkeley. Anyone from outside will be refereed out of existence."

In between playing sharks and crocodiles with Kiralee in the pool, Morgan told Eckersly about the Three-Stage-Model fracas at London:

"I understand now what was going on – though I didn't at the time. Hood and Somerton knew that that model was far too big for a potty little place like London Observatory. They may not have been aware of their own motivation, but that was it, as sure as eggs is eggs. A discovery of that magnitude in the wrong place would only cause pain, embarrassment and annoyance all round. If, for instance, George Field at Berkeley had made it then it would have gone straight into publication and every one would have said 'What a great man.' But as little Twm Morgan stumbled over it first, it was the general duty to see it stifled."

"What a cynical bastard you are."

Eckersly took Curly from his father's hands and began towelling him down. Curly screamed to get back in the water.

"No not really." Morgan dried himself off and dressed. "We human beings need some kind of social structure. That's how we evolved. Too much honour going to the babies in the troop would lead to anarchy and breakdown. Hood and Somerton were only well-behaved baboons keeping necessary order. We'll find ourselves doing it some day."

"God forbid!"

After Curly had been put to sleep for the night the two men resumed their arguing about science over dinner, which Eckersly had cooked.

"I'm dissatisfied with myself as a scientist" Morgan admitted "I'm an able opportunist – and that's it. There's no depth, no philosophy behind it."

"I don't see what else you, or any scientist can be, not at this early stage of your career."

"I started late Ron. I was almost twenty seven when I started my PhD, whereas most people have got theirs before they're twenty five. I'm thirty bloody four. Most people who are going to be any good have a well thought out scientific strategy by this stage of their lives. They have some coherent career program which will direct their scientific lives for the next twenty years. Look at me, dashing about like a brainless honey-bee from one pretty little flower to the next. Look at all that time I spent on 'Arrays', and on the astronomical television project."

"A lot of people thought they were bloody clever Tom."

"They were fascinating, yes – I'll grant you that. But I'm never going to be a telescope builder, or an electronics wizard. That's not why I came into astronomy. If there was any depth to me I would have been far too busy with the real McCoy to divert so much effort like that."

"It's just as dangerous for a scientist to put himself on tramlines too early in life." Ron disagreed. "You need to jump off and go down a more interesting side-road sometimes. Some of the saddest bastards in our game are those who've settled for a comfortable little niche where they hope to go on publishing comfortable little papers – which nobody needs to care about – for the rest of their lives. They're not scientists, they're careerists. If everyone was like that, science would come to an end within a generation. No, ten years would do it."

"Well I don't want to be a butterfly collector. " Morgan said decisively, as he dried the last dinner plate. "I'd much rather fail at something really big than succeed in a whole lot of small things. And I haven't found that something big , not yet, and it's beginning to frighten me. A man of my age needs to have a dream of his own. I was reading about Christopher Columbus. Apparently he found these exotic seed-pods washed up on the wester shore of Ireland. From that moment on he knew there had to be some giant, mysterious undiscovered continent out beyond the horizon for him to find and explore. How I envy that man. It was not that he succeeded or failed, but that he had a dream, a quest, a holy grail beckoning him forever from beyond the western ocean. I would far rather drown following a dream like that, than row comfortably from haven to haven. Wouldn't you?"

"May be." Ron thought about himself. "But it's given to few men to find a dream like that."

"Why else do astronomy?" Morgan snorted. "If we can't dream, with all the universe out there to find, then who can? That's what we're for. To dream dreams for our fellow men. To beguile them, to send them to sleep with big questions on their minds. Not to stopper up their curiosity with facile explanations for every little this or that. They want to be told, and I want to tell them, that there are huge continents out there that have yet to feel the tread of human feet."

"The Big Dreamer eh? Good luck to you Tom. I hope you find your exotic beans lying in the sand. But how you do that I don't know. Surely it's luck?"

"It may be luck to find, but not to search and search and search. Columbus wasn't in Ireland on a package holiday – you can be sure of that. He'd heard rumours I'll bet – and went to see for himself. The clues are out there Ron – probably all around us – we're just too blind, too timid, too busy to see."

"It's easy to say that, and I hope you're right Tom. I really do. But I'd want some kind of evidence, some encouragement to keep on searching for your Big Dream."

"Fossils" Morgan replied unexpectedly "Men had been finding fossils in the rocks for thousands of years before anyone confronted the issue of what they could really mean. Facile men spoke of 'The Flood' and brushed them away as of no consequence. They were too busy working out the chronology of The Book of Daniel. Might we not be doing the same thing?"

"You'll need to show me a fossil to convince me Tom."

"OK I will. Help yourself to some more wine while I check on Curly."

When he came back downstairs Ron was standing, glass in hand, in front of a small painting on an easel:

"I've been meaning to ask you about this. Looks like an early van Gogh."

"It is. What do you think? I stole it from the Art Gallery of New South Wales down in Sydney."

"Garn, pull the other one." Ron laughed.

"No really. Ann loved it. So I promised I'd steal it for her. Look here's the frame." He picked an ancient gilded frame out of a wooden box, handing it to Eckersly. Ron put his glass down to inspect it carefully:

"Jeez! You're serious aren't you? So what do you need an easel and paints for ?"

"Obvious. You can't steal a valuable painting like that without replacing it. So I painted a replica here, from a print they were selling in the Museum shop." He picked up the print, taped to a piece of hardboard, and placed it next to the painting. "Then I bought an old frame, that was the hard part, from an antique dealer in Paddington, and did the swap when no one in the gallery was looking. I was carrying Curly, so they wouldn't would they? That was six weeks ago. So far nobody's noticed."

" 'Strewth, I think you're serious." Eckersly stared at Morgan "What about all the alarms?"

"This is New South Wales – not the Louvre. It's a small state museum. They can't afford them. Or not many. I was counting on that. Their security relies mainly on bluff."

"They'll catch you you silly bastard."

"Oh no they won't. They might if I sold it. But I'm not going to. It's a present for Annie. I told you. I'm just about to post it off to her – sans frame. That might be a give-away. See it'll fit just nicely inside this calendar of Australian Birds which I'm going to post her. We don't want the old oil paint cracking. It's about eighty years since Van Gogh painted this."

"Are you really serious about this?" Eckersly was incredulous.

"Why not? I mean I'd never have gone through with it if Annie hadn't left. That would have been daft. But now that she has I felt I had to go through with it. Not let her down. Keep my last promise to her and all that. And it is beautiful isn't it. It was a study he did for his 'Potato Eaters', the masterpiece that ended his Dutch phase, before he went to Paris."

"I wish I'd never looked at this." Eckersly shook his head as he replaced the fragile painting on its easel. "I'd heard all these mad rumours about you Tom, about climbing, and about Malaya – but I never believed the half of them. Now I do. Christ, I'm an Accessory-After-The-Fact now." He turned away :"I'm going to pretend I never saw it."

"Good." Morgan sat down at the dining table. "You asked me a few moments ago to show you something in astronomy analogous to an ancient fossil. Something that doesn't fit. Something that ought to disturb us all profoundly. Well I'm going to. Ever heard of an astronomer Fritz Zwicky?"

"Sort of. Vaguely. Wasn't he something to do with Supernovae?"

"Yes. That's how I came across him first. He is the supernova hunter par excellence. He was a pioneer on the Crab Nebula back in the nineteen thirties, and the very first person to suggest neutron stars. He's still alive and quite a character. He was a Swiss mountaineer who went to Caltech in the nineteen twenties as a star physicist, but turned to astronomy. Very pugnacious apparently. Referred to all his colleagues on Mount Palomar as 'Spherical Bastards.' "

"Spherical? Why spherical?" Ron wanted to know.

"Because, so Zwicky explained, they were bastards whichever way you looked at them. Apparently they hated him back too. Listen to this." Morgan opened a thick tome: "This is from the introduction to his latest Catalogue of Galaxies, it's entitled "A reminder to the High Priests of American Astronomy and their Sychophants":

> '... the most renowned observational astronomers in the 1930s also made claims that now have proved to be completely erroneous. This eroded real progress in astronomy by several decades since the said observers had a monopoly on the use of the large reflectors of the Mount Wilson and Palomar Observatories, and inasmuch as they kept out all dissenters, I myself was allowed the use of the 100-inch telescope only in 1948 , after I was fifty years of age, and of the 200-inch telescope on Palomar Mountain only after I was fifty four years old, although I had built and successfully operated the 18-inch Schmidt telescope in 1936, and had been Professor of Physics and Astrophysics at the California Institute of technology since 1927 and 1942 respectively. E.P. Hubble, W. Baade and the sycophants among their young assistants, were thus in a position to doctor their observational data to hide their shortcomings and to make the majority of the astronomers accept and believe in the erroneous presentations and interpretations of facts.'

"Sounds like a paranoid to me." Ron chuckled.

"I rather like the sound of him" Morgan said "But paranoid or not he was certainly a genius."

"And what's this fossil you spoke of?"

"OK, back in the nineteen thirties Zwicky got interested in Clusters of Galaxies. They're the largest structures in the Universe, typically a couple of million light years across. Most of the Elliptical galaxies we've been talking about today live in Clusters. We, that is to say The Milky Way, the Magellanic Clouds and the Andromeda Galaxy live in a small cluster or Group containing about twenty galaxies in all. The biggest clusters contain thousands of galaxies, mostly Ellipticals."

"And Zwicky?"

"Zwicky got interested in the nearest really big cluster – The Coma Cluster – about three hundred million light years away. And what he did was use a really ingenious technique to weigh it."

"How did he do that?"

"The Coma Cluster looks like a swarm of bees, but with each bee being a giant Elliptical Galaxy. Zwicky reasoned that the whole swarm would fall in upon itself due to forces of gravitation acting between all the galaxies. But obviously it hasn't fallen in, otherwise it wouldn't be there today. It can only remain uncollapsed if the various bees in the swarm, the various galaxies in the cluster, buzz about fast enough."

"It's like the planets going round the Sun too fast to fall into it." Eckersly drew a parallel.

"Good example. And just as you can weigh the Sun by measuring the speed of the planets, and their distances from the Sun, so you measure the entire weight of the Coma Cluster from measuring the speeds of a few of its galaxies, which you can do with a spectrograph on a telescope, as Zwicky did , using the Doppler Effect."

"I'll buy that."

"But here's the extraordinary result. The Coma Cluster weighs hundreds of time more than the weights of all its individual galaxies added together. Hundreds of times! Zwicky had found that The Coma Cluster must be dominated by mysterious invisible 'Dark Matter'."

"S'trewth. What did his contemporaries think?"

"I'm not that old Ron. But I suppose it was like the proverbial eight-hundred pound gorilla in the bedroom. Everyone knew about it, but nobody wanted to talk about it – in case it stirred into life."

"Didn't they question the data?"

"At first they did but then another chap called Sinclair Smith found the same result in the Virgo Cluster – which is right next door to us."

"There must be some reasonable explanation. Surely?"

"Nope. Zwicky himself didn't see anything surprising in it. 'Why' he asked 'Why should everything finish up in nice big, easily visible galaxies? Most galaxies may be dwarfs, far too faint to see individually at that distance. Or, as he surmised, galaxies may tear each other apart as they pass in the night, scattering their contents of stars into space, and individual stars would be far far too faint to be seen in even the nearest Cluster. But such explanations aren't tenable any more."

"Why not?"

"No matter how you break galaxies down, the stars inside them must still give off the same amount of light. That's fundamental physics. So if the Coma Cluster, for instance, were made up of dwarf galaxies and individual stars, the total amount of light would be undiminished, and should show up as a diffuse glow detectable with modern telescopes."

"Are you sure?"

"Apparently so, yes – though it's a tricky measurement."

"So where do we go from here?"

"That's just it. Nobody knows what to do next: or what to say. So we optical astronomers more or less keep quiet. It's not a conspiracy or anything. We're a bit ashamed I'd guess. Here we have this eight hundred pound gorilla, and we go round whispering 'Dark Matter' and then tip toe away."

.

Shortly after Kiralee started walking Karen turned up again next door. Morgan, who had no legal rights to Curly, was worried she'd want her son back. He needn't have worried. Karen was very curious though. Kiralee showed very little interest in her.

He doesn't remember me does he?"

"Are you sad?"

"Yes – in a way. But it's better so. I don't feel anything for him. All I remember is him screaming, screaming......" She covered her ears at the memory. He looks so calm now. That's what I can't get over. What have you done to him?"

"I'm calm, so he's calm. And I don't have to breast-feed him like you did. How long are you staying?"

"Not long. I'm going back to PNG. I'm studying this really untouched tribe up in the Highlands. It's a fascinating study for my PhD."

"What about Curly?"

Karen looked at her son with no particular interest:

"I couldn't take him if I wanted to – infant mortality up there is sky high. But honestly I don't want to – take him I mean. He's yours for keeps – if you want him."

"Of course I do – don't I Curl?" Curly wriggled out of Morgan's grasp and tottered off into the garden.

"Where's Ann?"

" That's a good question. She left me about an hour before you did."

"Jeeze Tom! You mean to say she's never been back? "

"Never answered a phone-call or a letter."

"That's ridiculous!" Karen stood up and paced furiously about the room: "I can't believe it. You and Ann were just made for one another. A marriage made in heaven." She stopped and stared at Tom. "Jeeze if I'd have thought, even for a second, that it would ever come to this, I'd have….I'd have run all the way to Melbourne. She must be mad! I've got to write to her. Tell her how it really was. And how it wasn't. We weren't having an affair behind her back were we?"

"I didn't think so. Not like that. But then there's Curly."

"Curly was an accident for God's sake. If I'd been serious I'd have been on the pill."

"Why the hell weren't you? "

"God knows. It's too late to worry now. I don't want Kiralee. It'd frighten the bejesus out of me to think I'd be responsible for him for twenty years. Part of the reason for me coming back here was to get the legalities settled. You should get back with Ann as soon as you can. I'm going straight back next door to write to her. This is ridiculous." She marched out indignantly as if the situation would never have happened – if it had been anything to do with her.

Letter from Karen Painter:

Dear Ann

I thought this would be an easy letter to write. But it isn't. I've thrown dozens attempts away in the month I've been back in Canberra. I'm just going to say a few things:

1 Morgan loves you to death. Anybody can see that, every moment of the day. He writes to you, he talks about you – he even stole that bloody painting for you. What a mad thing to do. All he'll say is 'I promised Annie.'

2 Kiralee was a stupid accident, in more ways than one. Tom was mad angry at you – something he'd read in a letter you sent him from London, and I asked him round here to calm him down before he cut off his bloody foot with the wood chopper. Yes things went too far – I imagine they often do after a bottle of wine. But if we'd been planning anything I'd have surely been on the pill. Believe me Ann we didn't even kiss one another – or spend the night. To think that your's and Tom's marriage should end over such a trivial incident – and that is what it was so far as I'm concerned – is beyond my understanding.

3 I didn't want a baby, and I don't want Kiralee. I might be a bad woman, but I never had strong feelings for him, except blind panic. I can't bear the thought of ever losing my freedom again. It may have something to do with the evil sect in which Roy and I grew up. I've heard other 'escapees' say the same thing. Motherhood is just not me.

4 Tom is amazing with Kiralee. Everybody says so. The kid doesn't recognise me – why should he? I'd rather he didn't. I don't want to feel any more guilty than I have to. I'm making him out legally to Tom. If he ever has a mother it will be you. Certainly I can't imagine Morgan ever marrying anybody else. I'm

not going to plead for him. You must know, far better than I ever can, what a fine man he is. What you can't know is what a beaut father he's turned out to be too – under great difficulties, considering his job. Everybody's doing their best to help Tom, but there have been times when Kiralee has had to be left alone in the bush out at Tidbinbilla, with no one to look after him but little Kylie's Kelpie dog. Kiralee seems none the worse for wear though, and follows his dad in everything, as well as in looks. He's going to be a dark sultry Welshman, not a blond Northern Italian like me. Take him and bring him up with the children you and Tom should have, must have, together.

5 Whatever you do don't blame Tom. He never made a pass at me though, to be honest, I always found his farouche looks attractive. You know I never had a proper sex life with Roy. That may well have contributed to it. An unfulfilled woman's body may do things her mind would never condone. What Tom did to me was probably a kindness on his part more than anything else. It was just a casual little thing for both of us at the time. Only the accidental consequence, Kiralee, is important.

What more can I say? It would be dishonest to claim that I'm filled with remorse. I only regret the consequences for you and Tom – if you're foolish enough to let them spoil both your lives.

I'd like to think we'd be friends again one day Ann. We had so many interests in common; and those don't (underlined) include Tom. I'd just love to tell you about my work in PNG with the Malinga tribe, to whom I shall be returning in a few weeks time. Meanwhile I'll do the baby-sitting at nights when K is asleep. Tom has been getting by on three to four hours sleep a night – and you can see it beginning to tell in his face. He looks older, but he's ruthless, absolutely ruthless about his bloody astronomy. Even K isn't allowed to get in the way of that.

I leave Kiralee to you, while Tom was always, and will always be yours.

Karen.

Jack Cockle's job on the UK Schmidt telescope, just reaching completion at Siding Springs, took him back and forward to London. Returning from one such trip he stopped over with Morgan in Canberra.

"Did you see Annie?" were Morgan's very first words when he opened the door with Kiralee in his arms.

"Of course I did. She's fine and…….". Cockle had been preparing this lie for twenty seven hours on the plane "…she sends her love." The truth was she had absolutely refused to discuss either Morgan or Kiralee with Jack.

"Hello Curly. Remember Uncle Jack?"

Kiralee put out his arms and Cockle took him:

"God what a weight. Are you going to be a monster like your dad? A monster who keeps his mate outside the door without so much as offering him a cup of tea?"

That afternoon they went over to Tidbinbilla for a barbeque. Greg Anson and Morgan, aided and abetted by all the kids, Kiralee in Kylie's arms, built a giant bonfire down by the river, with several of the big old Shire horses looking on and Picton barking his approval. Jack, who hadn't met Jenny Anson before, helped her in the kitchen with the food.

"I wanted to get you aside" she said "To ask about Ann. It's so awkward in front of Tom."

"Don't I know." Cockle agreed, forking a string of sausages.

"Ann's my good friend." Jenny went on.

"I know that." Jack said "She talked about you several times – though she couldn't have known I'd be coming to Tidbinbilla. She said she really missed this old farm 'The only place in Australia where I really felt at home'."

"How is she?" Jenny stopped scrubbing the potatoes in the sink and looked at Cockle directly. "You don't have to beat about the bush with me. I won't tell Tom anything you don't want me to."

"Promise?"

"Cross my heart and hope to die."

Jack wiped his hands on a tea cloth and pulled on his beer:

"To tell the truth it's a relief to talk frankly. It's so difficult with Tom right now. His need for Ann is so great he only wants to be told one thing. That Annie's coming back."

"And is she?"

"God alone knows. I don't. She never said so and she refused, point blank refused, to talk to me about Tom."

"That doesn't sound good." Jenny resumed her scrubbing.

"It doesn't does it."

"Is she happy do you think?"

"You have to remember I don't really know Ann. But yes I'd say she's happy. Loves her work. Has got a flat of her own now, in Kensington. Never mentioned Oz at all. Loves London again. And, I'd hate to say this in front of him, knowing how Tom feels."

"Go on." Jenny looked at him again.

"I think Ann's moved on. She's put her marriage behind her."

"What makes you think that?"

"She's constantly in the company of another man."

"Oh no!" Jenny was aghast.

"It's worse than that. This man is not just anybody. He's Tom's best friend Frank Cotteridge."

"Are you sure?"

"I can't be positive. But both times I arranged to see Ann, Frank turned up with her. And both times I arranged to see Frank – he's a close friend of mine too – who should turn up with him but Ann. I couldn't get him on his own, not for a second."

"Couldn't she just be looking to him for consolation?"

"Jenny Frank is in love with Ann. He has been for years. Told me ages ago. He wouldn't be seeing so much of Ann, I can tell you, simply on Tom's behalf. And that idiot Morgan has fallen out with him again – unfairly accused Frank of all sorts of nefarious dealings. So Frank won't have any inhibitions about stealing Ann now. And he looked damned pleased with himself, happier than I've ever seen him."

"But Tom and Ann were such lovers Jack. Such lovers."

"I know Jenny. Christ don't I know. I had a blow by blow account of their courtship from day one because Tom and I shared an office. But you know Ann looks happy with Frank. In some ways they are better suited to one another than Tom and Ann."

"How do you mean?"

"Frank can share Ann's work for a start, hush-hush stuff. That was a huge problem for Tom. And for Ann. Huge."

"I know. Ann told me several times. Poor Tom."

"And then they're temperamentally more alike. They're both Christians while Tom is a pagan – and proud of it. And he's such a clumsy, thoughtless lout at times whereas they are both, what's the word, yes 'civilised', to their fingertips. They actually think before they speak, and certainly before they act – a notion totally alien to Tom."

"But Tom is in Ann's blood. I never met a woman more in love than she was. She worshipped him."

"I would have agreed. Until I saw her with Frank. Frank's quite somebody, you know Jenny. He's even taller than Tom. Cleverer – if anything. Very handsome, though going bald – it suits him actually. Multi talented. Musical like Ann. Perfect manners. Glides through life on an ocean of talent. It's sickening. I should have thought any woman could adore him."

"I knew there was something. Here, you can peel these onions Jack."

"OK – it'll give me an excuse to cry. That's what I want to do when I see what's happening to Tom."

"You love Tom don't you Jack? Ann told me. What is it about him?"

"I've often ask myself. He's arrogant, he's hot headed, he's rude, he's pugnacious, he's insensitive, he's bossy and he's always causing trouble for himself – and his friends. But, but... there's not a mean or calculating or boring, or materialistic, or faint-hearted cell in Tom's body. When you're with Tom life is exciting; it's a quest, an adventure, a challenge. Tom goes out after dragons – that's it. He's the champion, the dreamer of dreams, … every tribe needs one. But not two. Tom lives a fairy story. When you're with him he conjures heroes, ogres, dungeons and goblins out of the air. I feel six inches taller when I'm with Tom. And so does everybody else – even Frank. Tom makes you feel that life is…..homeric. He's in touch with the gods. He behaves as if Jupiter is an old mate. But he must be hell to live with."

"Why? Ann didn't think so."

" I'm not a woman. And I never had much chance to see him as a husband. But he hardly bloody sleeps. He's always thinking, thinking, thinking. Nothing's good enough. He flies into rages at the slightest silly inanimate things. And just when you think he's happy he dashes off on another wild goose chase. He's interested in every bloody thing under the sun – except little details like where the next meal is coming from. Or repairing the taps. Or buying clothes…… The trouble is he thinks he can do anything – if he wants. He sets no sensible limits. At school he formed this club, six of us. We were going to build a yacht out of plywood, and sail it round the world. He had the plans and everything. Made me learn astronavigation. Frank had to go to carpentry classes. We all had to learn splicing for God's sake."

"What happened?"

"Tom went off to Malaya to fight, three blokes had to get married in a hurry, and when Tom got back he was mad about mountaineering instead. He went to Bangor University so that he could spend every moment in Snowdonia. I suppose it's quite simple really. Tom was born a hundred and fifty years too late. He's an explorer at heart. He should have been out there with Livingstone, or Raffles or Cook. He's an astronomer only because the stars are the last frontier – even if he doesn't realize it."

"So where does Ann fit in?"

"She's his one and only true love. His touchstone. His Penelope. And apart from that she's bright enough to keep up with him. He'll never find another Ann. If he loses her now he might crack up. He's dying for me to say 'OK Tom, all will be well. Your love will return.' But I can't. I don't think she will now. Do you?"

Jenny, who was chopping salad, paused before she spoke:

"I used to be so certain that Ann would come back. She was utterly possessed and satisfied by Morgan. He was everything to her – including his bossy personality. And I'd say she's a very 'moral' person – that is to say she wouldn't do something dramatic out of spite, or on the spur of the moment. But it's how long now?"

"Ten months."

"Quite long enough for her to get over her initial shock, and decide what to do. And, from the odd letter I've had, pretty calm about things. Especially since she got her own flat. Her father was pestering her to get an immediate divorce apparently."

"Well that's hopeful isn't it?"

"I used to think so. But now you tell me about……who is he?"

"Frank."

"Frank may be the reason she's got away from her father. Ann badly needed to get back her sense of self-worth. She needed her job back. She needed someone to tell her she's still desirable. Above all she wants to know she can have babies. She's obsessed with babies – as who wouldn't be after three miscarriages. If she has a baby with Frank then that could be the end for Tom."

"They're certainly thick as thieves."

"The one thing going for Tom, in an odd way" Jenny said "Is that she's never written him a Dear John. She would have done so by now I should have thought. Perhaps she can't bring herself to give him up."

"You know" Jack said " He writes to her every single day. And he stole that bloody Van Gogh for her."

Jenny laughed for the first time:

"So he fooled you too? What a rogue that Tom is. I don't see how any woman could resist him."

"Didn't he steal it?"

"Of course not. Tom's not that much of a fool. He painted a perfect replica, a 'forgery' he calls it, and bought an old frame to put it in. Ann's got the forgery, not the real thing, that's still in the gallery. Tom was sure Ann would see the joke. Apparently his best mates didn't."

Jack Cockle looked aghast as Jenny laughed aloud.

"But I've been haranguing him to put it back again. I even offered to help."

Jenny laughed so hard she had to wipe the tears away on her sleeve:

"I can just see you being arrested when the alarms went off. You thought you'd be doing the decent thing but the police would catch you with a forgery under your arm –which you were just about to substitute for the real thing…." And she went off into another set of giggles.

"You rotten bastard Morgan! I'll get you back for this."

Jenny had to sit down and bury her face in her apron she was laughing so much.

Cockle glared out of the kitchen window at Morgan who could be seen down by the river organising a stone-throwing competition. He had to laugh himself. Nobody, except Morgan, really knew which version of the Van Gogh story was true. For all Jenny knew, the masterpiece might be in London now, with the forgery hanging in the gallery.

"So what the hell am I going to say to him? I mean about Ann."

Cockle stayed for several days in Canberra, mainly to baby-sit while his friend did a four night run on the 74 inch telescope.

"Look at that Jack." Morgan showed him the latest spectrum of AP Lib, on a small microscope he'd brought down from the observatory.

"It's certainly featureless" Cockle agreed "I've never seen anything like it."

"Now look at this one." Morgan mounted another small glass slide into the microscope and focussed it by eye:

"The last spectrum I trailed along the slit, and you can see nothing but the nucleus. On this one" he stepped aside to let Jack look "I didn't trail. The nucleus is in the middle, the light above and below must come from the surrounding galaxy. If I can get a redshift for that galaxy then Bingo!"

"I don't see a feature in that either" Jack said "Except man-made atmospheric lines. I see Mercury 3568 from city lights."

"Yes, worse luck." Morgan conceded. "But I'm going to take a dozen spectra if I can, and then add them together; faint galaxy features which you can't see on a single spectrum like that, might then show up."

For the whole of his stay Cockle pondered whether to tell his friend about Ann and Frank. Not to tell him might remove from Tom his one last chance to go to London and fight for his wife. On the other hand to tell him about Frank might overstrain a man already stretched to breaking point. Either way it was a hideous responsibility. He sensed too that there was a part of his friend that suspected the worst – but that Morgan couldn't acknowledge it. It was telling that, after the first time, he never again mentioned the subject of Ann in London again, as if he suspected something bad was going on.

Not only did Morgan write to Ann every day, he wrote to many of their mutual friends. What he hoped to achieve by this he couldn't say but it comforted him to exchange reminiscences about Ann, as if it brought she and he closer together.

Bob Salt wrote back to say he was a bloody fool, that Ann was too good for him, but he was glad that he was looking after his baby, and that he would go up to London and plead Morgan's case.

In his second letter he confessed that Ann had refused to listen to him, and threatened to walk out if he persisted:

"She's going to make up her own mind up in her own good time."

Pat Gilkey, who could scarcely write legibly any more because of her eyesight, also cursed him for a fool – but in much stronger language than Bob Salt. She and Walter were in Long Beach but hoped to go to London for their usual summer in Dolphin Square:

> "And when we do I shall be sure to see that poor mistreated gel. She's too good for you Tom Morgan. On the other hand she'll find it nigh on impossible to find a better man. Some women can forgive a philanderer. I couldn't and I fear Ann may be like me. If you want her back then you had better keep your pants tightly buttoned up. Your son looks like a real Morgan – and just like you as I recall when you were a baby. Walter and I are leaving money to see him through a decent college education when he grows up. Love. Patti.

To bring up Curly, while maintaining a full blooded astronomical career, would have been impossible without a lot of help from his friends and neighbours, particularly the Ansons and the Cockles. But they all had children of their own, who naturally had to come first. Even Kylie had to go to school two days a week, a special school for Downs' kids to prepare them for an adult life in shelters with others of their own kind. So there was only so much help he could expect, or wanted to ask for. His salary wouldn't run to child care, not even for one day a week. So he cut down his sleep to less than four hours a night, supplemented by odd cat naps during the day when Curly was sleeping. He undertook heroic amounts of baby-sitting amongst his neighbours, in return for payment in kind. He fitted research into the oddest crevices of the day and night. He skimped on housework, ate raw or fast food, learned to do several unlikely things at once and took risks with Curly which, in normal circumstances, he never would have dared.

Observing runs, particularly at Mount Stromlo, stretched his ingenuity to the limit. Kylie needed to sleep, while Curly still woke up in the middle of the night for a feed. There were very strict rules about who could be allowed in the telescope at night, and babies obviously weren't included.

Morgan's solution was to put Curly to sleep in the van, and park it just outside the dome. He could nip in and out to keep an eye on his son, and feed him during a hopefully slack moment of the night. Curly, by now quite vociferous in his own interests, protested vigorously, and had to be put in a harness to prevent him from escaping if he woke. Nothing else could be done. Unfortunately nights on the mountain could be cold, extremely cold in winter. Morgan bought half a dozen hot-water-bottles which he distributed around Curly, both inside and outside his crib. He also kept a thermometer in the van to monitor the temperature. Occasionally, on really clear winter nights, the thermometer would plummet way below zero, threatening Curly with hypothermia. On such occasions Morgan would smuggle the crib into the dome – which itself was perishing cold. Apart from the control room – where the night assistant worked, the only warm place was the tiny darkroom where Morgan developed his plates. The control room, with it's dim lighting, and someone to keep an eye on Curly, would have been ideal, but Morgan didn't want to compromise the night-assistants, who were directly responsible to Bacon for the safe operation of the telescope. Had Bacon found out that a Night Assistant was complicit in Curly's presence he would have been dismissed at once. In practice they all came to know about Curly, and even kept an eye on him, outside or in, during long exposures, but keeping him in the control room would have been an unacceptable risk for them. In any case, knowing Bacon's animosity towards himself, Morgan wanted as few people as possible to know about Curly.

His luck was bound to run out in the end. And it did. Defying the forecast the temperature plummeted one night. Curly was even crying with the cold in the van so Morgan furtively tucked him into the darkroom, lulled him to sleep again, and climbed back up onto the observing platform.

At one stage, during a long exposure on AP Lib, he heard an unfamiliar voice below him in the pitch darkness. Sound echoed incoherently round inside the big dome so that he couldn't make out who was there, or what was being said.

When he reached the ground the night assistant Dunc apologised:

"I'm sorry Tom. I couldn't stop him. It was the astronomer in the thirty-inch telescope. He'd run out of Kodakl IIIaF plates and knew there were spares in the darkroom. I didn't know where they were so he had to go in himself."

"Who was he?"

"Don't know his name. One of the students I think. Young feller anyway."

Morgan looked at the telescope schedule hanging from the wall:

"Bugger! He must be one of Doolan's students. Did he say anything?"

"No. Thank God. If he had then I would have had to report Curly."

"Let's just hope he keeps his trap shut."

Almost a week past before Morgan was summoned by phone to appear in The Director's Office. He knew he was in trouble when he found Doolan grinning in the ante-room, with a student looking uncomfortable beside him. Morgan was ushered straight into Bacon's presence.

The great man didn't even look up, but continued writing. With his fat little hand he pushed a piece of typed paper across the desk at Morgan.

It was a confession by Morgan that he had '….without the director's permission, taken an infant into the 74-inch dark-room at such a time and such a date whilst he was the astronomer in charge of the telescope'.

He read the confession, which was factually correct, and returned it to Bacon.

"Sign it." Bacon still didn't look up.

"No I won't – not without the addition of a paragraph explaining why the baby was there."

"I'm not interested in your private life."

"The baby would have frozen to death if he hadn't been taken inside."

"Then it shouldn't have been on the mountain in the first place."

"But unfortunately it was. And a choice had to be made between life and death. Had I taken the baby down to Canberra the 74-inch would not have been used on a clear dark night. That would have been a criminal waste. Would you have wanted me to waste the telescope time?"

Bacon now looked up, his eyes barely visible as tiny dots through his thick spectacles:

"Whether you sign that or not, you have behaved in a thoroughly unprofessional way and in so doing risked the safety of a major telescope."

"Horseshit!" Morgan laughed. "Do you think the baby would blow up or something? Babies are harmless you know. They're tiny helpless little things."

"Spare me the sentimentality. You're trapped and you know it Morgan. If you don't sign that paper I've got witnesses as to your dishonesty. You will be suspended and dismissed."

"And if I do sign it?"

"The result, in the long run, will be the same." Bacon smiled for the first time in Morgan's acquaintance.

"You absolutely refuse to consider the circumstances in which the baby was there?"

"There could be no circumstance of an extenuating kind."

" In that case I will sign your paper."

Morgan snatched the paper back, took a pen out his shirt pocket and wrote:

"The baby, my baby, was taken in to the dark room from my camper outside the dome to save him from freezing to death when the outside temperature, as the records will confirm, fell without warning to below minus ten degrees centigrade. The move in no way compromised either the safety or efficiency of the telescope. The director, Professor Bacon, has just stated that 'There can be no circumstance of an extenuating kind'. I therefore appeal to the common-sense and decency of the Vice-Chancellor."

Then he signed and dated the confession. But instead of giving it to Bacon he took it back to the outer office and asked the secretary to make two photo-copies, which she did. Then he marched back in again and threw the original on Bacon's desk:

"I should read that if I was you. It could be your job on the line as well as mine. I can just see the headline in the Canberra Times; 'Director orders baby to freeze.'"

Bacon coolly took up the document and read Morgan's amendment before signing it. Then he took a second typed paper out of his drawer and handed it across the desk. It read:

"You are hereby suspended from your fellowship pending a hearing on full dismissal. Pending that hearing, which will take place within 60 days, your salary will be paid in full. However, on pain of instant dismissal, against which there will be no appeal, you are banned from appearing on observatory premises, either at Mount Stromlo or at Siding Spring.

In the mean time you are advised to consult your legal adviser.

Signed

The Registrar,

Australian National University.'

"You really are a turd aren't you?" Morgan smiled at Bacon "Twice round the pan and pointed at both ends."

"Thirty minutes." From which Morgan gathered that that was the time which he had to gather his papers. It was vital to leave nothing behind which might be vital to his research. His brain was so busy calculating what he would need that he barely registered the wolfish grin on Brucie Doolan's face as he passed.

The Union representative was moderately helpful. He advised Morgan to hire an employment lawyer. Morgan refused:

"There are no legal or technical issues in dispute. As charged I am guilty. I shall plead mitigating human circumstances, with a veiled threat of unfavourable publicity. Bacon will never be able to prove that his telescope was in any jeopardy. But I do request the longest delay possible. I've got papers to write while I've still got a salary. But don't say that. Plead 'Time to prepare his case.' What sort of people will be at the hearing?"

"Mostly academics. A politico. A union rep. One or two real outsiders – probably J.P.s. They are usually pretty fair."

"And what are my chances?"

"Depends very much on the chairman. If he insists on sticking to the narrow case at issue, then you're sunk. If they permit a review of the wider context, you might be OK. I've never heard of a case like this with a baby in the spotlight. Basically academics are cowards. They won't be concerned about you, or the baby, or Bacon for that matter, or his ruddy telescope. All they'll want is for the university to come out smelling of flowers."

"Press allowed?"

"Nope. But an appeal against a verdict of dismissal has to be open."

"OK. Do what you can to get a humane chairman."

"We'll do what we can mate. But human beings are thin on the ground in a university. I still think you'll need a lawyer. You strike me as a bloke who could easily lose his temper."

Morgan found, with no other distractions beside Curly, who now spent several hours every day at the local nursery, that he could sleep more and work rapidly. He finished off the Ellipticals paper and sent it off to Ron Eckersly, his co-author, for typing. The pulsar paper he typed himself on a machine 'borrowed' from the observatory by Greg Anson. With forty-five free days on his hands he decided to take Curly to Tasmania.

Letter from Karen Painter:
        To Ann Morgan.

        Dear Ann,
                You will have heard of Tom's suspension from the university. He decided to go to Tassie and I blackmailed him into taking me part of the way as I needed to spend time in the Hobart library researching the confidential files on the rounding up and extinction of the Tasmanian aborigines by white settlers. I'd like to talk to you about that some time. It's a complicated story, based as much on fear and ignorance as on race prejudice. White settlers were simply 'vanishing' without trace in the bush and, all other explanations failing, it was presumed that the poor aborigines were responsible. So they were all rounded up in a grand sweep of Tasmania and exiled to the small Flinders Island, partly for their own protection because farmers were shooting them out of hand as presumed cannibals. The whites never understood how much land hunter-gatherers need, so the aborigines rapidly died out, as much from hopelessness as anything else. But it's a terrible story – never completely told. The locals are extremely sensitive about the records, as you can imagine. And anything I write, based on such records, has to vetted by the State government, which is a bummer and explains why the tale still needs to be properly researched.
                The terrible irony was that after the fatal sweep and after the last aborigine had been transported from the main island, white settlers continued to vanish in the bush just as they had before. The truth only emerged when a man escaped alive to tell the tale. There was something out

there far more deadly than any aborigine. He was walking his paddocks one day with his sheepdog, in search of some lost woollies, when he simply vanished into the earth: literally into the soil. The sheepdog ran back to the farmhouse and roused his wife. She returned to to find a small tear in the ground. She was mystified. But when she tried to leave, the dog barked frantically and wouldn't let her. So she returned to the 'tear' and tried to look into it. When she lay on the earth and put her face to the hole she was astonished to hear her husband's voice calling for help from far below. She fetched her sons and between them they widened the hole, which led into a gulf of absolute blackness. The smallest boy was lowered into the gulf with a lantern and reported that he was hanging amongst the uppermost branches of a dead forest so thick that its canopy had grown together above his head to form the apparently false layer of 'ground' upon which they were now all standing. He was lowered to the true ground where his father lay injured in total darkness.

That man was the first ever to escape from a peculiarly Tasmanian phenomenon called 'Horizontal Scrub', in which the trees of the temperate rain forest grow so thickly together that the leaves cannot fall and eventually form a layer of humus or 'false ground' overhead. It was this treacherous 'Horizontal Scrub' which had swallowed up so many unfortunate settlers and which accounted for the genocide of the Tasmanian aborigines. I tell you all this to prepare you for what happened to us.

Tom, by the way, didn't want to take me but, until the legal formalities over Kiralee are complete, I am in a strong position to have my way with him. I tell you this (Tom made me) in case you should think we are lovers again – which we certainly are not. Tom slept in the van with Kiralee while Karen slept in her little tent in the bush.

As I said before, Tom is a natural parent. Although such an impatient and irascible man in other respects, he never resents attending to Kiralee or playing with him. Kiralee has an amazing 'vocabulary' , which is not surprising since the two of them are talking to one another all the time in their own language. Kiralee sat in the front with Tom, commenting on the passing scenery, while poor Karen sat right in the back practically ignored by both of them. Ann you really should have babies with Tom, he has turned parenthood from a nightmare, as it was for me, into a constant stream of fun. Life's so unfair isn't it? Kiralee has a dream of a father, while mine was a nightmare. Kiralee is pretty good fun too but he refuses to go to bed before Tom does. A great little passion killer I'd say.

The other thing about Tom, which will be no surprise to you Ann, but which was a revelation to me, was his complete obsession with his research. No matter where we were, no matter how busy he had to be about the camp, or looking after Kiralee, he never spent less than four hours a day with his astronomical papers, his notebooks and his slide-rule. He'd go into the van to get Kiralee off to sleep then creep out again and work on the camping table by the light of the Tilly lamp, with the moths swarming round his head. God knows how long he went on because I'd nod off in my tent with his lamp still visible through its canvas canopy. And when I got up with the dawn chorus as like as not Tom would be working there still, or in the van beside Kiralee, covering page after page with his funny equations. I presume he'd slept some time during the interval. It made me realise that research isn't something you do instead of work, but a wonderful obsession which you cannot avoid, and would never want to. When he was in such a trance I could put a mug of tea by his side and come back an hour later to find it untouched. I hated it when he looked through me as if I wasn't there. And even when Kiralee cried out for attention you could see the enormous struggle Tom had to escape from some deep and utterly fascinating region of the universe to join us poor mortals up here in the mundane world. For a wife to live with such a man she would have to share him with a ruthless and demanding mistress. I asked him who she was and he said 'Dark Matter'. Lucky you!

Anyway we went to the Wild West first where the temperate rain forest is far thicker than any jungle I've seen in PNG. Roads through it were wild and far between, usually logging tracks to ship out the magnificent big trees to pulp factories and mills on the coast. Looking one night for a camp site up one such forlorn track we found we simply couldn't get off the road. The bush, which thereabouts consisted largely of tea-trees, grew so thickly together that I literally couldn't thrust my fingers more than a few inches between the twigs and branches.

It was growing dark and we'd passed the nearest settlement hours before. If we'd camped on the road then quite likely a huge logging tractor and trailer would have run us down – without ever noticing. So we had to find a way off.

It was pitch dark before Tom found a thinning of the trees to one side; it wasn't much but it did allow us to drive a few yards off the track. I lit a fire while Tom fed Kiralee. As I put chops on the grill drops of rain began to fall through the treetops causing the fire to spit. It always rains on the West side. Suddenly there was a bang; we were plunged into total darkness because the fire had disappeared. Totally disappeared! We couldn't believe it. Kiralee cried a little from fright. Somehow Tom found the torch. Where the fire had been there was a gaping hole. Peering into its blackness along the beam of the torch we could pick out the branches of dead standing trees disappearing down into the gulf below.

"Cripes " Tom said "This must be your 'Horizontal Scrub'! We're camped on the bloody stuff. The van could fall through at any moment and take us with it. Here, take Kiralee and the torch and walk back exactly on our wheel tracks to the road."

This I did, and I can tell you it was relief to reach solid ground. Then I used the torch to direct Tom as he tried to reverse the van over its own tracks.

Horizontal Scrub though was the least of our excitements. I don't know how much Tom has told you about the Night of the Monster Waves? Not much I suspect, seeing how he nearly killed himself and turned Kiralee into an orphan.

We were camped on our own in a field not far from the village of Bicheno on the East coast. The sea was half a mile away and Tom had arranged to go out for tuna with one of the local cray-fisherman at dawn next day.

During the night I was woken in my tent by an unfamiliar thundering roaring sound. . I crawled out of my bag to investigate. It was a beautiful windless night with a full summer moon etching the landscape in silver and black. Surge after surge of thunder, which even shook the ground underfoot, seemed to be coming from the direction of the shore.

It even woke Tom inside the van. He picked up Kiralee and we tip-toed through the moonlit bush to investigate. When we reached the low cliff and stared out to sea the sight that greeted our eyes was of awe inspiring, terrifying beauty. Gigantic, enormous, indescribable seas, some of them thirty or forty feet in height, were rearing up in the moonlight, vertical walls of water that seemed to hang up there like nightmares, before toppling over in slow motion to break in a wrath of foam and thunder. Closer in to the shore the whole bay was a maelstrom of moonlit foam. The row was deafening – one might as well have been standing immediately behind the curtain of the Niagara Falls. The uncanny lack of wind meant that spume and spindrift rose high into the sky where it cast moonbows against the summer stars.

Never in my travels, and I had once been a surfer, had I seen, or even imagined, seas as gigantic as these. So high they were that they were breaking far out, well beyond the headlands. It was just as well because had they broken any closer to shore they would have overwhelmed the land.

At this point Tom's sanity left him. He handed Kiralee to me , but although we screamed at one another from inches away nothing whatsoever could be heard. He walked off, went down onto the beach, removed his pyjamas and leaped into the surf.

I assumed he was committing suicide because he was immediately sucked out in the retreating surf for about two hundred yards. Even in the bright moonlight it was difficult to see a white body in the white foam, but from time to time we could see his head emerging and his arms flailing in a desperate crawl.

Then he was buried under the next monster breaker as it raced towards the shore and I thought he was lost. But as it retreated there he was standing in the shallows braced like a statue in the moonlight. He was trying to resist the outgoing torrent which raced round his body like the bow wave of a speedboat. Suddenly he fell and was sucked out into the tumult again, struggling in vain to regain his feet. This happened again and again, sometimes he almost made it, losing his footing only when the water was a few inches deep, and he was but feet from safety. At others he never got closer than waist deep before he was dragged out again. I was screaming and waving while Kiralee was screaming too – I could see his face – but of course neither of us could hear each other above the thunder.

I could see Tom was weakening – he must have been buried under water three quarters of the time. I thought he was gone when two or three times he was washed in and out again without any attempt to gain his feet. He waved to us once, which I thought meant that he had given up. But actually, as he told me afterwards, he was looking and thinking in order to give himself one last best chance.

The next time he was hurled in I could see him swimming like mad on the very crest of the inrushing torrent, and as it paused to turn back again he stood and managed to regain his feet. For a brief moment he was standing on the sand, and then he sprinted to safety before the next monster could seize him in its tow, which it very nearly did.

It was a miracle he survived. Only his great strength and weight saved his life and, he said, the need to come back for Curly. I don't know why he did such a foolhardy inexplicable thing, but then Tom is Tom – perhaps he explained it to you in his letter next day?

Later that morning we went into the village of Biceno and down to the harbour. What a scene of devastation! Monster waves were still breaking over the rocks which form the natural breakwater there and every boat had long since been smashed into matchwood. Tom went into the pub where his cray-fisherman told him that such freak waves come in every few years and wreck everything. Apparently they've been diverted Northwards by some storm out in the Roaring Forties , or even the Antarctic. Only the extreme richness of the fishing pays for the regular annihilation of the fleet.

Morgan never could explain his foolhardy action to himself. What he wrote to Ann was :

'I was hypnotised by the moonlight and thunder. I was drawn towards the surf like a moth to the flame. To go out there and body surf down those monstrous toppling walls of seawater seemed the most desirable, most inevitable thing in the world. And the most frightening.

I cannot imagine now, or explain to you, why I did such a foolish thing, but I took off my pyjamas and threw myself into the foam. Immediately I was tumbled head over heels and buried in the roaring tumult. I knew at once I was fighting for a life I had recklessly thrown to the gods. As the foam from the last wave receded I was sucked out at twenty miles an hour, catching gulps of air between being buried alive. And then the next wall of roaring white foam towered overhead before snatching me up like a beetle in a storm-drain.

As my body was tumbled helplessly inward and outward in the maelstrom, my mind looked coolly on from somewhere above and outside. The same mind that had foolishly taken me into the surf now searched for a way to save my life. I had to conserve my strength and wait for a probable lull in the procession of great waves. Sometimes I was carried to within ten yards of dry land. I'd then stand up but the giant suction as the water receded first tugged the sand away from under my toes and then tore my legs from underneath me, sucking me back into the maelstrom

In a moment of respite I looked to see Karen standing there in the moonlight with Curly clutched in her arms. He looked like an orphan already. I thought 'I've got to try and save the poor little fellow'.

Eventually the lull came. I surfed in on a lesser wave then dug my toes into the sand and paddled madly with both arms. Suddenly the freezing water was down round my ankles and I could run up the beach, sobbing with exhaustion and relief, thanking providence for the possession of a second life which I certainly didn't deserve. Somebody is no doubt saving me for something worse.'

The hearing on Morgan's dismissal was held in the main campus of the Australian National University overlooking Lake Burly Griffin. It was a formal affair with microphones recording every word electronically as well as a trained court stenographer hired from the Federal Courts of Law. The dismissal of an academic was a rare and very serious matter which had to follow procedures laid down minutely in the founding statutes of the National University, statutes borrowed from much older institutions such as Oxford and Harvard. Everybody, except for Morgan who didn't possess one, was dressed in a dark suit and was concealing a sense of human anticipation underneath an artificially solemn demeanour.

In fact this was the first such hearing in the brief history of the ANU, so considerable trouble had been taken to see that it was attended with the maximum solemnity. The Judicial Board, drawn from the University Council – itself made up of academics and distinguished layman in equal proportion – sat at a long baise table on a raised dais, facing the body of the court room.

The chairman of the Board, Professor Donnison, Deputy Vice-Chancellor for Academic and Administrative Affairs, brought the hearing to order by banging the table with his gavel. He was a fussy little man of a kind Morgan loathed on sight, almost certainly one of those academics who covered up their failure, both as scholars and teachers, by busying themselves with the administrative minutiae of university life. Like mice eating crumbs fallen from the High Table they were to be found in their hoards on every committee in the institution, where their main purpose was to multiply more sub-committees to attend to matters which they misconstrued to be of paramount importance. Morgan's worst fears were realised when Donnison used ' it behoves us' no less than three times during his nervous opening address. He was clearly a man for the formalities, especially so in a case like this where there was no local precedent, and where the statutes were so accoutred in ancient legal phraseology, much of it in Latin, as to be virtually incomprehensible. His guiding attitude seemed to be that unless a procedure was specifically authorised in the Statutes, then it must be forbidden.

Having made this much clear and warned everyone that he would allow into the proceedings no matter not already specified in the written statements submitted to the university by both sides some sixty days before, Professor Donnison introduced the members of the Judicial Board one by one. Where they weren't from the university they were largely drawn from government, business and law. Three of the eight were women, all rather serious looking and elderly.

The next business was to eject from the court all persons who did not possess a formal invitation to attend. Witnesses, including Bacon and Doolan, were required to wait in the ante-room until they were called by the usher. Thus the body of the courtroom was largely cleared, except for a surprisingly large number of members of the University Senate, composed of senior academics, who could attend by right. In the front seats on the right, facing the Board, Morgan sat with his union representative, while on the left sat two barristers, both in wigs, who would be representing the university.

Having thus cleared the court Donnison, in a ringing voice, called upon the senior barrister to make the opening address, which would outline the case, and name the witnesses the university would call.

The barrister was brief and to the point. The accused had concealed an infant inside the dome of the 74-inch telescope on Mount Stromlo. This was specifically against the Standing Orders signed by the Director of the said observatory, Professor Oliver Bacon, and constituted a risk to the most powerful optical telescope in the Southern Hemisphere, one operated by the National University on behalf of the government, and costing, in modern terms, millions of Australian dollars. He was proposing to call Dr.Bruce Doolan, an expert on the telescope, and Mr Mark Hackforth, who had actually found the infant. He understood that Dr Morgan was not disputing either the presence of the that infant, or it's identity as his son. Then he sat down.

Donnison fussed about, checking to see that the address had been correctly recorded both by the sound technicians and the court stenographer. He explained : "In the event of an Appeal, should the accused be found guilty, an accurate transcription of the proceedings could prove crucial." He then went on:

"The accused academic, Dr Twm Ianto Morgan, a research fellow at the aforesaid Observatory, has chosen to represent himself, although he had been advised by the university in writing, that it was unwise so to do. Before calling upon Dr Morgan to make his own opening address, I want to warn him that in acting as his own advocate he must stick as strictly to the procedural rules as any qualified legal professional, and that if he chooses to step outside these rules then I, as chairman, will intervene immediately."

Morgan rose to his feet nervously. But as soon as he began to speak the nervousness vanished completely:

"Members of the Board, I represent myself because, as a junior academic, I can afford to do nothing else. However I do not ask for any extra consideration on that score for in this case, or so it seems to me, there are no legal niceties in dispute. Indeed the facts are not in dispute at all. I did have my baby son in the telescope darkroom during the second half of the night. The outside temperature had plunged to below minus ten degrees centigrade and there was a real danger of him dying of hypothermia, asleep as he was, in my camper van just outside the dome. I can produce evidence, if required, as to that temperature drop."

"Of course it will be objected that the baby shouldn't have been on the mountain in the first place. In a strict sense that is true. But all of you who have had children will recognise that, however careful the planning, sometimes things will go awry. And in that case of course it is the parent's instinct to see that his child is safe. In this instance, as I shall evidence, my wife had to be away in London on vital Admiralty business. I made arrangements for my son to sleep in our camper van just outside the dome, where I could nip out and cast an eye on him from time to time. This I had done several times satisfactorily before. But I hadn't anticipated, how could I for it wasn't forecast, that the temperature that night would fall as far and as fast as it did."

"I am an experienced observer and I have used telescopes far larger than the 74 inch. Therefore I understand just how valuable such an instrument is, particularly one sited in the Southern Hemisphere where astronomy is, relatively speaking, in a backward state. The choice open to me was this: to bring the baby into the darkroom where he would constitute zero risk to the telescope; or to take the baby down the mountain and close the telescope for the night. But for the very same reason that the 74-inch is valuable, so much more is a clear moonless night's observation on that same telescope, and no conscientious astronomer should or would consider closing it down on account of a private family matter. As evidence of this note that all professional telescopes, including this one, are scheduled for full use on the nights of Christmas Eve. It is an earnest of our dedication to the profession. I took the decision I did both to save my son and to make best use of a very valuable scientific facility, one which is entrusted to this university by the Australian Federal Government."

"Why am I here at all? I am here because my director Professor Oliver Bacon refused to exercise his own discretion, or discharge his responsibility to the university which employs him."

"I'm going to stop you there." Donnison intervened. "This is no place for personal abuse".

"But sir, this isn't a question of personal abuse. I assure the Board that it is not. I refer you all to a copy of my 'confession' contained in my submission."

There was a good deal of paper shuffling while the Board sought the paper in question. When the shuffling ceased Morgan said

"May I quote from that paper Sir?"

"I suppose so, though matters of detailed evidence are not generally to be brought up in your opening address."

"I understand Sir. But this in direct response to your own interruption."

"Proceed." Donnison snapped.

"I quote from the letter signed by me, and countersigned – that is the point – by Professor Bacon, in his office one week after the incident. It reads 'The baby, my baby, was taken into the darkroom to save it from freezing to death when the outside temperature fell below minus ten degrees centigrade, It in no way compromised either the safety or the efficiency of the telescope. The director, Professor Bacon, has just stated that 'There can be no circumstances of an extenuating kind.' "

"Of course it is for the Board to decide, but I contend that I shouldn't be standing here at all, faced with dismissal. In any sanely run observatory I might have been ticked off by the director, even lost some of my observing privileges. But I would never have faced dismissal, never. So the Board might like to ask itself why such a vindictive course has been pursued here, and why Professor Bacon failed in his duty as director. There are actually very strong reasons – but I will not bring them up – unless asked to do so by the Board, as a witness, and under oath."

"Would you kindly conclude Dr Morgan." Donnison ordered.

"I will Sir. I point out that the real issue here is that I endangered the 74-inch telescope. If I did so then I am guilty. But the burden of proof is on the university to prove it so. The telescope is a very massive, very strong machine, weighing tens of tons. My baby weighs not much more than twenty pounds and was fast asleep in a restraining harness. If you dismiss me I will not only have lost my job I will, to all intents and purposes, have been thrown out of my highly competitive profession for good and all. I don't think I deserve that. Really I don't."

The proceedings continued all day, fussily conducted by Donnison. Ann hadn't written, as Morgan had begged her to do. However a direct appeal to the Admiralty had resulted in a letter from The Director of Naval Intelligence Sir Timothy Saumarez KCMG, the key sentence of which read:

'Mrs Ann Morgan is an irreplaceable member of Admiralty Intelligence. Although temporarily on leave of absence in Australia it has always been understood that she would return to Whitehall when matters in her provenance, involving the National Interest, are at stake."

It was suitably vague about whether such matters of National Interest were at stake in the present instance, but the Board were too overawed to quibble.

The only moment with a potential for drama came when Brucie Doolan was called by the prosecution as an expert witness on the telescope, and on potential safety issues. He grinned and fawned on the Board a great deal but it didn't do him any good. Morgan simply rose to ask him:

"Doctor Doolan, can you sketch to the Board a single practical scenario in which a sixteen month old baby, asleep in his cot in the darkroom, could jeopardise either the safety or the efficiency of the 74-inch telescope, or any of its vital equipment."

Doolan huffed and pontificated but the increasingly plain truth was that he could offer no such plausible scenario. The Board itself began asking increasingly sharp questions, which he couldn't answer satisfactorily. Eventually he was dismissed by Donnison.

At the end of the afternoon, and rather to his surprise, Morgan was himself called by the Board as a witness under oath. One member of the board in particular, a Justice of the Peace from New South Wales, asked most of the questions, while Donnison himself looked uncomfortable:

"Dr. Morgan, we, that is to say some us on the Board, would like you to elaborate on a remark you made in your opening address upon 'strong reasons for the director, Professor Bacon, to act unfairly towards me.' I remind you that you are under oath, and that we are interested in ascertainable facts not in personal feuds and vendettas."

Morgan sketched out the enmity that existed between Australia's three major observatories, and described how he had, unwittingly, walked into it. And how, as a result, Bacon had threatened to see "that you never get another job in astronomy". He admitted there were no witnesses to that threat but pointed to people like John Bolton who would be able to substantiate the broad picture.

The Board, after some discussion amongst themselves, wanted to call Bacon. The awkward fact was that Bacon was Morgan's witness in the sense that it was Morgan who had effectively subpoenaed him to give evidence as to his own actions. As a result Bacon had been fuming in the ante-room all day with the other potential witnesses.

Donnison called the court to order and explained the awkward predicament.

Morgan thought hard before rising to his feet in an act of apparent magnanimity:

"I realize that it would be awkward to be here while the Board questions Professor Bacon. Therefore I consent to him being called as my witness. But I will step outside while he is testifying. I do so on one condition. That his testimony be confined to the state of enmity that exists between the three Australian observatories, and my role in it, such as it is. I will leave my union representative here to see that it does not descend into a personal character assassination whilst I am absent."

The Board hastily agreed.

Bacon was gone some time while Morgan sat in the ante-room overlooking the artificial lake which formed the centrepiece of the city of Canberra. Round it were gathered the embassies and the Governor General's residence. He tried to look nonchalantly confident simply to annoy Brucie Doolan.

Morgan was called back to hear the closing address of the prosecution, and he made his own. He had decided to be very brief:

"In this case the burden of proof lies on the university to prove, beyond any reasonable doubt, that the safety or efficiency, of the 74-inch telescope was compromised by a wilful action on my part. The only witness called to that effect was Dr Bruce Doolan the deputy director. I submit that he didn't offer any convincing scenario in which my baby son, sleeping in the darkroom, could have jeopardised either the telescope, or its efficient operation. That being so the Board must surely find me innocent of any crime serious enough to warrant dismissal – which would also entail the loss of my profession."

"Professional Astronomy is the world's largest village – consisting of more than a thousand souls scattered around the globe. Like any village it is rife with gossip. By now nearly every villager will know that one of their number stands on trial for endangering a major telescope – almost the greatest crime they can imagine. If even the slightest suspicion remains of my guilt then I am finished, for I will never get another astronomical job. The competition to remain in the profession is extremely fierce, fiercer even than the competition to get into the Australian test cricket team – if you can imagine that. Therefore I think it only fair to ask the Board to point out in its written judgement, supposing me to be found innocent, that this case should never have been brought against me, for the telescope was never at risk. To say less would be to condemn me by omission. I would be found innocent, but punished all the same by the loss of my profession – a profession I live for and for which I have fought with all my heart and sinew. So long as there lingers even the slightest suspicion that I endangered a major telescope, so long I am a condemned man. I know it will be much easier for the Board to wash their hands of me and to say in effect 'Not Proven.' I beg you all to believe that, for me, such a verdict would amount to a sentence of professional death. Thank you."

The court was cleared, the witnesses were sent home and Morgan was left with his union representative and the two lawyers to watch darkness settling over the lake. Sandwiches were brought with a tray of drinks, and they sat talking round a friendly fire – about everything except the case itself. Morgan was worrying about Curly, who fiercely resisted going to sleep unless his father was present.

It was almost nine thirty pm before they were finally called to hear the verdict. Donnison read it out with the harassed manner of a man who had just lost a long argument.

"The Board recommends that Dr Morgan be not dismissed from the university. We find that neither the telescope, nor its efficient operation, were ever in jeopardy. Though the course of action he took clearly did breach the Director of the Observatory's Standing Orders, it was forced upon him by unforeseeable meteorological conditions. Therefore no stain whatsoever attaches to Dr Morgan's reputation as an astronomer and we recommend that the university extend his fellowship by at least two months to compensate for the research time he has lost due to suspension."

339

"The Board further believes the university was unwise to bring this case at this level. In doing so it has subjected itself, and others, to a great deal of unnecessary trouble and expense. The matter could have been, and should have been, dealt with at the observatory level."

CHAPTER 15

DARK MATTERS.

The busiest time of year out at Tidbinbilla farm was the haymaking. The old Shire horses, weighing a ton each, needed a lot of hay to see them through the winter and the only way it could be afforded was to make it on the farm themselves. Volunteers of all ages came up from Sydney to help and to handle the gentle beasts, who wanted to be involved in the heavy work themselves. They pulled the mowers, and the rakes which tossed the hay, and in pairs they dragged the heavy old wains which brought the hay back to the farm to be built into stacks.

There was so much to be done that Greg and Penny were at it from before dawn until they dropped from exhaustion well after dark. Morgan took Curly out to the farm and worked with his friends almost as hard as they did. All the equipment had to be taken out of the old woolshed and made ready for the work; there were wagons to be oiled, repaired and painted; harnesses to be thoroughly checked and softened; implements to be de-rusted, sharpened and oiled. Then the woolshed had to be converted into a temporary 'hotel' for the visitors, with bunks, mattresses with new hay, and canvas screens hanging from the rafters to provide some privacy. The wood stove which provided hot water for the shower and the tea-urn had to be brought to life again, while the great table, where twenty shearers had once been fed, had to be set up again to feed the troops.

Once the harvest started Greg was out in the paddocks all day training the newcomers and supervising the work. He galloped about on a huge black Shire over eighteen hands high called Cromwell. Cromwell could get up a good head of steam, as behoved an animal bred to carry a knight in full armour in a cavalry charge. The sight and sound of him approaching at a full gallop, hooves thundering on the hard Australian ground, nostrils snorting, harness jingling, white feathers flying out behind leg and hoof, Greg bouncing about on his back – barely visible above the great creature's rocking head, and with Picton tearing along behind barking furiously, would have struck terror into any poor Saracen ordered to withstand the charge.

The old Shires loved working. Morgan, who'd never thought about horses in his life before, was touched to see even the feeblest ones jostling to have a place in the fun. The visitors, who were mad horse-lovers of both sexes, were given the task of seeing that each old horse felt it was contributing to the harvest.

"They're like us" Penny remarked "They feel that their lives have to have a meaning too."

Since he was too unskilled to help Greg, Morgan took over as much of the domestic work and cooking as he could, in order to relieve Penny to work with the horses, which was her love and her skill. He scarcely saw Curly who was out and about with the other kids all day, though he did worry about one of the giant Shires stepping on him by accident. The Vee Dub came into its own as he drove back and forth to Canberra to fetch mountains of food, drink and other necessary supplies. He usually had one or two helpers in the kitchen or at the barbeque while he cooked commercial quantities of bacon and eggs, roasts, pastas, curries, rissoles, pies, stews, gravies, potatoes and vegetables. He made fruit salads and fruit jellies for afters, all of which were transported over to the woolshed in a trap drawn by an old mare called Daisy who was led by fifteen year old Diana from Paramatta who fluttered her eyelids and wiggled her bottom quite shamelessly at Morgan. The high point of Morgan's day was dinner in the woolshed with all the others. Curly would be down the other end of the table with the rest of the kids. He could take off his apron at last and join the adults sinking schooners of Greg's home-made brew whilst volunteers did the dishing up from a side table.

All the doors and windows of he woolshed would be open to let in the cool evening air, which would have been a great idea, except that the old horses crowded their heads through to watch the feast, their eyes shining in the oil lamps hanging from the rafters, their teeth munching on whatever they had in their muzzlebags.

"You're a good man Tom Morgan" said Penny, kissing him shyly one morning when he was frying bread "I hope Ann never forgets what a great husband she had. If she ever does, some other woman will snap you up. Just look at that Diana. I'm surprised she hasn't crawled into your van one night."

"How do you know she hasn't?"

"Because you're still head over heels in love with Ann, and you want her back."

"That's certainly true. And we don't want any more silly mistakes – though I do love Curly."

"How would you feel if Ann never came back?"

"She will. I know she will. I'm a part of her – just as she's a part of me."

"People divorce you know. Split up all the time."

"Not me and Annie."

"Then why hasn't she written Tom? It must be a year and a half now."

"I don't know. I wish I did. Perhaps she's waiting for me to come back. If she was going to leave me she'd certainly write. But she hasn't."

"How can you be so sure? Perhaps there's another man back in London?"

"Perhaps. I wouldn't blame her. But it won't last."

Morgan put the last of the fried bread into the oven and began breaking three dozen eggs into a bowl for scrambling.

"Oh God!" Penny put her face in her hands and turned away. "Somebody's got to tell you."

"About Frank you mean?" Morgan sounded quite calm as he added salt and began whisking the eggs with a fork.

"You knew? " Penny looked up sharply. "Add water otherwise they'll go all rubbery."

"Tom Cockle told me ages ago that Frank was in love with her. I didn't know that. And Ann's very fond of Frank: she's always thought he's wonderful." He put quarter of a pound of butter into a large frying pan to melt. "Frank's got a lot more in common with Ann than I have. They're both very clever, very sociable people. And they're both religious. Above all they both 'fit in' and are very successful. Which I am not. Here, pass me the pepper. I'm a loner if ever there was one. I don't mean solitary. I'm a friendly sort of chap, as you can see. But I have to go my own way. I always have and I always will. I can't follow the crowd. It's not in me. It's not that I despise them – or care much what they think. But I only feel really alive when I'm striking out on my own, taking risks. That's why Ann loves me, and in the end why she couldn't love Frank. Ann needs a man who's got his own star to steer by. And Frank hasn't."

"I hope you are right Tom. I hope to God you're right, because Jack Cockle told me the pair are seeing a great deal of one another."

At that moment Diana came in and glared at Penny:

"Daisy's ready to go up to the woolshed Tom. Shall I put the hot plates in the trap?"

"Yep. And the bacon and fried bread. But cover them with cloths to keep the flies off. The scrambled egg will be just a jiffy. And do me a favour will you Di. Cut up Curly's bacon for him before he swallows it in one piece and chokes."

"I think Curly's wonderful." Diana fluttered an eyelid. "He's going to grow up just like you."

Penny dug Morgan furtively in the ribs.

Although he was too busy during the harvest to do much research Morgan was mulling over a paper by Franz Kahn and Lo Woltjer that had come out in 1959. They had devised an ingenious timing argument to claim that even the relatively close-by space around the Milky Way must be filled with massive dark material. Their argument was almost too simple to take seriously. They noted that that the closest giant galaxy to the Milky Way, the Andromeda Nebula, was, according to its spectrum, falling toward the Milky Way at a hundred kilometres a second. Since the Universe as a whole was expanding this falling-together of two giant galaxies could only come about through their mutual gravitational attraction. But judging from their visible contents of stars and gas they were far too light to reverse the local expansion and turn it into infall. Either the Universe was far older than it appeared – or else the two galaxies were far more massive, at least six times more massive than their visible contents would suggest.

Here it was again, arrived at by a rather different argument; Fritz Zwicky's concept of a Universe dominated by massive, dark and totally mysterious material. What were the invisible agents pulling galaxies, and clusters of galaxies, together? Were they dark stars too undermassive to shine? Or whole dark galaxies? Or mysterious atomic particles that had so far eluded detection on Earth ? Or planets without stars? Or rocks? Or meteorites? Or gas, either frozen into snow, or so hot and diffuse that it gave off no light, but a thin whisper of undetectable X-Rays? What could be more exciting for an astronomer, Morgan wondered, than to devote his life to the search for Dark Matter. Such a man would be like Columbus standing on the Irish shore and finding there exotic beans which could only have come on the current from some giant continent far out there beyond the horizon. Here was a task worthy of his ambition, commensurate with his wildest dreams. A man could hazard his life on such a quest and not complain if his voyage ended short of The Fortunate Isles. Damn Pulsars, damn Red Giants, damn The Interstellar Medium, damn even Quasars. Here was the epic journey, the saga , the quest, the mission that had been beckoning all his life. He would provision his barque, set her sails, and voyage out beyond the rim of the known world.

Easier said than done. Christopher Columbus had only to find some backers, a ship and a doughty crew. He Morgan had to have an original idea. He decided to open a notebook on Dark Matter and write in it every day. It would be his confidante, his fellow dreamer, the grit in his oyster, the hair in his shirt.

Up at the Observatory the gossip was rife among the staff, some of whom were thinking the previously unthinkable. Even the worms who had previously referred to him as 'Oliver' were crawling out of their holes and wondering, ever so quietly, if it wasn't time for Bacon to go. After all he had deployed the full majesty of his directorship against a humble research fellow – and lost. And worse, far worse, he had lost the headquarters of the Anglo Australian Telescope, which everyone had assumed would come to Mount Stromlo, to Sydney, the home of the old enemy. The defeated and unpopular leader, coming up for the renewal of his directorship, was, for the very first time, in a vulnerable state. If Bacon was to go, only his cronies like Bruce Doolan had anything to lose, and even Doolan, it was rumoured, was out of favour with the Great Man, who blamed the Morgan fiasco on Doolan's ineffectual performance on the witness stand.

The directorship became a regular subject for fierce debate. It was amazing how people who had knuckled under silently for years suddenly recalled resentments they had apparently felt all along; resentment over the way Bacon had hogged all the foreign-travel funds; resentment at the food insultingly served to them at Siding Springs; resentment at the lack of dark observing time on the 40-inch – which again Bacon had hogged; above all resentment at the elevation of despicable and incompetent toadies like La Bulstrode and Doolan.

According to the constitution of the university the staff were going to be a given a say in the director's re-appointment, but not of course the final say which would rest with a committee of anonymous big-wigs advising the Vice Chancellor down on the main campus. Thus to openly speak out against Bacon now was to risk his revenge if, over the objections of the staff, he was to be re-appointed.

Morgan, the only one on the staff who had nothing to lose, being doomed anyway, suddenly became popular. People who had ignored him for years suddenly called him 'T-Bone' again. He was even asked for advice:

"If you don't get rid of Fat Sow now he could get this place closed down. Then you'd all be out of a job. After all why should the government pour money into a place like this, an observatory increasingly affected by city lights, when it is building the great Anglo Australian Telescope at a much better site and with its headquarters in Sydney? Thanks to Fat Sow's unpopularity and incompetence you've missed out on that. If you don't slit his throat while you've got the chance he'll take you all down with him, then bugger off back to his chair in California."

"Yer off yer flamin' heads if you think Bacon's going to go." Doolan riposted. "He's got friends in 'igh places. I should know. Anyway, all this so called 'democracy' is bullshit, window dressing. When did they ever get rid of a director who wanted to stay on – and Ollie certainly does. Why, if they got rid of him their own comfortable positions might also be at risk one day. No way José ! Youse fellers, if you value yer skins, had better stay in line. Ollie won't forgive anyone who plots against him. Not anyone. Don't listen to Morgan here. He's a dead man walking. You're out of here T-Bone the minute your contract's up. And Ollie's fixed your chances of another job in astronomy. I happen to know. If I was you mate I'd take evening classes in … in bus conducting, or something else you're more suited to."

The other astronomers were confused. They knew Morgan had a point – but then so did Doolan, and Doolan had the ear of powerful people in high places – such as his uncle, Senator Mickey Doolan. Or did he? They only had his word for it. And if Bacon stayed on as a disastrous director – which everyone now recognised that he was – they might all have to pay with the loss of their careers.

Greg Anson told Morgan that Doolan had come into his office and threatened him directly:

"We all know you're muckers with T-Bone Morgan. If you want my advice sport you'll keep away from that Bolshie Pom. Believe me Ollie knows everything that goes on in this observatory, out in the open or behind his back. He can hear a cockroach fart. And you're in no position to start a flamin' mutiny Anson. We had a good look at your contract this morning. It was a special deal worked out by that old fool Bok when he was director. You are to stay so long, and only so long as your G-Dwarf study needs completing. And who decides that? Why the current director of course. So you keep your nose clean sport, and away from that blighter Morgan, or else you'll be looking for another job – and smartish."

"I wanted to hit him Tom, I really did. What a beastly creep. But then I thought of Kylie, and the horses, and Tidbinbilla, and my G-dwarfs. But I swear I'll choke that swine one day."

"Hostages to fortune. You don't have to publicly associate with me at the observatory Greg. It won't effect our friendship. Why risk your position – and so much else?"

"Because we've all got to make up our minds. We can't just sit here doing nothing, hoping for the best. If you think Fat Sow is incompetent, and most of us do, then we've got to get rid of him before he brings the observatory crashing down about our heads. It's self preservation really. But most of the astronomers aren't going to help. They're hoping somebody else will take the risks."

"Of course they are. They're academics." Morgan was scathing. "Why most of them are just grown-up swots and brown-noses. They've never done anything but study all their lives, tried to please teacher, never taken a risk. They're too old to behave like men now."

While Morgan was getting breakfast one morning the phone rang:
"Jim O'Leary here. I'm over in Sydney on R and R from Vietnam." Morgan struggled to recall the gung-ho graduate student from Arizona who'd volunteered to go out and 'Waste the Cong'.

"Jim! What a surprise."

"Can I come up and stay with you?"

" 'Course you can."

"I'll be there this evening."

The brash, rootin-tootin' Texan bantam cock was a changed man. Subdued, distracted, he spent most of his time on the floor playing with Curly and his toys.

"Ah doan wanna talk about 'Nam Morgue. It's a mess." Now that he was out of the States Jim's Texan accent seemed exaggerated. "Ah need to git mah sanity back. Ah wanna hear all about astronomy man. What's been going on since I left? You never git to hear nothin' out there. Tell me what you been doin'. Bring me Helmut's latest papers from your library. Show me a telescope. Make me feel like an astronomer again. Ahm goin' straight back to graduate school when ah can git out o 'Nam..... if ah get out of 'Nam. Let's start with quasars; they were the hot thing when ah left Tucson."

Morgan described the latest developments and in particular the 'Superluminal Sources'. These were quasars with radio jets spearing out from them at many times the speed of light.

" But ah thought that that was impossible. Ah thought that Einstein proved that the velocity of light was the absolute maximum."

"Exactly. That puts the whole quasar-distance problem into sharp relief once again – which is what I'm working on. The super luminal speeds are based on the assumption that the sources are at their redshift-distances. If instead they were ten times closer, then the jet velocities would be ten times less, and there'd be no conflict with Einstein."

"So how you tacklin' the quasar distance problem?"

Morgan told O'Leary of his quest to find among the Bolton radio galaxies a single miniature quasar close enough to have its distance measured spectroscopically by two different means: by the redshift of its emission lines coming from the nucleus, and by the redshift of its ordinary stars out in the halo:

"If the redshifts are exactly the same I will have proved that quasars are at their redshift-distance – their 'cosmological distance'. After all there shouldn't be anything dodgy going on in the spectra of the stars. They'll just be normal stars buzzing about in the parent galaxy – not subject to any exotic physics that might be going on in the intense gravitational field of the quasar nucleus."

"Ah'll buy that. So how you doing?"

Morgan took him up to the observatory and showed him the dozen or so good spectra he'd accumulated from AP Lib:

"The nucleus is varying rapidly – on a timescale of weeks or months. When it's bright I can't observe for long without saturating the nuclear spectrum. When it's faint I can go on for longer and accumulate far more signal from the dim halo. If I get lucky and catch it one night when the nucleus is really faint I'm sure I'll catch enough light from the halo to pick up the stellar spectrum."

"You must be mighty close already." O'Leary agreed, screwing up his eye at the microscope eye-piece "Ah kin definitely see some kind of a spectrum from the halo. But it's a tad too dim to pick out any stellar features. But you're awful close Morgue, awful close."

"I know. Tantalising isn't it. One of the great problems of astrophysics hanging by the very thinnest thread, just waiting to fall into my hand. All I need is an hour or two of exceptionally good atmospheric seeing. And you get them occasionally at Mount Stromlo. What's preventing us seeing the stellar spectrum out in the halo is nuclear light scattered out into the halo by the atmosphere. With two hours of good seeing on a night when the nucleus is in a low state I'm pretty sure I could get it. Exciting isn't it?"

"Ah kin see a snag." O'Leary was still looking through the microscope,, "Ah cain't see no quasar lines in the spectrum neither."

"That's true," Morgan conceded. "And we need those too. Right now they're swamped by the continuum light coming from the nucleus. But when the continuum is in a low state we ought to see them standing out too. They shouldn't vary, at least not as rapidly."

"Seems to me you need a lot of luck Morgue."

"Luck comes to those who persevere. Isn't that what they say? I've been persevering with this bugger for close on three years."

"Wha' don't you add all them spectra together? Any weak signal might show up above the noise then."

"I've thought of that. But we don't have an analogue to digital spectrum scanner at Stromlo – or indeed in Australia. I thought of taking the spectra to the States. But there's no travel money for the likes of me. Our revered director spends it all on himself."

"Hell that's a shame Morgue. This is really Big Science you got here. Bigger even than your Crab Pulsar. You don't do nuthin' easy."

"I know. It's really frustrating. What I have done is trace out each spectrum onto a long roll of graph paper. Here, let me show you."

He took a long roll of paper from a shelf and the two of them spread it out on the floor of the corridor, for it was too long to fit into Morgan's office. It revealed a trace twelve foot long of the original one-centimetre spectrum in the microscope. It was a long wobbly ink line with no obvious features.

"Ah cain't see nuthin' convincin'."

"Nor me. But if I lie ten traces from ten different spectra, on top of one another, and shine a light though them, then something faint, not visible on a single spectrum, might show up."

"It's a long shot. If ah was goin' back to the States, which I ain't just now, ah'd take them spectra and git 'em traced for you digitally. Then you could add 'em properly in a computer. Boy, you could be sitting on something mighty big here! Why don't you send 'em back to Helmut back at Kitt Peak. You could trust him."

"I know I could. But would you trust this precious scientific data, on fragile glass plates, to any postal system?"

"Nope."

"It's bloody frustrating isn't it? Quite possibly I've got the data to solve one of the greatest problems in science and I can't get the fare across the Pacific. And I could be out of a job any day too. The Director has got it in for me."

O'Leary was obviously in an odd state of mind, but quite how odd Morgan didn't realise until he found Curly's baby-food disappearing from the refrigerator. Nobody else but Jim could have taken the jars of strained carrots, or apricot puree with emulsified rice. And experiments proved that it was so.

O'Leary had brought a bottle of Bourbon so Morgan planned to get him drunk one night, which wasn't difficult since a double whisky poured into his tiny frame amounted to a quadruple for someone of Morgan' size. When he was good and truly soaked O'Leary began to babble about Vietnam:

"We lost it Morgue. We well and truly have. Would you believe? Uncle Sam beat all to hell by a bunch of skinny peasants in black pyjamas? All we're doin' is cowerin' behind hah walls. The gooks control the countryside out there – and the towns. What in hell we're doin' out in 'Nam any more ah cain't tell you. Tryin' to fool ourselves, or the folks back home?"

Then he began to cry:

"You know how proud I was to go Morgue. Faht for my country an' all. Now ah'm ashamed. Yew know what ah do?"

He burped and dried his eyes on his sleeve.

"The only thing we do naow is mount the odd 'Aggressive Patrol'. That's what they call 'em. We put five hundred guys in fifty vehicles, armed to the teeth, then we open the gates and go lahk a bat outer hell. We don't stop fur nuthin'. We daresn't. We don't stop for chickens. We don't stop for pigs. We charge straight through their villages at fifty miles an hour and don't stop for nuthin'. If we did, some gook hidin' in the crowd, would lob a grenade through a truck window, or launch an RP – a rocket projectile. No sir we don't stop fer nuthin'. Not for an old lady crossin' the road. Not even for a little chahld like your Curly playin' with his friends. No Sir. Jesus Shit!"

He began crying again.

"You know what ah do Morgue? Lootenant O'Leary of the United States Infantry? Honest Jim? Practically the only graduate stoodent patriotic enough, or stoopid enough to faht voluntarily for his country? Know what ah do Morgue? Ah follow in the last jeep of the convoy. Ah got wads of dollar bills packaged up in to five hundreds, thousands and two-thousands. When ah see a kid dead or dyin' beside the road, knocked over by Uncle Sam, ah throw out a five hundred. That's mah orders.

An old lady's worth fahve hundred too. Women and old men is a thousand. And a dead or dyin' peasant man's worth two thousand. Them's mah orders."

Then he began sobbing again:

"Thank the fuck ah ain't drivin' the leading truck – that's all ah kin say. Thank the fuck."

The 'democratic meeting' organised at the Observatory by the main university to discuss the Director's reappointment, turned out to be a farce. Everyone somehow crowded into the seminar room, from the senior astronomers to the tea ladies, nearly two hundred in all, many standing in the aisles or round the wall.

As the Deputy Director, Doolan commenced the proceedings by shouting above the hubbub:

"Come on. Pipe down! This isn't a bloody Two-Up at Randwick racecourse."

When some silence had been secured he introduced a man in a dark suit:

"This is Professor Simons, who is representing the Vice Chancellor. He will chair the meeting to hear your views on the Directorship of this Observatory and Siding Springs. Professor Oliver Bacon our present director has volunteered to continue in his post – which is the normal state of affairs. However if some of youse out there are daft enough to disagree, now's yer chance to speak out and state yer views. My secretary Josie will be taking a record of the proceedings. Professor Simons."

Professor Simons rose to his feet, looking rather uncomfortable:

"I don't think it would be appropriate to take a record of the proceedings. After all we're all friends here. Aren't we?" He didn't sound too sure. "It is my duty to convey a sense of this meeting back to the Vice Chancellor. No names no pack drill. Hah hah."

There was no response from the audience.

"And I don't think that Dr Doolan presented the situation as uh….as accurately as one could wish. You see there's no presupposition that your present director, Professor Oliver Bacon, will stay on – or indeed leave. There is no, shall we say, no normative expectation in these circumstances. While Directors are appointed as permanent professors, the actual office of director is a temporary thing, renewable, or not, as the case may be, by the Vice Chancellor in concert with his many advisers. And amongst his advisers he counts the staff of the institution concerned, in this case the university's astronomical observatories. Do I make myself clear?"

Josie, Bruce Doolan's secretary, was writing furiously.

"I'd rather you didn't my dear. Really I would. After all the VC wants these proceedings to be free and easy. People must not feel that any remarks they may choose to make are being recorded, and may later be used…… against them….if you ah follow what I mean. Ha ha."

Josie looked at Doolan, who nodded. Then Doolan slipped out of the room.

"Well then, I think we should start. Who's got anything to say?"

He looked around. Nobody spoke. When his eyes rested on this or that individual they looked away, or down at the floor. A minute passed. Almost two.

"Am I to assume then that you are all happy with the situation as it is then?"

Again there was along silence. Eventually Morgan got to his feet:

"I don't think you can sir. If I am any judge of the feeling here among the staff, especially among the astronomers, then Professor Bacon is generally regarded as a failed director."

"May I ask why?"

"Certainly. First and foremost because he has made enemies of practically every Australian astronomer not at this observatory. That can easily be corroborated. We are thus completely isolated."

There were gasps all round the auditorium. Doolan had returned with Bacon himself waddling in tow. Everyone stared at Bacon, apart from Morgan who apparently hadn't seen him, and Simons who was listening to Morgan, and scribbling in his notebook.

"Just as bad," Morgan continued "He has managed to alienate the British astronomical community with his foolish plan to take over the new Anglo Australian Observatory. As a result the headquarters have gone to Sydney instead of coming here, as we all naturally expected."

Simons jotted something in his note book. Greg Anson, who was sitting three rows in front of Morgan, tried to mouth a warning at him but Morgan was too busy selecting his words to notice:

"Second because his man-management, if you can call it that, is appalling. I can assure you that in the British Army he would never make the lowest grade of non-commissioned officer, that is to say a Lance Corporal."

"I'm afraid you have to be more specific." Simons interrupted.

"For a start he doesn't get out of bed until about two in the afternoon."

There were more gasps around the auditorium.

"Go on." Simons jotted in his notebook.

"Then again he promotes into positions of authority people utterly unfitted to the task."

"Be specific please."

" I could start at the top. However let me concentrate on a matter where the records can speak for themselves. Bacon recently appointed as Chief Engineer a young man called Wayne McGarrity – who turned out to be an imposter. McGarrity persuaded Bacon, through his deputy Doolan, to mortgage the observatory's entire engineering budget for three years ahead, in order to purchase a new and totally unnecessary computing network, and a digital television system that will never do, could never do useful astronomy. As a result the observatory is now virtually bankrupt."

"I take it you can back up such accusations?" Simons continued busily jotting. The whole audience stared from Bacon's face to Doolan's and back to Bacon again.

"Oh yes of course. As I could demonstrate, as many here could, the total incompetence of his second-in-command Dr Bruce Doolan, who has just sidled back into this room with no less than Professor Oliver Bacon in tow."

Uproar broke out. Doolan screamed at Morgan. Simons tried ineffectually to shut both Doolan and Morgan up. Many got up and escaped through the rear door, hoping they wouldn't be seen – especially by Bacon. People were arguing with one another. Nobody had realised that Morgan had been aware of Bacon's presence all along. Simons tried to establish some sort of order:

"I really must ask for you all to speak only when called to do so by the chairman. That is to say by me. Continue Mr ...Mr...?"

"Morgan. Dr Twm Morgan. Astronomer."

"He's just a bleeding Pom." Doolan screeched. "He doesn't speak for any of us Aussies!"

"I must ask you" Simons did a bit of screaming himself "I must ask you, especially you Dr Doolan, who ought to set an example, to stick to the procedural rules. Otherwise I shall have to clear the room and so end this meeting. Do I make myself clear?"

The hubbub gradually subsided.

"Continue Dr Morgan if you please!"

"There's a lot more I could say about the unsuitability of Professor Bacon as a director. For instance that he appropriates to himself the observatory's entire foreign travel budget – which is an absolute scandal, a scandal."

"Yer liar." Doolan couldn't control himself.

"That he has installed his mistress Mrs Bulstrode as the Superintendent up at Siding Springs. It wouldn't matter quite so much if she could cook, but even he agrees that she can't because he has himself fed a separate diet while we have to try and digest her dinosaur gristle and......"

Roars of laughter and ribald suggestions greeted this last sally

"And look at him!" Morgan, who had a very loud voice, turned dramatically and pointed an accusatory finger at Bacon :

"Just look at him. Utterly shameless! Even I find it hard to believe that he would butt into a meeting designed to discuss his own directorship. His presence here, Mr Chairman, can have no other purpose than to intimidate his staff, to prevent the full and fair expression of the general opinion. We ask you to eject him! Eject him!"

There were roars of approval from some of the audience. Simons who'd been staring at Bacon in amazement, took some time to come to his senses.

"Well I have to say this all very irregular. I would have thought..... I mean , so far as I am aware there is no formal ruling.......No precedent. While I understand your concern Dr Morgan I have no power, no power that I am aware of, to ask Professor Bacon to leave. Though his presence here is a circumstance which I shall have to report to the Vice Chancellor."

He wrote pedantically in his notebook.

"Have I the right to continue?" Morgan asked.

"Yes .Yes." Simons was tetchy.

"Keep it short you bugger." Doolan was apoplectic.

"Then I would suggest": Morgan continued, loud enough to be heard above the hubbub "That by his presence here today, Professor Bacon has singularly proved himself unfitted to be the director of this, or indeed any other observatory. Therefore I wish to put a motion to this meeting. May I do so?"

"Yes sir you may."

"I move that, since there can be no free discussion of his position while Professor Bacon is present among us, that all members of staff who so wish should convey their opinion as to his continued directorship, in writing and in confidence, to you as the Vice Chancellor's representative. I so move this motion."

Silence fell. Simons jotted in his notebook, then read the motion back to the meeting:

"Now who will second Dr Morgan's motion?"

Nobody moved. Doolan and Bacon glared around the audience. Finally Greg stood up:

"I second the motion."

"Your name please."

"Anson. Dr Greg Anson. Astronomer."

"Not for long you won't be feller." Doolan hissed, only partly under his breath.

"If this motion is passed I think we can assume the meeting will be over. Over, that is, apart from administrative arrangements. So I am going to ask for a show of hands. Those in favour of Dr Morgan's motion raise your hands."

More than half the audience raised their arms. Hardly any dared look at Bacon.

"Those against?"

A much smaller number of hands were raised, but those that did looked at the director.

"I therefore declare the motion is carried. We need to arrange how the letters shall be forwarded to me. I propose they be sent, sealed of course, to the observatory secretary here within seventy two hours, and he or she will forward them to me. Is that satisfactory?"

To general relief most nodded, and the meeting broke up.

A few nights later, while Morgan was working on his Dark Matter notebook at home, the phone rang. It was Greg Anson. He sounded shaken:

"You'll never guess what's happened Tom."

"I'll never guess."

"Bacon just rang me. He and Doolan had been reading my letter to the Vice Chancellor."

"Christ they can't do that. Those letters were sealed and confidential."

"Well they have. There can be doubt of it. He even quoted a passage back at me."

"My God! It beggars belief Greg. What else did he say?"

"He said my job was over. He's terminating my contract at one month's notice."

"He can't do that!"

"Apparently he can. Mine was always a special contract – me being a geophysicist by rights. My contract was to last only so long as the Solar-Star project was vital."

"Which it is for God's sake."

" I know. But that's for him to decide. He's decided."

"But, but……." Morgan was aghast at Fat Sow's behaviour. And yet, he realised, he shouldn't be surprised. Bacon had never exhibited the slightest sign of either shame or conscience.

"He's given me an alternative." Greg continued. "If I turn up in the morning and ask for my letter back, all will be forgotten."

"Phew."

"What shall I do Tom? If I get fired Tidbinbilla will have to go. We've got a colossal mortgage. The horses will all have to be put down. That'll break Penny's heart. We'll probably have to leave the Canberra area. Kylie will have to be pulled out of her adult shelter program. God knows how she'll take that. Picton's a sheep dog. We can't take him to live in a city. It goes on and on."

"What Bacon has done is criminal." Morgan was thinking aloud. "If we could prove he'd done it he'd be finished. And not just as director. They'd have to fire him."

"How?" Greg interrupted "How could we prove it? He's no fool. My word against his? Innocent until proved guilty. No chance. My brain has been racing round that for sixty minutes."

"Have you spoken to Penny?"

"No way mate. No way."

"Why not?"

"Because Penny's solid gold through and through. She'd desperately want me to withdraw that letter. For Kylie's sake. For the horses' sake. For Tidbinbilla, for herself……. But she'd never ask. And she'd go to her grave would Pen, never reproaching me even once, if I went through with it and got us all tossed out and into the shit."

"I see your point. What a woman you've got."

"Haven't I just. So what am I going to do Tom? What would you do in my position?"

Morgan was silent.

"What would you think of me Tom, if I withdrew that letter?"

There was along silence before Morgan replied:

"I'm just bloody glad I'm not in your position Greg. Bloody glad. I'm not going to be sitting in judgement on anyone……"

The next morning Greg avoided him at the observatory. In the afternoon there was an unprecedented commotion. Senior police officers were seen going in and out of Bacon's office. Secretaries were questioned. Forensic tests were carried out. Rumours flew round the hilltop community: 'Bacon was to be arrested for fraud; no he wasn't, don't be stupid, thieves have broken into his office; rubbish – it was obviously those letters to the Vice-Chancellor – and they wouldn't be in his office would they?; large quantities of money were missing; no they weren't, Bacon has been forging his travel expenses – to pay alimony to his four wives back in California.'

Two days longer Greg avoided Morgan, while the output of the rumour factory grew ever more fantastical. Finally everyone was called to an emergency meeting in the seminar room – which was barely large enough to squeeze them in. They were all there: machinists, opticians, electronic engineers, night assistants, secretarial and administrative staff, gardeners, cleaners, draughtsmen, graduate students and of course astronomers.

At the front facing them stood Bacon, Professor Simons from the Vice Chancellors Office and, in full uniform, a Superintendent O'Rourke from the Criminal Investigation Division of The Federal Police.

Bacon, fatter than ever, and peering at them through his owl glasses, called the meeting to order. Greg was sitting three seats along in the same row as Morgan.

"Over the past few days you will all have been wondering what has been going on." Bacon's American accent was pronounced. "The fact is somebody broke into my office in the early hours of Toosday morning and removed some very important and confidential papers."

There was hubbub among the ranks with plenty of 'I told you sos' audible. Morgan immediately looked along the row at Greg who was biting his lip.

"Those papers" Bacon continued "Turned up in the Vice Chancellor's Office. They are the subject of a major police investigation, led by Superintendent O'Rourke on my left. Whoever stole those papers is a criminal, and he will now suffer the full penalty of the law. But before we go into the police investigation Professor Simons on my right will speak to us on behalf of the Vice-Chancellor."

The assembly fell completely silent as Simons started in his reedy academic voice:

" Let me begin by reiterating, in the strongest possible terms, what your Director Professor Bacon has just intimated. The Vice Chancellor regards this matter in the gravest possible light. The very gravest. The theft of confidential papers is, in any circumstances, a very serious matter, a very serious matter indeed. But when those papers deal, as they do here, with the possible replacement of a Director, the matter assumes an even darker aspect. Whoever took those papers intended to meddle with men's careers, with men's lives; to influence and cheat the course of justice and fair play. Therefore The Vice Chancellor is minded to regard this as a serious criminal matter. The culprit, whoever he may be, and I am assured by Superintendent O'Rourke that he will shortly be apprehended on the basis of forensic evidence, the culprit will be prosecuted to the full extent of the Law. The University will spare no expense to bring a trial about, and to ask for the severest punishment – which might include a Long Sentence in Gaol." He paused to let the threat, in capital letters, sink in. Morgan was still staring at Greg, who in turn was biting the knuckle on his thumb. Simons looked down at his notes before resuming:

"We've called you all here today to explain what is to happen next. Every employee of the observatory, regardless of status, will undergo a fingerprint test."

There was widespread consternation and muttering among the audience.

"There are two finger-print experts waiting in the foyer outside this room as you file out. You are obliged to supply your fingerprints, so our legal advisers inform us, as part of your employment contract. However, and I want to reassure you all of this, your fingerprint data will be destroyed as soon as this particular investigation and prosecution, is over, and will not go into the permanent police files. Superintendent O'Rourke can assure you of this." O'Rourke nodded.

"Now you will agree that this is all very distasteful indeed, particularly so in an institute like this dedicated to scholarship and impersonal research. But we are determined to apprehend the culprit, and the culprit has left his finger-prints all over the missing file." He looked at O'Rourke, who nodded positively again.

"However the Vice Chancellor would like to avoid, so far as he can, bringing the Observatory, and of course the wider university, into public disrepute. One can imagine the lurid stories if the gutter press were to make wild with this incident. Therefore the Vice Chancellor is minded to offer a measure of clemency to the culprit in return for a confession. Should the culprit stand up now and confess, so saving us all the unpleasantness of a police investigation, fingerprinting and so forth, the Vice Chancellor agrees to drop the criminal investigation. The culprit will however suffer instant dismissal. He could, of course, expect no less. So, I am asking the culprit to stand up."

People began looking round them. Those at the front craned their necks to look back. Those at the back looked to either side. Many stared straight at Morgan. Nobody rose to confess.

"I know this can't be easy." Simons resumed. "Let us all be silent and close our eyes for a moment to reflect. What was done may have been done in a moment of passion or fear, and is much regretted now. Let us not condemn. Let us silently pray that that person, who may have done what he did for good, if misguided, reasons will now reflect and face what he has done."

Simons closed his eyes. A few others followed. Doolan glared straight at Morgan. Anson clenched and unclenched the fists resting on the desk in front of him.

Morgan rose to his feet. There was a collective expulsion of breathe.

"OK, I want to say something."

All heads turned.

" Late on Monday night Professor Bacon made a telephone call. He said he'd confiscated and opened some of the sealed, confidential letters sent by us, regarding the directorship, and intended for the Vice Chancellor's eyes only."

The audience turned as one to stare at Bacon who waved his arm in dismissal. Then everyone began talking at once before Morgan stopped them with his stentorian voice:

"I haven't finished yet. Bacon threatened me with instant dismissal unless I withdrew my very critical letter the next morning. The thought of that man attempting to pervert the course of justice, sitting there like a blackmailer and steaming honest people's mail open, enraged me beyond endurance. But as you all know, he sleeps through the morning like a pig. It was easy for me to get into his office, to take those letters back and then deliver them to the V-C's office anonymously. So you don't have to take my finger prints. I did it. And I am proud of having done so. But the question you should all be asking, and in particular the V-C should be asking, is what were those letters doing in Professor Bacon's possession in the first place? He was the very last person who should have touched them or read them. The very last person on this Earth. He's the one whose' fingerprints should be taken. He's the one who has been meddling in the course of justice – and been caught red-handed."

During the ensuing uproar Greg Anson stared at Morgan, his mouth wide open. Morgan didn't look in his direction.

Morgan, who was put under instant suspension, collected his papers and drove down to Tidbinbilla to pick up Curly. Greg was waiting for him, sitting on the bonnet of his ute at the farm gate, which was well away from the homestead.

"What on Earth did you do that for?" he demanded as Morgan stepped down from his van. "I reckon they were bluffing. You can't get decent fingerprints off a cardboard file. I was going to call their bluff."

"We couldn't take the chance." Morgan responded.

"*We* couldn't take the chance? It was my chance to take, not yours."

"It was brave thing to do Greg. I admire you."

"You do do you? Well I don't. I didn't mean to steal the bloody things. I was going there to rat. To pull my letter with nobody knowing. But when I saw those letters all laid out on that bastard's desk – he even had a kettle there for steaming them open – and razor blades, I thought 'Damn you, I'll be ashamed all my life if I let you get away with this'. So I stole the lot, wrapped them in newspaper, dropped them anonymously with some girl in the V-C's outer office. And I've been shaking in my shoes ever since."

"How did you get into his office? In case the police ask me."

"No problem. Jemmied it open with a claw hammer. There's no one about at six am. But why did you have to take the flamin' blame?"

"Because you have too much to lose and I haven't." Morgan waved his hands about at the farm, and at two old Shires who had come to make friends with them over the gate. They went over and nuzzled one each. Greg took two cubes of sugar out of his pocket and gave one to Morgan:

"I don't know how I'm ever going to thank you mate."

"Well I do Greg." Morgan let the great horse take the sugar off his palm with its lips. "You finish your solar-star project. That's what I was thinking of. Never let anything or anybody stand in its way. All mankind needs that. And let's not talk of this ever again. Not to Penny. Not to Annie. Not even to each other. Come on, Curly'll be screaming for his tea."

Morgan wasn't dismissed instantaneously. The university, in the person of Professor Simons, was too much interested in the circumstances leading up to the burglary to dispense with their chief witness. At Morgan's instigation they also interviewed Greg Anson about the telephone call he had received from Bacon, and Greg was then reassured that his position was safe. It seemed that Bacon, as much as anyone else, was now under investigation.

"You can't leave that creature in charge." Morgan protested to Simons. "Even if I hadn't burgled those letters the staff knew what he was up to. The Administrator's secretary apparently told everybody that he'd come into her office and confiscated the letters. She was shocked and distressed; knew it was immoral and told everyone. Do you know what they call him up there now? 'Steamer Bacon.' He's a laughing stock, as is his revolting girl-friend up at Siding Springs, Mrs Bulstrode. If you'd ever eaten any of her dinosaur gristle you'd know that not only is she not a trained cook – for which no doubt you are paying her a good salary – but she is also misappropriating the catering funds. That should be easy to check."

"I hardly think that is any business of yours."

"Oh isn't it?" Morgan told Simons the story of the T-Bone steak. He went on:

"If you're going to dismiss me then I've got nothing to lose have I? I can go to the papers and tell them the whole tragi-comic story. They'll love it. I bet I could sell it in episodes to The Sydney Morning Herald. They're no friends of either Canberra or The Australian National University. They'll love it. The Wayne McGarrity story alone will make your entire administration look like a laughing stock. Yes I think I'll write that up. Apparently I'm going to need the money."

Simons looked uncomfortable. The University apparently hadn't thought through the full consequences of dismissing Morgan, who obviously wasn't about to make life any easier for them. Realising his advantage Morgan went on:

"I suppose you're going to dismiss me in the end. After all, the burglary is public knowledge by now. But I want my pound of flesh too. I need to finish off my research in Australia, to use my office and to use the library. If you don't lift my suspension and let me get on with it then I'll have to go public."

"But Professor Bacon......"

"Steamer-Bacon – my bloody eye! Suspend him instead of me. He is, in any case, a dead man walking. Who is going to take any notice of him now?"

Simons, who was not unsympathetic towards Morgan, agreed to talk to the Vice – Chancellor, and in the mean time agreed to leave his salary in place. Morgan would need every penny because he would lose his house on the very day of his dismissal. Moreover he would lose his fares back to the UK, which had been a part of his original contract.

Although he put on a brave exterior Morgan was in fact deeply apprehensive inside. He was beginning to regret his over-hasty quixotic act. A junior astronomer, publicly dismissed for theft from his own observatory – for that is how it would look, that is how it would be recorded and remembered, with the extenuating circumstances excised – would be in a hopeless position to get an astronomy job in a ferociously competitive market. And that was the prospect he now faced. All he could do, all that he had done at the prospect of losing Ann, was stick his head in the sand and get on with his research. At least that was an all-consuming consolation.

He was also in a tricky situation over Curly. The formalities of Curly's legal parentage weren't complete, while Karen was lost in the Highlands of New Guinea. He wrote her a letter, pointing out the urgency of the situation, emphasising that she would certainly finish up as the full-time mother if he was thrown out of Australia. After all, his permission to be in the country depended entirely on the work-permit obtained for him by the university. If that was revoked he would be an illegal immigrant, subject to instant deportation, and without Curly. This began to prey on Morgan's mind. If and when he was deported he'd never stand a chance of getting Curly back again. Morgan buried his head in astronomy. There was nothing else he could do.

Morgan's Dark Matter notebooks became his favourite retreat and consolation. In it he was collecting together all the scraps of information that might have a bearing on the eight-hundred pound gorilla: all the observations of Clusters of Galaxies, all the suggestions for wriggling out of the implications, all the observations on the masses of individual galaxies –which turned out to be far skimpier than he had supposed. You could estimate the mass of a galaxy from the amount of starlight it emitted – but that supposed that it contained nothing much else beyond stars, and moreover that those stars were much like the stars in the Milky Way – neither supposition incontestably true. To actually weigh a galaxy you had to measure the gravitational pull it exerted on some other body, say a star on its outskirts, or a dwarf satellite companion galaxy. The trouble was that at the distances of even the nearest galaxies, they, and the stars within them, were exceedingly faint, too faint to make the needful velocity measurements. All that could be done was to measure the rotation rate of the starlight in towards the centre of a galaxy where it looked much brighter. The snag with that was that it measured the mass of the galaxy only interior to the point of measurement, with the great outer part of the galaxy unplumbed. For instance the speed of the Sun in its rotation about the centre of the Milky Way had been ingeniously estimated by Jan Oort from the relative motions of other stars. The Sun was apparently moving at two hundred and fifty kilometres a second in a circle around the centre of the Milky Way, a circle fifty thousand light-years across. It took two hundred and twenty million years to complete a single circuit, from which it could be inferred that the mass of the Milky Way, interior to the Sun, comprised little more than the visible stars. In other words no Dark Matter was called for in the centre of our own galaxy, in flat contradiction to Zwicky's results for galaxies in clusters. And our galaxy wasn't unique. With great difficulty and patience the rotation speeds of other spiral galaxies had been measured revealing that they too were lacking any of the mysterious Dark Matter – in their cores at least. So if the Dark Matter was there – as the cluster observations so clearly suggested that it was – then it had to lie either in their outer halos, or in the totally dark spaces in between galaxies.

The existence, or otherwise, of Dark Matter, had dramatic implications for Cosmology, the study of the Universe as a whole. Cosmology had fascinated Morgan ever since his early days at school reading Einstein's papers on General Relativity. According to Einstein's Field Equations the curvature of Space on its largest scale was intimately related to the amount of mass within it. The more the mass the greater the curvature until, at a certain critical mass, the space would curve right round and close on itself. In other words the Universe would be a giant, but nevertheless finite space. You could start off in a rocket in one direction, travelling in a straight line, and find yourself, billions of years later, coming back to your starting place from the opposite direction, just like a seaman who had circumnavigated the globe.

This idea of a closed finite space was both intriguing and appealing: appealing because the alternative of an infinite Universe, stretching in all directions for ever, seemed utterly incomprehensible and abhorrent.

The intriguing fact was that the mass-density in space required to make the Universe finite wasn't much greater than the value measured for Giant Clusters by Zwicky and his successors. Surely this was too much of a coincidence. Surely, after coming so close, the extra Dark Matter had to exist to bend the Universe into a satisfactorily finite volume? This extra Dark Matter required, or seemingly required by the mathematical theory of curved Space-Time, was referred to as "The Missing Mass.". The Missing Mass was about a thousand time greater than the mass of all the gas, the stars, the galaxies and the Clusters of Galaxies that astronomers could see.

The more Morgan thought about Dark Matter the more fascinated Morgan became. Surely Dark Matter wasn't just the greatest problem in astronomy, it was the greatest problem in all of science. Out there, buried in the sky, there had to be a thousand times more 'stuff' than mankind could presently see. Who else but an extragalactic astronomer like himself was ever going to find it? To spend his nights searching for this Missing Mass, succeeding perhaps, or failing gloriously, seemed to Morgan the most exciting, most desirable life imaginable. What a quest! What an ambition! And that exciting life lay not so very far beyond his grasp. He was perfectly suited to it too – as very few other astronomers were. He had the mathematical background to understand all the Einstein stuff about curved Space-Time, but he was becoming technically proficient too. He had thought as deeply about designing the telescopes and television systems that would be needed to carry out the voyage of discovery as anyone on Earth. Giant arrays, fitted with supersensitive digital cameras, might pin down the elusive Missing Mass at last. If only he could find a job in astronomy, a permanent job free of any short term constraints, he would devote every second of his working life, every fibre of his imagination, to prosecuting the great search.

But there lay the rub. Time was running out on him, and so apparently was luck. His future in Australia must be measured in weeks – possibly days. And where to go to from here? Who would want an astronomer in his mid thirties, indicted for theft, a single father to boot, with a young baby?

But that was the least of it. He had to have an idea too. You couldn't just say 'I'm going to find the Dark Matter' any more than Columbus could say 'I'm going to cross that ocean.'

Columbus had needed a vessel – indeed a small flotilla. Morgan needed an idea, some notion as to how he would set out. And you couldn't just order up ideas out of the dark. Nor was there any point about thinking about darkness itself. He was a scientist, and scientists had to detect and measure things. They had to work with light. And the only light out there coming from the darkness, came from galaxies, those inscrutable question marks in the sky. If he was going to find an idea, stumble across a clue, surely it would come from the galaxies themselves. It had to. There was nothing else out there to speak. So his Dark Matter notebooks were gradually becoming a diary of his exploration among the galaxies. He read, and questioned, anything about galaxies he could find. He used the bibliography in one paper to follow the paper trail of its antecedents back into the past. Back from the 1970s to the 1930s, the 1930s to the 1890s, so on back to William and Caroline Herschel struggling with their home made telescope to catalogue thousands of nebulae from their garden in Bath. Somewhere out there in the darkness, somewhere back there in the mists of Time, someone had surely seen a clue, a small thing perhaps, barely remarked upon at the time, but clear enough perhaps to a detective like Morgan searching backwards from the perspective of the late twentieth century.

What kind of a clue could it be, he wondered. It might be an anomaly, something that didn't fit in with everything else, analogous to the fossil of a creature not present on the Earth any more. Or it might be a pattern, scarcely noticed at the time, analogous to the succession of gradually changing fossils seen as one mined down a geological excavation, from the upper beds toward the bottom. From such tiny clues men like Hutton and Smith had deciphered the history of the Earth. And Charles Darwin had stumbled upon Evolution from an even tinier clue, the variation in a Finch's beak from one island of the Galapagos archipelago to the next. Extensive exploration and painstaking observation – these had been their watchwords, as they now had to be his. He was an impatient, lazy man, always eager to move on. An explorer? Yes. But a painstaking recorder and appraiser of all he saw? No. That would have to change. He had to re-grow himself. His Dark Matter Notebook was a start. Indeed it had already grown into three volumes, each one recording his reading, and his reflections on what he had read. The frenetic rushing from one project to the next – which had marked his astronomical life so far, would have to change too. He would have to follow the example of the old masters like Alfred Russell Wallace. Brought up at Usk in Wales, a poor man with none of the advantages of Charles Darwin, twice a millionaire, Wallace had made his meagre living collecting plants and butterflies in the remotest jungles of Amazonia and the East Indies. Waking in his hammock from a malarial fever he had realised, quite independently of Darwin, that plants and animals had evolved from one another under the pressure to survive and, braver than Darwin, had submitted his outrageous ideas to public scrutiny first. And he'd gone beyond Darwin, far beyond in one critical respect. He had recognised and recorded the stark bio-geographical boundaries that sometimes existed between one chain of islands and the next. How could islands so apparently close in geographical terms, be so entirely distinct in the populations of plants and animals that inhabited them? It was a crucial stepping-stone towards the idea of Continental Drift which was only now becoming respectable, a whole century later. Morgan had to become more like Wallace, more like Darwin, more like Hutton and Smith, a recorder of trifles, and a reflector on what they meant. Where was the hidden pattern, where the unconsidered clue? To give him inspiration he read about such mens' lives; they became close to him, closer even than his friends in Australia. They became his companions and guides in a search which would, above all, require fortitude, patience and imagination. After collecting for four years in the Amazon rain forest Wallace took his whole collection on board ship in 1852 for the voyage home. The ship caught fire and every single item, every precious orchid, butterfly, bird and animal, all his hopes of remuneration, even his notes and diaries were lost to the sea. Wallace gathered himself together and set off alone for another lonely eight years collecting in the East Indies. What a superman, and what a gay, modest one at that. From now on Morgan determined to travel with the great men only, to measure his own standards by theirs, to forget his mundane colleagues such as Doolan and, if necessary, to carry on alone. Whatever else his life turned out to be he determined that from now on it should never be petty, even in its tiniest respect. If the rats stole his lunch he would never, as he would have done previously, attempt to go down the hole after them and snatch it back. A big man, he decided, had to be big in all matters. He felt that every pettiness in one aspect of his life would diminish him in all.

The real challenge he faced was that galaxies were hardly brighter than the dimmest parts of the night sky. Accordingly, very few men had had the persistence, the good luck and the right technology to make any progress in their study. William Herschel had, by 1750, constructed the world's finest telescope, which he used to find, and with his sister Caroline to catalogue, over two thousand galaxies, or 'nebulae' as they called them, without knowing what they were. It had taken another hundred years, and the invention of photography, to really 'see' galaxies for the first time as anything more than smudges of light. The next step surely had to be the electro-optic detector, the digital television camera about which Morgan had thought so hard. Not only would such devices be a hundred times more sensitive than the photographic plate, they would never saturate either. You could, in principle, expose them to the night sky for ever, and so go deeper and deeper and deeper. Moreover they had the potential to see radiations beyond the spectral range of the photographic plate or the human eye, ultraviolet and infrared signals bearing entirely new information about galaxies. And all this would happen during the next ten years of Morgan's life. The prospects were heady.

Technology though would not be enough. He still had to find a guiding idea – as Columbus had with his exotic beans in the sand. Stars were understood because of an unexpected pattern in their properties, discovered back in 1913. Ejnar Hertzprung and Henry Norris Russell had independently discovered that there was a one a one-to-one correspondence between the luminosity of a star and its colour. Morgan wondered whether a similar such correspondence, or 'correlation' as it would be called technically, was to be found among the properties of galaxies. He itched to get back into the library – but he was now banished from Stromlo. So he rang up Ron Eckersly and drove down to the CSIRO Radiophysics in Sydney.

The jungle drums had been at work and Morgan found himself something of a hero among the radio astronomers, who all loathed Bacon. As before they found him a cabin on site to stay in, while Curly was temporarily accepted into the same day-nursery as the Eckerslys' two children. Curly had howled most dreadfully when Morgan left him there for the first time, but when he peeped back at lunchtime father found son playing with the other kids quite happily. Morgan fled back to the lab, and to its extensive library, and immersed himself in galaxies.

He found that the most extensive list of spiral galaxy measurements had been made by a Swedish astronomer called Erik Holmberg back in the 1940s. Holmberg had gone to work in California and there been given access to the extensive plate material taken at the Mount Wilson Observatory by Edwin Hubble and his colleagues. There he had measured the luminosities, sizes, shapes and colours of hundreds of galaxies. Unfortunately he had then returned to Sweden and published his material in the obscure, extremely obscure 'Archives of the Lund Observatory'. No copy existed in the Radio Physics Library and, so far as Morgan knew, none existed on the continent of Australia. He went to the librarian for help. She explained that a world-wide system of Inter-Library Loans existed. That scholars from one continent could, with patience, and a fee, get their hands, or at least their eyes, on archives existing in dusty vaults in another. Impatiently Morgan payed the fee out of his own pocket and asked that a photocopy be made in Lund and forwarded on to him via Ron Eckersly in Australia.

The next item of interest was the discovery, or rather re-discovery of a paper written by Robert Fish, a student at the University of California Berkeley. Wagoner had pointed the paper out to him back in Arizona where Morgan had ransacked it for a particular number, without paying much heed to the rest. Now he re-read it carefully. Fish had taken plates of thirty Elliptical galaxies and found a rather remarkable result which Morgan explained to Eckersly over sandwich lunch:

"This guy has shown that the Binding Energies of Elliptical galaxies rise as the three halves power of their masses. What the hell could that mean?"

Eckersly wanted to know exactly how Fish had measured his two quantities. Morgan explained.

"If you ask me Tom he hasn't measured either – I mean either masses or binding energies. He must have measured some other things – and used them as proxies."

As soon as Ron said it Morgan realised he must be right. There was no way he could measure either the mass or the binding energy of a galaxy directly. So how had Fish inferred those properties, and were his inferences justified? He took out his fountain pen and began doing algebra on his sandwich bag. He was interrupted when Eckersly gripped his arm and hissed:

"Look who's just come in Tom. Bill Kretchmaier."

Morgan looked up to see a large middle-aged man standing in the lunch queue talking to several others.

"So?"

"It's Kretchmaier you drongo. He's just been appointed Director of the Anglo Australian Telescope."

"I didn't know."

"Well you do now. It was announced last week. He's just come over from California for a couple of weeks to get things going. He could be our new boss – yours and mine – if we're lucky."

Morgan looked at the legendary instrumentalist with new interest. Blond haired and blue eyed he was extravagantly handsome. And well dressed, unlike your typical scruffy astronomer.

As he and his companions brought lunch trays in their general direction Ron Eckersly stood up:

"Bill, this is Tom Morgan from Mount Stromlo, the guy you were asking after."

"Kretchmaier's eyes lit up with pleasure. He put down his tray and shook hands vigorously with Morgan:

"Just the guy I wanted to see. Just the guy. I was thinking of paying a flying visit up to Canberra just to see you. But this is better, much better. I'm busy right now. Can you come by my office at three? I'd appreciate it."

Kretchmaier was charming and friendly. When Morgan explained his awkward position at Stromlo Kretchmaier bust into laughter:

"Why everybody in astronomy knows about your little local difficulty Tom. It's the talk of the town back in California. You know what gossips astronomers are. More power to your arm I say. Bacon's a truly spherical bastard. So what research are you doing?"

Morgan explained about his radio galaxies, and his work on AP Lib with its connection to the quasar-distance problem, because he knew Kretchmaier was an expert on quasar spectra.

"Yes, John Bolton told me about that. If you can crack the distance problem it will make a huge difference to our whole subject. Right now it's *the* crucial issue. But it sounds tough, real tough. Did you know Bev Oke and Jim Gunn are trying to do exactly the same thing at Palomar – on a different but very similar object? 'BL Lac' they call it. They claim they've got a redshift for it – but I'm not convinced."

Morgan's heart fell – was he going to be pipped at the post again?

"But it's not that I want to talk about – it's this."

Morgan recognised a photocopy of his television paper on Kretchmaier's desk.

"Boy, this is a Lu-Lu. I picked it up as the plane took off from Frisco and I was still reading it when we let down into Sydney thirteen hours later. What insight. This s my field you know, but you're out on your own Tom. You've seen further into the future than anybody. This is the map. Do you want to come work with me on the AAT?"

"Of course!" Morgan's heart leapt.

"I want you to be my second in command."

Morgan couldn't believe it. He didn't know what to say. All he could do was stutter:

"B...But why me?"

Kretchmaier laughed loud and long: "A modest astronomer eh? I'm not used to those Tom. But look it's natural. You're a hot shot observer. That Crab pulsar stuff was amazing. Then, so I understand, you're the only astronomer in Australia who talks to all three groups. And that will be crucially important to me. I don't know shit from shinola out here. You'd be my eyes and my ears within the Australian astronomical community. And then there's this!"

He picked up Morgan's paper, stood up and banged the paper on his desk. Suddenly he looked serious:

"You know what we've got to do Tom? You know what the Brits and the Aussies want us to do? They want us to be the best goddamned telescope in the world; to overtake the 200-inch by a mile. And you know what that means? It means assembling the most sensitive detectors and instruments ever built. I know all about spectrographs, and the detectors to go on them. You'd lead the way with astronomical imaging. I know you could do it. You really understand this stuff." He banged Tom's paper again. "You could lead us so far out ahead that Palomar wouldn't catch us up in a generation. Come on, lets go outside – I'll show you where our new offices are going to be built. Then we'll go out and I'll treat you to the best goddamned dinner in all of Sydney because I'm off to see the telescope in the morning. I'd take you with me – if it wasn't for your little local difficulty." And he roared with laughter, slapping Morgan hard on the back again; "Boy we'll show those crumbs from Palomar. They won't know what hit 'em."

Over dinner Ktretchmaier explained that he wanted to offer Morgan a ten year contract, with a salary eight times what Morgan was getting now.

It all made Morgan giddy.

"But I can't offer you a hard and fast contract right now. All positions have to be approved by the Anglo Australian Telescope Board in six months time. But boy I'll be mad if they don't grant me this one. Hopping mad. As I see it Tom you're crucial to the AAT; in fact the key. Can you hang on until then? I only wish I could put you on the books tonight. But there's no salary money for now. Not even mine. This is just a temporary consultancy. But hang in there Tom, hang in there."

Absolutely elated Morgan went back to the Eckerslys to pick up Curly. Ron was thrilled for Tom, and woke up Kay to tell her the good news.

As he departed, with Curly wrapped up in a blanket in his arms, he turned back:

"I do wish Annie could be here to share this amazing news. It's only half real without her Ron. She so wanted to come to Sydney. And now she can. I'm going to stay up all night and write her the longest letter."

The following day Morgan received a telegram from Karen in Canberra saying she had come back from PNG especially to sort out Kirralees's status, and demanding his immediate return. Given Karen's attitude the matter was comparatively straightforward, though drawn out into a number of legal stages so as to provide incomes for as many lawyers as possible. Indeed Morgan had to employ a lawyer himself and was indiscreet enough to tell the man what an urgent plight he was in – with the possibility of being deported before the case was settled. The lawyer then decided it would be rather nice to demand all of Morgan's savings – a demand Morgan was now in no position to refuse. Expecting a letter of dismissal from the University at any moment he simply had to get Curly onto his British passport. By the time the lawyer had finished with him Morgan didn't own a penny in the world. Even the Vee-Dub had been mortgaged to the Bank to pay the second set of legal fees. The end of it all was a single line added to Morgan's passport under 'Children travelling with the holder…' which read 'Kiralee Ianto Morgan, born Canberra Australia……197….., and stamped by the British High Commission in Australia.

At the very last moment Karen showed some regrets, realising she would probably never see Kirralee again. But Morgan promised to keep in touch and to tell Curly all about his Mum when he was old enough to understand. Then they ran Karen out to Canberra airport where she cuddled her bewildered son for the last time, gave Morgan a hug, and disappeared back into Stone-age Papua New Guinea.

Greg and Penny Anson were thrilled to hear Morgan's news about the AAT job and even more thrilled to hear that he would be coming back to Australia one day, albeit to Sydney.

"I don't know what we'd have told Kylie otherwise." Penny admitted. "She's like a little mother to Kirralee isn't she? She carries him all over the place even now that he's old enough to walk. And she pines for him when he's away. Look at them now."

Kylie was holding Curly upright in her arms, talking to him in her Kylie tongue – which he seemed to understand perfectly – while the two of them watched her brothers convey a basket across the Murrumbidgee by the rope transporter they had slung between a gum tree on one side and a casuarina on the other.

"They're building another camp over there" Greg explained "So they can fossick for alluvial gold. I found them some old pulleys and they're working on a horse-powered ferry to draw them back and forth. Such ferries used to be common round here in the old days."

"What a life your kids lead." Morgan envied them: "I only hope Curly is half so lucky. I was brought up wild in a seaside village in Wales – and I realize now just how fortunate I was. Poor old Curly will probably grow up in some wretched suburb where the most exciting thing will be soccer on Saturday afternoon in the park. No dens, no tree-houses, no midnight fishing, no fossicking for gold, no rabbiting with your dog, no building forts and fighting with the enemy gang.....how can such boys ever grow up to be men? The truth is they can't. What the hell is the good of homework and 'The Muppet Show' instead?"

The dreaded letter from the University came soon enough:

Dear Dr Morgan

This is to confirm that your dismissal from the University will take effect from   197..... Seeing that you have confessed to the offence of stealing confidential University property, there can be no right of appeal. We have informed the immigration authorities of your dismissal and you have notice to quit Australia within 24 hours of the above date.

Although the University would be within its rights to revoke the privilege, we have decided, in view of the very short notice, to purchase single economy-class air tickets to the United Kingdom, for you and your family, provided only that they are used on or before the aforesaid date. You should contact the Bursar's Office immediately.

You are further served notice to vacate your dwelling as soon as possible, but certainly before the aforesaid date of dismissal. The University Housing Officer will be in touch with you urgently on the matter. Again, in view of the short notice, the new Director of Mount Stromlo And Siding Springs Observatories, Professor Bruce Doolan, has kindly granted you five days grace from the date of this letter to remove all your effects from the Observatory After that you will be persona-non-grata, and any effects remaining will be impounded.

In view of the circumstances the University would be within its rights to deny you any further emoluments. However the Vice Chancellor is minded, as an act of mercy, and under strict conditions, to pay you three months of salary beyond the date of your dismissal. The conditions being that you report to the Australian High Commission in London on or before   …th, with your passport stamped with its re-entry date to the United Kingdom. Once the High Commission has confirmed to us that you have so complied, the salary will be paid to the UK bank of your choice on a monthly basis. However note that the salary payments can be halted entirely at the Vice Chancellor's discretion if he felt you were bringing further dishonour to the University's reputation. I hope I make myself crystal clear on this point.

If you should require an employee's reference from us Professor Doolan has agreed to supply one which would not make specific reference to the precise circumstances of your dismissal.

Yours Sincerely ………..

Morgan sat at the breakfast table stunned. The letter was so cold, so immediate, so final. Somehow, childishly, he'd been hoping for a magic reprieve. He glanced at his watch. Within less than twelve days they would have to leave Australia. He looked at Curly who was half eating his egg soldiers, half smearing them all over his face. How he would miss Kylie and all his other two- and four-legged friends out at Tidbinbilla. Morgan glanced out of the window; it was a blustery Autumn day with pink galahs swaying about comically as they tried to cling on to telephone wires in the wind. Some of them had lost it entirely and were hanging upside down, flapping furiously. He'd miss them, and he'd miss the Vee Dub which was catching the morning sun on its white paintwork. They must have spent a hundred nights sleeping out in her in many a lonely camp in the bush.

He was so stunned that it took time for the bit about the new directorship to sink in: 'Professor Bruce Doolan' – was it a joke? And where was Fat Sow Bacon? He rang Greg up at the Observatory. Anson greeted him:

"Tom! I was about to ring you. They've just put this notice up in the foyer. You'll never guess what it says."

"Go on."

"It says; 'Professor Oliver Bacon has decided to return to the USA to resume his chair at The University of California. Dr. Bruce Doolan has been promoted to Full Professor and will take up the directorship of the combined observatories with immediate effect'. Signed by the VC. Fat Sow's been fired Tom. He's been fired. We've done it!"

"He's not the only one." Morgan explained his predicament: "But I couldn't stay on under 'Professor' Brucie Doolan anyway Greg. Isn't that a sick joke? That can only be Senator Micky Doolan's doing. Do you know 'Professor Doolan' has 'kindly offered to supply me with an employment reference'?"

Morgan broke into a mad laugh and slammed down the phone. He didn't trust his voice any longer.

"What's wrong Daddy?" Curly looked alarmed. Morgan lifted him out of his chair and gave him a cuddle, as much to comfort himself as to console his son:

"It's a cruel world out there Curly-boy. Don't you be in any hurry to grow up. We're going home to Britain. You'll see Aunty Annie, and Grandma, and Uncle Bob Salt and…..all sorts of nice people you've never seen before."

"I don't want to see Auntie Annie." Curly said perspicaciously, "I want to see Kylie."

"OK old chap." Morgan put him down. "You run upstairs and get Teddy. We'll drive straight out to Tidbinbilla and drop you off with Kylie. Daddy's got so much to do; so little time to do it in."

Indeed Morgan had very little time in which to sleep so long as he remained in Australia. That of course was the university's intention. They had no wish to leave him with time to contact the media or write articles. And once out of the country he'd be harmless.

Morgan's prime concern was to rescue as much of his nearly three years of research as he could. There were crates of data, and a dozen papers to be written somehow, somewhere. So he raced up to the observatory, only to find himself a pariah. The Australian astronomers, apart from Greg, were too mindful of their own skins to show any friendship to a man known to be the sworn enemy of their new Director. 'So much for Australian mateship.' Morgan snarled.

The saddest thing was to leave AP Lib and the quasar distance problem uncompleted: three years hard work with the end so near, and yet so very far. He thought of handing it all over to some other extragalactic astronomer on Mount Stromlo but couldn't bring himself to do it. Especially after they'd behaved so cravenly.

So, on his very last night, when he had only until dawn to be off the premises for the last time, he decided to have one last shot. All of the dozen best spectra of AP Lib, nearly all taken by him, but one or two by other astronomers, had been traced out on rolls of paper about twelve feet long. Since the office building was deserted at one in the morning he laid the sheets out in the corridor, one above the other, their ends held down with books. He stood back and looked down upon the wobbly ink traces. There were no obvious features in any of them. What he decided to do was mark the ten most prominent squiggles on each of them, then to measure the wavelengths of those squiggles with a ruler to see if any of them corresponded.

Careful to mark each spectrum out of sight of, and therefore uninfluenced by the rest, he quickly marked exactly ten of the tallest peaks and lowest dips on each tracing. Having done all dozen rolls he measured the position of each and every squiggle with a ruler, recording the results in his observing note-book. Lastly he converted the measurements into wavelengths with his slide-rule. To have done so earlier might have made him prone to bias.

The results astonished him. On each spectrum there were four or five squiggles which corresponded exactly in wavelength with squiggles in other spectra. Some of the commonest such features corresponded in wavelength with well known absorption-lines in the atmosphere. They were no help astrophysically but at least they were real, not chimerical figments of his imagination. Most of the remainder corresponded with no wavelength with which he was familiar. But that was as it should be. The object would certainly be redshifted, thus altering the original wavelength to its measured value. But the redshift would not alter the *ratio* of the wavelengths to one another. So Morgan worked out the ratios of all the squiggle-wavelengths to one another with his slide-rule. Then he looked in his note-book for the wavelengths of all the best known galaxy and quasar spectral lines and worked out the ratios of those too.

Bang! The result hit him like a thunderbolt. Many of the squiggle-ratios corresponded exactly to the wavelength-ratios of real spectral lines. So they *were* real!

It took but a moment to calculate the redshift of the galaxy lines, and another moment to calculate the redshift of the quasar lines. The two redshifts were identical! He'd solved the quasar redshift problem. The quasar redshifts were identical to the redshifts of the stars in the surrounding galaxy. Both must therefore be redshifted by the expansion of the Universe. No exotic physics, as he had supposed back in Worcestershire, was needed to account for the redshifts. Quasars *were* far out there in the cosmos, at their full redshift distance. There was now no escaping the inference that huge amounts of energy were being generated in tiny volumes. A ten-year battle that had sucked in some of the best scientific brains in the world, was now settled once and for all.

As he carried the last of his dozen cardboard cartons of papers and books out to the Vee Dub, dawn was breaking. A magpie in the tree on the lawn was yodelling towards the East, its breast catching the first roseate hues of the morning sky. Morgan paused to listen, and to whistle back at the bird. Soon they had a duet going. Across the lawns, on the far side of the observatory gardens, he could see the dome of the 74-inch turning pink, the dome of the old British telescope which had gathered all the light from AP Lib.

"You haven't lived in vain." Morgan said to the telescope "But then neither have I."

CHAPTER 16
REVELATION
1974

Cycling through the southern suburbs of Birmingham at quarter to ten at night reminded Morgan viscerally of the days, ten years before, when he used to work the nightshift at the Austin car factory in Longbridge. London might never have happened, nor Arizona, nor Australia. It was if he'd never been an astronomer. The Dunlop dynamo whined against the front tyre with exactly the same sound, the front lamp cast as pathetic a beam into the gutter as the one he'd had back in 1964 before the climbing accident. And here he was going to work the nightshift in another Birmingham factory. As he passed under an orange street lamp he glanced at his watch and realized he was going to cut it fine. It was a hard ten mile pull to the Factory Centre from the Salts' house in the country where he and Curly were staying. Usually he could rely on a Souwesterly wind behind him but tonight it was mostly in his face so that by the time he reached the green at Kings Norton he had only five minutes left before clocking in. As he raced past the public library where he'd spent so much time as a boy, the orange glare from the lights of the furnaces reflected off low cloud, picking out chimney stacks belching black smoke. He was panting hard by the time he'd locked his bike to the railings and run through the door to take his time – card from the rack and put it into the clock to be punched. In his worst nightmare he'd never imagined that such wage slavery would reach out and entrap him again.

The truth was he and Curly badly needed the money. Morgan was happy to live with Bob and Valerie Salt – but he wasn't going to sponge off them and, after his abortive interview with the Vice Chancellor in Canberra, he was damned if he would accept their three months of extra salary as a bribe.

"You've been able to sack that fool Bacon – thanks to me." he'd told the V-C. "Now I ought to be reinstated."

"Professor Bacon wasn't discharged. He went of his own volition."

"No one will believe that."

"No one could prove otherwise."

"Perhaps not. But don't you owe any moral obligation to me?"

"To condone a theft so widely known would be to invite chaos. In any case Professor Doolan would never have you on the premises; he's said as much."

"Another crass appointment."

"You are in no position to comment."

"Oh no? It was I who originally found out that Doolan had appointed an imposter called Wayne McGarrity to a senior position at Stromlo, where he cost you a cool two million bucks. Every single astronomer and engineer and technician at Stromlo knows it was Doolan's blunder. He's a laughing stock, and so will you be now."

The V-C got to his feet decisively:

"You've had your promised ten minutes Dr. Morgan. When I want your advice I'll be sure to ask for it. Meanwhile remember that your three months continued salary is at my personal discretion, has strings attached to it, and can be revoked without notice."

It was the worst possible thing to say to an already enraged Morgan:

"You shove your hush-money up your jaxi. I'll make twice as much publishing this scandal in The Sydney Morning Herald. What's Senator Doolan promised you eh? A knighthood?

I'd forget that if I was you. Early retirement is more on the cards. I'd brush up your flower arranging."

That defiance had been all very well at the time but now he was paying the price for it, or rather trying to earn it.

Morgan's new employer BKL Alloys made high grade Aluminium and Magnesium alloys, mostly for the aircraft industry. They bought scrap aeroplanes, broke them up in the yard at the back, and melted down suitable pieces in open hearth furnaces. Morgan's job was to analyse the melt from the furnaces, and to tell the workers what pure metals had to be added to produce the required alloy. Sometimes they had to add small quantities of trace metals such as Nickel, Zinc or Cobalt, at others reduce the proportion of some deleterious metal such as Silicon by adding ingots of pure Aluminium.

To analyze the small billet which a worker would bring in to the lab, still warm from the furnace, Morgan had a spectrograph which, in principle at least, worked like the ones he was used to on telescopes. Having machined the surface he would pass high voltage sparks into it through a carbon electrode. The brilliant blue sparks evaporated the metal into a glowing vapour whose light was focussed into the spectrograph. Each of the trace metals he was looking for emitted a strong, characteristic emission line, whose strength could be measured with a photo-electric eye. Simple in principle it required conscientious care to get reliable results. Unreliable measurements could lead to the pouring of a whole furnace-load, hundreds of tons of valuable alloy that was 'outside specs'. Unsaleable, it would have to be remelted, ingot by ingot, and reworked all over again.

He'd taken the job because it was reasonably well paid, was only every other week, and because, in principle at least, it would leave him time in between tests to read and think about Dark Matter. The job was both solitary and monotonous, the only excitement being an occasional foray to watch the men at work. The furnace was a glowing swimming-pool of bubbling molten metal, its surface bobbing with filthy dross. Gangs of workmen, some with fork-lift trucks, hauled and hurled clumsy bits of aeroplane into the cauldron, at seeming risk of their lives as splashes of molten metal flew in all directions. Although they were all supposed to wear dark goggles, asbestos helmets and thick protective clothes, the heat was so intense that men stripped off and risked agonising burns. They would boast and show off their terrible scars to one another in the canteen.

When, according to Morgan's measurements, the mix was right, the foreman would order the pouring of the melt and would himself tap out the plug underneath the furnace. In a subterranean hell, the molten liquid would run out along troughs and runnels to where gangs of half naked, sweating workers used giant tongs to heave moulds in and out of the fiery stream. The whole melt would sometimes be poured in a single operation involving hundreds of tons and tens of thousands of ingots. The heat, the clangour, the flickering light, the unrelenting labour of the men, the ordered chaos and the swearing were all on a heroic scale. It was, Morgan imagined, like working the carronades on the lower gun deck of a ship fighting at Trafalgar. But in Birmingham it happened every single night. He experienced a certain pride in being part of such an operation, providing the ultra light, ultra strong metal alloys without which modern jet aircraft could not fly.

Originally Morgan had intended to stay with his mother back in Wales – to which she had returned with his stepfather Maurice. They had bought a house inside the old walls of Tenby town. Morgan had always loved Tenby with its colourful harbour, its two gorgeous beaches and its views East across St Brides Bay towards Monkstone and Amroth, West towards Caldey Island

and the Atlantic approaches. Curly loved the beaches and the boats – which were being readied on the slipways for the coming season. But he didn't like Grandma Blodwen, and Grandma Blodwen certainly didn't like him. It was antipathy at first sight. Naturally Curly was exhausted and fretful after the ghastly twenty-seven hour flight from Australia, but on Blodwen's side the unmistakeable antipathy was inexplicable. She took one look at him and started criticising. He had no manners, he was disobedient, he was noisy, untidy, messy and disrespectful. In fact poor Curly couldn't do a thing right and Blodwen quickly let him know about it. She ticked him off, brushed his hair savagely and stopped him from doing everything he liked doing and was accustomed to.

Morgan was devastated. He had naively supposed that Blodwen would adore her one and only grandson who, everyone said, was the spitting image of his father. Instead she turned into a hectoring, irritated shrew. At first he only remonstrated with his mother, tried to laugh it off. But the tensions became unbearable. In any case Curly, used to a good deal of adulation all round, wasn't having any of it. Normally amenable he now turned purple and shrieked back at Blodwen. If she disliked him he quickly grew to loathe her, and to act as Morgan had never seen him act before. He screamed, he hurled plates of food, he glared at her like an angry Winston Churchill, he broke her ornaments and in general did everything he could to reinforce her already low opinion of him.

The strain on Morgan became intolerable. He loved his mother and he loved Curly. Now he had constantly to intercede between the two. But the two of them hated one another like poison, and Curly, it appeared , was more than capable of giving as good as he got. There were rows, reconciliations, then more explosions. Blodwen sobbed and Curly screamed until Morgan nearly ran away. He roared at both of them, but particularly at Blodwen who was supposed to be grown up.

"If you ask me" his stepfather said, in the pub where they had taken refuge after a particularly frightful eruption "Its pure jealousy. Both of them are used to having your undivided attention. Now they're having to share it. Blodwen's probably too old to yield an inch while Curly is certainly too young. You'll have to move to the caravan."

"What caravan?"

"Your Mum's caravan. It's by the sea near Cardigan.."

"I'd forgotten that. She did write about it."

"She bought it as a seaside retreat when we still lived up near Birmingham. Now that we live here we scarcely go any more. She'd probably let you have that to yourselves."

"What a good idea. We can't stay here Maurice. I'm not having Curly bullied – he's a great little character. But I don't want to break irrevocably with Mam either. But one more blazing row like tonight could do it. I'd be grateful if you'd seed the caravan idea in her mind."

"Unfortunately you can't move in until the official summer season begins. That's one of the regulations with caravans."

"Oh hell! Then we'll have to move out anyway."

Under pretence that it was temporary, Morgan repacked everything and took train for the Midlands where Bob and Valerie Salt were absolutely delighted to see them. They took to Curly at once and the feeling was cautiously, but with growing strength, reciprocated.

With the Wild Goose project flourishing Bob had moved the whole operation to a remote farm. He and Val had moved in to the farmhouse while 'The Skunkworks' was concealed in a large barn labelled 'Aeromodelling Hobbies'.

" As yow can see " said Bob "This house is far too big for oos. We only took it 'cos of the barn. The Yanks'll pay for anythink. And so they bleedin' should an all. They been tryin' to snitch our secrets and undercut our operation. I ain't havin' none of that, They may 'ave their secrets but 'oive got mine an all."

"Don't start on that again our Bob." Valerie ordered "Yow finish a'telling him about the rooms."

"Oh ar."

"What he means" Valerie interrupted "Is some of the rooms upstairs is never used. Some ain't even furnished. Why dain't you and Curly take 'em. We'd be delighted wouldn't we Bob? It'd be loovley to have young faces and young voices around us again. Loovley! We can easy pick oop sticks of furniture for nothink in sales. Please stay."

And so it was arranged. Curly adored people who 'did' things, unlike his father who stared at pieces of paper all day. He trailed around everywhere after Valerie and Bob, Bob in particular.

"The little bastard" as Bob referred to him in wonder "Sticks 'is 'ead into everythink. What a one for askin' questions. I can't answer 'em half the time meself. Why yesstidday he wanted to know why one of our models hadn't got 'fevvers'. Not a bad idea when yow coom to think on it: streamlined, light – no radar reflection. I bet the Yanks never thought on that."

A self-employed chief executive for several years now, Bob Salt was a lot cockier man than Morgan remembered:

"We'm in the front line of the Cold War now Tom." He said proudly. "The Yanks have built that amazin' Blackbird reconnaissance aircraft what can fly at Mach Three and 'as broke all the records. But they wouldn't be showin' it off if it was any damn good now would they? They'd keep it a dead secret – like our stooff. The fact is they daresn't fly it over Roossia – the Russkiis would shoot it down with an even faster missile. So we'm the ones as goes in under the clouds and photographs all their secret installations: air bases, missile sites, nuclear plants, submarine pens… Yow name it, Bob Salt an 'is boys 'ave bin there – at second hand loike. Our Mark Nine is a little beauty, an I mean little. She can fly in at ninety knots for near on seventy hours. She's dead reliable – with the radar signature of a gnat's turd. She joost drops out of the cloud near the target, then pops in again to fly 'ome. We've lost one or two behind the Curtain, probably in turbulence, but they carry demolition charges so any bits what hits the ground would be unrecognizable. That Yankee Blackbird is joost a cover operation, costing billions of dollars, for our stooff."

"It must be a big business now Bob."

"Ar it is an all. We only do the Research and Development stooff 'ere. The operational teams what flies out to Finland or the Arctic, or Alaska, or even Greenland, are based at Boscombe Down in Hampshire, ready to fly out with models at an hours notice. When there's a flap on the Yanks might demand several flights in a week. I only wish our Ernie were 'ere to see it all now. Makes 'is life worthwhile dain't it Tom? An I'll never forget as it was your formula as made this all possible."

"But without Ernie I'd have had no cause to think the formula up. It was Ernie who gave me those first books on aerodynamics. And he asked the crucial question: 'What is the maximum possible range?' In a sense it was more his formula than mine. I just used my mathematics."

"I ain't a goin' to argue with you Tom Morgan. I know 'oo done what. We all played a part."

"You know Bob your accent, and Valerie's, have improved considerably – or should I say 'changed' rather than 'improved'?"

Bob looked uncomfortable:

"It's true we've been 'avin elocution lessons – and we listen to a lot of BBC Radio 4. That slip of a girl Beth, oo's my history assistant, she suggested it. She says as how the British are so snobbish about accents as we'd be short changing ourselves if we dain't learn 'The Kings English' as she calls it – even a bleedin' republican like me. I can talk real posh when I want. But not fer long, and stupid bits of Brum gets a'mixed oop in it. I dain't know as it's a good idea altogether. We'll see. Tell yer what; I shall practice me Kings English on you. When I remember. Yow got a posh accent Tom."

"If you want to. Though personally I like the old 'Brummagem Bob'."

Of course England was Ann; his Annie. Or was she his Annie any more? A mere two hours away from the Salts' farm he could walk in on her any day and discover his fate. He scarcely thought about anything else for long. Everybody was full of contradictory advice. His mother had warned him that, under no circumstances was he to go anywhere near Ann just now 'because it is completely the wrong time'. Ann was seven or eight months pregnant, after yet another miscarriage in Britain, and could think of nothing else but bringing her baby to term. She'd even moved back in with her parents until the baby was born. Blodwen was contemptuous:

"If you ask me you're well rid of her Twm. What's so bloody special about Ann anyway? Men will always take a bit on the side if they get half a chance. It's Nature. They always have and they always will. Intelligent wives find ways to deal with it. Not run off like that and make love to your best friend. How little she must value you!"

"Oh Mam don't go on about it."

"It's about time somebody gave you the straight truth son. Mooning on over her for what – two years now? She's not good enough for you Twm Morgan – not by half. If she didn't realise what a fine man you were before – then she should damn well know now. Look how you've brought up that wretched baby – and ruined your career in the process."

"I haven't ruined it Mam."

"That's what you say. If they hadn't found that baby in the telescope you'd still be an astronomer, not unemployed."

"I've been promised this top job."

"Promises!" Blodwen was contemptuous, "I'll believe that when I see it. Who's going to employ an astronomer who has to go home every night to look after his baby – because his wife has run off and left him? Grow up Tom Morgan. I thought you were tougher than that. Look truth straight in the eye. Your father always could. Evan Morgan never blinked. Stop being daft. Even if they offered you the job – and I bet they won't, they'll find some excuse – you couldn't take it. Not with that wretched child to look after."

"Curly's not wretched Mam, I love him. I wouldn't be without him for the Earth."

"Never mind the Earth Twm Morgan. What about your profession? That was the making of you. You fought so hard for it through all that agony. We were so proud of you. And now it's all gone. All because of that flighty little Londoner. She hasn't lost her profession has she? Oh no! She's even taken your best friend away from you."

"That was all my fault."

"Rubbish! I can understand her flying off in a rage to London. I'd have done the same myself if I'd discovered your dad in bed with a floozy. Within six weeks – no three – I'd have been back again. Why? Because I loved him; really loved him. I'd have supported him through thick or thin – even, if necessary, brought up his bastard baby. That's what real wives do Twm – in case you hadn't noticed. You get yourself a real wife next time Twm. Preferably a passionate

Welsh girl, not some superficial metropolitan flipetty-gibbet. Why, you told me she left her first boyfriend for you didn't she? She's just done it again. And it's probably not the last time either. Poor Frank will be the next one – just you wait."

"You don't understand….."

"You're the one who doesn't understand Twm. Can't you see? It's daft what you're doing to yourself. You're like that tragic Cho Cho San in Madame Butterfly, mooning after her Lieutenant Pinkerton long after he'd married some other woman and was laughing up his sleeve. The trouble with you Twm Morgan is that everybody's frightened of you. They won't tell you the truth: tip toeing round you and pretending it's all right – in case you get angry. Well I'm your mother and I'm not going to do that. Go and see that Ann if you must. But wait until she's had her baby. The one thing I'll say for her is that all those miscarriages could unbalance any woman – for a time. Go and see her then by all means. When you see her you might find you are no longer in love with her, or she with you. One conversation could be enough. A long enough absence can break any love-spell, however magic. It did so for so many husbands and wives during the war, believe me. Propinquity matters. Then move on and find a real wife. In the mean time you'd better fight for your profession. Without that my boy you'll be nothing. In the long run it will matter to you more than either love or parenthood, because you are one of those odd people who were born to think. Your father and I could see it in you from the age of two. 'Mr Why' we used to call you. Astronomy allowed you to think for a living. It was your guiding star in the night. If you take your eyes off it you'll be lost."

"I know that Mam. And I never will."

Although he quarrelled about Ann with Blodwen at the time, Morgan respected his mother. She was usually right about people; she'd fought hard to bring him up as best she could, and she knew him better than anybody else. So, by the time he was working at The Factory Centre, Morgan was beginning to rethink his feelings for Ann. Certainly her failure to communicate with him, or respond to his blizzard of letters, was unnatural, inexplicable and, depending on one's point of view, unforgivable. And on his side lay fear. He'd buried his head in the sand for so long that he was petrified to pull it out and face the truth; to face the truth that she'd ditched him permanently for Frank. But Morgan found that hard to believe too. He was still proud enough to believe that no man, least of all Frank, could take his girl away. And she was still his girl, at least in his own heart she was. They'd been like two children together; shared every thought; enjoyed every intimacy; dreamed each other's dreams. They'd reacted identically to other people, laughed extravagantly at each others jokes, resented moments apart when the other was not there to share. Only that wretched Admiralty secrecy had stood between them, allowing Frank to slip between their sheets. How could Morgan compete with the bloody Official Secrets Act? That was it, from the very beginning to the very end. He would never have gone round for dinner with Karen, and she would never have offered herself, if he hadn't been so mad about that letter from Ann. That had driven him absolutely mad with jealousy, far more than her sexual liason with Frank. Morgan sometimes wondered if he was undersexed. Other people murdered each other because of it. Morgan could murder somebody over love yes; but sex? That would be ridiculous. Any physically non-repulsive human being could find a sexual partner as easily as purchasing a joint of beef. Look at Bacon and Bulstrode. It might be expensive – but it wouldn't be hard. But stealing your mate – the one person you loved – that was different.

Morgan didn't even blame Frank any more. Frank was in love with Ann – as who wouldn't be. It was his, Morgan's, furious letter to Frank about the Admiralty thing which was responsible. He could see that now. Frank must have been very very upset. And Frank's story rang true. Despite all the corruption in Britain involving the Oxbridge Old Boy Network, corruption that had so blindingly come to light in the Burgess-McClean-Philby affair, Morgan couldn't quite believe that Frank, for all his questionable Oxbridge pals, could quite worm his way into the Admiralty without being asked. If that was possible then the West was as good as lost – and Morgan didn't yet believe that. If people like Ann were prepared to risk their marriages over secrecy, and she had, then there was till enough honour out there to keep the British going, despite Oxbridge and its creepy priest-hood-ridden cloisters.

Morgan's tribulations over Ann were interrupted by the arrival of the Gilkeys for their annual four month stay in London. Pat rang immediately to command Morgan down to their service flat in Dolphin Square Chelsea:

"And bring that boy of yours." she screamed over the telephone, deafer than ever: "I want to see if he's turning into a proper Morgan like his grandfather. And I want to talk to you about that wretched gel of yours. Walter and I are going over to Kew to see her tomorrow. You had better come up at the weekend. There's not much room here, but you can sleep on the couch in the sitting room." And the phone banged down without the chance for Morgan to explain the complications.

Forty-eight hours later she rang up again:

"Tom, you come up here immediately. Immediately you hear? We're in trouble. Walter's fallen off a bus and is in hospital with a badly broken hip. And me – ah can't see a thing. Or hear much neither. And there's all these people in our apartment interfering. I want you to come up here, throw 'em all out and take me to see my darlin'. Walter's in pain and he needs to see me, and I need to see him. You hear? We both need you right now."

'England expects every man to do his duty.' Morgan thought. Fortunately it was his week off and as he was very fond of the old couple he left Curly with the Salts and raced up to Chelsea.

As Pat had described, the tiny flat was crowded with people, mainly elderly friends and acquaintances who were trying to help. But it was all too much for the old lady who was sitting cross legged on her bed in her nightie, wig awry, as blind as a bat, and chain smoking her half-cigarettes on the end of a hat pin.

"Get 'em all out of here darlin'" she shouted, loud enough for everyone to hear. "Pack 'em all off, bless 'em. Ah just need you to help me. Walter's in St Thomas's just the other side of the river."

When the last friend had been ushered out, some of whom Morgan recognised as famous, Pat revealed the other source of her agitation:

"Tom I want you to open the wardrobe and find our pill bottle, Walter's and mine. Ah don't trust some of them churchy busybodies…. They might take 'em away – or flush 'em down the john."

Morgan found a large jar, filled to the brim with multicolour pills, which he handed to Pat. She opened it eagerly and, unable to see any more, felt inside with her bony little claw.

"They're our escape pills, Walter's and mine. Nobody's going to separate us. Not for a moment. When the time comes we're going together, Walter and me. In here Tom is enough Sodium Amatol to kill off a squad of marines. It's taken us years to accumulate 'em. We don't want no goody-goody taking then away cos we're 'mentally incapable', or some such childish nonsense. Now you hide 'em real good, tell me where they are, then take me to St Thomas's."

He helped Pat into some clothes – she wasn't the least embarrassed – then into a wheel chair, then down the lift to a waiting taxi.

In a darkened ward, which Walter shared with three others, the old man was lying on his back, half comatose with drugs, but still very obviously a gentleman. Pat, assisted by Morgan, got out of the wheel chair, climbed ever so slowly onto the bed beside her husband, put her arms round his neck and kissed him passionately.

"Oh my darlin'. Your Patti's come to love you…."

Morgan pulled the curtain round them, his eyes stinging, and tip-toed away.

They operated on Walter next day, trying to pin the broken pieces of his hip together. Walter had climbed onto the platform of a double-decker bus outside Fortnum and Mason's in Piccadilly, with a hamper for Patti in one hand, his other holding the bar, when the conductor had pressed the bell prematurely. The bus took off, jerking Walter over, and throwing him violently into the roadway. The surgeon admitted to Patti that at his age, over eighty, the prognosis for the hip knitting properly was none too good.

Morgan stayed to see the two old people through the worst of the crisis and to take Pat in to see Walter at St Thomas's twice a day. She, being an awful snob, agitated for him to move to a private clinic. Walter, a staunch supporter of the NHS since its inception, and believing that America needed the same thing, adamantly refused to move. She was persuaded only when he put the question direct:

"Where do you think the best doctors work Patti? In a private clinic for the extra money? Or in a public hospital where they can do the best medicine and surgery, irrespective of their patient's wealth? At my age I need the best doctors in London don't I darling? Not second or third raters, who do it for the money."

So Pat conceded, though not without a good deal of grumbling and swearing at the other patients, as if they had no right to be sharing the ward with her Walter. Morgan could never understand how such an otherwise intelligent woman could be quite such a snob. He tackled her directly. Her answer was straight:

"Mah mother, by her brains and determination alone, escaped out of an Irish bog. Boy, she was never going to fall back in there and, by thunder Tom, neither is Patti. Egalitarianism is a misconceived child of the French and Russian revolutions – and just look what failures they were, and are. D'ye know what Leonardo da Vinci said? He said:

"How many there are who could be described as mere channels for food, producers of excrement, fillers of latrines, for they have no other purpose in this world; they practice no virtue whatsoever; all that remains after them is a full latrine."

Morgan protested that the aristocratic world from which so many of Pat's British friends came was no guarantee of either ability or worth – on the contrary. He quoted Bob Salt who had pointed out that that the current British aristocracy was largely descended from the pimps and prostitutes of the Restoration, who had taken stolen titles and stolen lands from Kings Charles and James in return for the sexual favours of their wives. Others, hardly more fastidious, had married American heiresses and bargained money into status.

"And produced men like Winston Spencer Churchill." Patti retorted.

They both loved to argue, and as neither of them slept much, there was plenty of time for it. Then of course there was Ann:

"If you ask me Tom, she loves Frank Cotteridge. Ah saw them together two days ago. But she's not *in* love with him, not like she was with you. Why that gel's eyes never left your face.

You were the Sun and Moon to her, like Walter is to me. A woman don't forget a passion like that, it don't come but once. If you play your cards right she could be yours again one day. But not now. That gel's obsessed with her pregnancy – as who wouldn't be after her history. That's the crime you committed in her eyes. Rushed to have a baby with some other woman when she was tryin' so hard to have yours."

"But I....."

"But me no buts Tom. It may not be rational, but that's what any woman in Ann's position would feel. Ah know ah would. But here's another item in the equation: that creepy father of hers."

"Henry?"

"Svengali you mean. He hates you with a passion. Why you took his little gel away – and could do so again, whereas Frank, Frank is no rival. Svengali knows that, deep in his sick bones. So long as Ann's with Frank her father feels safely in possession. And Ann is in his thrall, is his Trilby."

Morgan told Pat about Blodwen's opinion of Ann's superficiality, which Patti dismissed as 'Maternal Jealousy.'

"Your mother's a pretty good hater herself. Why she certainly took against me. Cain't blame her for that. But she can't quite forgive Ann for taking little Tom Morgan so deep into her own arms. Why you could be a real bore about that little wife of yours."

"Who I want to have back! D'you think I can get her?"

"Ah reckon you'll have to wait until she's well and truly settled with Frank's baby. Then she'll calm down and move back to her own apartment, her own space. Then you might be able to snatch her out of the dragon's lair again. You done it once. Why not twice? You're more than a match for Svengali Tom. He knows that. That's why he's so bitter, and boy he is. Are you sure he hasn't been snitching your mail?"

"My God – I never thought of that!" Morgan was dumbfounded.

"You wouldn't. It's way beneath you Tom. But not beneath that creepy father of hers. He's in love with his own daughter, his own little creation. His wife – what's her name?"

"Gwendolyn."

"Gwendolyn knows it, and she don't like it. I may not be able to see much these days Tom but I could sense that. She could be an ally of yours."

"She was before."

"She might be the ace in the hole that you are going to need."

Morgan suddenly burst into roars of laughter. He explained to Pat about the Van Gogh:

"If he's been opening my mail I bet he's been in touch with the New South Wales Police. When they go to the gallery and find the original still there they'll think he's totally barmy."

Pat enjoyed the Van Gogh story:

"Boy you're some lover Tom Morgan. What wife could ever give you up? A woman adores a man who can make her laugh. I don't reckon Frank can. He's more the faithful adorer. A woman can grow fed up with that. They like a challenge – leastwise the red blooded ones do. You gotta find a way to get letters to Ann which her father cannot intercept. Try Gwendolyn. Van Gogh eh? Boy I can make a great anecdote out of that." She embraced Tom:

"I got a little bit of you darlin' haven't I? At the end of my life. And that's somethin'. And you be sure to bring that Kirralee or Curly up to see his great grandmamma Patti before it's too late. By all accounts he's going to be another Morgan heartbreaker. Walter and I have a mind to leave him something in our will – enough to go to a decent college, enough to send him to

Harvard or Chicago. But they say nowadays that Swarthmore College in Pennsylvania is the best university in the world – for students that is, not for faculty."

Then she began crying gently. Morgan had never expected to see such a thing. He got her a box of tissues. She quickly dried up:

"D'you know what ah was crying for? Not for an old woman like me. Not even for Walter. Ah'm crying for the loss of my faith in America. D'you know what happened in Long Beach, not two weeks ago?"

Pat and Walter had decided to sell their beach house – they couldn't get up the stairs any more – and move into a small apartment with elevators and overlooking the ocean. There was no room there for all their furniture and their collection of mementos from around the world. So Pat had sent cards to all their closest friends to come one morning and each select an item to take away as a memento of Walter and herself.

"And you know what Tom? Some of 'em came with vans. And they fought over our belongings. Some of 'em actually fought. You remember that old Chinese lacquered orangewood desk of mine, the one I bought off the quay at Shangai?"

"It's gorgeous."

" Not any more. Some of them tore it in bits. One took one drawer, another took the next. Ah bet they'll go to law over it. They just tore the whole place apart whilst Walter and I looked on helpless. Finally I rung the police and had the whole brew of 'em thrown out. And they were supposed to be our friends. Ah don't think I can face Long Beach again Tom. And that was our home for more than forty years. That's why I'm shedding a tear. Won't happen again darlin'. Now let's go see Walter. Boy I miss that man, old as I may be. But not old in my heart. Ah'm still a girl inside you know, and Walter's still mah boy."

In the Worcestershire countryside the English Spring arrived in all its glory. The broad leaved oaks and elms of The Forest of Arden burst into such greenery as one never saw in Australia. The chiff chaffs and the swallows arrived from Africa, building their nests in the hedgerows and eves. The doves cooed and the cuckoos called from distant copses. The rooks built high in Bluebell Wood – omens of a good summer to come, while flocks of jackdaws tumbled in the breeze overhead causing Morgan to look up and wonder if one of them was his Jack, now ten years old. He would walk, with Curly on his shoulders, along the deep country lanes, banks of primroses and anemones climbing high on either side. They would follow the towpath beside the old canal through Alvechurch, and stop by the secluded reservoir where the moorhens, the mallards and the grebes were raising their chicks among the reeds. Britain was as beautiful and eternal to his inner eye as ever, more beautiful in fact. The constant drip-drip of anti-British propaganda in Australia, something the colonials seemed to need, presumably to reassure themselves that they'd made a good move, had done its work. Every bad story about Britain had been gloated over, every good story suppressed or ignored. Britain had 'lost its empire', been over taken by the Americans and taken over by the Europeans. The Blacks had ruined it – no it was the Indians. The Brits couldn't play cricket any more. And look at us mate. We just won ten gold medals in the Olympic swimming. How pathetic that all was – he could see it now in retrospect. But at the time it had been pernicious. Who cared about a bunch of teenagers with outsized feet who had nothing better to do all day than plough up and down chlorinated, urinated swimming pools? How could you possibly set that against The Battle of Britain, Dunkirk or Trafalgar? Milford

Haven was every bit as beautiful as Sydney Harbour; more so in fact, and larger. And what had Australia to set against Newton, Tallis and Shakespeare? Britain had created modern society, now the model for the civilised world, and defended it against all comers, from Napoleon to Hitler. He agreed with Bob Salt about that. And she was still here, shorn of her imperial pretences perhaps, but what did they matter? They had impressed foreigners far more than the British themselves, proving to be an economic disaster for the home country. So good riddance! Who the hell but a few newspaper proprietors, and jingoistic politicians, cared about 'dominion over palm and pine'? Not when you've got oak forests and beech groves of you own. Morgan wouldn't have given Savernake Forest away, or Pembrokeshire, for the whole continent of Australia with its million million grey gums. He rediscovered his love for the lush dampness of his native country. It was natural to health and vigour and produced, so the astronauts said, the greenest landscape on Earth. And the seas around her island coast teemed with so much plankton that it fed more sea-life than anywhere else on the globe.

"This is your country Curly" he said, lifting his son high to the sky "Sniff it, glory in it . Be a part. You're a lucky boy: a Briton like your dad, and his dad, and dads going back to the beginning of time. All the rest of them envy us. And why not? We've got History and Geography. We've got Literature and Science. We've got fantasy and fortitude. We fought to find them, we fought to keep them, and if we have to we'll fight again. You might anyway. So revel in it son!" He threw Curly down in the long grass and rolled him over and over until Curly was helpless with giggling and giddiness.

Life on the old red-brick farm was good. Apart from the 'Airfield' most of the fields were rented out to neighbouring farmers. But Valerie kept chickens, ducks and geese on the big pond, and half a dozen pigs who, to Curly's delight, often came into the house. They loved to lie in front of the fire toasting their bellies.

"I can't see over the boogers they're that fat," Bob complained. "'Ere Curly let's take a hot poker to 'em. That'll shift 'em."

Morgan was amazed to find how clean pigs were.

"Course they are" Valerie said. "Given half a chance what animal would wallow in its own shite? It's them ignorant farmers who lock 'em in filthy cells as is to blame. I'd like to lock some on 'em up in pens the same size theirselves and yow'd soon see how smelly and filthy the boogers would get. 'Ere Doreen, get your 'ead off me lap, yer drooling on me apron."

The pigs were supposed to be for bacon, but somehow Valerie couldn't bring herself to order in the slaughterer.

"It's a sanctuary for obese pigs is this house." Bob complained. "Why, they can't even lay eggs. Leastwise I aint seen any. Have yow seen any pig-eggs Curly? Thank God they'm too fat to git up the stairs. Otherwise they'd be in our bed; the 'ole lot on 'em at once."

Sometimes he'd take out the carving knife and sharpen it in a bloodthirsty manner on a stone:

"Now Curly, which one shall it be? Oo's going to get the chop first? Nelson or Boadicea?"

Curly would scream, trying to stop Bob's menacing hand.

"Dain't yow worry Curly." Valerie would reassure "He'll not touch a hair on their hides. And if he did slaughter 'em he wouldn't eat a bite. Not a rasher, not a pork chop, not even a sausage."

"Yow just try me missis. Yow just try. I could murder a plate of faggots and gravy."

Valerie, once in awe of Morgan, came out of her shell after he came to stay. Unlike her husband she was no great reader, but she still had well articulated opinions of her own, including a strong respect for Royalty and the Anglican Church – which didn't extend so far as attending services herself. She ran the farm, did all the now extensive Wild Goose accounts, and kept Bob from 'getting above hisself' with a line of deadly banter which he was seldom quick enough to resist. For instance she thought his History Project a ridiculous indulgence:

"Ee's rewriting 'istory Tom with all the bits he dain't like, sich as Kings and Queens, left out. Them perfessors will laugh their 'eads off when they reads it. *If* they reads it at all."

"I'm only doing what every other historian does….."

"Ar I know – rewriting 'istory so as the Bob Salts o' this world come out on top – smellin' much better than they really does, better 'n the Bishops and the Dooks and the Kings."

"It's about time."

"Yow should stick to what yow know Bob Salt; engineerin'. When it cooms to owt else yer a babby. Yow can't even keep them 'istory assistants of yours under control. They keep on puttin' the Kings and Queens back in Tom." she giggled with delight.

In truth Bob was having great difficulty exercising 'editorial control' over his own project – not least because he could spend only a small fraction of his time on it. Every other Monday his two PhD assistants, Beth from Manchester and Adrian from London, would come to spend the day in Bob's 'History Library' arguing over the latest drafts and the latest 'finds'. Believing ardently in democracy as he did, Bob was distressed to find himself all too often out-voted and over ruled by his two young assistants.

"Beth is all right" he would explain afterwards "It's that fellow Adrian. Just cos he's been to Oxford he thinks as he's a right to be in charge. Well he ain't a going to be. It's my project and it's my money."

Valerie roared with laughter:

"It's your toy you mean Bob Salt, and yow dain't like anyone else a'playin' with it."

"What yow think Tom?" Bob asked "Yow met 'em and sat in wi' us for a bit."

"I'd fire Adrian. Forthwith. And not because of his opinions or his probably false lah-di-dah accent."

"Why then?"

" Because he's more interested in persuading others than in getting at the truth. I never noticed him change his mind once, or be persuaded by the evidence. You know what my definition of a good scientist is?"

"Go on."

"He is someone who prefers losing an argument to winning one. If you lose you've learned something. If you win then you are stuck where you started. And Adrian's either too stupid, or too callow perhaps, to realise that. He thinks scholarship is persuasion, or salesmanship if you like. It's very much the Oxbridge way. It doesn't work with me – nor should it with any decent scholar. Unless you've got the time and money to completely re-educate the fool I'd give him the sack."

There was silence round the table. Valerie looked at Bob.

"That's joost how I feel in me bones." Bob said "But I dain't like to be a tyrant meself. What yow think Val?"

"Well it's your 'obby."

"It's not a 'obby."

"Yes it is. It's like me keepin' pigs. If yow dain't enjoy it give it oop I say. Or change it so as yow do enjoy it. And that Adrian's been keeping yow awake and 'grumblin' this last six month. Yow'm the boss. Mek oop yer mind. Joost think on the fun you'll 'ave when he's gorn, choppin' out all them Kings and Queens what he put in."

Adrian's services were dispensed with and Bob looked five years younger overnight. Valerie henceforth referred to him as 'The Tyrant':

"Ere he cooms. Keep yer eyes down Tom else ee chops yer 'ead off."

While he was looking for a new history assistant Bob paid Morgan's salary, in the weeks he wasn't at the factory, to teach him mathematics. He'd been so impressed by the Wild Goose formula, and by Morgan's contention that mathematics was probably the unacknowledged mover, the hidden hand that governed much of history, that Bob was determined to learn.

Morgan bought him Kasner and Newman's four-volume masterpiece 'Mathematics and the Imagination' and set to work filling in the systematic background. Despite his age Bob turned out to be a quick learner. For a start he was highly motivated. And then, as an engineer, he was used to numbers, tables, trigonometry and graphs. Thus Morgan could move straight into algebra and thence to calculus. Bob had been in awe of calculus all his life, but when Morgan explained that it was only the 'Language of Graphs', graphs being familiar to Bob, the pupil picked up Differentiation and Integration in no time. Bob was entranced by the concept of Maxima and Minima and was thrilled to calculate for himself the optimal shape for a gasometer.

"I wish as how I'd learned this as a nipper" he said in awe "I could have finished oop running Rolls Royce Aero-engines."

But his delight in gasometers was as nothing compared to the impression left by Morgan's demonstration that history was necessarily unstable:

"Think of a single continent, with a roughly constant population-density all over, split into a number of nation states, some big some small. The total population of a state will thus go up with its area – that is to say with the square of its distance across. If it's twice as long, given the same shape, it will have four times the area, and hence four times the population. Right?"

"Right."

"But the length of the boundaries will be proportional to its total length, that is to say be twice as long. Right?"

"Right."

"So it will have four times the population, but only twice the length of border to defend. Hence it can afford twice as many soldiers on each mile of border to defend itself – or attack. Got it?"

"Yep."

"So you see a big country will always be able better to defend itself against its neighbours than a small one. So big countries will grow while small ones shrink – or disappear altogether. Thus there is a mathematical pressure on every country to grow at the expense of its neighbours, because if it doesn't grow it will be gobbled up by some larger neighbour that has. I think that must be the driving force of history. Expand or die. Mathematics has forced bands to become tribes, tribes to become principalities, principalities to become nations, nations to become alliances, and so on. Even if men were fundamentally peaceful, they couldn't afford to be. Mathematics would be prodding them from all sides: 'Grow or be doomed'."

"The bigger you are the faster you can grow." Bob looked shocked.

"And the smaller you are the quicker you'll be swallowed up. It's mathematics – not some dastardly side of human nature."

For days Bob Salt wandered about in a dazed state, clutching Volume Two of Kasner and Newman under his arm : "This Mathematics –it's like a new and different pair of eyes. If yow ain't got 'em yow'm more than half blind. Mooch more'n half. Why dain't I know this before? Why dain't everybody?"

When he'd overcome his shock he was delighted:

"Now I'll show those history professors what Val is always going on about. Bet none o ' them can understand calculus. Means they can't understand most of history neither. Yow salary is the best investment I ever made Tom. Now I want to know about Differential Equations. Says 'ere as they'm the real guts of the subject."

"All right. But not before you've completed your home-work."

Salt was eager to show Morgan over The Wild Goose Project, now in full flow. He had half a dozen people, mostly young ex- aero modellers, working in the barn or out at the airfield. There was a wind-tunnel, an electronics shop, an engine testing rig and a lab where a chemist worked on fuel additives. There was even a small computer 'to impress visitors':

"I dain't know how to use it but some on the lads has showed Val how to do the accounts and the 'Word processing' on it, which is a posh phrase for 'Typing' I think. Anyroad she loves it, even if I dain't."

Bob explained that the real breakthrough had come with the development of a stabilising device called "Dumbo' which was so secret that even their American paymasters didn't know how it worked.

"We used to lose a lot on 'em in the early days. Couldn't find out why. So I hired a two-seater motor-glider and pilot and followed our models in flight for hours. It were turbulence. Yow gerra lot of that near the bottom of clouds where we'm aiming to fly. A vertical gust would hit 'em too fast for 'em to recover. They'd flip over on their backs then go into an irrecoverable spin. So we tried spin-recovery software in the on-board micro-computer – but it dain't work well enough. Then I asked meself 'How do birds do it?' They use the same balancing method as we use: three fluid-based semicircular canals perpendicular to one another, one for each plane. So I built meself a large system out of transparent plastic pipes containing linseed oil to see 'ow it worked. We fitted sensors inside, wired 'em to the electronics, and built in a feed-back loop. After some fiddling it worked a treat. Yow couldn't turn it over no-how. Steady as a rock."

"How ingenious."

"It were Nature, not me. I'd never of thought of it on me own. But we 'ad a big problem."

"What?"

"How to fit it in a Wild Goose. My model covered a whole table and weighed a stone. We 'ad to microminiaturise the whole thing. An' I 'ad no idea how to do it. So you know what I done?"

Morgan shook his head.

"I went down the road to The Royal Radar Establishment, which 'appens to be in Malvern. According to the Yanks they've got the biggest collection of scientific brains in Europe there. More'n fifteen hundred PhDs. I got meself an introduction through the US Air Force. Saw the boss and he sent down 'alf a dozen of the brightest young chaps as yow'll ever meet. And all on 'em signed up to The Official Secrets Act. They was fascinated by Wild Goose, and they agreed to do it, or at least to get it done by the most suitable people – 'biophysicists' they called 'em. An' they did an all. Charged me a bomb – but I passed the bill on to the Yanks. After that we could fly Wild Goose even in to thunderclouds and she come out the other side dead straight and level, though sometimes iced up."

"But how do you know where you actually are – in relation to the ground?"

"Ar, that's the Yank's big secret like. They gi' us a tiny box, no bigger'n a ten-fag cigarette packet, very light too, and skimpy on power. It's summut to do wi satellites is all I were told. It knows where it is within twenty yards, anywhere on Earth they say. Bloody clever! And it emits no radio signal. It gives course corrections to our control circuitry every ten second. They gi' us that and they gi' us their tiny electronic cameras and storage devices. The rest we do ourselves."

"When Morgan was shown the latest Mark IX Wild Goose he could barely recognise Ernie's original design. For a start it was much sleeker and heavier, though somewhat smaller.

"We goes for speed now as much as endurance." Bob explained. "The Yanks prefer us to get in fast and get out fast. And the 'igher the speed the less susceptible we are to headwinds."

Morgan stared at the deadly little toy in wonder. Everything looked so precision made, so professional, from the smoothness of its aerodynamic surfaces to the almost perfect camouflage.

"Ar it is professional an all." Bob agreed "Ought to be with all the manpower what's gone into it. It's like a watch inside."

"I'm surprised the Americans haven't taken over the whole project." Morgan said.

"They tried alright in them early days: like everything else British – from penicillin to radar, they wanted to pinch it. Did yow know that pinching European patents was one of the main motives for their so called 'War of Independence'? It makes me blood boil. Do yow know Tom as some idiot in Whitehall sold all our jet engine technology, what Whittle 'ad developed over twenty year, for eight 'undred thousand bloody pounds to the Yanks? Wouldn't buy yow a single big engine today. That was the stoopidest business deal in all of history. And it weren't even 'is to sell. It were Whittle's. Got hisself a KBE I dare say, and ruined Britain in the process. Makes me blood boil!"

Morgan had to stop Bob going off into one of his rants.

"So how did you stop them getting their hands on Wild Goose?"

"I went to see the Prime Minister. 'It's better' I said 'If this is run as a British operation. If the Roosians ever do find us out they won't need to blame the Yanks and start a third world war. The Yanks can tick us off in public and everybody'll be 'appy. He must've agreed because the Yanks laid us off after that."

"How on Earth did you get to see the PM?" Morgan was incredulous.

"Easy! I sent 'em a close-up image of the Kamchatka submarine pens. Had me own camera on board that time. Here Tom I'll show yer."

What an extraordinary story, Morgan reflected, it all was. In the midst of nuclear aircraft carriers and intercontinental ballistic missiles this jaunty little genius, who may have, if Ernie Salt was right, played a decisive part in winning World War Two, was also winning the Cold War from his pig-farm in the Worcestershire countryside. And how on Earth had he, Morgan, got involved with two people, Ann and Salt, so central to Western Intelligence?

"Oh that's easy." Bob explained. "This is a democracy ain't it? In times of emergency the right people often slide into the niches where they'm most needed. That's why we allus have won against the dictators, and why I think we allus will. So me and Ann and yow, all bein' really clever boogers, we find ourselves floating side by side into Intelligence, which is the front-line at the moment. Ann was allus going to fall for a bright feller like you. And you? Yow was lookin' fer a father figure bright enough to kick your arse occasionally. And that's me. 'Ere, turn round." Bob laughed.

Curly didn't enjoy 'Wychal End', as the farm was called, quite as much as Tidbinbilla. For a start he missed Kylie, and there weren't older boys about to build dens and light fires. But 'Grandfather Bob's barn was full of fascinating things to watch and young men to talk to: model aeroplanes were being sprayed and tiny engines being run in the soundproof enclosure. And although he missed horses the pigs were actually more interesting: they were always being naughty, pushing themselves into the house, or digging up places they shouldn't have with their snouts, and squealing when they were hungry. Belcher had the habit, when he wanted his breakfast, of picking up a pail on his nose and hurling it upwards against the tin roof of the pig-shed to deafening effect.

"I'll fetch the butcher to you yow devil" Aunty Val used to threaten him when she'd been woken thus by Belcher at dawn. But she never did. And she had a rotivator, which Curly found fascinating, a noisy beast of a thing for turning over the earth in her large vegetable garden. So what with the pigs and the geese and the model aeroplanes, and the out-houses and Aunty Val's rotivator and Grandfather Bob's Landrover to ride in, Curly was kept pretty busy at Wychal End, leaving his father plenty of time to think about the Universe, galaxies in particular.

Morgan kept returning to Fish's Law, one of the very few pieces of systematic information discovered about galaxies. In 1959, as a graduate student at the University of Berkeley, near San Francisco, Fish had discovered a tight relationship between the Binding Energies and Masses of Elliptical galaxies. Furthermore, at the end of his thesis, Fish had offered a most ingenious explanation for his law in terms of the opacity of the hot gas out of which the galaxies must have formed in the first place.

Ron Eckersly had however been highly dismissive of Fish's observations when Morgan had explained them to him in Sydney:

"He can't measure the Masses, and he can't measure the Binding Energies. So how the hell can Fish find a relationship between two things he cannot measure? It doesn't make sense to me."

When he had the time to think about it again Morgan realized that Eckersly had to be right. Furthermore Morgan knew a lot about the theory of collapsing gas in the cosmos; after all that was what he'd worked on, in different guises, both with Hood and Wagoner. And when he went over Fish's ingenious explanation again Morgan realized that it didn't actually work because Fish had forgotten something.

So here was a fascinating problem to think about at Wychal End: neither Fish's observations, nor his explanation for them, made sense. And yet he'd obviously discovered something systematic, something really fascinating. So what had he really discovered? Morgan tried to reconstruct from Fish's paper the actual measurements he had made and the thread of his subsequent reasoning. This wasn't easy because he hadn't found the space in his paper to include all the intermediate steps in his argument. Morgan even rang the Astronomy department at Berkeley, only to be told that Fish had long since left astronomy to work for Eastern Airlines.

In the normal course of events Morgan would have abandoned the trail at this juncture. There were usually better things to do in science than try to locate one of a hundred thousand employees of a large company. The trouble was that so little systematic was known of galaxies that abandoning Fish's unquestionably intriguing clue would be criminal. So Morgan tried to think himself into Fish's mind, tried to imagine all the steps he must have followed in his thesis investigation. For a start, what raw data had he had to work with? It turned out that he had three photographic plates for each galaxy, taken with the 120-inch at Lick Observatory in California. Morgan had taken just such plates of Ellipticals with the 36-inch at Steward Observatory, and the 40-inch at Siding Springs. To look at, Ellipticals were rather featureless objects, fuzzy blobs of light, bright in the centre, getting dimmer towards the outskirts until they merged imperceptibly into the darkness of the background sky. Sometimes they were circular, most often they were slightly flattened, which gave them their 'Elliptical" label. There was little or no sign of the spiral arms, the opaque dust lanes, the rotation and the bright star clusters which made Spiral galaxies so much more complex to look at, and so much more interesting. And yet Fish had inferred a Mass and a gravitational Binding Energy for each of them. How on Earth had he done that? The fact was that there were only four things he could have measured for each galaxy: its distance, inferred from its redshift – already published in the literature; its apparent brightness as seen on the plates; its apparent size and its ellipticity – that is to say how far off round it looked on the sky. Evidently he hadn't used the ellipticity and he'd used the distance only to convert apparent brightness into intrinsic Luminosity, apparent size into true Radius. So, in the end, the only two quantities he'd had to work with for each galaxy were its true Luminosity and its true Radius. Everything else would have to be inferred from just these two quantities. Fish explained quite openly that the masses had been inferred from the Luminosities simply by assuming that all Ellipticals were composed out of the same kinds of Red Giant stars. Given that Ellipticals were all roughly the same colour this seemed to Morgan to be a very reasonable assumption. Fish had obtained his masses by multiplying the measured luminosities by a conversion factor appropriate for a population of Red Giant stars. Given that he had only one other measurement – Radius, he must have inferred his Binding Energy from that. Unfortunately he hadn't tabulated his measured radii, so Morgan was forced to work backward and reconstruct the Radii from Fish's tabulated Binding Energies. So finally Morgan had a table of his own, listing for each galaxy its Luminosity and its reconstructed Radius. And like any scientist with such a table he plotted all the data on a graph. All the data-points, one for each galaxy, fitted perfectly to a smooth curve. Here in its rawest, purest unadulterated form was the truth that Fish had stumbled upon. The more luminous a galaxy was the larger its radius. That made sense. The question was 'How much larger?" If the galaxy was twice as luminous, was the radius twice as large – or what? This was the kind of question children were trained to answer in the labs at school. Instead of the original quantities themselves you took the logarithms of the quantities of interest and plotted those logarithms on a graph. Then the curve on the original graph would turn into a straight line on the logarithm graph. And from the slope of that straight line on the logarithm graph you could infer what was going on. Morgan did this, and out popped the indubitable, but puzzling result: "The radius of any Elliptical galaxy is strictly proportional to the square root of its Luminosity." – that was Fish's Law in its purest form.

Here, felt Morgan, was something simple and unexpected, a cosmic truth hitherto unknown, a key into the innermost profundity of galaxies. He'd never been more excited in his career. He was a Stone Age hunter again. He could hear the rustle of truly Big Game nearby in the bush, but he didn't know what it was. Would a mastodon emerge, or a sabre – toothed tiger?

It was anyway exciting to be back in the bubbling cauldron of world astronomy again. After Britain, and in particular after Arizona, Stromlo had been so isolated, so lacking in stimulation. Whereas in Arizona he could go to an interesting seminar practically every day, at

Stromlo they were lucky to get one a year. And with Fat Sow guzzling up all the foreign –travel funds there'd been no possibility of travelling abroad for inspiration. No wonder that, in such a barren landscape, choking weeds like Doolan thrived.

From Wychal End Morgan cycled over to Selly Oak on a regular basis to see Martin Johnson. Still mentally spry and curious Martin wanted to know all about Morgan's astronomical adventures in Arizona and Australia. In return Johnson regaled him with all the astronomical gossip on the British side:

"You won't be pleased to hear this Tom but Fred Hoyle's just resigned from Cambridge. Apparently some other professors there outmanoeuvred him whilst he was away in Australia attending the AAT Board. They've effectively seized control of The Institute of Astronomy which, as you know, he built up himself. Goodness knows what's going to happen to Hoyle himself now. He hasn't even got a salary any more. But he's lost his power base, which means that your old friend Sir Adrian Bellfounder is now effectively in control of the whole of British astronomy. His tentacles reach everywhere: into the government via the Science Research Council and the Royal Society, and into all the important journals through their editorial boards. He controls the purse strings, and he controls the appointments. There's no one left to say him nay. As his scientific stature has waned, thanks in part to your work on Red Giants and Star Formation, so his appetite for power has grown. He's a favourite with the public on the BBC – they never see his talons unsheathed – while his right-wing elitism plays well in Whitehall nowadays. Scarcely an astronomical sparrow can stir on this island at present – unless Sir Adrian approves. He's even put his placemen into the Anglo Australian Telescope Board."

Morgan's heart sank when he heard this last news. He'd been relying on Bill Kretschmaier's promise of a key position on the AAT. That promise was all that made his current unemployment bearable. But would Kretschmaier now be strong enough to stand up to the cunning and vindictiveness of a man such as Bellfounder ? Bill, with his American innocence, would have no idea of the corruption he would be up against on this side of the Atlantic. Morgan woke up at nights sweating about his future in astronomy. He was practically unknown in Britain ,whereas Bellfounder's Cambridge tentacles reached into every tiny department across the land. He'd sent his written application for one of the half dozen advertised British Fellowships on the AAT. If Bellfounder had any say in matters, which it seemed he now inevitably would, then Morgan was finished.

On the other hand he'd just settled the Quasar distance problem hadn't he? His AP Lib paper had recently come out in The Astrophysical Journal in America and was surely causing a stir. If there were any justice in the matter, then that paper, along with his part in the Crab Pulsar discoveries, and his work on astronomical television, would make him a top, if not *the* top contender. Cambridge or no Cambridge, Bellfounder or not, surely there had to be some rationality in British astronomy, if not much decency.

The weakness of his position in Britain was fully brought home to Morgan at an all-day meeting of the Royal Astronomical Society in London to discuss "The Physics of Quasars." Jointly organised by Frank Cotteridge and Professor B..... – one of Fred Hoyle's most distinguished associates in California – Morgan submitted a short talk on AP Lib and its consequences for the quasar distance problem. It was rejected. He went to the meeting anyway. His first thought was to look for and speak to Frank. Frank was there, now totally bald on top. But when Morgan approached him Frank turned away in disgust.

The meeting was very well attended; there were several key speakers from the United States; Bellfounder – as articulate and hawk-like as ever, was very firmly in the Chair. The mere sight of his Assize-Judge-like visage set Morgan's heart palpitating with a mixture of nervousness and loathing. He knew it would be very difficult to keep calm, which he would have to do if he was to make the impact he was aiming for.

His opportunity came early when an ex-Cambridge astronomer, Professor S......,, also now based in America, gave a review talk on the quasar-distance problem. He reviewed first the feeble astronomical evidence in favour of the of cosmological distances, then the strong physics arguments against, emphasising the near impossibility of squeezing so much radiation out of such small volumes, if indeed quasars were at the enormous distances the cosmological hypothesis supposed. There was no doubt where his prejudices lay. To Morgan's amazement and indignation he never once mentioned AP Lib.

When he sat down, to considerable applause, Morgan shot to his feet. Bellfounder stared at him in amazement, no doubt surprised to find him back in the UK, and then turned away to call on another member of the audience to speak. And after that member he called another – and so on. Morgan bobbed up and down to no avail, before the meeting moved on and his opportunity was lost.

The only chance he was granted to speak came at the very end, when most of the audience had strolled into the library for tea, and `Bellfounder had vacated the chair in favour of Professor B.....,, Fred Hoyle's henchman from California.

"The distance problem" Morgan finally claimed "Has already been solved. The object AP Lib, formerly known as Parkes 1514-24, has all the characteristics of a quasar, including optical variability on a timescale of weeks, as well as a flat- spectrum radio source. And yet it lies close enough for us to detect spectra of both its nuclear light, which is continuous, with faint quasar-like emission lines; and of its halo light, which has the spectrum of a normal population of old Red-Giant stars. And here is the clincher: both spectra have identical redshifts. The redshift of the quasar is unquestionably cosmological, and so presumably are all the other redshifts. The paper is now out in Astrophysical Journal. I'm surprised Professor S... didn't mention this crucial evidence in his review."

The Chairman looked to Professor S.... who was still in the audience. S.... got to his feet and turned back to face Morgan and the rest of the audience:

"I was aware of that evidence, of course. The question is how seriously to take it. After all, the data were taken with a smallish telescope, using a non-digital detector, and by a group with no previous track record in this very difficult and competitive field. Moreover the claimed lines are very weak, and many were unidentified."

It was clear to Morgan that S.... was not aware that he was the lead author.

"So altogether," S...continued "I don't think we should take the AP Lib paper seriously, any more than we should take the analogous data from Gunn and Oke at Palomar for BL Lac, an apparently very similar object in the North. This distance problem is far too important to be settled by marginal data of such a kind." And he sat down.

Morgan jumped to his feet again:

"As the lead author on the AP Lib paper I have to strongly disagree. We may have used a moderate sized telescope, but the spectrograph is modern, and more than a dozen spectra were taken over the course of three years. I can assure you there's not a possibility in hell that the paper's conclusions are wrong. I did all the measurements blind. The redshifts popped out with no possibility of premeditation or collusion. I'd be prepared to place a heavy bet that the paper is right."

The chairman looked back at S .. for his reaction. S...rose to his feet:

"OK, I'll take you on. At a hundred to one."

The audience roared with laughter, for some reason they thought it was funny.

S…..continued:

"I'll pay you one hundred dollars if Bill Kretschmaier, with his digital spectrum- scanner, can be persuaded to look at AP Lib with a decent telescope, and confirms your result. And if he doesn't, then you pay me one dollar."

He sat down amidst more gales of laughter.

"I'll back that up." the Chairman added, before dismissing the company for tea.:

"I will give you another hundred dollars – if by chance your results should turn out to be right."

The audience thought this last jibe was absolutely hilarious.

Morgan was too angry and humiliated to stay for tea. He'd forgotten how easy it was to impress the British with a cheap laugh. It was a tactic he'd used himself to great effect.

Walter Gilkey's hip didn't mend well. At his age brittle old bones were reluctant to knit. He still couldn't stand after six weeks, and he was in considerable pain both day and night, pain that he bore like a gentleman, but which Pat could not. She blamed it all 'on those goddamned socialist doctors', forgetting that, like Walter, she'd been a staunch supporter of the NHS since its very inception. The surgeon at St Thomas's admitted that the operation hadn't fully worked, and that the multiple fracture which he'd tried to pin was still partially loose. But he was reluctant to operate again at once, wanting to wait until Walter had got his strength back.

"Well he ain't getting it back, and that's a fact", Pat belligerently announced when Morgan took Curly up to Chelsea for the weekend to see them. The visit wasn't a success because Walter was so obviously suffering, Pat was a tirade of complaints, and Curly hated being cooped up in the tiny flat, screaming to go back to Wychall End, to Val and Bob Salt, and to the pigs. Morgan decided to depart early for Curly's sake though he hated to leave the two old people in such a helpless state. With Pat's blindness Walter had literally done everything for them both, and now he could do nothing. Fortunately they weren't starving, since it was a service flat which supplied meals on demand. As far as Morgan could see the food was fine although Pat complained about every single dish. She was undoubtedly a very spoiled old lady, and a tyrant to boot. Her life had so far been greased by Walter's charm, and his readiness to hand out bonuses to all whose feathers had been ruffled by Pat's bullying. Now he couldn't do that any longer, and the strains were showing. Morgan did his ineffective best to explain to Pat that room service went only so far and that if she wanted the best for Walter she'd have to negotiate with the staff, and not hector them the whole time. But Pat was far too set in her ways to change now, and instead of listening went into a tirade of indignant abuse. Walter, lying grey on the bed beside her, winked at Morgan as if to say 'You see.'

He phoned them regularly and suddenly it seemed as if things were literally on the mend. Pat announced that they were going down to a friends house in Surrey for a 'country weekend'. Yes Walter was feeling a lot better and she'd phone Morgan when they got back.

Morgan did get a phone call, but it wasn't from Pat. It was from the pastor of The American church in London:

"I'm sorry to have to tell you that Dr and Mrs Gilkey passed away over the weekend. I'm afraid their affairs were in a mess and I had great difficulty locating you. There is a memorial service in our church at noon tomorrow, followed by a private service at the crematorium, to which you are particularly invited. They left a note to that effect."

The American clergyman refused to be drawn, but it was pretty clear, reading between the lines, that it must have been the suicide pact which Pat and Walter had been planning for themselves all along. After recovering from the shock, and a profound sense of loneliness for Ann – who had shared the Gilkeys with him, Morgan reflected on his role in their suicide and decided that what he had done was absolutely right. They had had a wonderful life together, and a life-long romance. Holding on to the bitter shards of life would have served no good purpose at all. On the contrary. Anyway they were, or had been, far older and wiser than he, and had evidently thought it all out long before the end, when they were in a perfectly fit state to make a sane decision. His one surprise was to find the Church involved, considering what outspoken atheists they both had been, particularly Pat. Morgan suspected that their more 'respectable' upper class friends in London were responsible.

Leaving Curly behind he went up to London by train, straight from his night-shift at The Factory Centre. He wore his working clothes, for they were all he had, though he did don a psychedelic tie from his days in swinging Bayswater.

He reached the American church in Mayfair just in time. The road outside was packed with Rolls Royces and long American limousines, out of which debouched a procession of elderly people, many of the women in veils, and all dressed in black. Pat had evidently been as much the doyenne of the American community in London, as she had been in Southern California, and the community had come out en masse to pay its last respects.

He managed to squeeze into the packed church, the only one in the congregation not arrayed in mourning. Trust Pat, he thought, to go out in style.

The two coffins lay side by side at the front of the church, completely buried in flowers. The parson and his entourage entered, the congregation rose to sing 'The Battle Hymn of the Republic'. The religious side of the service was perfunctory but a series of distinguished sounding people went up into the pulpit to pay tribute to the remarkable pair, both as individuals and as a couple. For instance an ex-cabinet minister, now in the House of Lords, gave thanks for Pat's role in supplying food parcels to Britain, millions and millions of them, during the Second World War. She'd also been responsible for starting the California branch of the Spitfire Fund which had raised the money to buy a whole wing of Spitfires before the War's end. And after the war she and Walter together had initiated a foundation to supply German libraries and schools with translations of books on democracy and civilisation. And Walter came in for eulogies too. His heroic behaviour in risking his life to evacuate so many patients in the Mayo Clinic fire was described at length, as were his distinguished contributions to paediatrics.

Morgan was listening to all this in surprise when he noticed a tall figure with a bald head at the front of the congregation. Frank! It had to be Frank. But why would Frank be there? Of course. He should have guessed. It was Ann, barely visible between the figures behind her, dressed in black with an unfamiliar black hat.

Morgan nearly fainted with the shock. He had to cling onto the pew in front while he gazed upon his wife, or what little he could see of her back, for the first time in over two years. It was all he could do to prevent himself running down the aisle and grabbing hold of her.

The rest of the memorial service passed in a blur. All he could think about was what he was going to do next. Should he shrink out of sight? Should he step out and confront her – or them? Her baby, Frank's baby, must be about due now. He'd been thinking about that every day. He couldn't let this opportunity go – he couldn't. Pat for a start would never forgive him nor – more importantly – would he ever forgive himself. But if he leapt out into the aisle in front of her it might precipitate another miscarriage. Or would it? He'd read that foetuses at this stage of maturity were very hard to lose.

Speech followed speech, with the odd genuflections and the odd hymns in between, whilst Morgan's brain raced back and forth between the alternatives. None seemed right, and yet to do nothing seemed worst of all. He tore a page out of the hymnal, to the disapproval of the respectable mourners on both sides, took a pencil out of his work-shirt pocket, and then didn't know what to write. The 'Dear Annie' was easy, after all he'd started a thousand letters to her with those same two words. But what next? He was paralysed completely. Only when they'd sung an incongruous 'Jerusalem', and the congregation were filing down the aisle, starting from the front, and led by the parson, did he scribble a few desperate words:

Dear Annie
I've written to you every day since you left. Because
I love you. Why didn't you write back? I've missed you so much. Twm.

He couldn't see Ann when he stepped into the aisle; she was hidden by taller people in the foreground, but he could see Frank's bald pate approaching above the crowd. He waited on Annie's side of the aisle until suddenly there she was, red eyed, very enceinte, and much older than he remembered, with streaks of grey hair under her broad brimmed black funeral hat. She was looking down as she came, her left arm in Frank's. Then she must have seen his rough work shoes pointing in the wrong direction, facing the flow of the oncoming people. She looked up, straight into his face, her free hand flying to her mouth, her eyes wide open in shock. Evidently she'd had no idea, no idea whatsoever that he would be there. Frank moved across to intervene, to protect her from Morgan. Morgan didn't resist, simply pushed the folded scrap of paper in between the fingers still covering her mouth. Then he stepped back into his pew, leaving them to pass out of the church together among the crowd.

Somehow, he felt, in an indefinable way, that it was all over. Whether it was his fault, or Ann's, or Henry's, or just simply the passage of Time, it didn't matter, but he knew that things could never be quite the same again. He was Curly's father, she, within a few days, would be the mother of Frank's child. She was a woman now, not his girl Annie any longer. The past two and a half years had changed them both, almost out of recognition.

From the caravan window Morgan was staring across the Teifi estuary to Poppet Sands which were still wet from the receding tide. But he wasn't thinking about the sea, or the black and white oystercatchers poking about in the shallows for cockles, or about Kirralee his son, still fast asleep in the bunk beyond the door, or even about his lost wife Ann, now the mother of Petra, Frank Cotteridge's daughter. Morgan was thinking about the Universe, and in particular about galaxies, those dim islands of stars, like the Milky Way, floating in the vast immensities of space. For weeks now, ever since they'd left Wychal End Farm and come down to Wales, he'd been thinking relentlessly about Fish's observations, and what they could possibly mean. His instincts all told him he was close to something big. He couldn't see it in the darkness, he couldn't feel it with his hands, but all the same he knew it was there. Some hunter's sixth sense had located it in the bush. All he had to do now was flush it into the open and aim true.

Back at Wychal End he had realised that Fish's observations of thirty Elliptical galaxies implied that their Radii were proportional to the square roots of their Luminosities – a vary odd fact indeed. But it was true. He looked back over another set of Ellipticals which he himself had observed with Ron Eckersly back in Australia. Their two hundred measurements also conformed exactly with Fish's weird law. But what did it mean? The obvious thing to do was to square both sides of the equation to get rid of the square root. Now it made more sense: the Radius squared, or area of an Elliptical galaxy, was proportional to its Luminosity. Or put another way the Luminosity divided by the area, or the *Luminosity per unit area*, or 'Surface brightness ' as it was called by astronomers, was more or less the same for every giant Elliptical galaxy measured by Man.

Surface Brightness was an intrinsic quantity for a galaxy, one that was independent of its distance away, and therefore fundamental. If a galaxy were moved to say twice the distance away, its apparent luminosity would fall by four, but so would it's apparent area , and so the ratio of the two, that is to say the 'Surface Brightness', would remain the same.

Surface Brightness too was vital to the Visibility of a galaxy – that is to say how easy it would be to see it against the night sky. For instance if a galaxy were too dim, dimmer than the foreground sky, it would be virtually, perhaps wholly, invisible. And given that the Earth's sky was, for one reason or another, bright in cosmic terms, this dimness could be a serious problem. For a start the Earth lived inside a fairly bright spiral galaxy – the Milky Way. Then, even at night, the smoke floating in interplanetary space, smoke that could 'see' the Sun even at night, because it lay out in space beyond the Earth's shadow, also lit up the moonless sky with unwanted 'Zodiacal Light'. Finally came Man himself, with all his street lights, and his pollution in the air to reflect that glare back down, even from cities that were seventy miles away. All these unwanted sources of light in the foreground could thus mask any dimmer galaxy in the background. The astronomer would be like a man in a lighted room looking out through a window at night. He would see the street lamps, the lighted windows in the house opposite, but not its walls or its roof. The trees wouldn't be visible, nor the unlighted buildings, nor yet the hills beyond. He'd be blinded to almost everything out there that was less bright than the room in which he lived.

The awful suspicion was creeping into Morgan's mind that here lay the explanation for Fish's Law. Fish's Ellipticals all had the same Surface Brightness, only because galaxies that were any dimmer wouldn't be seen; that the galaxies known to Man were only a tiny subset of the whole population, that tiny number whose signal was bright enough to make itself visible against the terrestrial sky. If that was true then the implications were breath-taking, absolutely colossal. It might be true that for every such visible galaxy there were a hundred, or even a thousand more, lurking out there hidden just beneath the brightness of the sky. Fritz Zwicky's mysterious Dark Matter that had haunted extra-galactic astronomers for a generation, would be explained at a single stroke. Morgan suspected there was a hidden universe of dim galaxies, lurking out there just below the night sky, a universe waiting for the astronomer bold enough to land his feet on its shore.

It was a staggering thought, but one alas, that didn't quite fit, 'a beautiful hypothesis killed by an ugly fact', one of what T.H. Huxley had referred to as 'the tragedies of science'. The ugly fact was that Fish's observations were too precise: they didn't say "All Elliptical galaxies have a Surface Brightness of more than such and such – the critical value which enables them to be seen above the terrestrial sky." Oh no! They said "All Elliptical galaxies have exactly the *same* Surface Brightness, never less than that critical value, but never more than it either. It was the extra 'never more than it either' that constituted the ugly fact. It was easy to see why galaxies too dim would remain undetected by Man, but why would ones too bright be invisible as well? Fish's

Law was so precise: all known giant Ellipticals had the same Surface Brightness, neither too dim nor too bright.

And yet and yet......the "Visibility Hypothesis" as Morgan was beginning to call it in his own mind, was so compelling, so beautiful, so natural, so dramatic that it surely had to be right. It had to be! He was just missing something. As he stared across the Teifi estuary he was trying to imagine what that tantalising something could be. For several days now he had felt the merest glimmer of a solution hovering just below the level of consciousness. He felt as he had looking for the Crab Nebula through the 36-inch at Steward for the first time many years before. Something had stirred out there in the blackness, at the very periphery of vision, a tantalising wraith of light, only to vanish the moment he stared at it directly. But when he looked away, there it was again, trembling on the edge of consciousness. So it was with his Visibility Hypothesis now. Or so he felt.

It had been thus for three weeks, ever since they'd come down to his mother's caravan at Gwbert. Night and day he could barely think of anything else, barely do the chores, barely attend to poor Curly who was bored here and wanted to go back to Wychal End to be with Valerie and Bob Salt on their busy farm, not here with a father who was too distracted even to tell him one of his usually fascinating bed-time stories.

With no one to test out his ideas on, not even Bob Salt, there were times when Morgan felt he was teetering on the very lip of sanity. His 'Visibility Hypothesis', the idea of a Hidden Universe just below the grasp of detection, was just the kind of obsession that mad men were supposed to have, the delusion that they, and only they could see the world as it really was. After all he'd been under such a colossal strain recently. Perhaps the glimpse of Ann, the loss of his beloved after such a long hope of clinging on, had finally proved too much? Perhaps he'd given up the real world for a more attractive one, one that he could conjure out of the astronomical darkness – Morgan's World, the imaginary world of delusional galaxies that only he could see, the world where he was king? They would put him in an institution where he would walk about with an enormous grin, babbling to whoever would listen, of a great Hidden Universe up there beyond the clouds, beyond the countable stars?

And yet and yet! He didn't feel like a mad man. Yes he felt unutterably alone without Annie to talk to in his mind any more, to write letters to in at least the hope that she would read them, if never reply. Those dolphins now, out in the estuary, they were surely real, a small family who often came inshore on the tail of the falling tide, looking for sewin. Yes they were real. And looking down on the table the Hewlett Packard calculator, the amazing little computer he'd bought for himself in the Duty Free at Singapore airport, and which was now his pride and joy, yes that certainly was real too. He switched it on and the red LEDs flickered to life. And his note pad, now covered all over, page after page, with doodles of imaginary galaxies and algebraic calculations, that surely was real too, even if the man who had scrawled them was wondering if he was still sane.

Kiralee stirred next door, emitting the funny little gobbling noises which he did when he was having a bad dream. Morgan went into the bedroom, picked his son out of the hot bed and held him over his shoulder. Curly whimpered, half awake now, then emitted a sharp cry, confronting demons of his own.

"There there Curly boy. It's all right. Daddy's here. They've all gone now, just a dream, just a dream."

Curly sighed deeply, rested his head back on Morgan's shoulder, and fell asleep again in a trice. Morgan lowered him gently back into the bunk, pulled up the blankets and admired his sleeping son by the dim light filtering through the crack in the caravan curtains. Here was reality. Here was something to cling on to in the furthest wasteland of melancholia. Curly needed him, because Curly didn't have anyone else. His mother was lost to him in the jungles of New Guinea, and Kylie was back at Tidbinbilla, on the banks of the Murrumbidgee, twelve thousand miles away. Curly had Morgan, and he had no one else at all. Morgan had Curly, and Curly wouldn't let his father slip over the edge. Morgan tiptoed out, certain of his own sanity again, and returned to his notebook. There had to be a solution. There had to be.

Morgan took an imaginary galaxy, for the hundredth time, and put it into a dark, but not totally dark, imaginary sky. Then he used imaginary hands to stretch it further and further, keeping its total Luminosity, in other words the total number of stars in it, constant. As it grew in size so its imaginary Surface Brightness grew dimmer and dimmer until....until...then what happened? Obviously it would disappear, lost beneath the sky. But would it disappear all at once, lost to view in a sudden vanishing trick? No it wouldn't. A galaxy was always brighter in the middle than the outside. So the outside would grow too dim to see first, whilst the inner part would still remain visible to the eye. In other words as the galaxy grew in physical size its visible image, the bit brighter than the sky, would actually shrink.

How strange. Morgan played the imaginary game in his head over again. He stretched the galaxy with his imaginary hands while keeping his astronomers eye on it. First it *appeared* to stretch, then it reached a maximum size, and then it appeared to shrink, as all its outer parts were swallowed by the sky.

He played the imaginary game in reverse. He started with a galaxy so stretched out that all of it was hidden beneath the sky. It was totally invisible. Then he squeezed it inward until a little pip of light, the nucleus, appeared at its centre, just brighter than the sky. He squeezed some more and the galaxy actually appeared to grow as more of it was bright enough to be seen. He squeezed more until virtually all of the galaxy was visible. What happened if he squeezed even further? Obviously the galaxy would shrink now because it was all visible, yet truly shrinking in size. Eventually, if he squeezed too far it would shrink into a point of light indistinguishable from a star.

Suddenly there it was. The magnificent beast had emerged from the bush, its flank exposed to Morgan's spear. More alive then he had ever been, or ever would be in his life again, Morgan raised his spear and hurled it, deadly and true, through the ribcage and into the pumping heart.

Of course, of course of course! He leapt into the air, banging his head with his two fists. There was an optimum Surface Brightness for any galaxy when it *looked*, that was the important point, when it *looked* biggest in the sky. If the Surface Brightness was too low most of it would be hidden beneath the sky, leaving only a little pip visible to see. And if the Surface Brightness was too high it would mean the galaxy really had to be small, and would *look small* too. In between there was an optimum Surface Brightness when the galaxy, to an Earth bound explorer, would look its biggest size. And that optimum Surface Brightness, Morgan was now prepared to bet his life, was the very Surface Brightness that Fish and he had measured.

The beautiful idea wasn't dead! The 'Visibility Hypothesis' was alive and well. The vast majority of all nearby Elliptical galaxies were hidden beneath the sky, either because they were too small to be picked out from the multitude of stars and tiny background galaxies in the sky or because they were too dim to show up above the sky. Only those with a most particular value of the intrinsic Surface Brightness would appear big enough to be recognised as true galaxies in the neighbouring night sky.

Columbus's beans were nothing compared to this. Columbus had found only a neighbouring continent. Morgan had tripped over ninety nine percent of the Universe, or even more!. How he wished Ron Eckersly was here – to tell, to argue with, to share the excitement. What would Ron say?

Morgan stopped in his tracks. He knew only too well what Eckersly would say:

"Neat idea Tom. Now prove it! It's far too vague as it is. Where's the evidence?"

Morgan deflated like a balloon. Yes, where was the evidence? What could possibly convince someone as sharp and sceptical as Ron of such a fantastical idea? And it was fantastical. To claim that ninety nine per cent of the Universe was lurking just out of visible reach, because it's Surface Brightness wasn't quite right, was the most fantastical idea, come to think of it, that any astronomer had had since Copernicus had claimed, also on the flimsiest evidence, that the Earth travelled round the Sun, and not vice versa. How was Morgan ever going to convince himself, let alone the Eckerslys and Bellfounders of this world, that such a fantastical, improbable, incredible, tantalising idea was right?

It didn't take him long to figure out how. He could calculate from first principles, using mathematics, what the optimum Surface Brightness *should* be. It would be some exact number, X say. Then, working backward from Fish's observations, and his own, he would calculate the Surface Brightness of all the *observed* Elliptical galaxies. That would be some other exact number, Y say. If, and only if, Y turned out to be exactly equal to X, would the Visibility Hypothesis be very probably true. It would be far too much of a coincidence for the two numbers to be equal, and yet for the hypothesis that generated that equality, to be wrong.

Suddenly Morgan was terrified. What if the two numbers didn't agree? Then his Visibility Hypothesis would be wrong. Unquestionably wrong. You could rarely prove, beyond a doubt, that a scientific hypothesis was true. But you could falsify it at a single blow by showing that one of its predictions was numerically wrong. Elated a few minutes before, Morgan was now terrified of the elaborate calculation he would have to make. It was straight 'Do or die'; the Moment of Truth. Get the sword right down in between the beast's shoulder blades, or get the ripping horn straight into the groin.

The calculation wouldn't be trivial either. He would have to derive a number of tricky mathematical equations, work out their numerical consequences with his new calculator, then plot them out on a graph. And, Oh shit, he hadn't got any graph paper with him; he would have to go into Cardigan. They'd need to go in the boat. The tide was running in fast now and lapping up towards the caravan. Poppet Sands, on the far side of the estuary where the oystercatchers had been feeding had vanished. It was a Spring tide, running hard, with no wind for the sail. They would need to catch it on the Flood, and come back down the Teifi on the Ebb.

Curly tottered into the room rubbing his eyes. Morgan lifted him up and sat him in his lap: he smelt strongly of urine.

"I'm 'ungry" Curly complained in the thick Australian drawl he's picked up in Canberra. "I want a 'nana."

"We've run out of 'nanas old chap. What about a bit of toast?"

"Orright then. Vegamite, like Kylie makes."

Morgan had to break the news that Vegemite was a purely Australian concoction, completely inedible to many Brits. Curly burst into tears:

"Never mind" Morgan cuddled him, "You'll soon see Kylie. We're going back to live in Australia again. Not in Canberra but in Sydney. But I'm sure you'll see Kylie all the time. And Kylie can come to stay with us. And you'll see all the horses."

"Grumbo?"

"Yes you'll see Grumbo."

"And Picton?"

"Of course. He'll bark like mad when he sees you again."

"And Cromwell….." Curly ran through a long litany of names while Morgan changed his nappies. Morgan had had his interview in Whitehall for the AAT job a month ago and was expecting to hear any day The interview had gone smoothly. No sign of Bellfounder, while Bill Kretchmaier had winked at him at the end, as if to say "All's Well".

After breakfast Morgan hauled the wooden rowing boat down the beach and into the shallows. What a wonderful way to go shopping, he mused, as he always did when they were setting out. They didn't have any other transport and it was too far for Curly to walk up to the bridge which crossed the estuary. He tied a life jacket round Curly and lifted him into the stern sheets. Then he leapt into the boat and pushed off.

As he rowed up the estuary, the morning sun on his back, Morgan tried to forget about galaxies. Herring Gulls called round his head while Curly gave a running commentary on everything to be seen, from Cardigan Island to the old castle. They tied up at the quay from where, not so long ago, sleek Welsh schooners had carried Welsh slate to the far corners of the Earth.

They climbed up the stone steps into the busy little town, Aberteifi as it was called in Welsh, the market town of Ceredigion. He was lucky enough to find a book of graph paper in the stationers, presumably stocked for school children. They wondered round the 'supermarket' picking up groceries, with Curly calling out at favourites recognised on the shelves. Then to the butcher, the baker and the greengrocer until Morgan was loaded down with plastic bags. He couldn't help thinking about galaxies.

As they were making their way back to the quay through the jostling Saturday morning crowd, half made up of locals and half of holiday makers, Curly cried out in distress:

"The post office daddy, post office…."

Curly liked the post office because they sold delicious ice cream.

So they turned back and bought him a vanilla cornet. Absentmindedly Morgan picked up his post. And there it was at last, the letter he'd been waiting for, with 'Anglo Australian Telescope Board', proudly embossed on its envelope.

They went outside where Morgan perched Curly on the stone wall to eat his ice cream. Then he slit the envelope open impatiently with his thumbnail:

" Dear Dr Morgan

We regret to inform you that you were unsuccessful in your bid for a post on the Anglo Australian Telescope.

The successful candidates were…………."

and there followed a list of names, only one of which Morgan had ever heard of, nearly all from Cambridge University or the Royal Greenwich Observatory. But the real sting was in the tail:

"Dr Frank Cotteridge has taken 5 years leave of absence from Trinity College Cambridge to assume the position of Deputy Director.

Yours sincerely………….."

Morgan was stunned. Frank! And not even one of the lesser five fellowships, not even a junior fellowship for him. Kretschmaier had been so certain: wanted him so much in the senior post. What had happened? What could possibly have taken place behind closed doors? He was finished! And Ann would be going to Sydney after all, as she'd always wanted to do; but not with him, with Frank! Morgan was staggered; found it hard to breathe. He'd been counting on the AAT job so much; been virtually promised it by the Director. And now there was nothing; not even a measly two-year fellowship to tide him over. He was unemployed; now he was unemployable. Finished in Astronomy. After all that fighting, all that success, he wasn't rated in Britain even for a junior fellowship. It was incredible. It was a bad dream. He looked at Curly licking his cornet contentedly on the wall. Poor Curly too. He wouldn't see Kylie again; probably never ever revisit Australia. How could it have happened? It was too cruel, too unforeseeable, too unexpected. He glanced at the list of undistinguished names again. Who were they? Protégés of fucking Bellfounder no doubt. But there had to be an explanation. Then he recalled that there were two other letters. One had Bill Kretchmaier's name scribbled bottom left. He tore it open:

Dear Tom
I know what a terrible disappointment it will be to you. Almost as much to me. It had nothing to do with astronomy believe me. You were well on top there, and I thought you were safely on board. Then this professor from Cambridge, with a double barrelled name which, of course, I'm not allowed to disclose, brought up this fight you'd had in the 74-inch telescope with Ken Freeman over 'spectrograph design'. I have to say it sounded highly unlikely to me. But he insisted on the truth of it, and the rest of the Brits on the committee backed him up. They said 'We can't have a service astronomer, one responsible for helping visitors, who is a violent and powerful man like Morgan'. Put like that it was difficult for me to argue, though Boy I tried. I guess you'll have to learn to kerb that explosive temper of yours. But it shows you really care about instrumentation!
All the same the AAT will far the weaker without you. If there's anything I can do, short of offering you a job, let me know.
Best wishes
Bill Kretchmaier
PS As you asked we looked at AP Lib with the new electronic spectrum scanner on the 120-inch at Lick. It took us the best part of two whole nights. But boy you were bang on right. I'll send you a copy of the paper as soon as it's writ. I guess you should collect that hundred dollars each from….. and …... . Don't give up Tom. You are one hell of an astronomer!"

They rowed back down the estuary, this time against the tide. Morgan, his veins bursting, bent the ash oars until they nearly snapped. Every so often he stopped and screamed invective at the sky, while Curly cowered in the stern sheets, never having seen his father in a battlefield rage before.

"You Fucking Liars! You creeping crawling cheats! Is nothing beneath you? Fighting in the dome with Ken Freeman? A total fucking, bleeding fabrication!" He stopped, stood in the boat, almost toppling it over, and crashed an oar down onto the water with an almighty splash.

Curly howled, howls which calmed Morgan down a bit. But Morgan was shivering with rage as he cradled his distressed son in his arms.

Who could possibly have made up such a malicious, such a ridiculous fabrication? Who ever fought over spectrograph design? Why would he fight with poor Ken Freeman, who was barely five feet tall? It was all lies lies lies! But it was too late of course now. They'd never reverse an appointment once it had been publicly announced.

As the tide floated them back up the estuary again towards Ceredigion bridge, Curly clutched in Morgan's arms, Morgan realised what a fool he had been. First Schweinhunt, then Bacon, now Bellfounder. Every one had said, without exception, that Bellfounder would get him in the end, and now Bellfounder well and truly had. The Old Boy Network, that hadn't built the British Empire, or defended it, had built a malignant tumour instead, a tumour whose poisonous tentacles spread out from the public schools and the old universities, into the clubs, the courts, the committees and into the corridors of power. You could hear them, the Adrian Bellfounders and the Alec Douglas-Humes, sucking on Britain's blood. They'd taken his job, they'd taken his wife, and now they'd taken his profession. They may not have built Britain those Old Boys, they hadn't participated in the Industrial Revolution, or won Trafalgar, or developed the Jet Engine, but they controlled Britain now, and so long as Britons were snobs, they always would.

All that night, and the following night too, the caravan lights cast their yellow glow across the moving water. They could take away his profession, they could take away his wife, but they couldn't take the Universe away, not entirely. Perhaps soon he would be working in an insurance office or a factory, an ex-astronomer who'd failed to succeed in his field. But so long as he had some savings he could continue to dream, to fight and to think.

By dawn of the first night the calculations were complete. The calculations based on the Visibility Hypothesis revealed a maximum apparent size for an Elliptical galaxy which peaked sharply at a Surface Brightness of 15.7 Blue magnitudes per square arc second exactly. Scarcely daring to breathe he turned back to the folder containing Fish's observations and his own. It took some time with the new calculator to turn those Surface Brightnesses into the same units. But when he'd done so the answer was identical ! X equalled Y. The prediction of his Visibility Theory, and the observations of hundreds of real Ellipticals by Fish and himself, agreed exactly. It was beyond the bounds of probability that this was a coincidence. The Universe had to be stuffed with Elliptical galaxies, all but a few invisible to Man with his current techniques. It was a revelation worth more to him than all the jobs in all the observatories across all the world.

He went out on to the beach and wearily stretched his arms and shoulders, staring as the sea came to life under the rising Sun. What had Kepler said when he discovered the Laws of Planetary Motion?

"I have attested it as true in my deepest soul and I contemplate its beauty with incredible and ravishing delight."

But he wasn't finished yet. During the night he'd had another damned good idea. If Visibility Theory was good for Elliptical galaxies it must surely be good for Spiral galaxies too. And that thought had triggered a memory, the memory of what had seemed, at the time in Arizona, an extremely boring seminar in which the speaker had claimed that all Spiral and Irregular galaxies had the same Surface Brightness as each other. That evening, as soon as Curly had gone to sleep, Morgan set out to repeat the original calculation, but this time for Spirals, where the algebra was quite different. Again total success. An even sharper peak culminating at the exact Surface Brightness of famous measured Spiral galaxies such as The Andromeda Nebula and The Milky Way, a peak value quite distinct from Ellipticals. The Universe must be stuffed with as many invisible Spirals as it was with invisible Ellipticals. The Hidden Universe, his Hidden Universe, was waiting out there on the horizon, just like Columbus's continent. Maybe he wouldn't reach it now. Maybe some other man would first set foot on the Promised Land. But he had had the enormous privilege of seeing it first. No other would be able to stand first at the cross-trees and yell out:

"Land Ho! Land Ho!"

Later that morning, after a second night without a wink of sleep, Morgan lifted his son onto his shoulders and skipped along the beach, kicking at the surf with his bare feet. Curly gurgled with laughter at the fun of it, and so did Morgan . He didn't have a job. He didn't have money. He didn't have a wife any more. He didn't have prospects, and worst of all he had no partner to share his triumph with. But for that one day Morgan was, and he knew he was, the happiest man in the Universe.

DISCLAIMER

Everything *scientific* in this book happened either to me, to a close colleague, or to an immediate predecessor. In that sense this is an unadorned portrait of an astronomer during that unique epoch between 1960 and 2010 when space science was opening up the Universe to full view for the first time. There is no need to exaggerate, or embellish, for imagination could never keep up with the mixture of high adventure, low villainy, and everything else in between, that characterised that place and time. On the other hand this had to be a novel because most of the adventures were going on, not in their telescope domes, nor on their launch pads, but in men's minds. It would be impossible to convey the dreams, the gambles, the surprises, the all too common disappointments, and the rare sweet garlands, if it were not done from the interior point of view. In that sense the book, and all its characters, though here and there they may have stolen garments from real people, are entirely imaginary. The author, although he is a Welsh astronomer, is not Morgan the central protagonist, nor does he share many of Morgan's views. Nor are Morgan's wives and children my own. Nor, I am glad to say, were Morgan's enemies and his misfortunes all mine. Nevertheless, without exception, they were, severally disguised, the enemies and misfortunes of one or another real astronomer that I knew, just as were his astronomical delights, and very occasional triumphs.

"

Printed in Poland
by Amazon Fulfillment
Poland Sp. z o.o., Wrocław

55785344R00237